WORLD OF THE VISCEREBUS

BOOKS 1-3

OZ MARI G.

Published 2024 by Next Chapter

CONTENTS

THE KEEPER

DAWN OF THE DUAL APEX

RISE OF THE VISCEREBUS

THE KEEPER

WORLD OF THE VISCEREBUS BOOK 1

ACKNOWLEDGMENTS

The Keeper is my attempt at telling a sweet love story set in a fantastical world. It is also my first YA novel. The book contains elements that I truly love. But it would have ended up as boring were it not for the following people.

My eternal gratitude to:

My best friend for life, Maricar J, for the unwavering support and encouragement, for being always open to read a first draft and point out what my stories lacked.

And the rest of the beta readers who gave me objective feedback.

I dedicate this book to:
My son, Joshua, the inspiration for everything I do.
Finally, to my two cats, iO and Laki, who journeyed with me with little complaint.

PROLOGUE

It has been told that Prometheus, the creator of all creatures on earth, gave life to two types of being in the likeness of the gods.

The first was the humans who he moulded from clay and earth. He gave them fire as a gift. This generosity infuriated Zeus. He bound Prometheus at Mount Caucasus where the latter's punishment was to have his liver eaten every day by a giant eagle, another titan named Aetos. The liver would regrow every night, and the torturous cycle was to be for thirty thousand years.

Prometheus, legend said, created a pair of second beings as his companions during his suffering. They were not just made in the image of the gods, but from its true essence.

Prometheus added a piece of his liver to the soil and rocks he used to fashion the new creatures, thus bestowing them with superhuman strength, speed, slow aging, and super senses. He also gave them the power to shape shift into animals to enable them to hide from Zeus.

However, he was unaware that the saliva of Aetos tainted a portion of the liver. And his second creation inherited the need to consume viscera.

He called them Viscerebus, or viscera-eaters.

Once Prometheus was free, he bid the Viscerebus to live among humans. Thus, begun the conflict between the two.

The Viscerebus hunted the humans for their viscera, and the humans hunted them back for survival.

For decades, they were locked in a fierce battle for supremacy. The Viscerebus were stronger, faster, and more powerful, but the humans had centuries of head start in population. They outnumbered the Viscerebus, and it shifted the balance of power.

To protect their own, the Viscerebi formed a Tribunal and engineered a system that ensured the survival of their kind.

They set up a process of procuring fresh viscera without the need to kill humans; the distribution of the victus to their kind to stop them from hunting humans; and the campaign to convince the humans that the Viscerebi were creatures of lore.

They perfected the strategy for millennia, and the Viscerebi thrived, hidden in plain sight among human societies all over the world.

Their success hinged on keeping the Veil of Secrecy intact—the hiding of their existence from the humans at all costs.

But like air, secrets could only be contained through insulation. And like all insulation, it would never be permanent.

When two different beings coexist, their imperfections could create either conflict or cohesion.

1

ASWANG, ERDIA AND HUMAN

Veren stood in the middle of the forest. He breathed deep, trying to pick up the scent of the wild boar he heard foraging. The thick foliage overhead filtered the remaining sunlight, making the forest darker but not dark enough to trigger his night vision.

A breeze blew by him. It carried the smell of the trees, the rotting leaves, the decaying fruits on the forest floor, and the musky odour of the boar. He scanned the direction of the scent until he saw movement two hundred meters away. The animal was digging for something by the roots of the banyan trees.

Veren looked around to see if any of his fellow cadets were close to his location. He centred his senses, listening for human voices, and smelling for them. He could not detect any. With his gun slung behind him to keep his hands free, he lowered his centre of gravity and sprinted towards the unsuspecting boar; the wind whizzed past his ears, the wet squish of the leaves on the ground muffling the sound of his feet.

His speed was too much for the boar. It was a mere split second before the animal realised he was coming. It lifted its head from the ground just before it found itself raised by the hind legs. He swung the boar against the tree trunk, crushing its skull with the force of the blow.

He crouched down and inspected his kill.

Oh, damn... I shattered one tusk.

With a sigh, he took out his handgun and shot the dead boar in the head where the tree had done the most damage. It would be hard to explain to his superior the true cause of its death otherwise. It required tremendous strength to shatter a pig's cranium. A gunshot would be the easiest way to avoid questions.

Inherent caution coloured all of his interactions with humans, just as it did with every single one of his kind. By nature, his kind avoid any potential exposure to their existence. There was no need to alarm the humans and create suspicion.

As he walked back to their camp in the woods, the dead boar slung over his shoulder, he encountered some human hunters along the way. He avoided crossing paths with them. It was easy enough, as he could hear them and their heavy treads on the forest floor. He found himself replying to their conversation in his head.

"*I think we should hunt close to that military encampment,*" one human male said to his companions. There were three of them.

"*Why? There are no bandits in these woods.*"

"*Yeah, maybe not, but I heard there are Aswangs.*"

Yes. There is. Me, he thought.

"*Well, we have guns.*"

"*I am not sure if guns can kill Aswangs ...*"

Sure they can, if you pump enough bullets in us and we bleed to death before our ability to heal and regenerate catches up.

"*Well, what do you think those military men carry as weapons? Guns. And I'm sure they don't use silver bullets.*"

It was funny how humans had melded one tale of legend into another. For most people, their legends were part of old beliefs, stories passed on through generations and told to scare children. Not one of those tales was accurate.

"*I can't believe you still believe in Aswangs ... In this day and age, we would have heard of attacks on humans. We all know what they're after.*"

To hide their existence, and their need for human viscera, the *Tribunal* had perfected a system of securing much-needed organs without having to kill any humans. Veren believed that it was pure genius to operate most of the funeral parlours, morgues, and mortuaries all over the world. It gave Aswangs access to fresh viscera without the humans' knowledge. The process became seamless over centuries of experience.

"*Yeah, not to mention that our military would definitely go after them if they attacked humans. They like nothing better but a reason to kill.*"

Yes, I agree. And it would be catastrophic to our kind.

Thinking about what the *Tribunal* did for him, how they took care of him, never failed to make his heart swell with gratitude, Veren's vow to serve the community that nurtured him remained his driving goal. And his path to that goal was to become an *Iztari*.

Nothing could be nobler than protecting his kind from the peril that surrounded them all within the human communities. It was a necessity to be in proximity to them, as their need for human viscera was critical to their daily survival.

Military academies all over the world were the natural training grounds for people like him who desired to belong to their elite law enforcement. There were always a few of his kind who graduated every year. Several staffs in the Academy were *Aswangs,* including the Commandant, who took care of supplying them with raw human viscera every three days.

"It's creepy enough in these woods. Stop your horror stories or we'll be too scared to hunt later."

The words of the hunters faded into the distance.

As he walked back to rejoin his troop, his thoughts replayed the discussion other *Aswangs* in the Academy were engaged in last night. There was no one in his class to discuss his opinions with. He was the only *Aswang* there, and he was not close with anyone in the lower and upper classes.

Some of his kind favoured surfacing and showing their might and ruling over the humans. In his opinion, to play on the humans' fear of *Aswangs,* scare them into submission, offered limited value. Fear could be a powerful deterrent, but it tended to wane in potency given enough time. History was littered with toppled governments through revolutions orchestrated by terrified people.

The *Viscerebus* might be stronger, faster, and superior to the humans, but at the odds of thirty to one, even their superior traits could not survive an attack, whether in retaliation or fear. Humans had the numbers and weapons to kill them.

They were safer if they remained hidden in plain sight, unnoticed by the humans and thought of only as a relic of a superstitious past.

Humans were less likely to attack an enemy they did not believe to exist.

Manila, same time, same day.

Anza watched her classmates giggle over selfies with the boys they met at the mall during the weekend. They were on their midday break, waiting for the next class to start. The thought of the boys waiting in the parking lot later excited the three girls. They talked about hanging out with them at the Cosy Café located across the street from the main gate of their school.

The tall and slim Elyse, half-Filipino and half-German, led the girls. The other two were attractive and stylish: Rizzi with her mixed Arabian blood, and Summer's half Chinese heritage. All three were popular and fit the mould of archetypal it-girls. But what really made them unique was they were not mean, hurtful, or selfish, as one might assume.

On the surface, Anza fit the group well. She was petite, slim, and had been told multiple times that she was attractive. She preferred to think these girls wanted her in their group because she tried to match their kindness whenever she could, to compensate for every time she rejected their invitation to go out, and not for her looks.

She wanted to be friends with them, but her father and the laws of the *Viscerebus Tribunal* would not allow it.

"Anza, come with us. They will bring their friend with them. He's interested in meeting you," Elyse prodded her. "He's also into music and photography," she added with a smile.

"Interested in me? How does he know about me?" She had been very careful not to get her pictures on any social media.

"I posted our year-end class photos on my Instagram. He saw it and asked Kirk for an introduction to you," Elyse replied casually.

For her classmates, this was commonplace. Nothing to worry about. For her kind, it was always a concern. It was a footprint to be erased, a snapshot of time that could come back to haunt a slow-ageing *Aswang*. It shouldn't have been an issue for her, because she would age just like a normal human, but she grew up trained in the same rules as her family. It became a habit for her.

"I'm not sure ... My dad won't like it." Her usual alibi was a hundred per cent true.

"Well, they're arriving twenty minutes early, so come with us and chat with them," Elyse implored. "You can leave once your father arrives. Please ..."

All three girls begged her to say yes. It would be embarrassing to say no, and the temptation to give in was strong.

"Okay," she said with a nod.

"Great!" Elyse jumped up from her seat and gave her a quick hug.

She must like that Kirk guy a lot for her to be that excited to make me say yes.

As she watched the three girls chat about their weekend activities, a sense of envy pierced her heart. She wanted to join them. Just once. They asked her every time, and she kept saying no. It was a wonder that they hadn't given up on being nice to her.

Maybe being seatmates helped. She sat behind Elyse, and whenever the trio chatted with each other, she was within hearing range. It was convenient and natural for Elyse to include her in the conversation. As Elyse was the leader of the three, Rizzi and Summer accepted and followed her example.

Two hours later, as she put her things away, she debated whether to tell her father about the early class dismissal today. This meant she wouldn't have to talk to the guy, but Elyse interrupted her thoughts.

"Are you nervous, Anza?" Her smile was gentle and concerned.

She nodded. "A little."

"Why? You're very pretty." Elyse sounded surprised as she looked her over from head to foot.

"It's not my looks that worry me," she began, but Rizzi interjected.

"Anza, with your baby-doll looks, just bat those lashes and you'll have the poor guy eating out of your hand." Rizzi giggled at her own statement.

"Or, you can jam with him. We heard he's a sucker for girls who can sing," Summer added.

Elyse and Rizzi smiled in agreement.

Her classmates misunderstood the source of her reluctance. They didn't know that meeting the boy, no matter how much she liked him after, would never lead to anything. It would be a pointless exercise.

And apart from being forbidden to tell them the truth, they would not believe her even if she broke the *Veil of Secrecy*. They would think her crazy if she told them her entire family was *Aswang*.

That afternoon, for forty minutes, she had a sample of the life she would lead if she inhabited her human heritage. The boy, Mark, was good-looking, charming, and endearingly nervous.

The girls flirted with the boys, laughed at jokes, shared some drinks, and assured that they would see each other again during the coming weekends—the simple joys of connecting with people her age. It was fun, enriching ... and in principle, harmless.

She left them reluctantly. She wanted to stay longer. Not so much because of Mark, but she felt greedy for the moments shared with humans. She had seen what her life could be if her parents allowed her to live the life that her humanity could afford her. She didn't have the long life her parents enjoyed, but they didn't seem to realise this.

Her family was due for *Transit* soon. This meant they would move somewhere far away and new. She would have to go to a new school, meet new people, but couldn't make friends with any of them. And that would repeat in another twenty-five years.

Her life with her family was destined to be limited and lonely, with no one but her parents, uncles, aunts, and cousins as contributors to her experience. She would never fulfil her full potential. She could never have her photos published, her songs sung in airwaves, her poetry read. Just like the contents of her social media, it would just be for her own eyes, like a digital diary.

And this grieved her—the premature death of her potential, the wasting of her life.

Manuu Soledad, the head of his household, came home from a meeting with the *Matriarch* and the *Patriarch* of their *Gentem's Tribunal.*

They discussed the logistics of the *Transit* of Manuu's family, which comprised his daughter and wife.

Normally, this would be a simple arrangement if it just involved his immediate family. But his wife's family, whom they had gotten very close to during the past twelve years, wanted to join them. That required a more extensive logistical setup.

One small family moving into a new community would be unnoticed, but three moving to the same place at the same time would attract attention. The local *Tribunal* decided they could all move to Auckland together, provided they would not live in the same community. Their homes would have to be at least four kilometres apart. At least for the first five years.

For the *Viscerebus,* a *Transit* was a normal part of existence. It was a requirement that they go through every twenty to thirty years, to hide their slow-ageing and longevity. The humans would notice, otherwise.

He was glad the rest of the family would *Transit* with them for the sake of his only daughter, Anza. This was to be her first, and it would be difficult for a teenager like her to cut ties from all her human friends and classmates, to leave behind everything connected to her life in the Philippines.

To have someone close to her age, like her cousin Xandrei, who was so fond of her, would make the process easier on his beloved daughter. She had been quiet and withdrawn for the past few months, especially since the day he did not permit her to attend her school fair. He knew then that she was missing the company of young people.

As his car passed along the coastal road, he thought of the house that he bought in Auckland Bay. His Anza would love it. It offered plenty of photo-worthy scenes. His daughter's poetic soul would appreciate the scenery and the view.

At least, Anza would not have to get used to a new name and identity. He kept their current one. Next year, after Anza finished Year 12, they would fly to their new *Gentem*, to start their *Transit*.

The whole of New Zealand was picturesque. No doubt Anza would enjoy taking photos and writing songs in their new home country.

2

AWAY FROM HOME

Veren slung his duffel bag over his shoulder. They had called him to the *Iztari* head office for a quick briefing. He was planning to take his bag home first, but it was no hardship to pass by the office before going home.

They instructed him to go straight to the office of the *Chief Iztari*, which was on the third floor. He walked into his mentor's corner office with a thrill of anticipation.

Edrigu Orzabal was waiting for him, a smile of satisfaction on his face. Edrigu gave him a tight hug and a thump on the back.

"Congratulations, Veren! Papa told me you graduated top of your class," Edrigu said.

"Thank you, Sir! It was the least I can do," he replied.

He couldn't help but to grin back. It flattered him that his achievement pleased his mentor and Don Lorenzo Ibarra, his sponsor. He thought he owed it to them to do well. They were his only family in this world.

"So, how long do you have before they give you your first deployment?" Edrigu asked.

"I don't know, but we have about a month-long break before we report back to camp for more training," he replied.

"Okay. What do you plan to do with your month?"

"Can I spend it here at the office?" He was hopeful Edrigu would say yes.

"You do not have to. You're allowed to take a break, you know," Edrigu said. He got up and walked to the corner of his office, where a small bar was installed. He pulled out two bottles of cold beer and handed him one.

This surprised him. He didn't realise they could drink in the *Iztari* office. He hesitated.

Edrigu chuckled. "It's allowed during special occasions, and today qualifies," he said in a manner of explanation.

"Thank you, Sir." He accepted the beer.

They clinked their bottles together and toasted to his graduation from the Military Academy. They had spent few companionable moments together.

Veren's heart swelled as he gazed at his mentor, and around the room they were in. The entire building felt like home to him since the first time he stepped into the premises sixteen years ago.

"I prefer to spend my summer break here," Veren said after a moment. "I've always wanted to become an *Iztari*. So, if it's okay with you, Sir, I would love to do this."

Edrigu looked at him, his expression paternal. At least Veren would like to think that was how a father would look at a son—indulgent, patient, and caring. His mentor also seemed to read deeper into him than he cared to think about himself, much less reveal to anyone. Only self-discipline stopped him from looking away.

"Don't you want to spend your summer doing carefree things, like being with people your age, partying, meeting young women, getting a girlfriend, and all those sorts of things?" Edrigu asked. "The opportunities to do that once your work begins will be slim."

"No, Sir. I've spent all my life with people my age. I'm not interested in parties, and while I don't mind meeting girls for a laugh or two, I think it would be unfair to any potential girlfriend of mine to be in a relationship with a man like me, who has no plans of getting serious," he said, and he meant it.

"Okay, if that's what you prefer," Edrigu said, then nodded. "I will train you myself. Come here in the morning at eight a.m. For now, go home and rest. You deserve it." His mentor patted him on the shoulder and gave him a shove toward the door.

"Thank you, Sir. I'll see you tomorrow," he said, giving Edrigu an *Iztari* salute. He took his leave, his duffel bag slung over his shoulders once more.

Edrigu watched his protege walk out. It was a pity the boy was too young for his granddaughter, Yuana, and that she was already deeply involved with a human. Otherwise, he would set them up. Veren was the type of man that any grandfather would want their granddaughter to meet. Smart, intelligent, driven, and with his heart in the right place.

And as he was an *Aswang*, everything would be easier for his granddaughter.

One year later.

Anza wasn't looking forward to today's itinerary. Her father and stepmother, the entire extended family, would go on their quarterly holiday to their mountain lodge. It would be a very long drive, and she had nothing to be excited about for when they would get to their destination.

They would leave her alone in the cabin when they all went out, giving vent to their natural inclination to transform and be themselves.

She couldn't take part in the activities they all looked forward to, which were all geared towards a demonstration of supernatural skills that she didn't have: super strength, super speed, super senses, and shape-shifting. She was the only one in their midst, an *Erdia*, a half-Aswang who shared their bloodline, but none of their powers.

The only thing of value she had for her father's kind was that her viscera could power them better than a human's. At times, she fantasised about incidents where they would need her to give them her liver to save their lives.

But the reality was, the scenario would never happen, and if it did, her father would never allow it.

She was her father's princess, and he treated her like one to a fault. Her parents loved her, and that blinded them to the fact that she was not like them. They treated her like a *Viscerebus,* and raised her to follow the laws and the codes of their world, including the *Veil of Secrecy*.

When they went for their *Transit,* they would expect her to go with them. They would have to move to an unfamiliar country where no one knew who they were. It would be a complete severing of connection with any humans from their previous life.

They seemed to have forgotten the fact that she was as human as her late mother and most of the people in her school. She would age like the humans. And eventually, she would look older than her parents, and she would die long before her parents were halfway through their lifetime.

In the meantime, she would live the Viscerebus life. With no permanent roots, with no longtime friendships or relationships with any non-*Viscerebus*.

She sighed and got into the car beside her Momstie. She leaned back and closed her eyes, the plush leather comforting, the floral scent of the air freshener familiar. Her parents chatted quietly about the *Transit*. That suited her. She was not in the mood for conversation.

It would be a few hours before they arrived at their destination. A convoy of their families' cars followed theirs. Memories of how she felt as she listened to her classmates talk about going to the movies during the weekend, and of their sleepover tonight, were still fresh. The piercing sense of envy and longing hurt. They invited her, but she had to decline. Her father never allowed her to hang out with her human classmates.

She understood her father's reasoning, always followed his dictates, never doubted that he only meant well, and she used to agree with him. She wasn't so sure anymore.

Four hours later, their car entered the gated compound of their mountain lodge. A thick growth of trees surrounded the property like a wall closing in. The sounds of the forest—the crickets, the birds, the wind that rustled the leaves—were unusually loud. Anza found the familiar fragrance of the wilderness cloying. Everything about it made her uncomfortable. It highlighted the feeling that she didn't want to be here.

Her room in the lodge was unchanged. The caretakers had cleaned it, as expected. The bed and the linens were fresh. They had aired it, for it did not have the musty smell of a room long unused. They would have done all this within a day. Their *Erdia* caretakers lived in the lodge year-round and went on holiday during their visits, leaving them to their privacy whenever they'd come. It was a neat arrangement her family preferred.

With a deep sigh, she looked around her room, her sight landing on her bag. She couldn't be bothered to unpack, so she left it alone. There was nothing much in it, anyway, just the essentials for a three-day break.

She could hear the cacophony of her family outside. They were all in high spirits. Her step-uncle's booming voice dominated as he said something funny. A chorus of laughter followed it. Momstie would be in the kitchen now, supervising the supplies they brought for the weekend - the food, the wine, and everything they would need to spend a memorable family event.

Like before. Like always.

An unwelcome knock pounded on her door. She trudged towards it. It was her cousin, or more correctly, her step-cousin, Xandrei.

"Anz, we'll set up the barbecue outside. Would you like to join us?" The smile on his face was wide and cajoling.

She nodded and followed him out to the verandah.

Xandrei looked down at her, one arm rested against the door as he regarded her. Despite the two-year gap between them and the difference in interests, they were close. Or, as close as she allowed herself to be with him. Xandrei was always attentive to her. He had a depth to him that most people would never know. They bonded over their common love for poetry, which seemed incongruous as Xandrei looked every bit the jock.

And they were both unhappy with their *Viscerebus* trait. In her case, the lack of it. For Xandrei, he found his inability to use his full strength and speed in the sports that he loved, frustrating. There was nothing he could do, because it would violate the *Veil of Secrecy* if he did.

Xandrei compared it to fighting one-handed: it was fun in the beginning, but it became less and less so. Their shared exasperation on this impediment was another reason they had gotten closer in the last five years.

The grill sat on the uncovered portion of the long verandah that wrapped around the lodge. Its position allowed the smoke to waft out into the air once they started cooking. Beside it was a small table laden with raw steaks, marinated chicken breasts and drumsticks, prawns on skewers, corn on the cobs, pineapples, plantains, and pre-baked potatoes wrapped in foil, all ready for the grilling.

Xandrei fired up the grill, while Anza hung back and waited for it to heat. She could see his surreptitious glances. He seemed to sense her disquiet, but he would not ask her directly. He would wait for her to open up. That was Xandrei's way.

He may have to wait for a long time, though, because she didn't know what was wrong with herself, or the source of her unhappiness and dissatisfaction. Her heart was heavy with a combination of grief and anger, a sense of injustice that grew bigger every day.

She was like a keg of gunpowder awaiting contact with a lit fuse that was crawling ever closer.

Anza watched as her cousins horsed around in the gated backyard of their lodge. The ancient trees that surrounded the area seemed bigger and lusher. It added security to the walls that fenced their property. Laughter came louder as the older ones teased the younger ones to the point of annoyance. Immature tempers flared and her younger cousins shifted into their *Animus* out of frustration.

Her fourteen-year-old cousin, a rascal named Caleb, had been making fun of his sister's crush with Caleb's human friend. The twelve-year-old got so fed up with the antics of her older brother that she, Shelagh, transformed into a hyena. She snarled, growled, and snapped at her older brother. The elders laughed it off. However, their father intervened when Shelagh clamped her jaws on Caleb's calf muscle. He cried out in pain, unable to shake her off.

"Enough, Caleb! Shelagh, stop! You're drawing blood!"

Her uncle's stern voice arrested Shelagh's fury. She let go of her brother's leg and shifted back into her human form. She was teary-eyed out of wrath and frustration. Her brother's blood rimmed her lips.

Caleb glared at his sister. His hand pressed against the bleeding calf muscle that was almost torn off. The bite looked deep, but it would take less than an hour to heal. Her uncle gave Caleb a handkerchief to bind the wound. Shelagh stood with a sullen pout over her brother as she wiped her mouth on the neckline of her pink T-shirt dress and left a streak of a bloodstain on it. Her mother shrieked in exasperation. Blood was hard to remove from cotton fabric.

It's funny that what this household considers commonplace is probably horrific to a human.

Tomorrow, her family would venture into the woods, then shape-shift into a land-based predatory animal to hunt or merely to run around. And by habit, they would leave her alone in the house. It was like being the permanent designated driver when your family and friends went out to get wasted. She was the only one sober, and not by choice.

In the past, she didn't mind. The solitude afforded her time to write songs or poetry, read a book, or take photos. This time, the prospect of being left behind was distressing. She felt... excluded.

She didn't realise the pasted smile on her face had faltered and that she was fidgeting, until Xandrei nudged her side with his elbow.

"Should I hunt him down, Anza?" Xandrei asked, his expression calm. But his eyes bored into hers.

"Who?" She looked up at him, startled.

"Whoever it was who put such a grim frown on your face," he said. Xandrei touched her forehead and stroked the lines away.

"No one did this to me. I was just ... preoccupied."

She walked away and sat in one of the six rattan chairs that lined the verandah. She didn't want to talk about her restlessness, but Xandrei followed and sat beside her.

"Something is bothering you. And if I would hazard a guess, it's your 'otherness,' as you call it. You're back to thinking you're out of place, again," he said, his eyes on her intently.

The truth in his words stabbed at her heart. He read her right. Her discontent had bubbled over the surface. The desire to understand became overwhelming. "How does it feel, Xandrei?"

"Feel what?" Xandrei looked at her, a frown on his forehead.

"To shape-shift. But more to the point, why do you want to?"

It took Xandrei a long moment to respond. His eyes narrowed as he examined his own thoughts. "It's hard to articulate, Anz, but it's like a growing constriction. At first, you hardly notice it, but as the days go, you become uncomfortably trapped, until it becomes a driving need. So, when opportunities to let loose are available, we view it with full enthusiasm."

"Like removing your socks at the end of a long, hot day?" Her lame attempt at analogy made him laugh.

"Yes, actually." Xandrei was still laughing and shaking his head, "It's a very precise analogy, if I may say so."

In a strange way, she could relate to what he described. It was how she felt exactly—trapped. And she wanted to be free. Being unable to do so was driving her to the point of rebellion. Xandrei could remove his proverbial socks, while she could not.

"So, what's bothering you, Anza?" Xandrei's question was serious this time.

"I'm just tired, Xandrei." She avoided his gaze and picked on the loose rattan weave on the chair instead.

"Tired of being the only *Erdia* in a family of Aswangs?"

"I guess ..." It was the closest to admission she could give to him.

To reveal more might give him an idea of what had been brewing in her mind for months now. She wasn't ready to have anyone find out about it, as her plans had not crystallised yet.

Her reticence should have made it clear to Xandrei she was not ready to discuss what was in her heart, but he continued to stare at her with watchful intensity. Her cousin was worried. She patted his hand in reassurance, got up, and went inside to help her stepmother in the kitchen. She needed to go somewhere in which she wouldn't be the discussion or the focus of intense scrutiny.

Her Momstie was preparing the family's *sustenance* for tonight. It was a raw human liver. Her father kept her stepmother company and was gazing at her with soft, loving eyes. She took a seat beside her father, and together they watched Momstie portion the liver in neat, even slices.

Everyone would have a slice, except her. She had seen her parents and her extended family eat raw human viscera countless times, and she was used to the scene. It never bothered her before, but now, her 'otherness' intensified.

She absentmindedly picked up a napkin, twisted it into a thin strip, and fed it into the flame of the lighted cinnamon candle. The napkin burned in slow degrees; its cinnamon scent took on a burnt smell. The rising smoke mesmerised her and took her out of her own mind. It calmed the chaos in her. The curling smoke unravelled into nothingness. She wished the path to her decision would solidify in contrast.

On impulse, her stepmother's soft hands reached out and stopped her. Momstie never liked this habit. She considered it a nervous tick. Her father didn't mind it. He looked at it as a self-soothing habit. Her dad intuitively connected her tendency to set little things alight when she needed to sort out something in her mind.

With a sigh, she dropped the half-burned material at the base of the candle holder.

"Are you okay, Anza?" Her father's gaze was intent. "You're kindling again."

She nodded and said, "I'm okay, Dad. Just bored." She smiled at them both. She didn't want them to probe. Her stepmother had always associated smiles with a positive frame of mind. Hopefully, her Momstie could influence her father. But even she seemed unconvinced.

The voices of their family floated into the kitchen. Everyone was back and had congregated in the living room. It was *sustenance* time. Her Momstie walked off with the bowl of the human liver to where the family waited.

Her father kept looking at her, assessing her. He was wavering between asking her and waiting for her to open up to him. Half of her wanted him to press her, but her other half knew that his response would remain the same. He would, with a gentle and firm voice, tell her she was too young to know her own mind.

Her stepmother popped her head in through the door a moment later. "Anza, the ice delivery guy is coming tomorrow morning. Can you handle it while we're away?" It broke the tension in the air.

"Yes, Momstie," she replied, her tone cheerful.

She didn't mind the errand. It was something to do in a day full of nothing.

That night, in one corner of the living room, the male adults were playing cards while the females were engaged in gossip in the kitchen. The younger ones busied themselves with a board game in the breakfast lounge with more passion than could be expected from the game. Her teenage cousins were, like her, occupied with their gadgets.

Her rambunctious Uncle Heydar, a burly man whose clean-cut look was a complete opposite to his personality, went around the room singing in a deep baritone. The lyrics annoyed the women, but it entertained the young ones.

Her family filled the house with chatter, laughter, and activities. They kept each other entertained with their own antics and stories. Her family was content being themselves. They were complete.

It was beyond her to pretend to be upbeat. She kept to herself, with her headphones on. Music floated in her ears and drowned the hum of noise surrounding her. It helped as everyone was in full volume.

She sat at the corner chair and put up a pretence of chatting with her friends on the phone, looking at social media posts, scrolling past photos and articles, and watching videos. She was the picture of engrossed.

In reality, she was drowning in misery.

"You need not feel like an outsider, Anz. Don't set yourself apart. Choose to belong," Xandrei murmured on her forehead as he dropped an affectionate kiss on it. He left her to her own company and proceeded to his room.

His words made her sit up. It drove the clouds of melancholy from her mind. It sparked an idea of how she could end her inner turmoil.

Choose to belong. Of course!

I have always had a choice, but I never thought about taking the step to claim it.

And I might just have the perfect opportunity tomorrow.

Then, she took in her first freeing breath in months.

Early the following day, the sun was just rising, but their kitchen was already abuzz with activities. Every single one of her family members was preparing for their day out. They would spend the better part of it running in the woods in their *Animus,* hunting for deer, wild boar, or whatever took their fancy.

She would have preferred to stay in bed, to pretend that she was still asleep, so she wouldn't have to see them off. She didn't want to be discouraged from her plan. A knock on her door forced her to get up, to open it and engage with whoever was outside.

It was Xandrei.

"Your mom is calling for you. I think she wants to leave a few instructions."

She knew he didn't miss the signs that she barely slept, but was wise enough to keep his opinion to himself. Her cousin was the soul of diplomacy and tact.

She followed him out to the living room. Everyone was waiting and raring to go. Each one wore a tracksuit and a snapped-on bag strapped diagonally around one shoulder. The bag would keep their clothes and shoes while they were in their animal form, so it would be within easy reach when they'd return to their human forms.

"Anza, the payment for the ice is on the kitchen table. Have them put the twelve bags of ice cubes in the big freezer and the big block in the smaller one," her stepmother said.

"Yes, Momstie," she said.

Her heart had been picking up its beat as the seconds bled away. A plan had crystallised in her head last night, and being left alone was crucial to its execution. She noticed Xandrei had hung back. He didn't seem ready to leave like the rest. He could ruin her plan or remove her time advantage if he stayed.

"Are you not running out with everyone?" she asked.

"Are you okay being alone here, Anza?" He ignored her question, a frown on his face. "I don't want to leave you here by yourself."

"Oh, don't be silly," she said. She pushed him toward the rest. "I'll be fine." She added a lilt in her tone to reassure him.

"No, truly, Anz. I don't mind staying in today," he said.

He stared at her, trying to assess her sincerity. But she heard the reluctance in his voice. Xandrei loved running in the woods in his *Animus* since he never got to do it in the city.

"No, I won't let you pass up this chance to unleash your *Animus*. Don't worry. I'm okay," she insisted.

"Are you sure?" Xandrei's uncertainty was fading.

"Yes," she said, her tone emphatic. "I'll lock up behind you, so I'll be safe. Find me some wild guavas and we're even." She offered him her most reassuring smile. "Go and take off the proverbial socks."

He grinned at the quip, a touch of relief on his face. He dropped a kiss on her forehead, snapped on his own leather bag under his right arm and around his left shoulder, then headed out after the others.

Soon, everyone ran full tilt to the woods. They disappeared behind the thick cover of trees, their shouts of goodbye fading. She rushed to Xandrei's room to get his backpack. She would borrow it without his permission, as it was much better for travelling than her own. It would keep her hands free.

She found it on the chair by the bed, opened but still full. Her cousin, like herself, didn't bother to unpack. She dumped his stuff into a drawer in his wardrobe and slid it shut. A quick search of the many pockets of the bag ensured that she had taken out everything that belonged to him.

She took the backpack into her room and loaded the contents of her own bag into it: extra jeans, two t-shirts, a bath and face towel, toiletries. As an afterthought, she took one of Xandrei's t-shirts from his wardrobe. She would use that as her nightclothes, as she didn't bring her own during this trip. She was in a hurry to finish this before the iceman arrived. With house keys in hand, she took the backpack to the kitchen to wait for the ice delivery.

She had enough time to write her parents two notes. The longer one explained her plan. That should lessen their worry. But she placed it in her father's wallet, where he wouldn't find it as soon as they had returned.

She needed as much time as she could get to cover more distance before they looked for her. Her second, shorter note was a decoy—it said she went to the nearby creek to take some photos. This one she left on the kitchen table, propped against the coffee maker.

She had just finished having breakfast when she heard the approaching truck. Her heart pounded like a giant woodpecker. She stuffed the two water bottles and the sandwiches she packed into a plastic container into her bag.

Ten minutes later, the ice was loaded and stored in the freezer. She paid the men and asked them for a ride to the city. She told them she needed to buy something, and the old driver obliged. When asked how she was going to come back, she told them her father was going to pick her up.

With the house locked up and a last look around, she hurried out and got into the front with the driver and his assistant for a ride to the city. She wanted to cry, but held herself in check. She had chosen her path, and she needed to follow it. This was where she belonged—with the humans.

And she needed to learn to live as they do.

It surprised Veren when he picked up his phone to find it was Edrigu calling him. He just got home from the *Iztari* office. There must have been something he had forgotten to do.

"Hello, Sir?"

"Veren, can you come back to the office? I have a case for you." Edrigu's voice was even, but there was a sense of urgency in it.

"Yes, Sir. I'll be there in twenty minutes," he replied. He grabbed the backpack he had dropped on his bed just a minute ago.

Sixteen minutes later, he walked back into Edrigu's office. He was on a video call with a worried-looking gentleman.

"Take a seat, Veren," Edrigu said, then turned back to the gentleman on the screen. "Manuu, this is Veren. I think he is the perfect person to find your daughter. As we agreed, we will have more success in getting to her and convincing her to come back home if she doesn't feel threatened by the *Iztaris*."

The man on the screen looked at him closely. He seemed unconvinced. "He looks so young, Drig."

"Veren is twenty-three, well-trained, capable, and he has my complete trust, Manuu. The office will use both approaches so we can recover her in the quickest time possible. But I think Veren will be more successful at this," Edrigu said. "I will send a second team to cover other areas."

Edrigu's trust and open endorsement warmed his heart. But Veren kept his face impassive, his posture erect. He listened and kept all questions to himself. He wanted to receive the full instruction from his mentor before he asked them.

"Okay, I trust your judgment. You know best how to do this," Manuu said, his fatherly concern palpable. "But please hurry, Drig. She's only sixteen and an *Erdia*. She cannot protect herself."

"Don't worry, Manuu. We will get her back. She cannot have gotten that far. Now, send me a copy of her letter to you," Edrigu said. The man nodded and hung up.

Edrigu turned to him. "As you heard, I'm assigning you to this case. Manuu is a good friend of my father-in-law, and his daughter, an *Erdia*, ran away. We need to find her ASAP."

Veren nodded. "She ran away with her boyfriend?" he asked. Such cases were common.

Edrigu shook his head. "No, Manuu does not think so. According to him, Anza has been despondent for the past few months. She didn't seem to want to go in *Transit*. Her cousin said that she was feeling like she doesn't belong with them. She is the only *Erdia* in their closely knit family." Edrigu pushed a copy of the printed picture of the missing girl to him.

He picked up the photo and inspected her image. She was pretty. Long black hair, enormous eyes, innocent-looking face. Almost no makeup. Slim and petite. Around five foot three, at most. She looked younger than her sixteen years suggested.

Could this be an old photo?

She might look different now. Most sixteen year-olds he had met looked far older than their age because of how they dressed and all the makeup they would wear.

"Is the picture recent, Sir?"

"Yes, that was taken a month ago, on her sixteenth birthday," Edrigu replied. He printed the attachment that he'd just received from the email. It was the letter from the runaway girl to her father.

Edrigu read it aloud.

"Dear Daddy, please do not be angry. Do not worry. I went to live with the humankind where I belong. I love you and Momstie with all my heart, but I am not like you and the rest of the family. Time will separate us anyway since I do not have your long lives. Let me establish a root here this early. Allow me to find a family that will be like me, mortal and human, while I

have the time to do so. This is not forever. When you leave for your Transit, keep our post office box open. Send me a letter there so I know where I can get in touch with you. I will write to you to let you know how I am doing, that I am well. I love you and you will always be in my heart, Anza."

The antics of the runaway girl annoyed Veren. It was too bratty of her to leave her family on a whim, just because she was feeling insecure about being an *Erdia*.

To make her parents worry like that was just petty and inconsiderate. This girl did not know how it was to be an orphan, to be at the mercy of other people's generosity and kindness. She had no idea what it meant to be truly alone.

"How can she be the only *Erdia* in her family, Sir? Her mother should be like her, at least, right?" he asked.

Edrigu shook his head. "No. Her biological mother was human and died of complications during childbirth. She was referring to her stepmother, an *Aswang* who married her father when she was three."

"Okay. So, what do you want me to do, Sir? From what I understood, you want me to find her. Why me and not the *Iztaris*?"

He wanted to get the full picture, the objectives for this case, and what Edrigu expected him to achieve.

"The simple aim is to find her and bring her back. I believe she could relate to you better than my other *Iztaris* because Anza is closer to your age. We don't know for how long she has planned this. Her father said she's smart and organised, just a tad emotional. No doubt because she's still a teenager," Edrigu speculated. "So, if she had planned this well, she would be harder to find. She would factor in our presence and the possibility that the *Iztaris* will try to recover her. She might have prepared for that." His brows knitted in concentration.

"So, does it mean that when I find her, I must bring her back without telling her the *Iztari* office sent me?" he asked.

Edrigu smiled. "Without telling her that an *Iztari* found her."

His eyes widened with disbelief in what he heard, "*Iztari*? Am I one now?"

Edrigu's smile widened. "Yes, this is your first official case. You are the youngest *Iztari* in the history of this office."

"And if I don't find her? If I fail to bring her back?" He still couldn't believe it.

"Don't say that. And you won't fail. But even if you do, the outcome will not affect your appointment. When you return, you will begin your Iztari fight training. Welcome to the team." Edrigu held out his hand to shake his.

He clasped it tight. In his gratitude, he shook his mentor's hand with vigour. "I will not let you down, Sir," he said, too excited to say more.

Edrigu laughed. "I'm convinced you won't. So off you go. I gave you access to her file. Learn about her tonight, and you will be off to the area where she was last seen—Tuguegarao City. From there, you will figure out where she could have gone to hide."

"Okay, thank you, Sir. I appreciate this opportunity," he said, giddy and fired up at the same time.

With a quick *Iztari* salute, Veren left the office. He had to stop himself from jumping with joy. His blood was afire with excitement, ready to begin the preparation for the case.

He was confident he would find her and bring her home no matter what. Even if he had to sedate her the whole way back.

3

A NEW MISSION

Veren sat in a local coffee shop in Tuguegarao City. He didn't expect it to be so dense with low-rise buildings and people. The streets were typical of small cities: tight four lanes of concrete with almost no sidewalk. Old homes made of wood and stone and semi-new buildings made of glass and cement stood side by side along the road. Cars, jeepneys, and tricycles roamed the roads in a noisy parade, but there wasn't much traffic. Their pace was slow, but steady.

He was waiting for the man who delivered ice to the household of Anza Soledad, the last person who saw her. According to Manuu Soledad, the man gave Anza a ride to the city and dropped her off across the street. Then, he drove away. Still, Veren wanted to interview the man himself to see if he could pick more clues that the Soledads missed.

While he waited, he reviewed the digital file of his subject, everything about her on record and whatever else he had learned from her family. Aetheranza Soledad, or Anza, as her parents Manuu and Leire Soledad called her.

Interesting name.

If there was one dead giveaway for an *Aswang* parentage, it was their name. Their kind had a penchant for very ancient and unusual names for their children.

He was glad that his target had social media. As an *Erdia,* she had an advantage over *Aswangs* like himself—their Tribunal allowed her the leeway to create a social media account, for as long as there was no exposure of her *Aswang* relatives in it.

The photos of her showed a well-dressed young girl, fashionable even.

Her social media was as extensive as any average human teenager. She filled it with pictures of her travels, the books she read, movies she watched, places she dined in. There were brief clips of her singing songs she wrote herself. Her voice was sweet and clear, almost angelic.

The contents of her pages were engaging. She could easily be a popular influencer, if not for one specific thing—she did not have followers. It was like she designed her social media to be a journal; it was private and exclusive to herself. A record of the moments of her life, to be reviewed later in old age.

That struck a chord in him.

Her family said that she was good at school. She was passionate and strong-willed, but otherwise a dutiful daughter. Her father and stepmother gave him differing opinions on her personality.

According to Manuu Soledad, she was a book-loving, introverted girl. Reserved, observant, and content to be by herself.

Her stepmother disagreed—she claimed Anza loved poetry and music, but she craved affection and social interaction. It would seem her stepmother was correct in that aspect.

He thought about the other information provided to him by her family. He knew she carried little, as she came to the lodge with a small bag. And she borrowed her cousin's backpack. This meant that more than likely, she saw an opportunity to leave, that this was impulsive rather than a preplanned action.

"Mr. Albareda?"

An older man stood by his table. He looked to be in his mid-fifties, with sun-browned skin and thinning hair. He smelled of the sun, sweat and a tinge of coolant. The man had one arm darker than the other, which told Veren that he drove with the said arm propped on the window of the truck.

He nodded in acknowledgement, "Mang Andong?"

Veren stood up and offered his hand to the man, who shook it after a moment of hesitation. The older man's grip was limp and weak; the hand was dusty.

Mang Andong took the seat he offered, and after their order of coffee arrived, the man asked him, "What can I do for you, Mr. Albareda?"

"Our family asked me to look for my cousin, Anza. I believe you gave her a ride from the lodge and dropped her off here?"

This was the practised spiel he agreed on with the Soledad family.

"Yes. I told them that already," the man said with a nod.

As Manuu Soledad told him, Mang Andong seemed very open and cooperative. Veren's tablet was open and ready to note what Mang Andong would say. He was also taping their conversation, so he could review it later.

"Yes, Sir. My uncle told me you did. Did you notice anything about her?

Did she say or ask you about anything during the ride? Was she carrying anything with her?"

Mang Andong was quiet for a moment as he dredged his memory.

"No, I don't think so. She just said thank you when she first got into the truck and thank you when she got off. She saw this coffee shop and asked to be let off here. That's where I dropped her off." He pointed to the open space across from the coffee shop.

Veren looked out at it. There was nothing of note on that side of the road.

"Did she ask to be dropped off at this coffee shop in particular?"

"No ... not really ... I guess I just assumed. It was early morning, and this coffee shop is popular with the local teenagers. I thought she needed breakfast," he said.

Veren looked around and realised that Mang Andong was right. It was now getting filled with young people, coming in small groups of two or three.

"Did you see her go into the shop?" He wanted that clarified.

"No, but I looked at the side mirror and I saw her cross the street. That was it." The man took a careful sip from his styrofoam cup. "I hope you find her. She's so young," Mang Andong said, his face serious, his tone touched with concern.

"I hope so, too, Sir," he said. "Thank you for your help." He shook the kind gentleman's hand for the second time.

When Mang Andong left, Veren got out to the front of the coffee shop and surveyed the area. There was nothing of note until he realised there was a small travel agency three doors away. It was closed at the moment, but it could be worth looking into later.

When he got back to his table, the manager of the coffee shop hovered near it. He had requested to speak to her earlier, but she was not in yet. She was here now.

"My staff said that you were looking for me?"

A human female in her mid-thirties asked this with a slight frown on her face. She smelled of cinnamon, baked bread, and the coffee powder that dusted her right-hand sleeve. She must have ground some coffee beans and transferred them to a jar.

He nodded.

"Yes, I just want to ask some questions about my missing cousin. We believe she may have stopped here two days ago." He handed her the picture of Anza. "She looks like this."

The woman looked at it, trying to recall. "I'm sure I didn't encounter her—I'm good with faces. Approximately, what time do you think she might have come in here?"

"Around eight to eight-thirty a.m."

"My assistant may have come across her. I was on the afternoon shift two days ago. He won't be here until after lunch, around one p.m. You can come back to ask him later," she suggested.

"Thank you, I'll do that," he said, nodding.

"Anything else I can help you with?" she asked. Her unremarkable facial features changed into something pleasant as she smiled.

"Ah ... What time does that travel agency next door open?" he asked.

"Oh, you mean the Travel Bug? That office has been closed for a few months now. They transferred near the City Hall," she replied.

"Oh, okay. I'll check them out." He stowed his work tablet into his backpack, zipped it close, then slung it over his shoulder. "I will return here at one-thirty p.m., if that's okay."

"Sure. See you later," the manager said.

He left the shop and walked to the nearby Travel Bug to examine it. Faded stickers of airline logos and posters of tourist sites and destinations covered the dirty glass doors. There was a sign on the wall that said, 'WE TRANSFERRED TO OUR NEW LOCATION.' A map of the new address was included. He snapped a photo. This was where he was going next.

If Anza came here, she must have looked at the window display. He noticed the most prominently displayed picture was Batanes island, and remembered the destination shots she had posted on her social media.

The island might appeal to her poetic soul.

He had a gut feel about it, and was convinced she went to Batanes, but his mind told him not to jump to the conclusion. He didn't know her very well. Batanes Island might not meet her standards. She grew up in comfort and luxury. The island's rustic reputation might have dissuaded her.

He walked to the travel agency's new location, a mere four blocks away from their old one. Their new office was cramped, with mismatched tables and chairs, set back-to-back with each other. Two old metal file cabinets were set against the far wall. It had the usual chaos of phone ringing, a pair of dusty computers, and plastic inbox trays piled high with various documents. Though the staff accommodated his questions, the interview yielded nothing. Anza didn't go there at all.

He spent that morning walking around the area. He noted the structures he passed by: small stores, and some middle-sized houses in between commercial spaces. Anza would not take up residence here, he thought. It was too close to their mountain lodge. If she had wanted to disappear as she stated in her letter, she would go somewhere else. The city would only be her jump-off point.

He asked some locals who he encountered along the street where the bus station was, and they directed him to it. It was another couple of blocks away. He found a big, covered area with greasy, gravelled ground. The air stank of petrol and burnt tires. There were about ten buses parked. He noted the various destinations the bus company covered, and his spirit sank a little.

If she took one of the buses from here, she could be anywhere.

He interviewed the ticket officer, a man in a grimy brown shirt and a paunch. While the man was sure he had never encountered Anza, he was kind enough to call in the bus drivers and their assistants to ask if they saw her on any of their trips. No one had seen her. Of course, it was possible they just didn't remember seeing her.

"Maybe she went to Batanes," the ticket officer said out of the blue.

It made Veren's heart jump. "How do you get to the island from here?" he asked.

"You fly. There's no other way." The ticket officer shrugged. The man turned to the line of ticket buyers that accumulated behind him during their discussion.

Veren walked back to the coffee shop to have lunch and waited for the assistant manager. His thoughts were full of the possibilities of Batanes. He would need consent from Anza's parents to secure her flight information if she flew there. The airlines would never give it to him otherwise.

The coffee shop was full of diners when he arrived. A smiling manager welcomed him as he entered.

"You're back. My assistant will be here in half an hour. Will you have lunch while you wait?" she asked, her smile turned expectant.

"Yeah, that's the plan," he said, and smiled back in response.

"Good. Thank you for contributing to the local economy."

She looked around for a second and found him a seat in the shop's corner. He ordered coffee and meat pie.

Forty-five minutes later, the manager brought the assistant over and introduced him. He was a younger man, though older than him, with a pleasant, round face.

"Mr. Albareda, this is my assistant. Clyde, Mr. Albareda here wanted to talk to you about his cousin. He's looking for her and was wondering if she came here during your shift two days ago," she said in a manner of introduction.

He shook the man's hand, and they both sat down together at his table. He showed Clyde the picture of Anza, who looked at it, his brows knitted together.

"I think she came in here and bought a drink," he drawled.

The information raised his hopes.

"Did she say anything? Mention anything at all?" he asked, mentally crossing his fingers.

"Not to me. But she spoke to the guard briefly before she left. I think she was asking for direction," Clyde said.

"Can I speak to your guard?" Impatience rode him.

"Sure, let me call him." Clyde raised his hand and beckoned the guard over, who approached them.

"Yes, Sir?" The guard inclined his head to Clyde.

"Manong, do you remember this girl?" Clyde showed him the picture of Anza. "She was here two days ago."

"Oh yes, I remember." The guard's face brightened in recognition. "She asked me where the airport was, and how to get there," he replied.

Veren's heart jumped in excitement at his words. That was a solid lead.

"Did she say anything else, Sir?" he asked, wanting to make sure.

The guard shook his head.

With a thank you, he left them and hurried to the airport. He knew where it was. Half an hour later, he was in a queue at the ticketing office. As expected, the airline staff would not divulge details of Anza's flight. He expected it, but it was still frustrating. He would lose some time to secure the required affidavit.

With one last effort, he tried to get the cooperation of the counter staff. A female human who, he realised, was flirting with him. He gave her his best smile as he pleaded his case. She shook her head regretfully.

"I really can't—it's company policy. Besides, Mr. Albareda, she would have needed a written consent form from an adult to book her flight. She's a minor."

That information made him sit up.

"Is there any other way that she could have gotten a seat without the consent form?" He was so sure in his gut that Anza took this route. She would not travel by bus anywhere.

"Hmm, well, if she booked through a travel agency, then we can only check her in. And the only thing we would require during check-in is her ID," she said.

"Where is the closest travel agency?" he asked her, his own smile conspiratorial. Hers widened.

"There are three in the building next door," she replied. "Try the first one on the left," she added.

He took her hand and clasped it tightly in gratitude. "I will look for you when I check-in," he said.

She looped her hair behind her ear, looking up at him from behind her lashes. For a moment, he was thankful for the genes he inherited from his parents, whoever they were. To be decent-looking had definite benefits.

Veren rushed to the building next door and went to the one the ticket officer hinted at. He got lucky. He encountered the woman who handled Anza's airline reservation and ticket. She confirmed his hunch. Anza flew to Batanes Island that same day. She was lucky to have caught that day's flight by chance.

Veren booked himself for the following day. He was fortunate the low season made it possible for him to secure a seat, as flights to the island were only three times a week. The travel agent said that during peak periods, the seats would be booked to capacity weeks in advance.

With a satisfied sigh, he contacted Anza's father to inform him where he was going. It took him a few minutes to pacify Manuu Soledad and convince him not to fly to Batanes, as they do not know exactly where she was, and she might just bolt again if spooked.

He took a room in an inn close to the airport and to spend the rest of the day researching about the island Anza disappeared to and reviewing her files.

Batanes Island's population was too small to support an Aswang, much less a community. No viable source for *victus*, or fresh human viscera that he needed to stabilise his human form. With his consumption of *sustenance* yesterday, he would have five days to find and bring Anza home before he would need to fly back to the mainland to secure his *victus*.

It was best to focus on his target.

He needed all the information he could find out about Anza. His mission required him to approach her incognito. Her father didn't want her to be returned by force or by guile to the family, he wanted Anza to come home voluntarily. Manuu Soledad was afraid that if forced, she might run away again, never to be found.

She could not know that he was an *Iztari*. Based on what he found out about her, she could be wilful. This meant he needed to be as cunning as he could be to convince this girl to come home on her own accord. Sedating her into unconsciousness was not an option.

It's a pity... That would be easier.

Anza looked around at her rented room. The room was neat, with pastel-coloured walls, floral curtains and bedspread. Everything about it appealed to her, especially the beautiful garden view and the cosy verandah. The breeze that wafted from the open door brought the fragrance of jasmine, which covered the garden below.

She really liked it here. It made her feel safe and at home, but she would have to leave this place to find cheaper accommodation and a job.

When I find a stable job, I will come back to this room and rent it for a day as a reward. Hopefully, it won't take long.

She needed to find a job before she ran out of cash. The money she had withdrawn from the ATM two days ago would not go very far. She would have taken more if there was no maximum limit, and she didn't want to make another withdrawal here, as that would pinpoint her location. Her father would trace her through her credit card and ATM use. Paying in cash was the way to go for her.

She missed her father and stepmother. And she was guilt ridden for ruining their holiday. By now, her parents would be frantic. And for sure, they had already deployed the *Iztaris* after her. Hopefully, she had covered her tracks well enough. She hoped that when they'd find her, she would be settled and have a good job to convince her father that they could leave her behind to live on her own and be independent.

With a heavy heart, she picked up her backpack. Another day of looking for a job. A glance in the mirror startled her, her look still unfamiliar. She had her hair dyed a lighter brown, cut shorter just past her shoulders from its usual waist length. She styled it in a more sophisticated way.

The negative feedback from the jobs she applied to was mostly because of her age. No one wanted to accept her because she looked too young. Today, with her new hairstyle and the full make-up, she looked older. Hopefully, this would also help hide her from the *Iztaris*.

On her itinerary today: quick breakfast first, then an entire day of job hunting.

Four hours later, she was unsuccessful, tired, and demoralised. She didn't have any experience and couldn't provide any references from any of the locals. They gave her pitying looks, advice to go home and focus on her studies, and sent her off. No one wanted to hire a strange girl who looked like she had never done a day's work in her life.

Her footsteps were as leaden as her heart as she sat down on a plastic chair outside a small, local eatery. She was hungry, thirsty, and close to tears. A prepubescent girl approached her with a laminated menu.

"Miss, what would you like to order?" she asked, without glancing at her, her focus on the small pad of paper in her hand, pen poised to write.

Anza took a deep breath to steady her emotions and glanced at the menu. She had scrambled eggs and toast for breakfast, which was not adequate fuel for all the walking she did this morning. She ordered noodles and a boiled egg for protein. She must learn to live and eat simply until she could afford it.

Her food arrived, served hot by the same girl. The server also placed a cold, light brown beverage on the old, Formica-covered table.

"I didn't order this ..." she began. She wanted to keep to her budget, to stretch her cash as far as she could.

"It's free with every order. It's house iced tea." The girl informed her, her tone dispassionate, and then left her to usher in a couple who just arrived.

Anza mumbled her thanks to the girl's departing back. She felt overwhelmed by a stroke of good fortune, and a wave of self-pity followed in its wake. Her chest tightened as she tried to control the expanding pain that bloomed in her heart. Hot tears pricked at the back of her eyes. She breathed deep and tucked into her noodles to stem the desire to cry.

But she couldn't stop the tears from running down her cheeks. She was truly alone, in a situation she made for herself, one she still believed was necessary for her future.

It was hard to chew when her jaw was taut with the effort to keep her sobs in. She was thankful that the noodles, aided by the broth, just slid down her throat. The hot broth warmed her stomach and soothed even her throbbing heart.

It fortified her.

She took a deep, shuddering breath. Crying would not help her situation. She wiped the tears on her face, resolved to continue her search for a job. She forced herself to finish her noodles and the egg. Her appetite left her two spoonfuls ago, but she needed to eat and didn't want to waste food. She had the rest of the afternoon to accomplish her immediate goal. She needed fuel.

With renewed faith in herself, she considered what her new strategy would be. This time she needed to find a reference, and she had an idea who she would approach. A glance in her hand mirror told her she needed to fix her face. Her mascara smudged when she wiped her hand across her eyes, and her tears created tracks on her cheeks. She didn't know how to fix her makeup without her kit.

She got up and proceeded to the ladies' room.

Ten minutes later, fresh-faced and determined, she went back to her inn. She needed her landlord's help. Hopefully, Mrs. Bassig would be generous enough to extend her a helping hand.

Veren wanted something to perk him up. His flight was an unpleasant experience. It was delayed and the voyage itself was bumpy. He was hungry, and he lost time. Anger borne out of frustration tightened his chest, but it was useless to fume about the wasted morning.

He would have to make up lost ground in the afternoon.

The outdoor seating in the coffee shop provided an ambience that suited the area and his need for a calming influence. It reflected the spirit of the island—quaint, cosy, and relaxed. The wide cream and brown awning overhead softened the sun's glare, and the breeze that ruffled his hair was lukewarm.

He sat outside to drink his coffee and was savouring the first sip when he noticed a young woman across the street. He watched her walk to the local eatery, her shoulders slumped, head bowed—her posture telegraphed defeat and misery.

Seeing a familiar emotion in another person called out to some part of him.

He averted his eyes to shake away the sentiment that resurfaced in him, because he had no time to feel sorry for a stranger. He had a job to do, and he needed to focus. To find his target might take more than the time he had on his hands, and he did not want to fail.

But he found himself drawn to the woman. He could see how upset she was. Her shoulder-length hair could not hide the tautness in her jaw as she fought against her pain, or the movement in her throat as she swallowed down her emotions. Tears glistened on her cheeks as she hunched over her bowl of noodles. He noticed the struggle in her as she tried to control her shoulders from shaking.

And his heart contracted in sympathy.

Then her spine straightened, her chest expanded as she drew a breath. Fascinated, he saw her pull herself together and wipe the tears with the back of her hand like a child. He heard the deep indrawn breath as she fortified her courage. And he could not help but admire the way she recovered so fast from whatever devastation she had suffered earlier. She looked less like a child and more a woman at that moment.

He wished, for an instant, that his quarry, Anza Soledad, was as evocative as this unknown woman across the street.

She continued eating with the grim determination of a soldier who decided to plough into battle. Her fighting spirit showed clearly in the straightened line of her back and the stubborn jut of her jaw. Then she stood up and went inside the local eatery, presumably to fix herself. He waited with anticipation for her to come out again. For a second, he thought he lost her through a backdoor and was disappointed, but when she came out, his heart stopped.

Her face wiped clean, her hair tied in a ponytail, he recognised who his crying lady was—Anza Soledad.

His target.

I found her.

A thrill of satisfaction ran through him.

Veren jumped up and followed her as she crossed the street. He kept a decent distance between them, making sure that she was always within sight.

Her eventual destination was an inn that looked like a renovated ancestral home. She walked into the lobby with purpose and familiarity. She approached the counter. The staff seemed to recognise her, their manner familiar, their smiles welcoming. He saw her sit on the couch. She looked like she was waiting for someone.

He didn't want to book a room until he was sure that she was staying here. He took a brochure, chose a seat close to her, and pretended to peruse the material. Then an idea struck him. He turned to her with a slight smile.

"Miss, are you staying here?" he asked. "How are the rooms?" He kept his tone and facial expression neutral and mild, so as not to alarm her.

"It's nice here. Clean, secure, and the staff are friendly," she replied, her expression polite, but not inviting any further exchange. Natural restraint ruled her interaction with strangers.

Her parents trained her well. She didn't confirm if she was staying here.

A buxom older woman, her grey-tinged hair set in a loose bun, came out from behind the reception counter and drew Anza's attention. The front office staff pointed at Anza. The woman smiled from a distance and beckoned Anza over.

Anza stood up and hastened towards her. He followed on the pretext of inquiring for a room. Their conversation reached his ears clearly.

"Anza, what can I do for you?" The older woman asked, her gaze soft.

"I have a favour to ask, Mrs. Bassig," Anza replied. Her tone was hesitant, almost shy.

The older woman looked surprised, but smiled just the same. She invited Anza into her office. Anza complied and followed Mrs. Bassig to the room behind the reception desk. The door closed on his ability to eavesdrop.

He trusted his instinct and booked himself a room. The only way for the manager to know Anza, and for Anza to have enough confidence to ask for a favour from the older woman, was because she was staying here.

He took his time filling up the registration form. And when he got his key and Anza had not come out yet from the office, he asked the front desk staff for tourist site suggestions. With the tourism brochures in hand, he stood by the counter and made a show of studying them with careful intent.

A few minutes later, Anza came out of the office with a bright smile and sparkling eyes. She looked both relieved and excited. She thanked Mrs. Bassig profusely.

"So, when do you want to start, Anza?" the older woman asked.

"It's up to you, Mrs. Bassig, but I'm ready to start anytime."

"Why don't you check out the place that I recommended to you first? Get yourself settled and then we can start your training on Monday. Iza, the one you will replace, will not be available to train you till then," Mrs. Bassig said.

"Okay, Mrs. Bassig. I'm very grateful. I don't know how to thank you," Anza said. There was a slight tremble in her voice.

"Do your best, Anza—that will be the thank you I want," Mrs. Bassig said, and with an affectionate pat on her shoulder, the older woman left Anza, who stood teary-eyed as if she still could not believe her luck.

"Congratulations!" Veren said in a soft tone, startling her.

"Excuse me?" she asked, blinking her tears away. "It looks like you got the job," he said, pointing back towards the reception area. At her silence, he added, "Sorry, I can't help but overhear. I was checking in."

"Oh ... Yes. I did," she replied. Her earlier relief coloured her voice and tinted her smile.

"Well, I took your recommendation and got a room here. So, thank you," he said.

"You're welcome. How long are you staying?" Her response was automatic, out of politeness rather than from genuine interest.

"I don't know yet." He shrugged. It was the truth.

"Long holiday?" she asked. Her question, this time, carried a tinge of curiosity.

"Yes, maybe," he replied. "How about you?" He wanted to keep his lies to her to a minimum. Perhaps he could pick up some more information about her.

She just gave him a sad, brief smile. A spark of fear and determination glowed in her eyes. The flash of pride and protectiveness rose in him, and it took him by surprise.

"So, I'll see you around?" she asked, but her tone carried no expectation. She was being polite once again.

"Yes, definitely. Hopefully this afternoon?" He turned on the charm now, his smile friendly and harmless. Now that he found her, she was in his keeping, and would remain under his protection until she returned home.

"This afternoon?" she asked, a slight frown appeared on her brow.

"Yes, I would like to invite you for coffee. For helping me find good accommodation," he said with a deeper smile.

"Ah ... I'm not sure." Her rejection sounded like an automatic reaction. "Um ... I need to check out a place that Mrs. Bassig recommended to me," she said, reluctant and regretful at the same time. Her smile dimmed.

"Can I come with you?" he asked. "I have nothing else to do ..." When she didn't respond, he said, "I would like to explore the area, mingle with the locals, and I don't want to look like a loser by walking alone ...".

She hesitated for a while, regarding him with careful intent. He kept his expression benign and waited for her reply. Finally, she gave him a shy smile and nodded. "Okay."

He couldn't hide his obvious delight at her response. "So, what time are we leaving?"

"I was thinking of doing that now," she said.

"Well then, let's go," he said, and held her elbow.

She threw him a speculative glance. He could see her prudent side warred with her desire to socialise, to connect with another human being. He gave her another reassuring, friendly look, to tip the balance in his favour.

She returned it, and walked towards her destination. He took a relaxed step beside her, pleased with this minor success.

4

CROSSING OF PATHS

Anza was very aware of the man walking beside her. She watched him through her peripheral vision. He was lithe and fit, like an athlete. If she was to guess, he would be a swimmer, based on the width of his shoulders. And he was tall; her head came up to the middle of his chest. His skin had a slight tan, a sign that he enjoyed spending time outdoors. And while he seemed relaxed in his manner, he moved with a certain controlled gait that reminded her of soldiers.

"My name is Veren—Veren Albareda," he said.

He offered his right hand to her. She stopped, looked up at him, then grasped his offered hand. His grip was warm, his hand big enough to envelop both of hers. Manual tasks had roughened his palm.

"I'm Anza," she replied.

Her voice faltered as she took a full look at his face. His eyes were almond-shaped, their colour an odd light brown with amber flecks, framed by straight brows that almost didn't taper at the ends. There was a slight, natural bump on his nose. His lean cheeks and square jaw reminded her of her father. There was nothing remarkable in the individual features of his face, but combined, the result was striking.

It was hard to guess how old he was. He seemed both young and mature, but if she would warrant a guess, he would be in his early twenties.

"Do you have a last name, Anza?" he asked. His lips curved in a crooked smile.

The sight of it made her retract her earlier description of his facial features. His lips were remarkable. They were full, yet masculine. Most of the men in her family had a thin upper lip.

"Sol ... Soledad," she replied. She was uncertain if it was a good idea to tell him her last name. She glanced at him again, gauging her own instinct about him. He looked too young to be an *Iztari*.

"I'm very pleased to meet you, Anza Soledad," he said. He seemed pleased with her response.

"Likewise," she replied.

He covered her hand he still held with the other, and shook it once again. She pulled her hand away—his warm grasp made her fingers tingle. She resumed their walk to mask her nervousness. He fell beside her with effortless grace, shortening his gait to match hers.

"So, are you from this region?" he asked.

She shook her head. "No, I'm from the ... south," she replied. She didn't want to reveal more information about herself.

"South, like Batangas? Or like Cebu?" Veren's eyebrow raised in inquiry.

"Not as far south as Cebu. Closer to Batangas," she replied. She braced herself for more questions, but Veren surprised her by dropping the topic.

"So, where are we going?" he asked instead.

"Ah, it's a bed space place. Mrs. Bassig recommended it," she replied.

"Bed space? You're no longer staying at Mrs. Bassig's?" He seemed alarmed at the thought.

"I can't afford to stay there. My future salary will not be enough to cover my cost of living." It was painful to accept that she was no longer the Anza Soledad who never had to worry about basic survival needs like food and shelter.

Veren touched her elbow, halting her step. He stared at her, as if trying to understand why she needed to work.

"Are you in trouble, Anza?"

His question startled her.

She shook her head. "No," she replied. She didn't know what else to say.

"Okay, but if you are, let me know. I'm your bodyguard, after all," Veren said, his tone light, almost joking, but she could detect an underlying seriousness in his statement.

She didn't know what to think, so she walked on. They found the house exactly where and how it was described by Mrs. Bassig. It was a medium-sized structure, made of stone and wood, old but well maintained, with a colourful garden in front and surrounded by a white wooden fence made of driftwood.

Low, thick bushes with tiny red and white flowers reinforced the fence. There were clucking chickens roaming and pecking around the garden, and a small triangular roof-like structure on the ground with a rooster perched on top of it. The wooden gate was low, with a number 32 painted on it.

The thin, elderly owner named Teresa ushered them into her living room. The windows to the house were all open, the short flowery curtains that swayed with the breeze providing privacy to the residents. The house smelled of fried bananas and ginger tea. Her furniture was made of similar driftwood material, upholstered in green floral fabric.

"Hija, I have no available bed space today. The next available one would be on Tuesday. I can reserve that for you if you want to wait," she said after she set the ginger tea and bananas covered in crispy batter in front of them.

Her heart sank. A week away. That would mean she would have to spend more of her money on her accommodation, something she would rather not do.

Could there be other options?

"Do you know of any other bed spaces here?" At least a temporary one until Tuesday.

"My brother operates one. It's in the next barangay, so it's quite a walk from your workplace. Plus, he accepts male bed-spacers, too, so you might not feel comfortable with that." The elderly woman glanced at Veren beside her; she seemed to gauge what their relationship was.

Veren's gaze was intent on her. His face was impassive, but Anza sensed that he didn't like the idea of her sleeping in proximity with strange men. She didn't like it either. However, the landlady was looking at her expectantly, waiting for her response, and she didn't know what to say.

"Manang Teresa, can you give us the phone number of your brother? And yours as well. Anza needs to think about it," Veren suggested. The old lady nodded and wrote the numbers down on a piece of paper, then handed it to him.

They took their leave and strolled back to their inn. Her mind juggled her options. A week's stay at her current accommodation could cover five months of rent in the bed space place.

Maybe I could stay at the other bed space for a week and then move to Manang Teresa's after?

She was so preoccupied with her own thoughts that she didn't notice when Veren pulled her to a small cafe. At her puzzled look, he pointed at the sign and said, "Coffee, remember? I owe you one."

"Okay." She allowed herself to be pushed gently to a chair.

"What would you like?"

"Mocha or latte," she replied.

He nodded and approached the counter.

Moments later, Veren came back with two lattes. They sipped their respective cups in silence. Out of habit, she pulled out a paper napkin from the holder, twisted it into a thin strip, and fed it into the flame of the lit candle on the table. Calm settled in her as she watched the smoke spiral upwards. With it, the earlier dismay for the situation.

Veren set his cup down. It startled her out of her reverie and made her drop the napkin on the table. She looked up to find his eyes on her.

"Anza. I hope I don't appear a presumptuous prick to you ... Granted, we just met, and I still fall in the category of a stranger, but ..." His statement faded, and an awkward silence followed.

"But?" She wasn't sure what he wanted to say.

"I'm not comfortable with you sleeping in a house where there are strange men. It sounds dangerous," he said, face serious.

She didn't know what to say to that, given that she had the same concern. "It doesn't seem so different from having a room in an Airbnb like Mrs. Bassig's." Her defence to justify the plan was half-hearted.

"It's different. You get your own room in Mrs. Bassig's. In a bed space, you'll end up sharing a room with others. Hopefully, all women, but you might be unlucky enough to bunk in with a man. How will you be able to sleep when you have valuables to guard?"

To hear him say it made her feel worse that she had even considered staying there for a week.

"Veren, an extra week at Mrs. Bassig's is equivalent to five months of rent at Manang Teresa's. I think I can handle a—a week." Her voice faltered at the look of alarm on Veren's face.

After a moment, he said, "I have a suggestion."

"What is it?"

"If I hire you as my tour guide for a week at the cost of what you pay for your current room at Mrs. Bassig's, would you do it?" he asked.

"What? I'm not qualified to be a tour guide ... I'm also a visitor here. I just arrived and I don't know the area at all." She said this weakly—his offer had her heart pounding with hope.

"Okay, as a travel companion then," he suggested.

His offer was perplexing, and his persistence baffled her. "But ... why? Why are you helping me?"

"Why not?" He shrugged. "To travel with friends is always better than travelling alone," he reasoned.

She looked at him, trying to find a reason to say no. His offer was so tempting as a much-needed lifeline.

"But I can't afford the cost of travelling with you. The transportation, the food, the entrance fees ..." The reality of her financial status dampened her hope.

"I'll take care of all that. So, don't worry," Veren said, confidence reassuring.

"It seems... unfair to you. Taking me with you as you go around would double your cost, then add what you would pay me every day. It sounds excessive." She was unwilling to take advantage of him, even if his offer was god-sent.

Veren considered what she said for a moment, thinking.

"Okay then, while we're travelling together, would you consider telling me about you? I'll pay for your stories and that would cover the cost of the travel. Your daily fee will be for the companionship." The matter-of-fact way he explained this made it sound like a fair trade.

"What happens if you tire of my company, or I bore you with my stories?"

"That's a risk I am willing to take ... So, is that a deal?"

There was no reason to decline his offer. It would solve her problem, and she had another week of staying in relative comfort. As much as she wanted to ignore it, he had been pleasant so far, and he intrigued her.

She took a deep breath and decided to trust him. She offered her hand, and they shook on it.

"When do we start?" she asked.

"Today is good," he said. There was a crooked smile on his lips and a twinkle in his eyes.

"No, it's almost the end of the day. You won't get your days' worth. Why don't we officially start tomorrow?"

"Well, I'm already enjoying your company now, so I'd be the one taking advantage of you if we don't count today," he said.

"Take today as an activity between friends. It costs you nothing." It was the least that she could give him.

"So, can we spend dinner as friends as well?" he asked.

She felt the full blast of his charm, and a frisson of thrill went through her. In her panic, she nodded. Her throat was a little constricted for words.

Veren felt pleased with himself. He secured Anza's safety and gained her trust. Now, he found a way to get to know her and discover the best way to convince her to go back home to her parents.

He debated whether he should tell her father that he had located Anza. But Manuu Soledad might preempt his plans and ruin his chance of fulfilling his mission in full. However, he would have to say something to Mr. Soledad later, or the man might just fly in and show up unannounced. He settled on sending him a text message to inform him that he was still looking for her. He got lucky when he chanced upon her so quickly—he would take advantage of that.

Edrigu Orzabal was a different matter. He didn't want to lie to his mentor. Edrigu knew he was flying to Basco. His mentor would assume that he was still looking for her today, and if he didn't call, Edrigu would assume there was nothing yet to report. Veren had a few hours before he needed to call him.

For now, he had to shower and change. He would meet Anza at six p.m., which gave him two hours to prepare for eventualities. While he had consumed enough human viscera to last him a week, it didn't hurt to cover all the bases. He must convince Anza before the week was out, because he would need to be back on the mainland to get his *sustenance*.

He sat down with his tablet to record the details of the day, his observations and what he learned about her so far. Anza was not what he expected. He assumed she would be bratty, and half-expected her to give up and go home before he could find her.

It was the foremost reason he was in a hurry to beat her to it. To find her was not enough of an accomplishment. He wanted to be instrumental to her decision to go home, so there would be no doubt he did his job to its fullest extent. He wanted to earn the resolution of the case, rather than get it resolved by default.

Based on what he saw from her yesterday, before he realised it was her, he thought she had grit and the fighting spirit to continue. This girl would not give up, and if he hadn't been lucky yesterday to have been in the right place at the right time, he probably would have run out of time looking for her.

Anza was still in a daze. She was breathless with the idea of having dinner with Veren. Her pulse hadn't slowed down even after she showered on autopilot. She wasn't even sure if she shampooed her hair. She relied on the texture of her tresses as she wriggled her fingers through, drying them upside down under the blast of the electric fan.

No boy, human or *Aswang*, had ever expressed this much interest in her before. And Veren was no longer a boy. She was unused to the attention shown to her by an attractive man, and it created this heady emotion.

Come to think of it, it's similar, although a little more intense than what I feel for Xandrei.

It was different because Veren was a stranger. He was just a decent guy who was sorry for her, and maybe she reminded him of his sister.

I don't even know if he has a sister.

With a sigh, she straightened up and flipped her hair back. The electric fan had dried it enough. The method gave her hair the body she wanted. She brushed it back into place, then secured the front pieces behind her head with a barrette. The baby hairs that grew around her face refused to be tamed without the aid of hairspray, so she gave up. This would have to do.

She couldn't behave around Veren like her giggly classmates whenever they saw a boy. It would be humiliating. She would embarrass him and make their daily interactions awkward.

I must regard him as an older brother.

She would treat him like how she treated her cousin Xandrei, since there was nothing different in how Veren treated her from how her cousin did.

She spent the next couple of hours on an emotional seesaw between diverting herself from getting too excited about the dinner to imagining different scenarios, then chastising herself.

After a week, Veren could leave Basco, and she would have to focus on her goal to be independent. His friendship, the first-ever outside of her limited sphere, one formed naturally, was a good beginning to her new life. Hopefully, the memories that would come out of it would be worth remembering for the years to come.

She felt human already.

Veren was already waiting in the lobby when she arrived. It surprised her because she had left her room early. She was expecting to wait for him. He waved at her from the distance. A wide, delighted smile was on his face. He had changed into faded grey jeans and a dark blue T-shirt under a grey hoodie that was unzipped at the front. He looked carefree and young.

"Hungry?" he asked as she came closer.

She nodded in response. It was the best explanation for her being early. And it also explained why he was earlier than her. He must have been hungry, too.

He took her hand and pulled her with him. Like an older brother pulling his younger sister along. He walked her to a motorcycle parked at the side of the entrance and handed her a helmet.

She hesitated, unable to hide a slight alarm at the idea. A jolt of uncertainty struck her heart. She had never ridden a motorcycle before. It looked dangerous. She met Veren's gaze. The helmet was still in his hand as he waited for her to accept it. His happy expression was both encouraging and challenging.

Take a chance, Anza. It's just a motorbike ride.

With a deep breath, she took the helmet and put it on under Veren's approving gaze. He fastened the strap under her chin. Her sense of bravery kicked up a notch, and the anticipation of the motorbike ride replaced some of her fears.

As she straddled the bike behind him, she didn't know where to attribute the added thrill that coursed through her, whether it was from the upcoming ride or the unfamiliar sensation of being pressed close to a male body—one that belonged to someone not related to her.

"Hold tight, Anza. And relax. Just lean on me. Don't worry, I'm an expert at motorbikes. I won't let you fall," Veren said over his shoulder.

He must have noticed my death grip around his middle.

"Ready?" he asked.

She nodded.

With a small jolt, they zoomed into the road towards the mystery destination of their dinner. She forgot to ask him where they were going.

Five minutes into the ride, she relaxed. Veren did not lie: he *was* an experienced rider. After the initial starting jolt, the drive smoothened into a fluid motion. The hum of the engine became noticeable to her, together with the feel of Veren's firm and warm back.

It was a brief ride, but with the newness of the experience, it felt drawn out yet fleeting. The surrounding sights went past in a blur of old houses, native vegetation, and people. Her focus was on the sensations rather than the view.

When they reached their destination, it came as a surprise. She was expecting a simple neighbourhood eatery. Instead, the place looked like a must-go for tourists.

Perched atop a hill, the restaurant offered a stunning view of Vayang Rolling Hills. In the waning light, she could see the building was made of packed earth, bamboo, and wood. It had the thatched roof characteristic of the native Ivatan houses in the area. The flowering plants and green hedges that surrounded the restaurant compound gave it a homey yet magical quality.

The sea breeze that rolled from the ocean cooled the place. There was a small blackboard by the entrance that had the specials for the day: grilled flying fish served on Kabaya leaf, and coconut crabs cooked in coconut milk.

The wait staff ushered them to a table near the window. There were about eight tables in the restaurant, four already occupied. The air had a slight flavour of turmeric, coconut, banana leaves, and sea air.

"I don't know about you, but I find today's specials hard to resist. Do you like seafood?" Veren asked, his eyes gleaming.

"I love seafood. I've never had flying fish and coconut crab before," she said, unable to curb her own excitement.

"Okay, let's get those, and ... some Luñis," he said.

"What's a Luñis?" Everything on this island cuisine-wise was new to her, but that couldn't have put her off, as nothing could be stranger than what her *Aswang* family partook in regularly.

"It's an indigenous dish of preserved pork, usually served fried, crispy, and paired with turmeric rice," he replied.

"How do you know all this?" It amazed her that he knew so much about the island in such a short time.

"Internet searches. I do them before I visit any place," he said, a smug look on his face. "Did you not do the same before you came here?"

"No. My decision to come here was ... an impulse."

"Why? What brought you here? It seems such a long way away from where you were from—the south close to Batangas."

"I'll tell you tomorrow when I'm officially in your employ." She would avoid answering questions about her identity for as long as she could and evade it with every means she had.

He looked at her, eyes narrowed in speculation, then he shrugged his shoulders. "Fair enough."

He got back to perusing the menu. She did the same.

Veren was glad he had already chosen what he wanted to eat when he saw the blackboard earlier. He wasn't reading the menu—he was trying to sense Anza's mood. She came out relaxed, fresh-faced and every bit the sixteen year-old that she was. There was something about her that appealed to him —a mixture of vulnerability and fire. She made him want to tease her, challenge her to take chances, and keep her safe and take care of her in equal measure.

She was reluctant to get on the motorbike earlier. He expected her reaction. It was not the safest form of transportation for most people, and she was a sheltered young woman who was used to the chauffeured, four-wheel kind. He liked bikes but would have rented a car for her if there was one available. It was the spark of courage he saw in her earlier that made him goad her. He had a feeling she would accept his challenge.

And he was right.

He was glad to have chosen this restaurant. Anza did not expect it. He smiled to himself when he recalled her expression. She liked this place. He noticed that his efforts to develop her trust in him had kept her off-balanced and it was proving effective. She needed to reach the point where his words would have enough sway in her decisions. She needed to heed his advice to come home voluntarily.

"Are you ready to order?" he asked.

She said she was hungry earlier. She only had noodles for lunch, and because she was upset then, she might not have eaten well. As far as he knew, she only had a cup of coffee aside from that. She smiled and nodded at him, putting her menu down. He beckoned the server over and ordered both the coconut crab and the flying fish, plus an order of Luñis.

"What would you like to drink?" he asked.

She didn't respond. Instead, her eyes were full of speculation.

"Will you order a beer?" she asked.

"For you? No, you're too young." He wasn't about to corrupt her with bad habits.

"Not for me, for you," she said, her upper lip curled in mild annoyance.

That made him smile. That one action displayed sparks of her inner fire.

"Well, yeah, I am having a beer ..."

"I'd like to take a sip out of yours ... Just for the experience." Her tone was hopeful, like a little girl asking for ice cream, but the gleam of naughtiness in her eyes was adult.

"Ah, I guess that's okay. I'll give you a sip. But what would you like to drink?"

He felt pleased and somewhat guilty for enabling Anza, for allowing himself to be used to test her new independence, to sharpen her claws. On the plus side, this would deepen her trust in him.

"I will have Kalamansi juice," she said after perusing the drink menu.

The server came with their drinks five minutes later. She was looking expectantly at his beer, which arrived ice cold. Her glance flew to his face when he made no move to hand the bottle over. With a chuckle, he pushed it to her.

An excited giggle escaped her as she lifted the bottle to her lips too quickly. He didn't have time to warn her as she took a huge gulp and swallowed the icy liquid. She spluttered and snorted the beer out of her mouth and nose, her body wracked with coughs, her eyes watering.

He found it impossible not to laugh even as he patted her back gently and gave her his handkerchief. Anza glared at him through teary eyes. As her cough subsided, she took a sip of water from the glass he handed her. He held the bottom to control the amount that she could take. She didn't resist. That pleased him. Already, she trusted him more.

The server hovered with a rag to wipe the splatter of beer on the table, but he motioned him away. He wiped the table dry with the napkins himself. He didn't want Anza to be more embarrassed. Her cheeks were delightfully red as she looked across from him and saw the people on the next table watching her. The flush of colour spread to her face and neck.

"Are you alright?" he asked as she dabbed her cheeks and eyes with his handkerchief. Her coughing had stopped.

She nodded, looking mortified still. He grinned at her. He couldn't help it. She looked so adorable with her red-rimmed eyes, the flush of high colour on her face and neck, defiance in her jawline. She looked incandescent with life.

"What do you think of the beer?" He tried to keep his face straight.

"It was painful, especially up the nose." Her tone and expression went deadpan. Her lips quivered, and for a split second, he thought she would cry. His gaze flew to her eyes in alarm. Mirth sparkled in her eyes as she tried to stop herself. Their eyes met, and they both burst out laughing.

"You weren't supposed to snort the beer, Anza," he said after he calmed down, in a tone reminiscent of a professor.

"The beer had a mind of its own. I wanted it to go down my throat, but it travelled up instead," she said. The humour of the incident lingered in her gaze.

As he looked at her face, the inner fire he saw in her seemed to have set her alight from within. She glowed. At that moment, he had a glimpse of what she could look like when she had grown into her womanhood. And it kindled something in him that expanded in his chest.

He felt glad that he was here, with her, tonight.

Their server arrived with their food, breaking the electrified moment. The aroma of the grilled flying fish came with the fragrance of heated banana leaves and a hint of citrus. Their crabs looked deliciously rich, the orange shells bathed in coconut cream. The golden-brown pork dish looked crunchy and mouthwatering.

They tucked into their food in relative silence. Anza was hungry as he watched her eat with complete absorption and enjoyment. She savoured a new dish with singularity—she would put it in her mouth, close her eyes, inhale deep, then hum under her breath as if she was engaging all her senses in one go. Her eating habits entranced him.

She didn't just eat her food, she experienced it.

This revealed more than words ever could as to why she rebelled and ran away. Her thirst to experience life to the fullest was deep, and her family, without conscious thought, hindered it.

It amused him to see her suck the flesh out of the crab claws. Her delight in it was so contagious that he ended up copying her. It became a game of who slurped the loudest. This was the first time a meal transcended into an event. It etched itself into his memory.

The sparkle in her eyes told him all was right in her world at that moment. She was happy. It sent a glad note to his heart and with it a sliver of apprehension. She might get used to this human life and that would make it hard for him to convince her to come home to her parents, to their kind, their world, and its veiled existence.

With their bellies full of food and in their hearts, merriment, they capped the night with coffee and enjoyed it over at the lookout point. The rhythmic sound of the waves crashing on the shore, the slight chill in the air paired well with the hot coffee. The result was very calming.

"That was a wonderful dinner," Anza said, glancing up at him. "Thank you."

Her hair was down from its earlier ponytail. The elastic seemed unable to hold it in place. The wind whipped it about her face, making it a challenge for her to drink her coffee in peace. He couldn't resist lifting the strands off of her cheeks and mouth and tucking them behind her ears.

She handed her cup to him as she self-consciously gathered her hair back in a low ponytail. She tucked the shorter baby hairs that grew around her face behind her ears. In that instance, she looked like the sixteen year-old that she was, and he felt a twinge of regret. She was still a baby. And the object of his mission. It was unseemly for him to develop a crush on a high-school student.

This must be how a crush works—the object of your interest seems to blossom right before your eyes, making her more beautiful, more compelling every second.

"What was your favourite dish?" he asked, to keep his mind off its present preoccupation.

She paused, her head tilted, eyes narrowed. "Hmm ... I can't decide. I like them all."

"If you can order only one dish when we dine next time, which among the three would you reorder?" He was unsure why he wanted to find out her answer to his question, but it felt essential.

"I think ... the crab," she replied with a smile.

He was reminded of their slurping game and smiled back. "Yes, me too. It's a pity that it's an endangered species and we can't eat them regularly." They had tried to reorder another, but the restaurant limited each table to one order.

"Yes, that's sad. But I heartily support that rule. It's for the good of the coconut crab population," she replied.

"Are you a rule-breaker or a law-abiding citizen?" He now faced her as he handed her coffee back.

That gave her pause, although her stance was still relaxed. She took a sip from her cup and sighed. The sound was like a breeze on a scorching afternoon.

"I've never broken a law. I've always abided by it ... but ..."

He waited for her to continue. She seemed unable to.

"But not today?" he suggested. He kept his expression non-judgmental. He wanted her to open up.

She looked thoughtfully at him, as if gauging if she could take the step of trusting him with her secrets.

"Exactly—not today," she said.

His heart jolted a beat faster. "So, will you tell me why you came to be here? Why you're so far away from home?" he asked, staring at her.

She tucked the strand of hair the breeze had freed from behind her ear before she replied. "I ran away from home and came here to learn ... independence."

"What made you run away?" He needed to understand what drove someone like her to leave a family who seemed to love her, to put herself at risk in an environment she was unfamiliar with.

"I can't tell you," she whispered.

She spoke as if her heart was tight. He knew she was hoping he would accept her response and leave it at that.

"Is it something that can't be resolved?"

"I don't know," she replied.

The sigh that preceded the words was heartfelt. He wanted to probe, but he couldn't press her. Not yet. Then a dreadful idea dawned on him. There might be another reason she left home; one they did not consider.

He frowned. "Anza, were you getting hurt? Are you in any danger?" He prayed it wasn't so.

She looked touched by his concern. And he was glad when she shook her head.

"No, Veren. I'm not in any danger. And I wasn't getting abused at home. I ... just can't live the same way. I'm different from them, and I have to face that fact. Eventually, I'll have to leave them anyway. I just want to have an early start and not get too dependent on their presence. It's better to do it now while I'm young and able," she said.

He knew it was the most she could tell him. It was very difficult not to reassure her that he understood what she was going through. Silence reigned between them as he digested what she revealed. Her cousin and her mother were right about her and what made her run away from home.

Anza looked up and was struck by the expression on Veren's face. It was like he just saw her for the first time. And yet the way he angled his head as he fixed her with a penetrating stare made her feel like a revelation to him.

"Do you not think your parents will be anxious about you?" Veren asked. His frown was etched with concern.

"I had planned to send word to them that I'm okay. Hopefully, it will suffice," she said.

"That wouldn't suffice. You're very young, and pardon me for saying so, but you don't strike me as someone who is used to this ... spartan kind of life," he said.

She couldn't contradict him. Mrs. Bassig made the same comment to her earlier, and it was her obvious naivete that convinced Mrs. Bassig to offer her a trainee position as front desk and guest relations officer for the next six months.

"Is it that obvious that I'm inexperienced?"

"Hell, yeah! You look like a child, a sheltered child," he said. His voice had increased in intensity. He sounded annoyed, almost angry.

"I'm not a child. I'm already sixteen. Most people call me a young woman!"

Veren sighed, reaching out to take her icy hands between his. He shook his head as if he regretted having raised his voice earlier.

"Anza, for most parents, sixteen is still a child. And you look younger than sixteen." His tone was gentler.

"Well, I can't help that I have baby face genes in me..." She felt like stomping her feet, but that would just prove his point. Instead, she pulled her hand from his and turned away.

There was silence from Veren. She waited for his comment, but there was none. And when she glanced back at him, his lips quivered from the effort not to grin.

"I suppose declaring that I'm an adult, then throwing a tantrum to prove it, is counterproductive," she said.

Veren grinned.

Her own smile broke through her lips and spread to her heart.

5

THE DEVELOPMENT

He had been staring at his phone for almost an hour now since he returned from walking Anza to her room. He had been trying to decide what to report to Edrigu. Why he put himself up to the goal of convincing Anza to go home was beyond him.

A call-in for his progress for the day was due, and he didn't want to lie. If he told Edrigu that he found Anza already, he might wonder why he had not told Anza's father about it. He could use Manuu Soledad's own desire to have Anza come home at her own choice as the reason, but Edrigu might point out that Manuu would want to do the convincing himself. All he had to do was let Manuu know Anza's location.

With Manuu, he could pretend that he misunderstood his instruction, but with Edrigu, there wouldn't be any ambiguity. If his mentor gave him an order, he could not go against it.

Unless ...

An idea came to him. He dialled Edrigu's number, pulse picking up. His mentor answered in two rings.

"Good evening, Veren. How are you coming along in Basco?" Edrigu's voice was clear despite the distance.

"I'm good, Sir. I just called in to report on my progress." He kept his tone controlled to tamp down his own uneasiness at the minor deceit he would play on his mentor.

"Okay. Do you have solid leads about Manuu's daughter's location?" Edrigu asked.

"Yes, Sir. I found her this afternoon," he replied.

"Wow! That was fast. Have you told Manuu? What is the arrangement? When are you due back here?" Edrigu's questions made his heart race.

"I have not told Mr. Soledad that I found her. Ms. Soledad still does not know I am an *Iztari*, and I'm afraid if she finds out, she will disappear again. Her father wants her to come home willingly and telling him might not achieve that—he might show up here and spook her away." He hoped his voice wouldn't give away his exaggeration of the facts. "And, if she disappears this time, we may not find her again."

Edrigu was silent on the other line. He had the impression that his mentor knew what he was doing. With luck, Edrigu would consider the logic in his explanation.

"So, you want to convince her yourself?" Edrigu asked. The tone of clarification made Veren's heart skip a beat. His mentor read his intention with ease.

"Yes, I was hoping to do that, Sir." He held his breath as he waited for Edrigu's response.

"Okay. So, what kind of help do you need from me?" Edrigu asked.

Veren felt his relief like a loosening of a tight band on his chest.

"Help me reassure Mr. Soledad that he need not worry about his daughter, that I can convince her to come home voluntarily," he said.

"How much time do you need to accomplish this?"

"A week, hopefully, since I would need to go to the mainland for *sustenance* by then," he replied.

"Okay. I'll take care of Manuu. In the meantime, I will give a heads-up to the *Sustenance Supply* in the mainland to prepare for your needs," Edrigu said. "Just in case."

"Thank you, Sir. I truly appreciate it." His chest loosened with relief.

"You're welcome," Edrigu said, then hung up.

He was sure, at that moment, that his mentor knew exactly what he was up to and was giving him the latitude to do so. He felt better and guiltier by the end of that conversation. He fell asleep justifying to himself that he just wanted to complete the mission in its entirety.

Anza had been running through the night's events again and again in her head. The exhilaration she experienced tonight was all new to her. The mental back and forth of being hopeful and cautious, in giving meaning to each word and action that was part of this experience, had kept her unbalanced.

This must be what having a crush is like—being in constant awareness of his presence, his words, and actions.

Veren was the first male human she had spent this much time with. Her father's rules had prevented her from forming friendships, even with her classmates, limiting her to brief conversations and tepid, trivial pleasantries. The warnings of potential separation pain when they *Transit* was never far from her mind.

She blamed her own inexperience for her susceptibility to Veren's attention. But her father did not raise an airhead, so it would be an insult to him if she allowed a crush to sway her within a few days of being independent. Veren may be human, but she was not about to exchange a dependency from one species to another.

Besides, depending on a man's affection as a source of joy would be counterproductive for her search for true happiness.

Tomorrow, I will look at all the actions and words of Veren to be nothing more than those from an older brother.

Or a good friend ...

No, an older brother ... Nothing could develop outside of a brother-sister relationship.

She walked into the lobby, expecting to see Veren, but he was nowhere. She was looking about for him when he came out of the gift shop at the corner. He was carrying a bottle of sunblock, which he handed to her.

"Are we going to the beach?" She looked at the bottle in her hand.

"We're going to a lighthouse. I don't know if the beach that comes with it is good for swimming, but I thought it best to be prepared," he said. "Do you want to get your swimsuit? Just in case it's possible to swim there?"

"I didn't bring one." There was a lake and a creek on their property, but like the previous trips, she was not expecting to swim, since her family always left her behind when they ventured into the woods.

Veren glanced at the gift shop, and she saw a rack of swimsuits inside. She stopped him before he turned back towards the shop.

"It's okay, I ... don't want to swim today. There will be other opportunities. We *are* on an island ..." She turned away and slid the sunblock in her backpack to avoid any more conversation about the topic.

Veren's eyes narrowed. He looked like he wanted to insist, but she stopped him with a question. "Shall we go?"

"We're leaving in a while. I'm still waiting for something," he said, a small smile on his face.

She nodded and sat down on the couch. She was a tad hungry but didn't think she would have enough time to order a sandwich. Veren might be on a schedule, and she didn't want to cause a delay.

A coffee shop worker came out with a small picnic basket just as she was thinking to buy a bottle of water to tide her over. She handed the basket to Veren, who thanked her with a smile. The girl blushed and tittered.

"Shall we?" Veren inclined his head to her, and she followed him out to where he had parked his motorbike. He secured the basket at the back of the bike while she picked up the helmet she used the day before and put it on.

"Do you have a jacket?" Veren looked at her flimsy T-shirt.

She shook her head. Veren took off his own backpack and fished out a long-sleeved shirt.

"Put this on—the ride is long. You'll get cold," he said.

He helped her slide her backpack off, holding the cotton shirt as she pushed her arm through the sleeves. It was soft and well-worn. It carried his natural fragrance and something citrusy. The man smelled good ... and familiar. Yet, she couldn't identify it.

She was picking through the catalogue of scents in her memory when Veren grasped the front of the shirt and buttoned her up into it like a child. His action startled her into stillness, allowing him to do the task quickly.

The sleeves seemed a foot longer than her arms when she held it up. Veren grinned and folded it back to allow her fingers to show.

"Shall we?" He nudged her chin with a knuckle. She nodded and followed, straddling the bike behind him.

I'm a little sister to him.

He's like the big brother I never had.

She repeated the words to herself as they zoomed along the country road, her arms wrapped around his waist, her thumbs hooked on his belt loops.

They drove through cliff-side roads that offered stunning views of the sea, and interior rural streets that oozed with quaintness. They zipped past towns humming with country life: women sweeping front lawns and hanging laundry; kids playing with sticks and well-used traditional toys; men walking with a purpose towards somewhere, and domestic animals and livestock meandering about.

It was such a simple, very human existence. She was both sad and glad to be in the middle of it. Life on this island contrasted sharply with her previous one. It was almost poetic that she had ended up here to start her new life as a human. It was a perfect representation of back to basic and starting from the bottom.

But if she was to start her life with this new beginning, she could not have chosen a more appropriate location. She was far safer here than if she had chosen the big city. A simpler life was easier to achieve among simple people and surroundings.

The ride took three hours. Her butt went numb, her throat dry, her stomach protested in hunger, yet she didn't ask for a break. She didn't want to inconvenience Veren. Her job was to be his companion, not a dependent. She was wondering how much longer the trip was going to take when they turned right into one of the country roads, and there it was: the Basco Lighthouse.

It gleamed white from the distance, standing solitary and imposing at the edge of a hill. It reminded her of the immobile Beefeater that guarded the Tower of London. Maybe because it appeared as dependable? This concrete guard looked like it watched and waited for passing ships in perfect patience for decades.

Their bike purred to a halt by the parking area in front of a building with a blue roof. It was a closed café. She hopped off to allow Veren to kick open the bike stand and secure it in place, then she removed her helmet to better view her surroundings. The sea, a deep aquamarine that blended into the intense blue of the sky. The hills were lush and emerald, like undulating pillows of vegetation.

And the air tasted of sea salt and adventure.

On impulse, she ran closer to the safety railing that protected the visitors from falling off the cliff. A wooden stairway with thick ropes for support snaked across the face of the hillside down to the beach.

The exceptional beauty and serenity of the scene drew her eyes in. The sound of the waves in a perpetual race to the shore, the bright blue sky that forced her to squint, and the light breeze that swept in from the sea soothed her ragged spirit. It seemed like the world had given her permission to dare. To live.

She looked back to check where Veren was. He had untied the basket from behind the bike and carried it with him as he approached her. He led her towards the lighthouse. They stopped by the grassy area in front of the circular tower. Veren unfolded a fabric she recognised to be a tablecloth from the coffee shop at their lobby. He knelt and unloaded the contents of the basket: bottled water, sandwiches, and packed garden salad.

"Let's eat first." He tugged at her hand to make her sit down. She slumped beside him, almost landing on his lap. Veren chuckled and gave her a bottle of water, cap loosened. She drank it down to half and sighed in relief as the cool liquid soaked the parched tissues of her throat.

"I figured you were dehydrated," he said. Amusement glittered in his eyes.

"How could you tell?" She picked up a sandwich.

"Your lips were dry." He tapped the bow of her lips with a gentle finger.

Her gaze flew to his as her fingers covered her lips in defence. "It was a long ... and windy ride," she mumbled, focusing her gaze on the sandwich in her hands to will away the heat that bloomed on her cheeks.

It was a long roll that looked like a hotdog bun. She opened it to examine the filling. The scent of lemon and dill wafted from it. By the look of it, this was a lobster roll sandwich, the specialty of the coffee shop, but one she had yet to try.

"Eat. That looks delicious," Veren said. He was holding a big cheeseburger.

She took a bite and almost moaned—the chilled lobster meat was fresh and sweet, with a hint of mayonnaise, celery, lemon juice, and dill. The bread was soft and the combination of flavours sublime.

Veren shook his head at her, his expression a mixture of regret and amusement as he took a bite of his burger. She realised Veren might have ordered the lobster roll for himself, and she took what she wanted without care, without asking him.

"Oh, did you want this?" She felt guilty that she hadn't even asked Veren before she took the lobster roll.

He laughed. "It doesn't matter. It's just ... your appetite is contagious."

"No, truly, we can share. I *cannot* finish this." She set down the bun to search for a knife to cut the roll in half. Veren stayed her movement, his cool hand on hers.

"No need to slice it. Eat and enjoy it. I'll finish the leftovers if there are any," he said.

"Won't that be off-putting ... to eat my leftovers?" she asked.

"You don't have rabies, so I'm not worried," he said. He stopped her protest by lifting her chin to close her mouth. "Stop arguing, little one. Just eat. I know you didn't have breakfast this morning."

Little one?

"How did you know?" She hoped she didn't look starved.

"I asked. They said you hadn't come down to breakfast."

"Oh ..."

She didn't know what to think about that. Veren had a mischievous twinkle in his eyes as he continued to eat. She followed his lead and finished her lobster roll.

Little one, really?

Like a puppy?

Veren watched Anza surreptitiously. She ate like a child, with full enjoyment. She was prim and proper when she was conscious of what she was doing, as if she had to stop herself from being too enthusiastic, from immersing herself in the moment. Yet, when she forgot herself, when the experience overcame her reserve, she soaked it all in, full senses deep.

It was stirring to behold.

Is this how she lived her life? Like a flame trapped in a glass jar, slowly suffocating at the lack of oxygen?

Anza reminded him of the young elephant he saw in Thailand a few years ago. It grew up tied to a metal pole, so it got accustomed to the limited movement of the length its leash allowed. The animal was so used to being bound that it stayed within that range even though it had doubled in size and could uproot the pole if it so desired.

Anza was the elephant who walked beyond the range and uprooted the pole. However, the experience was so new to her that it scared her. She could still feel the imaginary leash of the *Vis* world and its restrictive power. She would never be free until the muscle memory of being reined in faded and left her completely. That would require exposure to the other side of her world, beyond her comfort zone and into unknown dangers.

In that moment, Veren could empathise with Manuu Soledad.

Anza roused something soft and intense in him, a sense of protectiveness that he had never felt for anyone before. She was like a kitten, all fluffy fur and claws; like a filly, ready to bolt anytime she got spooked. And Anza was a hair's breadth away from bolting deeper into a surrounding she was unfamiliar with.

Anza reclined on the picnic cloth, stretched her arms overhead, and arched her back. Her actions were almost feline. He realised she must have been sore from the ride. She was rigid that whole time, despite the relaxed hold she had around his waist. It disappointed him that she wasn't comfortable enough to lean on him. But then, they had only known each other for less than twenty-four hours. It would be odd if she lacked caution.

With her eyes closed, he could observe her face. She looked very young, a bud still far from full bloom. Her youthful features, her size, her physique, her vulnerability called to his masculine protective instinct. He understood why her father sheltered her the way he did.

Anza stirred as he was putting away the remnants of their lunch. She got up and collected the cloth, folded and placed it into the basket. She was going to take it to the bike, but he took her by the hand and towed her toward the lighthouse. He placed the basket on a wooden bench by the circular stairs.

"Ready?" He smiled at her and pointed to the top of the tower.

"We can go up?" Her eyes rounded with undisguised excitement.

"Yes, we can. The view is best on the top."

She hesitated for a moment, gazing up. Her expression was a mixture of apprehension and thrill.

"Let's go." He tugged more firmly at her hand and made her choice easier.

With a giggle, she followed him up the narrow, winding stairs to the top. Their ascent was rushed. Halfway through, Anza stopped and gripped her sides, bent at the waist.

"Hang on," she gasped. Her face was flushed and glistening.

He gave her a couple of minutes' rest. Then, he pulled at her hand and said, "Hurry, while we have the lighthouse to ourselves. You can take pictures to your heart's content."

"How do you know I enjoy taking pictures," she asked, curious but without even not a tinge of suspicion.

Oops!

"Don't all teenagers?" He kept his tone neutral. Anza trusted him, and he needed to keep that trust. "Don't you have any social media?"

"Sure, I do, but it's private. Only for my consumption," she replied.

The familiar sadness flashed in her eyes.

"Don't you have followers?" he asked. He wanted to keep her talking. They were in the last five steps to the top.

She shook her head.

"Will you allow me to follow you online?" He made room for her to step onto the platform, to the view. It unfolded before her, leaving her mouth agape, eyes wide.

"Wow!" she breathed out.

That drew a wide smile from Veren. Her delight gave him pleasure.

"Wow, indeed!" he said, following her gaze towards the horizon.

The sun was no longer overhead. The sky, where gaps between patches of thick clouds showed, was a clear blue, but he could sense an oncoming rain. He felt the change of pressure in the atmosphere and smelled it in the air. Anza had better take her photos soon.

A quiet sigh escaped Anza's lips, and regret flashed in her eyes. He realised that, since he met her, he had never seen her use her cell phone.

"Don't you want to take pictures?"

"No." She shook her head. There was a slight downturn at the corner of her lips. "It's all right. My social media isn't that important right now."

"You don't have to post it until you're ready." He wanted to capture this moment for her. "It may be a long time before we return here, so take the pictures now."

She looked even more crestfallen. "I don't want to turn my phone on," she said.

"Why?" He frowned.

"My father could be tracking my phone ..."

It surprised him that she knew about how cell phones worked. He didn't expect it. Also, she was right. The *Iztari* office was tracking the transmission from her phone. Once again, he felt chagrined at his quick misjudgment of her capabilities.

He took out his own phone and handed it to her.

"What's this for?" Her eyebrows quirked.

"Use mine. And click away," he said. "I'll transfer the photos to your phone later."

"Oh, thank you!" On impulse, she bounced on her feet and launched herself into his arms.

"You're welcome." He hugged her back. The jolt in his heart made him uncomfortable. "Now go, while the light is good. The clouds are rolling in ..." He pointed at the sky.

"Yes, boss!" She gave him a gleeful salute and a wide smile. Her face beamed with pure joy.

Anza spent the next fifteen minutes taking shot after shot. She deleted those that didn't meet her standards and showed him the images she liked. Her innate talent for photography was on full display.

"Are we going somewhere else after here?" she asked as she handed him his phone.

"No," he said, sliding the phone in his pocket. "Sunset is beautiful here. The locals highly recommend it."

"That would be awesome," she said, eyes lit up once again.

"Let's hope the rain doesn't come before that."

Luck was with them. The rain came as the sun sank across the horizon. Anza had just finished taking photos.

It started as a drizzle, then turned into a sudden downpour. The wind drove the rain towards them and forced them inside the lighthouse for shelter. They sat together on the floor by the glass window, as the dark columns of rain undulated with the wind and lashed against the transparent barrier.

Rainwater had soaked Anza's jeans, and the hem of the shirt he loaned her. Within minutes, she was shivering. The tremors that ran down her slim body travelled from her shoulders to his, where they touched.

"You're cold," he said, and pulled her closer to keep her warm. His arm curved around her.

Her discomfort was significant enough that she didn't resist. In fact, she gladly leaned into him, sighing as she did. He anchored her better, her head cradled in the crook of his arm and shoulder, her cheek pressed against his chest.

The hum of the wind and the hiss of the downpour was hypnotic. Mother nature expressed its raw power in the churning waters of the sea, by the vertical drive of the wind, and the darkening of the sky. Veren knew Anza had dozed off. Her weight had settled on him. He centred her body and head on his chest, to make her more comfortable.

The rain droned on for hours. With her limp, warm body nestled against his, both of his arms around her, a cocoon of contentment enveloped him. He was at peace. He held her to him, this delicate creature with the tensile strength of titanium now temporarily in his keeping.

Gladness seeped into his soul and lulled him to sleep.

Anza surfaced from her nap in slow degrees. Her awareness first centred on a familiar scent, then the warm, hard flesh under her cheek, and a steady beating of a heart. It took her a moment to realise she was half reclined on Veren, his arm curved around her.

He was still asleep. She was reluctant to leave the comfort of his arms, but she eased herself out, trying not to wake him. She sat up and looked around—they were on the floor, leaned against the concrete wall of the lighthouse.

The slow flash of the light overhead reminded her of the cameras of old. The glass window mirrored her image back at her in intermittent flashes. It showed her hair in disarray. She pulled the hair tie off, then combed her fingers through her tresses, massaging her scalp.

The rain had stopped. The air smelled salty from the sea and tasted sweet from the wet grass. They should probably be heading home now. It was already dark, their ride was long, and she was hungry. Maybe she could ask Veren to stop by a convenience store for something to eat and drink. She gave Veren a gentle prod to rouse him.

"Hmm?" He blinked awake, looking up at her. He seemed disoriented and stared at her for a while.

"Shouldn't we go now? We have a long way to go," she whispered.

"Don't you want to wait for dawn? You can take photos of the sunrise to match your sunset shots," he murmured. Then he sat up and stretched his long limbs, a slight wince on his face.

"I would if I wasn't so hungry," she replied, and got up. Blood rushed to the numb places in her limbs, making her groan. "Pins and needles ..."

That made Veren smile.

"Do you think we can stop by somewhere for food?" She asked this to distract him from her embarrassment.

Veren's smile turned indulgent. He glanced at his watch. "I can do better. There's a cafe nearby." He jumped up and helped steady her on her feet.

"The blue and white building?" She gathered her hair back to tie it in a ponytail. "Isn't that closed?"

"It opens at 6 p.m.," he said, then stayed her hand. "Leave your hair down—it will help keep you warm." With a light touch, he smoothed the strands away from her face.

She found the affectionate gesture sweet.

Hand in hand, they walked down the circular stairs. They were the only two souls in the lighthouse. The weather discouraged tourists. The picnic basket was where they had left it, the motorbike still at the front of the cafe that was now open. A white car was parked nearby. After securing their basket on the bike, they proceeded inside.

There were three people in the cafe, two boys and a girl. They all swivelled and gaped at Veren and her as they walked in. She felt self-conscious, as the two boys' interest was fixed at her. She glanced up at Veren. His face was impassive, but he was looking at the boys as well. A slight tension emanated from him. Veren seemed wary and on guard.

The server greeted and ushered them to a table at the other end of the room. Veren pulled the chair where she could see the three in her peripheral vision. The guys were still looking at her. Veren sat beside her with a direct vantage point to the other table. His relaxed pose was misleading.

She wanted to look at the other table, to see what had caused his stress, but she didn't want to be obvious about it. The menu proved to be a useful shield, as she peered at them from behind it. The boys were still throwing glances her way.

She then noticed the girl with them had her eyes on Veren. She was older than her, with waist-length, shiny, straight hair and a self-confidence that made her feel uneasy. Her interest in Veren was as obvious as the interest her companions directed at her.

A stirring of animosity against the woman rose in her. She glanced at Veren. He was busy reading the menu, uninterested in the woman's gaze from across the room.

"What would you like to have, little one?" Veren asked, his eyes still on the menu. "How starved are you?"

She was, earlier. At the moment, her annoyance had lessened her appetite. But she wouldn't let the other woman ruin her dinner.

"Very," she said, "I would like this one," She pointed to the chicken dish on her menu.

He lowered his menu and looked at what she pointed at. "Okay. Is that enough?" he asked. His gaze went back to his menu after a cursory glance at hers. "No soup or salad?"

"No. The chicken is enough." The bite of satisfaction lessened her growing irritation. Veren didn't even glance in the woman's direction.

Veren signalled the server over and placed their order. She kept her eyes on him as she thought of ways to keep Veren from exchanging looks with the woman ogling him. The odious girl was now waiting for a chance to catch his eye, a small, ready smile on her face.

"You look irate, little one," Veren said. He reached over and picked up a lock of her hair and tickled the side of her nose with it. "Is that hang-ger?" His tone was teasing.

"Hang-ger?" She frowned in confusion. "You mean hunger?"

"No. Hang-ger. Hunger-induced rage." His eyes twinkled in mischief.

"Oh ... No, I'm not ..." Anza began, her temper heated. She realised it was a better explanation for her attitude, "I guess I am." She smiled at him apologetically.

"A bit of patience, little one," Veren chuckled.

He reached out and playfully pinched her cheek. Pleased with their exchange, her brain scrambled for ways to keep him engaged. None of her previous experiences with her father or cousin Xandrei seemed applicable. She had never had to manipulate her father or cousin to keep their attention on her. Then she remembered their deal.

"Don't I owe you stories for the meals?" she asked.

"Oh, yeah." Veren's smile widened. He looked pleased to be reminded of it.

"So, what would you like to know?" She was thrilled her ploy worked.

"Tell me about your childhood." Veren scooted his chair closer, an encouraging smile on his face.

She hesitated for a bit as she thought how much she could divulge without giving too much, without revealing her true identity.

"I'm an only child. My mother died of birth complications. My dad raised me alone for the first three years of my life, and then he married my stepmom. I call her *Momstie*," she began. She paused as the server arrived with their drinks. She wanted no one else to hear of her life story.

"Momstie?" Veren asked as he unwrapped the straw and pushed it into his drink.

"Ah ... Momstie, short for stepmom ..."

Veren nodded. He seemed impressed with the nickname.

"How was your relationship with your parents? Your dad, in particular." He blew on his coffee.

"It's a great relationship. My dad doted on me, but he was ... overprotective." She stirred the straw in her iced tea.

"How so?"

She felt a twinge of guilt at the thought of talking about her father to a stranger. She sighed, "I'm not allowed to make friends, not even with my classmates."

"You have no friends of your own age?" Veren's focus was solely on her now.

"None ... Just my cousin, rather, my step-cousin Xandrei. He's eighteen. He's the only one I'm ... close to," she said.

"Did your cousin know?" he asked, his expression appraising. "Your plan to run away, I mean."

She shook her head. "No, he's overprotective as well. He would have told Momstie." She took a sip of the iced tea to loosen the knot in her chest, buying time should he ask for more details. As a compulsion, she reached out for the paper straw covering; the flame of the lit candle on their table beckoned.

"Okay." Veren seemed to understand. He reached out and covered her fidgeting fingers with his. "How about your stepmom? Do you get along with her?"

She nodded. "Yes—she treats me like her real daughter. Momstie is cool. Nothing bothers her. In short, we're very different."

Veren said nothing. He just continued to look at her and seemed to wait for her next words.

The arrival of their food interrupted their conversation. Veren's eyebrows knitted in a quick reaction, but his face became a pleasant mask when he turned to the server.

The tone of their dinner changed. Their interaction had always been lighthearted, but now there was a depth, an added layer to their relationship. It was almost tangible, the finest of threads, yet strong. She waited for him to ask questions, to cue her to return to their previous topic, but he kept their conversation friendly and casual.

Veren ordered grilled lobster for himself. It reminded her that she stole his lobster roll sandwich earlier.

"I'm sorry ..." She felt driven to apologise again.

Veren looked up in surprise. "For what?"

"I took your lobster roll this morning." She pointed to his dish.

He shrugged. "It's no big deal. Actually, after seeing you eat the roll, it made me crave lobster." He scooped a chunk from the shell, dipped it in the lemon butter sauce, and popped it into his mouth. "Oh ... that is good ..." His voice deepened in appreciation.

"So, you really bought the roll for me, and the burger for yourself?" she persisted, wanting reassurance.

Veren chewed and swallowed before he replied with, "I bought both for either of us. If you had chosen the burger, I would have happily eaten the lobster. It was a simple matter of getting something I thought we would both like."

"Really? Are you—"

He cut her off. "Anza, eat your food. It's getting cold."

She smiled at him. In return, he gave the lock of her hair a slight tug and continued with his meal. There was a noticeable increase in the camaraderie between them during the rest of the dinner. They shared each other's food. She cut him a portion of her chicken and placed it on his plate. He reciprocated with his lobster but insisted she take a bite from his fork.

In her head, that last act could be sexy and romantic, just like in the movies.

Or platonic, like a big brother feeding his kid sister.

With her luck, it was probably the latter.

With two steaming cups of takeaway coffee, Veren drew Anza to her feet. The coffee shop would close soon. They would drink their coffee outside where they had lunch earlier. As Veren opened the door, a blast of frigid night air hit him. Behind him, Anza shivered.

He gave Anza the coffee cups to hold and pulled her into his jacket. Anza sighed, and it made him smile. They made their way back to the patch of grass in front of the lighthouse with a brief stop by their bike. He took the tablecloth from the picnic basket and tucked it under his jacket.

The downpour left the grounds wet. The tablecloth would not have offered protection. They ended up huddled on a dry patch atop a low boulder, their backs against the stone walls of the caretaker's house. The structure shielded them from the icy wind that swept inland from the sea.

"What brought you here in Batanes?" Anza asked as she blew on her hot coffee.

He took a sip before he answered. "Nothing in particular. Part of a bucket list ..." He wanted to avoid this topic. He didn't want to lie to her. It was a good thing she was too inexperienced to know how to probe for information.

Anza looked up from her cup and stared at him. "Will you tell me about your childhood?" she asked.

Fuck!

His heart leaped at the question. No one had asked him that question for years.

"Not much to tell. I was an orphan," he said. "My mentor took me under his wing when I was five, sent me to school, then gave me a job. He gave me everything a young person with no parents needs to survive and thrive." He adopted a relaxed posture to hide the fact that discussing his past was not a pleasant subject for him.

She didn't seem convinced by his facade. There was a frown on her face, but her eyes were devoid of her usual emotions. He couldn't tell what she was thinking. His little one had learned to mask her feelings.

Not good.

"It must have been hard," she said, her eyes never leaving him.

Darn!

He took a deep breath before responding. "Yes, I guess it was." Giving brief replies might discourage her from asking for more.

"So, what do you do now?" she asked, her head inclined to the side.

Holy Aquila! She's persistent.

He took a big gulp of his lukewarm coffee to buy time to plan his response.

"I'm in between jobs," he said. That was technically true. "I return to my new one in a month," he added.

"A month? Are you staying here for that long?" Anza was looking at her own cooling cup, her voice stilted.

"Maybe ... although it depends," he replied to the top of her head. He wished he could see her expression.

"On what? I thought this trip was part of your bucket list."

Wish granted—she was looking at him again.

"Well, the items in my bucket list are not simple, one-layered things to be ticked off," he replied.

Anza's nod was slow, but whether she accepted and understood what he said was unclear. It seemed to be an automatic action she did when she was trying to make sense of the information she received.

They both turned towards some voices that were coming closer to them. The group of humans at the coffee shop were now going their way. Anza glanced at Veren with a frown. She couldn't make out what they were saying. Thanks to his superior hearing, the conversation of the incoming party was clear. The three were looking for them. The boys were keen on meeting Anza, and the girl was interested in him.

He sighed. They would have to deal with these juveniles unless they left the lighthouse. But he promised Anza the sunrise ...

"Oh ... do you think they're coming this way?" Anza asked, her nose wrinkled in disapproval.

"I'm afraid so, little one. You'll have to put effort into being sociable," he said.

She shook her head. He pulled her closer in a mock headlock.

"I don't know how to be sociable," she replied from beneath his arm, then untangled herself from his hold. He could almost imagine her pouting, except she wasn't the pouting kind.

"Then this is a good time to learn," he said, and released her.

Anza combed her hair back and twisted to face him. There was a worried crease on her brow and fear in her eyes.

"You did well with me. You weren't shy," he reminded her.

Her frown deepened. "You're different. You didn't give me time to think, and I forgot I didn't know how to be sociable," she said.

"Well, do what you did with me. Just answer their questions ... and don't frown." He touched her forehead to ease the creases. "And I'm here. I'll help you."

Three minutes later, the group caught up to them.

"Hi, guys! Are you waiting for the sunrise, too?" The only girl in the group was leading the pack. She wore a wide, friendly smile.

"Yes," he answered casually.

He surveyed the group standing ten feet away. She was carrying two bottled waters, one in each hand. The guy behind her was carrying an extra bottle. A quick look at the bottle caps told him that both were unopened.

"Can we join you?" she asked, then paused right in front of him. Her question was just for him, despite the word 'we'. She stood with a stance seemingly meant to emphasise her curvaceous hips. The girl apparently knew she possessed a splendid figure and was using it to her advantage.

Veren glanced at Anza to make sure she was okay. Her face showed no emotion, but he could feel the slight tension emanating from her. He almost said no.

"Sure, join us." He gestured toward the space in front of them. The soldier in him wanted them where he could see them.

"I'm Charisse," the girl said, waving with the bottle in her hand.

"I'm Veren."

"Hi—I'm Anza," Anza said. The tension in her shoulders increased, but her voice was calm.

"I'm Diego," the taller of the two boys said. He had short shorn hair at the back and the sides, but the front was longer and styled up. His smile revealed a pair of dimples and nice teeth.

"Hey—I'm Charlie," the other boy said. This one had longer, slicked-back hair. "Would you like some water?" Charlie asked, offering the bottle in his hand to Anza.

Veren intercepted it. He wanted to make sure it was safe. The bottle was chilled. He unscrewed the cap and handed it to Anza.

The boy's expression was telling. Charlie was unsure of how to react to Veren's protective gesture. Veren didn't care—he wanted this boy pre-warned that he was here to protect Anza.

"Thank you," Anza said, directing her remark to Charlie.

"Can we sit with you?" Charisse asked. She eyed the space in between

Anza and him. She seemed to want him to scoot a little, to make room for her.

He nodded, but before Charisse could act on it, Anza moved nearer and covered that coveted gap. She took the option away and made her opinion about the situation clear.

Charisse, to her credit, was unfazed. She sat in front of him, cross-legged, her back to the view. The two boys copied her. The rock could only accommodate two-and-a-half people. Both Diego and Charlie positioned themselves right in front of Anza.

Time to do due diligence on the three. "So, where are you guys from?"

"We're from Baguio," Charisse replied with a disarming full smile. "Diego and I are cousins. Charlie here is Diego's friend, frat brother, and my classmate."

"What brought you here?" Veren asked.

"We're on holiday," Charisse replied. Her free hand now played with her own hair, twirling it like most young women do when trying to be overtly feminine.

"Which school do you go to?" Anza's question sounded relaxed.

He glanced at her and noticed that her posture was rigid and almost defensive. Anza was asserting herself. His little one was flexing her confidence muscle.

"Oh, U.P. Baguio," Charisse said. She looked at Anza for the first time, her smile tight at the corners. The girl clearly saw Anza as competition.

"How about you, Anza? Which school do you go to?" Diego asked, his tone open and friendly.

"I don't know yet. I haven't decided where to go," Anza replied.

His little one was cool under pressure. When it came to hiding her background, Anza's years of practice as an *Erdia* showed.

"So, are you from here, or are you visiting like we are?" Charlie asked, glancing at Diego, a challenge in his gaze.

Veren could read the competition between the two boys. And he didn't like it. Their antics to win her regard might prove enough of an inducement for a young girl like Anza to want to stay with the humans longer.

"We're visiting." Anza's curt reply was guarded, not encouraging.

Veren inwardly smiled. So far, the boys hadn't enticed her. She was too inexperienced to use their attraction to her to her full advantage.

"How long are you here for?" Charisse asked. Her gentle touch on his knee ensured that he would look at her.

He turned to Charisse, who was smiling at him as she waited for his reply. Anza's interest in his reply to Charisse's question gleamed in her gaze, which had turned on him.

"For however long it takes to accomplish what we want to do here," he replied, answering for them both.

"Are you ... together?" Charisse's asked, her tone tentative, one eyebrow arched.

It was clear to him that she wanted to know her chances. The two boys were also keen to find out if Anza was available. He chose to misunderstand the question. He wasn't about to divulge the nature of their relationship.

"Yes. We came here together," he replied, and glanced at Anza.

Anza gave him a slow blink of annoyance. A quiet huff followed as she turned to Diego. He was unsure what caused her ire—he thought that she wouldn't want her circumstance known to strangers.

"So, Anza, are you going to University this coming school year?" Diego asked, outwardly glad to have her looking at him.

She shook her head. "11th grade."

"Oh, you're about ... 17?" Diego asked. "I'm 18, turning 19."

"I'm sixteen." Anza's admission came out reluctantly.

"Wow, you must have started school early," Charlie interjected, unwilling to stay in the background.

"No, I skipped first grade." Anza's response was automatic.

That was news to Veren. Her records didn't mention it.

"You must be smart, then." Charlie's comment had a hint of condescension.

Veren felt Anza's defensive barriers rise, annoyance in her eyes. His little one had claws and was preparing to use them. Charlie was still smiling at her, unaware of the effects of his words. *This would be interesting to watch.*

"There are worse things than being smart," Anza said, her tone clipped.

Charlie's face fell as he realised his mistake.

"I agree with Anza. Being a basketball jock, for one." Diego wisely picked up the opening that Charlie's gaffe created, and gave Anza a conspiratorial smile.

Anza smiled back at him. Diego scored a point there. Veren felt a kick of irritation and a stirring of dislike towards Diego.

A cool breeze swept over them, making Anza shiver. She was the only one among them unprepared for the cold temperature. The thin shirt he loaned her was not enough to keep the chill away.

"Do you want my jacket, Anza?" Charlie offered, poised to remove his windbreaker, and redeem himself from the earlier mistake.

"There's no need," Veren said, stopping Charlie. He took the picnic cloth tucked inside his jacket, shook it out, and draped it over Anza's shoulder. The cloth retained the heat from his body. He took advantage of the opportunity and placed his arm around her, pulling her closer to him.

He could better protect her like this.

6

IN KEEPERSHIP

If I was a full Vis, a true Aswang with shape-shifting skills, my animal form would be a cat. No doubt about it.

The cosiness of being cradled by Veren was purr-inducing, and she would have purred if she had been capable of it. His left arm was draped behind her, cushioning her back against the stone wall. She had laid her head on his chest. He smelled of that unidentified yet familiar scent of himself and night air. She closed her eyes to savour and drown her senses with the sensation of being close to him. It was also useful to pretend to doze off to avoid engaging with the three people who invaded their private moment.

She was comfortable, both inside and out. She could stay like this until morning. No conversations, just being together. The sound of the waves, the cool breeze that wafted from the sea, and the comfortable semi-darkness had a mellowing effect on her. Nothing Charisse or Charlie could say or do tonight could rouse her temper.

"Aww ... she's so sweet. The poor kid fell asleep," cooed Charisse.

Except that.

"Has she?" Veren asked with laughter in his voice.

She knew Veren was aware that she wasn't sleeping, that she just didn't want to socialise and this was her means of escape. The tension in her body would have been impossible for him to ignore.

A lull in the conversation followed. Her hair tingled at the sensation of eyes resting on her. Perhaps they were making sure she was indeed asleep.

"What do you do, bro?" Diego asked, breaking the silence.

Anza thought, *That's a good question*. She also wanted to know Veren's answer.

"I'm into asset recovery," Veren replied, a hint of mirth in his tone.

Asset recovery? That made her peek under her lashes.

"Cool ..." Diego clearly didn't know what Veren meant.

"You're in finance, then?" Charlie piped in.

"Not quite."

Veren's reply made her want to press him for more explanation herself, but she couldn't because she was pretending to be asleep.

"What type of assets do you recover? Properties? Vehicles?" Charlie persisted.

"Only those of extreme value," Veren replied. He rearranged the cloth that had slid down her back.

She wondered what valuables he was referring to. His response to the question didn't make his position clear.

"How long have you three been friends?" Veren asked, effectively ending that topic.

She could almost see his raised eyebrow, a habit of his when asking questions.

"Years," Charisse replied. "Diego and I have hung out together since grade school. Charlie and I met two years ago through Diego." Charisse sounded glad to be directly conversing with Veren.

She heard Charisse shift in her position, maybe to find a more comfortable one, or to move closer to Veren.

"Are you and Anza related by blood?" Charisse's question was bold and direct.

Veren stiffened. Either it surprised him, or he didn't like the question.

"We're not." Veren's response was curt. It discouraged further probing.

She wondered if Veren's clipped response told Charisse he wasn't about to divulge any information about them. Hopefully, the woman was smart enough to pick up on the nuance.

"What *is* your relationship with her?" Charisse asked.

Apparently not.

"At the moment, I'm her keeper," Veren said. The muscle in his arm flexed. It felt like it tightened around her.

"Keeper? What is that? Like a babysitter?" There was a slight smirk in her tone.

"Or a bodyguard?" Diego asked.

"Anza doesn't need a sitter, and she can take care of herself," Veren said.

There was a tinge of pride in his voice, and a touch of disbelief, like it was a revelation to himself. It warmed her insides.

"So, what does it mean to be her keeper?" Charisse persisted.

"I'll let Anza answer that," Veren replied, evading the question.

"But she's asleep ... Can you just tell us?" Charisse cajoled.

Under her lashes, she saw Charisse reach out to touch Veren's knee. She wanted to slap it away, and didn't realise her hand, sandwiched between them, was clenched until Veren chuckled and squeezed her shoulder.

Veren shook his head. "No, that would betray our keepership," he replied, chuckling.

Charisse released a slow breath of frustration. "How old are you, Veren?" she asked.

"I'm ... 23," he replied, surprised at the turn of Charisse's question.

"I'm turning 20," Charisse said, with a note of glee. "We only have three years' age difference between us," she continued. "My cousin and Charlie are closer to Anza's age," she added when Veren didn't respond.

Anza sensed Veren's puzzlement. He didn't seem to understand where Charisse was going with the question and statement. But she did—Charisse was using the age gap between Veren and her as a weapon. It sparked her temper and incinerated her natural inclination to be prudent.

"Are we comparing manufacturing dates? Measuring shelf life? Or counting down to our best before?" Anza questioned.

All eyes swivelled in her direction, their expressions of surprise identical.

Except for Veren—amusement danced in his eyes. A slight warning entered it when she roused herself. With hands linked, she stretched them overhead, pulling on the muscles of her back. The hard rock and the cold air made it sore.

"We were discussing birth dates ..." Charisse's tone sounded defensive, and a touch antagonistic.

"Were you?" she asked sarcastically, not caring if she offended the woman.

"Was that a good cat nap?" Diego asked in a pacifying manner. The smile on his face seemed genuine.

"Yes, it was ... stimulating," she replied, smiling back. Of the three, Diego was the only one she liked. Marginally.

"Was there enough time for a dream?" Diego appeared to be bent on easing the tension that had built up between her and Charisse. He was a peacemaker, a true gentleman. Anza appreciated it.

"Alas, no," she replied.

"Would you like to stretch your legs?" Diego had stood up, offering her his hand. She hesitated. Her muscles were tight, but she didn't want to leave Charisse to monopolise Veren.

Charlie got up, too. "That's a good idea, Diego." He faced Veren and said, "With your permission, Veren, can we accompany Anza for a walk?"

Veren looked at her, waiting for her to decide.

"Let them go, Veren. My cousin and Charlie are harmless. They'll take care of Anza," Charisse said, touching Veren's knee again.

"Why don't we all stretch our legs?" Veren suggested, standing up and pulling Anza to her feet.

She didn't realise her butt had gotten numb from sitting for so long. She winced and gasped as the blood resumed its restricted flow through the veins at the back of her thighs.

Veren heard her. "Are you okay, little one?"

"Pins and needles," she said, trying to rub the sensation back on her rump. Veren grinned as he watched her. "I'm ready." She shook off her legs.

With her hand curved into Veren's arm, they walked toward the end of the ridge, their steps slow and meandering. Diego had situated himself beside her. Charisse, as Anza expected, had slid her own arm through Veren's other arm. Charlie, it seemed, had lapsed into silence, and walked a step behind them all.

She wished the three would leave them alone. She wanted to ask Veren some questions, specifically what he meant when he declared himself her keeper.

Was he just joking?

What does it mean?

Veren's patience was running thin. These three humans and their normal ways shouldn't have bothered him, but they did. He didn't like how Charisse treated Anza, or how Charlie insulted her. He was glad that Anza's reaction to a crushing comment made her hackles rise instead. Her first instinct was to fight.

But the most bothersome thing was that Diego got on Anza's good side. Veren didn't want to look too deep into why it displeased him, since Diego wasn't as obnoxious as the other two, and making friends would benefit Anza.

During her brief stint here in Basco, she would have a chance at every human experience to create enough memories to last her a lifetime—so, she wouldn't want to do this again. The most ideal situation was for her to make them while Veren was around to protect her. He could help her assess which ones she could trust, and which ones she should stay away from.

Anza's instinct with people was good, but her youth and perhaps her desire to make connections would make her vulnerable. And, if tonight was an example, she was attractive in every way a teenage girl could be. She would draw that kind of attention wherever she went, especially when she learn to use her feminine charms.

He wondered now if her father ever taught her how to defend herself. Most females of their kind, at least the *Vis* he knew, had some basic training. It was part of the drill.

Anza didn't look trained, her body slim and slight like a normal human teenager. She didn't strike him as athletic, either. Maybe it was the combination of her physique and innocent face that made him want to make sure she was safe, unharmed, unhurt.

Anza's chuckle drew him out of his own musings. She was laughing at whatever joke Diego told her. The boy was getting more successful in drawing her out by the minute. It chafed at him, but he didn't react. He would let Anza enjoy herself. This was temporary since she wouldn't see Diego again after tonight.

"I think my cousin and your ward are getting along fine. Don't you?" Charisse's comment was pointed as she leaned closer to him.

He could smell the pheromones emanating from her, but her wish would remain unfulfilled. He wasn't into one-night stands, and his work ethic forbade playing while on a job. Unlike the other males of his kind, he wouldn't dally with female humans just because it was common practice. *Brevis Amorem* may be a habit to most *Viscerebus* males, but it was not his.

The *Tribunal*'s rules may justify the indulgence for brief affairs, since they were expected to keep relationships with female humans brief and impersonal, but it was not something he liked to do. He wouldn't add more parentless children in this world. No child of his would be a *Vondenad* left to survive alone in this world.

Charisse tugged at his arm, prompting him to respond to her earlier question.

"Anza is a friendly girl," he said with a glance at Anza and Diego. Anza's hand was still hooked on his arm, even if her attention was on Diego. That made him feel connected to her still. On an unconscious level, it anchored her to him.

"My cousin likes her very much. Charlie does, too. But, since Anza seems to prefer Diego, Charlie has stepped back," Charisse observed.

"We'll see. In the meantime, Diego had better behave himself. Anza is under my care." He said it loud enough for everyone to hear. It was a warning that he wanted Charisse to know, and for Diego to heed.

Anza and Diego stopped at the edge of the ridge and looked at him. Then, Anza pulled off the tablecloth draped around her shoulders and laid it on the grass. Charisse was quick to sit at Anza's right side after Anza took the first seat. With Diego at her left, they sandwiched Anza between them.

Charisse's intention was obvious: the vacant space beside her was for Veren.

Veren opted to be behind Anza. An exasperated Charlie sat beside him.

Undeterred, Charisse twisted around to face him instead. Her disinterest in the incoming sunrise was made clear. Veren sighed, finding her persistence tiresome, although he couldn't help but be impressed by her extreme self-confidence—she ignored all the signals he was giving her. She seemed like a woman unused to getting rejected. Either that, or her manner of succeeding with them was by railroading their objections.

"So, Veren, do you have a girlfriend?" Her forwardness wasn't unexpected.

"No, I don't have a girlfriend."

Anza overheard his response and twisted to look at him. He placed his hands on her shoulders and made her face forward with a light pressure on her shoulder blades to keep her there. He rubbed gentle circles to reassure her.

Of what, he wasn't sure.

"What traits do you find attractive in a woman?" Charisse asked in a tone so saccharine, it was cloying. All her affectations were so unnatural—it was off-putting.

His response was a gentle shake of his head and a smile. Charisse pouted, unable to hide her irritation at his evasion.

Rays of sunshine started peeking out from the horizon, lightening the dark sky. The midnight blue hues transitioned to red violet. They were all transfixed at the sight. A welcome spate of silence enveloped them. Veren dug out his mobile phone and gave it to Anza, handing it to her from over her shoulder without an exchange of words. She glanced back at him with a grateful smile.

Another blast of cold air swept through them, making Anza shiver. Without a word, he grasped Anza's waist and pulled her back to him, close to his chest. His bent legs served as her armrests. She leaned back on him. His body protected her from the wind, warming her. Her silent sigh of contentment echoed his.

His chin rested at the top of her head, her back flat on his chest. They watched the sunrise on the horizon in complete silence. Anza held his mobile phone, her elbows propped on his knees. His arm hung loosely around her middle.

As the half globe of the sun showed, Anza aimed the camera at the view, watching the sun through the screen. The colours of the horizon transitioned from varying shades of violets to reds and yellows. Her eyes focused on the display, her fingers clicking at a furious pace.

"Two more minutes, Anza. You have enough beautiful shots," he whispered in her ear. A puzzled frown formed on her face as she glanced at him.

"Why?" Her question came a breath away from his cheek.

"So you can experience the sunrise—the photos can never capture that," he replied. "Be present, little one."

She nodded and lowered his cell phone. And for the succeeding minutes, they watched the sunrise until the whole globe of it emerged. The rays of yellow radiated from the centre sphere and painted the surrounding areas, layering them with red and orange.

It was breathtaking.

Anza took a deep breath and released it in gradual degrees. He felt her smile on his cheek, which triggered a smile of his own. "Shall we go?" she whispered.

"Yes. Let's get some breakfast along the way," he said. With a swift motion, he got up, pulling her too to her feet.

The rest of the group got up with them. Anza seemed surprised at their presence. He couldn't blame her. The complete silence and their shared moment earlier made him forget them, too. That wasn't a good thing if he was to become a great *Iztari*. Losing awareness of the surroundings could be deadly to a warrior.

"Are you guys leaving?" Charisse asked, stepping off the cloth as Anza tugged at it.

"We have to be on our way," Veren said. He took the cloth from Anza and folded it.

"Where are you off to next?" Diego's question was directed at him, but his eyes shifted to Anza.

She shrugged. Anza was waiting for him to speak for them.

"We'll decide along the way," he replied. He understood that Anza was as eager to leave their company as he was.

"Can we tag along?" Charisse asked.

He saw the spark of temper in Anza's eyes. She was close to saying something rude. He squeezed her fingers to stop her.

"We have a few things we need to accomplish. So, goodbye to you now. It's been a pleasure." He held out his hand to Charisse. She looked at it, unwilling to accept his handshake of farewell. Charlie grasped it instead.

"The pleasure was ours. Thank you, too," Charlie shook his hand. "Guys, I believe we have to get going, too. We've imposed our presence on them long enough. We don't want to take up more of their time."

Veren's dislike towards the guy lessened. It seemed he wasn't *that* self-absorbed.

Diego offered his hand to Anza, saying, "It was great meeting you and spending time with you, Anza."

She shook his hand and replied with a benign smile, "Likewise."

"Can I ask for your number? Maybe we can get in touch when we get back to civilization?" Diego's gaze and crooked grin seemed hopeful.

Anza hesitated.

"Anza doesn't have her phone right now. Give me your number and she can get it from me later," he said.

Diego hesitated for a moment, but dictated his number anyway. As he saved it on his phone, he wasn't sure if he could be selfless enough to give Diego's number to Anza after. He could only hope that Anza would forget to ask for it later.

"Can I have yours, Veren?" Charisse asked, her phone at the ready.

He gave her his number without hesitation. It was a burner phone, with a burner SIM card. Training protocol required that they destroy the phone and the SIM card after every case.

The three walked them to their bike. Just before Anza got on the bike behind him, Diego stopped her. "Call me, Anza, okay? I'd like to get to know you better as a... um... friend," he said. His hand clasped hers once more.

The warrior in him didn't like the feeling that bloomed in his chest at the sight of Anza's smile. It made him impatient to leave. The feeling faded as they zoomed out of the parking lot and onto the road, away from Diego, Charlie, and the persistent Charisse.

Veren stopped at a roadside eatery half an hour later. On the menu were fried rice, eggs with fried flying fish and the crispy, dried pork dish they had the night before. The meal came with dark coffee and brown sugar. It was served outdoors—the weather was perfect for it.

As they set the plates down, Anza's mouth watered at the aroma of hot, garlic fried rice. Intrigued, she watched Veren pour a quarter of his coffee on the rice. Veren laughed at her expression.

"You should try it. It's fantastic. I learned this from the Batangueños. They all pour coffee on their fried rice." With an excited lift of his eyebrow, he tucked into his food with enjoyment.

She copied him with more caution. She spooned some of her coffee over a bit of rice. Combined with the egg and flying fish, she had to agree with Veren. The smokiness of the coffee complimented the flavours and neutralised whatever oiliness there was in the fried rice and egg.

"That was delicious!" she said as the first mouthful assaulted her taste buds.

It was such a simple variation of a commonplace dish. Just a tweak. And yet, it brought her a new understanding of it, a new appreciation that made it more enjoyable.

"That's what travelling does to you. It enables you to experience other cultures. And the best way to do that is through their food," Veren said. "Have you travelled outside of the country before?"

"Yes, every year, with my parents." Somehow, her trips with her parents didn't have the feel of a novel experience or an awakening. With them, it was conventional, like a continuation of a routine, just in a different location.

He frowned at her lacklustre response. "Did that not make you perceive the people and their cultures in a different light?"

"It's hard to learn more about people when you encounter them at a distance, or to appreciate something new if your parents restrict you the whole time." She sighed. "It doesn't matter where we go, which attraction we visit, which restaurant we eat in: I feel like I still view my world through the narrow lens my parents set me up for."

Veren's intent gaze revealed his contemplation, as if her viewpoint was something he hadn't considered.

"I think we view the world through a narrow lens of our own experience," he stated, "and for most of us, each lens is different, but the size of that lens is within our individual control. Yours is a distinct case, I've got to admit."

They ate in silence for a minute or two as she weighed whether she would raise her next question now or later. Her impatience won.

"Veren, why did you say you were my keeper?" She had been itching to ask him the question since she first heard him say it.

Veren chewed, slow and prolonged. It appeared deliberate, as if he was buying his time to think of a decent response. "Well, that's the role I see myself having in your life..." It was a very casual response; it was almost evasive.

"What does it mean ... to be my keeper?" That he saw it as a role in her life implied permanence. Considering the limited time they had together, the statement confused her.

"Like a bodyguard, I guess. A mentor, a guidance counsellor, a friend ..."

"All of those require a constant presence." She had to point that out. When he left Basco, she would still be here. *How could he be my keeper if he's somewhere else?*

Veren stared at her. There was a line of strain around his mouth, as if he was in pain. It disappeared when he smiled at her, yet there was a touch of sadness to it.

"That's true, but with technology, there's really no way to lose contact with anyone you care about," he said.

A stab of sadness hit her. Once he leaves here, there would be no way they could keep in contact with each other. For as long as she was hiding from her parents, she couldn't turn on her phone. She planned to hide for a year. She doubted that Veren would still remember her.

"For some people, yes. In my case, that wouldn't be possible," she said.

Veren's frown deepened. "Why? Don't you want to be friends with me?"

"While I'm in hiding, I *cannot* turn my phone on. That means I won't be able to text you, either." Even if she went back home, her parents would never allow her to form a relationship with a human like him.

"What about when you return home? Can't we keep in contact then?"

"No. My parents would never let me be friends with any human ... being." In the *Vis* world, she would go back to her isolated life. She didn't want to go back to that.

Veren was quiet once again. He turned contemplative, then took a deep breath and continued eating. When she didn't do the same, he prodded her. "Eat up, little one. Your food is getting cold."

She complied, but she had lost her appetite. There was no resolution, but it was no use forcing him to respond if he didn't want to. She had heard and witnessed his evasive moves last night. He was skilled at it.

Ten minutes later, as they were preparing for the ride back, a thought came to her: "If you are my keeper, does it mean that I'm your keeper in return?"

Veren paused from fixing her helmet. "When I'm ready to have a keeper, you'll be my first choice," he replied. "There you go—all done." He avoided her gaze and turned to straddle the bike.

She had no choice but to follow his lead. She got behind him, like before, with her arms around his waist, her thumbs hooked inside his belt loops. But this time, while it was the most natural thing to do yesterday, today it felt awkward.

Just before he put his own helmet on, Veren looked back at her and said, "Little one, you need to hold on to me a little tighter. You've had no sleep and I don't want you to fall off during the ride."

"Okay." She leaned closer to him, her stomach pressed to his lower back, arms firm around his midriff, hands crossed and thumbs hooked on his belt loops. Her action became automatic; the awkwardness faded with his command.

Veren strapped on his helmet and away they zoomed along the picturesque country road. Like yesterday, they zigged and zagged past the stone, earthen and wooden homes; the mixture of blue sea and sky, the lush green of the hills, and the local people going about their daily chores.

She was content—something fundamental to her well-being settled in her heart. The hum of the motorcycle hypnotised her, and her last conscious thought was the hope that she could smell him through the helmet. His scent reminded her of home.

The silence and the stillness woke her up. Disoriented, she realised they had arrived back at the inn. She was still pressed along Veren's back, and his left arm was pressed on her right, left hand clasping her elbow.

Veren straightened when she moved. His hand loosened, but he didn't remove it, anchoring her to him still.

"You awake now, little one?" He asked over his shoulder.

"Yeah—Sorry. You were right. I needed the sleep ..." She straightened up. Her legs were wooden. She gasped when the rush of returning sensation attacked her limbs. Veren looked back at her in alarm. "Pins and needles," she muttered.

"Don't move," Veren said.

He manoeuvred his long legs off the bike, removed his helmet and then hers. The strap had left a mark on her chin, and Veren massaged it away. He then grasped her by the waist, lifted her, and set her gently on her feet.

She winced as the painful sensation of recirculating blood flowed to her veins, making her hop on each foot. Veren's hands remained on her waist, steadying her. Soon the prickles faded, allowing her to stand on her own. Veren's gentle fingers combed through her hair, ruffling it.

By instinct, she touched his hand, but before she could ask him what he was doing, he said, "Helmet head," and his hands dropped away.

"Thanks." Her hair must have looked like a bird's nest. "I think it's time to hit the shower. I'm starting to stink..." She needed a brief respite from her rioting emotions. Her resolution to treat him like an older brother was melting like ice cream in the midday sun.

"Yeah, me too. It's a wonder you were able to fall asleep on me like that. You must think I smelled like hell and the devil's ass combined." He ruffled his own helmet-flattened hair.

"No, the helmet was on the way," she blurted.

Veren laughed. She felt her cheeks heat up.

"Okay, so that redeemed this helmet from its hair flattening flaw." He chuckled.

"I guess," she said. "Are we going somewhere else later?" she asked to divert him from the reddening of her face and neck.

It was mid-afternoon. There was still the rest of the day, and Veren might have other plans for them. She needed re-energising. She felt lethargic.

"None for the day, but I'll meet you here later at six. Let's go out to dinner," he said.

"All right, I'll see you later ..." She proceeded to her room. She had a ton of things to do and so little time.

Her clothes needed to be washed, or she would have nothing to wear tomorrow. She had worn her two t-shirts, and if she wore this pair of jeans one more time, it might grow its own culture. Perhaps she would have enough time to go to the town centre and get a dress. She could afford one if she didn't spend over five hundred pesos.

As she got into the bathroom, she realised she was still wearing Veren's long-sleeved shirt. She rushed into the shower for a quick rinse. She wanted enough time to wash the clothes, go out to buy a dress, and come back in time for dinner.

To save time, she washed her shirt, underclothes and Veren's shirt under the shower using the hand soap that was provided in the room. It took a while as the soap wasn't foamy or meant for washing clothes. But it was all she had. She hung them on the verandah of the room to ensure that they would dry by morning. She would return Veren's shirt clean.

With her wet hair combed into place, she rushed out. She needed to get to the town square as fast as she could. It would be a good fifteen-minute walk, and she had about three hours to get ready for dinner. She wanted to have as much time as possible to make herself presentable.

Veren jogged down the stairs, checking the piece of paper he had and the written instruction on it. The front desk staff had given him directions to the town centre's best shop. He wanted to get Anza her own jacket. As he got out of the lobby and turned left, he saw Anza up ahead, hurrying towards somewhere.

Where is she going?

He followed her.

She might get into trouble.

Three blocks on, Anza turned left to the main street. The shop he meant to visit loomed over the horizon. He had kept the one-block distance between him and Anza, but lessened it as he realised he might lose her inside.

She just entered a clothes outlet when he got to the entrance. Anza disappeared through the door. He stayed out of sight and watched through the windows as she flicked through the hangers in the clothes rack. The racks were shoulder-height, and he could see every expression that crossed her face. There was an impatient frown on her forehead.

She was looking at dresses.

He realised Anza was a dress-wearing kind of girl, even if he hadn't seen her wear anything but jeans and a T-shirt since he met her. He supposed that, when she came with her parents for their holiday in their log cabin up in the mountains, a dress would have been inappropriate.

Anza had picked up a beautiful light and flowy, grey sleeveless summer dress with a tank top bodice and soft pleats under the breast. It had a profusion of tiny red, yellow and blue flowers embroidered on the hem that looked like it spilt from a basket.

Her eyes sparkled as she held it against her to check the fit. It was in her size. Then Anza looked at the tag. Her face fell. With a sigh, she put it back on the rack and walked away, but she glanced back with longing at the dress one more time. In her characteristic grit, she squared her shoulders and continued on to the rack closest to the wall.

He watched her pick up a short, blue eyelet blouse and a skirt set. She held it against herself and examined her reflection in the mirror. She asked for another colour. The saleslady informed her there were three choices—blue, yellow, and green, then came back with what looked like a sea-foam green pair. The lady pointed to the dressing room to her left. Anza walked over and disappeared inside.

I should let her shop in peace and not spy on her like this.

Yet, he was compelled to keep watching. But his vantage point was bad. He couldn't see her well from this location. He entered the shop and headed towards the male section, then navigated between the racks of clothes for women and children. The shop was crammed and dusty. Grimy, beige linoleum covered the floor. The place smelled of plastic, floor wax, and packaging. The men's section was a little further at the back, close to where various shoes were on display.

"Good afternoon, Sir. How can I help you?" An eager saleslady approached him.

"I want to browse first. Can I go around for a bit? I'll call you when I need you." When the saleslady didn't respond, he asked, "Is it all right?" while exerting his charm. The saleslady blushed, nodded, and left him.

He positioned himself among the hanging clothes. Not looking, but waiting with bated breath for Anza to come out. To his disappointment, she wasn't wearing the new dress when she got out. She smiled at the waiting service staff and confirmed that she would get the set.

After she paid, Anza walked out, but not before throwing one last longing glance at the grey dress she had looked at earlier. With a sigh, she left the shop.

With her gone, he bought what he came here for—something warm for Anza to wear. He found a blue hoodie with a zipper closure on the front. It was the thickest he could find. On impulse, he bought the dress that Anza liked.

Satisfied with his purchase, he tucked the shopping bag inside his jacket and got out of the store. He hurried back to their inn, and within minutes, from a distance, he spotted Anza going the same direction.

He remembered the blouse and skirt pair she bought and wondered if she would wear it at dinner.

An hour and a half later, he sat in the lobby, waiting for Anza to show up. He was looking forward to seeing her in her new purchase.

Ten minutes in, he wondered what was taking her so long. She was uncharacteristically late. He approached the counter to call her room, but no one answered.

She could be on her way down now. It's a pity that she's not using her cell phone.

After another ten minutes without her, he got worried. He knocked on her door. There was no answer. For a moment, he felt tempted to kick the door in. Instead, he got the lock picking set that he always carried with him. A remnant of his childhood and a reminder of his troubled past, of what he had escaped from, what he overcame.

Every time he looked at it, it made him grateful for what he had, where he was, what he had achieved and the people who helped him. Today, he was grateful for it for a practical reason.

Within a minute, the door opened. Anza was lying on one of the two beds in her room, curled on her side like a child. Asleep. He felt a quick rush of relief to find her safe, but he saw the flush on her cheeks and realised she was running a temperature. He approached her and touched her cheek. Her fever was high. Heat emanated from her body.

She had laid out the clothes she bought at the edge of the other bed, and beside it were the jeans she wore earlier. She was wearing the same oversized T-shirt. *It must be the one she borrowed from her cousin.* It was a good thing, as it was long enough to cover her. She was lying on the top of the sheets, shivering.

He whipped the cover from the other bed and draped it over her. He was tucking her in when Anza woke up, disoriented. She looked confused when she saw his face. Her eyes darted around.

Alarmed, she rasped, "Am I late?" She tried to get up but swayed even in a seated position.

"You're fevered. We're not going anywhere, so you're not late for anything." He pressed her back to the bed with gentle force and tucked her in.

"Give me a few minutes' rest, then I'll be fine," she said weakly, her eyes already closing.

"Have you taken any medicines?" He prodded her.

She shook her head. Her body trembled.

He phoned the reception and asked for some fever medicine. He didn't carry any—something he must rectify in his first aid kit. While he waited, he lay down behind her and pulled her close, infusing her with his warmth to stop the tremors that wracked her body.

The doorbell rang. It was the front desk clerk, with two paracetamol tablets in hand.

"Sir, these are the only two tablets we have. Do you need more?" the clerk asked.

"Yes, please," he said, giving a nod. "Can someone buy them for us?" He didn't want to leave her. The clerk nodded. "Is there a doctor on the island, just in case?" He didn't want to think about it, but it was best to be prepared.

"Yes, Sir. Should we call him?" The clerk peeked over his shoulder to ogle Anza.

Veren moved to block his view. He felt protective, and ... possessive.

"Not yet. Let's see first if the medicine works. If we need to call him, how soon can he come?" He wanted to plan, to prepare.

"If he's not at another house call, around ten minutes. His home clinic isn't very far from here."

"Okay. Thank you very much." He dismissed the clerk. Anza needed the paracetamol in her system as soon as possible.

He lifted Anza's upper body and slid behind her, leaning her back on his chest. Her body was scorching.

Holy Prometheus, she's on fire! This medicine better work.

He roused Anza with a gentle shake. She blinked up at him, her lids heavy. "Take this, Anza. It's for your fever."

He pushed the tablets through her lips. She complied, but it seemed to have taken most of her strength. She could barely swallow the tablets and the gulp of water.

He kept her pressed close to his chest until her shivering subsided. But her fever was still raging. He eased out from behind her. His body heat was adding to her temperature. She needed to cool down.

He realised she had unplugged the air conditioner in her room. No doubt—she didn't want to use it to save money. He turned it on to full blast, hoping it would help cool her down. He toed off his shoes and sat on the other bed, to stand guard and watch over her.

This was how it was to be someone's keeper—to be in charge of their physical, mental, and emotional welfare. It was such an enormous responsibility; he was unsure if he wanted it, but at that moment he had no choice. And, if he was honest with himself, he would have no one else care for her but himself.

For half an hour, he waited for the medicine to take effect, to control her fever.

Anza twisted in a sudden movement and flung the covers off. A long moan came out of her mouth. Fear struck his heart. He tried to rouse her, but she was insensible. She was close to convulsing. He picked her up and hoisted her over his shoulder to keep one hand free.

He went to her bathroom, turned the shower on and tested the water. She was burning up to a dangerous level, but the water couldn't be ice cold, just a few degrees cooler than her core temperature. He let her slide down his body until she was on her toes and anchored against him, his arm around her to support her limp body.

Heedless of his own clothes, he stood with her under the shower. The water flowed over both of them for a few minutes. One big hand held her head by the neck, so the cooling liquid could cascade from her crown to her feet without getting into her ears.

The water drenched them both, clothes and all. But it worked—Anza's fever abated, although she remained unconscious throughout. He reached behind her and turned off the shower. Still clasped against his chest to keep her upright, he pushed the hair off of her face. Anza stirred and briefly opened her eyes.

"Veren," she mumbled, then fell back into unconsciousness.

He walked her out of the stall where her towel hung. Beside it was the bathrobe provided by the inn. He took both. He wrapped the beach towel around her, and laid her on the bed. Her feet dangled over the edge. He knew he would have to get her out of her wet shirt. While he was concerned about her sensibilities, right now it was more important to keep her dry.

Without a second thought, he took the damp towel from her body, revealing the soaked T-shirt that was almost transparent. With his eyes averted, and with quick movements, he pulled the shirt off of her, and her underclothes followed. Her wet clothes landed on the floor with a splat. With determination, he pushed away every thought that had nothing to do with Anza's welfare and covered her with the dry bathrobe.

He didn't realise he held his breath while undressing her with averted eyes until he had to inhale. The air conditioner was blowing fiercely at him and sent shivers up his frame. He also needed to get out of his own sodden clothes. He peeled them off and pulled on the second bathrobe that was hanging in the wardrobe. It was thin, but it would do.

He collected their soggy clothes and dropped both sets on the bathroom floor. He towelled Anza's hair dry and ran her comb through the wet tresses. Tangled hair would greet her in the morning, and he was sure she wouldn't like that.

He fit her properly into the bathrobe, lifted, and placed her back on her bed. He pulled the covers over her and spread her damp hair on the pillow. She still had a mild fever, but her temperature was under control.

Thank Prometheus for that!

He was on his way to her bathroom to take care of their wet clothes when the doorbell rang. It was Mrs. Bassig, and she looked scandalised when she saw him in a bathrobe.

"Please, don't jump to conclusions, Mrs. Bassig." He stepped aside to let her in.

Mrs. Bassig walked in, speechless. She looked at him from head to toe, the raised eyebrows laden with questions and judgmental thoughts she dared not voice out for fear of having it confirmed.

"No doubt you came here because you heard Anza is sick." He glanced at Anza, still deep in slumber on the bed. "Her fever spiked so high, she was a second away from convulsion. I had to put her under the shower to lower her temperature."

Mrs. Bassig continued to stare at him. He could tell that she was trying to curb her own initial assumption. The older woman's considerable bosom heaved.

"Mr. Albareda, as far as I know, you just met Anza the other day in my lobby. Why are you suddenly so close to each other? What are your intentions towards this little girl?"

Mrs. Bassig's questions were direct. His impression was that she would not swallow a lie, and nothing would get past her sharp eyes and instinct.

"Mrs. Bassig, my intentions are pure. I assure you, I have done nothing, nor will I do anything that would harm her. All I want is to protect her and keep her safe." He infused his truth with as much sincerity as he could.

"But why are you doing this? What are you to her?" Mrs. Bassig asked.

"I'm her keeper." His reply was quick, automatic.

He could utter no truer words at the moment. And no one could make him unsay it.

Not Mrs. Bassig. Not even Anza's father.

7

THE REVELATION

"Who are you, really, Mr. Albareda?"

Mrs. Bassig's tone told him she wouldn't leave the issue alone until he answered all her questions to her satisfaction. At his hesitation, Mrs. Bassig's hands went to her hips. She bristled with authority.

"And don't tell me you're her keeper. *I* can take care of our young patient. She's staying in *my* inn. *I* have offered her employment, she's more *my* responsibility than yours."

Alarm streaked through him at her words. She threatened to cut his access to Anza if he didn't tell her the truth of who he was, why he was here, and what his connection to Anza was. He needed to tell her an acceptable variance of the truth.

He sighed. "Okay, Mrs. Bassig. You win ..." He sat down so he was at eye level with her. "My name is Veren Albareda. Anza's father, Manuu Soledad, sent me to find her, watch over her, and convince her to go home."

"Her father sent you?" Mrs. Bassig raised a disbelieving eyebrow. "How come she doesn't know you? She told me she met you here when you first checked in." Her tone sounded thick with suspicion.

"Because we have never met before." He glanced at the bed to check if Anza was still asleep. He didn't want her to overhear anything.

"Why send you? Are you a private investigator? You look too young to be one," Mrs. Bassig questioned.

"Do you mind if we move outside to talk? I don't want to disturb Anza." he said.

Mrs. Bassig gave his attire a pointed look. He shrugged. His clothes were wet, and he couldn't care less if people saw him buck naked.

After some hesitation, Mrs. Bassig nodded and opened the front door. He followed, barefoot and in a bathrobe. They stood in the hallway.

"Anza's father is a friend of my ... family. I just graduated from the military academy. I've been away for my studies. That's why Anza and I never met. Her dad asked me to convince her to come home. They didn't want to send anyone they don't trust."

He didn't create that brief explanation on the spot. It was part of his training to cover all kinds of situations. He had thought about this scenario before, except in his head, he was saying this practised statement to Anza.

"I gather Anza doesn't know yet who you are, and you don't want her to know..." Mrs. Bassig guessed correctly. Her objection to his strategy was plain in her voice. "So, what *is* your plan?"

"I want to ensure her safety while she's here and convince her of the merits of going home. She'd be more receptive to a neutral viewpoint. If she finds out who I am, that I'm part of the family, she'll put a wall between us. She'll dig her heels in, out of stubbornness." The reasoning was sound, and true. That had always been their concern about Anza.

Mrs. Bassig's indecisive stance softened. He could see that his explanation made sense to her. Finally, she nodded and said, "Okay. I'll keep your secret. But you can't take care of her dressed like ... that." She gestured to the bathrobe; her own thoughts had scandalised her.

"I was going to hang my clothes to dry and put them back on later. This was the only thing I could use for the moment. I wasn't planning to walk around your establishment wearing this robe. I just need this for the meantime."

"Give me your clothes and I'll have someone run it in the dryer."

Mrs. Bassig shooed him into the bathroom to get the wet clothes. He scooped them out into the damp towel and handed the entire load to her. Arms full of sodden clothing, she called something out over her shoulder, then added, "I'll send up some hot soup in an hour ... or so."

"Thank you, Mrs. Bassig."

He closed the door.

Anza was still deep in sleep. He touched her forehead. Not bad. He sighed and sat down on the bed, his back against the headboard. He wondered what caused the sudden onslaught of fever. The high temperature was the body's response to an infection. Hopefully, it was just a minor one.

His stomach rumbled. He was hungry. They both missed lunch earlier. He also wanted to get a spare change of clothes from his room, but the need to keep Anza in sight, not to leave her alone, was stronger. He would have to be in this bathrobe until Mrs. Bassig returned with his dry clothes. Maybe

"Better?" he asked. At her nod, he touched her cheeks and forehead. She was cool to the touch.

"You need to eat—you're weak." He grasped her hand as it shook when she tried to reach for the bottled water again.

"I'm not hungry. I'm just thirsty," she said shakily.

"No, let's give you something easy to eat." He called the front desk to order some Arroz Caldo, a chicken and rice porridge for her, and some bacon and eggs for himself.

"Did you watch over me the entire night?" Her voice came out soft, her expression one of curiosity and concern.

"Yes, little one, I did." He nodded as he sat on the other bed. "I came looking for you when you didn't show up and found you asleep, and burning hot. Don't you remember?"

"No." Anza was trying to dredge her memory, but it must have come up blank. "The only thing I remember is taking a nap."

He pushed the limp hair off her pale face and pressed the cool, damp towel on her forehead, cheeks, and neck. Her eyes closed in bliss.

"Do you have any injuries? You might have an infection," She frowned in confusion at his question. "I'm trying to find out the source of your fever," he explained.

"No injury, but ...... my throat is sore," she replied, and swallowed. "It feels swollen, too."

He tipped her face up by the chin. "Say ahh."

She opened her mouth wide as he peered down her throat. Her tonsils were red and inflamed.

"Okay. Let's see if the swelling goes down within the day." It didn't look too bad. He was relieved. The island wasn't equipped for serious medical cases.

"Veren ..." she called as he stood up to go to the bathroom.

He looked back and waited for the rest of her statement. "Yes, little one?" he prompted.

"You don't have to pay for my fee, since I can't accompany you on your trip today," she said.

"Oh, don't be silly. You're keeping me company."

"No, you're nursing me. There's no need to charge you for the privilege," she said. Her attempt at humour made him smile. She was on her way to recovery.

"Let's discuss that later, little one—when you're strong enough to argue with me."

There was a knock on the door. Their food had arrived. He strode to the door and took the food tray in. "For now, you and I will eat."

Anza insisted on eating by herself. Despite her pronouncement on her disinterest in the food, she almost finished the porridge. This pleased him. As expected, she got sleepy after the meal. He was reading a book while Anza rested when his phone rang.

Edrigu was calling.

"Good morning, Sir." His mind debated with his heart whether to tell Edrigu about Anza being sick.

"How's everything, Veren? I'm due to call Manuu in half an hour, so I need an update from you," he said.

He understood Edrigu was asking not just for the truth of the status of his mission, but he also wanted a plausible statement they could give to Manuu.

He stepped out of Anza's room for privacy. "I have established a rapport, Sir. But I'm not yet confident that I can influence her enough to make her change her mind."

This was an accurate statement. Anza's reason for leaving was rooted deep, and he didn't think he would have enough influence on her decision.

"Is there anything you need to hasten the process? Manuu is worried and restless," Edrigu said.

"Yes, I think there is. I think it might be the only thing that would convince Anza to return and ensure she won't run away again. I need a commitment from him, Sir." He needed Edrigu to champion his cause, Anza's cause, to ensure her safety.

"What kind of commitment?" Edrigu sounded intrigued.

"He needs to promise to allow Anza to make friends with humans, to establish long-term friendships and ... relationships," he said. There was silence on the other line. "Sir?" he prompted.

"Is that what Anza wants?" Edrigu asked.

"Yes, Sir," he sighed. "She feels out of place in her own family, being the only Erdia among them. She can't take part in any of the things they do as *Vis*. Even so, her father treats her like a *Vis*. They all do."

He had to sway Edrigu to this cause. "She's not at all like us. She doesn't want to live her brief life unanchored, as our kind does. We have the longevity to do this, she does not. She does not want to waste her short lifespan living the *Vis* life when she doesn't have the years to sustain it."

"I see ..." Edrigu said.

Those two words carried so much understanding, it made his heart pound.

"Can you help me, Sir?" He heard the plea in his own voice. "I don't think Mr. Soledad will listen to someone like me, but he will with you."

"Veren, Anza is sixteen. In *Vis* years, she's practically a baby. She is his father's only child, daughter of his great love, the centre of his life. Therefore, he is understandably over-protective. While I see your point, a father's love is something we cannot question," Edrigu said, his tone gentle.

"Sir, it is the only thing that would convince her to come home, and stay home. Without that promise, Anza might just run away again. I believe Mr. Soledad is due for *Transit* next year. Anza might just do it again then. And this time, she might get lucky enough to disappear completely. It's the only way to keep her safe." The desperation in his voice was obvious to his own ears.

"Okay, that's a good argument. I will do my best to persuade Manuu to give her that." Edrigu sounded convinced.

An enormous rush of gratitude flooded his heart. "Thank you, Sir!" He could breathe easier now. Anza would be safe when he'd return to his training. He could focus on the rest of his life goals and not worry about her while away.

"So, what update can I tell Manuu?" Edrigu asked.

"You can tell him I have covered leads in Naidi and Vayang, and I have not found her there. I'm going to Valugan next," he said. This was half true. Those were the locations that he intended to visit with Anza.

"Okay. That will work. I don't expect him to say yes immediately, but I will convince him of the merits of your plan," Edrigu said. "I'll call you in a day or so. Earlier if I succeed with Manuu on my first try."

Waves of confusing emotions washed over him when he realised that if Edrigu secured Manuu Soledad's commitment tomorrow, he could reveal himself to Anza and convince her to go home. And, if she agreed, perhaps in two days they would part ways.

My time with her would end.

I should be glad.

I should be happy that I'm so close to completing my mission.

Instead, he felt deflated.

Anza woke up in the dim lamplight.

Did I sleep all day?

She glanced at the other bed and saw Veren asleep, an opened book lying face down beside him. He looked peaceful and boyish.

This must be what he looked like before the troubles he took upon his shoulders weighed on him. At twenty-three, he struck her as more serious than he should be. Despite his light-hearted manner, there was something grave that underpinned his actions.

She stretched out and her tight muscles protested. She had been abed for far too long and needed a shower. It propelled her to go to the bathroom.

After a short, cool rinse, she put on the same bathrobe she wore earlier. The feeling of cleanliness and the scent that lingered in the bathrobe gave her a sense of well-being. She sniffed at the robe, trying to remember where she had smelled it before.

She padded out to the verandah and sat on a cushioned rattan lounger. The cool sunset breeze soothed her. The fresh and fragrant scent of sea, jasmine, wet grass, and some unfamiliar vegetation perfumed the air. Day birds had changed shift with their nocturnal kin, their call now dominated the night air. The cricket chirps accompanied their song.

She sat curled up and hugged her knees close, enveloped by the comforting darkness. The first week of her journey for independence had been eventful. Fate seemed determined to show her, at first instance, what it would be like on her own. If Veren didn't show up, she would have been sick alone, in a bed space, with no one to help her.

Her life wasn't in danger, but if something direr had occurred, it would devastate her father. If he never ever found her, or her body, he would suffer for a long time not knowing what became of her. Her impulsive action to run away was irresponsible, and selfish. She knew that she needed to rectify it, that she must relieve her parents' anxiety about her health and safety.

The door behind her slid open with a thud, startling her. A frantic Veren followed. His eyes were wild and furious.

"What the hell, Anza!"

Veren loomed over her. His body vibrated with menacing energy. She looked up at him, confused by the anger on his face.

"What did I do?"

"I woke up, and you were gone. You ... I looked all over for you ... I thought ..."

"I'm sorry, I wanted some air. I didn't realise you would worry ..."

He stood looking down at her for a while, fists clenched. He exhaled, and the tension bled out of him. With a sigh, he tapped her leg to make her scoot over so he would have room to sit down. She did. Veren dropped beside her.

"Why didn't you wake me?" His tone was calm. The light from the bedroom no longer illuminated his face, darkness hiding his expression from her.

"You were sleeping. You needed your rest too." She tucked her legs under herself to hide her toes. The night air had turned cold.

Veren scooped her into his lap. One hand covered her bare feet. The heat from it warmed her toes. She went rigid for a moment, but soon settled into him. She curled into his chest and laid her head at the curve of his neck. This felt right, being cradled in his arms. It was safety, comfort, affection all rolled into one warm cocoon.

Ahh. The smell is Veren. He wore this before I did.

This realisation made her heart hum. It still had that elusive whiff of something familiar yet unknown embedded in the robe, but she was too content at the moment to delve deeper into her memory bank.

"You scared me, little one," he murmured.

"I'm sorry. I didn't mean to." She inhaled deeply. With this breath, a decision solidified within her, borne out of the insight that came to her tonight. "I seem to have a habit of unintentionally scaring the people who care about me."

Veren's body tensed. She could sense his eyes on her.

"Did you come to an epiphany during your fever?" he asked.

That made her smile. "Not quite an epiphany. Just a realisation that I've been selfish. I didn't think about how much my father and my family would worry about me when I left like that."

"Wait—does this mean that you've changed your mind about your plan? To be independent and live away from them, I mean."

There was a hitch in his voice that she didn't quite understand, but she let it go.

"Not quite. I still want to achieve independence. But I need to amend my methods, so I won't worry my parents unnecessarily. I guess they still see me as a child."

"You can do it gradually, Anza. Not like this—not cold turkey."

"Right," she yawned. "Not cold turkey."

Veren felt Anza's weight settle on him as she fell asleep. The hand that rested on his chest slid down to her lap. Her breathing became an even cadence. She slept like a child—complete, trusting, vulnerable.

This had become a habit between them. Him watching over her slumber as she dreamed. He wouldn't have it any other way.

He took in a deep breath, then released it. Every molecule of air flushed away the remnants of the fear that had gripped him earlier when he thought she'd wandered off in a fever-induced sleep. He went on a frantic search for her in the hallways. And the stairs, half afraid that he might find her broken body at the bottom.

He was in the garden when he looked up and saw someone smoking on a verandah. He realised he didn't check the one in her room. The only thing that stopped him from climbing the verandahs from the front was the smoking guy. It would shock the man to see him scale the building one verandah after another. That could cause a ruckus.

He rushed back to her room. His relief when he found her curled on the small couch overwhelmed him. Then he got angry at himself for overreacting.

Anza had carved a space in his heart, a fact that he found alarming. She was too young for him, and he had no time for love in his life right now. Her impulsiveness, her drive for independence, required someone who would watch over her constantly while allowing her to grow.

He couldn't afford to be derailed. His path was set and the timetable for each milestone, fixed. This case was supposed to be a stepping stone, but she turned out to be a divergence from the direction he had chosen since childhood.

His frustrated sigh echoed her sleepy one. She shifted in his lap and straightened her legs. He looked down at her sleeping form and cradled her closer, rocking her. Holding her like this, entrusted in his keeping, somehow soothed his anxiety. It made him believe that life would sort itself out in the long run.

It gave him hope.

Their conversation earlier showed him the time to convince her to go home had come; she was ready for it. She had loosened her grip on her idea of independence. She was ready for a compromise.

He knew he could convince her to go home before the end of the day tomorrow if he applied himself. And they would be on her trip back home the day after. She would be with her father then, and he would be on his way. It would be 'Mission Accomplished' with a day to spare. His schedule would return to normal, but the rest of his life never would.

Anza sneezed. It alerted him to the dropping temperature and reminded him that she was still recovering. He stood up and carried her with ease back to the room, then laid her down on the bed, tucking her in.

He stood by her door as he fought the desire to stay. The knowledge that he had another day with her made him close the door and walk away.

If he must learn to let her go, he might as well start now.

Pangs of hunger woke Anza up. She was disappointed when she saw the empty bed next to hers. Veren must have decided last night that she didn't need to be watched anymore.

The sky was just lighting up now with the morning sun. She wondered if the kitchen was already open. Her stomach growled. She felt normal, but her hands trembled a little. *Must be my hunger.*

To revive herself, she took a full shower to wash away traces of her illness. She put on the sea-green eyelet dress she bought the other day. She was going to wear it the night she fell ill. Now that she felt better, she wanted to look good.

She got downstairs and found that the coffee shop had just opened for the day. The staff was turning on lights and setting tables. The kitchen wouldn't be ready for another hour. They offered her coffee while she waited. She accepted it and took it with her as she walked to the bakery located two blocks away. An hour was too long to wait. Also, she wanted fresh air—the walk would do her good.

A block in, she was out of breath and reconsidering the wisdom of her decision. She rested and weighed the pros and cons of continuing to the bakery—she was halfway there already—or going back to wait for the kitchen to open.

She was gauging the distance between her two options when she saw Veren hurrying her way. His expression was thunderous. And she knew the reason for that look. She waited for him to come closer and as he loomed over her; she gave him her best heartfelt smile. It worked as intended. Veren faltered mid-step and forgot whatever he intended to say at the sight of her beaming face.

"Good morning, Veren. What brought you out this early?"

He blinked at her. Twice.

Resigned, he asked, "Why are you out this early, Anza?"

"I was hungry. I want to buy bread." She pointed to the bakery.

"You're not recovered enough yet to be walking this distance." He led her to a wooden bench at the corner of the street. "You wait here. I can get you what you want. Anything in particular?"

"I can go with you ..."

"No. You're already breathless. Just sit there, and I'll be back shortly."

He sounded like her father whenever he didn't want any argument or negotiation. It made her smile.

"So, what do you want?" Veren persisted.

"Some pandesal? Or anything with meat in it, like meat pies, or sandwich buns. Anything savoury ..." Veren's eyebrow raised in surprise. "I'm hungry," she said in her defence.

He reached out and touched her cheek, smiling. "That's a good sign. Your appetite is back. And your temperature is normal." With one last appraising perusal, he departed.

She watched him jog to the bakery. Her heart fluttered. How exactly did Veren see her apart from as a little sister? His affection and concern for her warmed her soul.

The sound of jogging feet made her turn her head. It seemed there was another early riser today. To her surprise, she recognised him as Diego. He skidded to a stop in front of her, jaw going slack in surprise.

"Anza!" The delight in his face was clear.

"What are you doing here, Diego?"

"Jogging. We're staying four blocks away from here." He pointed in the bakery's direction. "I'm on my way back to our hotel."

"What a coincidence!"

"Where are you staying? And why are you here?" Diego's questions were tripping over each other.

"I was going to buy bread from the bakery. Veren is doing that for me."

"Oh ... So, he's still with you?" His frown seemed wary.

"Yes. He's my keeper, remember?"

"Yeah, I remember. Although, I still don't know what it means," Diego said, his tone inviting an explanation from her. He would be disappointed, as she had no inclination to do so—she didn't know how to define it herself.

In perfect timing, her keeper approached, a brown bag full of bread in his hand.

"Good morning, Diego. It's quite a coincidence to find you out and about this early in the morning." Veren's deep voice lacked much intonation, but still sounded thick with meaning.

"Good morning, Veren, and I agree. It's quite a pleasant shock to encounter Anza here. But it makes my day."

"It looks like you were out jogging, so we won't keep you. Anza needs to eat and rest for now." Veren may have been polite, but he was also dismissive. He grasped Anza's elbow, clearly intending to bring about her eating and rest as soon as possible.

The highhandedness annoyed her, but she had no energy to argue with Veren in the street, and certainly not in front of an audience. "Bye, Diego," she said in a cheerful voice as she waved at him. "It was nice to see you again."

Diego had no choice but to nod. His expression reflected his unvoiced protest.

She and Veren walked back to their hotel, bag of bread in hand. They settled on a chair set outside of the coffee shop. Veren took out the contents of his purchase. The smell of freshly baked bread made her mouth water.

A pandesal and a beef bun later, she was a new woman. The coffee was the perfect pair for the pieces of bread. Veren consumed the rest, and when the staff informed them that the kitchen was ready to take their order, he asked for scrambled eggs.

"You're still hungry after all that bread?" His appetite amazed her.

"I'm a growing boy," he joked. "Plus, the jog to the bakery sapped my energy."

"Oh, that reminds me ..." Her earlier annoyance at his domineering manner returned. "I dislike it when people decide for me."

His eyebrow raised. "Did you not need to eat and rest earlier? You braved the distance just to get something to eat, and you were breathless in the effort. That shows you were both hungry and tired."

"Yeah, but that's beside the point."

"Well, you can discuss your point when you're well and have enough breath to argue," Veren said, ending their discussion on that topic.

It was hard to sustain her annoyance when he had a valid argument. She would let it slide, for now.

Anza and Veren spent the morning by the garden under the shade of the trees, with Anza dozing off a few minutes at a time. But she was on the mend, and her recuperation satisfied him. He wanted her recovered for their talk about her homecoming.

The day was breezy; the garden was fragrant with jasmine, the sky blue and cloudless. His heart felt full of emotions as he watched her nap against him. Anza looked better in a dress. She looked less like a child in it than in jeans and oversized shirts. She was on the brink of blossoming into full womanhood. It pained him to think he wouldn't be there to watch it happen.

For now, he needed to finish his mission, to fulfil what he meant to do when he came looking for her; to convince her to come home.

The opportunity came over lunch. He had food delivered to her unit and set it all up on her verandah. He wanted the perfect ambience and privacy for their talk.

Anza ate well. She even had a hankering for dessert, so he ordered some fruits for her. Over her ginger tea and his coffee, he raised the question that was at the surface of his mind.

"Anza, last night you mentioned changing your plans to achieve independence. What changed?"

"I want my parents to know that I'm well," she said.

"How would you do that?"

"I'd like to borrow your phone for a start, so I can text them and tell them I'm okay." Her eyes held an appeal for him to say yes. "I plan to send them regular messages later, perhaps once a week, once I get a new phone."

"Anza, a text message once a week won't stop your father from worrying. Only one thing would do that. And you know what that is." He could relate to her father's anxiety. The thought of leaving her here alone and unprotected was knotting his gut into pretzels.

"I can't give up on my independence, Veren. It's crucial to my future ..." Her response carried defiance, desperation, and regret.

"You wouldn't have to give up on your quest. There's a better way to do this."

"How?"

"Negotiate with your dad. Tell him why you want to do this and then ask him to allow you to make friends and establish relationships with people outside of your family."

Anza digested his suggestion, determining the viability of it. "Do you think my dad would agree?" Hope glinted in her eyes.

"You're in a better position to answer that, Anza. I don't know your father ... as well as you do." He took a gulp of his coffee. "But, given his bitter experience this past week, he would know you're serious and that it's worth considering."

Anza went quiet for a while, chewing on the inside of her lower lip as she contemplated her circumstances and the options available to her.

"It might work ..." She nodded to herself, then sighed. "I wish I had asked him before I ran away."

"Well, look at it this way. The pain of the past week added weight in your favour to sway him to your cause."

She smiled. "You have a good point there."

"So, are you ready to go home tomorrow?" He wanted to bring her to her father himself, to ensure that his last image of Anza was that of her surrounded by the people who loved her.

"Yes, I am," she said with a nod. "How about you? When are you planning to leave here?"

"I was thinking that we can travel together; fly back to the mainland tomorrow."

"Why would you cut your visit here short?" She was perplexed.

"I want to make sure you get home safe and sound."

"Veren, I don't want you to cut your holiday short on my account."

"I can come back here anytime," he reassured her. "Besides, I need to go to the mainland tomorrow. There's something I need from there that I can't get here." He needed his *sustenance*, since his *vital hunger* was surfacing. He could feel his *Crux* weakening. The telltale tightening of his core had begun this morning.

"Are you sure?" She looked doubtful. "You're not just saying that because you're taking your role as my keeper seriously, are you?"

"No, I'm not saying that because I'm your keeper. However, I *do* take that role seriously." He pressed her mouth closed with his forefinger when she was poised to argue. "So, it's settled. We're flying out together tomorrow."

Anza looked unconvinced, her eyes narrowed as she seemed to be readying herself for an argument. And he remembered their last exchange. His chest tightened with the effort not to coddle her, like her father did.

"Anza, I am not deciding for you in this instance. I am choosing for me. And I really want to fly with you. Will you let me?"

She looked at him intently, then a slow smile appeared on her lips. She nodded. "Okay." She went back to eating her fruits.

Warm feelings invaded his heart as he watched her eat. He wondered if he should tell her who he was, why he came here. It was an unnecessary barrier between them.

Will she be angry at me for deceiving her? Maybe I should warn her father not to divulge who I am to her.

"After lunch, why don't you go take a nap? I'll go to the airport and buy our tickets."

"Okay, but let me give you money for my fare." She jumped up to rush off.

He held her arm to stop her. "It's okay, little one—I can take care of it."

"I insist, Veren. Besides, I don't have to pinch pennies now. I'm going home." Her mouth had a stubborn curl to it.

"Okay." He let her go; the determined glint in her eyes brooked no argument.

Anza came back soon after and handed him the money.

"I should call my dad first. He could be in Manila," she said, thinking aloud.

"He won't be," he said on impulse.

Anza looked at him, surprised. "How would you know?"

"Well, um... if I was your father, I would stay where you left me, in case you return."

She paused and considered that. "I guess so."

He got up and kissed her forehead. "Bedtime for you, little one. I'll take care of our tickets."

On the way to the airport, he battled regret, sadness, gladness, hope, and some other emotion that he couldn't name. It was too alien for him to identify.

All he knew was that it stemmed from the reality that he was parting ways with Anza by tomorrow.

8

THE KEEPER, THE VISCEREBUS

The mixed feelings that ruled him as he completed his task weighed in his heart. He had secured the tickets. The inevitability of their parting was now tangible. He was both reluctant to hurry back and wanting to take his time. With the moments ticking by, he wanted to squeeze every second with Anza, and yet, not seeing her felt like he was holding back time.

As if Fate wanted to rub it in, his phone rang. It was Edrigu.

"Good afternoon, Sir," he said. Edrigu's call was another dose of reality.

"Good afternoon, Veren. How are you doing with your mission?"

"We're flying to the mainland tomorrow. Anza agreed to go home." His heart weighted down by that declaration.

"Congratulations. I knew you could do it." Edrigu's pride in him should have lifted his spirit, but it didn't. "Did she make a fuss?"

"No, Sir. She came to her own resolution when she got sick. But the idea of negotiating a measure of freedom from her father convinced her, ultimately."

"Well, she won't have a hard time. Manuu agreed." Edrigu sounded smug.

That was welcome news, but that information was like the closing of a door.

"What did he agree to, Sir?"

"We didn't discuss the details. Just that he would allow Anza to make friends with humans, and keep in contact with them. I trust Anza can handle it herself. Based on your reports, she's got pluck."

"Yes, she's got that in buckets." He was proud of her. Anza would hold her own against her father.

"So, does she know who you are? Have you told her?"

"No, Sir. To her, I'm a friend she made here on the island. Her first human friend. A temporary keeper."

"A temporary keeper ... I see." A brief silence ensued. Edrigu seemed to have understood the pain in Veren's heart. "Should I expect you to be back here by tomorrow as well?"

"Yes, Sir, I booked a flight in the afternoon."

He had today and tomorrow with Anza, and he planned to make the most of it.

He was perusing the tourist brochure for a place to take Anza to dinner later that evening when someone tapped him on the shoulder.

"Hi, bro." Diego stood beside his table, uncertain yet defiant.

"Diego"—Veren stood up, surprised—"What brings you here?"

"I was looking for a place to eat, and ..." Veren's direct look made Diego falter. "Fine. I came here looking for Anza. I saw you guys go in here earlier."

"Why are you looking for Anza?" There was no use in prevaricating, in pretending he was unaware of Diego's interest in her.

"I'll be honest with you, Veren. I like Anza very much and I want to be her friend." Diego's straight reply and unwavering gaze impressed him. Most guys wouldn't challenge another male if they could help it.

"Diego, I can't stop you from pursuing her. Only Anza can, frankly." This truth was obvious to them both, but he knew Diego wanted to hear it from him.

"So, you won't stop me?"

Diego was asking for his permission, he realised. As much as Veren would have liked to deny Diego the pleasure, he didn't have it in him to impede what would be beneficial for Anza.

"Of course I won't, but you must accept the responsibility for what your actions would do to her. Anza's young—a sixteen year-old. She had a sheltered upbringing and she's naïve. If you take advantage of her, if you hurt her, you'll colour her view of life and men from then on." He paused only to take a breath. "So, are you prepared for that?"

He was daring Diego to give him his word, to prove to him that he was as honourable as he seemed to be. Diego stared at him, gauging his sincerity, it seemed.

"Yes. My intention is pure. And if friendship is the only thing she wants at the moment, I'll be a friend to her." Diego's statement conveyed that he wanted more.

Part of him wished Diego had backed down. Emotionally, Anza was a blank slate. If a human like Diego showed her kindness, she might just fall in love with him. Veren felt a twinge of fear. But he couldn't put his self-interest above Anza's. Her welfare was more important.

"What she wants and what she needs might not be the same thing." Veren couldn't help but stress the point again. "Are you committed to putting her needs above your own?"

If Anza was going to go out into the world, it would help that she had another human in her life who wouldn't take advantage of her lack of experience. Especially since he couldn't be with her, to watch out for her.

"I have never taken advantage of anyone in my life, Veren. I'm not about to start with Anza." Diego's defensive response was empathic, but not enough for him.

"Diego, Anza needs someone who would allow her to experience life. She needs to make many friends, to develop relationships that would expand her horizon. Would you allow her to grow into her own person before making her yours?"

Diego stood still for a long moment; his eyes never left him. The understanding that dawned on Diego's face chafed at Veren's insides. It made him feel raw and exposed.

"Is that what you're doing, Veren?"

Diego's question struck him with the force of a sledgehammer. His jaw tightened. He had to swallow to loosen the knot in his chest.

"Can you do it?" He asked, ignoring Diego's question.

Diego nodded and released a long in-drawn breath, then held out his hand—a man's offer of his commitment. Diego had just accepted to take his place in Anza's life as her keeper. Veren shook the other man's hand; it was the sealing of a pact, the passing of a baton.

And it was a blow to his heart.

"When can I see Anza?" Diego asked, clearing his throat.

"Not today. We're leaving Basco tomorrow." He wanted all of Anza's remaining hours here to be only his. Every single second.

At Diego's expression, he took a piece of paper and wrote Anza's phone number down. "Here you go. Anza's number. Her phone is off at the moment, but she'll turn it on when she returns to Manila." He handed it to Diego. "I'll tell her to expect your call."

Diego looked at it and considered him, "Thank you, Veren." He pocketed the paper. Then, with a nod, he turned and left.

His borrowed time with Anza was bleeding away fast. With grim determination, Veren proceeded to where she was.

Anza was still napping in her room when he entered. He watched her for a while, memorising the curve of her shoulders, the relaxed, half-opened mouth, the lashes that threw a slight shadow on her baby-soft cheeks, and the gentle rise of her body as she slept. He would commit this to his memory, etch it in his heart. This child-woman that destiny threw in his path continued to create chaos in his soul without knowing it, and with so little effort.

He laid down the dress he bought for her a few days ago at the foot of the bed. He hoped to see it on her tonight.

It would be his one and only chance.

Mrs. Bassig allowed them to use her vehicle when she found out he was planning to take Anza to Fundación Pacita for dinner. She didn't want Anza exposed to the chilly night air, which she would be if they rode his rented motorbike.

When Anza showed up wearing the grey rayon dress, it rendered him speechless. She fixed her hair into relaxed waves, and she was wearing makeup. She gave him a glimpse of what she would be like as a woman, when she'd be old enough for him.

Emotions choked him up.

"You look stunning, little one," he said through a tight throat. His voice sounded rusty, even to his own ears.

"Thank you," Anza said, throwing him a bemused look. "And thank you for this dress. How did you know I wanted it?" The glitter in her eyes was challenging, and a tad suspicious.

He swallowed a kick of panic in his constricted chest. "I saw you look at it in the shop a few days ago."

One delicate eyebrow quirked with warning. "You were following me?"

"No. I was going to the same shop... to get you a hoodie, so you won't be cold when we travel." His pulse was rioting while he waited for Anza's response.

Her eyebrow lowered and erased the suspicion in her eyes. She smoothed the dressed down. Her smile was shy, and grateful. "Thank you, again."

"You're welcome." He gulped down his relief. "Shall we?"

She took his offered arm and walked with him to the waiting car.

"No bike tonight?" Anza asked, surprised. She looked around for the motorcycle.

He smiled at her. "No. Mrs. Bassig doesn't want you to get too exposed to the night air."

"Oh! Does that mean we're going somewhere far?" Her eyes were alight with excitement.

"Not far, but somewhere special," he replied, and ushered her to the passenger seat.

"Where are we going?"

"You'll like it. You'll see."

A garden glittering with hundreds of tiny fairy lights greeted them. Fundacion Pacita was perched atop rolling hills, with a three-hundred-sixty degrees of amazing view. The beautiful stone building made her think of a small castle ruling over a compact kingdom. It had an otherworldly ambience.

Veren booked a table for them on the verandah with the view and the sound of the wind-swept ocean. Their illumination came from the glass lamp set on one corner of the table. They sat side by side, allowing them to enjoy the scenery and talk at a comfortable level.

Few words were exchanged between them during dinner. Veren seemed content. He gave her smiles, affectionate little touches, and pleased looks. As for her, she was just happy being there with him, in this peaceful setting. Time was fleeting, and words seemed to make the clock move faster. Silence was the best way to savour the moment.

She recalled when she woke up earlier that day, thinking of the grey dress that she regretted not splurging on. It was like a miracle to find it there, draped at the foot of the bed. For a moment, she thought she dreamt it. It could only be Veren who got it for her. She thought it an odd coincidence that he picked up the one dress she really liked in the shop. But then, the shop was small, the choices weren't varied and the grey dress was the best among the selection.

It was not the most expensive dress she had ever owned. Not even close. But to her, this dress was invaluable. Veren gave it to her at the time she wanted it most. It made her look and feel like a woman, or at least older than her current age. And, with the aid of make-up, she felt worthy of the opportunity to breach the age gap between her and Veren tonight.

As she glanced his way, she caught him studying her, a look of indecision on his face. But he took a deep breath and his smile chased it away.

"Why were you looking at me like that?" She wanted to know what was on his mind, to see if she read him right.

"What do you mean?"

The flickering light of the lamp made it hard for Anza to read his thoughts as the shadows danced across his face.

"Earlier," she explained, "you looked like you were weighing your options, and whatever it was, you decided against it."

"I was weighing ... whether I was going to order dessert or not, but I had enough ... food already. It was just ... greed," he replied.

She sensed he wasn't referring to food, but she let it pass.

"What's our plan tomorrow? What time do we leave?" The thought of going home and seeing her father again gave her butterflies in the stomach.

"Eleven a.m. We need to leave the hotel by eight. Will you be ready by then?"

"Yes—all of my possessions fit in my backpack." Packing her bag had brought the finality of her decision home. "Where are you staying in the city?" She was compelled to ask him. She didn't want to cut their connection short.

"I don't know yet, but I can escort you to your home, to your father." He covered her hand in assurance.

"You don't have to. I can call him. He'll want to pick me up at the airport." She didn't want him to feel obligated.

"I want to do this, Anza."

Why? "As my keeper?"

"As your keeper."

"How long are you going to be one, Veren?" She leaned closer to read his expression better.

He paused before answering, "For as long as it takes."

It was still a vague, unsatisfactory response, but the promise of a future reassured her. If her father agreed to her bargain, Veren would be her first official human friend. And she couldn't have done better. Her father wouldn't fault her judgment on Veren.

An icy breeze swept over them, making her shiver. Veren took off his jacket and draped it over her shoulder, grasping the front of it close.

"Shall we go?" he asked, tapping the end of her nose.

She nodded.

As she stood by the entrance, Veren stopped. She glanced up at him, wondering why.

"I've got a request, little one." Veren smiled down at her, tucking the wisps of hair behind her ear.

"What is it?"

"Can I take a photo of you?" He held up his phone, crooked half-smile on his face.

She didn't expect that. *Veren wasn't the selfie-taking kind.*

Bemused, she nodded. With the fairy-lighted garden as a backdrop, Veren took a photo of her on his phone. The seriousness in his face as he took the shot made her smile—the satisfied glint in his eyes as he looked at his picture widened it.

On the leisurely drive back to their hotel, Veren stopped by every lookout point along the way and took more photos. It was like Veren was trying to capture all their moments together as much as he could, cram as much of it in the remaining time they had together, and record them all in his phone for posterity.

"You have to give me copies of those shots, Veren," Anza said in jest. It was her attempt to drive out the unsettling emotions from her heart.

"Of course. I can transfer them to your phone later. Have you turned it back on, by the way? Or called your father, for that matter?"

"No, not yet. I was planning to do it tomorrow when we're at the airport." The thought of calling her father made her stomach ache.

Veren squeezed her hand. "Everything will be okay, little one."

Somehow, she believed him. His certainty gave her confidence.

They got back to the hotel just before the wind changed. The downpour that followed made their shared coffee on her verandah cosy and heart-warming. There was something soothing about being together while watching a storm rage outside. It made the turmoil in their hearts seem inconsequential.

They spent the late hours of the night and well into the early hours of the morning talking about life, anything, and everything. During the moments of silence, they were in accord. No conversation was necessary.

Veren held her close to him for hours. They remained awake and witnessed darkness turn into light. They listened to the whispering wind that turned into a howl as the morning came and the rain intensified. Flashes of lightning made the swaying streams of rain visible. Stormy weather had never looked as fascinating or compelling. Dark clouds hid the sun, giving them the illusion that night refused to give in to morning, that it was here to stay and prolong their remaining time together.

The moment was broken when Veren received a text message. His serene expression turned into alarm as he read it. His grim silence and the hardness in his expression unnerved her.

"What happened?"

"They cancelled our flight because of the poor weather." Veren's flat tone scared her. It seemed to have created a panic in him.

"It's not too bad ... isn't it? We can re-book tomorrow, or the next day ..." Her voice faltered as the dread in his eyes grew. He didn't seem to hear her. Her heart hammered violent beats against her chest.

"Anza, I have to go ... somewhere. I need to do something. Stay here. I'll be back later," Veren said, then rushed out of the door. He didn't wait for her response.

For the first time in her life, she was frightened. Of what, she didn't know. It was a premonition of something terrible, and it settled like a boulder in her stomach.

Veren phoned Edrigu multiple times, but the signal was bad. He sent him a text message, just in case. It was a disaster to be stranded here today. There was no *Tribunal* source of *victus* here in Basco. The population was too small. No morgue or hospital to steal fresh human heart, liver or kidney from.

His *vital hunger* was rising. His *Crux* was strong because of practice and training, but he didn't know how long he could delay the *Auto-morphosis* into his *Animus*, his animal hunting form.

Once he turned into a panther, his vital hunger would force him to secure the viscera he needed. Hunting humans remained a capital crime in their laws, and he didn't want to unleash his beastly nature in this island paradise. It would ruin the peace.

The weather, which seemed beautiful earlier, now appeared like a sign that all things that could go wrong just did. His only consolation was that people would be less likely to come out in this storm. There would be fewer victims and potential witnesses to his crime.

The safety of the people on the island would depend on the protection that he would erect around himself. He hoped his text to his mentor got through and *sustenance* would be on its way within a day or so. He would try to hold off the *Auto-morphosis* for as long as he could.

If help failed to arrive in two days, he dared not think about the choices left to him. To kill a human, a capital crime punishable by death; consume his own liver, which would make him insane; or end his own life.

The result for him would be the same—death.

For now, it was time for his defensive plan. He had scoped the area the first day he arrived for a potential shelter just for an incident such as this. The old grain barn, made of stone and clay tucked at the back of the compound just behind the hotel, was the ideal place. And as was his training, he brought everything that he would need with him. His *Impedio*, some sedatives, and a muzzle. He would restrain and barricade himself there until *sustenance* arrived.

His pounding heart threatened to deafen him. He took deep breaths to calm himself down, to slow his heartbeat and tap into his *Crux* to determine how many hours he had left before he would lose complete control of his *Animus*.

Six, maybe eight hours before my Crux breaks down.

He needed to be away from Anza before then. He had enough time to prepare the barn, to protect the people from him. And hopefully, he would have some time to spare to reassure Anza.

She would be alone during his confinement. He didn't want her to think that he had abandoned her.

Veren had been gone since six a.m. It was past noon now, and he still wasn't back.

He wasn't in his room, nor was he in any of the public areas of the inn. No one had seen him, and they doubted he went anywhere outside since it had been pouring rain since dawn.

Where is he?

Anza couldn't shake the hunch he was in trouble. Something dark loomed, and it would affect them both.

The verandah, which she grew fond of because of the moments she had spent with Veren, was now restrictive. A single text message wiped away the serenity they had enjoyed just a few hours ago. She could not stay there, just waiting and worrying about him.

Despite their connection, she knew little about him. He could be a fugitive from the law or a psychopath. But even as she enumerated every possible dire and dangerous scenario about him, she couldn't disregard the fact that he had been nothing but caring to her.

She was a runaway, and he knew about it. He could have done anything to her, and no one would have found out. He could have taken advantage of her many times—at the Lighthouse, when she was sick, and even last night. There were plenty of times she was alone with him, and if he had wanted to do her harm, it would have been easy for him.

She was pacing in her room when a knock sounded. She rushed to open it, but to her disappointment, Mrs. Bassig greeted her.

"Good afternoon, Anza. I heard they cancelled your flight." Her cheerful voice grated on her nerves. Mrs. Bassig was carrying folded bedsheets, towels, and pillowcases.

"Good afternoon, Mrs. Bassig." She stepped aside to let her in. "Yes, Ma'am. I think they rescheduled it for tomorrow."

Mrs. Bassig handed her fresh bedclothes, and paused by the bed when she saw the backpack.

"All packed?" Mrs. Bassig said over her shoulder as she stripped the bed of its sheets with a quick, efficient motion. "You must be excited to go home to your family," she continued as she took one of the fresh sheets from her and redressed the bed.

"Yes, I am."

"I'm glad Veren was able to convince you to go home. While I would have loved for you to work with us, I was quite worried about you, as you are very young." Mrs. Bassig prattled on as she stripped the pillows' old cases and replaced them with fresh ones.

"And thank you for your generosity, Ma'am. I truly appreciate that you offered me the job." She would never forget how the older woman came to her rescue with no qualms.

"Did you call your father yet? He must be waiting for your homecoming," Mrs. Bassig mumbled as she stripped the second bed and peeled the cases from the pillows.

Anza shook her head. "Not yet, Ma'am. I need to charge my phone still. It might be flat." She found the tediousness of their exchange grating. She was worried about Veren and would rather go look for him.

"Oh, I'm sure Veren has informed your father already," Mrs. Bassig said as she fixed the new sheets on the bed. "He's an efficient emissary," she added as she tucked the ends of the sheets under the mattress.

Emissary?

"What do you mean, Mrs. Bassig?" Anza had taken a step closer to the older woman, unable to believe her words.

"I'm sure your father made the right decision in sending Veren ... I like that boy," Mrs. Bassig continued, unaware of the upheaval she created. She was busy shaking a pillow into a fresh case. She fluffed it and dropped it on the bed.

Anza's heart, already beating fast because of her anxiety over Veren's unknown whereabouts, stopped and sank like a leaden weight inside of her stomach.

My father sent Veren after me? That can't be true.

She had to find Veren to talk to him, to hear the truth from him. Maybe Mrs. Bassig misunderstood, or Veren just said that to protect her. There were a thousand other reasons that could have prompted Veren to say that to Mrs. Bassig.

She rushed out of her room to search for him and left Mrs. Bassig without a word, driven by undefinable emotions. The horror that Veren might have played her echoed in her head as she rushed to his room, but he wasn't there. His backpack was also missing.

Did he leave me? Her heart pounded even harder at the thought.

She ran down to the lobby. Like earlier, no one had seen him. She felt crushed and bewildered, but told herself not to jump to conclusions until she had spoken to him.

Where did he go?

Short of running around in the rain, where else could she search? She had no choice but to go back to her room.

Just as she turned the corner of the stairway, she noticed movement in a small stone building at the end of the hotel compound, close to the herb garden. Someone slipped inside the structure. She didn't see who it was, but her gut told her it was Veren.

She sprinted downstairs and ran the distance from the back door to the stone building. The pouring rain drenched her, but she didn't care. The heavy wooden door was ajar. She pushed it in, just enough so she could squeeze through. It was dark, musty, and smelled of grain and damp stones. A barn.

Unable to see the interior, she cautiously paused by the entrance and waited for her vision to adjust. But she sensed a movement inside, which raised the hairs at the back of her neck.

The sound of a panting man echoed from inside. It was Veren. Then another sound came from the depths of the dark interior. It was something unknown to her. It sounded like the whimper of a wounded beast.

She took a step forward, but faltered when a harsh voice stopped her.

"Anza, no!" An agonised call came from the corner, behind sacks of grain piled high like a wall. "Stay there!" The guttural command wasn't enough to dissuade her.

Her eyes adjusted to the dark, and she could now see the heavy sacks that had partially barred the door. It looked like Veren had created a floor-to-ceiling barricade, to keep himself inside. Judging from the uneven height of the stack, it was unfinished, likely from a lack of material.

"Veren," she whispered.

"Anza, please ... leave me ..." Veren's harsh voice reverberated against the stone walls.

His plea went straight to her heart. It propelled her to climb atop the unfinished stack. Veren was curled on his side. His entire body shook—it looked like he was in horrible pain. He had a dog muzzle on, and he had shackled himself to the stone wall with chains attached to a thick leather vest strapped tight around his torso. That familiar contraption, an *Impedio*, one that she had seen in every *Viscerebus* household, explained everything to her.

Veren is a Viscerebus.

An Aswang like her entire family.

That one item confirmed everything Mrs. Bassig said to her earlier. Anger bubbled up inside her, threatening to explode. In its wake, the pain of betrayal.

He was her keeper because her father sent him. He meant to take her home because it was his mission to do so. And he was to gain her trust, her friendship, to convince her to come home.

She stood there, rooted on the spot by the competing urge to lash out, and to leave him, never to see him again.

"Anza, please go ... you can't be here," he pleaded through pain that roughened up his voice.

The tortured tone broke through her fury. She realised he was protecting her from his *reflexive transformation* because she was the closest viscera source around. Her thoughts cleared like a cloud blown away by the wind.

If she ran to hide and left him to his fate, he might break away from his shackles. His wall of grain sacks was incomplete. Escape from this barn would be possible. If that happened, he would be in danger of attacking one of the staff in the inn. The humans would go after him in retaliation. They would kill him.

But even if he escaped them, an attack like this, in a place like this island, would make national news. The *Tribunal* would consider this a direct violation of the *Veil of Secrecy*. They would end his life, because he had just exposed the *Viscerebus*.

Veren would be in trouble no matter what.

By instinct, she knew what had to be done. All her life, she had prepared for and imagined doing this to her family members—to give out the only valuable thing she had to offer them: her viscera.

The clock had run out on Veren. There was no way for the *sustenance* to arrive on time.

She was his only chance.

She jumped down from the sack and rushed to Veren's side. He recoiled, crawling away from her. He held out his hand to ward her off.

"Anza, no! Stay away ... Go to your room. Please, I can't—"

"Shut up, Veren! You need my help."

She started looking around for tools to use. She might need to go back to the kitchen and get a sharp enough knife, and the first aid kit.

"How much time do you have before you shape-shift?" She heard the urgency in her own voice.

"I don't know ... An hour or less," Veren replied, giving her a confused look.

"Okay, I need you to hold on. I'll go to the lobby and ask for their first aid kit. And a knife." She turned away from him. "Hopefully, a very sharp knife," she muttered.

Veren's hand shot out and captured hers, stopping her.

"I have those in there," he gasped out, pointing at his backpack. It was lying unnoticed behind her.

She reached for it and dug for the kit inside, conscious of the time constraints. She took out two soft bags marked with a big red cross. The smaller one contained two small bottles of pills. Sedatives and antibiotics. She zipped that one shut.

The bigger one was what she was looking for. Inside it, she found three hard plastic cases. The biggest contained a scalpel, some surgical clips, clamps, a pair of scissors, and various suture needles and surgical threads.

The middle-sized one was the heaviest. It held a bottle of antiseptic, a smaller bottle of alcohol, plastic-wrapped bandages, and cotton pads.

A longer but slimmer case carried two individually packed sterile syringes and needles, and two tiny glass vials.

"Anza, what are you planning to do?" Veren asked. His face reflected his dawning suspicion and was aghast.

"You're going to *absorb* me, Veren. It's the only way to save you."

The firmness of her tone hid her own misgivings. She didn't want him to doubt her intent, or to argue. If he fought her in this, she could lose her nerve.

"No ... Anza, you don't have to do this." Veren's weakened denial was hopeful, contradicting his words.

"Veren, don't argue. I've made up my mind. This is the best option. You'll end up killing a hapless human if we don't do this. And they'll murder you in return."

She had taken out the scalpel and bottle of antiseptic, then hiked her t-shirt up, exposing her abdomen. She realised she didn't know how to start.

"Veren, I need you to help me, too. You'll have to guide me on where to make the incision."

Veren's sharp intake of breath made her pause. He must have seen the determination in her eyes, saw her fear of what she needed to do, and her anticipation of pain.

"Okay," he said. "Let me do it."

He took off his muzzle and fumbled at the straps of the *Impedio*, but he stopped. He kept the *Impedio* on. After a moment's hesitation, he took out the bottle of alcohol from his kit and squirted it on his hands, rubbing them vigorously. Then he grabbed the bottle of antiseptic from her. With shaking hands, he ripped open a package of cotton pads, twisted the cap off the bottle, and moistened the pads with it.

"Lean back, Anza, and hold your shirt up."

She half reclined against a sack of grain. He wiped her upper abdomen, under her right rib cage with the antiseptic-moistened cotton pad. With efficient motion, he took a syringe, fitted a needle in it, and took one glass vial from his kit. He began siphoning the contents into the syringe.

"This is anaesthesia," he muttered through gritted teeth.

Thank Prometheus for that.

She nodded in acknowledgement. Her breathing became shallow.

"Are you sure, Anza?" he asked again, his expression pained.

She swallowed and nodded once more. "I am. Hurry, before you run out of time."

She was conscious of the possibility that he could transform at any moment. She wouldn't have the strength to stop him should the *Impedio* fail to keep him restrained.

The first puncture was quick, like an ant bite. He dispensed a quarter of the contents of the syringe. She felt the liquid spread through her muscles in tiny tentacles, radiating outward from the puncture point. Three more injections followed, then it was done.

She breathed out in relief. Sweat beaded her forehead.

"How long before the anaesthesia takes effect?"

"A few minutes... I'll make this quick. But I have another vial if we need to ..." He was unable to finish his sentence.

While they waited in the pregnant silence, Veren busied himself by preparing the suturing needle he would use later. He fished out a towel in a sealed bag from the bottom of his backpack. She marvelled at his level of preparation, despite her efforts to regulate her breathing to arrest her growing panic.

"How come you have all these medical tools with you?" she asked to distract herself and lessen the tension in the air.

"It's part of an *Iztari* medical kit. A standard issue." He couldn't meet her gaze. "Tell me when the area feels numb."

Finally, she felt the numbness in her upper stomach.

"Veren, it's time."

He poured antiseptic on his hands and rubbed them together. He then took the scalpel from her, squirted alcohol gel on it, and spread it all over the blade.

"Ready?" he asked. His thumb and forefinger pressed on the area where he would make the incision.

She swallowed and nodded. "Yes." She took a deep breath; braced herself for the cut and averted her face so as not to see the blood.

The sharp end of the blade cut deep into her flesh. She winced, not in pain, but at the strangeness of skin and muscles getting sliced, and the flow of warm blood that poured out of the cut and ran down her torso. Then she felt a sharp twinge of pain as the blade reached deeper and cut through the sheath that surrounded her liver. It made her gasp and jerk.

"Sorry," Veren mumbled, his voice as pained as hers. One hand held her down to minimise her movement.

Her hands clenched on the t-shirt she held up while her body trembled at the pain, her abdominal muscles locked with tension. Tears leaked out of her tightly squeezed eyelids.

It was unlike any pain she had ever experienced.

"Relax, Anza. Deep breaths ..."

Veren's calm voice alerted her to her shallow breathing. With extreme effort, she followed his direction. He widened the cut to expose a bigger portion of her organ. Thankfully, the cutting of her muscles didn't hurt, giving her reprieve.

However, when he cut through her liver, though it was quick, she screamed. The sound reverberated in the barn. The pain almost made her lose consciousness. Through her fading alertness, she heard Veren slurp the piece he had taken from her. She was vaguely aware of Veren pinching the wound close; of his warm tongue as he licked the wound to stem the blood flow.

Cold sweat covered her body, her efforts not to hyperventilate forgotten. Every puncture of the curved needle as he sewed her up made her appreciate the power of the anaesthesia. But at every moment, she expected the return of the pain.

Veren worked quickly. His movements were practised and quick.

After what seemed like an eternity, he cut the excess suturing thread from the wound. With a gentle touch, he wiped her torso clean with the towel, then poured antiseptic on the cut. The last thing she remembered was Veren pressing a square bandage on the wound.

Then everything faded.

Veren panicked when Anza's body slackened. His thumb touched the pulse on her neck. It was strong and fast, but it slowed down to its normal pace after a while. He breathed a sigh of relief. She was fortunately unconscious.

His awareness of their surroundings came back. It was still pouring rain outside; the howling wind would have masked Anza's scream. His strained muscles loosened somewhat. The effects of Anza's liver strengthened and energised him, fortifying his *Crux*.

Then the enormity of Anza's sacrifice dawned on him. Gratitude and something else he couldn't comprehend engulfed him. It was his undoing—his tears flowed.

His bloodied hand picked up hers, and he kissed it with reverence. Every emotion he had inside him, he poured into that kiss. This child-woman in his keeping became his keeper. He was supposed to save her, and yet she became his saviour.

She did not know it, and she probably never would, but she would always own a part of him that no other person in this world ever would.

He unshackled himself from his *Impedio*. There was no need for it now. Her liver gave him a week before he would need *sustenance* again. He got out and washed the bloodied towel in the rain. He returned inside the barn to make sure Anza was comfortable. While she slept, he put away his things in the backpack and started dismantling his sacks of grain barricade, returning it to its previous location—stacked at the back of the barn.

He kept a close eye on her wound. It had stopped bleeding. When the rain abated, he slung his backpack on over his shoulder and lifted Anza in his arms. He was thankful that they didn't encounter anyone along the way as he carried her to her room.

He realised this was the second time he would have to undress her. Her shirt and jeans were damp from earlier. Like before, he kept his eyes averted, but this time, he didn't dress her in a bathrobe. He covered her with the sheet. Her cut bled a little. The blood seeped into the bandage, staining it. It would be easier to dress her wound if she had no clothes on.

After replacing the bandage, he took the shirt to her bathroom and washed it. There were spots of blood on it. He hung her jeans and wet underclothes to dry. His mind was occupied with worry and prayers that her wound wouldn't get infected.

He was thinking of getting to his room to change out of his own damp jeans when his phone rang. It was Edrigu.

"Veren, I have been trying to call you, but you were out of range. I was informed that your flight was cancelled. How are you doing?" His questions came out in a barrage. Edrigu knew he was due for his *sustenance* today.

"I'm well, Sir," he replied. "The storm made it hard to get a signal." He didn't know how to tell Edrigu what Anza did for him.

"Can you still hold on for another day? I will try my best to fly in *victus* for you tonight. Although, I'm not sure if our team in Tuguegarao can brave the weather," Edrigu said, forewarning in his tone.

"There's no need for it, Sir," he began. "Anza offered ... her liver to me." He choked down the emotions that rose in him.

"What? Wow!" A low whistle followed his words. "How is she?" Edrigu asked after a momentary silence.

"She's resting," Veren said. He didn't want to voice out his concern about infections, for fear he might manifest it into a reality.

"Do you have antibiotics in your supplies?" Edrigu asked, his perception of the situation clear. His calm tone implied that everything that happened was commonplace.

"Yes." Edrigu's question had bolstered his confidence.

"Good. Give her two doses as soon as she wakes up. Now, you need to call Manuu to assure him you're taking Anza home in another two days," Edrigu said.

His mentor's brisk manner reminded him not to be emotional, to think like an *Iztari*. That sobered him up.

"Should I tell him ... what Anza did for me?"

"I think it is Anza's decision to make. Ask her when she awakens," Edrigu advised.

"Okay, Sir. Thank you," he said. The load on his shoulder lightened with the support of his mentor. "By the way, Sir, if I need a chopper, just in case, would you be able to arrange one?"

"Yes, just let me know if, and when, you need it. I'll have one on stand-by," Edrigu assured him.

After he ended the call with Edrigu, he took a deep breath and dialled Manuu Soledad's number. Their call was formal, his emotions held in check, no trace of the agitation that ruled him. He assured Anza's father that Anza agreed to go home and that he would arrange it in two days when the weather improves. As expected, Manuu was impatient and wanted to send a helicopter to pick them up, but he told him the weather could make the trip dangerous.

Manuu asked to speak to Anza, perhaps to reassure himself. He got out of it by telling him Anza was still unaware of him being an *Iztari,* which was technically true. He pacified Manuu with two promises: that Anza would call him after she learned the truth about him, and that he would call Manuu by tomorrow afternoon to reconfirm they got a flight back to the mainland for the following day.

Anza stirred awake a few minutes later. He rushed to her side. She tried to get up, but the wound on her abdomen made her flinch and flop back on the bed.

"How are you feeling?" he asked. The pallor of her skin worried him.

Anza touched the bandage and realised she was naked underneath. Her cheeks flamed in embarrassment.

"Anza, on my honour, my eyes were closed. I kept you undressed because it's easier to change your bandage, should I need to," he said in haste.

His agitation calmed Anza as she looked back at him. Her abashed expression faded and transitioned to a serene, assessing one.

"Veren, I need an explanation." Her quiet words were loud in his ears.

He sighed and nodded. "Yes, you do. I'm an *Iztari,* and your father sent for me to find you ..."

"My father asked for you specifically?"

"No. The *Chief Iztari* appointed me because I was the closest to your age. Your father told us you know how the system works and you would expect *Iztaris* to come after you. Your father didn't want to force you to come home. He doesn't want you to run away again. They ordered me to work undercover."

"So, the friendship ... all to get me to trust you? To convince me to go home?" Anza's tone was clipped.

"No ..." He swallowed, took a deep breath, and grasped her hand in his. He wanted to be completely honest with her. She deserved nothing less. He caught her gaze and held it. "In the beginning, the goal was to get your trust. The friendship came naturally." He hoped that his sincerity got through her defensive wall. The indecisiveness in her face hurt. He rubbed his chest to ease the pain of it—losing her regard might be the price he had to pay.

"Is that why you called yourself my keeper?" Her question came after a long silence. She sounded uncertain.

"No, Anza. That, like our friendship, was unplanned, unexpected. It just happened, and I wouldn't have it any other way."

Anza's eyes held his. In earnestness and without words, he pleaded with her to believe him. He felt tears prick behind his eyes, and he swallowed hard to push them back. Anza's gaze softened. She smiled and reached out to touch his cheek.

He closed his eyes at the relief; the gratitude at whichever god in the universe had gifted Anza with such a generous heart. He caught her hand and pressed a kiss at the centre of her palm. Her hand closed on that kiss and pressed it to her own heart.

To him, that small action was the most beautiful, most excruciating thing he had ever seen in his life.

9

THE HOMECOMING

Veren watched Anza sleep in silence. He had given her antibiotics and pain medication from his kit; and requested the front desk to get some ibuprofen from the doctor nearby for her use in the succeeding days. He told Mrs. Bassig that Anza was suffering from a bad toothache. It was an acceptable reason for her not to question why Anza would be in her bedroom for most of the next two days.

The next morning, with the sheet wrapped around her, he assisted her to walk around her room for a few minutes. The surgery exhausted her, so Anza spent a lot of time sleeping. Her wound was healing well. Her *Erdia* genes helped heal her cut faster. Not as fast as someone like him, but it was still quicker than a human's.

He spoon-fed her, even when she refused. He also made her do breathing and coughing exercises every time she was awake to ensure that she didn't develop pneumonia. By the evening, Anza was begging him to allow her to take a shower. He would hear none of it.

They compromised with a partial sponge bath.

Just before bedtime, he convinced Anza to call her father. He moved to the verandah while father and daughter conversed. He wanted Anza to have the time and privacy to express to her father how she felt about her life, and what she wanted to do.

The call wasn't long, and Anza was crying by the time it ended. Worried, Veren went back to the room to comfort her. A tremulous smile accompanied her tears.

"Did everything go well with your father?" His heart was full of hope for her.

"Yeah, I apologised. He accepted it. I told him we'll go home the day after tomorrow. He wanted to send a helicopter for us, but I convinced him not to—I told him the flight is confirmed," She said, her tone light. She looked relieved.

"Did you tell him about the *absorption*?" He wanted to be ready when he faced Manuu Soledad.

"No." She shook her head, her eyes intent on him. "That was my decision. It remains mine alone," she whispered.

"Okay." He wasn't altogether sure if he agreed with that decision, but as Edrigu said, this was her province since it was her liver. *Absorption* was always a personal decision. He realised he hadn't thanked her yet, even if he felt it in his soul.

"Veren, what happens after?" Anza asked, her eyes focused on the corners of the sheet she was twiddling with her fingers.

He understood what she was asking about, what she was asking for.

"I don't know, Anza. I have to go home, and I have military training to focus on." He had three more weeks of holiday before he was due. He was torn between spending it with her or using the time to fortify his emotional defences against her, which she had demolished with ease.

"Will you keep in touch?" Anza asked after a while. She seemed to have accepted the fact their lives would diverge, if not the day after tomorrow, soon after.

"Yes. I will," he said, response automatic. "If that's what you want," he added, not knowing if she wanted this friendship to continue.

The slowly widening smile on her face soothed the ragged edges of his bruised heart. "Yes, I would like that. Very much, actually."

He knew what the promise would cost him, but there was no question about giving it to her. He would keep in touch for as long as she wanted him to. The power to dictate how much of him she wanted in her life would be in her hands. He wouldn't hinder the spreading of her wings, no matter how it might lead her away from him forever.

Hopefully, she would need him until she was ready for the kind of love that he could give her. And she would still be there when he became ready to love her the way she deserved to be loved.

Loving an *Erdia* like her would be a short-lived bliss for an *Aswang* like himself. Most of the males of his kind knew this. That was why most of them avoided it—why he should avoid it still.

It was a heavy price to pay for the surrender of one's heart for eternity.

The hour of their flight back to the mainland flew by despite Anza willing for time to slow down. Veren was solicitous, almost overly so. He refused to let her carry anything, not even her backpack. He hovered over her like a mother hen. She allowed him to, because she knew it was his way of thanking her.

Her wound was healing well. It still stung, but compared to the remembered pain of the surgery, it was negligible. Apart from the inner soreness behind her ribs, no doubt from her traumatised muscles and injured liver, there was nothing wrong with her.

They had left the wound free of the bandage after the first night to allow it to heal faster. Today, Veren placed a plaster over it so it wouldn't get chafed by her blouse during travel.

She thought about what she did and asked herself if she regretted it. Her response was an easy no. The reason she did it had a logical justification for it, but why she gave it to Veren was harder to answer. It just felt instinctive. No rhyme or reason to it.

They sat in silence, side by side. Her head rested against his bicep by force of habit. It was the most natural thing to do when she felt like dozing off. Her heart hummed with her head on him like this, surrounded by his familiar warmth and smell. As she inhaled, she recognised the elusive scent she had been trying to identify in Veren—the telltale musk of a *Viscerebus* male.

Her heart smiled, and something settled in her like a missing puzzle piece found.

After a few minutes, Veren lifted his arm, settled her head against his chest, and pulled her close. His action was spontaneous, and nothing new between them. What she didn't expect was Veren's larger hand clasping hers up as soon as they sat down. He linked their fingers together, palm resting in palm. His hand tightened on hers periodically during the flight, as if he was reassuring her and himself.

Two hours on, they both declined meals. She wasn't that hungry, and she didn't want to relinquish his hand. He didn't seem inclined either.

The jolt of the touchdown registered in her heart, like a final curtain call. Her father would be at the airport to pick her up. Veren would wait for his connecting flight to Manila. And, they would part.

They kept to their seats until they were the last passengers in the aircraft. They had no check-in luggage, nothing to delay the parting. As they walked on, they slowed their steps as much as they could. Before they turned into the arrival area, Veren stopped her.

"Anza"—he dropped her hand as he dug his phone out from his backpack—"here's my number. Take it as we might not have time to exchange numbers later when we see your father."

She grabbed her phone from her bag and typed it into her phone. "Shall I give you mine?"

"Text or call me later and I'll save it." He wanted to keep to his internal vow to let her take the lead in their relationship.

She dialled his number, her eyes on him. The phone rang, confirming the number he gave her. That was a burner phone, with a burner number. Normally, he would discard it after a case, as was their training, never to use it again. This time, the phone would remain in his possession. It would be his lifeline, a part of him that only she would own.

She smiled at him, satisfied. Then, she took a step forward, but he stopped her with a hand on her elbow. There was one more thing he had to do, and it required going against his own interest.

"Anza ..." He inhaled then let out his breath. "Remember Diego?"

She nodded. "Yes. Why?"

"He might call you in Manila ..." he mumbled. "I just wanted to warn you." He couldn't look her in the eye. He had given Diego the chance to usurp his position as her keeper. He could only hope that Anza wouldn't take him up on it.

"Okay." Her response was dismissive.

She took the information like it was of no consequence to her. He didn't know how to process her reaction. Then Anza grabbed his hand and pulled him toward the arrival area, where he knew her father would be waiting.

Her welcoming entourage was a party of four: her father, stepmother, a male cousin, and an uncle. They all enveloped her in warm hugs, their circle complete and exclusive.

And Veren was outside of that circle. Out of place. He watched them admonish her gently in between kisses and hugs. These people clearly loved her. She would be safe and well-cared for.

"Mr. Albareda?" Manuu Soledad broke off from the group to shake his hand.

"Yes, Sir," he said. He kept his face impassive to quell the pain inside of him.

"Thank you for all the help. For getting her back to us. We owe you an enormous debt of gratitude that we cannot repay. If there is anything I can do for you, just say the word." Manuu Soledad's effusive gratitude rubbed him raw.

"Please, don't mention it, Sir. No gratitude is necessary." It was time to restart his life. "I have to go, Sir, as I have my Manila flight to catch." He shook Manuu's hand.

He turned towards the departure area, his back ramrod straight. As he walked away, he kept his eyes forward—he didn't want to look back and see Anza's face. He felt panicked at the idea of saying goodbye to her, and mournful for not being able to.

One regret was eating at him, he just realised.

He had wanted to kiss Anza, maybe since the first time he saw her. He never allowed the thought to surface, to even consider it. Her age, his age, their situation—all had stopped him.

At this moment, he would have given anything for that one brief kiss. But it seemed the kiss would have to wait for the right time, the right circumstances.

Just as he turned the corner towards the departure area, compulsion made him steal a last glance towards Anza. Her family still surrounded her, but through the gaps between the multiple arms wrapped around her, their eyes connected in the distance. There was a question in her gaze and a promise in his.

For his life, she willingly gave him a piece of her liver, an organ that she could regenerate. For her sacrifice, he gave her his heart.

Unfortunately for him, he couldn't regrow a heart.

10

THE RETURNING HEART

Six years later.

Veren was on the third day of his first-ever holiday since he became an *Iztari*. They had promoted him: a reward for a hard two years of war to subdue a rebellion among their kind. It was an arduous battle. He almost died during two encounters, but he fought on. The vow he made to himself made him want to live.

The war ended, but the danger of another one was never far from their minds. It caught the *Supreme Viscerebus Tribunal* unaware and, as a result, it endangered the lives of every one of their kind from the humans that outnumbered them.

His mentor, Edrigu Orzabal, had formed a small band of *Iztaris*, designed to work in complete secrecy to spy, and to preempt any other potential uprising.

Before they started their official operation, they were all given a chance to rest, recuperate, and fulfil any unfinished business they had left behind. Veren intended to do all of that. If there was something the previous war had taught him, it was that time was fleeting, and he shouldn't let it bleed away without doing everything in his power to achieve the personal happiness that he craved.

He selected this location for his first Transit, not for the scenery or the lifestyle. His reason to be here was more compelling. He was on a search and recovery mission—a personal one.

And according to confidential records, Anza had moved here.

After the war, he needed to find her. He realised that he had searched for her every day in the most elemental of levels. His work may have occupied his waking hours, but she was never far from his thoughts. She was with him during the lull of each day, the minutes just before he fell asleep, and most often, she appeared in his dreams.

In the early months of their separation, her messages were friendly, sweet, and innocent. She filled it with accounts of her days, which made his heart ache with longing, and the worst parts were when she reminisced about their days in Basco. That broke his heart every time.

As he had promised himself, he adopted the same tone as her messages, but with fewer details. He didn't want to clip her wings as she learned how to fly, nor did he want to anchor her to the ground when she needed to soar.

The frequency of their exchange dwindled as the contents of her messages changed. It became filled with mentions of other people in her life, new routines and activities. She stopped communicating with him after one year. That is, after Anza's family left for their Transit.

He wondered if she had changed, if she was still into photography, music, and poetry. If she still thought about their days in Basco.

Now, six years after the fact, he was hot on her trail. One of Edrigu's gifts to him was access to the Soledad family's *Transit* file. He knew she was here in Madrid, but not her exact address. He would have to do some digging from the local *Tribunal*. One lead was the Biblioteca Nacional. He had a gut feeling that would lead him to Anza.

Intuition led him to her that first time. Hopefully, it would guide him to her this time.

Anza closed the book *The Matriarchy—Five Hundred Years of Progressive Viscerebus Existence in the 21st Century*. For the past five years, she read as much as she could about the lives of the *Viscerebus* to make up for the years she ignored that part of her heritage.

She grew up with her *Aswang* kin, bound herself to the *Veil* that ruled them, yet she had never attempted to get to know them deeper. That was a mistake. She limited herself to knowing her immediate family, but not into understanding them at a core level. She knew their laws, but not why the laws became necessary.

Her thoughts, as usual, dealt with Veren, her Keeper, whenever she touched upon the subject. She wondered what he was doing at the moment. They had lost touch five years ago when her old phone fell into the sea when they boarded the cruise ship to Europe. It was a holiday before they settled in New Zealand for their *Transit*.

She was frantic about it when it happened, but she realised maybe it was meant to be. His previous replies to her messages had become shorter and impersonal. The last one was a single word—"Okay," which took him two days to send. Perhaps he got busy with work as an *Iztari*. It could be that he moved on with his life. One that did not include her.

She then focused her attention on enjoying the freedom she won from her parents. It was hard fought, but it was well worth it. She now lived the life of a human. Her father had given her a reasonable amount of autonomy, with just one caveat—none of her family members would be photographed, mentioned, or recorded in any of her correspondence and social media, except in the most superficial of ways. Also, she needed to spend at least three months a year in Auckland with them.

When they *Transited*, she had a choice to keep in contact with her friends by phone, but not with her social media. She kept that account active for two years, hoping that Veren might contact her there, but at his continued silence, she relented and deactivated it.

Two years after they settled in New Zealand, she moved to Madrid to study. And here she had stayed since. She'd made close friends here, a circle of five girls including Elyse and Rizzi. They had maintained their friendship since high school. Elyse and Rizzi elected to study in Madrid and she found the idea attractive. Summer had been crossing over from Paris twice a year.

She spent her days on her creative endeavours—writing and composing songs for some upcoming singers in the country. Her life became more balanced, more satisfying. Richer and nuanced. However, the sense of contentment that she was trying to recapture remained elusive.

Veren resurfaced in her consciousness and had taken up much of her thoughts in the past two years, because of the political crisis that assailed the *Viscerebuskind*. The conflict had escalated to a degree that it almost became a full-blown global war. Her concern for Veren's welfare became constant. Reading the *Tribunal Journal* as soon as it got released became a priority. She scouted for news about the *Iztaris*, about him.

She put the book back on the shelf. It was time to meet her friends near Puerta de Alcala. A glance at the overhead clock in the library told her she was running late. She would have to walk as fast as she could to arrive on time. Diego, a long-time friend, had flown in from Manila and she didn't want to make him wait.

All her friends rooted for Diego. They thought it very romantic that he always came to Madrid at this time of the year for his annual holiday. Diego hadn't been secretive about his desire to be more than friends with her since the very beginning, but she felt she was too young for a relationship back then. Also, she had to admit that her memories of Veren hindered her inclination towards other boys her age. They all seemed too juvenile, too shallow, too insubstantial.

Diego was selfless enough to accompany her through her journey of personal growth and learning about the world and its human inhabitants. He had been a good and constant friend over the years, and he was one of the few humans she maintained contact with after the *Transit*.

Her close relationship with her cousin Xandrei balanced her view of the two kinds of people in her life, and she realised she was quite lucky. She lived between two worlds, allowed to cross either at will. Most of her *Vis* did not have that freedom, and the humans didn't even know of the other. Diego remained ignorant of her nature and her family, so trust between them never deepened.

As she walked down the stairs of the library, she thought that if she was going to have a boyfriend now, she could do no better than Diego. Attractive, smart, kind and steadfast. She trusted him, and she knew Diego loved her.

Her mind was preoccupied with the thoughts of the past, present, and wishes for her future as she rushed towards her destination.

Anza traversed the streets by instinct while she sent a text message to her friends to inform them she would be ten or fifteen minutes late. She was familiar with the streets of Madrid, and had walked them almost every day since she moved here. She slid her phone back into her bag and turned into the corner of an alley that would cut her travel time in half.

As Veren turned the street corner, a woman crashed into him, almost bouncing off of him. By instinct, his hand shot out to steady her. That simple touch electrified him. His entire being knew before the woman looked up.

Anza.

Her gasp of recognition echoed his sharp intake of breath. His brain reeled, dizzying him as his world staggered to a complete stop. He didn't know how long he stood there gazing at her. She looked equally stunned and thunderstruck. Her eyes locked onto his.

All his senses focused on her and her sweet face. Familiar, yet new. The baby soft cheeks were less so, her eyes were still as wide, and her lips had the same plump pout. All those years apart, the tame, friendly messages in the early months, and the complete silence in the last five years, came rushing back to him.

The pressure in his heart bubbled over, and a burst of instinct overpowered him. He pulled her flush into his arms, her hands flattened between them, palms rested over his pounding heart. His mind had only one overwhelming thought: to kiss Anza. *Finally*.

His iron control was stretched taut. His sense of honour compelled him to ask for permission from her. But the words wouldn't come. His lips were almost touching hers, his shuddering breath an entreaty as he waited in pained silence for her.

Anza's own breath trembled before she breached the hairline gap between their lips. Her agreement was like an explosion to his senses. That was enough.

His lips fastened onto hers like a man dying of thirst. It was a fierce, demanding, pleading kiss. Anza's indrawn breath was lost in his mouth, her head cradled in his hand as he anchored her for his kiss, savouring the texture of her mouth.

Her scent enveloped him; the softness of her clouded his vision. She still smelled the same, still felt the same. Except that she was a woman now. Ready for the love he wanted to give her. And his heart quickened as she kissed him back with equal intensity. The same longing flavoured her kisses. The same feeling of homecoming suffused them both.

All the emotions he had bottled up inside, so he could function during those years of radio silence, all the feelings he refused to shine a light on as a matter of self-preservation, converged into this one single moment.

He ripped his mouth off from her when the pressure on his chest threatened to burst. He leaned into her; their foreheads touched. His arms wrapped like tight bands around her. His very being wanted to absorb her into himself, never to part with Anza again. He kept his eyes closed. To look into hers would unman him.

"Anza," he breathed out into her mouth. His throat refused to move for the words he wanted to say to her. He swallowed to loosen it.

"What took you so long?" She rested her cheek on his chest.

"Life goals ... You needed to grow up, and I needed to be ready for us."

"And are you ready now?" Her voice came soft as a whisper.

"Yes ... No more wasting time."

Her sigh of contentment went straight to his soul.

And everything in his world righted itself. In her presence, he felt his heart grow back.

THE END

WORLD OF THE VISCEREBUS GLOSSARY

THESE ARE THE VISCEREBUS TERMS MENTIONED IN THE NOVEL.

Absorption—or ***Zurugatzen***—the voluntary practice of offering one's own viscera upon death to select Viscerebus loved ones. This is practiced by Viscerebus, Veil-bound Erdias, and in rare cases, Veil-bound humans. The offered organs are consumed or 'absorbed' by the Viscerebus recipient. This is an act of love and faith that once absorbed, the donor, or *Rugat*, becomes part of the recipient, or the *Zurugat,* forever. The ritual is usually between parent and child, siblings, life partners and lovers. (*See Zurugatzen – The World of Viscerebus Almanac*).

Animus (Heart or Instinct Animal) or Spirit Animal — the true animal form of a Viscerebus. All Viscerebus have one, although not all would discover theirs. An *Auto-morphosis*, or *reflexive transformation*, usually reveals to a Viscerebus their Animus. Some Viscerebus transform into one animal all their lives and discover that their Animus was a different form.

In some Viscerebus families, it was part of their tradition to deny sustenance to the child of twelve to force an Auto-morphosis. This is usually done under the supervision of the adults. The practice lost favour over the centuries because it often resulted in injury to the child and usually the said child would elect to transform into the animal form they habitually turn into, thus defeating the object of discovering their Animus.

Now, the term is used erroneously by modern Viscerebus to refer to their animal form, whether it is their true Spirit Animal or just their hunting form. (*See Auto-morphosis. See Spirit Animal, Reflexive Transformation – The World of the Viscerebus Almanac*).

Apex – A super shapeshifter. A very rare Viscerebus that can transform into a winged animal, either chiropteran (bats) or avian (birds) form. They can transform fully, or partially. Other special Apex skills that previous ones have manifested are echolocation, sound blasting, and magnetic field manipulation.

Natural facial alteration for disguise is a skill Apex Kazu Nakahara discovered. For an Apex that becomes skilled in turning on their brain's theta waves, they can read other people's brain waves and influence them.

It is said that the full skill set of an Apex has not been fully revealed yet because new skills keep getting discovered by each successive Apex. (*See Shape-shifting – The World of the Viscerebus Almanac, Dawn of the Dual Apex*)

Aquila—the other name for the giant eagle named Aetos Kaukasios, one of the two primary mythical gods to the Viscerebus. The other is Prometheus. The Viscerebuskind attribute the beginning of their race to the two gods. According to the legend, Zeus sent Aetos to devour the liver of Prometheus every night as his eternal punishment for giving fire to humans and for tricking Zeus to choose a less valuable sacrificial offering from humans. The Viscerebus' need to eat viscera is attributed to the saliva of Aetos believed to have contaminated the liver of Prometheus, which was used by the latter to create the Viscerebus.

Aetos was the offspring of two other Titans, Typhon and Echidna, the father and mother of mythical monsters in Greek Mythology. (*See Prometheus. See Origin – World of the Viscerebus Almanac*).

Aswangs – The Filipino term for Viscerebus. Of all the countries in the world, the existence of Viscerebus is the most entrenched in the Philippine culture for two reasons:

First, the Filipinos launched the most aggressive campaign against the Viscerebus. Their Venandis were the most experienced. The Venandi practice, which started as a family endeavour, became traditionally and habitually passed on to the next generation. There are still active—albeit a lesser number of—Venandis operating in the country.

The superstitious nature of the Filipinos allows them to believe that Aswangs still exist, albeit in exaggerated and erroneous form. Many books have been written, and movies made, featuring Aswangs as evil creatures, usually depicted as the minions of the devil.

Like every culture, the existence of the Viscerebus has been relegated into myth and lore, and the term Aswang is used as a blanket term for almost every man-eating and blood sucking ghoul in the country.

Second, the local tribes in the country were also the first to accept the Viscerebus into their midst and established a collaborative and symbiotic relationship. Native Viscerebus in the Philippines were the only ones sanctioned by the Tribunal to work openly with the human tribal members. Their Veil-binding applies only to humans that were not part of the tribe. (*See Venandi – World of the Viscerebus Almanac*).

Auto-morphosis – also known as *Reflexive Transformation* is the involuntary shape-shifting into the animal spirit of a Viscerebus. The vital instinct to hunt and secure *Victus* or *sustenance* triggers this transformation. It triggers the vital instinct when a Viscerebus fails to consume human viscera for over three days.

It is possible to induce an Auto-morphosis through practice and meditation. Some Viscerebus do this to discover their *Animus*. (*See Animus, Crux, Reflexive Transformation, See Shape-shifting – World of the Viscerebus Almanac*)

Brevis Amorem—or short love. A label used by the Vis community for a temporary romantic relationship or affair between a Viscerebus male and a human female. The chief characteristic is the initial intention of the male to conduct a short-term relationship with a female from the outset, regardless if the female is aware of or in agreement with it.

Most male Viscerebus use the Veil of Secrecy law to justify having multiple brevis amorems. It was normal and acceptable. The community called Viscerebus males who practise this as a ***Hedonis***. It had the same connotation as being a player, or a playboy in the human world.

In the most recent history, female Viscerebus embraced the practice as well, and claimed equal rights to conduct brief affairs with males, whether Vis or human. The fundamental distinction was their refusal to have kids with the males. It started as a way of rebelling against the societal expectations for females to give birth to a new generation of Viscerebus.

To call a female *Hedonis*, or a ***Hedonna,*** was derogatory. Most female Viscerebus resented the label. However, the stigma falls away the moment a female Vis gives birth. The Viscerebus society considers them to have done their duty in the propagation of their kind. A woman could return to Brevis Amorem practice and never again be looked down upon.

Recent times, however, revived the title, and the Viscerebus women wear it proudly. (*See Hedonna, Hedonis – The World of the Viscerebus Almanac*)

Crux—the subconscious inner control of a Viscerebus to stop or start shapeshifting into their animal form. A Viscerebus could call forth their Crux into consciousness to prevent an *Auto-morphosis* or *reflexive transformation.* A Viscerebus can strengthen their Crux through meditation and constant practice.

It is common training for *Iztaris* and some individuals to embark on regular vital fasting to flex and strengthen their Crux.

The Crux is similar to human willpower. (*See Auto-morphosis, Reflexive Transformation, See Vital Fasting – The World of the Viscerebus Almanac*)

Erdia—an Erdia is a half-blood, born from a Male Viscerebus and a Female human. Erdias are very human in their nature except they would be slightly stronger, faster and live longer than their human counterpart. They may inherit some enhancement on their senses. They don't inherit the shapeshifting and need for human viscera.

Most Erdias who use their enhanced strength and speed become athletes. Erdias who inherit a superior sense of taste and scent usually become renowned chefs, perfume makers and other professionals that maximise their abilities.

The knowledge of the Erdias about the Viscerebuskind would depend on whether the Viscerebus father tells his offspring. If the Erdia was told, they would be bound to the Veil of Secrecy just like their Viscerebus parent, and they become part of the Viscerebus world.

A significant number of Erdias are unaware of the Viscerebus world because the Viscerebus father abandons them from infancy. These Erdias, being non-Veil-bound, are treated as human. They live normal human lives, unaware of the existence of the Viscerebus. (*See Eremite, Mejordia – World of the Viscerebus Almanac*).

Gentem — (nation in Latin)–the current country of residence, or the immediate, previous country of residence of a *Transitting* Viscerebus. A Viscerebus can have between six to ten Gentems in their lifetime. This is not to be confused with ***Patriam***, which is the country of birth of a Viscerebus. (*See Patriam – World of the Viscerebus Almanac.*)

Impedio – a leather vest and chain contraption meant to restrain a Viscerebus from attacking humans during Auto-morphosis, or reflexive transformation. It is strapped tightly to the body of the Vis; the chains are attached to a firm foundation, like a wall or a tree. And when appropriate, a muzzle is part of the set. Every Vis is required to own one and carry it with them when they travel to remote places, especially if they travel for over three days.

The modern Impedio has a Tracking Device that is automatically triggered when the Distress Transmitter is turned on. The Distress Transmitter can be activated manually and automatically by the change of the heartbeat in a Vis during complete transformation.

The transmitter signals the nearest Iztari office that someone needs human viscera. The Iztaris are then deployed to rescue the unfortunate being.

It is illegal to activate a Distress Transmitter as a joke or a prank. The punishment comprises a huge fine, and a demerit point on their record. (*See Auto-Morphosis, Reflexive transformation, See Demerit System – The World of the Viscerebus Almanac*)

Iztari—the law enforcement of the Supreme Viscerebus Tribunal. They are embedded in the human armed forces, police and security community as a way of hiding in plain sight, acquiring military training and gaining knowledge on the human military and police system.

The Iztaris' main mandate is to implement strict adherence to the Veil of Secrecy. They are deployed to either a) hunt Harravirs or Harravis, b) implement the Veil procedures, c) defend humans or other Viscerebus from Harravirs and Harravises, d) Find other Viscerebus communities.

The Iztari system is unique, as there are no ranks among the Iztaris. However, there is a Team Head appointed when a team is deployed. The only figure of authority is the Chief Iztari. The Iztari office employs both Viscerebus and Erdias with the right skills. Erdias are office bound and do analyst and research tasks rather than fieldwork.

Only the Viscerebus may go on field because of the inherent danger of dealing with a vicious Harravir and Harravis. Iztaris are well-trained and well-equipped for combat. The Iztari office uses the latest technologies that the human and the Viscerebuskind can offer. Ten per cent of the Viscerebi population are Iztaris. (*See SVT – World of the Viscerebus Almanac*).

Prometheus—A Greek Titan and the god of creative fire and the creator of men. He was the son of Titan Iapetus and the Oceanids, Clymene. His siblings are Atlas, Epimetheus, Menoetius. He is known for his intelligence, as the author of human arts and sciences, and a champion of humankind. His name meant "Forethought".

According to the Viscerebus legends, while he created humans out of clay, Prometheus made the first Viscerebus couple from his own liver, the soil and rocks of the Caucasus mountain where he was bound and tortured.

With his DNA, the Viscerebus inherited godlike traits of super strength, speed, senses, healing abilities and long life. Prometheus also imbued them with the ability to shape-shift so they can hide themselves from Zeus.

It was said that he created them out of his need for companions to distract himself from the pain of having his liver eaten every day by Aetos, and the loneliness during the regrowing of the organ every night.

During the day, the first Viscerebus were in their animal form, a feline and a canine, but they transform into their human form at night to keep Prometheus company. This is also why cats and dogs were regarded as the closest companions to humans. (*See Origin – World of the Viscerebus Almanac*)

Reflexive Transformation – also referred to as *Auto-morphosis*, the involuntary transformation or shape-shifting into the animal spirit of a Viscerebus. The vital instinct to hunt and secure sustenance triggers this transformation. This instinct, in turn, is triggered when a Viscerebus fails to consume sustenance, weakening the Crux, the subconscious and internal control of a Viscerebus to retain their human form. Once weakened, a Viscerebus' human form becomes unstable. Once sustenance is consumed,

Crux control is regained, and the Viscerebus can shift back to their human form with ease.

It is possible to induce a Reflexive Transformation through practice and meditation. (*See Auto-morphosis, Impedio*)

Shape-shifting – one of the primary traits of a Viscerebus. This is closely related to their need to consume human viscera. The viscera stabilises the human form of a Vis. The prolonged absence of a victus, usually three days, triggers the vital hunger and kicks in vital instinct to hunt. Once vital instinct is triggered, the Vis transforms reflexively into their Animus. A Vis has a conscious control of their shape-shifting at most times, through their Crux. (*See Auto-morphosis, Reflexive Transformation. See All about the Vis – World of the Viscerebus Almanac.*)

Supreme Viscerebus Tribunal – or the SVT. This is the primary ruling body of the Viscerebus. It is composed of previous and current Matriarch and Patriarchs from different Gentems all over the world. SVT functions as both the main legislative and judicial body of the Viscerebi. The execution of the laws, however, is the responsibility of each Gentem's Tribunal. Members of the body meet bi-annual, where laws proposed by members are discussed and voted on. The main mandate of the Tribunal is to oversee the compliance of every Gentem in the upholding of the Veil of Secrecy. The SVT is the ultimate rule of law for the Viscerebi. (*See Veil of Secrecy. See 5000BCE Constitution, Implementing Rules and Regulations – World of the Viscerebus Almanac*).

Sustenance– or *Victus.* The blanket term used by Viscerebus to refer to human viscera that they take regularly. This is crucial to stabilising the human form of a Viscerebus. This is the term used by modern Viscerebus, as the term does not invite unnecessary questions and explanations. (*See Crux, Auto-morphosis, Reflexive Transformation. See Victus, Vital hunger – World of the Viscerebus Almanac*).

Transit—The program of relocating a Viscerebus and his/her family to maintain the Veil of Secrecy. A Viscerebus can be under a Life Transit, a mandatory, scheduled relocation every thirty years; or a Forcible Transit, unscheduled relocation because of the Viscerebus' violation of the Veil. A Forcible Transit is equivalent to an exile in human government.

A Transitting Viscerebus is required to cut contact with any of their *non-Veil-bound* human or Erdia friends, relatives and connections. But they can keep contact with other Viscerebus and Veil-bound Erdia friends, relatives and connections.

A Transitting Viscerebus may keep his or her old name and profession, or may take on a new one. The new Transit location has to be in a different country or continent. A Transitting Viscerebus can return to their *Patriam* or previous *Gentem* after 100 years to ensure that any human they had a relationship with before are already dead. Visits to the Patriam and previous Gentems are permitted on brief holidays and only once every ten years. Veil of Secrecy restrictions apply. (*See Veil of Secrecy. Gentem, See Patriam, Transit Program – World of the Viscerebus Almanac*)

Veil of Secrecy—the inviolable law of the Tribunal to keep the existence of Viscerebus a secret from non-Viscerebus. The Law made exceptions to a) Human spouse; b) Human kids. However, the exceptions apply only if the above people prove themselves loyal to the Viscerebuskind and to the Veil.

The strict adherence to the Veil guides every interaction of a Viscerebus with humans and non-Veil-bound Erdias. The violation or breaking of the Veil would entail severe punishment that could cause the death of the human or the non-Veil-bound Erdia, and the violator is expected to execute the punishment. (*See SVT, or Supreme Viscerebus Tribunal. See 5000BCE Constitution – World of the Viscerebus Almanac*).

Victus – colloquially called as *Sustenance.* This is the blanket term for human viscera, heart, liver and kidney, that a Viscerebus must consume regularly to keep their Vital Hunger at bay and prevent involuntary transformation to their animal form.

This term had become less popular than its colloquial counterpart as humans who overheard ask question what it means. The Tribunal encourages the use of the term *Sustenance* in a public setting to avoid the questions. (*See Sustenance, Crux, Auto-morphosis, Reflexive Transformation, Vital Hunger*)

Viscerebus/Viscerebi (pl.)—or Viscera-eaters, colloquially known as ***Vis***. They are a different species of human. They live two to three times longer than a human, are stronger, faster, and have quick healing abilities.

Physically, they look exactly like humans, but they can shape-shift into a land-based predator. The Viscerebus need to eat human viscera to stabilise their human form. To normal humans, they are monstrous man-eaters.

Viscerebi are known by many names in many cultures. And the descriptions vary because of the dilution of the truth engineered by the Tribunal to bury the existence of the Viscerebus under myth and lore. The common thread among these lores is the shape-shifting and the viscera-eating.

Most modern human societies have completely ignored the lores, but the belief persists in some pockets of rural communities all over the world. This is especially true in Asian countries, particularly the Philippines, where stories about Aswangs, the local name for Viscerebus, are still told to this day. (*See Aswang*)

Vital Hunger—the term used to refer to the need to consume *Victus,* or *sustenance.* The sensation is similar to physical hunger, but it pertains to the need of a Viscerebus to secure sustenance to keep their Crux strong and prevent an Auto-morphosis. This manifests if the Vis has neglected to consume sustenance for at least three days. This triggers the *vital instinct* to hunt, which, in turn, triggers the Auto-morphosis, or reflexive transformation.

The symptoms are usually a loss of energy and physical weakening of the Viscerebus. Some Vis develop physical hunger-like symptoms, like shaking and trembling. Vital hunger itself is not painful, but the accompanying pain comes from the battle between the body's Crux and the vital instinct. (*See Auto-morphosis, Crux, Reflexive Transformation, Vital Instinct*)

Vital Instinct—the basic survival instinct of a Viscerebus to consume *Victus,* or human liver, heart or kidney. While this could be interchangeable to the term *Vital Hunger,* this refers to the instinct to hunt rather than the hunger to consume. This surfaces when a Viscerebus fails to partake of human viscera for over three days. At this point, there is a battle between the Vital Instinct and the Crux of the individual.

The stronger the Crux, the longer the Viscerebus can control the transformation. However, inevitably, the Vital Instinct wins, thus forcing an Auto-morphosis, or the reflexive transformation into the Viscerebus' Animus. Once the Vital hunger is quenched, it restores the Crux control of the Viscerebus. (*See Crux, Auto-morphosis, Reflexive Transformation, Vital Hunger*).

Vondenad (Vondenada, f, Vondenado, m) – from the Dutch word "vondeling". The Viscerebus term for "foundling." This refers to the Veil-bound offsprings of any male or female Viscerebus and Erdias that were abandoned by their parents. Although the term used is not the same as an orphan (*Aulila*) or a runaway (*Reneweg*), they are all taken into custody and become a ward of the Supreme Tribunal.

Unlike in human practices, most Vondenados and Vondenadas are immediately taken into the custody of the Tribunal. And they are assigned a foster family, or a *Thetadom* within thirty days. It is illegal to treat a Vondenado/Vondenada as an outsider while they are within the care of a foster family.

Foster parents (*Theta and Thetos*) are expected to care for their ward like their own child and teach them the ways of life and the rules of the Tribunal. They function like a mentor and a parent combine. A Viscerebus or Erdia family could only take on a maximum of one Vondenado or Vondenada every five years. Exceptions are made for siblings. They are usually placed together in one home.

Most foster parents end up adopting the child in their care. Adoption would only be approved when the child reaches the age of eighteen. However, the choice is left to the child whether they would like to be adopted or remain to be a protégé. More than half the Vondenado/Vondenadas opt for the latter because they do not feel like they belong, or they prefer the independence. (*See Aulila, Reneweg, Thetadom, Thetas and Thetos – The World of the Viscerebus Almanac*)

Note: All novels in the World of the Viscerebus series contain a glossary of terms used in the respective books. The full glossary of terms and other information can be found in the WORLD OF THE VISCEREBUS ALMANAC.

AFTERWORD

Dear Reader,

I have built the World of the Viscerebus as richly as I could with stories that are exciting, entertaining and stimulating to the mind. Viscerebus is my global word for the viscera-eaters that are prevalent in various cultures, especially in Southeast Asia. They are known as Aswang in my country.

In this fantasy world, there is the main storyline, a trilogy: Rise of the Viscerebus, First Chronicle; Dawn of the Dual Apex, Second Chronicle, and InEquilibrium, Third Chronicle.

Then there are the companion novels namely Beasts of Prey, The Keeper, and two others that are still works in-progress.

To improve on this fantasy world further, your feedback is valuable to me. If you can please leave a review of my book on Amazon or through the email listed below, I would appreciate it very much.

Or, if you wish to be part of the select early readers of my works, please let me know via email at marigr8@yahoo.com. And follow me at Twitter @GraceGranlund, Instagram @Gogranlund, or Facebook Oz Mari Granlund

Thank you.

Oz Mari G.

DAWN OF THE DUAL APEX

WORLD OF THE VISCEREBUS BOOK 2

ACKNOWLEDGMENTS

To V, for being a loyal beta reader and for your brilliant comments and suggestions. I took them to heart.

To my son, Josh. Thank you for the patience and the support. You are my *Gabay*, my *Bantay* and my *Alagad*.

To the readers of the series, this book picks up where the first chronicle, Rise of the Viscerebus, left off. I hope the second chronicle keeps you interested into taking the journey with our characters further to the third and the fourth and until we reach the end.

For my first-time reader, if you happen to pick up this book first, thank you. I hope you would find this interesting enough to get the other books in the series.

If you want to be a beta reader for my books, or simply interested to get in touch with me, email me at ozmarigranlund@gmail.com. Or get in touch with me through my social media: Twitter: @GraceGranlund, Instagram:@ozmarig

PROLOGUE

Tomio Mori got off the elevator to the lobby of the six-star hotel he was staying in. He carried a small titanium case. Inside was a selection of the highest quality gemstones from his recent procurement trip. But the stones were not for selling, they were his tools for this meeting.

He saw her immediately as she entered the coffee shop. She was sophisticated in a crisp white shirt and dark blue pencil skirt. The patent leather shoes are the exact colour of her jewellery. A set of blood red ruby earrings and a necklace framed her beautiful, unlined face; pieces that most women wear on special occasions, she wore daily. It was the day's end, but she looked as fresh as if it was morning.

Renata Esqueraas' glamorous persona suited her as the owner and editor of *Deesee*, a prominent lifestyle magazine. No sign of her sad childhood about her. She was the only daughter of a former naval officer and a nurse, both *Viscerebus*. Her mother died young. And her father remarried to an *Erdia*. When Renata was fifteen, her father sank with the ship he captained when it was torpedoed by an enemy vessel during the war.

Renata's elegant form as she walked towards him would have set her stepmother's teeth on edge. Vinezza was a social climber who craved to be accepted into their kind's *Alta*. When her marriage to Renata's father did not achieve her entry into the high society, she became resentful. Vinezza, envious of her stepdaughter's *Viscerebus* blood, had placed the teenager in the care of a boarding school and refused to have a relationship with her.

Until Renata became a successful, influential adult through *Deesee*, which became a global number one. The place in the *Alta* that Vinezza coveted became possible with her association with Renata, and by extension, to *Deesee*.

Deesee's rise to prominence happened through his company's support. The patronage of a renowned luxury brand gave her publication credibility and attracted other affluent brands and readers, both human and *Viscerebus*.

This one-on-one meeting, the second since she became a cog in his Grand Plan, was crucial. The reason he invested in her and her publication boiled down to this moment.

"Ms Esqueraas..." He greeted her with a smile. Her citrusy perfume scented the area.

"Mr Mori..." She inclined her head in greeting. Her smile beamed. Her eyes assessed him; the appreciation in them showed she did not miss the image he presented – a successful investor and entrepreneur in custom Italian suit. Her interest in him was more than professional, but he would not reciprocate. It would complicate his plans.

They shook hands. In this guise, he did not follow the Japanese custom of bowing, as it attracts unnecessary attention from the people around them. He preferred to be unobtrusive at all times.

"Shall we move to the room I reserved for us?" He offered her his arm. She inclined her head in concurrence and looped her hand through.

The small private room was in a corner. The service staff closed the sliding glass door to keep the outside noise out and their conversation secure. Mori opened the case he carried and placed it between them. The gemstones were visible to anyone curious enough to look through the glass.

Renata picked up a ten-carat Morganite and made a show of admiring the princess cut and its pink radiance. Her face appeared pleasant and interested. That was not a pretense; jewellery was her weakness.

"So, have you thought about what we discussed?" His questions had nothing to do with gemstones.

She nodded and replaced the stone in its velvet bed and picked up a cushion-cut Alexandrite. "Yes. We have the same goals," she replied, her tone light, a small pout on her lips.

He expected the response. He knew her motivation. "When will you start?" His tone was even, but he gave her an answering smile of satisfaction. He picked up an emerald-cut Heliodor and handed it to her.

"I will send my plans to you in a few days. Then you can send me the buyers." She turned the yellow-green stone this way and that, holding it up against the light. She was not talking about gemstone enthusiasts, either.

"I have the list now." He fished out a slim catalogue of gemstones from his inside pocket and handed it to her together with a loupe.

She took them, flipped open the booklet, and trained the loupe into the stunning emerald on the first page.

At the edge of each stone, in the tiniest of font, hidden in the shadow cast by the shot, were the names of their target politicians of the pre-selected countries. Even with her keen *Viscerebus'* eyesight, she needed the custom loupe to read it.

"How many?" she asked as she leafed through the list.

"Twenty-three, to start with," he replied.

"And the individual casebook?" she asked.

He pushed a long and slim, black velvet jewellery box to her. "Your username and password are at the end of the last page." He said as she opened the box and took out a pendant designed like a pencil, made of titanium and black diamonds.

The exquisitely crafted pendant brought a smile to her face. He took it from her and pushed at the side of the pendant, revealing a well-concealed flash drive. Her eyebrows quirked in surprise, smile widening.

She replaced it in the velvet box and dropped the box into her bag with the buyers' list.

"So, have you made a choice?" he asked. Their business talk concluded. Her eyes glittered in anticipation.

"I'm partial to blue stones," she replied.

He smiled back and handed her a brilliant, oval cut dark blue stone. "This reminded me of you..."

"Thank you. This is beautiful. What is it?" she asked, amazement in her eyes when they met his.

"Tanzanite, twelve carats," he replied, handing her a small velvet gem pouch to safeguard the stone.

He gestured to the service staff hovering outside to summon him into the room. For now, business talk was done. Establishing a deeper bond was important. So far, she behaved exactly as he expected her to. Her agreement to be part of his plan was even ahead of schedule.

Later that evening, Tomio Mori lounged in his hotel room, satisfied with the outcome of his meeting with Renata.

She had proven herself to be a perfect *Zuriajah,* a formidable one among his *White Generals*. Her solid position within the human society ensured her strategic placement.

Within a few months, she would deploy her chief asset, a network of *painlokaas* – young, teenage-looking female and male *Viscerebus*. They would be the baits for the human politicians they wanted under their control.

His *White Generals* had been steadily penetrating various human governments throughout the years, through the corruptible elected officials. His *Zuriajahs* were experts at bribery, blackmail, and various other means. All these strategies were part of the Grand Plan, the full extent of which he had not divulged to anyone.

It was multi-layered to assure success. Secrecy was imperative in every facet of it.

1

THREE MEN AND AN ERDIA

Ximena and Emme sat across from each other, their wine glasses untouched. Rays of the midday sun glinted against the amber liquid, the room humid despite the air conditioning.

The awkwardness of their fractured friendship was as substantial as the day it was destroyed by the act they collaborated on decades ago. A mistake both their consciences had borne and suffered from ever since.

The tension broke when Emme laid a thick folder on the table. Martin Bell's file. Ximena leafed idly through the worn pages without looking. The sensation on her fingertips, familiar. They had kept Martin Bell's file manual; it was personal to her. And to Emme.

Ximena's thoughts were not on the pages, her fingers still touching the edges of the age-softened paper. The visions of the day Martin spoke her name for the first time in fifty years still shook her.

"He called out my name, Emme," she said.

"What? How? When?" Emme's mouth dropped in astonishment, awkwardness forgotten.

"During my last visit." Ximena's heart tightened at the memory and the need to talk about it. She took a sip from her wineglass to ease the pressure a little.

"Are you sure, Mena?" There was a hitch in Emme's voice.

She nodded. Perhaps Emme was as hopeful as her to find redemption from what they did to Martin. It did not matter their intention was good; the outcome did not justify the means.

Ximena handed her phone to Emme. On it was a photo of what looked like a painting of a stormy night. Emme did not understand; the gaze that met Ximena was questioning.

"Scroll to the next one. That's the distant shot of the same painting," she said.

Emme scrutinised the next photo; the emotions and thoughts that chased across her face were identical to Ximena's when she realised what Martin had painted.

The black, grey, reddish, dark blue blotches and the silver rain streaks created an image of her superimposed on the face of a dark grey wolf. Martin's plea and anguish melded in his work. His mind may have been gone, but his soul remembered.

Emme swallowed the lump in her throat as she raised her eyes and met Ximena's.

This was the first time in fifty years Martin had shown any semblance of recognition or remembrance of anyone. He revealed that in the only painting that featured her from almost a thousand artworks he made over those years. Hope bloomed in her chest when she saw it. And the magnitude of it almost stopped her heart then. The heavy sensation had not left her since.

"Mena, what do you want us to do?" Emme asked, eyeing her.

"Try to liberate him out of his own mind, to bring him back," she replied. It was the only option they would consider. "Maybe this time, we will make progress."

"Yes, of course." Emme's quick agreement contrasted with the look of doubt in her eyes.

They both did not know how to achieve it, or if it was even possible. Over five decades, they guarded and watched him closely, always looking for a glimmer of entry into his mind. There was still a lot of uncertainty about Martin's condition, but they were optimistic. It was a rare emotion, and while they did not want to expect too much, it was hard not to.

Silence followed as they sipped their wine in this picturesque bar that should have been a place of casual conversation between friends.

"Emme... thank you for coming." She realised she was indeed grateful Emme had not walked away all those years. And was still with her on this journey.

Emme offered a shadow of a smile in her eyes. "I have waited for that call for decades, Mena. There is no way I will not come." This could be the brick from which they could rebuild their friendship.

All the past hurts between them began to bleed out of her heart. Soon, they would talk about it and sort it out. But for now, their debt to Martin could be paid, the principal, the corresponding interest, and penalties. And pay they would, Emme and her.

And hopefully, they could forgive each other, and themselves after.

The urgency of *Project Chrysalis* had doubled. In the past years, despite the hopelessness of Martin's mental health, Ximena never entertained the thought of giving up. She focused on the experiments and the research for both projects with a manic dedication. With a crack in the impenetrable wall that encased Martin's mind, they were closer to success than ever before. They could not waste time.

Emme and she were committed to healing Martin's mind. Their failure on that score, year after year, was disheartening. Seeing all his *Aswang* paintings was a painful visual reminder of his torment and their incapacity. The *Project Chrysalis* became her panacea, her focus, her alternative route to make things right.

Martin's body grew feebler by the day, brought on by age and lack of physical activities apart from painting. The sign of recognition he exhibited buoyed her spirit.

She needed to work on this project more closely, more extensively. Martin and her quest to convert him into a *Vis* had run its course. Her goal now changed into prolonging his life by adding *V Genes*. Maybe the added years would allow them to rectify what they did to him.

Would Íñigo agree to it?

This is frustrating, thought Íñigo, as he leafed through the latest laboratory test results. They could not bridge the gap between the human and *Aswang* genes, even with the use of the *Erdia* DNA with the highest *V gene* count.

He looked up to find Ximena entering the lab, her brows knitted. She looked perturbed, her distraction so complete that she did not notice him observing her for a long time. It startled her when he cleared his throat to alert her to his presence. Her smile of apology was weak.

"Family issues?" He was privy to Ysobella and Yuana's situation. Ximena shook her head.

The De Vida women have been unlucky in their relationships over the decades. They tended to fall in love with humans, and they paid for it with considerable heartache. None more so than Ximena. Her heart remained locked from him, unable to move on because of what happened to Martin.

Íñigo waited for her to tell him what was bothering her. Ximena seemed unsure. But he could almost guess what was on her mind.

"How are the testing coming along?" Ximena asked to divert his focus.

For a moment, he was tempted to press her. He pushed the report over to her in response.

"Are there any breakthroughs?" Ximena asked without looking at it.

He shook his head. "None. The FE2-human experiment showed promise in the beginning, but we cannot seem to push it further to a successful result. The specimen genes were not stable enough. We are still missing a link." He riffled through the report and pointed to a diagram to emphasise his point.

"FE2? The offspring of a female *Erdia* and a male *Viscerebus* with 9.5 *V Genes*." She frowned. "Is this the highest we could get?"

"Yes."

Ximena sighed. "Would we ever find the closest source? It is looking impossible." She rubbed her temples, an action that screamed despondency. With a deep breath, she straightened. Inner grit bolstered her determination.

"Well, our other option is to find a process that would augment what we are missing..." he said.

"You're right. We have been doing this for over fifteen years now, and we have progressed quite a lot. The final breakthrough may just be around the corner. Synthesising the cure for *VM* may have been elusive for now, but the *Altera Project* is far from over," she said.

That pulled a smile from him. He could not help it. "Yes. And our goal is as noble today as when we first secured the approval from the *Tribunal*. Let us focus on finding that missing link. I believe we are close to finding that cure."

Ximena's nod of acknowledgement was incongruent with the flash of panic in her eyes. He knew, by gutfeel, it had to do with the *Project Chrysalis* – her goal to convert humans into *Aswang*. One human. Martin Bell.

While it pained him to join her in the project, he could not find it in himself to deny her plea for help. Their undercover collaboration had been a secret to everyone, including her powerful family. And he suspected her inner panic earlier had something to do with Martin Bell.

Something had happened to his rival.

I am in the house of creatures that eat raw human organs.

The thought of *Aswang* and their human viscera-eating nature made Roald's heart quicken, and panic rose in him again. His eyes closed as he breathed deep to quell his gut reaction. He found if he focused on his feelings for Yuana, he could dissociate her from this debilitating fear of the creature.

Roald shook his head to cast his anxiety away. He was here to win Yuana back. With determination, he looked around him, to find a more mundane focus to drown out his more unpleasant thoughts.

The house was old, but very well maintained, and judging from the furnishing in the room and the bathroom fittings, it had been judiciously renovated and outfitted with the latest convenience.

His room was beautiful in dark wood accents that matched the big, comfortable-looking bed at its center and the wide windows. The front garden was visible beyond it.

The swish of the leaves in the nearby forest and the chirping of birds accompanied the breeze that swept into the room. It kept the surroundings cool enough, with no need for air-conditioning.The place had the romantic and sensual charm of a honeymoon getaway.

Yuana was a mere three doors away, but her parents' room was in between theirs. This meant he would not be tiptoeing to her room in the middle of the night. Roald could only shake his head ruefully. For such a modern family, they seemed so traditional.

He peeled off his shirt to take a shower. When he came here, he was not sure how long he would be staying, or if he was even going to be welcomed. He did not want to presume. Now, he wanted to present his best self to her parents.

This felt like his first dinner with Yuana's family, even though he had dined with them multiple times over the years. Yuana's revelation shifted everything, and tonight would be the first since he had accepted the truth that Yuana, her mother and the entire De Vida clan were... not human.

Under the shower, the white noise of the water spray provided a calming medium for his thoughts. It would be hurtful to Yuana if he reacted in fear of her kind every time. He had to find a way to deal with it.

Perhaps talking to Galen would help. Yuana's father, a human like him, was in the same boat. Yuana's mother left Galen all those years ago for the same reason Yuana hid the truth from him. Now, both of them would have to deal and live with their women's beastly nature.

Refreshed and galvanised by a new purpose, Roald went to the living room in search of Yuana's parents. He found Galen and Ysobella by the verandah, enjoying a drink before dinner. The couple did not see him as they both gazed at the vast lawn and the imposing mountain on the horizon. They were holding hands – a relaxed resting of Ysobella's palm into Galen's, their fingers loosely interlocked – and the sight bolstered the hope in his heart.

Both turned towards him as he approached, a slight smile on Ysobella's face and a calm inquiry on Galen's.

"Can I join you, Tito, Tita?"

He glanced at an empty chair beside theirs. Galen inclined his head in permission, the older man's gaze assessing.

Roald sat down and faced the couple. He took a deep breath and decided to be direct in his approach.

"Tita, I would like to ask for help... some guidance on how to live in your world..." Her silence compelled him to add, "I want to do this very much, but I do not know how to go about it."

Ysobella stared at Roald, gauging the sincerity in the boy's eyes. He looked haggard, despite having showered already. The emotions within the depths of Roald's eyes echoed the pleading in his voice. His vulnerability and courage were commendable, and promising.

Ysobella nodded.

"We will help you as much as we can." She spoke for Galen and her. She knows Galen would do everything to help their daughter.

"What kind of help do you need?" Galen asked.

The slight softening in his eyes showed his approval of Roald's decision to seek their assistance. A problem would be easier to solve when laid out in the open.

There was a lengthy pause. They waited in patience for Roald to continue.

"I... have deep fears... And it makes me recoil... I do not want to hurt Yuana's feelings every time it happens..." he began.

Roald sounded unsure and helpless in his inability to explain his difficulties. There was a slight tremor on the young man's hands, and he looked crestfallen. The sight made her stomach tighten.

How would Roald handle the truth if he is this terrorized by it?

"What is it about us that scares you?" Ysobella asked. Her parents informed her Roald may have had a traumatic *Vis* encounter in his childhood, but she could not tell Roald what she knew. She was not supposed to be privy to it.

"I am not sure..." Roald faltered, unable to verbalise where the fear was coming from, to share the details.

"What do you see when you look at Yuana, when you think of her?" she asked. Her intent gaze on him tightened his jaw, but he did not look away. Deep in his eyes, she glimpsed the depth of his boyhood fear.

"I see her... as her... my Yuana. But I have nightmares now... and it includes visions of her as an *Aswang*..." His voice was a raw whisper, like it passed through a shredder.

"What are those visions?" Galen interjected; his eyes narrowed in keen interest.

"I am not sure... it is usually a confused jumble of terrifying images, of Yuana, of blood, of human internal organs... It made little sense, but it is clear to me when I wake up that I am petrified of *Aswangs*." Roald's pained expression underscored his tone.

"You would need to figure out what scares you, Roald. It will be difficult to overcome something you do not understand. You would not know how to fight it, or conquer it," Galen said.

Like her, he recognised the boy's torment. Roald had a lot to conquer before he could fully accept Yuana and their family's nature.

"I know, Tito. That is why I am asking for your help. I can do this in small doses," Roald said.

She glanced at Galen for confirmation. The flash of agreement in his eyes was all she needed. They both turned to Roald and nodded.

"Okay, we will help you," Ysobella replied.

Roald sighed with relief, and the taut line of his jaw eased. His determination to conquer the fear was written in the line of his spine.

And as if it was perfect timing, Yuana came down the stairs, her steps light. The blaze of emotions as the young couple's eyes met was telling. It seemed Roald would give anything to keep that look in Yuana's eyes.

It strengthened her maternal resolve to assist Roald through this. For her daughter's sake. Hopefully, he would give anything and everything to succeed, even his own humanity.

The early morning breeze that lifted the strands of loose hair about her face smelled of damp grass, flowers and fruits that abound the woods at this time of the year. The sun inched above the horizon, brightening the sky.

With hot coffee in hand, Ysobella basked in the calm of her surroundings. An invigorating breath added to her contentment, the primary source of which was the slumbering man in her bed.

The bedsheet rustled as Galen stirred. He lay on his side now, facing her, peaceful and boyish. She allowed him to sleep longer; he needed all the rest he could get. His energy was not as high as hers, being what she was. And his malady handicapped him. She was tempted to go back to bed and cuddle with Galen, when her phone vibrated.

Her mother called.

She walked out to the verandah so the conversation would not disturb Galen's sleep, sliding the glass door closed behind her.

"Good morning, Bella, how are things there?" Katelin's usual cheery voice came through.

"Things are great, Mama. I have news to tell you..." She didn't know how to broach the subject, her heart afire with excitement.

"Hmm... what news? Good or bad?" her mother asked in a teasing voice. Only her mother would think of being playful this early.

"Mama... Galen and I are engaged. Finally." She tried to sound less giddy.

"We expected that. I am thrilled for you, Bella." There was a smile in her mother's voice. "So, when is the wedding?"

"May tenth. It will be a small one, intimate." She expected support from her mother and was not disappointed.

"Naturally, but have you decided where the wedding is going to be?" Her mother's delight was unmistakable in the girlish rise of her tone.

"No, not yet. I am still savouring this – the reality that Galen and I will finally marry."

"You deserve this, my dear...You and Yuana," Katelin said.

The mention of her daughter's name reminded her. "Speaking of Yuana, Roald is here. And they made up."

"Yes, your Papa gave him the address, so we were hoping for this outcome. Has the boy been informed about the *Veil of Secrecy*? Has he committed to be bound by it?"

"No serious talk about the *Veil* yet. We will do that later at breakfast. But I am hopeful about him, Mama. He talked to Galen and me yesterday and asked for our help. He mentioned he was scared... but he could not articulate what it was he feared."

"Ah... yes. We have confirmed he had a childhood encounter with a *Vis*. When he was three or four years old, he saw a male feeding on a woman," her mother said.

"Papa mentioned something to that effect, but he did not give details. That explains his fear... Should we tell Roald?" Ysobella knew his psychiatrist could not validate that to Roald without exposing Dr Sanchez's nature.

"Yes, but maybe a little later, when we are completely sure Roald is committed to keep the *Veil*. He cannot find out how much of his life we infiltrated. He will not take kindly to that. Most humans are prickly about that kind of intrusion."

"Okay, Mama. But I will discuss the facts with Yuana. She needs to know. It will help her understand Roald's reaction." She could almost see her mother nodding on the other side of the line. In the brief silence that followed, she debated whether she should discuss the newly discovered *Apex* nature of Yuana.

"Is there anything else, Bella?" Her mother's instinct kicked in. Katelin's insight into how her mind worked was as strong as ever.

She braced for her mother's reaction. "Ma... Yuana is an *Apex*."

"What? Did I hear you right? Yuana is an *Apex*?" Her mother's words escalated in tone.

"Yes, she transforms into a black bird. She thinks it was a raven, but she looked more like a cross between a raven and a Haribon to me." She still could not believe it herself. Her daughter, the rare super shapeshifter, one in every two hundred fifty million *Viscerebi* after every two centuries. It was too mind-boggling to contemplate.

"A Haribon? The Philippine eagle... Oh, blessed *Aquila*!" Her mother's words came out through her teeth; stunned was too mild to describe her tone. "Wow! The only *Apex* in our lifetime is my granddaughter..." There was awe in Katelin's voice.

"I know, Mama. That's exactly how I reacted when I found out."

"When are you coming back here?" Katelin's tone was urgent, as if she planned to throw a grand party.

"Yuana wanted to keep it a secret for now," she warned. "She has too many things on her plate. Let us keep it within the family for the meantime. Global attention from our kind is the last thing she needs. Let us give her some time."

"Of course. It is not our secret to tell, anyway. But I will tell your Abuelo and Abuela. I want to shock them..." Her mother's glee was contagious. "I can't wait to see their faces..."

"Oh, I would love to see that, too." Movements in the kitchen gave her pause. "I have to go now; I can hear Yam-Ay getting breakfast ready. Give a kiss to Papa from me," she said.

"Mwah... *may abundance stay with you*, my dear," her mother said and hung up. Her mother's well-wishes warmed her heart.

Galen shifted on the bed, drawing her attention back to him. His eyes were still closed, but his hands crept to her side of the bed. His lids opened when he found it empty; his gaze darted around to look for her. Galen's dark gaze met hers as she opened the verandah door and walked over. She smiled at him, gladness pervaded her heart at the knowledge that he was here, with her.

She leaned over and gave him a quick good morning kiss. "Breakfast?" she murmured against his lips.

He studied her intently. "In a minute... I am still thanking the universe for my luck." His expression conveyed gratefulness. Her heart clenched in response.

Galen made her life worth more than she could ever value it. Abundance stayed, indeed.

Yuana sat in contemplation. Her parents advised her about Roald's request and his childhood trauma. It could aggravate his *Aswang* phobia if she revealed that her *Animus* was a winged creature. He might start imagining her as a *gorzati,* a *Manananggal,* the most feared, but erroneous image of their kind.

What else can they do to make it easier for Roald?

Like her father, he would not have to see her eat raw human viscera. So that would be half the obstacle removed for him.

How would she conduct her flight lessons? She could not do it during the day, it would be visible, and Roald would find it strange if she disappeared for hours.

Her best option would be very late at night while everyone was asleep. She would need her mother's help to ensure the Mangyan household remained unaware.

The clanking call of the Pokpok alerted her it was time to go down for breakfast. She waved at the colourful bird perched on the tree outside her window; the creature became her natural alarm clock since she arrived.

She found Roald, coffee in hand, at the ground floor verandah. He heard her footsteps and turned, a welcoming smile on his face. His free arm opened wide as she neared, and enveloped her in a tight one-armed hug, dropping a kiss on her forehead.

"Good morning, Yu," he murmured, his breath made warm and fragrant by the coffee.

"Good morning, Ro." She smiled up at him. His eyes focused on her lips for a while, undecided what to do. She pulled his head down and gave him a quick kiss.

Roald's breath hitched in surprise. His eyes glittered in response. He would have kissed her back, but the sounds of Ysobella and Galen's footsteps halted his intent.

Her parents exchanged kisses as they descended the stairs. Roald shot a glance at her, and his slightly aggravated expression made her laugh.

"Good morning, kids," Yuana called out to her parents. They both grinned at her like kids caught doing something naughty.

"Shall we breakfast?" Galen asked.

They nodded and followed her father and mother towards the morning room, where Roald found her when he arrived at the Villa yesterday. The sunny and airy room had become her favourite in this house.

Breakfast was convivial and relaxed in the bright room that smelled of coffee, cinnamon, and baked bread. A mild, morning breeze blew in through the windows carrying the scent of dewy grass, flowers, and trees.

Roald was aware of his avoidance of the topic that Yuana and her parents anticipated from him. For now, he wanted to ignore it.

"Roald, did Yuana talk to you about the *Veil of Secrecy*?" Ysobella said out of the blue.

His heart skipped a beat. *Veil of what?*

"No, Tita." He glanced at Yuana.

"The *Veil of Secrecy* is the oath that each of us must keep at all times and is the foundation of our laws. We are bound by it from birth. In a nutshell, no one must know the existence of our kind. Our laws require anyone we share the truth about us to be bound by the same *Veil.* Our lives depend on it." There was a tensed line at the corner of Ysobella's mouth, and a grim glint in her eyes.

And his heart skipped another beat.

"I understand, Tita. And I... am willing to bind myself to... the *Veil.*" He could not imagine anything that would induce him to reveal that information to anyone, except... "Tita, Yu, I... I told my shrink... during my sessions..." His heart had dropped to his gut.

"It's okay, Roald. I am sure your shrink will not divulge your words to anyone because of doctor-patient confidentiality," Ysobella assured him with a smile.

But he could not smile back. He also told someone else. "And Daniel... I mentioned to him that Yuana claimed to be an..." He was unable to complete his sentence.

"A *Viscerebus*... or *Vis*, for short," Yuana suggested, her tone gentle. "That is the non-colloquial term, the scientific name, if you will. We refer to ourselves as that, especially here. The word *Aswang* alarms the humans when they hear it."

"Okay... I told Daniel..." he repeated, still worried.

"It's alright. He is a good friend to both of us. I am sure Daniel would never repeat it to anyone else," Yuana reassured him.

Yuana was right; it would be in character for Daniel to keep it to himself.

"What happens if someone does not keep to the *Veil*?" The thought popped in his head, and he was afraid to learn the answer.

"There are measures we implement. I can tell you more about that later if needed. Just keep the *Veil* intact, and everything will be fine," Yuana replied.

He realised she did not want to give him more reasons to fear their kind. He felt a mixture of relief and anxiety, but he needed to know.

"Would I be placing you in mortal danger, Yu, if somebody else finds out?" he persisted. Did he inadvertently endanger her?

"Yes. And my entire family." Yuana's brief reply told him the answer he dreaded.

Roald took a deep breath. The knowledge he had placed Yuana and her family at risk did not sit well with him. *Maybe I should speak to Daniel, to convince him to keep the information in strict confidence.*

Yuana's gaze seemed to have read the thoughts running in his head. And she looked warmed and touched by it. She reached out and squeezed his hand. "It's okay, Ro. I trust Daniel, even with my life," she said. Her smile beamed with confidence.

Yuana's parents exchanged a satisfied glance. He must have convinced them that his love for Yuana was strong enough for him to keep the *Veil.*

Galen logged out of the *Supreme Viscerebus Tribunal's* archives and closed Ysobella's laptop.

The more he learned, the more he appreciated the common ground between humans and *Viscerebi.* The scientist in him was keen on finding out about the physiology of a *Vis,* especially their brain and the spine. Ever since he saw Ysobella transform, the ability had fascinated him.

Despite his shock when she shape-shifted, his logical brain registered the process, and it seemed to have started at her spine. He could still picture the rolling ball of muscle that ran up and down her back, the reshaping of each vertebra.

He wondered for a moment if there were any studies about the process that he could review more closely. Maybe he should ask Ysobella. He would love to read the research.

As to their differences, in culture and traditions, some of the *Viscerebus* practices awed him. One grabbed his attention – the *Zurugatzen* or the *Absorption* ritual.

Many human cultures in the world practiced similar ritualistic cannibalism. Some human tribes believed in channelling the superior traits of their deceased relatives and enemies by consuming their body parts, imbibing the power and spirit of the departed.

But the *Viscerebus* transformed the idea into a physical and spiritual expression of love – a tradition to ensure a departed loved one would be forever entwined with those left behind. It was eye-opening to realise the man-eating monsters of lore treated the same practice with more care and honour than their human counterparts.

It was past noon. Sweat dampened his skin at the increased humidity in the air. He got up and stretched. The muscles in his back tightened during the long research session and his body had developed aches and pains here and there. What used to be an occasional thing was now a regular occurrence and had increased in intensity.

He knew it would happen; it was part of his disease. He forgot about it for a while because things had been so wonderful. But he would not allow this fact to mar his joy, or let the ticking away of the clock to rush him through his time with Bel and Yuana and miss every single moment of it.

He searched for his Bel, who went to discuss the shopping list with Yam-Ay. They were going to have a rooftop barbecue later. He heard the shower running as he neared their bedroom. And the tantalising images of his intended flashed in his mind. The day was suddenly ripe with possibilities.

What better way to spend the time than showering with one's beloved?

2

HAUNTED PAST, UNCERTAIN FUTURE

Daniel woke up with a splitting headache, a stomach that felt like it contained enough acid to strip the paint from a car, a dry tongue, and an acrid taste in his mouth.

The streak of sunlight that streamed into his room meant it was midday and he overslept.

I should get up now. He could not keep the reality of his life at bay forever. His body protested as he picked himself up to bathe his discomfort away.

Twenty minutes later, showered and refreshed, Daniel padded to the kitchen to have something to settle his stomach. He found his father seated by his favourite place to read – the breakfast table.

Mateo was not reading, though, but leafing through an old photo album. A practice that, like the drinking of scotch, he would do only once a year – during the death anniversary of his mother and baby sister.

His father's expression was blank, but there was despondency in the slump of his shoulders that got to Daniel. For the first time in his life, considering that *Viscerebi* age slowly, his father looked old and worn out.

"Dad..."

His father looked up at the quiet mention of his name. "Dan," he sighed, the sound glum and tired.

Did his father spend the entire day drinking like he did and neglected to eat? "Have you had lunch, Dad?"

His father got up instead, walked to the stove where a small pot rested, took out a bowl and ladled two servings of what looked and smelled like beef stew. His dad laid it in front of him.

Daniel took a mouthful of stew. It was still warm, thick, rich, and as good as he remembered. His father had always been a talented cook, a trait Daniel did not inherit. The stew was one of the comfort foods of his childhood. It was a dish his father served him whenever he needed cheering up.

Daniel ate in silence for a few minutes, trying to ease the tension in the room. He wanted to get back to the old calm they used to have – a combination of mutual love, respect, and admiration. He did not know how to recapture the camaraderie after he walked out on his father – when the horrific truth came to light: that his mother shot herself in the head so his father could eat his little sister as a cure for the deadly disease that plagued him.

"Dan, do you have any questions?"

His father's quiet query felt loud. He understood what his father asked him. Mateo wanted everything about that tragic past laid out in the open, the wound lanced and bled until the poison of the experience drained out of their relationship as father and son. So they could move on.

Daniel looked up and laid his spoon down. Their talk was much more important than his hunger. His appetite had fled anyway; his stomach churned in tension.

It struck Daniel that he never gave his father's motivation a thought. He got stuck on his own reaction to the horrifying truth of his father's beastly nature. Some animals eat their young, but he did not want to think that of his own father.

"Why did you do it?" he asked. He could not look at his father, so he kept his eyes on the bowl of stew in front of him, at the spoon head that disappeared beneath the reddish-brown sauce.

Mateo's sigh sounded like he was expecting this question but was not happy when it was voiced.

"I had no choice. Your mother made sure of that. You would have been an orphan in two years because of my *Visceral Metastasis*, and I did not want that for you." His father's reply was toneless, but misery was etched on his face and roughened his deep voice.

Daniel had very vague memories of his mother, no reference to her character apart from snippets of her in old videotapes of family activities when he was very young. She seemed like a vivacious young woman.

"My mother killed herself, so you may live?" A bitter aspect of the truth he did not consider.

Did she possess a big enough heart to make such a sacrifice?

"Yes. She gave me no chance, or option to stop her." Anguish coloured his father's tone, the prominent jaw so rigid, he worried for his father's teeth.

"Was there no opportunity to take her to the hospital? To save her and the baby?" Daniel asked, even though he did not believe it to be so. His father would have done everything to save his wife and unborn child.

Mateo shook his head. "None. She shot herself in the head, and the closest hospital was twenty minutes away. It would have been too late to save the baby in her... Your mother planned it well. She made sure that I had no choice but to consume your sister." The bitterness in Mateo's voice was as sharp as a knife.

Dad resented what mom made him do. He still does.

He finally understood. In his selfishness, he judged his father's primal act unjustly. His dad did it for Daniel's benefit. The realisation of his cruel reaction to his father's revelation made him sick. "Dad..." He swallowed. Daniel wanted to apologise, to ask for forgiveness, but his throat tightened.

His father's shoulders squared, back rigid as if preparing for a blow.

Dan felt that in his gut. He hurt his father in the most fundamental of ways. He hung his head and muttered, "I'm sorry, Dad..." his voice hoarse. Daniel half wished for the tears to come, but his emotions seemed locked in so deep, there was no possibility of crying.

There was no response from his father, except a rumble in his throat. He saw his dad swallow a few times, eyes averted, jaw taut as Mateo Santino tried hard to rein in his emotions.

Daniel wanted to comfort his father but did not know how. The gestures of affection between them were limited to quick one-arm hugs and pats on the back. At the moment, neither one seemed adequate to convey what he wanted his father to know, how he felt.

A few deep breaths brought his father's renowned control back. Mateo looked as relieved as he. His dad stood up and poured out two glasses of wine from a bottle on a counter behind him. Daniel ignored the glass his father pushed in front of him; his stomach had not calmed down yet, and he wanted to remain sober for the remainder of the talk.

The silence that followed became a breather as they relished the partially restored camaraderie between them. A lot about it still needed clarification, but he knew it would take time. The one thing that was foremost in his mind was his mother.

He wanted to ask about her, to understand what drove her to sacrifice herself and his baby sister for him and his father.

"Dad, why did she do it?"

His father did not respond, his gaze focused on the wine that swirled slowly in his glass. He seemed to be choosing the words and how to answer him.

"I think your mother got scared of the responsibility of single parenthood. She knew I was dying..." His father's brows knitted in contemplation. "I should have paid more attention to her fears. Your mom led a sheltered life as an only child. She grew up having someone to depend on all the time. She was delicate, physically, and emotionally. I fell in love with her partly because she needed me, and I loved taking care of her. She made me feel like a powerful man, and she adored being cherished. I can understand why the idea of being the only parent to you and your sister frightened her."

"But she had grandpa and grandma to help her..." His grandparents did not pass on until he was in his teens.

"Yes, she did... But the situation was different. She would have been the primary caregiver for you and your sister, the one responsible for your well-being. It was a position that she had never taken on before. Edrigu suggested that perhaps her perinatal depression contributed to it, to why she did what she did," his father said.

"Did she suffer from depression?" That was news to Daniel.

His father nodded. "Yes, I think she did. Her mood was erratic while pregnant with you. Your grandmother had to stay with her while I was at work. She also suffered from baby blues for about a month after you were born, but she recovered soon after. I was told it was normal for any first pregnancy." His father's brows knitted in recollection of the events.

"Her mood during your sister's pregnancy was different, more jovial. It changed when she found out about my diagnosis. That was understandable, so I did not look into it too deeply. I only had two years at most, so my prime consideration was to put things in order before my end comes." There was a note of apology and regret in his voice. His gaze clouded with memories.

"When she requested for us to go on holiday, I was happy to give her anything she wanted... Looking back, she planned everything, including placing herself in an area where emergency services would not be possible. My preoccupation allowed her to blindside me." Self-recrimination thickened his father's voice.

"Dad, please do not blame yourself. You could not have known."

His father nodded distractedly, still deep into the bitter memories of that fateful night.

Daniel looked at the man in front of him; his father, and a *Viscerebus*, a creature who ate human organs, possessed superhuman strength, speed, heightened senses, and slow aging. A superior version of man.

He had not paid attention to his father's *Viscerebus* characteristics and appetites. He had never witnessed his father do anything *Vis-like*. Mateo Santino was human in every way. The only thing that betrayed his *Viscerebus* nature was his looks.

His seventy-five-year-old father could be mistaken to be in his forties only because he had taken to adding grey tint to his hair. It was to avoid the questions why father and son looked more like brothers.

In another twenty years, Daniel would look older than his dad. But before that happened, his father would *Transit* to disappear to a different country, where no one knew him. The life of a *Viscerebus* was such – they never build permanent roots.

The reality of having such a long life was the cruelest joke of nature – it meant living a long and desolate life among the societies of humans. His father was destined to bury his *Erdia* son.

As a half-blood, there were many traits from his father's genes that was not passed on to him, but what would he have done if he had the option to be a full *Vis*? He could only inhabit his human side, a choice that had no advantage.

Daniel's thoughts got interrupted when his father stood up and spooned some stew for himself. Mateo handed him the glass of wine he declined earlier and told him to finish his meal. Daniel complied, out of habit.

In silence and solidarity, they ate the stew. Daniel felt better for the first time since the revelation.

Daniel tried to contact Yuana for the past half hour, but she was not picking up. Perhaps she had a lie in wherever she disappeared to, although he could not imagine Yuana being abed this late in the morning.

He sent her a text message, hoping she would return his call. An hour later, his phone rang. It was Yuana.

"Hey, Dan. You called?"

"Hey, woman! You sound upbeat. All is well with Roald?" he asked. There was a brief pause, and an indrawn breath.

"Yes, he is here..." Her breathy response was giddy. A stab of emotion hit his chest.

"Oh, that's good. I'm relieved to hear that." He tried to inject enthusiasm into his tone. It was one less issue for him to worry about.

An awkward silence followed.

"Is something wrong, Dan?"

Yuana had always been perceptive, able to pick up on his disquiet. He wanted to speak, but he had no idea what to say, or how to say it.

"Dan, just out with it. I am too far away to beat it out of you," she said. Her voice turned stern, a warning that she would not let the issue go.

He sighed. Whenever Yuana used the authoritative tone on him, he obeyed like a boy of four. He wanted to talk to someone, anyway. It was why he called her.

"Yu, did they tell you about Roald's childhood *Vis* encounter?" he asked.

"Yes, they did... Why?"

"Did they tell you the complete story?" He did not want to be the one to explain to her.

"Well, Mama told me earlier Roald saw a male *Vis* feeding on a woman when he was about three or four years old. I believe the *Iztaris* are still looking to verify it..." she said. "What about it?"

"The story is true. It happened exactly as Roald had related to the shrink." He forced the admission through a constricted throat. "The man was my dad... the woman, my mom."

"What?" Yuana's shock was apparent in the brief pause that followed. "Oh, holy *Prometheus*..." she breathed.

He thought he heard her sit down.

"Yes, indeed..." He sat down himself, his knees wobbled, and a long-held breath escaped him.

"But why?" Her voice faded in confusion. And when he did not respond, "I am sure there's a valid reason... Are you okay?" Concern thickened her voice.

His heart squeezed in reaction.

"I am okay. Dad and I sorted it out, or as much as we could handle in one sitting. And yes, there was a reason. A justifiable one." He was torn between the need to explain and keep the matter to himself. Sharing the truth with someone was like etching it in stone. More permanent and less possibility for it to be a complete mistake.

"Do you want to talk about it, Dan?" Yuana's voice softened, her tone gentled. Her voice reached him like a hug. It warmed him inside.

"Maybe later, when all is well..." He swallowed, still unable to pinpoint or talk about what made him uneasy.

Silence reigned for a few minutes. "So, what else is bothering you?" Yuana asked as she picked up on the turmoil in his heart.

He took a moment. "I guess I feel guilty about it. I want to apologise to Roald..."

"It was not your fault. Not even your father's fault. I can't believe your dad did that on purpose in view of a four-year-old human child. It is not like him, and you know it."

"No, of course not..." he acknowledged, but it did little to ease his mind.

"But your guilt is not just about your father's accidental trauma to Roald, is it?" Yuana's question carried a dare for him to deny what she suspected.

His heart lurched; her words hit a mark that he did not realise existed. His instinct to defend and deny was instantaneous. "What do you mean?"

"I don't know, Dan... Why don't you tell me?" Her gentle tone dared him.

He did not respond, but Yuana was very close to the truth of where his guilt lay.

"Dan, you can always talk to Roald about it, if you wish. I haven't told him who you are, and I leave that revelation to you," she said after a while.

"I do not want to aggravate the situation, Yu. It might be too early to tell him."

Her silence meant she agreed with him. And he felt a tinge of bitter satisfaction that he turned the tables on her.

"Yu, I never really asked you before..." he began cautiously; he did not want to offend. "... have you ever wished, even for a moment, you were not a *Viscerebus*?"

There was a thoughtful silence before Yuana replied. "No, I never thought, or wished for that..."

"Not even with this situation with Roald?"

"No.... I wished, fervently, repeatedly, for him to be one of our kind, but I have never asked to be human. I am what I am, I do not know how to be anything else. And there are perks to having the *Vis* genes..." Her voice trailed off as if she realised something.

He considered what she said for a while. Yuana, despite having a human father, was a true *Viscerebus*. Full traits and all. She never had her human and *Vis* side tug at her in opposing directions. Unlike him. He was neither this nor that, not a *Vis* yet not quite human. His pulse quickened as the true reason for his disquiet dawned on him.

"Okay, I will let you go now, I just want to check up on you. I am glad that all is well with you and Roald." His mind and heart still abuzz with many confusing thoughts and emotions, and it was making him panic.

"Dan, are you bothered you are an *Erdia*?" Yuana was unwilling to let the matter go. Her spot-on comment hit him hard.

"Call me when you get back to the city, Yu. Say hi to Ro for me," he replied instead and hung up.

A text message from Yuana came a few seconds later. *My left kidney has your name on it, ready whenever you need it, Yu.*

This was an old childhood joke between them, between their kind. Kidney being a symbol of reciprocal love, friendship, or kinship. But the organ was also the center of fear and anxiety. *How apt!*

He texted back the usual comeback to the joke. *And my right is yours.*

He realised then that he meant it—this woman could literally ask for his organs, and he would gladly give it to her.

Yuana read Daniel's text with a sigh. Daniel's state of mind worried her, especially with what he revealed. That must have been devastating for him. She had always known Daniel disliked the *Viscerebus* side of his nature. It was the reason he dated no *Vis* women, despite his popularity with them. She thought he had grown out of it after all these years, especially since he was very involved in the *Iztari* operations.

It seemed Daniel distanced himself from that part of him, and it was easy to do since he was more human than *Vis*. And this revelation made it hard for him to deny his father's bloodline.

Fate had been a bitch to all of them, including Daniel and Roald.

On one hand, Daniel just discovered the stark reality of his father's *Vis* nature, and that his dad unwittingly caused irreparable damage to his best friend.

On the other, Roald fell in love with her and would have to deal with a deep-seated fear of her kind. A phobia caused by the father of his best friend was too vindictive a destiny.

As if on cue, she heard Roald's footsteps as he walked across the front gardens towards her. He must have spied her from his bedroom verandah.

He pulled her off the hardwood bench and into his arms, his hands running down her back in a gesture that conveyed longing. She smiled up at him.

"Work call?" His inquiry was mild, one eyebrow quirked.

She shook her head. "It was Daniel, catching up. He said hi to both of us."

"Should I be jealous? I tried calling you for days, you never picked up." His tone was teasing, but it carried an undertone of seriousness.

"No. I went off the grid during those days, and was not answering any calls, Daniel's included."

"How was he? I wanted to speak to him myself."

"Call him," she said. She did not want him to suspect something was afoot with Daniel. It was not her secret to reveal.

Roald shook his head. "Later... Can you give me a tour of the gardens of this magnificent villa?"

"Sure..." She breathed a silent sigh of relief.

They needed more time for Roald to adjust before they hand him another shock. Palm to palm, they meandered around the vast front gardens. They were both buying time and building up courage.

Roald showed interest in the various exotic flowers and plants in the garden, and she identified them for him, the properties and practical uses of each.

"I did not realise you knew so much about these plants..." Roald sounded impressed with her knowledge.

"My *Vis* sense of smell can pick up the chemical signature of each plant and flower. It is crucial to our survival to know which plant relieves pain, hastens or delays healing, and masks our scent from another *Aswang*."

Roald flinched at the mention of the word, and she winced inside. *I should wait for him to ask questions and not volunteer information.*

As they walked around, she waited for Roald to ask about her nature. But he seemed determined not to do so. She wondered if Roald decided to just ignore the truth and pretend it did not exist.

How long does he intend to do this?

This was not acceptance, but avoidance of the truth. But then again, maybe this was part of Roald's coping mechanism, and he just needed more time.

Meanwhile, Roald was kept awake by one thought—how to train himself to deal with Yuana's nature.

He had been avoiding any mention of it, and Yuana's parents were supportive. But he could not continue as if Yuana's truth did not exist. That would be unfair to her and would not do him any good.

His cowardice shamed him, his inability to face the boyhood monster that haunted his four-year-old self. The idea of it was enough to send his heart hammering out of his chest.

Memories of the childhood nightmares that woke him crying flooded his mind, followed by images of his mother coming to his room to comfort him. A measure of calm settled on him as he remembered his mother's soothing voice and familiar scent. It reminded him of the dreamless sleep that followed.

He dialled her number, to say hi, to assure her that all was well, and to hear her voice again.

"Hi, Mom!" He realised it was almost midnight, and he might have woken his mother.

"Hi, my boy!" came her cheerful response. She was still wide awake, judging from the high energy in her voice.

"How are things at home? How's Pop?" His small talk bought him time to set up his question – the true reason he called her.

"Oh... your father has a new project, so he's been working all hours again." There was resignation in her tone.

His father would get carried away with work when he loved the project. Her mother's comment meant this latest one interested his father very much.

"It makes him happy, Mom."

"I know..." she said. "That is why I let him do it. I may not agree as that much work is bad for his health, but as you said, it makes him happy..."

A momentary silence followed as he tried to think of a topic to discuss with his mother, to keep her on the line, but nothing came to mind. With a deep breath, he plunged on. "Mom, I need to ask you something about my childhood..." he blurted out.

"What is it?"

He imagined her frowning at the other end of the line.

"When I was little... did I used to have nightmares?"

"Hmm..."

"When I was very young, say, five years old?" he persisted.

A brief silence followed as his mother dredged up her memory.

"Oh, yeah!" her mother said, her voice rising in excitement. "When you were... I don't know, maybe three or four years old. You used to wake up crying because of horrific dreams and would be inconsolable for hours. You ended up sleeping in our room for weeks."

"What was the dream about?" His heartbeat thundered in his ears.

"Hmm... I think it was about *Aswangs*... You said you saw an *Aswang* eating someone. You were so scared to go back to sleep, so I had to cuddle you close. You demanded to sleep in between your Pop and me. All the doors in the house had to be double locked, and your Pop had to have a weapon beside him. You used to call it Aswing..." A small chuckle escaped her. She was, no doubt, picturing him as an adorable three-year-old.

"When and how did the nightmares begin? What triggered it? Do you remember, Mom?" He wanted confirmation of what he recalled from the nightmares.

"Hmm... Let me see..." She murmured, trying to recall. "It started in Mataas na Kahoy... during one of our holidays there."

"How did it start?" The scenes played in his head even as he waited for her to speak.

"Well, that night, there was a power outage. Your Pop and I were in the garden enjoying a nightcap while you napped in the tree house. But you slept through it... When the lights came back on, the power surge blew out the bulb in the outdoor lamp post, and you ran out of the tree house screaming. You were trembling like a leaf. I think the sudden blast scared you."

"How long did I suffer those nightmares?" He wanted the complete picture as he could not recollect the details beyond the scenes and the terror.

"Not long. It ceased as soon as we left Mataas na Kahoy and returned home. Your fear was attached to the holiday house. That's why we stopped going there until you were ten years old." her mother related.

She described a familiar scenario. His use of the beloved treehouse ended that day. It explained a lot why it became a place of unease for him even now. His childhood was marred, scarred by something he may not have a hope in hell of overcoming. The stirring of fury towards something intangible and unidentified rose in him.

"Apart from the power outage, did anything happen in the area that could have caused my nightmares?" he asked. "Did I see something scary? Or was I told some scary story by anyone?" His parents would have heard if something happened in the neighbouring house.

"I remember an ambulance came to the house next door later that night. You were asleep by then. It took me a while to calm you down. And we were worried the siren would wake you." her mother said. "Your dad inquired about it and the housekeeper said it was for the pregnant lady of the house."

"What happened to her?"

"I assume she may have gone into sudden labour... She was heavily pregnant."

Her statement was a letdown. "Thank you, Mom. Send my love to Pop..." He hung up, confused by the mixed feelings of disappointment and relief.

At least his nightmares had a basis. An actual event happened. He did not imagine it or dream it up. It made sense to assume that he witnessed something that frightened him. His four-year-old self may have misinterpreted it, but he did not doubt it was a bloody incident.

How real was it? Did my overactive imagination as a child made me believe I witnessed an Aswang feeding on a woman? Could it be that she was giving birth, and the man was helping her?

That would explain all that blood, including on the man's hand.

But not the blood stains on his face.

The wind rushed past Yuana's face, the same powerful element that provided the lift to her, made her squint her eyes protectively as she soared higher. She flapped her wings to achieve more altitude, then spread them wide when she reached her desired height, gliding over the treetops, circling lower in slow degrees.

And when her feet touched the tops of the highest tree, she flapped once more to increase her elevation. She was cresting and bottoming like an undulating wave above the canopy of the forest. Her tail feathers served as a rudder and helped her in the swift twist and turn while airborne.

Repeatedly, she tested the strength of her wings, the flexibility and maneuverability of her new appendages, and gauged her stamina for long-distance flight. She flew twice the distance she covered last night. Her chest expanded and adjusted to the thinness of the atmosphere as she reached higher altitude.

During the first night of her flight lesson, she understood why baby birds started with jumping up and down their nest in the beginning. She flew and flailed in the air like a newborn chick and almost broke an ankle in one bad landing.

Her first twenty attempts were limited to take off and landing by creating a lift of about twenty feet and gliding down. Open wounds and cuts were not something she worried about, but broken bones were another matter. Those hurt like the devil and could take a day to heal.

She also learned that, contrary to her assumption about bird flight, it was less dependent on the strength or the frequency of the wing beats but more about taking advantage of the differing currents and air flows in the atmosphere. It was a combination of flap, soar, and glide. It was like being a bird and a kite at the same time.

Once she realised the warm air created a higher lift, and her wings could detect the change in the air temperature and current in the air by instinct, it became natural to make use of it.

Tonight, was more about enjoying the exhilaration of being airborne, to relish the view afforded by being this high above. To her added delight, like all birds, she possessed a strong magneto receptor. Even with her eyes closed, her inner compass could pinpoint true north, which she used to guide her back home. She had flown miles away, across the other side of the mountain to test it, and it did not fail her.

The temperature in the air had become warmer, a signal that the sun was just about to break the horizon. Dawn was coming. It was time to go home.

Soon enough she could see the rooftop of the villa from a distance. Her launch point was a seldom used, open-air space meant for rooftop parties. The only covered structure on it was the toilet, shower and jacuzzi that provided a mountain view. It was a convenient location to leave her clothes.

The concrete floor absorbed the down draft her wings created, making her take off noiseless. Plus, it saved her the walk to the edge of their property and ensured the Mangyan staff who shadowed her would never see her leave, or return. It helped keep her *Apex* status a secret.

She landed quietly, her tail retracting the moment her foot touched the ground. She *syne-morphosed* back into her human form within two steps. Naked and chilled, she hurried to the bathroom to get dressed. A minute later, she was coming down the circular stairway that led to the hallway of the second floor. Dawn would break soon, and while adrenalin still pumped in her veins, Yuana knew she would sleep well tonight.

Something unfurled further in her while she was flying. It was like coming home and walking into something unknown. It was a discovery of something familiar, elemental, and authentic. That curious feeling was her last conscious thought as she fell asleep.

3

THE BEGINNING OF THE END

Three days later, fate made it easy for Ximena.

A *Viscerebus* hunter discovered a dead woman and a male foetus during a hunting trip in the mountains with his human friends. He picked up the scent of another *Vis* and heard a scream. By the time they found the cottage in the woods, the *Vis* was gone, but left a mutilated body of a woman and a half-eaten foetus. There was no sign of other human presence in the cottage.

The *Vis* hunter's confident pronouncement that it was a wild boar attack was accepted by his human companions as they have never seen one before. They were too busy gushing over their luck at finding a body to volunteer to call the authorities.

The local *Iztaris* were called in. The 'local police' arrived headed by their chief, a *Vis* working within the force.

The manner of death of both mother and child required an autopsy. The involvement of the *Iztari* meant they were using the GJDV mortuary. An attack like that would leave DNA traces of the attacker. And it was imperative they find the perpetrator.

The remains of the foetus landed in Ximena's laboratory for one reason —its cells were unique. And this brought both her and Íñigo running. A geneticist in their team had the slides ready for them to view through the microscope.

They examined them and observed the behaviour of the cells with bated breath. It was indeed almost *Viscerebus*-like. But it should not do that because the mother was human and the foetus, an *Erdia*. But the cells had behaved beyond any *Erdia* genes they had ever tested. They would need to sequence the genes to confirm what they hoped it meant.

The *Iztari* office deployed a team to investigate the case. They would start with the identity of the woman, as there were fewer clues to her murderer. If they discovered who she was, her killer might be easier to find. He fled in haste and left behind some personal items, and his DNA. His act of preying on a pregnant woman meant he probably had *Visceral Metastasis*.

For Ximena, the identity of the killer was of lesser importance than finding the father of the foetus. There was something in his blood that made his offspring's cells behave that way. So far, there were no clues to his identity.

In the meantime, Ximena was torn between excitement and caution. The research and testing still had a long way to go. And finding out the father would take time. She had to temper her expectation so as not to raise her hopes and convince herself there was something there.

But she could not suppress her optimism. Things were lining up. Maybe she would get as lucky as Ysobella. Her niece got a second chance at love. This could be her last opportunity to give Martin back the life she stole from him.

Galen woke up with a dull ache at the base of his spine. It had been a persistent nuisance for days now. It was manageable, but the pain was a sign that his cancer was progressing. The time to go back to Manila for checkups had come. He needed to take control of his disease if he wanted to live past the normal five years he was given.

After taking pain medication, he showered and dressed to find Ysobella, who he assumed was already down at the breakfast room. He guessed right. And to his delight, Bel was sitting with Yuana, who appeared too animated this early in the day. He caught the end of Yuana's sentence as he came in.

"What was exhilarating, Yu?" he teased, kissing both women on the forehead. "I hope you have not gone hunting last night."

"My *Apex* skills, Papa, it was indescribable. I have flown farther last night, too," Yuana replied. Her eyes glittered with vigour.

"So, should we forgo the land trip back to Manila and you fly us instead?" he joked.

"I could try, but it will take a few trips as there are three of you," Yuana said, half laughing.

"Don't forget we have luggage," Ysobella added, her tone dry. The corner of her upper lip quirked up.

"So, I am air cargo now." Yuana laughed. "That's the sole purpose of my being an *Apex*. A courier service for my parents." Her cheeks sported two flags of colour, her excitement and delight infectious.

Galen laughed.

Ysobella observed her daughter and Galen with an indulgent smile, a mask to hide her worry from them both. She had detected the chemical signature of pain killers from Galen's scent. This meant he was hurting. But she did not want him to know she noticed. Galen might avoid taking the medication so as not to alarm her. His visit to the hospital was now overdue.

"Is that a hint that you want us to leave this place? Shall we all go back home soon? Like tomorrow?" she suggested.

"I wasn't hinting at anything, my love," Galen said. There was a teasing glint in his eyes, and he adopted a mock British accent for laughs. "Mayhap you are. Are you tired of our paradise, Bel?"

"A bit. I guess I miss the smog and the city noise." She smiled to reassure him, to think she was raring to go home. He would never ask for it, otherwise.

"Then we will go home tomorrow as my queen desires," he replied, and gave her a quick kiss on the lips. There was a slight relaxation at the corners of his eyes, a telltale sign of relief. Galen welcomed the idea.

"Then I'd better make the most of my late-night flying session then," Yuana quipped. Her daughter, in contrast, looked slightly disappointed to have her nocturnal expeditions cut short.

"Well, you can try flying above the smog. No one will see you," Ysobella suggested in jest.

"And have our daughter come back with smog rings around her nostrils?" Galen said in simulated horror.

The image made her and Yuana laugh. The door to the morning room opened. Roald walked in with a smile.

"Good morning, everyone... whose nostrils?" he asked as he walked over to Yuana and dropped a kiss on her cheek.

"No one. We were discussing hypotheticals," Galen replied without missing a beat.

"And we were also discussing we might go back to Manila tomorrow," Ysobella said.

Roald looked at Yuana, a question in his gaze. The boy sensed that her daughter liked it here, and Yuana was not tired of it yet, so he was leaving it for her to decide.

"I am ready to go home as well," Yuana replied with a mild smile on her lips. Roald nodded and accepted her decision.

"Can we drive home together, Yu? There is a place in Batangas I want to visit, and I want to show it to you," Roald said to Yuana. His tone was even, but there was a discernible tension in it.

"Of course," Yuana replied, nodding.

Ysobella kept her thoughts to herself, but she had a feeling she knew where Roald would take Yuana.

After breakfast, Roald asked Yuana to walk with him. The seriousness in his tone signalled to Yuana that a significant discussion would be part of the activity. They strolled hand in hand until they reached the edge of the property.

Waist-high wooden ranch fences surrounded the 20-hectare property, making it private. Along this fencing were inconspicuous motion sensors connected to the main house. This place was well-monitored, but Roald need not know this.

They perched themselves on the wooden fence, side by side, their shoulders touching. A companionable silence followed as Yuana waited for Roald to say something.

"Yu, tell me how it is to be an... *As*... a *Vis*," he began. Roald aimed his gaze towards the house. Yuana glanced at his face. His jaw was taut, his head bowed. The muscles of his body were locked, and there was a slight tremor in the arm that touched hers.

"What do you want to know in particular?" she replied softly, looking ahead as well. "Ask and I will answer."

He nodded. She waited for the next question to come.

"What is your day like... as a *Vis*?"

"Just like your day... as a human. We are not so different," she said. "But that is not what you want to hear, right? You want to know how we differ."

Roald's silence was a confirmation.

"We eat raw human viscera, *victus* as we call it. Every three days, or longer if we consume over fifty grams, but you do not have to see it. My father prefers not to watch, you can do the same." She heard the entreaty in her own voice.

Fresh tension infused Roald's frame, the knuckles of the hand that gripped the wooden fence for balance was white. "Why do you need to...?"

He was unable to finish, but she knew exactly what he meant.

"Our bodies need it, Ro. It stabilises our human form. Our *vittalis* or vital instinct kicks in if we don't have any for two to three days. We transform into our *Animus*, our animal hunting form, and our survival instinct takes over. We are driven to hunt humans to get the raw viscera." She wanted Roald to understand that it was not blood lust that drove them to it, that it was essential to their survival.

"When I saw you... You were..." Roald faced her now, a shadow of horror in his eyes, his skin beaded with sweat.

She kept her expression blank despite the pain that lanced her heart. "Yes, I neglected my... *sustenance*, and almost *auto-morphosed*." She broke eye contact. Her *Apex* nature became another secret to keep.

"*Auto-morphose*?" Roald's brows furrowed.

"Reflexive transformation. It was something my kind can barely control when our *vittalis* takes over."

Roald took a deep breath, and her heart tightened. Silence reigned for long minutes. Both hyper-aware of each other but were waiting for the other to break the tension. The minutes dripped like a molten candle to the flesh.

"How many?"

The raw question came after a while, and it pulled her out of her anguish. She did not understand what he meant.

"To eat... did you have to...?" Roald's face was tortured, as if his stomach was in knots. He shut his eyes tight when she looked at him, as if he was shaking an undesirable image from his mind.

She realised he was seeing her as the monster in his nightmare and was doing his best to shake it off. The comprehension was a dagger to her heart – for herself and for him. The idea he thought her a killer was crushing.

She swallowed the lump in her throat to force the pain down and mask it. "No, I have killed no one, nor did my entire family. We secure our needs in a wholly non-criminal way." She did not want to elaborate. There was no need to sicken him further.

Again, Roald said nothing. He seemed intent on controlling his reaction to the facts, to the answers she provided. She glanced at him and saw that his eyes remained closed, his jaw still clenched. He was in agony.

To lessen the pressure on her chest, she jumped down from the fence to stop herself from crying in front of him. She did not want him to see the tears that threatened to flow.

Before she could take two steps away, Roald's hand on her shoulder stopped her. He turned her around and pulled her into his arms. His entire body trembled, his hold on her tight. His obvious distress diminished the ache in her chest. He held her for a long time until his heartbeat slowed down.

"You promised not to leave me..." His voice was hoarse at his feeble attempt at humour.

"I was not leaving. I was giving you space..."

He did not reply but led her back to where they were sitting earlier. "Yuana, I will feel like this for a long time. It angers me it is so, but I vow I will do my best to get over this." There was a small tremor in his voice but his eyes were fierce. The flush on his skin was high. "I give you my word on that. Don't give up on me so quickly,"

She nodded, words were not enough to express how she felt at that moment, so she kept on nodding. Roald stilled the movement of her head with a hand on her nape. He pulled her near, touched his forehead to hers, his warm breath mingled with hers.

It was a breakthrough in Roald's path to true acceptance. And the vice in her heart loosened a fraction.

Their last dinner included the wild boar she caught that first time they took her father into the woods. He bragged about her prowess as a hunter the whole evening and embellished the story for laughs.

Yuana spent the rest of the evening packing. It was about one a.m. when she became free for her last flight.

She did not venture far like the night before. She tested her maneuvering skill by weaving in and out between the trees. It turned out to be more difficult to execute than mere flying, as it required focus and strength. She had to flap harder because of the weaker air currents. The denseness of the trees limited full wing spread.

No wonder birds prefer to soar, she thought.

She zigzagged through the woods; her tail acted like a rudder, allowing her to cleave through the air and make sharp, tight turns with more ease.

Yuana ended by the river where she met Kazu twice. She was not expecting to find the enigmatic gentleman there but was not surprised to see him seated at the same fallen tree trunk by the bank.

"Good evening, Kazu," she said, smiling at him.

He smiled back. His delight in seeing her *Animus* was apparent. She had a distinct impression he was expecting her, even waiting for her.

"Good evening, Yuana. I see you learned to fly, and quite well too." Kazu sounded satisfied.

"I did. I have been practicing," she replied. She folded her wings and sat on the fallen trunk. He looked her up and down and nodded in approval, like a proud father.

"That is good. You should practise often," he said. He seemed satisfied with the speed with which she adapted to her wings and her *Apex* capabilities.

She looked at him, quizzical. "Were you expecting me?"

He smiled. "Yes."

"How did you know I was coming here?"

"I heard you. You will learn how to do that yourself," Kazu replied. "I can teach you a lot about being an *Apex*; how to draw out the special skills from your *Animus* form." A flash of interest and excitement glittered in his eyes.

She felt an answering thrill in her heart. Then the regret. "I would love to. But alas, we are going home tomorrow." Her sentiment was genuine.

Kazu said nothing, but she sensed he was not pleased with that information.

"Oh, I see..." His mouth thinned. "When do you return?"

"I am not sure yet... Is there a way for me to get in touch with you while I am in Manila, I may have some questions about our nature?" she said. When he did not respond, "You promised to help me..." she added with a cajoling smile.

Kazu smiled back. "I have a phone number; I give to you. You call me if you have questions." His tone was pleasant, but disappointment hardened his eyes.

Yuana did not have her mobile phone with her, so she ended up giving him her number instead. And with that, she flew back home to have a few hours of sleep before they leave in the morning, her mind already elsewhere.

The plan for tomorrow was for her mother and father to travel all the way to Manila by helicopter. She and Roald would take their car and travel by land. Roald wanted to pass by his family's rest house in Batangas.

She knew why he wanted to go there but said nothing as she was not supposed to know.

Kazu watched as Yuana soared away. Her early leaving posed a slight obstacle to his plan, an interruption in his schedule to prepare the young woman for the impending *Txandictus*, the *Shift* that would affect the future of their kind.

But it was a manageable delay. A slight change in his strategy at worst. He needed to train, mould, and expand her understanding of her capabilities. It was important that she learned her skills well, and most crucial, that she learned to work with him as one.

The fulfilment of their destiny, the future of their kind depended on it.

The day was hot and muggy; mosquitos buzzed around his head as they trekked through the woods and into a village clearing. His guide, Mr Coone, a human mountaineer, had arranged for him to meet the leader of the tribe, Mr Bidwell. The latter was a *Vis*, who served in the human armed forces. A percussion grenade accident which left him partially deaf cut his military career short.

Terror echoed in Tojo's heart at the idea. He suffered from sonophobia, a fear of loud sounds, and it had plagued him since childhood.

"This way, Mr Tojo." Mr Coone interrupted his thoughts with a touch on his elbow. He smiled at the small man with sun-browned skin. Mr Coone pointed to his right.

"Okay, after you." He put the sweaty hat back on his head. He used it earlier as a make-shift fan to cool himself.

Twenty meters on, he noticed a tall and muscular man standing by the edge of the village. He surmised by the man's posture and aura of authority that he was the chieftain, Mr Bidwell. The man watched their approach with slight interest.

"Mr Tojo, please meet Mr Bidwell; he is the chief of the tribe," his guide said with a smile of pride, his face flushed from the heat.

Mr Bidwell offered him a big, rough hand, his face serious but not unfriendly. Tojo took it and gave it a firm shake.

"It is my pleasure to meet you, Mr Bidwell. And thank you for allowing me to interview you and conduct a study on your tribe," he said.

The leader's grasp on his hand remained firm. He could tell the chieftain was immensely proud of his heritage, and protective of all the tribe members: *Viscerebus, Erdias,* and humans. Bidwell's *Erdia* and human tribe members were all *Veil-bound,* judging from the lack of displayed *Kxalyptra* in the area. He could see only one displayed above the front door of a cottage.

"The pleasure is ours, Mr Tojo. It would benefit our tribe to be part of your global study. Shall we go to my house so you can refresh yourself? I believe the trip took two days for you, right?" Mr Bidwell was mindful of his needs as a *Viscerebus*. "The sustenance would be here in two hours."

"Thank you, I appreciate it. Please call me Eiji..." He appreciated the chief's offer and wanted to establish a less formal relationship with him.

"And call me Dreyden." Mr Bidwell smiled at him. He gestured to two men from the group of villagers, who approached without hesitation. They both wore traditional garb, and symbolic tattoos decorated their bare arms and torso.

"*Dasan*?" the younger and taller of the two asked. The boy's use of the traditional title, *Dasan,* to address Mr Bidwell, made Tojo smile. It seemed the tribe still upheld their tradition.

"Jabal, please accompany Mr Coone," Dreyden Bidwell pointed to the tour guide, "to the guest cottage so he can rest." Jabal nodded and led the guide away towards the house that featured the large *Kxalyptra*. It seemed the village was used to having *non-Veil-bound* human visitors.

"Tikaa, please take Mr Tojo's things to the guest cottage beside the Chief's house." Dreyden nodded at Tikaa, who complied without a word.

"I see they refer to you as *Dasan*, perhaps I should use that as well." He wanted to accord Dreyden Bidwell the deference he deserved. At least in his host's territory. While he remained an independent leader of his tribe.

"It is unnecessary, but it is up to you..." Dreyden smiled. Tojo could see that pleased him.

Twenty minutes later, Tojo sat in the comfortable living room of his host. *Dasan* Dreyden's home could pass for a museum of culture and art. Various tribal artifacts covered the walls. There were wood carvings depicting ancient deities, both human and *Vis*; woven scenes of country life; metal plates etched with undetermined writings and meanings.

Dasan Dreyden's tribe, it seemed, had formed a powerful bond of loyalty between the two species. Tojo must understand how they interacted for centuries to find what motivation would be strong enough to weaken it.

He watched as his host conducted a lecture to a group of youth. It seemed they were due for a higher level of schooling in the city, and his host wanted to prepare them for it. The youths were nervous and worried about not fitting in, about not being able to establish themselves and form relationships with any of the people they would interact with. Being members of an indigenous culture meant that there was an added stigma they would fight against before the city folks considered them on equal footing.

The frown that appeared on *Dasan* Dreyden's brow and the slight tension in his jaw revealed the chief's genuine feelings about their place in the human society. A thrill of satisfaction ran through Tojo. He found the crack in the chieftain's armour.

If his assessment was correct, it would take him a couple of days to ease *Dasan* Dreyden into his viewpoint and discuss his potential contribution to the Grand Plan. For now, he would learn more about the mighty leader, then plant the seeds of enlightenment in his mind.

"Was that a common sentiment – the concerns of the youth of your tribe to assimilate and get accepted by human society?" Tojo asked when he joined the chief later.

"Alas, yes... it is doubly hard for us, of course. We are not just *Viscerebus*, we are also from an indigenous culture – one that society expects to be backward and unnecessary," *Dasan* Dreyden replied with a deep sigh. He sounded tired of the idea, resigned to it, and yet there was an edge to his tone that told Tojo the chief wanted to change the status quo.

"Wouldn't it be nice if our kind can come out in the open, so we could show them how we are as advanced, as necessary in the society, if not more so than they are? For centuries, we had to tone down our presence just to keep them feeling safe and secured." Tojo kept his tone wistful, the suggestion subtle.

The chief paused and looked at him with keen interest. *Dasan* Dreyden was assessing his words, weighing their value. "Yes, it would be good. It is a pity that our *Tribunal* have an archaic view of the human society." The chief said. "I think we can work with them, live in an open but symbiotic relationship. Just like we do in my tribe."

Tojo feigned slight surprise at the statement of the chief with the straightening of his spine, then a spark of remembrance with a smile. "Well, there might be a way to change that... if you are interested..." He took a sip of his teacup and watched the expression on the chief's face.

Dasan Dreyden put his cup down. "Yes, I am..."

Tojo smiled. He read the chief correctly. He was a perfect candidate to become part of the team. His host was a perfect tactical partner. An ideal *Jaurdina*, a *Blue General*.

4

THE PAST IN THE PRESENT

By nine a.m., he and Yuana were ready to depart. They would take the De Vida car, and it would come on board the roll-on roll-off ship. A Mangyan staff would drive his rental back to the city.

After many hugs and kisses to her parents who would leave later via helicopter, they departed the Villa.

The trip was uneventful. They stayed in the First-Class section, their car ensconced below deck. Yuana was sleepy this morning. Her head rested on his chest, his arm wrapped around her shoulders as he cushioned her from the undulation of the ship during the two-hour voyage.

He watched her sleep, his thoughts at rest and focused on Yuana. Her warm body curved against his side; her scent flooded his senses. He felt content. Everything was right in his world when she was nearby, when she was in his arms. He did not know he needed this calm until it settled on him.

During the talk with Yuana yesterday, while it was both a relief and a burden, he realised he failed to explain the root cause of his inner fear, why this was so hard for him. The visit to his holiday home would be significant to him. The house, where his trauma started, could provide a step to healing.

Truth be told, he was one acceptable reason away from not proceeding, but he refused to give in to the impulse. This was a winnable battle – a stride towards conquering his big fear. And he needed every minor victory he could get to bolster his self-confidence.

Two hours later, they were travelling on the highway from Batangas Pier towards Manila. His unease grew as they approached Mataas na

Kahoy. Every kilometre they covered added to his mounting panic and increasing determination to conquer his fear. The inner tug of war inside him left him exhausted by the time he stopped the car in front of his family's holiday house.

Transfixed at the sight of it, he sat frozen, his jaw ached, his fingers stiff from gripping the steering wheel, and sweat dampened the back of his shirt as the memories of that night washed over him in waves.

Yuana's cool hand on his cheek brought him back to his surroundings. His ears still rang from his own heartbeats. He glanced at her, disoriented. Her expression was soft with understanding and encouragement. She said nothing, allowing him the time to bolster his flagging courage, her support unwavering.

Yuana's arm around him anchored him to reality, the feel of her skin, a source of strength. Her scent became a calming balm that enabled him to walk into the garden, and toward the treehouse. His jaw clenched as he looked up at it. His legs refused to move, rooted to the spot, even as his brain urged him to go in. Yuana stood in quiet patience by his side, waiting for his next step.

"This was where I saw the gruesome scene that fuelled the nightmares, the source of my terror for your kind..." His voice sounded exhausted even to his own ears.

"Tell me..." she prompted him, her eyes never leaving his, her voice soft.

"I was three or four according to my mother, when it happened... We came here for a holiday, like we often did..." Remembering made his stomach clench as the same sensation of horror came rushing back.

He was certain now that it was not a birthing he saw. The image became crystal clear in his mind as soon as he set foot in the garden, the missing pieces of the puzzle snapped into place.

The man bent over the woman's body, her distended belly wide open, her innards on stark display. He had blood on his hands and face. His half-opened mouth, almost in a snarl, or a silent scream, had human flesh in it, dark red and oozing. His eyes were full of rage, and there were tears running down his face. The man looked ravenous, wrathful... and wretched.

Roald recounted the full story, a combination of his and his mother's recollection. It offered him excruciating relief, like lancing an abscessed wound. Without being aware, he found himself by the door of the treehouse, with Yuana beside him, viewing its interior.

It was much smaller than he remembered, but that was understandable, as he was a toddler when he was last inside. He could not bring himself to go near the glass window that overlooked the house next door, the exact location of where it happened.

Yuana's arms curved around his middle. Her hand ran in soothing slow circles on his back in a gesture of comfort. He turned and wrapped both his arms around her, absorbing more of her warmth and essence. He felt changed somewhat. His fear lessened, but his desire to eliminate the obstacle of their differing nature became more ardent. He wanted to weep but could not unlock his grief.

"Your family's home looks beautiful," she murmured.

"Yes, we used to come here every year..." His reply rumbled deep in his chest.

Yuana pushed away to look up at his face and touched his taut jaw. She stood on her toes, and slowly rained kisses on the sides of his mouth and chin, avoiding his lips altogether. She seemed on a mission to distract him, to change his state of mind. Her seductive teasing continued until his muscles unlocked and his breathing changed. The previous tension left his body and replaced by a different kind.

He caught her retreating head and held it steady for his kiss. It was deep, needy, and impassioned, one designed to erase and replace terrible memories. Her tongue urged him to kiss her deeper, and it fuelled his passion. She kissed him as if she wanted to change his association with this treehouse with something positive and wanted. She seemed more than willing to stay here and kiss him back in perpetuity.

He searched and reached into the inner recesses of her mouth; her tongue mirrored his own, her fragrance the added fuel that fed the fire inside him. The fever of his ardour rose higher, as her response drowned the previous images in his consciousness. It was a welcome respite.

Roald broke the kiss and burrowed his head at the crook of her neck, inhaling her scent to dispel the remaining clouds of terror in his soul. His heart thudded madly, but he did not want to take advantage of her generosity by pushing for more. He did not want to taint their relationship by using her like this, despite the need that coursed in his veins. He had to stop while he could.

As he lifted his head and took in deep breaths, a movement in his peripheral vision caught his attention. Someone walked by the front lawn of the house next door, his movements familiar.

It was Daniel.

"Yu, is that Dan?"

She followed his gaze; her astonished expression was confirmation enough. She was as shocked as he was to find Daniel next door.

He tried to think why Daniel was there, but Yuana took a more direct approach. She phoned him. He saw Daniel answer the call.

"Hello, Dan! What are you doing here in Mataas na Kahoy?" Yuana asked, her pitch high.

Dan glanced over to where they were at. He could see the amazement on Dan's face at the coincidence of being in the same place at the same time.

"Come on next door, Dan," Yuana said cheerfully; her tone rose another octave. She gave him an almost frantic, beckoning wave.

He saw Daniel nod and walk in wide strides out of the neighbour's front lawn, then disappear at the side of the house. Soon, he appeared at their front gate. They both came down from the treehouse to meet him by the door of the main house.

Daniel greeted him with his usual one-arm hug and a pat on the back. He kissed Yuana on the cheek.

"What are you doing here, guys?... I mean, I can't believe the coincidence..." Daniel sounded bowled over still.

"I know, isn't that weird?" Yuana's excited tone bordered on nervousness.

"Is this where you disappeared to, Yu?" Daniel threw a glance at the main house.

"No, we passed by here on our way home from Mindoro," Roald replied for them. "The question is, what are you doing here?"

"I was checking your place out," Daniel replied. "Do you remember I wanted to borrow it for my company's mid-year budget meeting?"

"Oh, yeah... but what are you doing next door?" He was perplexed about Daniel's presence in the neighbour's house.

"I guess I went to the wrong house." A slight grin accompanied Daniel's chagrined reply.

"Well, that was funny. Imagine if we were not here, you would have ended up with a trespassing arrest," He chuckled, then frowned. "But even if you ended up in the right house, how were you going to go in? You do not have the key..."

"I assumed there was a caretaker..."

"What were you doing out in front?" Yuana asked.

"No one was answering. The front doors and windows were locked," Daniel shrugged, "so I searched for another entrance."

"I told you ours had a treehouse." He thumbed at the tree behind them.

"It escaped my memory," Daniel said. "I only remembered when I didn't find any next door."

"Well, let us not stand here all day. Why don't we all go inside and have something to drink?" Roald led them both into the main house.

"I would rather eat, if you don't mind," Yuana said. He nodded. They missed lunch.

"Let's order," he said. "I am sure there is nothing in the house except alcohol... Maybe not even that."

Yuana requested a tour of the house while they waited for their food. She wanted Roald diverted from their current discussion. She suspected Daniel would rather not have his motive of being here examined closer. And she concurred. Not today, anyway.

She exchanged a glance with Daniel – they both know why he was next door. His gaze asked for validation he was doing the right thing; hers warned Daniel to say nothing for now. Roald was still grappling with his phobia. One fear at a time was enough.

They spent the afternoon as longtime friends do, relaxed and casual, and in complete silent agreement to enjoy the day and ignore the real reason they were all here.

Daniel waved off Yuana and Roald as they continued their journey back to Manila. He was not going home without accomplishing what he came here to do – to see where it happened all those years ago.

At the front lawn, there was a patch of cemented area on the lush green grass. There were no outdoor tables and chairs now, but he could picture it in his head.

According to his father, this was where her mother killed herself. He did not think he would find remnants of the event, but he looked intently just the same.

Every brown and grey smudge seemed like bloodstains as he searched for patterns despite knowing two decades of sun, wind and rain would have washed those away.

He walked closer to the dividing wall between the property and Roald's rest house. The glass and wood treehouse was visible from where he stood, cradled in the bosom of a huge, mature mango tree, its abundant leaves curved like an umbrella over its roof.

He had a vague memory of asking his mother if he could befriend the kid next door. He had glimpsed Roald from his second-floor bedroom while he played in the enviable treehouse. Daniel agreed to go to bed only after his mother promised to take him the next day. It was his prize for being a good boy.

The treehouse, a childhood dream for most kids, now had a morbid taint for Roald and himself. He could imagine what the young Roald witnessed that night, the horror that gripped his young heart as he watched a *Vis* feed on a woman. Roald did not know it then; they were the parents of his future close friend. Daniel felt bilious at the idea.

He remembered his room in this holiday house; it had the view of the lake and the garden below. And had he been awake, he probably would have seen the whole thing too. He recalled they left very early the following day, and he was upset at having to leave without meeting the boy who owned the treehouse. His father told him his mother could not fulfil her promise anymore as she had gone to *Zemaya*. He realised now that his five-year-old self thought she went to heaven because of his request.

The years had faded the memory; he barely remembered its emotional impact on him. He felt no anger, inadequacy, or lack of love and encouragement growing up. Mateo Santino might not have been the affectionate father most kids wanted from a parent, but his father's quiet, logical, patient way suited him well. He never doubted Mateo's love for him.

Yuana put a finger on the sorest part of his guilt. It was not just the secondhand remorse on behalf of his father that chafed at his spirit. If it was not for Daniel's presence, his father would not have gone against his own humanity and consumed his baby sister, then lived with the painful reality for so long. Daniel was certain if he was not in their life that night, his father would have ended his own suffering.

Fate was a malicious worker. Roald, Yuana and he had been part of fate's nefarious plans from the beginning. Since birth, by the looks of it. Their path had been intertwined from the beginning, and all because of the *Viscerebus* bloodline.

And now, with the gory truth of his childhood, he would have to tell Roald about this. Hopefully, Roald would not be too devastated with the reality that he was right in the middle of the *Viscerebuskind* without knowing it.

How would Roald deal with the knowledge that the object of his childhood nightmares is two hundred fifty million strong and he lives among them?

Ximena gazed unseeing towards the grounds of the hospital, her mind busy turning over the possibilities she and Emme were looking to use for Martin's treatment. Prying him away from painting could have severe repercussions. It was the only channel for his emotions, the sole window to his state of mind. Emme preferred the gradual approach, but Martin's advanced age did not afford them much time.

She had visited Martin yesterday, and while he did not say her name again, he was in a fever to finish his work. His sole focus was on the canvas. He barely ate or drank. They had to sedate him to keep him nourished and hydrated intravenously. The moment he woke up, his first action was to paint and that occupied him until evening. His frenzy worried her, as he had never been in such a state before. Martin seemed to be in a hurry, like he was feeling his lifetime slipping out of his fingers second by second.

A text message from Íñigo interrupted her thoughts. *URGENT. Come to the lab.* Her heart leapt. She hurried out of her office; the staccato beats of her shoes preceded her arrival. She found him bent over one of the microscopes that lined the table. His focus was so complete, he did not notice her approach.

"What is it?" Her heart hammered in her chest as she stood beside Íñigo. He gave up his seat for her to view the slide herself.

She did but was not sure what she was supposed to see. "What am I looking at?" She glanced up at his face. His excitement was unmistakable.

Íñigo pointed to the two slides on the table. "That's the control sample, the original blood of an *Erdia* foetus, with the usual six *V Genes*," he began. She nodded for him to continue. "The next one is synthesized from the blood of an E2 *Erdia*, with 9.5 *V Genes*... the highest concentration that can be found in a non-*Viscerebus*..." Íñigo went on, his pitch rising slightly.

"And that one on the microscope is the original *V Genes* of the dead foetus," Íñigo continued, his voice triumphant, confident that Ximena picked up his meaning.

They have viewed, tested, and experimented with various combinations of *Viscerebus* blood, *Erdia* and human countless times in the past years, and they could not find or achieve any results that generated past the 9.5 *V Gene* strains. They had never pushed past that genetic barrier to recreate the thirteen *V Genes* of a *Vis*. There were four elusive *V Genes* they could not replicate.

She re-read the report on the foetus' DNA. It seemed impossible as normal *Erdia* genes was always six. "How many starting *V genes* does this have? Nine?" She looked at Íñigo for confirmation. He gave her a brief nod, his elation barely controlled.

What kind of Viscerebus is the father of this child? How did it get those three extra genes?

"What are we missing? We know the mother was human and her attacker was a *Vis* suffering from *Visceral Metastasis*. Our team considered everything, including possible contamination, and took great care in isolating the DNA from each participant who came in contact with the samples and the site... What could have caused this?" Reciting the facts as she paced the laboratory was her thinking tool.

And then it dawned on her.

"The foetus had a *harravis* father..." She breathed, almost disbelieving, but knowing she was right.

"Yes, I suspect so as well," Íñigo concurred. "But we need to know how this was possible. We know that *harravis* potency weakens after twelve hours and gone after forty-eight."

"He must have had sex with her within forty-eight hours after he fed..." She voiced her thoughts aloud. "We have to get the list of every *harravises* on record who were married during their immersion in the habit. And we need blood samples from them including their spouses and children."

This recent development was more than promising. They never considered the possibility that *harravis* offspring conceived during that crucial time frame would yield a different strain of *V Genes*.

"What do we tell them? They will wonder why we are asking for their blood after all these years," Íñigo pointed out.

"Tell them we are experimenting with an alternative way of testing for *VM*," she replied.

"Okay... that will work. I will leave you to secure the signed memo from your mother, so we can start the blood collection as soon as possible," he said, galvanised.

This project was at the cusp of a breakthrough, and it was exhilarating. If they succeed, this would be the quantum leap to understanding their own biology. It offered many potential benefits. Maybe it would provide an ethical cure for *VM*, or even help them increase their number in this world. The *Viscerebus*' natural way of procreating severely restricted their population.

Galen and Ysobella arrived at the De Vida home with twenty minutes to spare for the brunch arranged by Margaita, Ysobella's grandmother. They came from his checkup at the hospital. The drive to the De Vida home had been quiet, with both projecting lightheartedness. Music played, and he purposely tapped his fingers in sync with the beat to mask his nerves.

His oncologist's manner was relaxed during the visit. The doctor did some tests, prescribed him painkillers for his hip and back, and discussed nothing alarming about his condition in front of Bel. Bel came with him, and Galen did not want her distressed, so he instructed the doctor to say nothing.

The oncologist was supposed to email him the findings, and waiting for the email made him anxious. Galen wanted to open his mailbox to check, but they were due for the De Vida brunch. He did not want the contents of the email to affect his mood. This brunch was important for their future as husband and wife, as a family.

Seated on the couch, with his first cup of coffee for the day, the aroma of the dishes in the brunch spread teased his nostrils – croissants, pancakes, bacon, eggs, coffee and freshly squeezed juices. The chatter in the room was buoyant – about work, business, political events, and every cheery mundane topic.

Ysobella placed a dish of his favourites in front of him. He gave her a grateful kiss. He surveyed the room and felt glad that everyone would soon become part of his family. Legally.

At the end of the couch, Yuana sat sipping coffee. The sound of Roald's car made her jump. This would be the first time Roald would join them for a family gathering since the revelation. The family had agreed for the benefit of Yuana to integrate Roald into their fold and make it easy for him to feel at home with them.

Yuana met Roald by the door and brought him in. She appeared nervous for Roald; it was expected given the circumstances of his last encounter with the family. Galen got up and welcomed Roald, demonstrating his overt support to both Yuana and Roald.

"Nice to see you again, my boy." He joked as he shook Roald's hand and thumped him on the shoulder.

Roald's answering smile carried obvious relief. "Nice to see you, too, Tito," he replied.

"Come, let's eat, I'm starved." Yuana tugged Roald toward the buffet, and the thankful smile she gave her father was reward enough.

The family, in their usual display of solidarity, made Roald feel welcome and part of the De Vidas. They acted as if the previous disastrous episode never happened, that Roald did not walk out the house in sheer terror upon learning the truth about Yuana and the family.

As Galen watched them in action, he realised it must be part of their strategy, because once you felt like you belonged, you would be compelled to protect the family secret. *It was a good tactic, come to think of it.*

Soon enough, the discussion centred on Galen and Ysobella's wedding. Comments and suggestions came flying in, the excitement so infectious his oncologist's email became a distant concern.

The family's skill in organisation, the extent of their vast network and resources, became apparent to him as they arranged venues, licenses, and the planning team within a five-minute call. He was both thankful and awed.

The sooner he and Bel could become man and wife, the better. He wanted his family to be declared his in every legal and canonical means in both human and *Viscerebus* world.

Across the room, Ximena observed her family engage with each other, their mood festive. She was happy for her niece and Galen, but her own concerns detached her from the celebration. She had asked her mother earlier to sign the memo requesting the cooperation of all the recorded *harravises* and their offspring for the *Altera* – the *VM* serum, project.

Margaita's agreement was automatic. Both as her mother and the *Matriarch* of the local *Tribunal,* she saw the benefit of the project. Tomorrow, the message to those people would go out.

Her parents secured the *Supreme Tribunal*'s approval. Together with several well-meaning individuals and anonymous donors, the *Tribunal* had been funding them for decades. The *Altera Project* acted as the valid front for what she was doing.

Their primary goal was to develop a cure for *Visceral Metastasis* using infant amniotic fluid from aborted foetuses. It was hard to do because abortion was illegal in most countries; thus, the raw material was difficult to procure. The potential backlash from the human public should it come to light, given the sentiments of the humans against abortion, was a constant concern.

At the moment, the best the human foetus' amniotic fluid could provide was a treatment rather than a cure. Their short-term goal was to manufacture it in commercial volume. It would eliminate the *harravir* practice of those infected. The illegal hunting and killing of pregnant humans would end.

Their challenge was the logistics of manufacturing in viable volume because procuring the raw material in vast amounts was problematic. Their progress in this was slow. Ximena's team was still hard at work trying to synthesise the chemical and hormonal make-up of the amniotic fluid of a human foetus.

Most of their kind thought they were still searching for the cure for *VM*. Little did they know, the true cure had long existed, but the *Tribunal* forbade the revelation of it to the public. They reasoned that very few mothers, fathers, siblings, or even the *VM*-infected themselves would ever sacrifice an unborn foetus of their own blood to secure the cure.

And they deemed the process too dangerous as it could bring about a spate of killings within their own. And they could not afford to lose their number.

Until they found a viable solution, *VM*, as far as their kind was concerned, remained incurable. Their only consolation was the disease was not easy to get. For most of the *Tribunal* members, there was no powerful motivation to push for a cure because the primary vehicle for *VM* infection was through a commission of a capital crime – *harravissing* – the killing of their own and the consumption of their viscera. The threat of an incurable disease and a death sentence once convicted was a deterrent to the *harravis* practice.

Their endeavour to synthesise the treatment, and eventually a cure, was for the unwitting victims of the disease: those who contracted it from their spouse through sexual intercourse, from their mother in utero, and those who were born with it.

She sighed. Her mother did not know of the *Chrysalis Project* piggybacking on the research and development of the *Altera Project.* Her goal was to transform Martin into an *Erdia,* if not a full-fledged *Viscerebus.* She knew transforming Martin into a *Vis,* with the state of his mental health, would not just be futile, it might even be dangerous. They had to wait until his mind resurfaced, and recent awareness in Martin made her hopeful about it.

As Ximena contemplated what they would do next, an idea struck her – it was so eye-opening that she gasped. Luckily, the surrounding chatter masked that sound, and nobody paid her any attention.

If the human-harravis foetus in the lab could carry fifty percent higher V Genes, what would it be if it is of an Erdia-harravis one?

She could barely restrain her eagerness. She needed to expand her mother's memo to include the *Erdias* in their community.

With contained impatience, she sat through the family gathering with a mock representation of relaxed countenance. Her excitement, while genuine, was not about the upcoming nuptial of her niece.

Two days later, Ximena excused herself from a meeting. It had been a waste of her time, as her mind was so far from it. She was raring to be in her lab.

Emme's latest report on Martin's progress added to the sense of urgency that hovered over her daily. Martin's brain scans had shown some development, and although his behaviour had not changed, his painting showed otherwise. His colour choices now included yellow, a color he previously ignored.

As she navigated her way to the lab, she encountered Íñigo in the hallway. He almost bumped into her; his focus was on the lab results in his hands.

"That must be something awesome, you almost mowed me down," she teased, smiling at him.

His face remained impassive. "Yes. This is the DNA test result on the saliva found on the dead woman," he said, handing her a document. "The paternity test of the foetus," he handed her another. "It matched."

Ximena's mind went blank for a split second.

"The father of the child is also the attacker? He consumed his own child!" The implication was staggering. "The *harravis* impregnated the woman on purpose to cure himself of *VM*. This is serious! This can become a practice of every secretly *VM-infected Viscerebus*."

Holy Prometheus! The Tribunal's fears were realised.

"Yes. That is why I am in a hurry to prepare the report for Edrigu, so the *Iztaris* can find the guy. We need to keep this story under wraps, too. It might give others ideas," Íñigo said, his face grim, his tone urgent.

She nodded. They both hurried to the lab.

Upon arrival, they saw their team cataloguing the blood and fluid samples from the former *harravises* and their offsprings. The drive to solicit the samples was underway. While they expected reluctance from those who would rather forget the family member that was a *harravis*, those who lost a loved one to the disease were forthcoming.

And the fact the process was anonymous made the voluntary donation of blood or saliva easier. They even started a door-to-door collection drive to hasten the process. The trust of the *Viscerebuskind* in the De Vida name was instrumental to the high compliance to provide the genetic samples.

Their next step was to sequence what they had collected so far to find and establish the link between humans and their kind. And once found, they hoped it would lead to her ultimate prize – the means to turn human into a *Viscerebus,* or at least, in her heart – one human.

Íñigo watched the play of emotions on Ximena's face. Others would not see behind the cool façade she wore like a mantle. But he had known her for so long, he could hear the gears in her head turn. And he would bet three months' worth of *victus* that she was torturing herself with the thoughts of Martin Bell.

He felt annoyed by it, but he tempered his reaction. Her experience with Martin blinded her to other options and possibilities. He waited for her to wake up from it. And more than a few times, he felt like shaking her, but he had no right to do so. His only consolation was that Martin Bell was human, and the end of his life was near. The man must be past eighty now.

"How is Martin?"

Ximena's mouth fell open in surprise. "Hmm... he's the same. Nothing new." She swallowed, unable to meet Íñigo's eyes.

Alarm bells rang in his head, but he decided not to ask further. To press her now would be counterproductive. There was a development on Martin's case, and Ximena was keeping it from him. Her withholding hurt and angered him. He would never have a space in her heart if she kept the part Martin occupied locked and hidden from him. He could not clear a space he had no access to. If Ximena would not tell him, he would find out for himself.

They worked in silence for the next couple of hours until Ximena received a call. She grimaced when reminded she was scheduled to bring home the *victus* for her family's *sustenance* tonight. Her determination to continue working was her priority.

"Why don't you go home and have dinner, Mena? You can come back here and work some more later," he suggested. "I will be here all night myself."

She looked at him, trying to read his thoughts. He smiled at her in reassurance. It was important for her to go home to eat, to give him time to do what he wanted to do.

The door buzzed, and Ximena's secretary entered with the small icebox that carried whatever human organ the De Vida's were having for the night. Ximena took the box from her and set it down by the table.

She opened the box, took a scalpel, and sliced an inch-thick cut from the fresh liver, handing it to Íñigo.

"Go on, have these..." She offered him the slice, a small smile on her face. Touched, he took it from her hand and swallowed it, his eyes following her movements as she washed her hands on the sink. The gesture was natural, like it had been her habit to share *victus* with him. Hope throbbed in his veins.

"Thank you," he said as she turned back to him. She smiled again.

"You're welcome," she replied. "I will see you later." She snapped the lid shut and moved to the door, the icebox in one hand, her phone in another as she called her driver.

He watched her leave, and knowing the dining habits of the De Vidas, he knew he would have about an hour before Ximena came back.

He had enough time to visit Martin and see for himself how the man fared. Martin may not be in his right mind, but as a rival, the man was more formidable than anybody he had ever faced in his life. Love and guilt were a powerful combination, and he intended to liberate Ximena from the latter, and claim the former for himself.

And he would do everything in his power to achieve this.

Íñigo watched Martin Bell, his rival for Ximena's heart for half a century, through the glass panel on the door.

Martin was oblivious to anything but what he was doing – painting with frantic energy. His paint-splattered hospital gown hung loose on his frame, his blond hair now silver. He looked as old as his years, as feeble as one could expect a human to look when close to ninety. But Martin seemed bursting with energy in a frenzy as he wielded the brush across the canvas. The strokes were sure and true, alternately firm, and gentle.

Ximena had told him Martin did nothing but paint. It was hard to tell if something changed about the man.

Perhaps reading Martin's charts would give him the answer that he was looking for. There was nothing of note. With a sigh, he turned away, disappointed, but still determined.

Íñigo returned to the lab to await the return of Ximena and prepare his report to Edrigu in the meantime. Afterward, he would think about his strategies. He needed to make a headway with Ximena, patience had not worked for him.

5

A TRIO OF SECRETS

Edrigu's mood turned grim after he received a call from Íñigo. His father-in-law Lorenzo must have noticed; he paused from pouring whiskey and frowned.

"Grave news about our latest mysterious case?" Lorenzo asked.

He nodded. "The father of the dead foetus and the killer is the same..."

Surprise registered on Lorenzo's face. He resumed his arrested task and sat down. "That is alarming. What else did he say?"

Edrigu took a swig of the spirit before answering. "He suggested we keep that bit of information confidential as it might give other secretly *VM-infected* among us wrong ideas... And I agree with him."

"Of course. That would lead to a spate of attacks against our kind. And create more justification for *harravirring*. It might even induce a drafting of new laws which would complicate the matters in the *Tribunal...*" Lorenzo sighed as he sat beside him and downed his whisky.

Edrigu poured himself another measure, the bottle landing in a thud on the glass top.

"The greater concern here is the identity of the perpetrator. How did he find out about the cure? That was not public knowledge," Edrigu said. His main concern surfaced. "He may have connections to the *Tribunal.*"

"Or he might have just heard about the old *Eremites'* tale about it and tried it because of desperation..." Lorenzo said.

"It is possible. But we cannot assume that. We still need to investigate and keep the crucial information from the public." Edrigu wished they were having this conversation in his office; as Chief *Iztari,* his security access to their computer system was highest there. His mind filled with the strategies they could employ to catch their killer.

Lorenzo nodded. "Yes, I agree. We cannot make this case known, or we might spook our target. He seemed intelligent and well-organised. He might just go underground."

"Our challenge is by keeping our kind in the dark, it would make it harder to find our murderer. We cannot ask them for tip-offs. That limits our source for leads. Our *Iztaris* would have to ask help from the humans, making the facts vulnerable to exposure," Edrigu said.

"We do not have to give them all the facts, only the acceptable version of it... Let us bring Mateo into this investigation. He can use a select human team paired with our *Iztaris* to handle this. He has done this before, although not in this capacity," Lorenzo said.

Edrigu nodded in agreement. Mateo had enough contacts in the military, and the Santino investigation agency was one of the best, if not the best in the country.

With a decision made, they joined the women having their aperitif.

The water ran in full streams down his body, the steady hiss from the showerhead white noise that focused his thoughts. The email from his oncologist was unsettling. His cancer had spread to his bones. The only good thing was he would not be in too much pain, and if he kept taking the painkillers, he could still live a full life, however short it would be.

He took his time to compose himself under the calming effects of the running water. He did not want to come to their bedroom and display his anguish. Bel need not suffer prior to his ultimate demise, so he would have to distract her. It would be difficult to hide the prognosis from her; she would know how to read the test results. The most he could do was to keep her at his side as much as possible and make her happy while they were at it.

If he had only five years left to him, then he would ensure those would be the best years of both their lives. He wanted to leave an indelible mark, something that would tide Ysobella and Yuana over for the rest of their very long *Viscerebus* lives.

It was bittersweet that this time, he was the one leaving them.

He turned the water off, patted himself dry, wrapped the towel around his waist, and with a determined smile on his face, he came out of the bathroom in search of his Bel.

With every second of his time ticking away, it was best spent with his wife-to-be.

Mateo looked out, unseeing at the view of the city through the vast window in his office. The morning sun made the steel and glass skyline on the horizon glitter in places. The faint sound of traffic provided a background drone that made thinking easy.

He and Daniel were on the way to restoring their fractured lives. His son was forgiving, and he felt gratified they had the type of relationship that withstood such a shock. Perhaps he did something right as a father.

He knew something else bothered Daniel, and he would guess it would be the burden of telling the truth to Roald. He would have to take that burden away from his son. It had nothing to do with him, since Daniel was a child himself when it happened.

As the man who committed the heinous act, he was responsible. He just needed to find a way and the perfect time to do it so as not to ruin Daniel and Roald's friendship.

His secretary's knock interrupted his thoughts. "Sir, Mr Edrigu Orzabal is here," she said.

He spun his chair around. "Let him in... And ask him what he wants to drink."

"Okay, sir. How about you? The usual Cuba Libre over king cubes?" she asked.

He shook his head. "Coffee would be good," he said. There was no reason to drink.

She nodded and retreated. Half a minute later, she came back with Edrigu in tow. She left them after to get their drinks.

He shook Edrigu's hand in welcome and gestured towards the couch. He had a feeling they would need the comfort of the couch today.

"This is a surprise. What can I do for you?" He wondered for a moment if the visit was about Roald.

"Let's discuss after your secretary returns with the drink. It is highly confidential," Edrigu replied, his jawline taut, and a grim gleam in his eyes.

Soon enough, his secretary arrived with two cups of coffee. She laid it down on the coffee table and left, closing the door behind her.

He waited for Edrigu to speak as the man stirred brown sugar into his coffee, just as he was doing with his cup

"We need your help with a recent case," Edrigu said.

"Anytime... What is it?"

Edrigu's body carried a certain restless tension, one that Mateo had not seen in him in the past. It intrigued him.

Edrigu handed him a brown envelope. Mateo took out a thick file of documents. It looked like a commonplace *Iztari* report, but it would take too much time for him to know what this was about if he read it.

"What is the case about?" He sensed Edrigu was waiting for him to ask.

"A *VM-infected harravir* attacked a human female. We want you to find him, use your human team as much as possible, because this case has got to be very quiet. Our kind must never learn about the crucial details of this incident," Edrigu said.

That puzzled Mateo, as they hunted *VM-infected harravirs* in the past. Pregnant humans were the target of those predatory *Viscerebus*, the amniotic fluid being the only treatment available for *VM*. It was a known, although uncommon, occurrence in their society. It was the primary mandate of the *Iztaris* like him to stop the attacks and catch them.

"Why the secrecy, Edrigu? This is not the first time we encountered this kind of case."

"The modus is different. This *harravir* purposely seduced, impregnated the woman, and harvested the foetus when the time was right. We suspect he did it to cure his *VM*." Edrigu's jaw was taut, his expression grim.

Edrigu's words struck him to the chest. "How did he know that? Very few of our kind do. It is not public knowledge." The cure was real. It liberated him from his own *VM*, but even he was not aware of it at the time. His late wife orchestrated the process after she heard about it from an *Eremite*. "Maybe he heard about it and took a chance..."

"That is possible, of course. But we cannot take the chance. We must investigate how he found out about it. There are two reasons this must be done covertly. We think he is part of the local *Tribunal*, or at least connected to a member who knew. We need to catch him, bring him to justice, and find out who gave him the information." The order in Edrigu's tone was unmistakable.

"Okay, I understand... And the other reason?" Mateo's mind hummed.

"We do not want this modus to become known to our kind. It will not take much deduction that this is the cure for *VM*. Someone will copy him, and we will then have a spate of attacks like this from those who are secretly *VM-infected* among us. The threat to our exposure will be greater," Edrigu replied.

Mateo nodded. This was grave, indeed. He understood the reason for confidentiality. However, the need for secrecy meant the human team he would deploy for this mission would be blind to the truth. Without complete facts, they would not be as effective in gathering data and evidence. It would handicap them against their target.

"Anything else I should know?" He glanced at his notes; there seemed to be something missing still.

"Yes, we believe he's an active *harravis*, so be careful." Edrigu's tone was ominous.

Now, that was alarming. His team, especially the humans, would be in great danger. It would be formidable enough for them to encounter a normal *Vis*. A *harravis*, stronger and faster than them, and by nature, a killer, would be even more perilous. No *Viscerebus* would commit a capital crime against their kind and not be willing to kill humans as well. A careful selection of his human team just became critical.

A surge of adrenalin pumped in his veins; his heart raced in excitement. The thrill of the case was akin to being in a battlefield. He did not realise he missed being a soldier until now. He welcomed the seriousness of the situation, a challenge that would take him out of his own head and focus on a cause that was worthwhile.

"I want to be closely involved in this, but I will leave all the field decisions to you. Is that all right with you?" Edrigu asked.

"That's not a problem. I think, though, that we need to include a couple of *Iztaris*, especially during the fieldwork. It might get... hazardous."

Edrigu nodded. "I agree. Give me a list of what you require and your recommendation. I will give the orders to the *Iztaris* of your choice."

Edrigu left shortly after.

Alone in his office, Mateo opened the files that Edrigu left for him. He would have to study their target and establish a profile. And if Edrigu was right, and most likely he was, their target would be someone they needed to keep in the dark more than the *Viscerebi* population. Not only could the perpetrator be physically more powerful, but he might also be more influential as well.

And there was no question he was lethal.

Roald held Yuana's hand as they entered the darkened bar area of the high-end restaurant Galen and Ysobella booked for their dinner. Yuana, in raspberry silk, stood out among the crowd dressed in monochromatic tones of black and grey.

They usually dined with Yuana's parents on Wednesday evenings, but tonight was special. This would be the first double date night for them.

He was unsure if he wanted to do this regularly with Yuana's parents on Friday nights because that had always been a date night for him and Yuana.

Galen and Ysobella were already at the bar when they arrived. Both were holding glass flutes of pink champagne-based cocktail. Galen raised his glass when he caught sight of them. After the usual exchange of handshakes, hugs, and kisses on the cheeks, they received the same drinks.

Galen gave up his seat to Yuana and stood beside Ysobella's chair.

"Shall we enjoy some cocktails before dinner? Our table is ready whenever we are," Galen informed them.

"Are you hungry, love?" Roald looked at Yuana, who shook her head as she sipped on her glass with a smile.

"So, what is the occasion, Mama?" Yuana turned to Ysobella who was stunning in a light blue dress. Mother and daughter looked more like siblings.

"I will let your father tell you, this is his doing," Ysobella replied with a teasing smile at Galen.

Yuana raised an eyebrow at her father, an expression very familiar to Roald – one that implied no evasion would be allowed, and a full, honest answer was expected.

"Well, this dinner is not for you, my lovely," Galen said, tapping the tip of her nose with his finger. "It's for Roald," he added and threw him a sheepish smile.

Roald looked back at Galen in surprise, not having a clue what this would be about. He sent a questioning glance at Yuana. A puzzled frown on her brows told him she was in the dark, too.

"I was hoping to persuade Roald to stand in as my best man," Galen addressed her, but he was looking at Roald.

It took Roald aback and rendered him speechless. "Me? Your best man?" he asked after he found his voice. He was still unable to believe what he heard. "Are you sure?" At Galen's nod, he added through a lump in his throat, "It would be my honour, Tito."

Galen's smile widened and shook his hand vigorously in gratitude. "You are the closest male friend or relation that I have here, so you are my first choice."

"Naturally." Yuana's delighted laugh echoed the sentiments in his heart.

Galen and Ysobella were getting married in a few months, and Roald felt touched and honoured to have a more prominent role in the wedding than just Yuana's plus one. He felt like part of the family. Dinner had not started yet, but he was already glad they came.

Ysobella watched as her small family mingled over drinks and dinner. Galen and Roald were getting on well. Roald seemed unwavering in his decision to fit into their world, despite his phobia. Yuana looked happy. And Galen was single-minded in his aim to enjoy every moment of his remaining years on this earth.

She would ensure Galen's plans happened as she continued to pretend she was oblivious to his pain and go along with whatever little pleasures he arranged for them. If that was what would take for him to have a blissful and memorable five years, then she would give him that and more indelible memories his soul could carry in the afterlife.

Her world may be imperfect, but she would never trade it for anything. Except perhaps a few decades from her own lifetime to add to Galen's. If there was a way to do it, if it was even possible, she would not hesitate to give up what fate would require from her to add more years to him. Even if it took half her lifetime for every year added to Galen's. It would be more than a fair trade.

The server approached Galen to inform them their room was ready; Galen looked at her for confirmation. She nodded and held out her hand so he could help her down from the high barstool. She was happy to take part in one of Galen's little diversions. With a twinkle in his eyes, he fastened both his hands on her waist and lifted her down.

Roald did the same thing to Yuana. The similarities in their situation struck her. Like being two peas in a pod. Hopefully, her daughter would have much better luck in the love department.

Arm in arm, they followed the server to the private room reserved for them for the evening.

Later that evening, as Roald drove her home, Yuana looked up at the cloudy sky and a powerful urge to fly assailed her. For days now, she noticed that since she discovered her wings, her desire to take flight had been coming often and stronger.

Tonight, the compulsion to take to the sky was near impossible to suppress. It was a good thing she did not drink too much tonight, or she might just have given in to the impulse.

As soon as she reached the house, she hastened to her room, took off her clothes, and proceeded to the balcony of her bedroom. It was a cloudy night with a slight drizzle. People would keep themselves indoors. The chances of exposure would be slimmer. A near perfect environment for flying.

She hoisted herself on the railing of her verandah. Her wings unfurled behind her. She cut through the water-soaked atmosphere, the moisture rolling off her feathers. She soared higher still, above the smog and the clouds, to obscure her from the view of anyone who happened to look up.

Her flight followed the path of the clouds. Her vision was strong enough to penetrate the haze and see the pinpricks of light that covered the city below. It was ironic that her *Apex* nature would be wasted because their laws made it impossible to be truly herself. Her *Animus,* her true representation, would have to remain hidden. One more disadvantage of being a *Viscerebus.*

A slight disadvantage that is easily outweighed by the benefits of being able to fly, she told herself as she let the air current lift her higher.

It was glorious.

As she glided over Makati, her thoughts shifted to Roald, and she wondered if she should tell him about being an *Apex.*

Come to think of it, he never asked to see my hunting form, so perhaps he is still not ready to see me transform.

She wished he would. It would be great to take him with her when she flew, to share the breathtaking experience of being high up. For now, she had no choice but to wait for Roald to be ready. At this point, it appeared it would take a while.

She noticed the clouds were thinning now; the drizzle dispersed her cover. It was time to turn back and fly home. It took just about ten minutes to return, but she had to circle overhead for a few minutes until a new cloud cover, perhaps a combination of fog and smog, rolled over their compound before she could descend.

She would have to do a fast dive to avoid being seen by the humans. Condominiums surrounded their compound, and the chances of being seen by people living on the top floors were a real possibility that she forgot to consider.

The speed of her descent meant that she would have to land on their lawn. She was not sure if she could land precisely on her balcony, so it was better to be safe than sorry. She had not done a sudden brake from this speed before, so she would have to focus. She had to use her tail feathers to break her momentum.

It was not a perfect touchdown. She skittered on the grass before she achieved a full stop. Her tail retracted the moment her feet touched the ground.

Yuana was about to transform back when she remembered she would be walking up to the house naked in her human form. In her *Animus,* her wings folded over and around her shoulders like a cape, the feather tips scoring parallel trails in the wet grass. She walked the distance between the garden and the house.

With care, she opened the sliding door to the family room that connected to the lawn and the pool. The house was dimly lit, as it was already past midnight. Everybody must be in their bedrooms by now. She was tiptoeing across the living room to climb up the stairs when she noticed her great grandparents were looking down at her from the top. Their faces had identical exasperated expressions on them.

She felt like a girl caught with her hand in the cookie jar. She sighed and trudged up the stairs, reluctant to receive the inevitable talking to. If she was not so concerned about being punished by her elders, she would find the scenario funny – her great grandparents scolding a bird woman sneaking up the stairs. She must look like a literal giant wet chick, with her dripping feathers and guilty conscience.

"You got the rugs wet," her great grandmother said.

"I'm sorry," she muttered, her head hung. She glanced up at them when no other comment came after that.

"Let us hope there will not be any news about a giant bird or worse, a *Manananggal* stalking the skies of Metro Manila tomorrow," her great grandfather said.

"Sorry, Elo, I could not help myself. But I assure you, I took care not to be seen, and the night was cloudy and dark..." She glanced up at him. His eyebrows were still drawn together. "Plus, Elo, Ela, no one will mistake me for a *Manananggal*. I have my lower half intact. At worst, they will assume I was a giant bird," she reasoned.

Her great grandfather sighed and patted her bent, feathered head. "Achhh, you're wet all over." Her Abuelo Lorenzo wiped his hand on his robe. "Don't you feel cold?" he asked as he eyed her up and down.

"No, the water is just on the surface of my feathers. I will wipe it down when I get to my room," she replied, relieved now. Her scolding would not happen tonight.

"Go and rest now, let's talk in the morning." Her great grandmother said and gave her a gentle push towards her bedroom.

She obeyed. She did not want to give them time to change their minds. But there would be a reckoning in the morning.

She said her goodnight and proceeded to her room. Once inside, in her human form, she shivered. It was the usual aftermath of any transformation. Without her feathers, there was nothing to insulate her from the rainwater now resting on her skin. She grabbed the bathrobe that she left on her bed, wrapped it around her and almost sighed at being warm again.

After a quick warm rinse under the shower, and her usual bedtime ritual, she went to bed, content and gloriously tired. It was an emotion that always came after her flight, one she now expected. It was like finding the right pieces of herself and the power of knowing she could complete the puzzle of who she was. Her last thought as she fell asleep was a question.

Which truth would Roald accept easier – Daniel's secret, or my Apex nature?

The following morning, Yuana got to the breakfast room early. She knew last night's deferred discussion would take place this morning. She did not want to add tardiness to her demerits. To her dismay, her great grandparents and her grandparents were already up and sharing coffee. Her involuntary sigh of defeat drew their attention. Four heads turned in unison, cups paused in mid-sip, forks in mid-bite.

"Good morning, Yuana," her grandfather Edrigu said, his voice tempered.

It was not a good sign they addressed her in her full name. "Good morning, Lolo... Lola... Abuelo, Abuela..." she greeted them as politely as she could. They nodded in acknowledgement. Their faces impassive.

"I'm sorry if I placed us in jeopardy last night... I could not help myself." She hastened her apology to avoid the drawn-out silence and the awkwardness. But the slight smiles on the faces of her elders reassured her.

"We understand... It is your *Animus,* and it is hard to control and tamp down. We were just talking about you, and your... situation..." Margaita, her great grandmother, said.

"What about my situation, Ela?"

"Unlike us, our extensive grounds are enough for us to answer the call of our *Animus*. The trees within the compound and the high walls are enough to provide us cover. In your case, we know that this urge to fly is part of you now, so we need to do something about it," Ela Margaita continued.

At her alarmed reaction, Edrigu interjected. "It means we need to minimise the possibility of you getting seen whenever you take off and land..."

"What do you have in mind, Lolo?" Her grandfather's even tone made her pulse settle down.

"We think it is best that you take off from the top of a tall building. The taller, the better. That would mean finding a penthouse unit for you in such a structure." Her Abuelo Lorenzo explained.

"I have to leave home?" A jolt struck her heart. The changes of her new reality dawned on her. *Would giving in to my Animus worth being away from my family?*

"Your compulsion to fly is something that cannot be helped or avoided. Being an *Apex*, we think the call of your *Animus* will be stronger than usual. That is the safest option." Her grandmother's words sounded reasonable and calming.

But it made her sad. She did not want to leave her family or live alone. The desire to be her true self was strong, and she was sure that resisting it would be hard to do. She understood the practicality of what her elders were proposing.

"Don't look so deflated, Yu. We do not have to do this now. You have time," Katelin, her grandmother kissed her forehead in comfort.

"Now, tell us what you can do as an *Apex*..." Her Elo prompted. His obvious ploy to liven up her mood did not quite hide his excitement.

She smiled, glad her family would always consider her welfare above all else.

She showed them her ability to do partial transformation on some parts of her anatomy at will, a skill not possible for normal *Aswangs*. Unless they have a gene mutation like a *Manyaxi* or an *Equubus*.

But apart from her newly gained knowledge about her ability to fly, her sharper than usual senses and her advanced *auto-morphosing powers*, their collective information about being an *Apex* was sparse. No one was interested to be an expert on a *Viscerebus* that shows up in their midst once every two hundred years.

Everyone agreed her great grandmother would investigate covertly. As *Matriarch,* Margaita wanted to get an indication of how the *Tribunal* would feel about having an *Apex* emerge in their midst.

The *Viscerebi* community had always elevated *Apexes* in their history to an almost godlike status, and it might threaten the *Supreme Tribunal* members.

Being treated as a deity was not a responsibility Yuana wanted to take on. She did not want to be exposed as an *Apex* until they determined what it involved. They agreed that only when Yuana possessed a full picture of the requirements, and only if she was willing to accept it, would they inform the world about her *Apex* nature.

Part of her wondered if she should mention to her great grandparents about Kazu Nakahara being another *Apex*. The information might be important to them as well, but then she promised she would keep his secret. It was not hers to divulge. And he seemed content with just enjoying the perks of being an *Apex* without the responsibility.

Maybe I will ask him the next time I see him.

Mateo, Edrigu and the Emme sat around the conference table. The afternoon sun streamed through the window, increasing the temperature of the room. Its rays bounced against the glistening jug of lemon tea and disappeared in the tangle of ice cubes that floated on the top.

They stared at the enormous glass whiteboard in front of them – Emme's psychoanalysis. They determined their perpetrator was an organised individual. It required patience to wait out six months and meticulous planning to cover tracks well enough not to leave any identifiable traces at the murder scene. And more than that, there did not seem to be any way to trace the identity of the victim and the killer.

Their perpetrator would be of middle-class or higher economic status because of his ability to rent the mountain lodge for a couple of weeks before the murder happened. He would be attractive and socially adept, charming on the surface. But he would have little respect for women, especially those of low economic status. On purpose, he targeted provincial lasses, because they would be more naïve, and their families would have no resources to mount an investigation if a woman disappeared.

That was as much as they inferred from the circumstances and facts known to them. The key to unravelling his identity was to find out the identity of the dead woman. As far as the report of the *Iztaris* who first responded at the scene, the owner of the lodge did not know who she was.

According to the landlord, the tenant booked via a local real estate agent and provided advanced full payment for the two weeks. Unfortunately, the only document the landlord had on hand was the signed rental contract. The name and ID turned out to be false, the phone number invalid. The landlord had never met his tenant; he did not care since the rent was fully paid. And the agent only spoke to his mysterious client via the now-disconnected phone number.

Mateo and Edrigu shortlisted the *Iztari* who would work with the human team members. The human investigators would hunt for the identity of the woman. Mateo asked for Daniel's help to do a digital sweep using facial recognition technology to find her.

The two teams would do the fieldwork, starting with the neighbouring areas of the lodge, especially the nearest town centre or city. Someone must have seen them that day.

"I think our team should canvas the area of the lodge a week or two before the rental contract date started. Our guy could have canvassed the area himself. I cannot believe that he rented it unseen," Mateo suggested, sipping the cool brew. The sharp lemon taste was refreshing.

"I agree. The location is crucial to his plan. No doubt its relative seclusion is key. But more importantly, he rented the lodge earlier and longer than he needed it. He attacked her the same day they arrived. She had not yet unpacked her bags," Emme said.

"Okay. My biggest concern remains – if this person is connected to one of the *Tribunal* members, this investigation cannot reach his ears. We are at a disadvantage here, since we do not know who he is, but he knows how our *Iztari* system works. He must know that we are going to investigate, so he would be careful. He would be extra watchful," Edrigu said.

"That is true... But we could use this to our advantage," Mateo said.

"How?" Emme asked, eyebrow arched. Everyone's gaze focused on him.

"He would be on edge, waiting for the investigative team to knock on his door anytime. He knows he left the murder scene in a hurry, so he could not be one hundred per cent sure he left nothing behind that could connect to him. If we let it 'slip' that there is an investigation about the case, but we keep the team in charge a secret, he could expose himself by trying to find out more about it. He would want to know the development of the investigation. If he is connected to the *Tribunal*, he would ask about it, wouldn't he?" Mateo said.

"Yes... he would... and might even use his *Tribunal* connection to get the information," Edrigu said, nodding. His gaze narrowed as he weighed the suggestion. "That is a brilliant plan. We will inform our community about the case, that we have created a task force to do the investigation. We will hide the identity of the investigating team or the perpetrator's paternal connection to the foetus. The community would only know of a female human and her foetus that was consumed by an *Aswang*. That should suffice, don't you think?" Edrigu's questioning glance shifted to him.

Both he and Emme nodded. That would be enough to alarm the perpetrator and perhaps panic him to a mistake.

"One last thing, as this is highly confidential, tell no one about this case. This should be within this team alone. The only other people I will inform are the *Matriarch* and the *Patriarch*," Edrigu said. Again, they all agreed. There was always a possibility that their perpetrator could be connected to an *Iztari*.

"Okay, which team would be suited to do the fieldwork for this case?" Mateo asked.

"Those who do not have close connection or interaction with any of the *Tribunal* members," Emme suggested.

Both men nodded. They created two teams, with one *Iztari* to lead each team. Daniel would help with the digital requirements of the investigation. He would be assigned to do the online search through the secured system of the company. It would be an extra precaution, just in case their perpetrator was technologically savvy. They did not want the searches to be traced back to Daniel.

By the end of the meeting, they had identified the strategies for the search and capture of the *harravis* who ate his own child for a cure.

6

NEW PATHS REVEALED, A PATH CONCEALED

Two days later, the *Viscerebi* communities throughout the Philippine *Gentem* woke up to a familiar ping. The digital copy of *Heraldaketa*, the *Tribunal Journal* had arrived in their inbox.

The headline reported a *Viscerebus* committed a *harravir* crime by killing a pregnant human and the foetus in her belly. And the *Iztari* office had appointed a special team to investigate the case. There was a request for information and tips. The email and phone number provided was direct to the Chief *Iztari*'s office. The *Tribunal* was encouraging the *Viscerebi* public to help.

The case headlined in a *Heraldaketa* was common enough, but to have it appear in human newspapers, albeit whitewashed, was noteworthy.

Edrigu assigned two of his oldest and most reliable secretaries to answer the calls and take the statements regarding the case. Their perpetrator must have a contact person to approach and ask about the updates and developments in the investigation.

With luck, the killer would be spooked enough to make the mistake.

To most members of the *Vis* community, the case became a coffee break sensation for a few weeks, since it was the first time a *Vis* case appeared in the local human newspapers.

Speculations ran rampant. Some declared the *Iztaris'* negligence for failing to cover up the incident; others touted the humans' efficiency and ability to be in the right place at the right time. A good number complained about the *Tribunal*'s lax implementation of the *Veil of Secrecy*, while a rest claimed that it was part of the ruling body's strategy to catch the killer.

Their initial pity for the woman and the baby did not last long – mother and child were strangers. No one among their family and friends knew her. And she was human.

Their tears for the dead foetus lasted for just a day since there were no cute pictures of the baby they could ogle. It was not real enough for them, just a clump of blood and cells. The death of the mother and the foetus was tragic, but shit happens.

Their morbid interest in the perpetrator's identity overshadowed their disgust towards the crime. Various theories of why and how the crime happened went around the *Vis* community. After a few days, some were taken as facts because it was repeated more often and pushed by a more passionate theorist over others.

Soon, the topic faded into irrelevance, and they switched back to discussing the lives and intrigues of human celebrities, politicians, and the latest goings on in their next-door neighbour's house.

Except for one individual.

His existence changed when the *Heraldaketa* issue came out. He could not rest or relax. He had scoured the *Tribunal Journal*, including the human newspapers, as he waited for news about the investigation. But nothing was forthcoming. He kept a close ear to murmurs around him, listened for any tidbit of information that would reveal how much the task force knew about the perpetrator.

The silence of the task force regarding the details might mean that they have little, but he could not bank on that supposition. He dared not contact the *Iztari* office to inquire. He wanted to maintain as much distance between him and the case as possible. Perhaps there were other ways to find out. One that was not so obvious.

For Ximena and Íñigo, there was a reason for jubilation and frustration as they reviewed the test results of the blood samples they had collected. They had been at it all day.

For the secret *Project Chrysalis*, it had been frustrating. They tried all kinds of genetic combination, *Vis* and human, *Vis* and *Erdia*, *Erdia* and *Erdia*, but they were still coming up short. They could not bridge the gap.

The genes of the former *harravis*, as they expected, had reverted to their former state. The results did not differ from a normal *Vis* blood and fluid test. It did not replicate the behaviour of the genes of the dead foetus.

They had tested children of former *harravises*, and their genetic makeup did not show any extraordinary result. They had a hypothesis it might make a difference if they tested the blood of a *harravis* and an *Erdia*, one that had been conceived during the crucial forty-eight-hour time frame.

"We need to get ahold of *harravis* blood while it still coursed through the veins of the donor." Íñigo threw down the medical gloves he peeled off on the cold steel laboratory table.

"I agree. But how? No *harravis* is going to admit to the habit. The last I check, it was still a capital crime punishable by death. And there were no reported deaths among our kind. So, apart from our unidentified killer, where do we get our samples?" Ximena sighed. They were facing a dead end again.

"How are we progressing with the hunt for the mysterious killer? I know we ventured into the human social channels to find our victim. Any development?" Íñigo frowned, a glass of whiskey in hand, a partial grimace on his face as he swallowed the spirit.

She shook her head. "None yet. They believed she was a provincial lass who just arrived in Manila. She definitely came from an underprivileged background. She does not have any social media footprint, which is almost impossible for a human teenager. They think she could not be over twenty years old. The *Iztaris* are confident that they will find a link to her identity soon."

Íñigo sighed and a portion of his frustration dissipated with it. "Finding this guy is crucial. He is the key for us to understand how the *harravis*' blood behaves at the point of infection, and whether the foetus retains the *harravis* genes once birthed, and if it affects the child's nature. I mean, would the child be an *Aswang* like us, or just an upgraded version of an *Erdia*. Which of the thirteen genes gets passed on to this new *Erdia*? And would it open a door to potential cross infection of diseases between humans and us?"

Ximena stared at Íñigo. She was much more interested to find out if all these would lead to her being able to synthesise the *V genes* and change the biology of a human into someone like them. If it could help prolong Martin's life.

Where else can we search?

She had a sudden inspiration. "Íñigo, are there any files of former *harravisses* on a classified status?"

Íñigo's eyebrows rose. Her question took him aback. "Yes, there are. The *Tribunal* applied confidential status to those who were cleared from wilful *harravis* habit. The law deemed them victims of whoever forced them into it," he said.

"Maybe we can secure special permission to contact those people." She would need to talk to her mother about it. It would require her *Matriarchal* authority to secure permission to access such confidential files. They might find gold in there.

"At least, the *Altera Project* had a breakthrough, and we can begin synthesising the foetus cord blood into a pill form. And no mother or child would die with our process..." Íñigo raised the glass to his lips, a crooked smile on his face.

"Yes..." She raised her glass and took a sip in agreement with his sentiment. "We just need to figure out how to secure the raw material in volume. We would need for the mothers-to-be to give up the cord blood voluntarily."

"Will our team test the process with our kind? Perhaps the cord blood of a *Vis* foetus could provide the ultimate cure, then the synthesised treatment would no longer be necessary."

"That is the goal. But the testing would be the challenge. How do we find a *VM*-infected patient and a six-month-old foetus that is the close genetic match of the patient when those infected hide their disease?"

That remained their major challenge. Legislative change would be required, and that would take time because they need to change the mindset in the *Vis* society and the old guards in the *Supreme Tribunal*. But for now, the delay was favourable to Ximena's personal agenda. She needed that time to accomplish her goal. She could not, in good conscience, split her focus between her selfish agenda and the cure for *Visceral Metastasis*.

Ximena had already formulated the plan to harvest cord blood from a lot of women. She confidently prepared the presentation for the approval of the *Tribunal*. It was too important, too beneficial to their kind for the *Tribunal* to delay. Her mother and father would support it. As *Matriarch* and *Patriarch*, they would push for it, would understand her need for haste. And with it, would be the requisite funding. That was fine. All of those would contribute to the fulfilment of Project Chrysalis. Her parents just didn't know it.

As Ximena drew a deep breath, she realised everything was going their way, despite the current drawback. She just needed a bit more patience. Haste created more mistakes and derailed her goals. Tonight, she would speak to her father first. Her mother was more intuitive and might suspect the true motives behind her actions.

Yuana and Roald proceeded to a Japanese restaurant. He had a hankering for some sashimi for lunch. They just came out of the fitting session for their respective roles in Ysobella and Galen's wedding. Yuana would be the maid of honour, Roald, the best man for Galen. The celebration was going to be a combination of human and *Viscerebus* wedding rituals. It should be interesting to witness the melding of traditions.

"How big is this wedding, Yu?" Roald asked, curious.

"Not big. We prefer small gatherings and limited number of photos. All for personal use. And those photos are strictly confidential. Not to be shared with any human," she replied.

"So, how many will be at the wedding?" he asked as he perused the menu.

"Maybe thirty at the most. I am unsure of the final number," she replied.

"Is Daniel's family invited?" He had not seen Daniel for a while now, not since they crossed paths in Mataas na Kahoy.

"I am not sure, but most likely he and his father would attend. The guest list is my mother's responsibility. She decides who gets invited to it. My father has no one on his list except him and his oncologist. I think the oncologist cannot make it," she replied.

"You know, I have not spoken to Daniel since we saw him last. I messaged him a few times, and he has stopped attending our weekly tech meetups. Has he said anything to you?" he asked. He found it odd that Daniel seemed to have taken himself out of their circle, like he retreated into his man cave. Something was bothering Daniel.

"Really?" Yuana's eyes rounded. "Have you tried calling him?"

There was something in her tone that was rather intriguing, but he was not sure what it was.

"We men are not in the habit of asking our male friends if something is bothering them. That was why I asked. He might have mentioned something to you," he said. "Have you spoken to him since we last saw him?"

She thought for a while, her eyes narrowed in recollection.

"No, not since that day. We texted, but it was about trivial things." Yuana laid her menu down and looked at him. "Do you want me to call him and ask?"

He did not reply. If Daniel had not said anything to Yuana before, he might not tell her if she called. As he considered it, she reached over and patted his hand.

"You should call Daniel. He might open up to you more." As usual, Yuana read his mind perfectly.

Edrigu came down to the living room ahead of his wife. Katelin was speaking to the wedding planner and told him to go ahead. He had a long day and was raring to have a drink.

He found his sister-in-law, Ximena, seated on the living room couch with a glass of what looked like sparkling Rosé, her drink of choice when she needed to de-stress.

"Hard day at work, Mena?" He poured himself the same drink. Not his usual first choice, but it was chilled, and it looked inviting. Plus, Mena looked like she needed a drinking partner.

"On the mental side, yes." She sighed and took a sip of her wine.

Ximena was the opposite of his wife. She was serious and analytical – a complete left brain. Katelin, in contrast, was cheery, intuitive, artistic, and always positive.

"Do you need someone to bounce ideas off?" he offered.

Ximena regarded him and sipped on her drink. "Do you think Papa would secure me access to classified files of the *Tribunal*?" she asked.

He did not expect the question. The *Viscerebus* in the medical field, like Ximena, seldom needed information from the classified vault. "Well, in principle, classified files require time and a long-winded process for declassification," he said.

"I do not need it declassified, I just want permission to look at the files," she said.

"That will be hard for Papa. *You* know how much of a straight arrow he is..." He was curious what kind of file she was interested in. "What exactly do you want access to?"

"Names of the pardoned *harravises*. It's research for my *Altera Project*, and I need it ASAP," Ximena replied as she looked down on the drink in her glass. A tightness at the corner of her mouth interrupted her usual collected demeanour.

He realised there might be a way he could circumvent the classification and help Ximena. "I may be able to help you..." he said. "I can request a 'Peek-thru' for an investigation. The process will allow me to access the system, search for names and details. But I cannot print it for you."

"Oh, that is brilliant. That would be enough. I just need the names and addresses," she said, excitement in her eyes and voice. "This would shorten the wait – our process considerably."

"Come and see me in the office tomorrow. I would have to show it to you on our company system. I cannot access it from anywhere else," he said.

"Great. Would nine a.m. be fine?" she asked.

Edrigu laughed at her haste. Normally, he would leave home at nine-thirty. "Okay, I will see you at nine tomorrow," he replied.

"No, let's drive there together in the morning."

He could only shake his head at her persistence.

At nine a.m. sharp, Ximena walked behind him into his office, notepad in hand. Impatience oozed out of her as she waited in forced patience while he turned on the system. Only her legendary cool stopped her from peeking over his shoulder or pushing him aside so she could do it herself. And perhaps her not having the right biometric and password to the system.

This must be important to her.

He logged on, searched the system for the files that she needed, and typed in his security clearance ID number to open the file. A second later, a short list of names came up.

There were sixteen names, and four were in the Philippines. The others were located elsewhere. They clicked on the names of each, and their addresses came up. Ximena took a screenshot of them all.

Ximena's back straightened as she recognised Mateo Santino's name on the list. She forgot Mateo was once a *harravis*, as she was in *Transit* during that episode in Mateo's life. Edrigu did not even remember it himself until that day Mateo and he drove to Mataas na Kahoy. Their family had been good friends with Mateo for decades, and they all took his past for granted. His *harravis* past was not his doing, and was a one-time thing.

"You noticed Mateo's name..." Edrigu said. It was not a question. He wanted her to tread lightly.

"Yes," she replied, her head in a questioning tilt. She expected an explanation.

"It's a sensitive issue to Mateo, so have a care," he said in a quiet tone. It was not his secret to tell, even if Ximena was capable of diplomacy.

"Thank you... I will..." Her nod contained a wealth of meaning: acknowledgement of his warning, and a statement that she had work to do and not a lot of time to waste.

He watched her walk in brisk, determined steps towards the door. She was on her way to her domain.

As Ximena walked into her office, she thought about how to approach Mateo to ask for blood from him and Daniel. Edrigu's forewarning lay at the top of her mind.

Edrigu did not elaborate why Mateo was sensitive about it, so she suspected it was something Edrigu could not divulge. Perhaps it was better to ask Daniel first. With that decision made, she called Yuana to get Daniel's number.

Two hours later, a satisfied smile lined her lips. She contacted the three men on the list. They were more than willing to give their blood and that of their children to help her cause to find the cure for *VM*.

Mateo was the only person she had yet to ask, but Daniel had promised to do so for her. Daniel was going to drop by her lab in an hour to give his blood.

Her day had just turned better.

Daniel rolled down the sleeves of his shirt to cover the bandaged puncture in his arm. He just came from Ximena's lab to fulfil his promise to donate his blood for her *VM* cure research. When she phoned him earlier to ask for his help, he thought it ironic. Especially if his blood, or his father's, turned out to be the catalyst for the cure for *VM*.

Roald had called him earlier and invited him for a drink. He had avoided Roald on purpose in the past weeks because his truth would be hard to keep inside, and he did not want it to come out in a drunken rambling. He wanted to wait for the right time until Roald had adjusted to Yuana's nature. But an insistent Roald would not accept no, so he relented and agreed to meet him.

In the meantime, he needed to call his father as he promised Ximena, to ask him to donate his blood for her research. It was one topic they both avoided. The wounds to their souls were deep and talking about the past was uncomfortable. But if it would lead to doing something good for their community, for the eradication of the disease that destroyed half of their family, then it was worthwhile. Personal pain notwithstanding.

Who knows, it could be the absolution his father's soul needs?

Five hours later, he drove himself with reluctance to the club to meet Roald. He had called his father and the other *Iztaris* for an update on the surveillance on Roald. So far, the status of Roald's case remained at No Contact. This meant they were still tailing him but must maintain a safe distance. This was a good thing. Roald was proving to be a safe bet for Yuana, and for him as well.

He arrived in time to see Roald enter the club. Daniel followed him unnoticed as Roald proceeded to the bar, their most preferred location when they hang out together. It provided the best view of the room and the best visibility to the ladies. He doubted Roald had lady-hunting on his mind; it was more a force of habit judging by how he sat facing the bar, rather than the crowd.

He tapped Roald on the shoulder and settled himself on the barstool beside him. He ordered a beer to fortify himself, tonight might turn out taxing for them.

"You went AWOL on us, D? Busy?" Roald asked after a while. He seemed uneasy, unwilling to pry.

"A bit. Work, my dad, some extracurricular activities." He kept his response vague, hoping that would suffice.

Roald's eyebrow rose in interest. "Extracurricular activities, huh? You mean, a woman?"

He smiled at that. "Nah, I have no time for that." That was true. With everything that had been happening in his life, it was the last thing on his mind.

"It's about time you make time for one, don't you think?" Roald was only half joking.

"Just because you are close to tightening the noose of matrimony around your neck does not mean that I have to do so as well," he scoffed.

Roald grinned. "Speaking of matrimony, are you attending the wedding of Yuana's parents?"

"Yes, of course we are."

Roald's eyebrow rose slightly at his dismissive tone. He obviously did not know about the close relationship of his father with the De Vidas. "My dad is very close to Señor Lorenzo. He was my father's mentor."

Daniel shrugged and took a sip of beer. Roald still had a lot of momentous truths to face about their world. And his father's secret would probably be the most devastating to his friend.

I have to keep my wits tonight. Alcohol might loosen my grip on the truth.

Roald thought about what Daniel said and tried to dredge his memory about Mateo Santino's background. He remembered Daniel said his father was an orphan, so it would seem the Santinos' relationship with the De Vidas go a long way back. And a small sensation, like an itch under the skin, one that had bothered him for a time, resurfaced, crystallisizing into a firm question.

"Mentor? Their relationship must have started in your father's youth?" Roald watched Daniel's face with close attention.

"Yes, since the GJDV Foundation took him in. My dad lost his parents when he was ten years old. The Foundation provided for his education, board, lodging, etc. My dad said that he even spent his school holidays with the De Vidas during his young adult life," Daniel recounted, his eyes narrowed.

A slight chill of confusion and suspicion clutched at him. *Did Daniel's father know the De Vidas are Aswangs? Does Daniel know? Is it possible...?*

He stared at Daniel's profile as his friend drank from the beer mug. Daniel's gaze aimed at the row of bottles behind the bar but looking at nothing in particular. He seemed burdened.

"Did you and your father know the De Vida's are *Aswangs*?" His blunt question made Daniel choke on his beer; he sputtered and coughed. The bartender rushed to their side, a box of table napkins on hand as he wiped splattered beer off the counter.

He gave Daniel a few thumps on the back as he rasped and cleared his throat. Daniel pulled napkins from the box and wiped his mouth and teary eyes. Roald waited in forced calm as Daniel composed himself. It took some time.

Daniel faced him after a while, his face red, eyes still watery, and throat moving reflexively as he tried to clear it. "Ro..." It came out like a croak. Daniel paused and took a sip from his beer.

"Did you? Do you know?" Roald asked again. His calm tone surprised him. His mind and heart filled with confusing feelings and thoughts he could not articulate.

Daniel looked at him for a while, seeming to weigh his options. Finally, he nodded. "Yes, I did." The admission came out in an exhaled breath. "I have known for a long time. All my life."

Daniel's words felt like a kick to the chest. An irrational fury rose in him, but he pushed it down. "Why didn't you tell me... when I told you about Yuana?" Roald asked, his fingers clenched at the beer mug like an anchoring tool.

"For the same reason, Yuana kept her nature a secret. The same *Veil of Secrecy* bound me," Daniel replied.

Roald was half expecting something like this, but Daniel's admission staggered him still. He was about to say something, but Daniel interrupted him.

"Ro, if you wish to talk about this in depth, we need to move to a more... secure location," Daniel said under his breath.

The implication of the sentence hit home. Daniel, being bound to the same *Veil of Secrecy*, meant he needed to take as strict a precaution as Yuana. Roald nodded and gestured to the table at the very corner of the room, one quite far from the bar. Away from the ears of the bartender.

They both sat down with a heavy sigh, beer in hand.

"Are you also an..." Roald asked, dreading the response, but Daniel's denial cut him off.

"No. I am not. I am an *Erdia*, a half-blood." Daniel sounded resigned, like he had been waiting to say this to him.

"A half-blood? You're part..." He could not say the word.

Daniel nodded. "Yes, I am part... *Viscerebus*. My dad is one, my mother was an *Erdia* like me," he said.

It was all too much to take in. His closest friend, one he treated like a brother was an *Aswang* like Yuana. He felt like smashing something, but their location was not a good place to vent the fury that was fogging his brain at the moment.

"One more round, boys?" The server interrupted his focused inspection of the bottom of his glass. He glanced at Daniel, who did the same. They nodded in unison.

The intermission was unexpectedly beneficial; it shook the knot in his chest loose, and he could take a deep breath and rationalise the situation, his anger controlled.

"What is the difference between you and Yuana?" he asked. The need to know what it meant was strong.

"I am just like you." Daniel shrugged. "I did not inherit the *Viscerebus* traits. Not their strength, speed, power, or the need to consume viscera. I am just like a human."

"It is just genetics..." Roald murmured. A germ of an idea came to him, a possibility.

"Yes, I guess so." Daniel frowned and sounded perplexed.

Silence ruled for a few minutes, as they both sipped on their beers, their minds engaged elsewhere. Despite the slight tinge of an unnamed wrath in his heart, he could not justify being angry at Daniel given the circumstances. If he was in the same position, he probably would have hidden such a fact about himself as well, *Veil* or no *Veil*.

"So does this mean that I can use this to wrangle a free drink from you now and then?" Roald joked to lighten the mood between them.

"One drink, max. Or I would have no choice but to kill you," Daniel replied in a mock serious tone.

No more discussion about *Viscerebus* came after that initial admission from Daniel. It was enough for the night. Roald needed to work through his feelings – something he was not in the habit of doing since he was a child. And the past few months showed him how lacking he was skills-wise in handling emotions.

Daniel appeared relieved and... frustrated. Like something still bothered him. And he wondered what it was. Maybe the truth was as hard for Daniel to say as it was for him to hear.

Yuana was reading in bed when her phone rang. It was Kazu Nakahara. A pleasant but unexpected occurrence.

"Good evening, Yuana," Kazu's polite voice came through clearly. He sounded more serious than she remembered.

"Good evening, Kazu," she greeted back. She was delighted to receive his call. "It is so nice to hear from you. Are you in town?"

"No, I am in Calapan. I wanted to check how you are doing with your flying lessons."

"Oh, It's okay. I have had little opportunity to fly, though," she said.

"Ah, that is sad." Kazu sounded like a disappointed father. She felt chastised. "You must practice much, Yuana. It is important."

"I am trying. It's hard trying to find the right conditions, so I do not get spotted in the evenings when I fly," she said a little defensively.

"Understandable. Inform me once you find a way," he said.

"Of course... but what is the rush?" There was something in his tone that made her wary.

"Flying, especially in very high altitudes, when you soar up, will reveal much to you about your *Apex* nature, Yuana."

His cryptic and evasive response made her uneasy. "What do you mean?"

"I cannot tell you, because only you could discover that. But it is crucial that you get good at flying before you try, or you might lose consciousness and fall," he said.

The image Kazu painted made her heart race. "Oh, that might take time," she said in a dismissive tone, but deep inside, she was curious.

"Yes. Fastest way is for me to fly with you. I will not let you fall," he said.

"That is nice of you, Kazu. I will call you once we find a way to train."

"We?" he asked. There was a slight alarm in his tone. "Your family knew?"

"About me? Yes, but I did not tell them about you," she replied. "Can I tell them?" she added. She sensed his disapproval before she heard his response.

"No, I would rather not, Yuana," Kazu's reply was solemn. "If you do not mind, I would like to remain in secret. I hide in the mountains for a reason. It was not for fun."

"Okay. If that is what you want." Kazu must have a valid reason to keep his *Apex* nature secret.

"I shall say goodnight, Yuana. Telephone me when you are ready to fly together," he said.

"Okay. Goodnight, Kazu."

She set her book aside. Her thoughts became filled with the possibilities of all the new skills she might find out about herself. She fell asleep researching about the previous *Apexes* and their powers, trying to get clues of what might be hidden from her, what could be discovered.

Kazu was satisfied. Yuana was primed for training. He would wager she was raring to take off. The urge to do so would grow stronger in her as the days went by. She had experienced being airborne, and her *Animus* had been awakened.

It was just a matter of time.

7

BREAKING THROUGH

Seven years earlier.

Damian Graves closed the file. His last patient just left. Should there be any emergencies later, their pregnant clients could ring the bell out front. All that was left was the *messis,* and he would not be required for that.

"Nurse Glenys, will you please close for the day?"

"Yes, Doctor." Nurse Glenys locked the front door of the clinic. The small side door and the back door would remain open for their special evening clients.

Nurse Glenys returned just as he was tidying up his desk. "What time is the *messis* tonight, Doctor?"

"The *ontzian* is arriving at nine p.m. What is the background of our *iturrian*?"

Nurse Glenys pulled out a folder from the filing cabinet and flipped it open. "The *iturrian* is a College student, 20 years old. Boyfriend is a medical student who cannot afford to become a father yet. The young lady is on a scholarship and would lose it once her sponsor finds out she is pregnant. This is her first *messis*."

"Okay. I will leave it all to your capable hands." Their established protocol was for him to be away when the *messis* happens, to maintain the illusion that he was unaware of any illicit abortions being committed in his maternity clinic.

His two assistants, both *Viscerebus,* were versed with the procedures. And they had been doing this for decades. Yet every time they had an amniotic fluid harvest, he felt nervous. There was no reason for it. The instances of death in their pregnant clients were well below the norm.

The *ontzian,* a university owner who had been suffering from *Visceral Metastasis* for about as long as they have been doing the illicit harvest, should have nothing to worry about. The procedure had always been beneficial to both the human female and their *Viscerebus* client. While the human sources would come in voluntarily to get rid of their pregnancies, they remained unaware of the harvesting process. Those women would be terrified if they knew.

My clinic is doing a good thing by solving a young woman's problem and providing treatment to prolong the life of someone from their kind.

The chirp of a bird made him glance at the wall clock in front of him. Eight p.m. He had better get going.

He opened the back door when he noticed a distinctive-looking woman leaning against the side of his car. She was slim, toned and tanned, and dressed in jeans and a crisp white shirt, accented by a colourful scarf. But it was not her features that made her striking, it was the casual confidence. The knowingness in her eyes as she looked at him made the hairs on his back tingle in awareness.

"Doctor Damian Graves?" the woman asked as he approached her.

"Yes. How can I help you, miss?" The woman was of their kind, a *Viscerebus.*

"In a big way, Dr Graves. One that can change the course of the lives of our kind, if you are interested," she replied, one eyebrow arched.

The statement intrigued him; he did not expect it. Normally, the *Viscerebus* visited his clinic because of either purposes; they were pregnant and needed his skill as a gynecologist, or they needed human foetus' amniotic fluid. In short, they came needing his help. This woman did not fit any of those.

"How?" he asked.

"Let's get in your car and talk elsewhere. You do not want your *iturrian* to see you here, do you?"

Her statement surprised and alarmed him. She seemed to know his modus operandi.

He hesitated, but she smiled at him. "Don't worry, your secret is safe with me. As a matter of fact, we want you to expand your operations. Globally. And we will fund it," she told him as she slid into the passenger seat of his car.

He took the driver seat, still astonished. "Who are you? And what do you mean by 'we'?" he asked.

"My name is Aristo Cohen, Dr Graves. And I will tell you who we are, and why we think you would benefit by working with us," she replied, an engaging smile on her lips.

Ximena could not believe her eyes. She blinked against the glare of sunlight that bounced on the glass slides. With a pounding heart and careful intent, she repeated the test again. For the third time.

Earlier, when she saw the first result, she assumed she made a mistake, that perhaps her sample had been contaminated. A validating test was required.

Amazingly, the second test came out with the same results. She cautioned herself to relax, not to jump to conclusion. She needed someone else to replicate the test, to be sure. Very sure.

Her heart was in her throat when she called Íñigo over to do his own test, so they could compare. The intensity of her tone no doubt communicated itself to him as he came within two minutes.

"Íñigo, can you do the gene sequencing test for this blood sample?" She repeated the request to lower her heartbeat and temper her excitement. But he knew her too well. He looked at her without a word and nodded, his gaze shrewd.

She watched as he took part of the sample and prepared it for sequencing, as carefully and as exacting as she did with her testing.

If the results come back the same...

The minutes dragged on. She was close to chewing her nails off, her back rigid as she kept herself from pacing, her mind unable to take in the reports in front of her. She could not focus on anything else but the upcoming result of the tests Íñigo did.

Only one thing could distract her from her preoccupation – a visit to Martin.

Twenty minutes later, she walked down the familiar hallway to the special ward of the Psychiatry Wing. The staccato beat of Ximena's heels echoed in the hushed hallway. A very faint shadow cast by the low afternoon sun against her form preceded her progress.

As usual, the tug of war between reluctance and enthusiasm rose in her, the sensation customary whenever she visited Martin in his room. She slid the tiny door covering the glass panel on Martin's door. Ximena was expecting him to be immersed in the painting, but he was nowhere near his easel.

Martin lay on his bed, on his side, curled in a fetal position. A frisson of alarm ran through her. It was midday. He should not be in bed. He should be in a frenzy of painting activity at this time of the day.

Is he ill?

She punched in the codes to his door and rushed to his bed. He was burning up and was shaking. He was mumbling something incoherent.

Ximena called the attending physician, not taking her eyes from Martin as he trembled like a leaf. Her heart beat like a bird trying to escape from its cage. *Not yet, not now,* she chanted over and over to herself as she waited for the medical team to arrive.

Within minutes, a flurry of activity took over the room as a team of nurses and the doctor attended to Martin. She felt shaken by it – Martin could not die yet. Not now, not after fifty years, not when she was so close.

As the team left the room, crisis averted, Ximena found herself unable to leave. She wandered to Martin's painting and realised it was almost complete. He was doing something on the painting of her face. One eye seemed unfinished. It was dull and muted, unlike the other one.

She moved closer to inspect the art that he made and marvelled at his undeniable talent. Only Martin could layer his work like this. The viewer would see the image on the surface, but when one looked closely, there would be another image behind it, and sometimes another one behind that.

As she scrutinised this one, she realised there was figure hidden behind the shading in the iris of the eyes. She stepped closer to examine it further, and it became obvious Martin had drawn her silhouette into the iris of her portrait. Like an image within an image, within an image.

Her heart thudded as she recognised the message in Martin's paintings. She had been on his mind all those years. Her image, the convoluted images of who she was. Maybe she was never far from his mind.

If only they had tried harder, perhaps they could have dug him out of his mind sooner.

Martin's weak voice floated to her in the quiet of the room – one word – *Mena.*

The pain of that word sent her fleeing the room, her throat tight with the tears she could not shed, locked like a vise on her heart.

Íñigo found Ximena in her office, staring at the vast expanse of the well-manicured garden. The man-made lake reflected the beginnings of the dusk. On her face was an intent look, but she was unseeing, her lips tight with undisclosed pain.

He cleared his throat to announce his presence, and she swivelled to face him. The slight smile on her face was for his benefit. But there was a touch of panic behind it, and a soul-deep sadness.

Once again, his helplessness to do something about her pain angered him.

"Do you have the results?" Her question reminded him of the reason he rushed over to her office.

"Yes." He handed the document he carried to her.

A satisfied, triumphant smile spread across her face as she finished reading. Her face glowed, brightened, and chased away the sadness that was there moments ago. And gladness seeped into his heart.

"This is remarkable. We found our link!" Ximena was breathless, her excitement infectious.

"Yes, I think so too. That blood sample showed a blending of a male *harravis* and superior *Erdia* blood, an E3. So, this donor was lucky enough to have been conceived during the crucial forty-eight-hour window. We need his help," he said.

"I agree..." Ximena's voice rang with confidence. "And I believe he will help us."

The glitter in her eyes made his heart flutter. "You seem confident. You know the donor?" he asked.

"Yes, Daniel Santino is family."

Daniel stopped short as he stepped into his office. It was a surprise to see Ximena De Vida at such an early hour. She was already waiting for him when he arrived. He had not even had coffee yet.

"Good morning, Tita. I have to say I did not expect to see you here first thing in the morning." He was curious and a bit alarmed.

"My purpose is crucial, highly classified, and a matter of life and death." Ximena's tone was pleasant, as if what she just said wasn't loaded with meaning.

"Okay... three clichés in one sentence. It must be truly important..." he said. "Can I offer you coffee, Tita?"

"Tea is more my thing, Dan," she replied.

"Tea it is, then." He rang for his secretary.

Minutes later, with a hot beverage in hand, both sat down on the couch in Daniel's office. This was not a business meeting. It was personal.

"Tell me what you need from me, Tita. I'm fortified by coffee now and ready to deal with any life and death situation." His reflex to lighten the situation with jokes had kicked in. The coffee intensified it.

In response, Ximena handed him a piece of paper that contained colourful graphs. He looked at it, perplexed. "What am I looking at?"

"That is the result of the gene sequencing we did on your blood, Dan. And at this exact moment, you are one of a kind," Ximena replied, her tone became more businesslike.

"One of a kind?" He looked at Ximena in confusion. "How, exactly?" He could not grasp the gravity he detected from Ximena's behaviour.

"Normal *Erdias* have 6 to 9.6 *V genes*," she said. Her body canted forward, her gaze intent. "Your blood has 11 full *V genes* and 2 mutated ones. If those two genes were normal, you would be a *Vis*."

He frowned, his brain having a hard time following what Ximena told him. "What exactly does it mean, Tita?" His heart pounded in his chest; dawning suspicion crept into his mind.

"On you, physically, we do not know yet. But for our experiment, it meant a lot. Your genes provided the link between human and *Vis*."

He still did not understand how he could help her in finding a cure for *VM*. Ximena was now talking about genetic links between humans and Viscerebus. "Tita, how exactly would my genes help in developing a cure for *VM*?"

His question took Ximena aback. And her reaction told him they were not referring to the same thing. Pregnant silence followed.

"Dan, I am doing another kind of experiment, and it has nothing to do with *VM*." Ximena's tone was tempered, as if she was gauging his reaction.

"Tita, if you want me to continue helping your project, you had better tell me what you're going to use my blood for." His tone hardened. He felt a sense of betrayal at Ximena's subterfuge.

Ximena sighed. "I understand. Before I tell you all," she said, "promise me you will keep this confidential."

"Is it legal?" He doubted if she would do something illegal, but the earlier prevarication made him doubt Ximena's intent.

"Yes, in both legal systems." Ximena nodded, her chin thrust in a confident and defensive manner.

He thought about how he felt about participating in a covert science project. But there was something in what she said that intrigued him.

"I will work with you on this... special project, but I have my own stipulations."

"What is it?" Ximena's voice and face were wary, but her gaze was resigned.

"That you make it part of your research to find out what having those genes would mean to me, how it affects me physiologically," he said. He needed to know. It seemed that he was more *Vis* than he thought.

Ximena stared at him like she was probing his thoughts. Then she nodded. "Okay, that is a deal."

They sealed their bargain with a handshake.

"Who else knows about this, Tita?"

"Me and Íñigo, and now you."

"Just us? How about your parents?"

"Just us. My parents are the *Matriarch* and *Patriarch*, they should have plausible deniability when it comes to the *Project Chrysalis*," she replied.

"So, they know about the *VM* cure project, but not this... *Chrysalis* one?"

Ximena nodded.

Do I want to know what Project Chrysalis is all about? Or do I just want to know more about my part of the project?

He was keen to find out more about the side of his nature once and for all. It had become impossible to distance himself from that side of his nature. And he also couldn't ignore the consequences of his participation in the project. He would have to know everything. It was his blood after all. "So, when do you need me?" he asked.

"Let's meet later today with Íñigo so we can discuss the additional testing that we need to include so we could give you what you asked for."

They parted that day with a firm understanding. Ximena's visit turned his day upside down, and he did not know what to feel or think about the information about him. It was a pity it was too early to drink. A strong one would be useful now.

The morning greeted Ysobella, bright and fragrant with promise. Her wedding day. Hers and Galen's. The jumble of feelings that she drowned in for weeks leading up to this day intensified – elated and slightly scared, giddy like a teenager. But there was no doubt she had been waiting for this day all her life.

Galen was still asleep, his face relaxed. The lines on it eased. He looked healthy, virile, and robust. As if the sands of his life's hourglass were not draining out of the vessel grain by grain. Ysobella shook the thought away, not willing to allow anything to mar this beautiful day.

Their wedding was going to be at midnight, a unique request Galen made. He said it was in homage to her *Viscerebus* nature. He liked the idea that a minute after midnight signalled a new day, a new beginning for them both. And that the dawning of the sun awaited them.

The traditional marriage hour for their kind was the hour just before dawn, but Galen's slight deviation was as meaningful and personal. And it was theirs.

Galen stirred awake. His hand crept to her side of the bed like usual. His first conscious thought, it seemed, was about her. The action never failed to warm her heart. His hand encountered her body, and he rolled over, his eyes still closed, to pull her closer and flat against him. His sigh of satisfaction echoed hers, as his warm, hard, hair-roughened body pressed close to her.

"Wake up, husband-to-be..." she whispered to his chest.

"Five more minutes, I'm still thanking the universe." He murmured to her tousled hair as he nuzzled and inhaled her scent. His gratitude bled into her that her own heart overflowed with appreciation for him and the fortune of having a second chance at happiness.

She and Galen ate a late breakfast when their daughter, Yuana, arrived with Roald. Her daughter was followed by her parents, Katelin and Edrigu. Yuana and her mother, Katelin, were there to whisk her away to the De Vida house, to prepare her for the wedding. They would pamper her, make sure she had nothing in her head but be ready for tonight.

Roald and her father, Edrigu, would stay with Galen, to subject him to the male version of pre-wedding preparations, whatever that may be.

"See you later, Bella. I will take good care of your bridegroom for the meantime," her father said with a twinkle in his eyes.

"Remember that you and Galen need to be at the house before seven. The cocktails with the wedding guests start then." Her mother said over her shoulders as she pulled her along. Yuana was already ahead of them.

It would be a long celebration tonight. It would start during cocktail and continue on until the actual ceremony at midnight which would be held in the garden of the De Vida compound.

Galen was right, their wedding would be mysterious, romantic, and dramatic in equal measure. It would be quirky and passionate, just like Galen. And she could not wait for it to happen.

Finally.

Ysobella looked down at the venue of her wedding from her bedroom verandah. The garden was awash with lanterns and more flowers than she had ever seen in her life. A gazebo covered with hundreds of white and purple blooms was in the centre. It looked like a giant topper on a wedding cake. White wicker chairs arranged in a half circle faced the bedecked pavilion.

The overhead lights bounced off the white tablecloths dotting the cocktail area close to the patio. It competed with the shiny tresses of the guests and their glittering jewellry. On the far-left side of the vast garden, they lined up several tables for the wedding breakfast tomorrow.

Celia and Nita led a small army of De Vida staff who were busy refilling the buffet table and serving the guests. Their family and their closest friends enjoyed the fare and the company.

She was with them earlier when they shared stories and teasing banter about second chances in life, and how 'young' the couple was. But now the moment was near, it was time she changed from her cocktail dress into her wedding dress.

The butterflies in her stomach had not left her since then, and yet she felt serene as well. In a few minutes, the ceremony would start. It was time to come down. She took one last look at her reflection and released all the bottled emotions in her – anticipation, fear, excitement, and the deep love she suppressed for years. The wedding was like the ultimate permission she had been waiting for.

Ysobella descended the stairs, her wispy gown flowing behind her, her heart filled with joy. Her eyes honed in on Galen, crisp, elegant, and handsome in his wedding finery. Her heart thudded faster as she came closer to him. Galen was teary-eyed, his jaw tight with the effort to control his emotion of awe. Her heart responded; tears pricked behind her eyes. She swallowed the lump in her throat.

Galen moved to meet her at the bottom of the stairs without seeming to notice. His hand stretched out to hers. The warm clasp of it transmitted to her palpitating heart and calmed her.

They both looked down at the beautiful aquamarine ring on her hand, the engagement ring Galen gave her when he first proposed. The memories the jewellery carried for them were bittersweet and searing. They both inhaled deep and smiled at each other in a mutual unspoken decision – they would waste no more time on regret. Now was more important, and the future was before them.

They walked hand in hand towards the pavilion, with her family behind them. Every step she took was like a step to heaven. Her body lightened as she and Galen got closer to the gazebo.

Their family, close friends and household members witnessed the ceremony. It was brief and solemn. Galen's vow moved everyone in attendance, and it reduced her to happy tears.

"Bel, loving you and our daughter for the rest of my life is not enough. My lifetime is shorter than yours, but I will make sure that during my time on

this earth, I shall love you every microsecond, and leave you enough happy memories to last for the rest of yours. I vow I will never be parted from you from this day forward. My soul will always yearn for yours, in my lifetime and beyond."

She had committed it to heart and recalling the words brought on fresh tears. Since the ceremony, Galen kept her hand on his, a touch replete with pride, possessiveness, and intimacy. Her heart responded and overcame her reserve. She no longer cared about what her parents and family thought about the acts of affection Galen displayed in public, or her reciprocal reaction to it.

They rejoined the party as a couple. Cheers from the crowd greeted them. The evening overflowed with well-wishes and the celebration continued. The sounds that surrounded them were as musical as the joy in their souls: clinks of silverware hitting china, glasses meeting glasses for repeated toasts, the bustle of their household team replacing dishes on the buffet for replenishment, liquids sloshing as the drinks flowed, laughter and conversations from the guests, and the tune the *Vis* quartet played in the background.

They were all waiting for the rising of the sun, symbolic to the new life she and Galen would now have.

As the sun peeked over the horizon, the crowd did something spontaneous she and Galen were completely unprepared for. No doubt fuelled by copious amounts of alcohol, each member transformed into their *Animus* to greet the rising sun. They became surrounded by a variety of predatory beasts, growling, howling, and clad in formal clothes. It would have been hilarious if it was not disconcerting.

For a minute, she almost shape-shifted with the crowd, but the gasp from Galen stopped her. There was a tinge of panic in his eyes.

A glance at Yuana, who kept her human form, and Roald's terrified gaze assured her it was the right thing to do. Their men were human in the middle of beings who could tear them to pieces. They had reason to be scared.

A glance at her mother told Yuana they were of the same mind. Roald needed her to remain human in his eyes. Panic kept him rooted on the spot, his back rigid, his eyes wide with alarm. Yuana focused on Roald's face, gripping his hand tight to anchor him to the present.

And from her peripheral vision, she saw Daniel walk closer to them. Daniel draped his arm in camaraderie and protection over Roald's stiff shoulders, as if they were watching something mundane. Dan's act of solidarity with Roald touched her.

Daniel's presence was a welcome added support. His casual action made it appear like it was commonplace. It was a good thing Roald already knew of Daniel's *Erdia* nature. It was one less unnecessary shock.

As the sun rose over them and lightened the sky, the guests transformed back into their human forms one by one. A chorus of laughter followed a moment of silence as the crowd realised the ridiculousness of pack transformation while wearing formal clothes.

The slight tension that infused the five of them lifted, as they got surrounded by guffaws and giggles. For most of the guests, that was the highlight of the night. They would be talking about it for weeks.

A squeeze on her hand made her look up. Roald's face gained some colour back. He seemed more relaxed. His hand lost its clamminess, and he was able to smile and respond to the surrounding conversations.

"You okay, Ro?" She murmured to him when they found themselves alone at the beverage table to get some fresh coffee.

He smiled and kissed her on the lips. "I'm okay now, Yu." A shadow of emotion crossed his eyes but said nothing else.

"Would you like to go home now?" she asked. They were waiting for the wedding breakfast, but she would make excuses for Roald if he felt uncomfortable.

He shook his head. "No. I am the best man and I still have to give a speech, I believe."

"Ro, my father would understand, and speech-giving is not common in *Vis* weddings..." She wanted to assure him it was okay, that his absence would not be a big deal.

He leaned down and kissed her again, his lips cool and soft. This time the contact lingered. "I am fine, my love. A bit shaken still, and half expecting any of the guests will turn into a beast at a moment's notice... otherwise, I am okay."

"Don't worry, Ro. Even when we transform, we do not lose our cognitive skills. And I can guarantee you that should a guest run amok, I and the entire family will protect you."

He grimaced at that. "I feel like a damsel in distress. It is causing a dent in my self-confidence." His tone was sardonic and with a tinge of bitterness.

"Would you feel better if you were armed?" She was half-joking, grasping at whatever it was that could make Roald feel in control.

Roald's eyes narrowed, his thoughts inward. "Actually... yeah... I would..." His tone was wondering, as if he recalled a coping mechanism from the past.

That made her smile. "Let me do something about it." She searched for

Celia in the crowd who was passing around more mimosas. When she came closer, Yuana whispered something to her. Celia nodded and left.

Roald frowned. "What was that about?"

"You wait. You will see..." She smiled at him as she sipped her lukewarm coffee.

Celia came back with the item that Yuana asked for. It was a small, curved knife that resembled a claw, a *karambit*, encased in a leather holster shaped like a triangle. It was from her grandfather, a gift for her twelfth birthday, the day she achieved shape-shifting in under three minutes. She loved the knife, trained with it when she was a teenager. Although she had not touched it for years, she kept it well-oiled, sharpened and maintained.

She handed Roald the leather holstered knife, a long silver necklace dangling from it. "There you go. That is the most effective weapon against us," she said with a small smile.

"What is this?" Roald asked, even as he unclipped the lock and pulled the *karambit* out. Recognition and appreciation dawned on his face as he unsheathed the knife. He whistled under his breath as he inspected the blade. "This is one handsome *karambit*, my love. I never told you before, but I collect them. And this one looks vintage and well cared for."

"That was a gift from my grandfather, when I turned twelve."

"Then I cannot take this..." There was regret in his smile.

"Keep it for now. Until you no longer need it." She pushed it to him, folding his fingers over it.

He chuckled and hugged her. "Thank you, my love. For today, I will keep it with me. Tomorrow, I will use my own, your *karambit* is too small for my hand." The arms that closed about her were relaxed. Most of his tension had seeped out.

"You're welcome..." she said, her heart light. "Now, put it away before the bartender stops serving you drinks. It's a weapon, after all."

"Yes, ma'am," he said and pocketed the knife.

Hand in hand, they went back to the rest of the party, where Daniel stood with his father. They were talking to her great grandfather. Mateo Santino was her Elo's protegee, and they looked like they were catching up on each other's lives. As they walked closer, she noticed the pensiveness in Daniel's face. Something was eating at him. She took a mental note to ask him the next day.

The morning sunrays drove the darkness away. The buffet spread was laid out; the breakfast tables readied. Everyone queued to partake from the variety of dishes prepared for the occasion.

8

THE MEJORDIA

Yuana found herself wistful as she waved her parents goodbye to their month-long honeymoon trip to Tokyo. They had just left, and she already missed them. She wondered if this was how her mother would feel when it became her turn to go.

Her first task for the day was a visit to Daniel. And the best way to do that would be to surprise him with breakfast. Daniel could never resist Nita's pancakes – the fluffiest and creamiest ones she ever had.

Half an hour later, with her car loaded with the breakfast hamper, a mug of her special coffee, and a black one for Daniel, she drove to his office.

She got there just in time to hear the receptionist order a cup of coffee for Daniel from the ground floor coffee shop. Yuana stopped her, pointed at the picnic hamper, and sauntered to Daniel's office unannounced. She did not want to give him the opportunity to evade her. He had just looked up from plugging his laptop when he saw her. His eyes widened in surprise.

"Good morning, D!" She placed the breakfast hamper on his table with a flourish.

"What is it with you and Tita Ximena with all these unannounced visits?" he muttered, his brows drawn in a mixture of exasperation and resignation.

That comment piqued her interest. "Tita Ximena came here? When? What for?"

Daniel's self-disgusted sigh told her he did not mean for that to slip out. "Yes, she did, yesterday... It was nothing." His tone was dismissive, but Daniel avoided her eyes. He busied himself with preparing his desk.

"Oh, that is the furthest-from-nothing denial that I have ever heard of, so stop it, D!" She flashed him a warning smile. "You know very well I will badger you until I get the truth out of you." She started taking the food boxes from the hamper and laid the meal in front of him.

Daniel stopped what he was doing as the fragrance of pancake wafted out. His face was a comical mix of expression – hunger, annoyance, and accusation as he looked back at her. He knew she used his weakness for Nita's pancakes to soften his defences. And she was not sorry about it.

She laughed at Daniel's dismayed expression as he watched her pour the vanilla-bourbon syrup with deliberation over the fluffy pancakes. Daniel's preference for the sweet concoction was not a secret to the De Vida household.

"Yuana, you are more lethal as a devious woman than as an *Aswang*. I hope you realise that..." Daniel said through gritted teeth, his tone tart.

"Yep... guilty as charged." She handed him the food box and the plastic fork and knife. "Unfortunately for you, I am both, and you like me just the same. And fortunately, I like you too. So, stop whining and eat up. And then, it's confession time."

Daniel took the cutlery with a grumpy expression. "You didn't have strawberries..." he said, trying to find fault in the situation.

She smiled with glee and showed him a small container of fresh, plump, and chilled strawberries. She opened it with great flair. "*Tada!*"

He tried to maintain his annoyance, but she could see him trying to stifle a smile. Strawberries were his other food weakness. She handed him his coffee and the bottle of whipped cream without words; goading him would be counterproductive at this point.

He stabbed at his pancake with a sigh of frustration, but she could see his anticipation. She was certain the moment he puts a bite into his mouth, his facade of displeasure would vanish.

And she was right.

They ate in silent camaraderie for a few minutes. She would not broach the subject until he had eaten the third pancake. But Daniel beat her to it.

"I am working with your aunt, for a scientific project, a highly confidential one," he blurted out as he took a sip of his coffee.

That made her sit up straight. "What kind of project?" And why was there a line of strain around Daniel's mouth? "And why is it bothering you?"

Daniel's eyes rolled. "What? No beating around the bush? No waiting for me to ease into it?"

"Our friendship never allowed for any bush to grow between us, so the beating around something non-existent makes little sense. Quit the delay tactic and tell me. What is this top-secret project with my aunt?"

"It is called *Project Chrysalis*. And your aunt Ximena and Uncle Íñigo head it." His voice turned serious and quiet. "It is top secret and there are only three of us – well, four now, including you, that know about the project's existence."

She nodded. "Okay, but what is it about?"

"Your aunt and uncle are trying to find the link between the genes of humans and *Vis*. My blood provided the missing link." Daniel's voice carried a tinge of bitterness. "If they are successful, in theory, they could turn humans into *Vis*, and vice versa," Daniel said. He allowed that to sink into her understanding, the implications, the possibilities of what her aunt and uncle were creating.

"Holy *Prometheus*!... Really?" The magnitude was hard to grasp. "Is that what they said they were trying to do?"

"No. But I think it is something not out of the realm of possibilities once your aunt succeeds. And knowing Tita Ximena, it is just a matter of time."

"How did your 'blood' get into the picture? And why your blood? What's in it?" His connection to the project was not clear to her.

Daniel didn't answer immediately.

"In a genetic game of chance... I hit the damned jackpot..." His tone was laden with irony. "My father and mother got frisky during that crucial forty-eight-hour window while my father had the *harravis* potency in his system. And my mother carried a superior *Erdia* gene. I am now called a *Mejordia*, a different *Erdia*. I am *Mejordia* 001, the first ever discovered." He heaved a heavy breath as he rubbed his nose bridge.

And in that sentence, she saw what was bothering Daniel.

"So, why are you supplying your blood to their experiment? What do you get out of it, Dan?"

He shrugged. He got up and turned to the window behind him. His gaze far away. His face a mask of dark emotions.

"I want to find out exactly what I am, Yu. I am not human, not a Vis either. It is hard not knowing where I belonged. I am tired of it." He said it quietly, but there was an underlying vehemence to it.

She got up and stood beside him, and by instinct, wrapped her arms around his middle.

"I understand, Dan. But I want you to know bloodlines would not give you that sense of belonging." Her eyes locked with his over their mirrored reflection. "It is the acceptance of the people you care about that gives you that feeling. And I do not care if you are a half this or half that. I care about you, all of you, wholeheartedly."

His arm came around her shoulders and squeezed hard. Daniel was never one for expressing his emotions, but his actions spoke more loudly about how he appreciated her declaration.

"Does your father know?" she asked after a while. Daniel had not mentioned his father's name in their exchange.

Dan looked down at her and shook his head.

Yuana nodded. "Alright." She glanced up at him and winked. "So, can I blackmail you with this when I need to?"

He smiled. The dark depths of his eyes lightened now. "Well, if you do not mind going against your aunt's edict of secrecy... go ahead." He knew full well it would be a folly to cross her very smart aunt.

Yuana smiled back and returned to her unfinished pancake. She did not want to waste the uneaten strawberries. Daniel followed suit.

"How's Roald doing?" Daniel asked as he finished the last few bites.

"I think he was doing better, apart from that ridiculous... flash mob transformation at the wedding..." she said. The memories of the stupid scene during her parents' wedding made her shake her head. "No wonder the *Tribunal* wants us hidden, you can't take us anywhere."

Daniel chuckled.

And the hilarity of the images; of wolves wearing gowns and tuxedos, big cats in suits, ties and belts, cocktail dresses and heels, bejewelled and beribboned, came flooding back to her.

Her eyes met Daniel's, and they both burst out laughing.

Ximena arched her back to relieve the tightened muscles there. She had been reviewing the *Project Chrysalis'* test results. They were closer to their goal.

Her excitement about the recent developments motivated her to push herself further, and a step more. With Martin's failing health, the sooner they achieved the results they were aiming for, the better.

A frantic rapping on the door turned her attention. Antonina, her lead scientist for the *Altera*, the *VM* cure project, came into the room in a rush. She clutched a bundle of documents.

"Dr Ibarra, the results came in, and it was more than we expected." Antonina's face was flushed, hair in disarray, her voice high.

She smiled and looked at the papers Antonina handed over. What she saw widened her smile.

"Every result validated?" she asked.

Antonina nodded vigorously.

"This *is* splendid news. Now, all we need to do is to test it with an actual person," Ximena added.

Antonina had not stopped nodding.

"I will secure the approval and the trial participants. Prepare all the serums so we can start as soon as possible," she told Antonina, whose eyes glittered with excitement. With a final nod, her lead scientist rushed out as fast as she came in.

Things were lining up. And it was not even noon yet...

Now, with the cure to *VM* almost at hand, she felt justified in using part of *Altera's* funding for her self-serving secret science project. She just hoped that Martin would live long enough for the *Chrysalis* to be a success.

For now, their theory about what made a *Mejordia* different from an *Erdia* and a *Vis* was clearer. The results were interesting, and eye-opening. She needed to inform Daniel about it so they could put their hypothesis to the test. And if she was proven right, they might just discover a new variety of *Vis*, or human, whichever Daniel chose to be called.

The boy might just find out exactly who and what he is, and with it, his life's purpose.

Roald opened his eyes against the bright midday sun. The temperature in his room was warm. He had overslept. Ysobella and Galen's wedding celebration ended mid-morning yesterday, and he only got two hours of sleep. A lie in today was not surprising.

As usual, the sound of the shower and the sensation of the water running down his body silenced the hum of activity in his busy brain and focused it at his core concern. And for months now, the greatest one was his *Aswang*-phobia. He felt unmanned every time he thought about it.

The mass transformation proved to him his fear was so great he did not even notice the absurdity of seeing tuxedo- and gown-clad beasts around him. It petrified him.

Only Yuana's tight grip on his hand stopped the panic from overwhelming him. And Daniel's casual reaction to the scene anchored him to reality. It was emasculating but also an enormous relief to have both at the height of his vulnerability.

The rest of the event, he did his best to man up and remained where he was, to enjoy as much as he was able, or at least present a relaxed exterior. And he did, to some extent, he calmed down enough while with Yuana, Daniel, and to some degree, with Galen and Ysobella. On purpose, he stayed near one of them, and he was almost sure that Yuana and Daniel stuck to his side until the very end to help him.

He remembered the knife that Yuana gave him and realised that it made all the difference. He was hypervigilant, aware when they were within striking distance, but he could be in proximity to the guests without recoiling, knowing he was armed.

Prior to having the knife, his first instinct was to flee. The knowledge he had a knife made his fight instinct rise to the fore. And that made him feel better, about his situation, about himself. His fear did not disappear, but the *karambit* acted like a talisman.

He could thank his grandfather's insistence to train him in Kali when he was little. The perfect coincidence that he was adept with the *karambit* was an added boost to his confidence. He felt braver and not so powerless.

It was time for him to take out Maximo Magsino's highly prized *karambit*. The blade's life purpose had been renewed.

An hour later, he was on his way to meet Yuana for an early lunch when he saw her car drive into the entry of the GJDV building. She was on the phone when he got into the lobby, standing just before the elevator.

The kiss he gave her on the forehead startled Yuana and interrupted her conversation. She finished her call abruptly, like she did not want him to hear who and what she was talking about.

"I hope you did not cut off your conversation on my account," he said.

She blushed a little, looking a tad guilty. "No, it was just... Daniel."

The slight hesitation in her tone made him uneasy. "Oh... what was he on about?"

"Not much. Just something for my Aunt Ximena." Her dismissive tone did not match the look in her eyes. He let it go for now. He did not want to add a jealous boyfriend label to his name.

"Why are you here so early? It's still an hour and a half before lunch." Yuana's change of subject was smooth. He almost smiled.

"I got up late, and have had no breakfast yet, so I was hoping I can convince you to have an early lunch." He smiled at her, hoping to cajole her into agreement.

She grimaced in apology. "I already had breakfast." At his disappointed look, she reached up and kissed him. "Sorry..."

"It's okay, my sweet. Can you join me for coffee, while I eat?"

"Of course."

They proceeded to the coffee shop next door.

"So, tell me more about the *karambit* that you gave me the other night..." he said as he ate his scrambled eggs. "I hope it is not an heirloom piece..."

"Oh, it was my twelfth-birthday gift from my grandfather..." A fond smile graced her lips as she recalled that day. "It's a tradition in our family for grandfathers to give a *karambit* to their granddaughters when they achieve shape-shifting under three minutes, or when they turn fifteen, whichever comes first. Grandmothers do the same for their grandsons. A sort of farewell to childhood and welcome to adulthood. I got mine three years early..." Pride flashed in her eyes.

"Wow, the sentimental value of this knife is priceless. I should return it to you." He handed it back to her.

"No. It's not an heirloom piece. Keep it for now. You can return it to me when you do not need it anymore." She said in a gentle but firm voice that brooked no argument.

"It's okay, my love. I have my own. Like yours, this was my grandfather's," he said and showed her his holstered weapon. The bone and mother of pearl embellishment on the dark wood handle gleamed silver like the thumb ring.

Yuana's mouth rounded in awe as she touched the handle. "This is a beautiful..."

The approach of her driver interrupted her statement.

"Ma'am, do you need me in the next two hours? Your mama sent me a text to pick up something from Sir Galen's hotel, to be brought to the house. Also, do you want me to take the hamper home, or do you want me to leave it at your office?"

"It's okay. I have no appointments today. You can do Mama's errand. You can take the hamper home as well," she replied to him. The driver nodded and left.

"Why do you have a hamper in your car?" he asked. It was a curious thing to have in a car.

"Oh, I brought breakfast to Daniel this morning." Her automatic response came easily.

Yuana was unaware of the stab of emotion that hit him with her statement. The seed of jealousy in his heart sprouted, but he squashed it. He would not add insecurity to their relationship. There was enough to deal with in his current difficulties in assimilating with Yuana's kind.

Maybe the early breakfast was a common occurrence between longtime friends.

He was convincing himself of the same as he found himself parked in front of Daniel's office. Deep inside, he knew that Daniel and Yuana would never betray him, but people fall in love against their better judgement and best intentions.

Daniel and Yuana belong to the same kind. Daniel was already part of her world; he had been since birth, just like her. He, on the other hand, was still striving to do so and not even sure if he would succeed at it, given his terror of their kind.

Roald pushed the thought away. Entertaining it would give power to the idea, and there was no reason to do so since it was all conjecture on his part.

What's with these unannounced visits?

It surprised Daniel when Roald showed up in his office – not so much his presence, but that Yuana and he came in the space of a few hours. He doubted Roald was here about his participation in the *Chrysalis* project. Yuana would not have told him. She was always good at keeping other people's secrets.

"Hey, bro! Is this a tag team game between you and Yuana to keep an eye on me?" Daniel asked in jest.

Roald's face broke into a smile, one tinged with relief. "Not really. Yuana mentioned she had breakfast with you this morning..." Roald placed his mobile phone on his desk, nudging its edge to a slow spin, once, and then a second time.

"Anything on your mind, Ro?" He could see there was something Roald wanted to ask or say.

Roald spun his phone one more time before he spoke. "Why did Yu come here this morning, D?" Roald's tone had an edge to it that surprised him. His friend sounded jealous.

Daniel frowned at the thought. "She came as a friend. She wanted to know what was bothering me." He kept his tone flat, still unable to believe that Roald could be jealous of him.

"What was bothering you?" Roald asked, his face still blank, but his gaze intent.

"It was about my work with Yuana's Aunt Ximena. It's a tad unpleasant," he replied, unwilling to reveal more to him. He did not want to burden Roald with his identity crisis, considering Roald needed to get a handle on his own issues with the *Viscerebuskind.*

Roald continued to spin his phone on his desk. For as long as he had known Roald, he was not the fidgety type.

"More to the point, Ro, what is bothering you?" He wanted to clear the air between them.

Roald grimaced, his gaze on the spinning phone. "I guess I was getting an attack of insecurity."

"Why?" *Can he not see how devoted Yuana is to him?*

Roald shrugged. "I guess my inner struggle with the... *Aswangkind* destabilised my usual sure footing."

"You are not the only one..." Daniel winced. He did not want his self-doubt to bleed through his words.

That halted Roald's fidgeting, and he looked up at him. "So, what are you grappling with?"

Daniel weighed whether he should tell Roald but decided Ximena would not approve. Telling Yuana was defensible, being her grandniece, but Roald, at this point, was not part of their kind yet.

He sighed. "When I find the need for a broad shoulder to cry on, I promise to call you." He reverted to his old way of avoidance, by making a jest. Roald would recognise it and would understand.

Roald's light chuckle established the mutual agreement to allow each other the space.

Roald left Daniel's office with more certainty that his friend would never betray him. But he sensed the connection between them could easily turn into something deeper. He would need to overcome his demons to make himself whole for Yuana. And make sure she would not fall in love with Daniel.

As for battling his fear, he found a way to do so. He would resume his *karambit* training and go back to practicing Kali. He would turn on his fighter side, dial it up to rouse the warrior in him. It was his best defence and offense to defeat his fear.

The zoom of his car's engine as he sped away felt like the strengthening of his resolve.

Doctor Emme Sanchez walked with a steady pace on her way down to the psych ward for her regular round. She also needed to check up on Martin, as he was sick from a respiratory infection a week ago, and he was still recovering.

He was back to painting again after that, but his weakened state slowed him down and lessened his painting time by half. It drove him into a frantic haste, not stopping even to eat. She had to put him on an IV drip for nutrition and medication so he would not waste away. They also had to sedate and restrain him so he could not tear the drip off his arm. It worked, and his appetite returned.

Martin's test results showed he was still fighting off an infection. Even though it was mild, his body had difficulty coping. She ordered a twenty-four-hour wellness watch on him since then. Martin had to get better, for Ximena's sake.

Emme had not told Ximena of her concern over Martin's health. She did not want to add to Ximena's troubles. The *Altera Project* kept Ximena busy and away from Martin. She knew her friend's last visit with Martin had shaken Mena to the core.

She found Martin napping in his room when she arrived. The nurse took his temperature. His nurse approached her when he saw her, his face grim.

Emme's heart plummeted.

"Dr Sanchez, he has elevated temperature, and he did not eat this morning." The nurse pointed to the untouched food tray.

"Okay, tell his physician that we need to resume Martin on sustenance and medication drip. He needs to get better." The nurse nodded and left in a rush, driven by the urgency in her voice.

Dread settled in her stomach as she watched Martin's gaunt face. It was difficult to find any trace of the handsome, roguish charm that captivated Ximena then. He used to be fit and athletic, vibrant, and carefree; he was now but a skeleton of his old self. Yet this man's power over Ximena's heart remained as strong.

Martin could have died fifty years ago for breaking the *Veil*. Ximena would have died with him then. They both thought they had an option with the experimental treatment she espoused. Instead, Martin remained alive but imprisoned in his own mind. And he locked with him Ximena's ability to live her life.

His art was the only window to his mind that was left to them. His latest obsession, the painting of Ximena, was propped on the easel; it seemed close to being done.

What would happen when Martin finishes it? Is this painting his swan song?

She was a small, slim, toned woman, graceful and blessed with youthful features, even for a *Viscerebus*. If Aristo did not know how old Calista McCann was, she would assume she was twenty-five in human years. She was fresh-faced for a seventy-year-old *Vis*.

Aristo watched the woman's impressive form as she warmed up to prepare for her afternoon *Kali* class. Ms McCann's students had yet to arrive. Calista's movements were elegant and fluid, as she whipped her wooden sticks in a flurry of hypnotic weaving patterns. Her flicks and strikes were clipped, precise, and fierce. It was mesmerising, almost like a dance, the cadence of her footsteps in sync with the zing of the sticks cutting through the air.

As Ms McCann moved across the room, Aristo could not doubt the other woman's incredible skills and the power of the blows. She could imagine how lethal Ms McCann would be if she were using a bolo and dagger instead of the sticks in her hands as she warmed up. The woman was a true *Lakambini,* a Grandmaster of the highest calibre the Filipino Martial Arts could confer to an instructor.

An hour later, with a towel in her hand, the woman approached her with an apologetic smile as she patted the sweat off her forehead.

"Hi, I'm Calista McCann." She introduced herself and extended a slim hand in greeting.

Aristo took the woman's firm grip and shook it. "And I'm Aristo Cohen."

"Nice name! It sounds Greek," Calista said as she led her to the coffee table just outside of the training room.

"Yes, it is. That was where my family originated from."

"Oh, are you in *Transit*?" Calista asked, her tone was curious.

"Yeah, but I have no complaints. I like it here, and I like my new front. It is something I am good at – Photojournalism," she replied with a smile.

Calista nodded in understanding. A smile on her face made the other woman look even younger. Based on her research on the background of Calista, she and her father had gone through *Transit* twenty-five years ago after her mother and two siblings died in a car accident. It was a perfect way to deal with their grief – a complete change of environment, a new life.

"So, what can I do for you, Aristo?" Calista placed two coffee cups on the table, one for each of them.

"Well, my boss and I are looking for a martial arts program we can use to train some underprivileged folks in indigenous communities. And based on what I saw, your system seems to be the most appropriate," she replied.

A gleam of interest sparked in Calista's eyes. "Okay... Am I going to train our kind exclusively or does it include humans?"

"Would there be a problem training the humans?" She realised that Calista's students, a small class, were all *Viscerebus*.

"No, I have no problem training them, but you cannot put them together in one class. Sparring will be a problem. The humans cannot compete with our speed and strength, and the chances of injury would be high."

"I understand. We will let you design the class yourself. But the priority is training our kind," she said.

Calista nodded. "Where do we conduct the trainings? And how many sessions do you have in mind?" Calista sat back as she waited for her response.

Aristo smiled in satisfaction. She had expected the question. "In various locations all over the world. And our offer is a long-term engagement. May even be a lifetime one."

Calista's intent gaze focused on hers. "That sounds intriguing. What kind of package are we talking about? As you can see, I have my school here. I do not want to neglect it."

"We will quadruple your annual earnings. Plus a bit more so you can keep your school running. We can discuss the details... if you are in." Aristo paused and waited for Calista to respond.

"So, let's talk." The gleam of interest in Calista's eyes deepened.

Aristo smiled, satisfied. This worked better than she had expected. Not only would they have an exemplary trainer for their fighting force, Calista McCann would be a prime *Jaurdina,* a general among their team of Blue Generals – she just needed priming to their cause.

9

TO THE HEAVENS

Yuana's great grandparents were in the living room when she arrived home. A spread of photos lay in front of them. She saw what it was as she came closer – real estate. Her heart leapt and plummeted at the sight.

"Is that what I think it is, Ela? Elo?" She sat down beside them; her heart thudded in her chest.

"Yes, Yuana. This is the penthouse of the tallest building in Metro Manila. It took us a while to buy it off the human owners. They had to be persuaded." Her Elo handed her the layout of the units. "There were two penthouse units on the top floor, and we bought both to ensure no one else can access the floor. We can combine the units into one or keep it as it is. Your parents can live in one unit and you can have the other."

"I think we should keep the two units separate. Mama and Papa can still have their privacy, and yet I would still be nearby. I like the idea of living near them. Ask Mama which unit she wants, and I will take the other." She did not mind waiting for her unit to be renovated. Her parents could start their life together as soon as they returned from their honeymoon.

Her Ela smiled in agreement. "Okay. I will send this to your parents via email."

There were photos of the interior. One unit needed to be furnished, but the other was fitted out in a minimalist, modern black and white theme. The layout of the two units mirrored each other, with outdoor areas that could be turned into a garden. Her imagination flowed, her emotions with it. Perhaps now she could begin exploring what else she could do as an *Apex*.

It would be exhilarating to take off from here every night.

"So, what do you think?" her Ela asked, prompted by her silence as she examined the photos.

"Can I inspect the site tomorrow?" She wanted to see if she would be comfortable in there. This would be her first time to live separate from her family, from her mother.

"Yes, of course." Her great grandparents exchanged a look. "Yuana, we need to talk about something else. About your *Apex* nature." The slight frown on her Ela's forehead dampened her excitement.

"What is it, Ela?" Her pulse elevated. Her great grandmother looked worried, and it was not usual for her to be so.

"Well, on the surface of it, if you decide to come out in the open, you will become the object of adoration, and will have a god-like status among our kind." Her Ela's keen eyes were focused on her. "And if you accept this, in the best-case scenario, the *Tribunal* will look to you to break deadlock decisions – that is, if they agree among themselves to make you a figurehead. The worst case is that some of them will use you as a political tool to boost their power within the *Tribunal*. They will manipulate and deceive you."

Dismay and apprehension crept over her heart. Her knowledge of the workings of the *Tribunal* was limited to her exposure to her great grandparents, being the *Matriarch* and *Patriarch* of their *Gentem*. Her assumption of the morality of the *Tribunal* members was shallow because she based it on how her great grandparents governed.

"I did not realise that there is politics in the *Tribunal*."

"There is always politics among people who hold power and influence, Yuana. There will always be someone who would want to rule over everyone else, one who would not want to share it." Her Elo said. "Just as there will always be a need for someone to accept their destiny. Time will come that one might need to take on the mantle to rule. That might be your path, Apo."

Her great grandfather smiled at the dismay on her face. She was expecting something like this, but to have it confirmed by someone who was a part of the *Tribunal* was not pleasant. She had never held authority of such magnitude. Managing a department for their company was one thing. She trained for years to be competent for the position. To be in charge of the whole of her kind would be another matter, that would be bigger than being a *Matriarch* in a *Gentem*.

And she was definitely not prepared for it.

"Elo, this *Apex* business does not sit well with me. My experience in life had been a series of mundane tasks. I have had no real challenges because I was born into a privileged existence. What the hell do I know about governing the whole *Viscerebuskind*? It's too big a bite to swallow!" Just the idea of it made her heart race.

"Relax, Yuana. The choice is yours. You can keep your *Apex* status a secret, if that is what you wish." Her Ela held her hand, her warm touch and the gentle tone of her voice calmed her rioting pulse.

"Ela, I just want to enjoy the ability to fly..." She felt almost willing to give up on all her hidden *Apex* skills if she could maintain the status quo in her life.

Almost. A part of her rebelled at the idea.

"Then, do that, Yuana. There is no great urgency to reveal your emergence to our kind," her Ela said with a reassuring smile. Her Elo's smile was not as comforting. The unvoiced caveat was in his eyes – that she might not be able to keep her nature a secret forever. And her Elo might be right.

But that time was not now. Not anytime soon.

"Ela, when I did some search in our archives, there was a poetry, a prophecy of some sort, about two *Apexes*." She remembered the ballad and raised the question to change the tone of their conversation.

"Ah, yes. Well, I would not worry about it so much." Her Ela smiled, the shake of her head was dismissive. "I believe ever since that was written, every *Apex* that emerged waited for the second one. There is something thrilling about fulfilling a prophecy, so even those past *Apexes* were not immune to some drama. Unless we see the emergence of the second one, you're probably the only one in our lifetime, my dear."

"Well, Yuana has over two hundred years to wait for the second *Apex* to emerge, Cara..." Her Elo tapped her cheek in a familiar gesture, as he did when she was a child needing reassurance.

"Is there any information about that... prophecy that you know of? I have found little." She was torn between telling them about Kazu and her promise to him to keep his secret.

Her Ela shook her head. "Not much. There were some speculations, and some study made about it a hundred years ago, but it has yielded nothing concrete. In the past, the emergence of an *Apex* signalled a momentous event, or a catalyst for change. Most of the time, the *Apex* instigated it themselves, so just make sure your program for change is something you are passionate about."

She smiled back but said nothing. She felt guilty for not mentioning Kazu. But without Kazu's permission, she could not expose his secret.

Maybe I can keep it a secret until there is a compelling reason to reveal it. For now, it served us both to remain hidden.

"Ela, have you raised the possibility of an *Apex* emergence to the *Tribunal*?" Their members might not want anyone to usurp the wholesale support their kind reserved for them. An *Apex* would achieve that with little effort.

"Not directly, Yuana. I called some of the *Tribunal* members and casually mentioned there were sightings of a winged *Vis* in one of the remote provinces of the country, and took it from there," her great grandmother replied.

"What did they say?" Yuana somewhat dreaded the response.

"We all agree it will be politicised. We can name three or four members that would do that most definitely. Their status as head of their *Gentems* is unstable. I believe they have great contenders to the seat." Her great grandmother's tone was indifferent.

Yuana nodded. Her next steps became clear to her – the *Viscerebuskind* would not know in the foreseeable future an *Apex* had emerged in their midst. Let alone two of them.

The door opened to a bright, well-ventilated space, and a stunning view. They were on the highest floor of the tallest building in the city. It took her breath away.

"Whew," Roald whistled, echoing what she felt as they took in the space around them, and the one hundred eighty-degree view the unit provided.

"I know. It's gorgeous, isn't it?" she said, unable to hide her elation. The five hundred square meter penthouse unit was impressive in its bare glory. This would be her new home. Right next door to her parents. Once furnished, this would be even more breathtaking.

"Your great grandparents bought this for you?" Roald frowned. "Why? The De Vida compound is closer to your office."

"Mama and Papa are moving here, and my parents wanted me close. And this isn't so far, just another ten minutes," she replied. That was a happy coincidence, and a believable explanation. Roald accepted it without question.

"Well, it is a beautiful unit, my love." Roald smiled. He wrapped his arms around her from behind and kissed the line of her neck. "So, does that mean that I can freely visit you here?"

"You would still have to sneak in," she murmured back, teasing. "My parents are next door, remember?"

Roald's groan was heartfelt. "Hmm... Maybe we can time it whenever they are out on date night?" he said against the earlobe he was nibbling.

"Their date night is the same as ours. So, are you suggesting that I give up my date nights for sex?" she asked in mock outrage.

"No... you're giving it up for a night of unbridled, mind-blowing sex," he murmured against her other lobe.

"But I can have that without giving up my date nights," she replied, adopting a coy pout.

"You can have it every night, including the date nights..." His voice deepened as he turned her around, his hands cradled her head, his lips fastened to hers. His mouth was firm as it moved on her lips, his tongue duelled with hers as he licked the insides of her mouth, tasting her deep. His kiss gentled. He nipped at her top and bottom lip alternately.

The kiss was leisurely and hot, like he had all the time in the world, yet could not get enough. After a while, he lifted his head and rubbed her swollen bottom lip with his thumb as if he was testing its plumpness. His pupils were dark and dilated, his breathing as strained as hers.

The muscles of his back were hard as steel, his body hot, his masculine scent permeating her brain. He hunched over her as he kept her close. Her hands ran in slow circles up his back and settled at the curve of his lower spine. She curled her fingers into fists, to stop herself from cupping his butt. She knew that if she did, Roald's control would break, and she might just end up on the dusty floor with him. Roald had kept his hands on her face for the same reason.

They stayed like that for a while, breathing deep. The oxygen expanded their chests, slowed their pulses, their eyes closed, foreheads touching. Eventually, their heart rates settled. With her hand in Roald's, they explored the rest of the unit, mindful of not stoking the fire between them. They both had meetings lined up after this site inspection, and it would not do to show up dirty and rumpled.

Ximena woke up with a start, her heart pounding from a nightmare so vivid she still remembered the sensation of running through the fields, the tall grass that lashed against her skin, the chilled air that whipped against her face.

Martin occupied her dream, standing at a distance, calling her name. It was the Martin of his youth, and as she ran closer to him, he started fading and aging until he diminished into nothingness when she got close enough to touch him. She called out his name, and the wind carried his response – *Mena*.

The grief woke her. Her heart tightened close to exploding. She tried to stop crying, but her sobs escaped, and the tears burst out of her, flushing out the poison of the decades of misery and guilt she had lived with all these years.

The release drained her, and in its wake came a premonition. Something happened to Martin. She hastily dressed and rushed to the hospital. The drive was a blur; she was only aware of her mental prayer to be proven wrong. She jumped out of her car the moment it stopped in front of the lobby, threw her keys to the startled guard, and ran to the Psych ward.

Martin's door hung open, a whole medical team inside. The flurry of frantic actions by nurses and doctors hovering over Martin dominated the room. They were attempting to revive him, and all she could do was watch. Her ears rang with her own heartbeat and the loud internal scream that reverberated in her skull – *No. No. No. Not yet. Not now.*

The scene in front of her unfolded in slow motion: Martin's body jerking with the defibrillator; the urgent instructions blending into the background; the defeated posture of the doctor as he gave up, as he pronounced the time of Martin's death – two seventeen a.m.; and the nurse pulling a cover over him. Ximena was not aware that her knees buckled until Emme's supporting arms wrapped around her, trying to keep her upright. She felt wrung out, burned out, numb and hollow.

Her mind was so vacant, she could not think. She did not know how long she sat on the cold, hard floor until warm, firm arms lifted her from the floor and enveloped her.

Íñigo.

The tightness of his embrace melted the ice around her soul and the tears locked in her heart burst forth anew. The soaked shirtfront, Íñigo's deep-voiced murmurings against her temple and his unintelligible words penetrated her grief in slow degrees. She became aware of the sunlight that peeked through the windows, the abrasive pain in her lungs as the hard reality reestablished in her brain – Martin was gone. She pushed out of Íñigo's arms. His arms tightened for a second before he let her go.

"How are you?" he asked as his thumbs wiped the tears from her cheeks with a gentle pass.

Ximena did not know how to answer that. Instead, she looked around the room. Martin's body was still on his bed, covered by a sheet. She wanted to touch him, yet she did not want to. It would be too much for her if she felt rigour in him – which did not make sense because she was a forensic pathologist. She handled countless dead bodies in the past. And that was the difference. They were mere bodies. This was Martin.

On shaky legs, she forced herself to approach; she needed to say goodbye. And to apologise.

She clenched her fist to still the tremor in her hand before she could pull back the sheet. The skin of his face was ashen, a bluish tinge underneath it. He looked as lifeless as a body could ever look. The manic expression was no longer there. He was at rest.

"Go and paint some stars now, my gentle warrior, just like you wanted. Your last masterpiece will be hung in the sky, among the other stars, just like you planned." She whispered and pulled the sheet over him. *I am very sorry I did this to you. I tried to fix it. But time has beaten me.*

As Íñigo led her outside, Emme called out her name. "Shall I send the painting to your office?"

Íñigo glanced at her, an inquiring look on his face. She had no energy to explain. She nodded at Emme.

"Yes, please... Thank you, Emme." She turned and went with Íñigo to the lobby of the hospital.

"Come, Mena, I will take you home," Íñigo said.

Ximena shook her head. "I don't want to go home." She did not want to lie awake on her bed.

"You will go home, and you will sleep." Íñigo's voice was firm, his tone hard. "Then I will pick you up when you have rested, and we will talk about what our next step is."

Ximena looked at him, bleary-eyed. Her head was throbbing as she nodded. It was easier to comply than to argue. She was too drained to fight him.

Ten minutes later, Íñigo took Ximena to her bedroom and handed her a glass of water. He did not allow her to say no, popped a sleeping pill into her mouth, and prompted her to take a sip of water to help the pill down her throat. He plopped down on the small leather couch in her room and waited until the pill took effect.

The low hum of the air-conditioner was the only sound in the room, and it lulled her to sleep. The last sound she heard was Íñigo's deep sigh and quiet voice.

"Finally," he said.

Íñigo reviewed the results of the replicated test they worked on. It confirmed the specific characteristics of Daniel's *Mejordia* blood that made him different from other *Erdias*.

Daniel's blood contained the full eleven *V Genes* out of the distinct thirteen every *Viscerebus* possessed. The other two, the *Metamorpho* and *Calyptratus,* the genes that separated him from being a full *Vis*, Daniel possessed in an altered version.

It was almost certain that Dan could not shape-shift. The female *Vis* afflicted with *Manyaxis* possessed similar mutated *Metamorpho* genes, and they could not transform unless the right conditions existed.

The changed *Calyptratus* gene could mean Daniel would not have the need for victus.

He must confer with Ximena first. Perhaps it was a good thing that their scientific breakthrough happened now, when Ximena needed something that would take her mind off her recent loss. He had the time to wait for Mena to be ready. There was no need for haste now. The whole reason for it no longer existed.

For now, Daniel was unique, the first *Mejordia* they had discovered. At a certain point, they would share this with the *Supreme Tribunal*, but not until they had a clear picture of what someone like Daniel could do. And not do.

Their discovery presented various possibilities for the future of their kind. Nature limited their ability to procreate, but Mother Nature itself may have found a way to circumvent its limitation.

If his supposition was correct, a *non-Viscerebus* female could give birth to this new breed that had all the physical attributes of a *Vis*, and none of the disadvantages. They would no longer have to depend on the females of their kind to increase their number. It could even allow them to modify their genetics and eliminate the need for human viscera.

The chime of the wall clock reminded him Daniel would arrive in half an hour. He would need to distill the results down to the bullet points for simpler explanation. He would elaborate if Daniel asked for clarification.

Fifteen minutes later, with the notes done, Íñigo's thoughts went back to Ximena. Had she woken up? Last night, he was glad that Martin had died because it freed Ximena. But he was not so sure now. Her devastation was hard to watch, to relive. Martin's ghost may linger in her heart, and a ghost would be harder to compete with.

To see the woman he loved shattered like that for another man was almost more than he could bear, but it was impossible for him to walk away. He intended to be Ximena's rock in the coming months, to be part of the foundation she would use to build herself back again. He would replace Martin in her heart. He had the time to achieve that, something Martin ran out of.

The receptionist ushered Daniel into the lab as Íñigo poured himself a drink. After they both settled down with a glass, he sat down with Daniel.

"Are you ready to hear the results?"

Daniel's response was a single nod and a slight grimace.

Íñigo handed him a copy of the result. Daniel glanced at it but kept his questioning gaze on him.

"Your blood test showed you have the full eleven *V genes* in your system," he said with a smile. He could not help it.

"What are those genes?" Daniel looked down at the paper in his hand. "*Dynamus? Sthenus? Exceleritus?*" He looked up at him in confusion.

"*Dynamus* and *Sthenus* are the two genes responsible for our superior strength and stamina. *Exceleritus* and *Megakymo* are the genes for speed and energy. *Juventu* and *Aesclepiu* are genes for slow aging and fast healing, respectively. Those six genes come in pairs and go hand in hand," he explained.

"And the rest?" Daniel glanced back at the paper. "Let me guess. *Auditus* is for hearing? *Odorius* for scent? *Spectu* for sight and... night vision?" Dan looked up at him for confirmation.

Íñigo nodded. "Yes. *Gustum* is for taste, *Intactus* for touch or intuition," he added.

"And the two that I am missing? I am guessing it's the shapeshifting gene? And the need to eat viscera, correct?"

Daniel's immediate comprehension surprised Íñigo. The boy inherited his father Mateo's sharp mind.

"Oh, you have those as well, the *Metamorpho* and *Calyptratus*, but in an altered version."

The frown was back on Daniel's forehead. "What does that mean?"

"Well, your guess is as good as ours. But we plan to find out... Would you like to?" He took a sip from his glass and looked Daniel in the eye. "Are you ready for more tests?"

Daniel nodded, a glitter of excitement in the depths of his dark, amber-flecked eyes.

"Have you noticed if you are stronger than normal humans? Faster, more agile? And do you heal fast?" he asked.

Daniel frowned and shook his head. "I don't know. There was no reason to pay attention to that before. I've always been athletic because of my dad and granddad. We did a lot of physical activities and sports together when I was young. I was good at martial arts, maybe marginally faster at running than my schoolmates. I have never been in a fight where I would need to test my strength against another person."

"Okay, we will conduct endurance, speed, agility, and strength test on you. But let us try the fast healing today. It will require a minor cut and we will observe how fast you heal. Are you okay with that?" he asked.

Daniel nodded once more. Íñigo sprayed some alcohol on Dan's forearm, took out a scalpel and some bandages. He gave the young man a quick, shallow slash on the forearm. Daniel's reacted with a quick intake of breath and a wince. Íñigo pressed the bandage on the cut to stem the flow of blood.

"On a normal human, a wound like this should heal within three to seven days," he informed Daniel.

"And on a *Vis*?"

"At this depth, ten to twenty minutes. A three-inch deep stab wound takes us about three hours to heal."

Daniel's eyes widened in surprise. Íñigo was sure that Daniel, like the humans, never paid attention to their healing abilities. For a *Vis*, this was vital knowledge taught by parents to their kids as young as five years old. It was crucial for their kind to know such information as their life depended on knowing how long they would need to survive a wound, how far to run away to allow themselves to heal.

To Daniel's astonishment, the surface wound disappeared within half an hour. There was a slight soreness and a tenderness underneath, but even that faded in twenty minutes. Íñigo's expression exhibited smugness and delight.

Then, an idea came to him. Íñigo, a *Vis* at the prime of his health, would be strong. He would test his strength against him. "Let's see how strong I am. Why don't we arm wrestle?"

Íñigo looked up from writing his observation on the document in front of him. His eyebrows quirked. "Sure, we can try that." Íñigo laid his pen down. "Here?"

Daniel nodded and rolled up his right sleeve. Íñigo did the same to the sleeve of his lab coat. They locked arms. Daniel placed every ounce of his strength into toppling Íñigo's arm, but he could not. They remained locked in a battle for supremacy for twenty minutes until Íñigo pressed his advantage and beat him. The older man's strength was so much more than his. His defeat dashed the initial excitement he felt earlier with his fast-healing abilities.

Daniel's arm muscles were sore, sweat beaded his forehead, and rivulets ran down his back. He picked up his cold drink. Although it was room temperature now, he gulped it down.

Íñigo smiled at him. "Don't be disappointed. You were stronger than a normal human. I can normally topple them in two minutes flat."

"Did you try to beat me immediately? I thought you were just giving me the chance to beat you."

"Oh, you put up a good fight. Your endurance was unexpected. I wanted to see how long you can sustain your efforts, and you did surprisingly well," Íñigo said as he pulled out a handkerchief to dab his damp forehead.

It gratified Daniel to see he made Íñigo break into a sweat.

"So, what am I? A midway point? Stronger than humans, but weaker than *Vis*?" He needed to know exactly what he was.

"If we base it on the two tests we just did, it seems so, but I think it is too early to make that conclusion," Íñigo replied, a deep frown on his face as if there was a puzzle in his head that he was figuring out.

"What do you mean?" he asked; a sort of foreboding came to him. And with it, a surge of hope.

"The eleven genes in your system are just like any *Vis* genes that we compared it to, including mine. But their reaction to stimulus is slower and I have no idea why. However, I have a test in mind..." Íñigo's words held a note of hesitancy.

"You have a hypothesis... and you are convinced about it?" Daniel prompted. "Tell me."

"You might not like it." Íñigo's gaze held a challenge and a warning.

Daniel knew before Íñigo told him he was going to agree to his proposition just to find out more. "Tell me."

"I think we need to trigger your *Vis* side," Íñigo said.

"How?" It intrigued him.

"Human viscera."

The reply rocked him back. The idea of eating raw human viscera was, in his mind, the one thing that separated humans from a *Viscerebus*. To eat one would mean he elected to abandon the human side of his nature.

Do I want to do that? What happens if I did, and it opens a hunger for human organs? What happens if I become addicted, unable to stop the craving for it?

"You do not need to consume human viscera yet, Daniel." Ximena's voice cut into their conversation. They both swivelled in her direction. She walked into the room, composed and cool as usual. But there was something different about her, and Daniel could not put a finger on it.

Íñigo was as startled at Ximena's presence as he was. The older man took a step toward her but hesitated after the second step. Íñigo's assessing gaze was so intent on Ximena, it made Daniel wonder if something happened to her.

She gave Íñigo a wan smile, then faced him. She gestured for him to sit back down. "As I said, Dan, you do not need to eat viscera yet, not until after we conduct an initial test," she said as she sat down beside him.

There were dark shadows underneath her eyes. She looked tired and lacking in sleep. He would even bet she was crying hours ago, her eyes slightly red rimmed and puffy. Daniel wanted to ask her, but did not want to be nosy, and she did not look like she would entertain the question.

So, he focused on the issue at hand. "What do you mean, Tita?" It was a relief to know there was an option available to him.

"We can do the test in the lab first, use your cells, and some viscera cells, and see if it works. Your consumption of the viscera can come later for actual validation." Her tone was matter-of-fact as she picked up the report and perused it.

Daniel glanced at Íñigo, who turned silent when Ximena arrived. He found the man still watching her like a hawk, as if he was expecting her to keel over. She was as solemn, as capable as she had always been.

What happened to Tita Ximena?

"Do we have what we need?" She turned to Íñigo. And while the man's face was expressionless, he nodded.

The tension in Íñigo puzzled him. Something happened with Ximena the day before. Daniel was sure of it, but he could only wonder what it was. *I will ask Yuana later.*

"Will the test take long, Tita?" he asked.

"A few days. We will call you once the results are in," she said.

They drew blood from him before he left, but the upcoming test put him on edge. Its result could be a point of no return for him.

With Daniel gone, Íñigo took the test tube from Ximena's hand to stop her mad but understated effort to distract herself from her pain. He would not let her bury it deep like before. She needed to grieve, to heal.

"Did you sleep well?" he asked.

She nodded, a small grateful smile on her lips. "Yes, the sleeping pills helped."

"What are you going to do next? With Martin? The *Project Chrysalis*? And the rest?" He wanted to know if her plans for her future were a step to moving on.

"We will have a memorial for Martin in GJDV. We do not have any contact with Martin's family. It was useful not to have it during his... disappearance. It will not make sense now if we do. They will ask questions."

He nodded. "What will happen to his body?"

"We will have it cremated."

"Will you absorb him?" Íñigo dreaded her answer, but he needed to know. *If she said yes...*

"No..." Ximena replied with a deep sigh. "It would not be his choice. I have no right. I have taken so much from him in life, I will not steal from him in his death."

The breath of relief that escaped him was drawn deep from his core. He felt light-headed.

"And *Project Chrysalis*? What will happen to it now that Martin is gone?" He wondered if they were going to bury the project along with Martin's body.

"Let us continue it. It has a lot of potential good, especially now that we have a reason to repurpose it. The least of which was Daniel's *Mejordia* status. And we promised him when he agreed to help us." A genuine smile appeared on her face. "I have to admit that this project has turned out to be much more interesting than I expected."

That drew an answering smile from him.

She was going to be okay. It might take time, but it was inevitable. And he planned to be with her when that happened.

Mateo watched his son walk into his office with a faraway look and a furrowed brow. Heavy thoughts engrossed Daniel; his son did not notice his presence in the room.

He watched as Daniel slid his backpack off on autopilot, set it on the table behind him, sit down and log into the computer system.

He was startled when Mateo placed a cup of coffee on his desk. Daniel apologized with a sideways glance.

"I hope it is a beautiful woman that has stolen your wits, Dan," Mateo said as he blew on his coffee.

"Alas, I am not so fortunate, Dad," his son replied, and raised the cup to him in salute.

Daniel took a couple of sips before he turned his attention back to the program running on the computer. It was a face recognition system, checking millions of photographs on the internet. Dan had been running it for weeks, with no luck so far.

They had been monitoring the system daily because the social media platforms add millions of photographs every day. They had not found a match yet, but they remain resolute. Every time they did this, he felt optimistic. He believed it was just a matter of time. The dead woman may not have her own social media, but some of her friends or acquaintances would have, and her photo might just show up on theirs.

Mateo was just contemplating asking his son what consumed his mind when the system pinged. At the sound, they both leaned closer to the screen. The program brought up three pictures. Daniel clicked on the first one. Their eyes shifted from the digital display to the printed picture clipped on the document stand beside the computer screen.

They went through the other two. The software identified two names that posted the dead woman's photo. They found a link to their dead victim. Daniel threw him a triumphant smile.

"Well done, Dan!" he said, clapping his son on the back. This development was thrilling. It could change the trajectory of their investigation.

Daniel leaned back in satisfaction. "Let us hope this is the break we need."

"Yes, let us hope so..." he said, as he typed the information of the two people into an email to Edrigu. These could lead them to the identity of the victim and her killer.

10

AN INVESTIGATION, A BURIAL, AND THE FLYING LESSON

Kazu landed with a soft thud on the small clearing in the woods adjacent to a local inn and the bus station. The night masked his flight and landing. He transformed and fished for the shoes and clothes from his custom-made, aerodynamic, black *Morphbag* he had commissioned years ago. He got dressed and re-fastened the bag around his waist.

Kazu walked to the bus station and bought a ticket to Manila. The station buzzed with the activity of buses arriving and departing, people waiting, loitering about. He climbed into the familiar bus and took a seat at the back. The ten-minute wait would be best spent preparing for his task.

A Mangyan from the community he worked with boarded his bus, proceeded towards the back and sat on the seat in front of him. They made eye contact, but the man did not recognise him. It did not surprise him. He did not want to talk to anyone tonight or have his travel outside of Mt Halcon known to anyone.

The tasks he needed to accomplish during this trip would be crucial in his prime goal to train Yuana, to uncover her *Apex* skills and release them. Her avian *Animus* provided strong clues, but her capabilities would depend on her. And that would make all the difference.

His abilities were bat-like, like every other chiropteran *Apex* in the past. He had the advantage of historical records, as there were more of his kind of winged super shape-shifter than Yuana's. She was only the second avian in their history.

The first, *Apex O'Cuinn,* did not *Ortus* until the last year of his life. While the first avian *Apex* was prolific in his writing, his main occupation after his *emergence*, he wrote very little about his skills.

Yuana would be the key to unlocking the powers of the avian form. Learning about Yuana's powers would guide him to what he could still uncover in himself.

In war, victory's most effective weapon and strategy were knowledge and preparation. If he was going to usher them to the successful conclusion when the *Shift* happens, Yuana must be made ready for the *Txandictus* and her role as the *Second Apex*.

Kazu closed his eyes and mind from the hum of human chatter and engine noises and searched with his senses for Yuana's location.

Images of her flashed through his mind – fleeting and vague. He tried to focus on an image, but it flitted in and out of his mind's eye, unstable and unreachable.

With his inner ear, he listened to her words. But they were unintelligible, like a radio with poor reception. He harmonised his inner sight and hearing and focused it on her. All he got were similar clouded snippets of images and garbled sound bites.

He could not see or hear her clearly. He was unsuccessful in *aurally* imprinting on her. It was not surprising since they had limited interaction. As an *Apex* like him; she would be less pliable than an average *Viscerebus*. Her training was now more important than ever.

He took a deep breath and tried a few more times to reach Yuana's mind, but the results were the same. He could not tap into Yuana's psyche because he did not have her full trust yet to enable an *Aural* imprinting.

The *Aztarimar* had to be done. Soon. The time had come for his life's purpose to unfold.

By noon, Mateo's field team leader, Ben Carrion, arrived in his office with his human field partner, Julius Santos. They walked through the door just as he placed the *Kxalyptra* hourglass on his table, a precautionary measure and a reminder to Ben to keep to the *Veil* while Julius was in the room.

They were calling in to tell him they had identified the dead woman. Her image appeared in a birthday party photo with a group of young people, and they traced her information from one of them.

"Her name is Narcisa Tabogon, she's called Narcie for short." Ben laid down a blown-up picture, one of the three Daniel found on the internet. A red marker encircled their victim's image.

"Okay, tell me." Mateo was keen to hear the rest of the information his team dug up.

"The person who posted this picture on his Facebook page did not know her very well. They just met that night. She accompanied one of his gay friends. According to the gay friend named Quinito Torres or Queenie, he met her at a café close to his salon. She was new in town and was looking for a job. She lived in a dormitory next to the café. The landlady had little information about her. Her registration form listed her phone number and her provincial address as Cebu City. No other details. She was a tenant in the dormitory for only about three weeks. Then she left to move in with her boyfriend," Ben said.

"She did not have any close friends; however, she made friends with one girl there, an HRM student. Her name is Elisa Cuardero. She remembered they went to a street party in a town fiesta. One of Elisa's classmates invited her, and she asked Narcie to come along. That night, they met a good-looking man, who showed an extreme interest in Narcie. Her description was that he was tall, *mestizo*, very charming, and sophisticated," Julius added.

"And the mysterious boyfriend?" Mateo asked, his eyebrow raised, ready to receive another dead end. His team's less-than-excited expression was not encouraging. "What was the name of this charming man?" he asked. "And don't tell me that this Elisa girl does not remember..."

Julius smiled. "She does. I think she had a crush on him as well, but the man was more interested in Narcisa. According to Elisa, his name was Jim Masters."

"That sounds like an alias if I've ever heard one..."

"Yes, that is what we think, as well," Ben said, nodding.

"Do we have a photo of him? A selfie or something?" he asked.

Both men shook their heads.

"So, we hit a dead end on that one," Julius said.

"Not necessarily..." Mateo's brow furrowed in concentration. "He kept a relationship with our victim. They lived together, according to the landlady. He must have used that name in some other venue during those times. Do we have confirmation they did that? Any proof?"

Ben and Julius shook their heads in unison.

"I am more inclined to think they lived together. If he took so much effort to hide his identity, I think he had taken this provincial lass and hid her. Unfortunately, we do not know where to look. The landlady has no idea where Narcie moved to. And Elisa Cuardero said she lost touch with Narcie after the latter moved out," Ben said.

Silence followed as all three of them mulled over the information, trying to decide which path they should take next. They were reviewing the information when the door opened.

Daniel walked in to see his father and two men stood in front of the whiteboard, their brows furrowed as they discussed the detailed chart on it. Then he noticed various documents spread on the table; beside it was his father's ornate silver and spinel *Kxalyptra* hourglass.

Interesting. They have a non-Veil-bound human within their midst.

"Whoa! Anything good?" he asked. All three turned to him. *Ah... that would be Julius.*

"Maybe. Right now, we are trying to rationale rationalize which path to take," his father said with a sigh of frustration. "We dead-ended on the location of the happy couple's domicile."

Daniel glanced at the whiteboard; they had named their perpetrator, but it could be an alias. "So, this Jim Masters is a Caucasian foreigner?" he asked.

"No," Ben replied, "Elisa Cuardero said he spoke in Tag-lish, but his diction on the Pilipino words was spot on, so he could just be of mixed parentage, or someone who had lived here a while."

Perhaps they could run his picture through the same facial recognition software they used to find their victim. "No picture? Or social media of this guy?" he asked.

Ben shook his head. "No. But we asked Elisa Cuardero if she can describe him to our sketch artist. She agreed to do it on Friday."

"Okay. It might not work on the facial recognition software. At best, it could give us a false ping," he replied. "But we can still try. Who knows, we might get lucky twice."

"Did the lady say if he had any accent? Especially his Pilipino?" Mateo asked, his frown deepening.

"We didn't ask. But we can, on Friday," Ben replied.

His father nodded, but his frown remained.

Daniel understood the potential clue it would give them. If the man had an accent in either of the two languages, it would narrow down the regional background of the parentage, his origin, his *Patriam* or most recent previous *Gentem*. It was impossible not to pick up a local accent if you lived in a country for at least two decades.

"No clues on where they moved to and lived together?" he asked, recalling the comment when he walked in.

"None. We have been trying to hazard a guess," Julius replied.

"Well, based on what we know so far about our perp, he was a careful planner. So, if he met her in Metro Manila, he would not live with her here, because his goal is to ensure that no one knows he is connected to her. He would not want her disappearance and death traced back to him..." Daniel thought aloud, but the three men stared at him.

His father's frown eased. Mateo stood up, walked to the whiteboard to note what he said. His observation must have triggered some ideas in his father.

"Good point, Dan. The likelihood of them moving to her province would be slim as well. He would have taken her somewhere else, where she has no friends or connections... And they may have lived in various locations to keep exposure to a minimum," Mateo said, writing it on the board.

"And if we follow that logic, they probably lived in a place that is a few hours' drive to the murder scene. Our perp may have possessed a fake ID to support his alias, but I doubt he made one for the victim. He would not choose somewhere where they would have to fly to reach the lodge, because he would avoid having both their names in the flight manifest," Daniel said.

"Correct, and it would not be close to the mountain lodge as well, because there will always be a chance that the locals in the nearest town would remember them, especially since he's an attractive man," his father said.

"I think they will stay in a city rather than a small town," Julius piped in. "They would be less noticeable there, because the population is bigger, and his presence would be less noted."

They all agreed.

Mateo pointed the remote control to the ceiling and a screen lowered. A minute later, they were looking at the satellite view of the mountain lodge.

"Gentlemen, we are going to do a thorough search of the major cities and towns within half a day's drive from the mountain lodge. According to the *Aswang*..." His father cleared his throat. "I mean, the man who found her body, it was around two p.m. when he heard the scream. We know they just arrived that day. They did not have time to unpack. So, given those facts, let us assume they left early from their residence. I doubt if it would be farther than four hours' drive. She was pregnant, and she would need a stop-over on the way. I have a feeling that he would avoid that. So, we are talking about four to six hours' drive at the most. Let us focus on cities and big towns within that range," Mateo said.

The marching order was settled and given to Ben and Julius and the three other teams involved in the investigation.

"Again, gentlemen, extreme caution, and secrecy, please..." Mateo reminded the two men as they prepared to leave for their task.

"Sure, we will also avoid calling the killer an *Aswang* so as not to panic the people..." Julius joked, oblivious to the truth.

His father winced at the reminder of his earlier slip. "Well, yeah. That would be wise... Although it seems fitting given the way he murdered the woman and the child," Mateo added.

Julius laughed and took the explanation at face value. Being a *non-Veil-bound* human, they kept Julius in the dark about the killer's real nature. It was a delicate balancing act for an investigation agency that handles both human and *Viscerebus* cases.

They all departed: Ben and Julius to their tasks, he and his father to Edrigu's office. They were meeting him for lunch.

Daniel realised he got sidetracked from the original purpose of his visit to his father's office. He wanted to tell him about his participation in *Project Chrysalis*, and his *Mejordia* blood. A few more days of delay would not hurt.

After all, he had only donated blood. So far.

The memorial for Martin was quiet and formal. The attendance was small: herself, Emme, Íñigo, Katelin, Edrigu, and Yuana.

Only six people knew of Martin's life and death. It was heart-rending. With his talent, he would have been world-famous, beloved internationally. Had she not stolen his mind away, his departure from this world would not have been this sad. But it was too late now. Ximena could not undo what she did. Martin had no relatives when he came to the country to follow her half a century ago. And they hid him from the world shortly after. He had no one but her.

To honour him, they arranged the most beautiful sendoff she could manage. It was a human ceremony rather than a *Viscerebus* one, with a priest, prayers, and songs.

They cremated Martin's body after the ceremony and laid his ashes in a niche Ximena bought for him at GJDV columbarium. Her father offered a place in their mausoleum, but she declined. She did not know if Martin wanted his remains to rest amidst their kind. She would force nothing unto him anymore.

The atmosphere afterwards was subdued, because she was. Her sister Katelin offered to stay with her while they waited for the ashes of Martin, but she refused. She was in no mood to talk to anyone. She did not realise Emme and Íñigo stayed behind as well until the ashes arrived.

It was in an alabaster urn, not the traditional wood, ceramic, or metal vessel their kind preferred. Martin's only attempt in sculpting was with alabaster. He used to say the stone called to him to sculpt, and the design came after he saw the stone. It was only fitting he rested in one. It was the stone's final summons to Martin.

Íñigo and Emme accompanied her to place Martin's ashes into his niche. Ximena placed the letters she wrote him for almost five decades, letters he never got to read. She sealed those with his ashes. It was time he received them. The act was almost the final farewell, and it was both freeing and binding.

With his crypt closed, Ximena had one last thing to do to put him to rest. She would sort through Martin's items and everything she had connected to him. Part of her did not feel up to it, but she could lose her courage if she delayed.

"Mena, where are you going?" Emme asked to her retreating back, concern on her face.

"I am going to finish everything today, wrap things up," she replied over her shoulder.

"Can I come and help you?" Emme said. There was pleading in her voice. "I need to help, Mena..."

She nodded. Together, they walked out of the hall. Íñigo, grim and silent, followed them. He seemed determined to be with her to the end. Íñigo drove them to an old but well-maintained 1920s-era house she bought decades ago. This was the first time Emme and Íñigo would see it. But this was a familiar location for her – the site of both comfort and torment, her penance and restitution. For forty-eight years.

Ximena's caretaker opened the gate to allow the car in. The five-bedroom structure housed all the paintings Martin did in his life. She had started with one bedroom upstairs and when that became full, moved to the other four. Every room was filled with vertical painting racks where each canvas hung. Not a single work was displayed on any of the walls.

They stood by the entry of the living room as they surveyed the extensive physical manifestation of Martin's mind. There was a single art propped against the wall. Martin's last – the one he was unable to complete. It was a painting of her face, one iris unfinished.

As she wandered around the room, the caretaker approached her, carrying a small file box.

"Miss Mena, your office sent me this. Your secretary said that it came from the hospital," he said, handing the box to her.

"Thank you." She took it and threw a questioning look toward Emme, who shrugged her shoulders.

"Go on, open it," Emme urged her.

She did. Inside it were Martin's brushes, the bristles hardened by the dried-out paint. The smell of solvent teased her nostrils. Underneath the brushes was a flat parcel wrapped in brown paper. She fished it out of the box and found the small yellow post-it note attached to it that said: *We found this under Mr Bell's bed.* It was a small painting the size of a magazine.

Ximena looked at it and recognised it with a jolt. It was the one she modelled for Martin when they first met in Paris, fifty-five years ago. She remembered the golden spaghetti-strapped evening dress, the jewelled gold combs that held her hair in place, and the red rose in her hand that he gave her that day. A rush of emotions accompanied the images that bombarded her, squeezing at her heart so tight it became hard to breathe.

"How did this painting come to be in his possession?" she asked Emme.

"I don't know. Maybe it was among his things when we brought his brushes to him?" Emme said.

That was possible. She did not sort through his things when she brought his painting paraphernalia to him. Ximena tried to recall those early days of his treatment, when they had to sedate him, when one of his attending nurses left a pencil by mistake, and he used the wall of his room to sketch an image. They discovered then that he could be pacified and occupied if he painted. And they have kept him supplied with painting materials ever since.

"You didn't change at all," Íñigo said over her shoulder, looking at the painting in her hand.

"You're too generous." She shook her head in disagreement. "I have grown older."

"No, you look the same. What changed was the lost sparkle in your eyes," Íñigo said. His finger hovered over her face in the painting. He looked at her. "You allowed sadness and guilt to determine how you take your conscious breath in the morning."

She sighed. There was so much truth in what Íñigo said.

"Are these all his works?" Íñigo asked as he looked around him.

"Yes," she said. "All five decades worth. Browse if you wish."

"What do you plan to do with these? Sell them?" he asked as he inspected the third painting hanging on the rack.

"No, I plan to keep them. I own them. I've been buying all his paintings over the years. If he had... recovered, he would have woken up a rich man," she replied.

The statement surprised Íñigo. He glanced at Emme for confirmation. Emme nodded.

Íñigo continued leafing through the hanging paintings. They were of the same colour scheme and dark theme. Martin Bell's work carried a certain eeriness, but the scenes were compelling. His talent, undeniable.

Something in them raised the hairs at the back of his neck. The scenes were all different, but there was a common thread in each frame. Íñigo flicked through one painting after another until he encountered one that had two burning wolf's eyes. Something drew him in. He leaned in to look at it closer. Then he saw the commonality in Martin's art. In the pupils of the eyes of the wolf, a silhouette of a woman – Ximena.

It was the same silhouette in the painting she posed for. He flicked back to the previous ones and a few of the succeeding ones. Every single one of them had the same shadowy figure in one form or another, reflected in the eyes of the wolf, hidden among the bark of the trees, the tufts of wolf fur, the dark shades in the leaves, camouflaged as a shadow or a cloud.

It was on every canvas.

Martin painted each one of these with Ximena in his subconscious – or *a conscious, running theme in his every brush stroke...*

Íñigo went to the last work of Martin, the unfinished one propped against the wall. He found the same figure in the eyes of the wolf. The iris in one eye that looked unfinished had a silhouette painted in muted grey and black. The other iris had the golden tone of the original painting that Ximena posed for.

He turned to Ximena and Emme, who watched him, their expressions puzzled and inquiring.

"He finished it, after all," he said and turned the painting around to show the two ladies.

Both women walked towards him, their eyes focused on the canvas. Their gasps of comprehension came almost at the same time.

"It is in all of his work," he stated quietly.

Ximena took in a quavering breath. Her face reflected her every thought and emotion as she realised she was more in Martin's head than she had ever thought.

"I am as human in Martin's inner reality, just as I was a monster in his outer. I am there, beneath the layers of his fear. He never lost touch with who I was, and perhaps what I was in his life," she rasped, tears glistening in her eyes.

Ximena looked at the painting again, and the confusion in her eyes cleared. Like him, she saw the menace in Martin's art fade and be replaced by melancholy. It now carried a cry of pain. A silent scream of love.

"It's in every canvas, Mena. In his every stroke," he said, every syllable was a stab to his heart, but it had to be said. Even he could not deny the stark truth.

Ximena nodded, as she flicked through the other paintings hanging on the rack. "Yes, I can see that now. It is the same message. His pain underneath the fear, the love behind his terror. It was like he had been trying to break free from the prison of his mind all those years. It was loud and clear but I never heard it, never saw it. Not among the thousands of paintings that I kept." Ximena's emotionless statement carried a ton of guilt, regret and self-recrimination.

And it scared him to hear it in her voice – the possibility that Ximena would continue to punish herself even after Martin had been dead and buried.

He must do something about it. He would not allow it to go further. Martin's death should be the beginning of the end of his hold on Ximena's heart.

Emme saw everything that Martin tried to say all those years, through every art he created. Her failure to understand him washed over her in waves of agony that broke through the tight control she placed on herself, and tears poured unhindered down her cheeks.

She approached his treatment with a stoic determination to wipe away her mistake. Guilt and injured pride prevented her from seeing the signs. He was there, just underneath the surface. She could have brought him out sooner if she had just paid attention.

All those wasted years.

She had failed Martin and Ximena. She allowed her own selfish love, one she denied over the years, to keep her heart and mind closed. The key to Martin's prison was in her hands all this time, but she allowed him to be trapped there until he died.

The consequence of her self-denial crashed into her. And it was magnitudes more than she could handle.

Roald knocked on Daniel's door, surprised when Mateo opened it. "Good afternoon, sir," he said.

Mateo's eyes widened upon seeing him, but stepped aside to let him in. "Good afternoon, Roald. Come in. Daniel is not home yet, but he should be here soon." Daniel's father gestured towards the couch.

"I know, sir. I spoke to him. He said he was five minutes away," he replied, and sat in the middle of the couch.

"Can I get you anything to drink?" Mateo called over from the kitchen.

"Beer is good, sir," he replied.

Mateo returned with two chilled beers and handed one to him.

"Are you and Daniel going out?" Mateo asked, taking a swig from his bottle.

Roald shook his head. "No, sir. I just want to talk to him about something."

Mateo regarded Roald with a paternal expression. "How are you doing, Roald? How are you coping with everything?"

He knew what Mateo referred to. "I am well, sir. Still adjusting." He chugged his beer to avoid answering more questions. It was not pleasant to be reminded of his cowardice.

"Just reach out if you need help, Roald. You're my son's closest friend, you are like a son to me," Mateo said in a tone he had not heard the older man use on him before.

And he felt touched and emboldened. "Thank you, sir. I might just do that soon." His desire to re-train in *Kali* and *karambit* surfaced. Mateo sounded sincere in his offer. He figured that, as a military man, Mateo must know the best training schools.

"Anytime, Hijo, anytime," Mateo replied.

"Sir, I am looking to return to *Kali* training, especially in the use of *karambit*. Can you recommend a trainer or a school?"

Mateo looked at him in silence for a moment and then smiled. "I will train you myself if you want. You can join Daniel and I; we train every week."

"Oh, that is generous of you. Are you sure, sir? I do not want to intrude in your father and son time..." He didn't know how Daniel would feel at his intrusion.

Mateo waved his hesitance away. "I am sure... And you would not be intruding."

"Then, I would love to train under you," he said, elated. Daniel once told him that his father was one of the best in the country, that Mateo travelled all over the world to train the special military forces of other nations, humans and *Viscerebus* alike. "I hope Daniel won't mind," he added.

"What won't I mind?" Daniel asked as he stepped into the living room, dropping his car keys on the side table by the door.

"I invited Roald to join us in our weekly *Kali* training," Mateo replied.

"Oh, I don't mind. It would reduce my bi-monthly beer blowout to once every three weeks," Daniel said. He got himself a beer, some potato chips, and sat down with them.

Mateo laughed at his raised eyebrows. "We take turns treating each other with beer at the end of every session," he explained.

"Oh... Okay, I can do that," he said. It did not sound so burdensome.

"It's not so bad if it is just us three but wait till your beer-buying schedule falls on the quarterly team training that my father does. You would not dismiss the responsibility so casually. It's a lot of beer, and it's free flowing." Daniel grinned.

"Oh, I am sure Roald can afford it," Mateo joked and patted him on the shoulders. "Forty or so people drinking for three hours would not break his bank," he continued.

Father and son laughed in unison at the look of alarm on his face.

Mateo stayed to finish his beer, and they bantered with each other like men do. There was something intense about the relationship of Daniel and his father, a camaraderie of shared experience and pain. He never noticed this in his past get-togethers with father and son. But then, his lens in life was uncomplicated then.

Mateo left them for his appointment soon after. Daniel told him under his breath that Mateo was going out on a date – with a *Vis in Transit*.

"What is a *Vis in Transit*?" His imagination pictured a winged humanoid with fangs and claws.

"Most *Vis* relocate to a different country at certain times in their life, usually at thirty-year intervals so the humans in their community do not notice how slow they age. It used to be every twenty years, but the popularity of cosmetic surgery allowed for a longer period to stay in a community. They could return to their *Patriam*, their birthplace, only when the humans in their youth have died out," Daniel explained. There was a slight grimace on his face and an edge to his tone.

"So, Yuana needs to do this soon?" He did not like the idea of her getting uprooted from here, from him.

Daniel shook his head.

"No, Yuana and their family did what most prominent *Vis* do in their youth. They never established roots to begin with. Like all her family members, Yuana had moved constantly, every six years since she was born. She does not have childhood friends, high school cliques, college circles."

That struck Roald as depressing – the idea that his Yuana never formed a bond of friendship as a child, never had sleepovers, or whatever girls do in their youth when they band together. No wonder she kept all her other relationships casual.

Daniel was the only real friend, the longest friendship Yuana ever had. They shared common experiences – a history together, a part of her past. And Roald couldn't quite decide whether he would be thankful or threatened.

"Dan, are you really not bothered if I join you and your father in your weekly *Kali* training? I do not want to disrupt your time with your father," he said, shaking the nip of insecurity from his mind.

Daniel smiled, a crooked, self-deprecating one. "No, don't worry about it. I believe my father feels, well, fatherly over you. He felt somewhat... responsible... like a parent would, since you are my closest friend."

"Responsible for what?" Roald didn't understand why Mateo Santino would feel that way. He waited for Daniel's explanation, but Dan merely shrugged and avoided his gaze. An awkward silence followed.

"Yuana is right. There is something bothering you. And I think it has something to do with me," Roald said bluntly.

A shadow of emotion crossed Daniel's face, and he looked hesitant for a split second. He got the impression that Daniel was battling with a big decision, and whether to tell him.

"Remember the work I am doing with Yuana's aunt?" Daniel said after a deep breath.

"Yes, you said it was unpleasant..."

"In a manner of speaking. You know I am a half-blood, an *Erdia.* I have been contributing my blood to Tita Ximena's top-secret experiment that traces the link between human and *Viscerebus.*"

"Why is it top secret?" Roald frowned.

Daniel's expression fell, like he could not believe he let that information slip. "Well, anything a *Vis* tells you, including from a half-blood like me, has to be a secret, and in this case, Tita Ximena does not want the information about the research to come out yet." Daniel's explanation was sound, a scowl on his face.

"So, what is unpleasant about it?" Roald asked half a minute later when no other information was forthcoming.

"I qualified for this project not because I am friends with Tita Ximena, but because I have a specific genetic strain, a perfect mix of human and *Vis,*" he said. A pause followed. "I live in both worlds, yet I do not belong to either. I am neither human nor *Vis.* And getting reminded about it every day is unpleasant." A heavy sigh followed Daniel's response. But Roald suspected there was more to it than what Daniel was willing to reveal.

"I want to say I understand, but obviously I will never be able to. What I can empathise with is being in pain, although it may not come from the same source as yours, it hurts just the same," Roald said.

A heavy silence followed. It was emasculating to reveal so much vulnerability to someone else. Daniel seemed to suffer from a similar difficulty in this emotion-baring exercise that neither of them were used to doing.

"If you ever tell anyone what I told you today, I am going to break your nose," Daniel said in a mock threat.

"And reveal to that same someone I am a drama queen? Not on your fucking life," he replied.

Daniel raised his bottle for a toast; Roald raised his. Both bottles met with a clink.

"To pain," Daniel said.

"To relief," he replied.

11

OLD FRIENDS, NEW FOES

Kazu looked out of the roof deck of the penthouse unit; the perfect launch pad for flying out at night. He surveyed the area beneath him, studying the lay of the land by the glitter of lights that peppered the streets. His night vision engaged.

Soon he would start Yuana's lesson, to establish and strengthen her trust in him, to bond auras with her. Once they become *aurally* fused, as her *Aztarim*, he could imprint her with his wisdom and influence. She would be his prime *Aztarima.*

Yuana and he, as destiny foretold it, must move as one to ensure the fated *Shift* would benefit their kind. And the looming change was already underway. Yuana remained unaware of its impending arrival, but she must be made ready when it comes. The element of surprise served them well for now – both during training, and for keeping them under the radar of those who would oppose and be threatened by their life mission.

Kazu sat down at the corner of the four-foot concrete security wall around the roof deck, folded his legs into a full lotus position, and closed his eyes. He inhaled and took in the smell of his surroundings, the hum of traffic and muted honking of a multitude of vehicles below. His breath released in slow degrees, his muscles relaxing with the exhale, his heartbeat slowing. Three more times and his mind shifted from thinking into knowing.

Within minutes, his brain settled into the familiar theta waves as he communicated his desires and goals out into the ether, to the rest of his *Aztarimas.*

Eventually, he received answering brain waves from the individuals he had imprinted, his disciples. Their auras flowed back to him and told him that everything he desired was accepted and would be put into action as he wanted it. He was satisfied. The place was high enough to broadcast and receive vibrations, and everything was going according to his grand plan.

Yuana looked around the haze of city life that surrounded her and the flickering lights carpeting the streets below. Her new take off pad presented challenges Mt Halcon did not have. The remoteness of their holiday home and the cover of the woods made her feel safe. Her parents' open-air garden on top of the highest building in the city did not have such natural defence. The difference could not be starker.

She had to wait for the workers remodeling her unit next door to leave for the day before she could take to the air. She did not have to do that in Villa Bizitza. Here, she was in the middle of a densely populated city, with millions of potential witnesses to her flying lesson. There, her only audience were the creatures of nature.

Yuana took a deep breath in, her abdomen and chest expanding, then released it in slow degrees as she squeezed the air out. She repeated it twice more until her nerves settled. She stood naked in the middle of the outdoor garden, and with one more breath, transformed.

The tingling at the base of her spine, the stretching sensation on her shoulder blades, the heat from her core that spread all over her body from head to toe, and the vibration of her skin – all the familiar sensations of shape-shifting. She could transform now in less than half a minute, but she aimed to achieve an instantaneous *syne-morphosis* next time.

Her wings stretched, flexed, and lifted her off. She flapped a few times to reach the altitude she wanted, then soared higher and surfed the air. She was to meet Kazu in midair over in Quezon City. Her unerring avian senses guided her.

Twenty minutes later, she sensed him long before she saw his figure on the horizon. They circled each other a few times before they flew together towards the tallest building in the area.

She landed on the rooftop. Kazu was not far behind. He wore a wide smile on his face as he landed beside her.

"You look strong out there, Yuana. Were you having fun?" He looked so pleased she felt an answering delight in her.

"It was unbelievable." She was breathless in her excitement.

"Did you have a hard time finding me?" Kazu's eyes glittered.

"No. I followed my instinct. I think I could sense true north. And then I saw you." As soon as she said it, she realised it was true. She possessed magneto receptors like most birds do.

Kazu nodded, satisfaction in his smile. "Yes, you have a natural avian ability to do that."

Her excitement doubled. "So, what am I going to learn today?" She flexed her wings, shaking water off her feathers.

Kazu laughed at her eagerness. "Can you echolocate?" he asked.

"I don't know. Shall we see if I can?" she replied. "What do I do?"

"You create sounds by vibrating your tongue with your mouth closed, like this," Kazu said, creating a series of high pitched, clicking sounds.

"Like this?" She copied what she heard. Kazu nodded approvingly.

"Now, try again, but close your eyes this time and listen with both your inner and outer ears for the echoes that come back to you. The bigger the object, the louder the echo waves. The longer it takes for the echo to return to you, the farther the object is," he explained.

"Inner and outer ears?" *I have them both? What is the difference?*

Kazu nodded. "Your outer ear lets you hear the sound; the inner ear makes you feel the sound. Now, do it again."

It was strange that Kazu seemed able to read her thoughts. She closed her eyes and clicked her tongue and was astonished by the result. Kazu was right. She did not just hear the echoing sounds; she felt its vibrations. It was as tangible as if she touched the surface of where her clicks bounced off.

Kazu's triumphant expression arrested the thrill that ruled her heart at the experience. He had an almost manic glint in his eyes.

"How does it feel to echolocate?" His excitement was palpable, as solid as a shared experience between two individuals.

"Indescribable... But will it not give our location away?" The sounds were so distinct she worried it would draw attention.

Kazu shook his head. "It is on a frequency that people could not pick up without sensitive equipment. Some animals could, though."

"Does it work on air?"

"Sure. I use it when I fly high, so I don't run into planes, or when I fly low enough to hit mountain peaks, tall structures and trees." Kazu's eyes twinkled in jest. "Come, let's see what else you can do..."

He taught her how to use the aerodynamic advantage of her *Animus*' physical design to achieve a faster speed and a more efficient use of energy.

Then he tested her newfound ability and agility as they sped towards each other in death-defying velocity, then swerving before they collided head on. With her eyes closed. It required nerves of steel. And during the rest break, Kazu gave her pointers on the various potential uses of her new skill.

When it was time for her to go home, with equal ease, they both took off from the roof and flew in opposite directions. It was her last opportunity to apply her echolocation skills as she flew within the thick clouds. She dived from the great height she was surfing on, low enough to detect the echoes from the buildings below. Her senses told her she had about an hour before she was to meet Roald at a bar close to her new unit. She needed to hurry.

Yuana hovered within the cloud cover, and with her vision, she peered through to check for people in her parents' open garden. She saw no one. Once more, she combined sight and echolocation. The reverberation confirmed what she saw. The sounds that bounced came from solid structures, not the soft flesh of man or beast.

It was safe to fly down. She waited until the cloud cover hovered above the tip of her building and plunged, headfirst. She hurtled down like a speeding bullet.

At one hundred feet from the penthouse's pebbled garden floor, Yuana righted herself, her wings and tail spread wide, to slow and halt her descent. She landed with a soft thump in the middle. Her human form returned by the time she reached the door. She was wet from the evening dew, and the night air made her shiver.

She would warm herself inside and change back into her clothes, then drive to meet with Roald.

Yuana stepped out of the hot shower. She had washed off the scent of night air and smog that clung to her when she came in. It was a lucky coincidence the previous owner of the unit had left some bath towels, perhaps by accident, in the bathroom of the second bedroom.

I must remember to furnish my parent's unit with new towels.

She fixed her make-up using whatever she had in her portable vanity kit – moisturiser, pressed powder, lipstick, lip gloss and mascara.

She was fifteen minutes late. Roald was already halfway on his first drink when she got to the bar.

"Sorry I'm late, Ro." She kissed his cheek in apology.

His arm snaked around her waist and pulled her close. His mouth nuzzled her collarbone, savouring her scent.

"Hmm. You smell fresh," he murmured. "What kept you?" He pulled away to look into her eyes, his arms draped around her.

"I had to consult with the architect on the changes I want in my unit, and it took the workers a bit of time to leave as well. Then, I had to speak with my parents about what they want done in their unit to get it ready when they return home. That would be in two days," she said, her alibi preplanned, rehearsed and half-true.

"Oh, are they? They were away for a long time," Roald commented as he handed her the drinks menu.

"Yeah. They extended their honeymoon."

"You miss them?" he asked, one arm still draped around her as he took a sip of his drink.

"Yes, of course. I am very close to my mother, and I have gotten close to my father as well." She picked on his bowl of nuts and chips, popping some into her mouth. "It upset Mama that she was not here when Martin died. She wanted to be here for Tita Ximena."

"Martin who?" Roald asked, a frown on his brows.

"Oh... ah... he's a long-time close friend of my aunt... he died a few days ago." She could kick herself for revealing that to Roald. She had forgotten that Roald was not privy to their family secret.

"Oh, okay. You never mentioned him before." Roald's gaze was intent, his face wiped of any expression.

"I never met him. And his death was quite sudden." She chewed more nuts to avoid meeting his eyes.

"When is the funeral?"

"Uhm... I think it was held weeks ago." She felt relieved when her drink arrived. She took a hasty sip so Roald would not ask more questions about it.

"Okay. I was just wondering if we need to attend it." Roald shrugged.

She shook her head. "No need. By the way, how's Daniel? Did you speak to him yet?"

Roald smiled and nodded. "Yes, we spoke, and he told me about his participation in your aunt's project."

His response gave her pause. "And did he mention what was bothering him?"

"Yes. He was being a drama queen, spouting about not belonging, being a half-breed." Roald exaggerated a dramatic sigh.

She chuckled. It seemed Daniel kept his being an Iztari a secret, and Mateo's part in Roald's trauma. "Half-blood, you mean. It's more politically correct," she said.

Roald smiled and nodded. "Okay, half-blood it is, then. But seriously, I did not realise it was a thorny issue for him." The frown that appeared on his forehead belied the levity of his tone.

"Yes. It is. I think all the travelling he did with his father when he was young contributed to that. He did not have friends growing up. It was hard to do that when you travel so much." She knew all about having a friendless, gypsy-like childhood.

"Just like you did," Roald said, his eyes gentle, his expression understanding.

"Yes... It was a price our kind pays for living such a long life." The bitter tang of that truth was no longer easy to ignore.

"Is this why your relationships before me were all casual?" Roald touched her cheek with gentle fingertips to compel her to look at him.

She chewed on her lower lip. "Yes, I think so. I am not used to forming long-term relationships outside of my family. I did not want to get hurt like my mom."

"All of those men would not have let you go... I speak from experience here," Roald said, a slight smile on his face.

"I will always be left behind, Ro. Even by you... because your lifespan is shorter than mine." Tears pricked at the back of her eyes.

That stopped him. Roald could not refute her statement. Instead, his jaw tightened. He swallowed as if he found the idea gut-wrenching. "Why did you decide to gamble on me, then? Why not someone from your kind? Just like your grandparents," he asked. His intense gaze went straight to her soul, not giving her any quarter.

"We cannot tell a heart who to love," she sighed. He said nothing, but his gaze remained fixed on her. "You got through my armour, like no man, human or *Vis* ever did. How you managed it, I have no idea."

"We were meant to be together. You were not the only one who had a wall around the heart." He pulled her closer, his forehead touched hers. "Time may not be on our side, Yuana, but we will make every single hour we have worth it for us. We will not leave room for anything but love and joy between us. Nothing." His whisper was raw.

She closed her eyes at the sweetness of his declaration. She still had secrets he needed to know. He shook her when she did not respond, prodded her to promise, to commit. She nodded, and that earned her a quick kiss on the tip of the nose.

Roald let go of her, his eyes glittering. He turned his head away and downed his drink, his throat working furiously as he chased his emotions down with the spirit.

"Miss, is someone using this chair?"

Startled, she looked up to find the inquiring gaze of the server. She nodded her permission. She could not speak as Roald's hands clasped her free hand. He kept it enfolded in his for most of the night. Captive, like her heart.

Ximena sank deep against the comfortable couch. The plump upholstery firmly cushioned her back, her bare feet elevated on the leather footstool, a glass of wine in her hand.

She felt emotionally drained, and physically sapped. It had been a long day. She had asked Nita to bring her a slice of the liver she brought from

GJDV. Her family would come down for their *sustenance* in the next half hour, but she did not want to wait for them for her portion. She needed a pick me up.

Nita was by her side two minutes later, the *victus* on a small plate. Ximena popped it into her mouth, savouring the warmth and the metallic flavour of raw liver as it slid down her throat. She washed it down with a gulp of red wine.

Within seconds, she sighed in relief as the feeling of well-being enveloped her – the warming of her insides, the loosening of tight muscles, and the tingling of electric energy that spread to her every nerve. Her eyes closed as the power of the human liver coursed through every fibre of her being.

She would think of Martin later. Familiar footsteps came down the stairs - her mother's lighter treads and her father's heavier ones.

A slight weight landed on her lap. Her lids flickered open. It was a thick parcel. Her mother had a small smile on her lips.

Her eyebrows quirked up in inquiry.

Margaita's smile widened. "Open it." Her mother sat down beside her and poured wine for herself.

She placed her wineglass down and slit the envelope open with her nails. The embossed gold and crimson logo of the *Supreme Viscerebus Tribunal* was the first thing that greeted her sight as she pulled out the document.

It was an approval letter – for *Viscerebi* trial for the *Altera* serums. The *Tribunal* approved it within a week of her submission.

Eyes wide, she glanced at her mother. She had expected the process to take at least six months at the earliest. "You expedited it?" she asked, still incredulous.

Margaita's smile had a tinge of smugness. "Well, I would not say that. I merely badgered them to decide on it faster than usual."

"Your mother kept the request top of mind among the scientific team, harassed them to read and study it and come out with the recommendation. And then she called every single one of the *Tribunal* members and cajoled each until they all agreed to approve it," her father said dryly as he sat across from her.

She looked at her mother in awe, speechless.

Margaita chuckled. "You're welcome, Mena."

"Thank you, Mama. It cannot come at a more perfect timing," she said, glad to have something monumental to keep her attention. Between *Project Chrysalis* and *Altera*'s *VM* cure, she would not have much time to think of Martin's death.

"I know, Mena, I know..." Margaita said, patting her hand, her gaze knowing.

Ximena could not wait for tomorrow to come. Íñigo would be pleased. *Should I call and tell him now? No, I will wait until tomorrow and surprise him.*

Five minutes later, she sent a message to Íñigo to meet her early for breakfast – her treat.

Íñigo was having a slice of fresh kidney with a glass of Black Velvet when Ximena's text came in. It was an invitation for breakfast. His heart leapt. They had shared many meals together in the past, but it was because they happened to be together during mealtimes. Ximena never initiated an invitation. This was the first.

With hope in his heart, he went down to the Spanish restaurant on the ground floor of his condominium. He would enjoy dinner tonight. If tomorrow morning proved to be the foot in the door of his lifelong goal, he would take up the open offer of Lorenzo to dine with them every night.

He seldom dined with the De Vidas because he did not want Ximena to discover his feelings for her, at least not until he was sure she was ready to receive him.

Íñigo brought a basket of blooms with him. He was going to call Emme or Katelin to ask what Ximena's favourite was, but he remembered she did not like receiving roses. He understood why after he saw Martin's painting of Ximena. Her dead lover could rest in peace with the roses. He would make his mark with daisies instead, the flower for new beginnings.

Ximena arrived about two minutes later. There was a certain calm about her that pleased him. She looked like a woman prepared to move on from her past. A woman with a purpose. He kissed her cheek in greeting and pulled the chair for her.

"Good morning, Íñigo. Did I make you wait?" There was a glint in her eyes.

"Good morning, Mena. And no, I arrived about a couple of minutes before you did."

He would match her cool composure and wait for her to tell him what this breakfast was about. But she picked up the menu and perused it at leisure. He did the same – or at least pretended to. His senses focused on her, aware of every page she flipped.

With an impatient huff, she laid her menu flat; her face flushed with excitement. "Oh, daimon! I can't keep a secret," she said.

That made him grin. He lowered his own menu down and inclined his head towards her. She harrumphed at his silence, jerked her purse open and pulled out a thick, folded document and handed it to him. He saw a glimpse of the *Tribunal* logo, and it wiped the smugness off his smile. He opened it and scanned it quickly. His eyes went to her as he understood what the document meant.

"Holy *Aquila*! We can start live trials this soon?" he whistled under his breath. Ximena's smile was wide and self-congratulatory.

"Yes, indeed! We can start the trials immediately. We just need volunteers. And we can send memos globally!" Ximena's excitement made her voice rise an octave higher.

"Hey, Mena, calm down a little. We cannot just do a global announcement of our project. If we fail, it will be a public relations disaster, not just for our company, but for your family. Not to mention our competitors. I have intel they are pursuing the treatment for VM using amniotic fluid. It would not take much of a leap for them to go the way of the cure like we did," he said, half laughing.

Ximena's lips pursed in annoyance. "Yes, you're right... as usual."

"So, let's plan how we can elicit the voluntary participation of pregnant women in our community. The procedure is not exactly calming," he said dryly.

She nodded. "Let's think through it over breakfast," she sighed and picked up the menu.

He fished out the flower basket from under the table and placed it in front of her. Her eyes widened in surprise.

The profusion of the white and yellow blooms in the blue basket matched her attire by coincidence. The desire to snap a photo of her and his flowers was followed by regret he could not do so.

"Oh, thank you! What is this for?" Ximena was delighted.

"For this morning," he said with a small smile.

Ximena watched him over her menu for a while. She looked intrigued, as if she was trying to understand the reason for the gesture. As she placed the basket on the chair beside her, she noticed the card attached to it. It said, *"To new beginnings."*

"How apt," she said.

He looked down at his menu, the smile on his face widening.

Yes, Mena, and you have no idea how relevant it is.

Íñigo and Ximena considered a few options to secure the source of their cure – cord blood. And how to convince the pregnant women of the *Viscerebi* community to donate them.

They surmised those with close family members who suffered from *VM* would be an easy source. The nobility of saving the life of a loved one would be enough inducement.

For the *Erdia* women, they would appeal to their vanity and desire to remain youthful to match the slow aging of the *Vis* women. It was a point of envy for them and had been for centuries. That, too, would be an easy sell.

However, to the *Viscerebus* women with no personal reason to compel them, they would need a stronger incentive.

They had eliminated the danger to both mother and infant because the harvesting of the material happens after birth. But to expand the efficacy of the cure beyond its current limit - the closest DNA match of the foetus - to one that would work on all the other *VM-infected Viscerebi*, they would need to overcome a bigger moral barrier. Their kind must stop looking at the procedure as something akin to eating their own.

They bounced ideas over cups of coffee and during the leisurely walk back to their lab. As they crossed the threshold, an epiphany came to Ximena.

"What if we collect and store the cord blood after every birth as a routine procedure? We would not need to secure permission from the mother." Her heart pounded at the potential of the idea.

Íñigo stared at her as if he could not believe what she was suggesting. "And you are okay with that? The missing consent?"

Íñigo seemed baffled by her statement and was doubtful that she meant it. She understood why. Ever since their underhanded experiment with Martin went wrong, she became an advocate for full consent. And what she just proposed was a departure from that advocacy.

Íñigo's gaze was still intent on her, waiting for her response.

Am I okay with taking away a woman's option to decide what to do with a part of her and her child?

She met his gaze dead on. "Yes. The material would be discarded after birth anyway. And this is for the greater good of our kind. It would also benefit humankind once we have developed the cure. It would eliminate the need for the *VM-infected* among us to hunt pregnant humans."

Íñigo was silent, but his gaze never left her face. She knew he gauged the sincerity of her statement. She refused to look away. Her chin jutted in defiance of his skepticism.

A flicker of emotion flashed in his eyes. And a shadow of a smile appeared on his lips. He nodded. "We need to make sure we tag every one of those births properly, including the *non-Veil-bound Erdias*," he said.

She smiled back. "We can thank *Prometheus* for Yuana's foresight and planning. She had lobbied three years ago to direct a portion of GJDV's Foundation budget to fund new hospital wings all over the country for maternal health care and women-centric medicine. We just need to extend the procedure to pregnant humans."

"That sounds like a plan. This would make it easy for us to get the raw materials. We can expand our operation with hospitals across the globe after a year. That would give us enough head start over our competitors. Then we can create the serums and make it easily accessible to our kind worldwide," Íñigo said, nodding.

She placed her basket of daisies at the centre of the floating shelves by the entrance to their lab. She held her hand out to him, eager to finalise their strategy. "To a wonderful new beginning..."

Íñigo took her hand in his and clasped it a split second longer before he shook it. "Yes, a new beginning..." he replied, his voice deep with satisfaction. A gleam in his eyes.

She wasn't sure what it was, but at the moment, she was eager to start with work. Íñigo was still rooted to the spot when she glanced back from her worktable, his expression unreadable.

Six years earlier.

Doctor Fari Wolff had a vague thought he needed his protective glasses adjusted as they kept sliding down his nose. It was quite annoying having to push the glasses back multiple times. The heat of the sun and the burner in front of him made his nose sweaty.

Maybe I need one that has a band that would secure it behind my head rather than this slip-on kind.

His team was busy generating liver cells in the lab using pig liver. They worked on a validating experiment by repeating their two previous successful results. If this one came out positive, the *Vivo Project* would begin its next phase – the experimentation with human liver. And he could not wait to start on that. The success of his work would supplement the need of the *Viscerebus*. They would not have to worry about the far-flung areas of the world where they could not operate because of the scarcity of the human population. Every one of his kind would not need to worry about human viscera shortage.

And finally, and more importantly, he would be more successful than Niko, his rascal twin. His mother would stop hounding him to marry a rich woman like Niko did. Their mother's hopes of having *Vis* grandchildren now rested solely on him as Niko married an *Erdia*. But with his limited social circle and lifestyle, he probably had slimmer chance of meeting a suitable *Vis* woman.

Sure, it would be good to find a life partner of his own, but he practically lived in the lab. And even if he did not, he did not have friends to socialise with. And he was awkward with women.

He was very lucky to get connected to his current sponsor, without whom their company and their project would not have happened. Mr Mori found him working at the University as a professor of Regenerative Medicine and offered to fund his dream project.

Now, hundreds of millions of dollars later, they were almost at the home base. The *Vivo* project would make him famous and very rich.

How am I going to find out who are the Iztari members of the investigative team?

His frowning face stared back at him as reflected by the dark whiskey glass in his hand. The temperature of his room was heavy as the humidity in the air. His thoughts hummed in sync with the air conditioner as he turned it on.

There were no public announcements except a vague statement from the *Iztari* office – they had found the identity of the woman, but no mention of her name.

Were the Iztaris bluffing? Did they even get the name right? Was it Narcisa?

It was tempting to visit the office of the *Iztaris* under a guise of some need, but Jacob could not think of a valid reason that would not arouse suspicion. And even if he did, it would be unlikely he would find out the names of those *Iztaris.* If it was a confidential case, it would not be common knowledge in their office.

There was a strategy to that secrecy. It could be a trap, and he did not want to make the mistake of walking into it.

He tried tailing Edrigu Orzabal, the *Chief Iztari,* for a few weeks, just to see if any of the *Iztaris* showed up to meet with him. But he never met with anyone outside the *Iztari* Office, except with a few who looked like they were businessmen, or *Tribunal* members.

He gave the idea up because it yielded nothing substantial. He could not spend his time following Edrigu, or any known *Iztari* commanders. It would require immense effort and resources to cover his bases. And it might expose his interest in the case.

What would I do if I were in their shoes, if I have the name of the victim and nothing else?

They would trace her previous whereabouts, the people associated with her. He believed he had that covered. It would be near to impossible to trace his movements after Narcisa moved in with him. He took great care to avoid any paper trails that could connect them.

Narcisa was the perfect choice; naïve and provincial. She did not have any friends or relatives in the city. He had forbidden her to use any social media and kept her isolated. For seven months, he had taken her travelling in the most remote places in the country. They never stayed long enough for her to make friends.

Poor Narcisa thought it was all romantic, that they were on a perpetual honeymoon. Her taste was simple, content to watch cable TV and read gossip magazines all day. Her little girl voice and uneducated views annoyed him. She was shallow, with little ambition and expectation in life; nothing of value in her except her girlish body. It was not a hardship to part with her. Still, she served her purpose – the vessel that provided his cure.

For now, his *harravis* habit called to him. His secret strategy made him smile. The *Iztaris* never knew, like his victims, that he had been indulging in his habit for over a decade. They were all too stupid to realise because there were no bodies to hide, no deaths.

And now, even the threat of *Visceral Metastasis* no longer held power over him. Now that he knew how to cure himself.

Thank Aquila for gullible women.

12

THE WARNING IN THE WIND

Yuana included regular late afternoon visits to her unit a few times a week. First, to view the development being done on it, then take off to fly. Today, she oversaw the cleaning of her parents' unit to prepare it for their return tomorrow night. She bought new bath towels, pillows, mattress, and bed sheets for them. Her mother would do the rest.

She waited until work time ended at five thirty p.m., and for the workers to leave. As usual, she locked up and moved next door, eager to be on air again.

The theory of combining her hyper-senses, echolocation and magneto receptor, then focusing it on a specific person or item was a thought that kept sprouting in her mind.

Will she be able to isolate and recognise individual sound waves? Or locate them from a distance? Perhaps she could run it by Kazu and see what he thinks.

She was waiting for the sun to go down, for the darkness to provide her cover, when her phone rang.

"Hi, sweetie," Roald's deep voice sounded cheerful.

"Oh, hey, Ro! Where are you?" They were to meet for a late dinner later, at eight-thirty.

"I'm very close to your building. My meeting finished early. I thought I would join you there and we can have dinner shortly, if that is okay?" he asked.

"Oh... sure. Let me call the guard now to give you an access card. Come upstairs when you arrive," she replied.

"Brilliant. I will be there soon. See you."

Flight lessons would have to wait till next time. This would be better if Roald knew about her abilities, so she did not have to sneak out. She sighed and phoned the reception to give them Roald's name and her instructions.

It was a good thing Roald called before she phoned Kazu. One disappointed *Apex* was enough for the night.

She debated for a second whether to open a bottle of wine but decided against it. They may not have the time. The outdoors beckoned. She opened the sliding door that led to the garden when she scented an unfamiliar human.

She sensed the stranger was just behind the side wall. She could hear his breathing and his elevated heartbeat. The odour of sun-browned skin and perspiration was strong. The stranger avoided detection with careful movements. Unluckily for him, she was not human.

Yuana weighed her options to step inside or deal with the stranger outside when the unseen man shifted. Her heartbeat picked up, adrenalin kicked in, and her muscles locked in preparation. She realised she was going to fight rather than run away.

The man shifted once more. He listened for her, waiting for her to come through the door. It may be more prudent to handle the situation outdoors to prevent any damage to the interior of her parent's home.

She stepped outside.

A burly man appeared from behind the big planter to her left. She recognised him. One of the workers in her unit. He must have sneaked in here earlier to wait for her.

"Can I help you?" she asked, her eyebrows arched.

He stared at her with a malevolent grin and took a step forward, his intent to do harm clear in the way he leered. His eyes were red-rimmed, his face oily, and he reeked of sweat, dust, and paint.

"You're beautiful... And I'm very lucky," he said and took another step closer. He was confident his body size, twice as wide, held the advantage over her slight form.

"Really? How so?" she smirked. She was tempted to transform into a panther just to scare him. But it would not do to have someone blabbing about that. He looked like the kind who would.

"I have not had an expensive woman like you before. You look clean and delicious." His voice was gruff and he was almost licking his lips. His hands fumbled on his belt as he took another step closer.

"Thank you, but I cannot say the same about you. You look smelly and disgusting." Despite her elevated pulse, she felt calm, her body poised for action.

The man's eyes narrowed in fury, and with a growl, he rushed at her, hands outstretched. Intuitively, her right foot stepped behind to anchor her as she drew her right hand back. Her fingers curled into a loose fist as she aimed the heel of her hand on his chest. She struck him dead center a second before his hands closed on her shoulders. The force threw the man backward, hitting against one of the huge potted trees. He slid down like a limp doll, unconscious.

A gasp and rushing feet from behind her announced Roald's presence. He stopped by her side, astounded. His gaze transferred to the heap of a man folded into himself a few feet away. She looked up at Roald, feeling both guilty and smug at the same time.

In silence, Roald turned back into the living room and lifted the phone to talk to reception.

"Please send security to the Pinnacle East Penthouse. A man tried to attack a resident... Thank you," he said dispassionately and replaced the phone.

Roald stared back at her, his eyes inscrutable. He seemed unable to voice whatever it was he wanted to say to her about what he saw. She looked at him closely – he did not seem scared, traumatised, or angry.

When the doorbell rang, Roald opened the door to let two security guys in. Each had one hand on their weapon, ready to draw it out. Roald led them to the still unconscious man out in the garden.

"Sir, what happened?" A guard addressed Roald, but his eyes darted between them. Roald looked at her; one eyebrow quirked in inquiry.

"He was hiding out in the garden, and he tried to assault me." She shrugged. Simple statements were always better in explaining away unnatural happenings.

"Do you know who he is?" the other guard asked.

"I think he's part of the team working on the other unit," she replied.

"So, he must have waited for you here, ma'am," the first guard said.

"Yes, I think so, too," she nodded.

"And, sir..." the guard threw a questioning glance at Roald, "here knocked him out?"

"Hmm, no... I pushed him, and he tripped on his own foot, fell back, and hit his head on the pot," she said, pointing toward the planter the man slumped against.

"Okay, ma'am." The second guard nodded, satisfied with her story. "We will take him from here and report him to the police." Both guards moved towards the fallen man.

"Are you pressing charges, ma'am?" the first guard asked over his shoulder as they hauled the man to his feet.

She shook her head, but Roald interjected, "Yes, she is," his voice firm and insistent. The taut jawline informed her that an argument would ensue if she contradicted him. She nodded in agreement.

"Okay, ma'am. We will ask the police to come and take your statement tomorrow," the first guard said.

The two guards lifted the insensible guy by the armpits, supporting his weight with their shoulders, and marched him out of the front door.

She walked to the bar and poured them both a drink – it was something to do while she waited for Roald to speak. He followed her and took one glass from her hand, then sat beside her on the couch.

"Did I witness you knock a guy down just by pushing him away?" Roald's voice was wondering, and awed.

"Well, it was more than a push. I aimed for his chest and took the wind out of him for a bit," she said. "That was my grandfather's signature move. He taught it to me when I was young. It was a precise spot on the chest..." she added when Roald remained quiet. She did not elaborate that the move required conscious control of energy to avoid fatal heart damage to a human recipient.

"But he flew back a few feet..." Roald said, still disbelieving.

"He didn't fly back, he staggered back," she corrected.

Roald frowned as if he doubted his memory of what he witnessed. "Still, that required strength," he insisted.

"Yes, it did... Does it bother you?" She could not tell if he was upset. Roald sounded unsure of what he saw.

He stopped and considered. "No, but it surprised me. I did not expect it since I have always seen you as a dainty little thing... I will not make that mistake again," he said, his mouth curved in a self-deprecating half-smile.

She leaned over and kissed him on the cheek, and settled her head on his chest, sighing with pleasure. This felt good, almost as good as flying.

"What did the guy want? To steal?" he asked. His long legs stretched out in front of him as he leaned back against the couch.

"I don't know if that was part of his eventual plans, but he had lascivious intent," she replied with a sigh.

Roald's muscles tensed when he heard that. She expected it, as Roald possessed a protective streak. She was prepared to soothe his basal instinct when he spoke.

"That poor shmuck was destined to lose consciousness tonight. If it wasn't by your hand, I would have pounded him to oblivion," he said, his frown dark and menacing. "I saw him rush at you when I came in; before I could reach you, I saw you fell him with one move," he added, looking down at her. "You've got a hidden Jolie in you, my sweet. Where did you learn that?" he asked.

"I would hardly call it that," she scoffed. "I'm no trained martial artist. It was just one move my grandfather taught me when I was fifteen."

"Why would he teach you something like that?" Roald sounded intrigued.

"I know some basic stuff. My mom does as well. We are strong, but my grandfather thinks that in the interest of safety and expediency, we should learn a few moves to leverage our strength. A few, precise moves meant to incapacitate the opponent quickly to ensure a quick escape from injury and exposure. He made me practise that move many times because if I apply full strength, it's fatal to a human," she said.

Roald's intrigue turned to alarm. "In the interest of safety? Were you in worse peril in the past? Worse than today?"

"It's for the safety of the human, not mine. If I didn't know a few strategic moves, I would act in panic and resort to my natural abilities – strength, speed, my *Animus*. Fear, strength and razor-sharp claws or fangs would be a gruesome combination. I would have harmed him more than what I did tonight if I acted out of fear," she explained, repeating what her grandfather drilled into her during those days of training.

Roald nodded. "Your grandfather did not want you to resort to animal instinct."

"Yes... and he was right. The knowledge calmed me, gave me a clear head," she said.

Roald hugged her, squeezed her harder a second longer, then kissed her temple and sat up. "So, shall we have dinner now? I'm starving and you probably are, too." He looked at her expectantly.

"Yes, let's..." She downed her drink and got up.

Roald did the same. He took both glasses to the sink and rinsed them. He then took the kitchen towel hanging on a hook and dried both glasses. She watched with a slight smile – he looked at home in her kitchen and at ease with domestic work.

Just as they were leaving, a text message came to her phone. It was Kazu and his message said, *'Are you flying tonight?'* She texted back her reply, *'Not tonight.'*

She placed her phone in her bag, took Roald's hand and walked with him out of the unit. Her disappointment at missing her flight lesson dissipated into the air.

Kazu took a deep breath to control the surge of impatience against Yuana. She was being irresponsible, allowing herself to be distracted by petty little things. He closed his eyes, quieted his mind, and tried to read her fixation from a distance.

In his mind's eye, he got snippets of her thoughts. The images were not as strong, as clear, or as fluid as he wanted, but it gave him an idea of what occupied her attention.

A man. And at the moment, she was more bonded to the human than to her destiny.

Kazu needed to do something about it. This man posed an obstacle to Yuana's full *emergence*. He would have to change his strategy to achieve *aural Aztarimar*, his imprinting on her consciousness, as soon as possible. The *Txandictus* was upon them.

First, he must know more about this man, and how crucial he was to Yuana, how deep their bond was. Second, he must intensify his training of Yuana, and hasten the imprinting. She needed to be committed to their mission before he revealed to the world her presence as the second *Apex*. Yuana must be one with him in heart and mind to fulfil their destiny as the *Dual Apex* of prophecy.

Ximena added human liver cells into the petri dish with bated breath. This would be the moment that would reveal if their theory on *Mejordia V genes* were correct. Within seconds, the thrill of confirmation struck her heart. The liver cells energised the specimen. Just like it would to any *Vis* cells. Except the specimen came from an *Erdia* and it behaved contrary to what a normal *Erdia* cell should do.

It should not react to liver cells, but it did. Just like the cells of the dead foetus. The next question that required an answer – would the reaction remain, or would it wane after a few hours?

The next few hours would be a long wait. But she knew in her bones her hypothesis was correct. Daniel's genes would need waking up.

Yuana and Roald walked into the restaurant hand in hand, towards the private corner they reserved. The restaurant was not busy yet, with three other tables occupied. As they sat down, Yuana had eye contact with a lone man seated at a table. He was a *Vis*, and he was ogling her with interest.

He nodded at her, and she gave him a polite nod back. It was a common courtesy among their kind – to acknowledge each other's presence among the sea of humans.

Roald went to the men's room after they placed their order. She was waiting for their drink when the man approached her. He was well-dressed and good looking, with shiny brown hair that fell over his forehead. He was slim and tall, although not as tall as Roald.

"Good evening," he said with a friendly smile on his face. He looked young, could be the same age as her, but there was something about his eyes that told her he was much older.

"Good evening," she replied in a pleasant tone. He could be a *Vis in Transit* and in need of connection to their local community.

"I would like to make your acquaintance while your companion is away." The man grinned, leaned closer, his hands on the table, a hard gleam in his eyes.

"Oh, you mean my boyfriend?" she asked.

"Your boyfriend? Why are you with a human and not our kind?" The stranger's tone was light, almost joking, his demeanour conspiratorial.

"Interesting... What makes you think that is any of your business?" She lost interest in helping him, no matter what his concerns were. She found his manners arrogant, inappropriate and presumptuous.

"Oh, I apologise. I did not mean to offend you. I was just curious." He raised his hand, palms flat together. His tone was apologetic, but his eyes flared at her tone. He was not sorry, and did not like her response.

She merely looked at him, one eyebrow raised, not wanting to say anything more biting. The man backed away, hands held up in a gesture of surrender, and walked back to his seat.

Roald returned just then. His eyes followed the man as he sat down.

"Who was that? Was he bothering you?" Roald's frown was deep. His legs splayed in a protective stance.

"He tried to. But I sent him away," she shrugged. She wanted Roald to relax. She did not want him to confront the man; the stranger seemed dangerous to her. And given the odious man was a *Vis,* Roald might be at a disadvantage.

"So, who was he and what did he want?" Roald persisted, still frowning.

"I don't know who he is. He wanted my name, so I made him go away." She kept her tone casual.

She tugged at his hand to make him sit down. Roald threw one last annoyed glance at the man, who was still looking at them with a petulant expression. She could feel Roald's temper rising. She was glad their drinks arrived at the right time.

"What a spoiled brat," Roald said, sipping his beer.

She smiled at him, taking a sip from her craft G & T. "He's no brat. He's older than us by at least a decade," she said.

"Really? How can you tell?" he asked, surprised.

"He's a *Vis,*" she said.

"Oh..." Roald glanced at the man again, who was now talking to a *Vis* woman seated at the next table. "He looks very young, he could pass off as a millennial," he added.

"Yes. We are like humans, you know. Some of us are gifted with youthful genes, just like some of your kind," she said, taking another sip.

"He's certainly good-looking," Roald commented.

She wrinkled her nose in distaste. "Not my type. I like my men manly looking. And I am already in love with one," she said.

He responded with a wide smile of pleasure. He reached out and ran gentle knuckles along her jaw, then took her hand and lifted it to his mouth.

"I am blessed that you are mine, my love, for you are a singular woman. Beautiful, smart, kind, strong and capable. You do not need me, but I am glad that you wanted me in your life." Roald's eyes glittered with emotion.

His words touched her to the very core. "You do not need me in your life, too, but you chose to have me in yours, despite what you have to...do..." And she meant it. Roald faced enormous mental challenge just to be with her.

"Allow me now and then to defend your honour, it is not good for my ego to be so... unnecessary." Roald's smile was lopsided, his tone almost sad.

"Sure, but you are wrong... You are necessary to me. Maybe not for defence, but for support, for love, for happiness. You are as necessary to me as air," she said as she touched his face.

He turned and pressed a kiss in the middle of her palm. His eyes darkened with emotion. The moment broke when the service staff approached them to inquire if they were ready to order.

As she flipped the menu pages, she noticed the *Vis* stranger got up and leave the restaurant with the *Vis* woman he was chatting with earlier. It seemed he picked up a date.

Jacob Montejo led his new target by the elbow towards his car. He had invited her to dine in another restaurant. He needed to take her to a place new to her. A place that she did not frequent, unlike the restaurant they came from. She was a regular there.

He turned on his full charm with a smile. She was an elegant young woman, witty, but too trusting. They chatted as they drove to a Greek restaurant, he knew his date had never been to. He tried to jog his memory as to her name – *Sally, yeah... it's Sally, a humanised version of her real name, perhaps.*

His success in getting her to where he wanted her soothed his aggravated temper when the other woman in the restaurant shut him down. *One of these days,* he promised himself, *I will have her. And not just as a source. She would pay for her insolence.*

They arrived at the restaurant where they spent an enjoyable evening.

He charmed her, plied her with drinks to loosen her inhibitions. And when she was not looking, he dropped a pill into her drink and waited for it to take effect.

Within ten minutes, she became dizzy. He paid their bill and played the concerned boyfriend. To the other patrons of the restaurant, he was a total gentleman, caring for his date who had too much to drink.

He ushered her to his car and drove her to his apartment. Then carried her limp form to the guest room. He laid her down on the bed, covered in an expensive waterproof material, a shower curtain he had custom-made for this purpose. Sally was unconscious now; the drug had taken full effect.

Satisfied, he took a dark blue towel from the bathroom and tucked it under the right side of her body. She wore a floral cotton dress and strappy sandals. He took off her shoes, lifted her dress, and pushed her undergarment out of the way, exposing her abdomen.

He went to a drawer in the wardrobe and unlocked it. Inside it was a metal box that contained sterilised surgical tools, antiseptic, and a china bowl. All clean and ready for his use. He brought it next to her on the bed, applied clear antiseptic on the upper right portion of her abdomen, where her liver was located. As an added precaution, he injected a small dose of anaesthesia.

A few minutes later, he made a careful incision, a cut about five inches long and deep enough to get to her liver. Warm blood poured out of the cut. He sliced a piece of her liver and placed it into a china bowl beside him. He pressed the wound closed with his fingers to stem the flow of blood, then licked it. Within ten minutes, the outer skin of the wound sealed, a red welt the only visible sign of its existence.

He wiped his hand on the blue towel and picked up the slippery raw liver on the china bowl and popped it into his mouth. His eyes closed as he savoured the metallic flavour of the *victus*.

The ecstasy that followed as the effect of her viscera coursed through his veins. It was indescribable, the power it gave him. He felt stronger, faster, and invincible. It was electric.

His victim stirred but did not wake up. Her hand moved to her injured side by instinct. He intercepted it; he did not want her to have blood on her fingers. With the towel, he wiped it from her torso and made sure there was no trace left. He pulled the towel and the waterproof sheet from under her and rearranged her clothes.

Her wound would need about three to four hours to heal under the surface. She would have a sore belly for a day and her liver would have regrown the missing piece by then. She would never realise what happened to her. Ironically, the fast-healing trait of a *Vis* made it possible for him to get away with a capital crime. Repeatedly. For decades.

He repositioned her on the bed to make her comfortable. He would have to watch over her tonight, to make sure she did not develop a fever. She was deep in her sleep, but her skin had turned clammy.

He then took his tools, the bloody towel, and the waterproof sheet to his utility room. The bloodstains had to be washed off the waterproof sheet, then hung to dry. He dropped the bloody towel in the washing machine and ran it. Jake had learned from experience to ensure the washing machine was on.

Next was the bowl and his surgical instruments – the scalpel, forceps, and retractors. He then placed the tools in his steriliser. He would run it for an hour and then seal it for his next use.

This was the part he liked least for its tediousness, but it had to be done to avoid any health complications for his victims. It would not be good for his viscera sources to be taken to the hospital. An x-ray would reveal what he had done.

With his task completed, he showered and went to bed. Tomorrow, he would play the perfect gentleman card, be solicitous and impress her. He would then take her home. Like his previous victims in this method, she would be grateful. He would be a hero in her eyes, blame the drink for passing out the previous night and the mild nausea that she would feel in the morning.

And like every woman before her, there would be no second encounter with her. He would not risk his modus operandi.

The image of the woman who spurned him in the restaurant came to mind – it was a pity he did not get her. She would have made him reconsider his rule of no second contact with his victims.

He would not have minded dating her after – after he had consumed her liver.

Mateo sat on the floor in a split as he stretched his inner thigh muscles, his hands on his flexed toes. He bent sideways to his left for some minutes until the muscles loosened. The long hours of sitting behind his desk had tightened his calf muscles. It was a relief to release them at the end of the day.

He was in that position when Roald walked into the training room, followed by his son, Daniel. Both carried gym bags. Roald had a *Kali* stick carrier slung on one shoulder. It seemed the two decided to come together. He greeted them both with a nod and continued his warmup.

The two young men were engaged in lighthearted banter and jostling as they prepared themselves for the training. Roald looked nervous, and Daniel's jokes were his son's attempts to put his friend at ease. The two pals started stretching, with Daniel setting the tone and Roald copying what he did.

Ten minutes later, they were ready to begin.

"What was your training in *Kali*, Roald? And when was the last time you trained?" he asked. His training was more varied and a combination of everything deadly in the arts.

"It was mostly the Luzon style *Eskrima,* double stick and *Espada Y Daga,*" Roald replied. "I have not trained for over two years," he added.

"You said you wanted to train in blades, especially *karambit*?" Mateo confirmed. Roald nodded.

Mateo reached into his bag and dug out the training *karambits*, the dull versions of the real ones to prevent actual damage during the sessions.

They started with an easy sparring combination of strikes, blocks, checks and counters to assess Roald's speed and skills. Both their hands moved in a blur, in a series of motions that looked choreographed, but it was a result of training and muscle memory. He was surprised the boy had a natural aptitude for the art.

He felt glad that Daniel was part of the training because Roald needed a sparring partner who had similar physiological capabilities. With more coaching and practice, Roald could hold his own against a *Vis* with no *Kali* training, but with someone like him or any of the *Iztaris,* Roald would not be able to match their speed and strength. Mateo did not want him discouraged.

The succeeding hour and a half was a flurry of slashes, stabs, parry, blocks, locks and taps, and the flow drills that characterised the hand-to-hand techniques of the famed Filipino Martial Arts.

The room echoed with the zings of fast swinging sticks, the thwacks and clacks as wood connected with wood in furious succession. By the end of the session, Mateo garnered a new level of respect towards the boy he unwittingly traumatised. Roald possessed natural talent, speed and power, and his body and footwork were fluid.

The guilt that made him offer personal training to Roald resurfaced. He would train this boy the best he could, teach him everything he knew until he could match the best of their *Iztaris*. He owed this to Roald because he could not undo what he did to him. Reparation was the only thing left to him.

If *Kali* proficiency would give Roald a measure of calm and confidence, then he would supply it.

Sweat poured down Roald's back. Both Daniel and he laughingly settled on the bench for some energy drinks.

With adrenalin pumping in his veins, a sense of satisfaction suffused his being. He was not as rusty as he thought, and Daniel's dad was very patient. He saw the glint of pride in Mateo and Daniel's eyes as they sparred. Both father and son seemed pleased with his skills and ability.

It gave him confidence and a manner of peace to know that he could defend himself. The feeling it gave him was addictive. He wanted to do this again soon, and as often as possible.

Even more exhilarating was the knowledge that, throughout the training, he was aware of Mateo's *Aswang* nature. After the initial jolt of panic, his fight instinct took over. During the training, he forgot his fear. Maybe because he had known Mateo for a long time, and he had been friends with Daniel. Even when Daniel told him he was an *Erdia,* he saw his friend and Mateo as human beings.

"Thank you for the training, sir." Roald could not express how much he appreciated Mateo's generosity.

"You're welcome, Hijo. Should I expect you again next week?" Mateo patted the sweat off his forehead.

"Definitely, sir. I would be glad to come anytime you have a training," he said. Roald felt a sense of pride that he made a well-trained *Aswang* and *Iztari* like Daniel's father sweat, although the older man was not as breathless as he.

"I will let you know through Daniel here," Mateo said and glanced at Daniel, who was busy wiping his brow.

"Dad, we are going out to drink after this. Would you like to join us?"

"Nah, you boys go on ahead on your hunting expedition tonight. I have my own... prey to pursue." Mateo winked at his son.

"It's hardly a hunting expedition, Dad. If it was, Roald and I are the prey," Daniel scoffed.

Mateo rolled his eyes. "I don't know where you inherited such conceit, Daniel..." he said, shaking his head.

Roald watched the easy banter between father and son, and he thought of his own father. Sandro Magsino was not the bantering kind, but an intellectual, logical thinker who enjoyed serious topics and stimulating conversations. Their interactions were casual and cerebral, not this easy-going kind. Daniel and his father treated each other like buddies. His father treated him like an equal.

Cielo Magsino was the funny one in the family; light-hearted, always smiling. His father referred to her as a horizon where the sun never sets. It was a perfect description of his mother. His father adored her. Roald saw the display of it every day. It was clear in his father's constant need to touch his mother whenever they were in the same room, the sketches of her in small cards that his mother collected, his refusal to eat ahead of his mom, his insistence in serving her first, giving her the choicest cuts. In contrast, his mom was a touchy-feely kind, very affectionate. She was exactly what his father needed.

His parents' relationship, the quality of it, was the kind that he wanted in his life. Roald waited a long time to find a woman who would trigger the same kind of wanting in him, the desire, and the need to make her happy all his life. He had dated a couple of women in the past that he thought had possibilities, but while he cared for both women, he realised they never touched his soul. Only Yuana managed it and with so little effort.

As he and Daniel walked out of the training room, all showered and ready to go out, he wondered what Daniel's mother was like. He knew Daniel lost his mother when he was five, so he probably remembered little about her. One of these days, he would ask Daniel about the woman who gave him his human side.

Ximena and Íñigo could not believe their eyes. Both reserved judgement until they were certain. They looked at the video and the actual specimen. The cells had not lost their strength. They now behaved like true *V Genes* do. The scientists had expected it to wane after forty-eight hours and revert to its former strength.

The control samples that Íñigo set up, those of human and *Erdia* genes, behaved as expected when human liver cells were added to the petri dish. It did nothing. Unlike the *primal V Genes*, which morphed and stabilised into their *hominum* form when the liver cells were fed to it.

Daniel's *Mejordia* genes behaved identical to the *V Genes*, but the remarkable thing was, while the *V Genes* reverted to *primal* form as the effects of the liver cells waned, Daniel's *Mejordia* genes remained in *hominum* state.

Would it translate outside of the petri dish?

It seemed Daniel could awaken his *Vis* capabilities if he consumed raw liver. And if the results of their experiment translated into real life, he would only need to do it once.

How much of those capabilities would be with him? And would he inherit the need to eat viscera just like them?

They had a lot of questions that needed answers and a risk assessment they must present to Daniel before they asked him to experiment with his nature, his life and future.

“Do you think it is moral to ask Daniel to do this for us?” She glanced at Íñigo, whose face remained blank.

“It will be up to him to decide. You and I can only hope for the best,” he replied.

She glanced at her watch – seven p.m. Her palms itched to call Daniel to tell him about the results, but Íñigo's pointed look and head shake stopped her.

“It’s too late in the day to invite Daniel over to the lab. The boy deserved a few hours of break, Mena.” Íñigo's tone carried a note of censure.

He was right, of course, but it was still a struggle to contain her impatience.

13

THE SHIFT IN THE HOUSE OF SANTINO

Mateo adjusted the neckline of his shirt. He was nervous. This date differed from all the others in the past. Maybe it was because his heart had a room in it now, after the poisonous truth that occupied it was flushed out of him.

As he entered the restaurant, he looked about and found her seated at the corner table he reserved for them. Her back was to him, and for a few seconds, he admired the slim length of her neck, bowed as she read the drinks menu.

He approached their table, and she looked up at him with a smile. He bent down to kiss her on one soft and smooth cheek. She smelled of jasmine and orange blossom. His mouth watered.

"Good evening, Aris, I apologise for being late." His pulse picked up at the sight of her face.

"Oh, I just arrived myself, so no harm done." Her dimples highlighted a smile that lifted the corners of her lips and eyes.

"You look wonderful." It was true. She wore a silk dress that had wispy straps, emphasising her toned arms and slim physique. She looked feminine but powerful. Aris was a retired military like him, and she now worked as a photojournalist, a very physical job that required her to travel the world.

"You are not so bad yourself. And I must admit I prefer you in this casual look." Her eyes travelled over his face and physique as he sat down across from her. She was as pleased to see him as he was to her.

"Have you found a place to rent?" he asked as they waited for their drinks to arrive. She mentioned looking for a place the first time they met.

A glint of surprise flickered in her eyes before she nodded. "Yes, there are two places I liked. I need to make a choice."

"What's the dilemma?" he asked.

"I like them both. They tick all the boxes, although one has better furnishing than the other. The one I prefer is owned by a human, and the other is our kind. I wanted to meet the owners first to see who I am more comfortable with," she replied.

"If the human owner manages at a distance, then it would not matter." He was familiar with renting from humans, as he and his late wife started their married life as tenants. He found there was little difference.

"Okay, noted." Her smile deepened. Again, her dimples were on display.

Their drinks arrived and interrupted his overt perusal of her. He found her to be engaging. Behind her casual demeanour, he could sense a deep passion that fuels the fire behind her eyes. She was a driven woman, and he liked that.

Aris was a total contrast to his late wife, who was sweet, dainty, and emotionally fragile. He had to admit that what attracted him most to Espie was her ability to stir the protective side in him. He wanted to take care of her. However, after Espie's death, he found those same qualities in women repellent, like a warning signal.

Aris was different. She did not need him in the manner that Espie did. She was her own self, and he found it compelling. And liberating. He told himself to take it easy; it was possible his subconscious made him averse to women similar to his late wife. And his attraction to Aris could be a misguided self-defence reaction.

"Are you here for work? Or for a long break?" He wanted to know more about her, and it seemed unusual for a photojournalist to base themselves in one country apart from their home.

"A bit of work, and I needed a base for a while, a resting stop in between as I travel all over the globe," she replied.

"Why here? Or is it because the global drama is happening in Asia?"

"Yes, in a manner of speaking. Asia has so many things going for it that make it interesting to be here. I am also writing a co-writing a book about tribal culture, and Asia has a variety of tribes and cultures that are distinct from each other," she explained, emphatic hand gestures punctuating her words.

Her energy and passion for life made him smile. She exuded electricity and vibrancy even in the quiet moments.

"Sounds like a grand project. Let me know if you need escorts or some help in getting access to the tribal villages in the country," he said, sincere in his offer. His military career provided him access and connections in various remote locations.

"I might take you up on that. And I will remind you of it when the need arises," Aristo replied, her eyes twinkling in mischief.

Aristo was unreasonably breathless. A novel experience for her. Her previous job did not afford any opportunities to bond beyond professional friendship and camaraderie with the men she met in the course of her work.

Having retired from that, her choice of second life path was not conducive to forming a personal relationship either. Her task for the Grand Plan left no room for it. Mateo's entry into her orbit and her reaction to him surprised her.

In every aspect, he fitted the profile of a perfect potential *Jaurdina,* a *Blue General.* She could have recruited Mateo, but she felt a bit... selfish about him and their interaction. A part of her wanted to keep him to herself for the time being. Perhaps time would tell her later how to approach the rest of this.

She had learned a great deal about him; he seemed very open about himself, or at least the easy information about himself. Normally, she would have ferreted out more from him. She had considerable skills and thirty years of experience to do it, but she did not want to. It was rather telling, and somewhat perplexing – her reluctance should be a cause for worry, but there were no alarm bells.

What she knew of Mateo, she liked. He intrigued her in some elemental way. He had the elegance of years of military service and training in his posture. His assessing gaze felt like he wanted to pry out her secrets, to understand her, to establish a connection.

He had an honourable air, a strait-laced kind who would always abide by the rules of the law. He would not bend them to suit his agenda. A complete opposite of how she flourished in her previous military exploits – legal in her country, but illegal in others.

Her records indicated she always skirted the law. That could be why he appealed to her. Mateo was the pristine version of what she always wanted to be.

As they shared stories, jokes, and flirty banter amidst drinks and canapes; she soaked in the experience of her true first date – the kind she might have imagined and wished for when she had her memory.

She could remember nothing about her past beyond the night she woke up in the hospital. Her memories of childhood, teenage years, and her years as a spy – nothing was left except the memory of a couple whom she knew in her heart, though she had no proof, were her parents. The faces of the couple were her only anchor to her lost past.

It was possible she went out with Mateo because she needed new memories. One that felt different from her old life, her previous self. She was an empty bucket when she walked out of her hospital room. It was unsettling not knowing what her core values were, the things she used to dream about, goals she aimed for, why she had taken on the life of a spy.

Everything she did now felt instinctive because she had no foreknowledge of what her skills were. It was a thrill to discover them when faced with a circumstance that required her to react in an extraordinary manner. It became an exciting way to live a life.

Daniel stepped into Ximena's laboratory at eight a.m. It was too early to be dealing with such a situation, but it would be useless to delay it. Ximena's text message last night seemed ominous or promising, depending on which outcome he desired. Since he was still confused about his feelings on the whole thing, he felt both the menace and the potential of *Project Chrysalis*.

Ximena and Íñigo waited for him by the reception area of the lab. He wondered if they even went home last night, but Ximena still looked fresh, and somehow, Íñigo struck him as someone who would not sleep on the floor. He was far too refined for it. Maybe the lab had a bedroom somewhere.

"Good morning. Do I get a coffee before you tell me the... news?" he asked half-jokingly.

"Of course. Coffee is ready and waiting," Íñigo said, pointing to the pot to his left.

Daniel poured himself a cup, the fragrance of the brew added to his inner agitation. After settling on the soft lounge chair across from both, he took a sip of coffee to drive away the cobwebs in his head. This conversation required full wits and a sober mind. He was a tad hungover from last night.

The pair allowed him to take his time to enjoy his cup, which alarmed him a bit. By his third sip, he put it down. The caffeine had his heart galloping. "Shall we get on with it, Tita?"

Ximena regarded him for a moment before replying. "The tests proved our theories right. You have dormant *Vis* traits in you, and it can be awakened by introducing liver cells into your system," Ximena said.

"Introducing? What kind of... introduction?" He asked, but he had an idea what Ximena meant.

A gleam of excitement flashed in Ximena's eyes. "The interesting thing is that it seemed once is enough and your latent *Viscerebus* traits would surface," Ximena continued, ignoring his initial concern.

That astounded him. The idea he had suppressed physical powers that could be brought to the surface was enticing. But all *Vis* eat viscera regularly, sometimes daily.

"What traits?" *Would it be worth the risk to trigger those traits?*

"All six secondary genes and five tertiary genes in your system. We are not sure with the mutated primary genes, though." Íñigo's reply carried forewarning, and Daniel's heart jumped.

It would be nice to be as strong, as fast, as powerful as a *Vis*, but did he inherit the incessant hunger for human liver, too?

"No shapeshifting?" He directed his question to Íñigo. The glitter in Ximena's eyes was contagious and alarming.

Íñigo shook his head. "Your primary *V genes* were altered, but it is the first time we have seen such mutation. We could be wrong..." Íñigo's supplied a non-commital statement. The older man wanted him to decide on his own.

It was unbelievable he considered what Ximena proposed, that he was tempted to unravel his *Viscerebus* side when he had always thought he preferred being human. It scared him to ask, to be disappointed, but he needed the truth.

"You mentioned introduction to liver cells. It means I would have to eat raw liver, right?"

"It would be faster that way," Ximena responded, her voice quiet and hopeful.

He nodded, although not quite agreeing with her. "One time... does that mean I would not... need to eat liver after the first time?" He wanted to confirm it.

The silence that followed was just a few seconds long, but dragged on like a bad year.

"In all honesty, the test suggests you will not need to do so after, but we are not sure. We could not guarantee it," Ximena said with a heavy sigh, an acknowledgement of the risk that faced him.

"There is a feeling that we get when we consume viscera, Daniel. No words can describe it. A sensation more powerful than taking cocaine. It is a combination of euphoria and relief. Like a homecoming." Íñigo said.

"In short, we want you to know it can be addictive. A certain percentage of our kind gets addicted to the sensations. It is also the same reason some of our kind turn to hunting our own – in pursuit of that. *Harravissing* gives you double the high," Ximena interjected.

Daniel could not say he was thankful for their honesty in presenting the risks. Part of him wished he was never told. He wanted to say no, to stop his participation right there and then. He had given them enough of himself to fulfil what they needed to do. It should be enough to know he had latent *Viscerebus* power. He could walk away now, and he would have lost nothing – except the opportunity to get to know the ultimate truth about himself.

But if he walked away halfway through the process, it would never give him peace.

"Dan, do not decide in haste. If you choose to do this, your life will change irrevocably, so give yourself time. Be very sure." Ximena's warm hand covered his, her tone maternal.

He nodded. He left dazed, his head full of indecision.

Yuana walked hand in hand with Roald as they stepped out of the elevator. They had breakfast with her parents that morning. Her new unit was a good half an hour away from the office, so she came in a bit late to work today.

It was a surprise to see Daniel in her office. He stood by the couch, his back to them as he gazed out into the vast garden that often offered her solace when she had some heavy thinking to do. She looked up at Roald in question. He shrugged. Roald also did not know why Daniel was here.

"Good morning, Dan," she said cheerfully, though she was unsure of Daniel's mood.

Daniel turned at the sound of her voice, his expression a mixture of surprise, mild disappointment, and apology upon seeing Roald with her.

"Oh, sorry, Yu. I did not think Roald would be with you. I can call later when you are free..." he mumbled.

"Oh, don't be silly, Dan. We will sort out what you came here for." She dismissed his suggestion to leave. He came here because he needed her counsel. "Sit down, you are not leaving," she added when Daniel hesitated.

"Do you want me to go, bro?" Roald asked, his tone hesitant, but understanding.

"No... it's okay... I was just... I didn't want to interrupt your plans..." Daniel said. He complied with her command and sat down on the couch.

"Do you want coffee?" she asked. Daniel looked like he needed sustenance. "Breakfast?" A moment's hesitation, but he shook his head.

She closed the blinds to her office to give them privacy and sat across from Daniel. Roald sat down beside her; a protective arm rested at the back of her chair.

"Okay, what is on your mind, D?" she asked. Daniel looked like there was a puzzle stuck in his head that he could not figure out. She had seen that look on his face – they solved many brain teasers together in their childhood.

"Yu, they have offered me a chance to unlock my *Vis* capabilities, to explore it, bring it out of me," Daniel said, his head bent, his tone soft.

What? "Tita Ximena's project?" The question came out in a squeak.

"Yes..." came Daniel's quiet reply.

She had always known deep inside Daniel felt bitter about not inheriting full *Vis* traits. This should have been an easy decision for him. "And yet you hesitate... because?"

He did not respond for a long time. She threw a glance at Roald, who was also waiting for Daniel's reaction.

"There are risks..." Dan muttered, looking up at her, his jaw tight. She could not tell whether he wanted validation. Or to be dissuaded from a decision he already made in his head.

"What risks?" she asked when Daniel was not forthcoming.

His sigh was deep and drawn out. "I may not be able to uncross the line, to come back."

"What do you mean?" Her brows puckered in an unwanted frown.

"I possess the eleven *V Genes* in full, and the mutated version of the primary pair. They think if I awaken those genes, the two crucial genes may react unpredictably. I could turn into a full *Vis* or something else. Who knows what would happen if I..." Daniel swallowed, his brows furrowed.

She understood. "Oh, holy *Prometheus!*" The experiment could turn Daniel into something he could not control. It was too huge a risk, and everything about her rebelled at the idea. "Dan, I don't think you should do it..." Her stomach knotted in anxiety.

Daniel's jaw tightened; his expression turned unreadable. She realised her reaction strengthened his resolve to do it.

"What is the reward... if you do it?" Roald interjected; his gaze intent.

Daniel looked back at Roald, almost challengingly, then released a deep breath and tension left his frame.

"This is driving me crazy..." Daniel rubbed his eyes, his voice laced with frustration. "When all your life feels like an uphill trudge and your path is obscured. Then the cloud clears. You see the risks, you know your capabilities, and you are unsure of both. What would you do?" Daniel's voice deepened in intensity. The pleading for understanding, for support, was distinct.

Yuana understood what Daniel asked of her as a friend, and her heart disagreed with her mind. She did not want to lose him to potential danger and would rather he remained an *Erdia.* But this was not up to her to decide. Dan was going to do this with or without her support, and it would be easier for him if she did.

She glanced at Roald and caught his gaze. He squeezed her hand.

"How can we help mitigate the risk?" She sighed. Maybe Tita Ximena could give them an idea. Daniel's answering sigh was a relief. It almost made her smile.

"I do not know. They told me just this morning. I have not had time to ask them," he replied.

"Are they aware that... we know?" she asked.

Daniel shook his head. "I have not told them. I was banking on your discretion. Both of you."

"Okay. Asking my aunt is not the way to go, then..." She did not have a scientific mind, so researching would not help her without conferring with the scientists in the family. She would be referred back to her aunt.

"Dan, why is this so top secret?" Roald asked.

"I am not sure. I never asked. But I would guess that it is the same reason drug manufacturers keep their research and experiments a secret – competitors, early backlash, proprietary process, etc.," Daniel said.

"You told me before this experiment was about finding a linkage between humans and our kind, so when did this turn into transforming you into one?" Roald's question surprised her. She was not aware Daniel had told him as much.

"It was the compensation I asked for when I agreed to give my blood," Daniel replied.

She felt a spark of temper at his words. "You have made up your mind before you found out what the risks were." Daniel had the grace to look contrite. "Okay, so how can we prepare you for this transformation?" There was no question she would let him go through it alone.

"Your Uncle Íñigo said that you get a euphoric feeling after eating viscera?"

She nodded and threw a glance at Roald before she replied, "Yes. That is an apt description. To me, it is like drinking a glass of cold water when you're parched on a hot day, or when a masseuse loosens a painful knot of muscle on your back. It is a distinct sensation of well-being that is hard to explain."

"Is it addictive?" Daniel asked. Roald's gaze swivelled to hers. Both men waited for her response.

Memories of when she forgot to have her *victus* and Roald saw her accidental transformation flooded back into her mind. She could not have forgotten about taking it if she was addicted to it.

"It is vital for us to have viscera. But apart from our inner hunger for it, I do not think I am addicted to it. I have forgotten to take it from time to time..." she said.

A frown appeared on Daniel's forehead as he considered the logic in her statement.

"My dad had forgotten to have some now and then as well," Daniel said.

"It may be similar to how some humans are prone to alcoholism and some are not," Roald said in a reasonable tone.

"Is that what you are afraid of? That you might get addicted to it?" she asked.

Daniel shook his head. "No, I am afraid that if I consume viscera, which is required to awaken my *V Genes*, that I may turn into one permanently."

His words struck her in the chest, drawing a small involuntary gasp from her. The two men did not notice. Today, Daniel's issue was more important than her hurt feelings. It seemed the two men closest to her outside of her family hated the idea of being a *Vis*.

That was a hard truth to hear.

Yuana sat in the middle of her new condominium unit. All the furnishings were as she specified. The city view was in direct contrast to the country charm she was used to. But her new home offered a unique appeal and certain advantages.

Roald was coming later for the joint housewarming dinner with her parents. On impulse, she invited Daniel, as well. She wanted her friend to feel he belonged, no matter how he perceived himself, human or *Vis*.

He hesitated when she called him, but she would not accept a no. She instructed him to bring flowers. Daniel would never flake out when he accepted a task.

She proceeded to her outdoor garden to inspect her take-off and landing pad. And just as she instructed, potted dwarf hinoki cypress and jacarandas lined the bordering wall, alternately set in between low rectangular herb patches, lavender and Sampaguita bushes. The explosion of dark green, purple, and white stunned her. The combined aroma of basil, rosemary, thyme, dill, lavender and Sampaguita was heady. It almost made her sneeze.

There was an outdoor bar made of granite in the corner, an outdoor couch, table, and other seating near it. She had one side of the concrete floor covered with weather-treated purpleheart wood boards for a softer landing. It had enough runway space for her flight lessons and was cosy enough for entertaining. The rest was covered in garden turf.

Yuana was on the verge of jumping up and down in glee when the doorbell rang. She opened the door to her parents. Her mother carried the familiar icebox that contained their *victus* for the day.

"Good evening, my dear." Her mother kissed her on the cheek. Her father did the same but paired it with a tight bear hug that lifted her off her feet.

"I see you have our *sustenance* for the day," she said. They had agreed their *victus* was to be delivered in her unit where she and her mother consumed it. So, her father would not have to witness the act.

"We encountered the delivery guy just outside. And don't worry about it, I will just close my eyes." Her father waved away her concern. His eyes panned around the area with appreciation. "Very nice, very cosy," he added, nodding in approval.

He walked around, inspecting the décor on the wall to give her and her mother the time to consume the viscera. He turned back when he heard the water running as Yuana washed the icebox.

"Do you want to see the rooms?" she asked her parents as she wiped her hands on the towel.

"Let us do that later, when Roald arrives, so you only do one house tour for all of us," her mother said. Ysobella paused as she noticed the table setting for five. "Who else is coming?"

"Oh, Daniel is joining us. I invited him too," she replied. Her parents nodded.

A minute later, the doorbell rang. Daniel and Roald were both at the door, chuckling at some joke. She received a kiss on each cheek from the two men. Daniel handed her a jasmine plant in a small decorative basket.

"Here you go, flowers and a house-warming gift in one," he said.

"Oh, thank you! This is perfect," she said, delighted. The scent of the small white flowers pervaded the room. She placed the basket on a corner table near the glass window; where there would be equal sun and shade.

A short time later, with canapes served, drinks poured, she showed them around her condominium. They had converted the middle bedroom into an office and library. The second bedroom, a muted grey and silver, remained a guest room. The master bedroom was light and airy in mint green; a glass sliding door led to her magnificent outdoor garden.

"Yu, I shall claim the second bedroom as mine when I come here to crash if I become homeless," Daniel declared.

"Sure, as long as the reason for your homelessness is justifiable," she replied.

"Woman, your standard for justification may differ from mine," Daniel said, making her parents laugh.

"That is true, so let's have Roald decide whether that justification is valid," Galen suggested, still chuckling at the thought.

"They're buddies, papa. Men stick together, so how would Roald be an impartial third-party judge?" she protested, feigning outrage.

"Sweetie, it is unlikely that I will be okay with Daniel staying here with you alone, so believe me, I would be more partial to the no-sleep over decision," Roald replied. His eyebrow quirked.

"Fine, be like that. I will claim Tita Bella's guest room instead," Daniel said, giving her mother a sad puppy dog look.

Her mother laughed and patted Daniel on the head, ruffling his hair.

During dinner, with everyone replete with food and drinks, the talk on the table became more serious. Her mother turned to Roald, genuine interest sparkling in her eyes.

"How are you, Roald? Are you coping better?" Ysobella asked, her tone gentle.

"Yes, Tita, I found a way to manage my fear, somewhat," Roald replied.

"Oh, that is good. So, are you able to be with our kind without... distress?" her mother asked further, leaning closer to Roald.

"I have no problem being you and Yuana's immediate family members. Maybe because I see you all as humans. I still have a visceral reaction, pardon the pun, to others," Roald said, his hand crept surreptitiously by his side, where the *karambit* rested.

Yuana recognised the reflexive action and squeezed his free hand. Roald's hand turned over as he claimed her palm, his need for reassurance loud.

"I am glad to hear that," her mother said. Ysobella directed a smile of satisfaction at Galen, who nodded in approval.

Her mother surveyed the table. Like a hen to her brood, her gaze landed on Daniel. Her mother had always treated Daniel like a wayward son – with extreme fondness. Before they came back to the Philippines, her mother had stated in the past she was in favour of Daniel, should their relationship progress past friendship.

"And you, Dan? What has been happening to you?" Her mother turned to him; her eyebrows arched in inquiry.

Daniel was taken aback, and his mask of casual playfulness slipped. A gleam of interest flashed in her mother's eyes. Ysobella inclined her head, her face patient and open. Yuana felt alarmed and grateful for her mother's perceptiveness and ability to see beyond Daniel's façade.

Daniel looked at her. A silent question, a request for confirmation that it was okay to tell her parents. Yuana gave him a brief nod.

"I... took part in a program that would... could awaken my latent *Vis* traits," Daniel began, his tone careful. He put his drink glass down and brushed the imaginary crumbs off the tablecloth.

Her mother straightened up from her seat, her gaze turned serious. Her father noticed her mother's reaction, and his body language automatically mimicked hers.

"How?" Ysobella asked.

"I cannot give you the full details, Tita, for security reasons," Daniel replied. He looked uneasy about divulging the program to more people than he already did.

"Will it put your life in danger?" Concern knitted her mother's brows. Her father noted it, and a frown appeared on his forehead.

"No, I don't think so..." At her mother's raised eyebrow, Dan added, "It is experimental, and yes, there are risks, but I think those are manageable ones."

"But it bothers you, Daniel. I can see that. You are worried about it," her mother insisted.

"I am, a bit... but I think, I can handle this. Don't worry, Tita..." Dan patted her mother's hand. His smile was strained at the corners.

"So, if I understand it correctly, this... experiment... will turn you into an *Aswang*?" her father interjected with a deliberate frown.

"Yes, Tito, in a sense," Daniel nodded.

"Hmm, if that succeeds, it will be revolutionary. And even more ground-breaking if they can do it on reverse," he said. There was a shadow of a speculative gleam in his eyes.

To Roald, the conversation sparked a gem of an idea that opened a possible solution to his problem. There seemed to be a way to bridge the difference between human and *Aswang*. The chance of making Yuana and him the same. If it could be done, it would fix the only thing wrong between them.

He needed to talk to Daniel in private.

Daniel walked into Ximena's lab with determined steps. He did not want to encounter anything that could put doubts in his already chaotic brain.

Íñigo and Ximena were already there. After greeting them good morning, Daniel poured himself a cup of coffee and sat down. Íñigo and Ximena wore twin expressions of expectation.

She looked like she had been waiting for him to arrive. Íñigo's gaze returned to her, a frown on his face, as if he had been studying her face for a long time. There was something about Ximena that bothered Íñigo.

Yuana mentioned Ximena lost a loved one recently. And yet, she was here, working with enthusiasm and drive. Perhaps Íñigo's concern was that Ximena never had time to grieve.

"I'm in..." Daniel said. He took a big gulp of the hot coffee, wincing as the steaming liquid scalded his throat.

"But?" Íñigo asked. He seemed to think the barest pause in Daniel's declaration meant something.

"There are no buts... How are we doing this? Oral or intravenous?" He was impatient to start the distasteful process. He took another big gulp of his coffee. His throat worked to push down the urge to hurl with the hot beverage.

Íñigo and Ximena exchanged a glance. Ximena sighed. "It is quicker to eat it, Daniel," she said.

His heart jumped and his gut churned. "Should I have something in my stomach first?"

"It is better on an empty stomach. And it will help if you close your eyes, and chase it down with coffee," Ximena replied, "or alcohol..."

"I prefer cognac myself," Íñigo said.

That made sense. The smoky flavour of the beverage should wash away the aftertaste of blood better than coffee. "Yes, please," he said.

Íñigo left and came back with a half full cognac bottle, then took out glasses from the cupboard and poured two measures. Íñigo handed it to him. Ximena gave him a covered bowl, a small dessert fork on top of it.

Daniel swallowed. Blood drained from his face, and his hands turned cold. His hands trembled as he touched the cover.

"Close your eyes. Do you need help?" Ximena said. At his silence, she took the bowl from his hand, took the cover off. "Now, tip your head back and open your mouth when I say ahh," she said.

Daniel complied. He heard the clink of the fork as it hit the bowl, then Ximena's fingers pinched his nose. She told him to open up. He did. She dropped the liver slice into his mouth. The cold, metallic taste of the slimy organ rested at the arch of his tongue for a moment, until it slid down his throat.

He took a big gulp of the cognac to push it further down. Daniel felt the liver travel through his esophagus, then dropped into his stomach. The cognac masked the flavour of human flesh, but not the smell or the texture. His eyes watered as he willed it to stay down.

Daniel wiped the sweat off his brows and upper lip, then felt the heat from his flushed face as he waited for the gag reflex to kick in. Nothing happened. Íñigo and Ximena watched him, waiting for his reaction.

Then a sensation of loosening started in his gut. It radiated from his middle until it enveloped his entire body and settled on his heart. His pulse picked up. His skin tingled with goosebumps. He shivered but he wasn't cold. In fact, his insides were hot, similar to eating hot soup on a chilly day. Then a sense of well-being spread all over him.

He felt energised, powerful, and mighty – there was no other word for it. Awed, he looked at Ximena and Íñigo. The glitter of excitement in their eyes was a confirmation and recognition. They were familiar with the sensation that overwhelmed him.

"Let's get your blood," Ximena said, almost in a whisper. Her eagerness was palpable.

He presented his arm to her. With quick and efficient movement, Ximena swabbed his inner arm with a cotton ball, wet with disinfectant. He fisted his hand, and a tight band was tied on his upper arm. Ximena found his vein and inserted a needle, drawing blood.

Two full syringes later, the band was removed, another cotton ball was pressed on his inner arm, and the needle slid out.

Ximena rushed to prepare the specimen. After a series of never-ending steps, she looked up from the microscope with a triumphant smile. She moved to give way for Íñigo to look for himself. He wore a similar expression after viewing the slides.

"So?" Daniel asked impatiently.

"We were right in one part of our theory. The viscera triggered your *Vis* traits," Ximena said. Her smile widened even more.

"Which part did you get wrong?" he asked, his heart thumping out of his chest.

"We need to wait to see if you will... need viscera later," Íñigo said, his face carefully blank.

"How long before we know?" Daniel asked, his face grim.

"Two to three days." Íñigo's quick reply was firm and confident.

He nodded. He knew that if the craving arose in him within those days, he would feel it. "Should I come here... if the craving returns?" he asked.

"Yes. We will both be here. We will keep a close watch over the specimens, but we expect nothing different to happen," Ximena said, her smile reassuring.

"So, am I a... *Vis* now?" He did not know what to think.

"Well, technically, you have always been more than half-*Vis*. We just needed to bring it out of you," Íñigo said. "But if you were referring to being a full *Vis*, we think it unlikely. We could still be wrong, but both Ximena and I are almost sure you cannot shapeshift because your *Metamorpho* and *Calyptratus* genes carried a mutation. And since those genes are intertwined, we are also ninety-nine per cent certain that you would not be needing viscera later..." Íñigo added.

Daniel nodded. He understood the risk. "Do you think this would work with the other *Erdias*? That theirs can be awakened if fed viscera?" he asked.

Íñigo shook his head. "We do not think so. They need the genes that you have."

He wanted to know what else they could do with this experiment he put his future in danger for, to believe there was something big that would come out of it. One that would be beneficial to so many. "Would it be possible to supplement their lacking genes? Like a bone marrow transplant?" he asked.

"Gene editing, yes, that is the next step, but that would take some time. If that is a possibility, it will take a few treatments. So, if you know any other *Erdias* who may want to volunteer, let us know," Ximena joked.

Daniel smiled at her. He knew more than a few *Erdias* who would give an arm and a leg to become a *Vis.* They would relish the power that comes from being one. In his opinion, those would be the worst candidates for the program.

"Where else can we go with this experiment? Like human to *Vis,* or even the reverse?" he asked.

Íñigo gave Ximena a curious look. Her face was wiped clean of emotions.

"The original goal of *Project Chrysalis* was to turn human into *Vis*. And certainly, we will look at the reversal process as well," she replied, her tone sombre. She walked over to the cognac bottle and poured herself a measure. She took a lingering sip, staring unseeing at the distance.

"So, do you want to test your new traits, Daniel?" Íñigo said, distracting him from Ximena.

"Sure. Do we wrestle again?" The idea of trying again thrilled him.

"Even better, we had rented strength, speed and endurance machines just for this purpose. We can test your performance daily and see if there will be a waning," Íñigo said.

"Okay, let's start."

He stood up and followed Íñigo to the room filled with various machines like the ones at his gym, all attached to an impressive-looking computer. He guessed the variety of performance sensors would be attached to his body.

"Where do you want to start? Strength? Speed? Agility? Healing?" Íñigo asked, his stance very doctor-like.

"Maybe we can put the healing test later. I don't want to sweat over my wound as I exercise," he said.

"Well, if our assumption is correct, and I am certain it is, the wound would be healed long before you even begin to sweat," Íñigo said.

It made sense. And the healing test would be the quickest one to do. He rolled up the sleeves of his shirt and offered his arm to Íñigo. The older man smiled, took out his scalpel, and wiped it with alcohol. He swabbed an area on his arm and warned him of the coming cut with a quirk of his eyebrow. There was a quick sting, then a pressure of cotton ball on the spot. Íñigo noted the time.

Ten minutes later, the wound had sealed. Only a faint reddish crease line was left. Dan focused on it, and detected a slight tingling underneath the skin, almost like an itch. His skin was healing itself.

The next test was the bench press. Íñigo tried his own strength as control and lifted four hundred kilos. Daniel's first attempt came in twenty kilos short of four hundred. His second was ten kilos more. It seemed that, like a human, he would have to train.

Ximena joined them as they measured his grip strength with a hand dynamometer. He registered eight times a normal human's, and standard for a trained *Vis* athlete. Agility and speed tests would have to be done in a different location as the human machines on site were not enough to measure the limits of his capabilities.

Now, all that remained would be to wait and see if he would lose his abilities and, more crucially, if he would develop a craving for viscera.

He still struggled with mixed feelings about the development in his life. The surge of power coursing through his veins gave a heady feeling. It was breathtaking. And he caught himself wishing the power never leaves him.

And that disturbed him.

Four years ago.

Tomio Mori locked the door to his condominium to ensure complete security. He would be speaking to one of his *Zuriahjas*, a White General. This young and driven *Erdia* grew up in a human political family.

Rex sat in the senate and suffered from a burning ambition to become a president. And Mori would make it happen because Rex was strategically placed and close to the seat of highest power. He was well connected and a motivated crusader for the Grand Plan.

Mori knew the phone was going to ring a second before it did. His *Zuriahja* was punctual – six p.m. on the dot. Mori expected Rex to be.

"Hello, Mori speaking," he said.

"Good evening, Mr Mori. Rex here." The slight, high-pitched but raspy voice came through.

The image of the other man floated in his mind's eye. Rex was making the call in a well-appointed bathroom, where the likelihood of being bugged was slim. The room had a silver and grey motif. The scent of aftershave and mouthwash lingered.

"Good evening, Rex. How are we doing with our strategies?" Mori asked. He knew the answer would be good, but he wanted the details.

"It is coming all according to our plan. The party had been... hmm, persuaded... to nominate me as the Vice President for the next election. We just need to secure the approval of the presidential candidate to choose me for his running mate," Rex replied, a smug lilt to his tone.

"What would secure the candidate's decision?"

"Donation might secure it, but the other contender will do the same to assure his position. What would tip it to our favour is emotional pressure. It will be more valuable and longer lasting. And his wife and daughter could provide that. He listens to them," Rex replied.

"What inducement can we offer the wife and daughter?" he asked. Rex should be within an arm's length from the presidency in five years' time.

"I need to be introduced to the daughter. I can take care of securing her endorsement. The wife is very much into charitable causes," Rex said.

Mori dredged his brain for the details of the dossier of the presidential candidate's family. The daughter was smart but emotionally malleable. And indeed, Rex would fit her type – attractive, charismatic, and powerful. Plus, her father would find the idea of her getting on with a political rising star like Rex to be an upgrade from her previous relationships.

The wife was deep into charitable causes for over a decade, but it was not for altruistic reasons. Her favourite charities were the ones attached to high-profile celebrities – glitz and glamour dazzled her. She failed at an acting career.

Mori felt the spread of satisfaction in his veins. All that would be easy to arrange.

"Okay. We will organise a high-end jewellery show, a fund-raising event for the causes dear to the wife. We will invite the presidential candidate to be the guest of honour. It will be glamorous and filled with celebrities. You will attend as a guest and donate 'anonymously'. We will leak that information 'accidentally' to the mother and daughter. That will be your entry," he said.

"When is this happening? What do I need to do?" Rex asked.

"Nothing. Just wait for your invitation in the mail. We will take care of the arrangements." The details of the plan crystallised in his mind. He would have the boy elected as Vice President in the next election.

This was crucial to the Grand Plan, and, therefore, a done deal.

14

THE NEW BREED

Yuana landed in her outdoor garden with a muted thump, shaking the moisture from her feathers. She had flown farther than she planned, and the sudden shift in the weather did not prepare her for the force of the wind.

The turbulence blew her off course a few times. The pressure above the storm clouds turned out to be very uncomfortable, but flying low was out of the question. She could have waited out the storm, but Roald was coming to her condo. So, she battled the onslaught of the rain and gale.

She slid open the glass door to her bedroom; the plush rug proved useful in soaking the rainwater that ran down her naked body. She grabbed the bathrobe from the coat rack by the sliding door. The thick cloth felt like heaven to her chilled skin.

A glance at the wall clock told her she had only ten minutes to spare before Roald rang her bell. He would be on time. Her shower was quick and necessary. She needed to warm herself up, and her body ached from the demanding voyage back. The flow of the hot water soothed her tight muscles, but it made her drowsy.

She saw the text messages her mother sent when she picked up her phone to call Roald. He was in her mother's unit. He arrived half an hour early and proceeded to next door when he did not find her home. Her parents knew she was flying and made excuses for her. They told Roald she went out for a bit to get something from the store. She texted her mother; she was back.

A minute later, she opened her door to Roald, who looked worried as he towered over her.

"Did you get caught in the rain?" he asked, noting her wet hair and bathrobe-clad figure.

"Yes, I did. I'm sorry you had to wait for me." She stood on her toes to kiss him on the cheek.

"No need to apologise. I arrived early. But I got worried when you did not answer your phone," he said as he followed her into the living room.

"I left the phone on the table. I was in a hurry," she lied.

"You look exhausted." He frowned, inspecting her from head to toe.

"A tad, and I was cold," she said. "Let me get dressed. Give me half an hour," she added, turning toward her bedroom, but his arm shot out to stop her.

"We do not have to go out tonight, Yu. Let us just stay in... Maybe watch TV," he said.

"No... I just need..." she protested, but Roald's gentle finger on her lower lip cut her off.

He shook his head. "No... I truly do not mind staying in. The reason for going out is to spend time with you. We do not have to go anywhere to do that. And your place is still new to us, so it is like going out, anyway," he said, his gaze warm.

"Okay," she murmured. She did not realise how tired she was until she felt her relief at his statement. "Thank you..."

"Now, I will make you something hot to drink. What would you like?" Roald murmured against her lips.

"Soup, pumpkin soup. I have some in the fridge. Just heat some of that." She breathed his scent deep into her lungs and revelled in the sense of contentment pervading her being. It was instinctive to lay her cheeks on his chest. His hands rubbed soothing circles on her back, loosening her muscles more. She sighed aloud in pleasure. She sensed rather than saw him smile.

"Come and sit... We will Netflix and soup together in a while..." He guided her to the couch. She sat and curled her cold feet under her. She was tired to the bone.

She was half asleep by the time Roald sat beside her with the hot soup and bread. They decided on a comedy flick to supplement the restorative power of the dish and help boost her flagging energy. Nestled at the crook of his arm as they watch, she fell into unconsciousness before it was done.

Roald knew the moment Yuana fell asleep in his arms when the tension left her body and her full weight settled on him. He adjusted her position for her comfort, then relaxed in contentment.

He should carry Yuana to bed to make her more comfortable, but he felt possessive and greedy for closeness. So, he sank deeper into the couch and wrapped his arms around her. Her scent, which blended with the floral fragrance of her shampoo, shrouded his senses, her firm bathrobe-covered body emanating warmth. She was heaven incarnate.

Half an hour later, it was still pouring rain. A flash of lightning and the roar of thunder startled Yuana, but not enough to wake her up from sleep. With reluctance, he carried her to bed so she could sleep properly. As he entered her bedroom, the billowing curtains drew his attention to the sliding door to the outdoor garden. It was open.

Did Yuana leave it open by accident? Or is there an intruder in her unit? His pulse quickened as he recalled Yuana's prior encounter with an attacker.

He laid her down on the bed, careful not to wake her. Roald listened for any movement within her bedroom. But it was quiet. To reassure himself, he tiptoed to her bathroom to double check. No one was there. Satisfied, he walked towards the sliding door to close it when he noticed the indentation on the chocolate brown rug on the floor.

For a moment, he thought it was a design, because it was perfectly shaped. Two huge, clawed footprints flattened a perfect pattern on the fibres of the thick rug. He knelt and touched it. It was as if a giant wet bird stood on it so it would not trail water in the room. He inspected the floor for other bird footprints, but the only other prints he found were human. Small and dainty, like Yuana's.

Terror gripped him at the thought that dominated his head. His hand went to the *karambit*, holstered at his side. In an instant, it anchored him to the present and eased the sudden tension that invaded his body.

He studied Yuana's sleeping form. She appeared peaceful and trusting, her face innocent and angelic. He took a deep breath and sat on the small red leather seat beside her bed. He watched his beloved as she slept on, letting the vision of her remind him that Yuana was as human as he. She was just... gifted... in some form.

He did not know how long he sat there, but he moved to join Yuana in bed. He toed off his shoes, freed the *karambit* holster from his belt and placed it under a pillow. As he lay down close to her, Yuana stirred and rolled over to his side, fitting her form to his. He closed his eyes at the sensation of her, one arm under and around her. His other arm half buried in the pillow, his hand curled around the holstered weapon. It gave him a sense of security.

The sound of the rain in the background lulled him to sleep.

At two a.m., Yuana woke up, disoriented. She lay there for a few seconds, trying to figure out where she was. She realised she was in her room, lying on the wrong side of the bed, and that she had company. Roald.

She levered up on her elbow and peered at his sleeping form on her right. He was dressed, socks still on.

She eased herself out of his arms and tiptoed to the kitchen to get food and something to drink. She was preparing a sandwich on the island counter when Roald appeared by the kitchen door, his hair mussed, his eyes still half closed.

"Good... morning, Ro," she whispered and smiled at him, her knife poised in mid-slice over the tomato.

"Good morning, Yu," he whispered back in a raspy tone. He pulled a bar stool towards him and sat down.

"Do you want a sandwich?" she asked.

"What kind is it?" He looked at the bread, the bowl of greens, the tub of cream cheese, and a plate of warm caramelised onions in front of him.

"Roast beef sandwich, with the works..." Her smile deepened. This was Roald's favourite.

A shadow of a smile appeared on his face. "That sounds good," he said. He watched as she sliced a generous amount of roast beef and piled it on the bread. Roald opened a bottle of red wine.

Fifteen minutes later, they sat on the couch in front of the TV, a plate of sandwiches, some crisps and a glass of red wine each. She scrolled the list of programs when she realised Roald remained quiet beside her. He stared at her with pained speculation.

"Something on your mind?" she asked.

"Yuana... I... I have never seen you transform. What do you shape-shift into when you... need to?" he asked.

His words doused her like a bucket of cold water. It drove the sleepiness out of her head and snuffed out the sense of calm in an instant. She considered, for a second, hiding her *Apex* form from him and just telling him about her other form, a panther, but there was something in his tone that made her ask, "Why do you want to know?"

Roald sat quietly for a while. "I saw some footprints on the rug."

There was no room for lies now. It was time to tell him everything about the kind of *Viscerebus* she was.

"I turn into a bird, a giant black bird," she replied. Roald heaved a deep and shaky sigh. It sounded like relief. "Hang on, Ro... what did you think it was?" she asked.

A slight, sheepish smile lined his lips. "A *Manananggal?*"

"I thought so..." she said, shaking her head. Her relief made her lighthearted. "FYI, *Manananggals* are a result of failed attempts at shape-shifting by my kind. They are not a different type, contrary to the legend," she added.

Roald smiled at her attempt at levity. "Why did you fly out tonight?" he asked.

"I wanted to practise flying, to train," she said.

"Train? Have you not been transforming into one since birth?" he frowned.

"No. It was a recent discovery... that I can transform into a winged creature. My *Animus* used to be feline. A panther."

"Recent?" Roald's frown deepened. "When?"

"When we... when I was in Mindoro..." She was uncertain how he would receive the information.

"Did our separation cause the... discovery?" he asked, a slight frown on his forehead.

She thought about it for a while, if the heartbreak contributed to her emergence, the *Ortus* of her *Apex* nature. She could not rule it out. "It may have, indirectly. Maybe it was just time." She shrugged as she remembered Kazu's words to her. "Do you want to see it?"

Roald's hand flew to his side, a slight flare of panic in his eyes. He shook his head. "Later, when I am ready." He looked as wretched as he must be feeling.

She understood his reaction, even though it hurt. Her appetite faded, but she picked up her sandwich anyway and took a bite. It was something to do; it helped stop her from crying.

Roald followed suit and bit into his sandwich. He did not look hungry, either. For a moment, they both chewed in silence. He swallowed, then turned to face her and took the sandwich from her hands and put it down on the plate. With his hands on her shoulder, he made her face him.

"Yu, I dislike having this tension between us. This is my fault, but I cannot help my reaction. And I hope I can fix it now. Please be patient with me... I am trying." Roald's voice and eyes begged for understanding.

The knot in her heart eased. "I understand, Roald. I do not hold it against you," she assured him.

"I hate myself for being this... helpless." Frowns of frustration etched on his face.

"Be patient with yourself. Give yourself some leeway. Your pain is deep, it will take time to stop hurting. Self-soothe if you can." She framed his face, making him look into her eyes. He nodded. The tension around his mouth eased.

He pulled her into his arms, his hold tight. She ran her hands in soothing circles on his back. Soon, his breathing changed. He pulled away, his eyes darkened with familiar heat, his body infused with a distinct tension. A sexual heat now filled her as she realised, she was clad in a bathrobe with nothing underneath.

He touched his lips on hers, waiting for her consent, but unable to ask. She gave it by parting her mouth. His breath hitched, and he pressed his lips to her in a passionate, needy kiss. The fierceness of his lips, the ardent strokes of his tongue in her mouth, were a plea for reassurance. The intensity and depth of his need as he angled her head, in the hand that cradled her scalp was a reminder all was well between them.

His warm breath struck her cheek; his eyes closed as he savoured her mouth. The bristles on his chin left a trail of prickly burns on her skin. One hand travelled down her back and settled low, then pulled her closer until her body lay flat against him, chest to chest. He shifted and settled her weight on him more fully.

His kiss gentled and moved to the side of her mouth, following the line of her jaw up to her ear. The contrast of his soft lips and roughened chin as it travelled along the sensitive line raised the hairs at the back of her neck. His sharp inhale and exhale stirred the hair on her forehead as he clasped her closer still.

"I hope I have not lost manly points in your eyes." His murmur was husky and deep.

"No, I think sensitive men are more masculine. Also, it is hard to cuddle someone with nothing but sharp edges," she replied, burying deeper into him. His arm tightened in response.

He felt warm. His unique scent surrounded her and soothed her bruised heart. Roald was not perfect; his flaws were rooted deep. But she was not, either. Her own imperfections were inherent in her genes. Roald could overcome his; she could never change hers. And if he was willing to fight against himself to be with her, her heart would not give up on them until they achieved their common goal.

"Is there anything else I need to know about you?" Roald asked after a while.

"Yes. Keep it a secret. I am not ready for the world to know."

Daniel sat with Íñigo in companionable silence as they waited for Ximena's arrival. His brain was filled with the agility and speed test results and the implications. With his *Vis* traits awakened, he was now as strong, as fast, as agile. There were no signs of it fading. It had been fifty-eight hours. And he did not feel any need to consume viscera.

Ximena arrived ten minutes later. Her clipped footsteps on the tiled floor of the lab announced her arrival long before she came through the door. He stood up upon her entry and kissed her cheek in greeting.

"Sit down, Dan," she said, taking a seat herself. He sat back down; his stomach knotted with tension as he waited for her to speak. It was a good thing his breakfast was light.

"I have briefed Daniel on the results of the tests already," Íñigo said.

She nodded and faced him. "Dan, your olfactory, vision and audiometry test showed these senses are sharper than human's but not of *Viscerebus* level yet. You would need to train them into full capability." Ximena gazed intently at his face.

He nodded. He figured as much. There was a change in his hearing, scent, and sight, but nothing dramatic. Just like muscles, his senses needed to be stretched beyond what they were used to.

"How long would it take, Tita?"

Ximena shrugged. "I am not sure. We are new to this. Young *Viscerebus* are born with human-level senses, except the sense of smell which is in hyper level upon birth. The full development of the rest does not happen until we are able to walk. So, it all depends on the physical development of a *Vis* child."

Daniel was not sure what that meant, so he glanced at Íñigo. That earned him a mild smile from the older man. "It means it could take about a year, unless you stimulate them," Íñigo said.

"Stimulate?" *How the hell does one stimulate their senses?*

It was Ximena's turn to smile. "You focus your senses. To one thing at a time. One sound, one flavour, one scent, one sensation. Then you do it again. And again. Repeatedly. Until you learn to isolate each note and chemical signature, then catalogue it in your brain that identifying it becomes second nature."

It rendered him speechless for a second. "Is that all?" he asked, incredulous. That sounded like a lot of work.

Ximena and Íñigo chuckled. It got him smiling as well. The moment of levity cleared the remaining tension in the air.

"So, what is next, Tita?" he asked.

Ximena's demeanour sobered. "We want to continue our project to its conclusion. This might take years. You could walk away now if you wish..."

Her statement dampened his lightened mood. The forewarning hidden in her tone sounded ominous. "What is the end goal of *Project Chrysalis*?"

Íñigo and Ximena exchanged a glance, and it seemed they were in sync. "The possibilities in this experiment would be endless. Just like technology, one answer could lead to a bigger question, Dan. And we want to take it as far as we can," Íñigo said.

He met Íñigo's gaze head on. "I could continue giving you my blood, but only if you tell me exactly what you need it for, what you will use it for." Daniel had to know if the consequences of his participation in the program would be palatable.

Once more, Íñigo and Ximena exchanged a meaningful look. Íñigo's quick nod seemed to give her both the support and the right to tell him. The depth of their partnership became very clear to him more than any other time in the past. The pair understood each other's motivation at the core level. They had each other's back.

Ximena got up and paced. "In the beginning, it was for a selfish reason. I wanted to change a man I loved... into a *Vis* like us, so we could be together. But... I ran out of time. And it made me consider the bigger picture. The *Veil of Secrecy* is the only thing that kept us alive and thriving, and the threat of exposure remains constant. We will always be in danger because the humans outnumber us thirty to one. The only permanent solution would be to increase our number. And this experiment might achieve that. If it does, it will be a good thing." Her voice gained in intensity; her eyes fierce.

"How exactly would you do that, Tita?" He did not want to think Ximena would inflict the changes to unwitting humans.

"There are *Erdias* who would want to become *Vis*, so we will start with them," Ximena said.

"Start with them? Does it mean your program would extend to humans as well?" It seemed such a dangerous proposition. Most humans would not want to become like them. And unwilling victims would be dangerous.

"No, no. Not the humans. Only the *Veil-bound Erdias*," she clarified.

It was a relief to hear that. "And those *Erdias* who want to remain as they are..." he asked.

"I will not force anyone. I made the mistake of taking someone's right to decide once, and I ruined his life. And that is something I do not want to repeat." The bitterness in her tone, the pain of her regret, was palpable.

"Okay, Tita. I am still in," he said, reassured.

"Thank you, Dan..." Ximena's smile of satisfaction was perhaps tinged with relief and gratitude.

And he wondered who she referred to, what kind of mistake it was, and why it became a pivotal point in her life.

Kazu glided over the buildings, just above the clouds, to avoid being spotted. With his senses, he searched for Yuana's location, but was unable to pinpoint it. He could pick up some of her thoughts; however, they remained just quick flashes of inaudible sounds and disjointed images. He was still having a hard time connecting to her *aura*.

After a while, he did it the human way. He landed on the roof of one building and took out his mobile phone from the *morphbag* strapped around his waist. He phoned Yuana.

"Good afternoon, Yuana," he said, his eyes closed to peer through his senses to find her location.

"Good afternoon, Kazu," she replied pleasantly.

"When are you free for training?" he asked. He was still getting the same disjointed images, but he sensed she was in a building.

"Oh... yes. I'm sorry, I have been busy. But I have been practicing what you taught me." Yuana was apologetic.

He caught flashes of her walking out to her car.

"That is good. But there are many more things to learn, Yuana." He kept his tone gentle, despite his frustration.

"I understand, but I wanted to perfect the skills you taught me before I learn new ones."

He heard the car door open and close and felt the movement in his body.

"Let me teach you a few more skills that would be best combined with the previous ones you have learned. It would work better together," he said. Images of her sat inside her car flashed in his mind's eye. Dark brown leather upholstery. The fragrance of lavender car air freshener. The jolt of a moving car.

"Oh, is that so?" Her excited tone floated to him. And he saw her check her calendar. "Okay, how about we schedule it tomorrow night? Around midnight?" she said. He could now see over her shoulder as she typed in their appointment in her planner.

"Tomorrow midnight, then," he said, satisfied with her response.

He was glad. Tomorrow night, he would imprint on her. She seemed unwilling to unravel the depth of her true nature, so he would have to help her.

As her *Aztarim*, he could prepare her without her realizing it. He would usher her to the fulfilment of her role in the coming *Shift* in the history of the *Viscerebus*.

It was time for their destiny to unfold.

Mateo sat down on the couch to enjoy his gin and tonic after a long day. The evening shift manager just left his office after the case update and briefing.

He gave himself half an hour to relax before he proceeded to the ground floor gym where he, Daniel, and Roald would train. He did not expect to see Daniel arrive early with a grim expression on his face.

"Anything wrong, D?" His son's demeanour was too sombre for his taste.

Daniel sat on the couch beside him, his shoulders hunched as he rested his elbows on his thighs, his eyes on the gym bag by his feet. It reminded Mateo of the incident when Daniel was twelve and took the car without permission to impress a girl, then promptly wrapped it around a tree. Daniel preempted his questioning by coming to him and confessing.

Today, Daniel resembled that boy. He had something to say and was unsure of his father's reaction.

"Dad, I need to tell you something..." Dan said, his eyes still averted.

He kept his tone even to make it easy for his son. "What is it?"

"I took part in the *Project Chrysalis* of Tita Ximena." Daniel began and glanced at him to gauge his reaction.

"*Project Chrysalis*? Is that her project about discovering the cure for *VM*?"

"No, the *VM* cure is the *Altera*. *Project Chrysalis* is different," Daniel replied.

He was still unclear why it bothered Daniel. "So, tell me. What is it and what is your participation?" He sat back. He wanted Daniel to relax and not worry about his reaction.

"It's confidential research about the linkage between human and *Viscerebus* genes. They need my blood for their experiment... I provided it," his son replied.

"Why your blood?" He could not help but frown.

A shadow of a grimace appeared in Dan's mouth. "As it turns out, I am the missing link. A... product of the right moment with the right gene combination of a *Vis* and an *Erdia*," Daniel explained.

"There are plenty of people like you in our kind. Why you specifically?" Dan's diffidence made him nervous.

Daniel scratched his temple, unable to meet his eyes. It was a nervous gesture that his son had since childhood.

"Hmm... I was... conceived within the crucial forty-eight hours of a *harravis'* potency." Daniel's voice trailed, expecting him to pick up on it.

It took him a minute before it clicked. Then heat crept from his neck to his ears. "Hmm... okay, I get it..." He could not look Daniel in the eyes. Sex with his late wife was not something he wanted to discuss with his son. "Ahem..." He cleared his throat to dissipate the uneasiness in the air. "So, what else?"

Daniel's sigh of relief was heartfelt. "We discovered something unexpected about me," Daniel said.

"What is it?" His brain jumped to an unwanted conclusion about Daniel's paternity.

"We discovered I have more *V genes* than a normal *Erdia* and it can be awakened by consuming viscera."

Mateo's brain reeled, suspending time for a moment. Then a jolt of joy surged in his heart, but Daniel's jaw was rigid still. Mateo realised he never asked Daniel how he felt about being an *Erdia.* He just assumed his son was okay with it. Dan just found out the circumstances of his mother's death, and now, it seemed he was more *Vis* than human. All this must have been overwhelming.

"And how do you feel about it?" He suppressed his excitement at Daniel's news.

Daniel's gaze turned reflective. "I am not sure, Dad. The idea of eating viscera repulsed me, but I needed to know about my *Vis* side, so..."

"So, you had some viscera? And?"

"It triggered my *Vis* strength, agility, speed, and healing abilities. I could develop the super senses as I have the genes for it, but I cannot shapeshift."

"Wow!" He did not expect that. "So, you're a super *Erdia*..." His son must be the first in the history of their kind to manifest such a genetic oddity.

Daniel shook his head. "Tita Ximena called me a *Mejordia*, a higher form of an *Erdia*. And according to her, I am *Mejordia* 001."

"*Mejordia 001*... You have become a milestone, my son. How do you feel about being the first?" he asked.

"I like that part..." Daniel said.

"But?"

"It is more than that to me, Dad..."

"Explain, then..." Mateo could see that Daniel wanted to express something profound. And perhaps, this would be the one and only time his son would say it.

Daniel took a deep breath before he began. "I never paid attention to being an *Erdia.* I was not a *Vis*, and I was more human. It was easy to ignore that until you told me the truth about mom's death. The reality of your nature became material, and my true feelings about it surfaced. I realised being in the middle of those two worlds had been the reason I could not establish emotional roots."

"I thought I resented your nature, that I did not want to be like you, but this showed me that deep inside, I wished I was. And my resentment stemmed from envy. It was hard to consider myself half-*Vis* when physically, I was just like any human," Daniel continued and released another deeply drawn breath.

"And did your feelings change now?" His heavy heart pounded as he waited for Daniel's response.

Daniel's small smile accompanied the nod. "Yes. Science confirmed that I am more like you than my mother. And now that my latent *Viscerebus* traits have surfaced, I cannot deny that I am more *Vis* than human."

His back muscles loosened. Daniel's admission unlocked something in his heart. He swallowed the emotions down. "So, you think you can take me on now?" he joked to stop the awkward buildup of feelings in his heart. His son, like himself, would be uneasy with the sentimentality.

"Yes, I definitely think so. You can try me," Dan said, his grin was wide.

He grinned back. "I'm going to school you, my boy. It is time I show you what your old man can do," he said, getting up to pick up his gym bag from the corner of his table. With his arm around his son's shoulder, they marched to the gym.

15

ANIMUS RISING

Roald watched Mateo and Daniel walk in together. They were the perfect example of the ideal father and son camaraderie. They trash-talked each other.

"Roald, do you mind sitting on the sidelines for the moment? I want to teach my son here a lesson he will never forget for the rest of his brief life," Mateo said, his eyes twinkling with mischief.

"Oh... by all means, sir. I would not miss it for the world... Am I allowed to place a bet?" he asked, finding their banter infectious.

"Sure, for as long as you bet on me," Mateo said, smiling, as he proceeded to the shower stalls to change.

"Don't take unnecessary risk, bro. I am younger and tougher, plus we are friends," Daniel said as went to his own shower stall to change.

"Your dad is a military man, Dan. He has more experience in ass-kicking than you," he called out.

"That is a wise observation. How long do you think it will take before my son taps out?" Mateo asked him as he walked back to the training area, wearing gym pants and a t-shirt. Roald grinned in response.

"Why don't we make that bet more interesting? Loser pays for the winner's next date," Daniel suggested as he joined them, dressed for the session.

Both he and Mateo laughed at the novel idea.

"I hope it does not mean that you will join the date itself to pay for it," he said.

Daniel's left eyebrow rose, and a smirk appeared on his face. "I see you assume I will lose... Do not be too hasty, because if you bet on Dad and I won, you are also a loser."

"So, the winner might win two paid dates, and the loser could pay for two as well?" Mateo said, an identical arch on his brow.

"Yep, so choose well, bro," Daniel said, his tone mocking.

Roald pretended to think about it for a while. "I think I will still bet on a military guy who is my *Kali* trainer."

"Suit yourself... You'd better be prepared to tell Yuana you would miss one of your date nights, as your spending money would pay for someone else's," Daniel said, grinning.

"Enough yapping, Dan. Let's see what you can do with your new skills," Mateo said and moved to the middle of the room.

That statement caught his attention. He realised what it meant. And his interest in their sparring became keener. Father and son circled each other for a few seconds.

Daniel threw the first punch, a straight. Mateo blocked and swiped it to the side. Daniel's other hand came up with a quick hook; Mateo's hand caught it, then counterpunched. Dan slapped it away. Thwacking sounds filled the room as the two exchanged blows that hit muscled arms, elbows, and fists.

They were equal in skill. The punches became faster and more vicious. Daniel exhibited speed that was almost a blur. Mateo's counters were swift, his skill and experience obvious with the ease of his attacks and parries.

They moved all over the gym floor, their movements graceful, almost like a dance. The first punch that landed was Mateo's, hitting Daniel's chin. Dan staggered back but remained unfazed.

Within seconds, Daniel retaliated and landed a punch on his father's lip, drawing blood. Mateo wiped the blood off, grinned at Daniel, and launched a volley of attack, this time including elbows and knees. Mateo demonstrated agility with fast footwork. Daniel countered them all.

The beyond-human speed Daniel displayed amazed Roald. His friend's newly gained *Aswang* traits were in full view. And it made him envious. His attention refocused on the pair when Mateo kicked Daniel in the chest. He fell with a thump, landing on his ass. Daniel groaned. Mateo stopped and stood over him. Daniel sat up slowly, rubbing his chest. Mateo pulled him up.

"That was impressive, my boy!" Mateo beamed at his son's performance.

"Well, I tried... but not good enough. You kicked my ass," Daniel said in disgust.

"You have never been in an actual fight, so your movements were predictable. It was limited to training and sparring," Mateo said, tapping him on the back.

"So, should I pick a fight now and then?" Daniel asked?

"With your *Vis* traits to the fore, any normal human cannot compete with you, but a well-trained human, like some of our soldiers, will not be easy pickings. So, you need to train smarter," Mateo said, still smiling.

As Roald listened to Mateo, his heart sank. He would have to train harder and better to defend himself from an *Aswang*. He told himself that he had some training, he just needed to get back to it.

"I would have to be one of those well-trained humans, then." Roald joined the conversation to mask his unease.

"Ah... I am glad you said that, Roald. I intend to train you to the very edge of your capability and then further. At the end of all this, I want you to be the best student I've ever trained," Mateo said; his smile was warm.

"Oh... I see I am no longer your best student, Dad," Daniel quipped in jest.

"I don't consider you a student. You're my son, an extension of me," Mateo said.

"So, can I join you on your next date, as your extension, and the one who would pay for it?" Daniel's eyes twinkled in an identical gleam of merriment as his father's.

"Sure, if you allow me, just one time, to set you up on a blind date," Mateo countered and laughed at Daniel's grimace.

"Well, Dan, as you said earlier, loser has a potential to pay for two dates. I shall take great pleasure telling Yuana our next dinner date is on you. I hope your allowance can afford lobster and steak, at least," Roald said, joining the ribbing of Daniel. Dan gave him a finger in response.

"Okay, let's get on with today's training. I'd like to start you with the tactical knife work my battalion is famous for," Mateo said, curtailing any more jesting.

Roald stood up, eager. The next half an hour became a demonstration of defensive and offensive techniques, then the practiced execution of each. Mateo sparred with him in a controlled manner in the beginning. They were using practice blades for safety, but it could still do damage.

The session became progressively more intense as the hour wore on. Mateo cranked it up by attacking him with more speed and power, challenging his skill, strength, reflexes, and stamina.

Roald focused on deflecting every thrust and stab, dodging each slash, and responding with varying degrees of parry, block, and traps. As they moved around the room, Mateo forced him to sidestep the flurry of attacks, stalked and lunged for him when he retreated. Mateo pushed him harder still by repeating the moves faster and stronger until his strength gave way.

The edge of the training *karambit* ended a millimetre away from his jugular. The thrust would have killed him it if was an actual bladed knife. It was a testament to Mateo's skill.

Roald's heart hammered with the effort and the realisation he could not match a trained *Aswang* like Mateo. He felt both dejected and driven. He looked at Mateo and recognised his expression as that of a proud father, with extreme satisfaction, and it soothed his bruised ego.

"Well done, Roald," Mateo said, a pleased smile on his face. Daniel had the identical expression as his father.

"Thank you, sir, but just in case you did not notice, if that was a real fight, I would already be dead," he said flatly.

"Maybe, but not all *Vis* are as trained as I am. You may not have my speed, but if you practise enough, your muscle memory would bridge that gap. As to the strength, you can improve on it, but you cannot match our natural abilities on that score. So, focus on the techniques. The beauty of the bladed weapon is that you don't need to be strong to inflict a fatal wound to even the strongest opponent. You just need to be precise. And for a human, your knife skills are impressive," Mateo said, his smile still wide.

Roald was reassured by those words. If practice was required, he would do it. Mollified, they continued training. Mateo taught the techniques to Daniel while he watched them spar. The father and son were well matched in natural abilities, although Mateo's skills and experience were clear. Once again, he found himself envious of Daniel's *Aswang* abilities.

"Do I take it you already told your father you are part of Tita Ximena's project?" Roald asked Daniel as they towelled their wet hair.

Daniel nodded. "He knew I was taking part in the program, but not the full details. I also told him what we discovered about me. We sparred because he wanted to test my new skills."

"How do you feel about it? Now that you are more like your dad than your mom," he asked through the neck hole of his shirt as he pulled it over his head.

Daniel's head popped out of his neckline. He looked contemplative as he pushed his arms through the sleeves before he turned to his friend, his expression one of calm acceptance.

"I have realised my resentment towards that part of my genetic makeup was because I did not inherit the traits that made them different from humans. Now that I have that, most of it, anyway, I am more at peace with it," he explained.

He studied Daniel's face and saw the truth in that statement. Once again, he felt a twinge of envy. Daniel had wrestled his inner demon and won, while he still could not face his without a security blanket.

Mateo looked on as the two young men walked out of the gym to go wherever they venture to after training. He felt paternal pride for both. His son's revelation that he had uncovered his own *Vis* traits was welcome news. He never knew Daniel harboured feelings of bitterness against being an *Erdia*. Now he was glad he came to terms with it and had accepted his bloodline.

Roald's issue was the one remaining thing from his past that he needed to put to rest. He had been weighing the best time to do this. He might assuage his conscience if he told the boy, but his honour demanded that he make amends.

The easier way was to continue with what he was doing – training Roald. It soothed his conscience to make Roald the best fighter he could be. And the process was enjoyable.

The boy possessed natural talent. It also seemed to help Roald manage his fear because it gave him confidence. If this was what would overcome it, then he would not stop until Roald's trauma no longer existed.

This was the right thing to do. Roald might recoil if he found out the truth. Mateo would pay up before he owned up to his son's friend. He would not want to cause a rift between Daniel and Roald because of what he did.

Restitution first, then confession.

Yuana sat on the couch in her robe, waiting for the night to envelop the cloudless sky. There would be no extra cover for both Kazu and herself. They would have to fly higher so their figures would be less discernible from any potential viewers below.

As the sun set on the horizon, and the hue of the sky met the ground, total darkness cloaked her unit, but it did not matter. Her night vision was working fine. Yuana got up and slid her door open to the outdoor garden. She was on her full *Animus* by the time she hung her robe on the coat rack. Her transformation was now instantaneous and as natural to her as breathing.

She had four hours to spend on her *Apex* lesson before she was due to meet Roald and Daniel later. The two would be in training themselves.

Yuana stepped out, unfurled her wings, and took off. Her tail emerged as soon as her toes left the ground. A few vigorous flaps powered her flight upward. She propelled herself higher, then higher still, until the people below could not discern her human shape. To them, she was just a bird.

She flew northward, to where she would meet Kazu. While airborne, she threw ultrasonic clicks at intervals to supplement her night vision as she travelled. The pinpricks of city lights below and the stars in the sky felt like being sandwiched between sparkles of fireflies.

As she soared on, her lids lowered to protect her eyes, her thoughts went to her family. Like a flash of lightning, she saw images of her mother and father, sitting in their living room, watching TV. That startled her. The vision was clear, like a scene in a movie.

She closed her eyes to try it once more. The vision came back, this time she could hear snippets of their faint conversation; some portions of it were unintelligible. This was not her imagination. Could this be a new power?

With her heart pounding, she channeled her thoughts towards the rest of her family. One by one, she saw them all; gathered at the dining table, enjoying dinner.

What about Roald? He should be with Daniel now. And she saw them both entering a restaurant, being seated by the service staff. They were laughing about something.

Then a distinct, high-frequency click reached her ears.

Kazu.

He was still about five hundred meters away, but she could pick out his figure as if it was a mere twenty meters.

Then, they were face to face. They circled each other, and just like their last flight together, Kazu pointed below, and they landed on the rooftop of the tallest building.

"It is a perfect night. Good evening, Yuana," Kazu greeted her with a smile.

She smiled back. "It is indeed. Good evening to you too, Kazu," she replied. "So, what am I learning today?" She was impatient to start, to take advantage of their time together, then get back home by eleven p.m. to meet with Daniel and Roald.

Kazu's gaze was assessing. "It is a crucial bit of learning, Yuana. It will open the door for all your mental powers, but it requires a supreme amount of faith from your end," he said. The half-smile was wiped off his face, and with a piercing look, he asked, "Do you trust me, Yuana?"

That gave her pause. *Do I?* She did not have any reason to doubt him. Kazu had done nothing to cause her alarm, but she had not known him long. Trusting him without proof struck Yuana as reckless.

"I have no reason to mistrust you, but faith requires more than that..." She thought she saw a flicker of disappointment in Kazu's eyes, but he smiled and nodded.

"I understand," he replied. He paused and looked over the horizon, seeming to think about what he would say to her next.

"I guess it would depend on what you are going to ask from me." She did not want him offended, and she wanted to learn more about herself. If Kazu would make it easier to do that, then she would take a leap of faith.

"Of course," he said, and faced her again. "What I needed to teach you requires you to put your trust in me one hundred per cent."

"What is it you wanted me to do that demands such a price? One hundred per cent trust is almost impossible to give outright," she replied.

Once again, Kazu paused and stared at her. He seemed to be weighing if she was ready for what he would ask of her.

"What if I told you if you commit to my teaching, fully and without reservation, you will discover powers you would otherwise never know. I can teach you to master the ones you already know, and how to combine them with those we will discover still. If you found a way that would magnify your power exponentially, would you do it, Yuana?" he said, watchful.

Excitement shot through her body with a thrill she could not explain. In its wake, a fear of the unknown. "What do you require from me?" she asked instead.

"Do you know what *ZeNading* is?" Kazu's grey eyes penetrated her.

"No." She had never heard of it before.

"It is short for Zenith and Nadir, the peak and rock bottom. This would require us to fly the highest we can go, *syne-morphose* into our human form, and plummet together to the lowest point possible, then shift back to our *Animus* before we hit the ground so we can soar again."

The imagery of what he said stunned her. "What? But...why?" Yuana's brain reeled at the idea. There had to be a justification for such a risk.

"*ZeNading* forces you to open your senses like nothing can. It will reveal your latent abilities and the full potential of your *Animus*."

"But... how do I know when to transform back? And what if I lose consciousness on the way down?" The whole idea intimidated her.

"That is where the trust comes in. I will hold your hand as we plummet, and I will tell you when to transform back. I will make sure you do not crash to the ground," Kazu said, his tone confident and reassuring.

She had done nose dives during her previous flights, but not in her human form. The thought of flying high up and letting herself fall so close to death, where only Kazu's word would save her, was daunting. And she did not know if she could do it.

She glanced at Kazu as he waited for her decision. Strangely, she felt challenged by him and pressured to do it. Yuana was an inch away from taking him on, but her heart and natural self-preservation resisted it. Thoughts of her parents and Roald came rushing back to her consciousness; the loves of her life and her instinct won.

"I am not ready to do it yet, Kazu. I'm sorry." She truly was, but she was not prepared to take a literal plunge.

Kazu's expression remained impassive as he nodded but she sensed his disappointment. As he turned away, she noticed his jaw had hardened. She felt embarrassed at her faintheartedness, and for a split second, she almost reconsidered. But she kept silent.

Their training was cut short since it hinged on the trust test. With an apology, she bid him goodnight.

Kazu, to his credit, accepted with grace.

She flew home. Her mind dwelt on her disappointment at her lack of courage. But it was not a simple task; it was life-threatening.

Yuana realised she placed herself in a dangerous position, with no backup, and nobody in her family knew. Her grandfather would have her head if he found out she disregarded his primary rule – always have a Plan B.

Her dissatisfaction with her shallow existence grew tenfold. She breezed through life without having to plan or think about her feature. When having a backup plan mattered the most, she had none.

Kazu remained on the rooftop of the building, his eyes closed. He was still getting flashes of the image of Yuana flying back to her home, but there was nothing else. He could not read her mind or sense her emotions.

His visions of her become less clear the farther she was. He had hoped to engage her competitive nature by challenging her, but it did not work. He would have to change tactics.

Yuana was more indifferent about her true nature and its accompanying responsibilities than he realised. He would have to engineer her transition for her own good.

If *aural Aztarimar* did not work, then *oral* it would have to be.

Yuana's uneasiness lingered the whole flight back. Her mind lingered on the conversation with Kazu.

It was natural not to entrust anyone with her life since her instinct was against it. But if her training required *ZeNading* before she could progress, she needed to mitigate the risk.

But how? The only way to prepare for *ZeNading* would be to do it.

Then it hit her.

She would try a few times by herself, progressively higher and lower, with her *Apex* senses open. So, when she trained with Kazu again, she would not be doing it blind. With a resolution in sight, she hastened home.

She was in her human form the moment her feet touched the turf of her garden. Barefoot and naked, she slid open her door and proceeded to the shower.

The warmth of the water, the shushing sounds of the shower quieted her brain and washed the tension away. A thought came to her. *Hmm, would I be able to use my Apex telepathic viewing skill in my human form?*

She closed her eyes and called forth the image of Roald and Daniel, but she saw nothing. She tried her parents – still nothing.

Hmm...so, that power is only accessible to my Animus.

She partially *syne-morphosed* and felt something inside her shift. Her spine tingled, and she felt a micro vibration behind her eyes. Then she saw Daniel and Roald seated down, drinks in hand. A service staff approached and handed them the menu. She focused on the image and heard their voices, like a badly tuned radio.

Then she realised she could only view the scene thru Daniel's eyes, not Roald's.

Why? Is it because he is human?

She turned her attention to her parents. Clear images flooded her mind's eye. They were together, chatting on the sofa, kissing. She focused on her father. But just like with Roald, she drew blank. It was only possible with her mother. Her remote viewing capability applied only to *Vis* minds.

How about other Vis minds outside her family?

She fixed on her uncle Íñigo. And snapshots of his location flashed in her mind. He was in the laboratory, looking at a computer screen attached to a microscope.

How about those I have no personal relationship with? Co-workers? Clients?

Half an hour later, she was confused. It worked with some of them, but not with others.

But there was no time to think about it now. She turned off the shower and got dressed in a hurry. Her parents were still having dinner, but not for long.

Yuana gasped for air as she wiped tears of mirth from her eyes. Her father was regaling them with anecdotes about his early days in medical school. The story of the superstitious patient, the woman's lack of hygiene during a pelvic exam, and its effect on her father had them laughing to the point of tears. They had been cackling for half an hour when the doorbell rang.

It was Daniel and Roald.

"We rang your unit, and when you did not respond, we came here," Roald said as he bent down and kissed her on the cheeks. "Hmm... you smell delicious," he murmured.

"And you smell like..." Roald's natural scent blended with artificial pine and lemon, "car air freshener..."

Roald grinned.

"So, what are you youngsters up to? Are you taking my daughter out tonight?" Galen asked.

"Nah, Daniel here cannot afford to spend money in the next three weeks. He lost a bet with me earlier. He needs to save his play money to pay for my next date with Yuana. I warned him it will cost him about three Friday night outs," Roald said, chuckling.

Daniel grimaced in response.

"Aha! I love that arrangement. You guys take the risk and I enjoy the reward," she said.

Daniel snorted. "Do not rub it in... What is our plan tonight, Yuana?" he asked.

"Well, let's stick to the original one and hang out here," she said.

"I'm game. For as long as you have the booze to make my loss easier to bear," Daniel said.

"Sure, we can provide you enough booze to cover the three Friday nights that you will forego."

"Is this party exclusive to you three? Or can we join in?" Her mother piped in.

"Ah, even better. We drink my parent's bar dry instead of mine." She clapped with glee as Galen grinned at her.

Ten minutes later, with drinks on hand, they were listening to another one of her father's medical school bloopers.

"... So, when she opened her legs, we were staring at this lady's privates. She had shaved her pubes everywhere except a thin line in the middle. And my buddy immediately stood straight up, his arm shot out in a Nazi salute and he said, 'Heil, Hitler!'"

They all burst out laughing.

"And then, the bewildered lady levered herself up on one elbow, and said, 'I'm Jewish,'" Galen continued. "She was looking at my buddy accusingly, and my buddy tried to apologise, but he was laughing too hard. And when he sobered up, he said, 'I'm sorry, madam, it was my mistake. It was Charlie Chaplin,'" Galen added.

Another wave of laughter echoed around the room. Daniel and Roald almost rolled off the couch.

"Oh, honey, I would love to meet your old buddy," her mother said as she wiped her eyes dry.

"Sure, for as long as it's face to face. I'd hate for him to have other thoughts about you..." Galen grinned.

Her father's comments reminded her of her earlier issue. "Hey, Mama. I need your opinion on something," she said. Her serious tone sobered everybody up. Her mother looked at her, one eyebrow quirked.

"Fire away, my little Aya," her father said. At her questioning glance, "It means little bird," Galen added.

The new pet name gave her pause, but she continued on. "While I was flying tonight, I discovered I can connect to Mama, to our family, in a... telepathic way," she said.

"What do you mean?" her mother asked, frowning.

"When I was in my *Animus,* I saw you and Papa, on the couch. It was like watching a movie." She glanced at Daniel and Roald. "And you two, as well. At the bar."

Both blinked at her.

"Wow!" her mother breathed. Her mother's stunned expression was identical to everyone in the room.

"Ah... that's a wonderful skill to have, right?" Her father's gaze shot to her mother's face, then back to her.

"It has limits. I could only see through a *Vis'* eyes. And only with some of them. I could not do it through Roald's, and yours, Papa."

"Why?" A deeper frown replaced her mother's awe-struck expression.

"I do not know, Mama. It worked with everyone in our family, and with some of our employees and clients. But not with others."

"You said it works with all of us, except your father and Roald. So, this was not an emotional link. Or perhaps it is, but it does not work on humans..." Ysobella mused, eyes narrowed in speculation. "Did it work with Daniel?" Her mother's eyes focused on her.

She nodded. "It did. That was how I viewed them earlier."

"So, which *Vis* did it not work for you?" her father asked.

"Some of our employees, clients, friends," she replied.

"Who among our team in particular?" her mother asked.

She named the people with whom she had remote viewing success, and with whom she failed.

“Hmm… that is quite a puzzle…” Ysobella said and lapsed into silence. Her mother’s frown deepened as she mulled the facts over.

Yuana could only agree with her. It was perplexing. There was no definite common thread or distinction between her relationship with them that would explain the anomaly.

“What exactly did you see?” Roald asked.

“When I viewed you and Daniel, you were entering the restaurant, and getting seated. And later you were laughing about something. And when I was viewing Mama and Papa, they were sitting on the couch, watching TV,” she said.

“Yep, you definitely saw us… Oh, god!” Daniel exclaimed, his eyes widened.

“What?” she asked, alarmed.

“Yuana, I just realised you will be able to view me anytime, even when I am doing… private stuff,” he said, aghast.

“Private stuff? Like what?” she asked, confused.

Daniel’s wide-eyed expression spoke volumes.

“Eww… That is gross, Dan! You flatter yourself if you think I would want to see you do number 2!” she said, repulsed.

Laughter erupted from the rest.

Daniel looked scandalised. “I wasn’t referring to that kind of private stuff… or bodily function.” His tone was dry, one eyebrow arched.

Her eyes rolled in annoyance. “Oh… that is even more presumptuous of you!”

Roald punched Daniel’s shoulder in jest. “Don’t give her ideas. She might just find something to use against you,” he warned.

Daniel’s eyebrows rose higher, now doubly alarmed.

“So, my being human renders me impenetrable to mind control of your kind?” Galen asked.

“You exaggerate, Papa. I never said I can control minds, I can just see into it…” she replied, but an idea sparked in her head.

“How is your relationship with these people compared to these?” Her mother interrupted. Ysobella had made a list of the names and divided them into two columns.

Yuana looked at the list closely. She had good relationships with all of them. They were all long-term employees of the company. There was no obvious determining factor. “I cannot say there is any difference in how I feel about each of them,” she said.

“Perhaps how you feel about them that is not the crucial point, but how they feel about you,” her mother said.

“Yes, it could be about trust. Maybe the minds that were accessible to you trusted you more,” her father said.

That made sense. There was a precedent in psychology. People open up more to those they trusted. Kazu's words returned to her. He had said earlier that without trust their lessons would not progress.

Is this ability to read minds the lesson Kazu wanted to teach me?

Is there more to it? Like mind control, as Papa suggested.

Do I want to learn it?

16

THE FORESHADOWING

Yuana sat in her garden, contemplating the best way to execute the *ZeNading* by herself. The soft morning light provided enough visibility for a potential audience.

The risk of flying low to test her plunge presented the possibility of being seen, but the danger of *ZeNading* at the proper height would be literally life and death. And she could ask no one to help her. Except Kazu – trusting him was the crux of her current concern.

She could not place herself in the vulnerable position of relying on Kazu for her safety. The only people she had absolute trust in were her family. But she could not tell her parents what she planned to do – they would stop her. So, while she felt an extra dose of guilt at doing something on her own without a Plan B or backup, she would have to do it alone.

Daniel or Roald were not options. The two would tell her parents to stop her reckless behaviour. She sighed.

How am I going to execute the ZeNading safely?

Maybe she could keep her eyes open so she would know when to transform back. But that could make her panic... If only her echolocation skill were accessible to her human form...

Unless... it was a partial transformation... just like what she did in the shower to test her mind-reading abilities. And she could try it while still on the ground. Now would be as good a time as any.

With a deep breath and closed eyes, the telltale tingle at the base of her spine began. It travelled upwards until it settled at the back of her skull and raised the tiny hairs on her neck. The warmth spread all over her head and the heat settled behind her eyes. Her *Animus* core now dominated, although her outward form still appeared human.

She sent ultrasonic clicks and listened to the sound waves reverberate off solid objects. Her brain created a picture of those obstacles. Each material created unique echo signatures based on density and distance. Her mind distinguished between the cement walls, earthenware planters, trees, turf, soft cushions of the outdoor seats, and glass doors.

She stayed there for hours and moved around. She focused on each obstacle, learned the distance of each barrier, from the farthest to the closest. Over and over until she could pinpoint exactly what the object was and how close. She echolocated beyond her garden, mapped the surrounding areas, the surrounding buildings, and created a virtual diagram.

It was time to put it into practice.

She shed her clothes, *syne-morphosed* and took flight. Her wings cleaved through the air and pushed against it, increasing her altitude. Adrenalin pumped through her veins and gave her a shot of reckless energy. She flew even higher. At twenty thousand feet, the atmosphere thinned.

Yuana took a deep breath and shifted into her human form, with her *Animus* still at her core. Her ascent stopped with the loss of her wings, her body suspended in the air for a split second before the fall began.

It was swift and breathtaking. Panic reigned over her and froze her mind. She was a flurry of flailing arms and legs as she plunged. She shifted back into her *Animus* in an instant. Her wings unfolded and flapped in frantic beats, arresting her fall and flipping her upright. Her heart pounded so loud against her ears and chest it felt like a cardiac arrest. Yuana looked down and saw she was still about ten thousand feet away from the ground.

She hovered a bit, fighting with herself to continue. If she gave up now, she would lose her nerve. And if she postponed it, time would magnify the nerve-wracking moments. Yuana inhaled a deep, shaky breath to fortify her courage and steady her galloping pulse. She increased her altitude to create more space between her and the ground.

At thirty thousand feet, with her heart in her throat, she repeated the exercise. This time, as soon as she lost her wings, she tightened her abdomen and controlled her body, keeping it upright. She concentrated on the swiftness of her drop and the expanding ground waiting to receive her body.

The vibration on her inner ear shifted her focus and jolted her into a realisation – she was unconsciously echo-locating. The knowledge steadied her.

The wind whistled past her ears and chilled her naked body. Her hair whipped up over her head as she hurtled down feet first. Then she picked up a very faint ricochet of the sound waves. Yuana closed her eyes and listened until the reverberations became stronger, almost tangible. Her senses told her that the gap between her and the ground diminished every second.

At a thousand feet, she sprouted her wings and tail. Her massive wings flapped in tandem with her heartbeat, her tail spread wide to slow her descent. She hovered a foot above the ground for a moment before her toes touched the tufted surface of her garden, her landing soft.

Her sense of accomplishment did not come until her pulse slowed. She was astounded at her own daring. Even if she completed just half of the *ZeNading*, her confidence to execute a full one grew.

Her heartbeats doubled as she pondered what she had done, and what she was about to do. Yuana took calming breaths to slow her pulse down enough to execute a full *ZeNading*. She was about to take off when she sensed her mother and father. They were both in the living room, staring at her in surprise.

"Are you flying out, my little Aya?" her father asked as her parents walked closer to her.

She nodded and smiled.

"Can we watch?" Ysobella asked. The excited glimmer in her mother's eyes made her hesitate. Yuana did not want her parents to watch her. It would terrify them. But their expectant look made it hard to disappoint them.

"Okay."

She decided against telling them what she was about to do. With ease, she took off. Once more, the colder air at ten thousand feet enveloped her. It turned icy at thirty thousand. At over forty, her lungs strained, making it hard to breathe. It was the highest she could reach without losing consciousness.

She hovered for a moment, her wings spread wide, and then dove like an Olympian – headfirst. With her arms clipped to her side to avoid drag. She morphed into her human form as she sped towards the ground like a bullet.

This time, the filo feathers on her brows kept her eyes protected from the wind. Adrenalin pumped fierce and steady in her veins. The ground grew ever bigger, rushing towards her at breakneck speed. She panicked for a moment. The image of her parents' petrified faces, horrified at the sight of her falling like a meteor, flashed in her mind's eye. The sensation of their agitation centered her.

She echolocated to gauge the distance to her open-air garden – she was about a thousand feet away from it. Two seconds later, she *syne-morphosed* to her *Animus*, her wings spread wide by instinct as she righted her form and halted her descent. She had a glimpse of her parents' faces before she reversed course and gained altitude again.

She repeated the exercise thrice, the last more audacious than the one before it, returning to her *Animus* closer to the ground each time.

On her last dive, at one hundred feet from her rooftop garden, she transformed back to her *Animus* to land. Her feet touched the wooden board silently, a few feet in front of her parents who were white as sheets. Spots of colour rushed towards their cheeks, and their shock was replaced by dark censure.

"What the hell was that, Yuana Sofia Orzabal?" Her mother's furious words matched the scowl on her face, her arms akimbo.

She smiled at them and almost transformed back into her human form when she remembered it would scandalise her father. Yuana walked back to her living room to get her robe, retracting her wings along the way. The feathers on her head morphed into hair. She regained her full human form the moment the robe covered her body. Her parents close at her heels.

"Don't think you can get out from answering your mother's question, young lady!" Her father glowered at her, wagging his finger. He looked as furious as her mother.

"Relax, Papa. I will tell you both in a minute. Let me just get something to eat and drink. That made me hungry and thirsty." She proceeded to her kitchen. "Can I get you two anything?" she added, throwing the question over her shoulder. She needed the carbo load and the time to structure her argument.

Her mother's scowl eased a little, but her father grew more furious by the minute, high colour on his cheeks. They allowed her the time to prepare her meal, though. They both sat down at the dining table as they waited for her to finish.

"Okay, now tell us what that was, Yuana." Her father's stern voice matched his expression, impatience written all over him.

"That was *ZeNading, Papa*. It is short for *Zenith* and *Nadir*. It was something the *Apex* of old used to do," she replied, after taking a big gulp from her cold drink.

"What was the purpose of that?" her mother asked. Ysobella's tone was calm and measured. Her assessing eyes focused on hers.

"Can I eat while we talk? I am starving," she asked, looking at them both. They would not scold her too much if she was eating. Her father's brows knitted closer, his expression darker, but her mother nodded and sat next to her.

"Don't change the subject, Yuana Sofia Orza... Aurelio!" Galen said, trying to hold on to his anger. He faltered when he saw her mother's amused glance. "What? She is an Aurelio now," her father said in defence.

"Yes, my love, she is," her mother said, patting his hand. "But this is not the time to discuss her family name."

Her parents' bickering gave her the chance to eat half of her sandwich and plan how she would explain to them what she was doing and why – without revealing Kazu's identity.

"Okay. I'm fortified now. What do you want to know?" She dusted the crumbs from her fingers.

They both turned to her, expectation on their faces. Her mother's eyebrow arched in question; her father's head inclined to one side. There was no getting out of it.

"As I said earlier, that was *ZeNading*. *Zenith* and *Nadir*, or peak and rock bottom. It means flying to the highest high and plummeting to the lowest possible low," she said. And as Yuana expected, they were confused. So, she took a deep breath and prepared for their question.

"Why do you need to fly to the highest high? And more to the point, why plummet?" Her mother's pitch rose higher in alarm.

"It's a ritual, Mama. I believe the *Apex* do it to test their personal limits, to discover their hidden skills. Much like how humans throw their kids in the water, so they learn how to swim." Yuana kept her tone dispassionate. She wanted to lessen their alarm.

"Wh... Can you not do it in a safer way? Like using a proverbial swimming instructor?" Her father's incredulous tone was almost funny.

"There is no such instructor around, Papa. Remember, *Apexes* come once every two hundred years. Besides, how can I live up to the image as the supreme idol of the *Viscerebus* if I do not have such death-defying antics to prove my mettle?" she joked.

That brought the scowls back on both their faces and wiped her grin off.

"Yuana, please tell me you are not trying that stunt just to learn a few party tricks." Ysobella's tone carried a note of warning. One well-shaped eyebrow quirked in displeasure.

"Mama, no. Seriously, it was meant to open my senses and reveal what I can do, what I am capable of as an *Apex*," she replied. In her mother's mood, it was not advisable to make light of her distress.

"And what have you learned so far?" Her father asked. It was now his turn to soothe her mother. He was caressing her mother's hand.

"A few skills. I can echolocate. I am accurate to a thousand feet and less. My magneto-reception capability is very strong. I suspect I cannot lose my way. You already know that I can tap on other *Vis'* minds at a distance." Her excitement flavoured her tone as she enumerated the skills.

"What else is there to discover?" her mother asked.

"I think I have thermoreceptors and electroreceptors, too. I want to see if those are well-developed like my other new senses. And I also want to explore the remote viewing thing, to see how far I can take it," she said.

"How does... *ZeNading* help, exactly?" her mother asked, confusion in her voice.

"The plunge helped me focus my senses during extreme circumstances." At her mother's admonishing glare, she felt her nervousness rise.

"Can you not find another way to focus your senses? Try something more... safe, like... meditation, or yoga," her father suggested.

"That will take too long, Papa," she said.

"What's the rush? It is not like you need to fly blind at night to hunt small living things for food," her father said, annoyed.

That made her chuckle.

"Yuana, that scared us. Seeing you fall from the sky... We thought..." Her mother shivered a little at the remembered scene.

"She was not merely falling, Bel, she was hurtling down like a comet!" Her father's anger resurfaced; jerky hand gestures punctuated his statement.

"It was all controlled, Papa. I knew what I was doing. I have done it before..."

"Holy *Prometheus*, Yuana! It was truly terrifying. Especially since you did it three times. The succeeding times should have been easier to watch, but it was not."

"I understand, Mama." She hugged her mother and felt the slight tremor in her body. "Don't worry. I know what I am doing. I need to hone my new skills, and it won't happen without considerable effort from me." She needed her parents to give her their support.

Their deep sighs came in unison. "Promise us you will take extreme care when you do it again," Galen said.

She nodded. Her mother gave her a peck on the forehead, but there was a contemplative look in her eyes.

"Yuana, I sense that there is something monumental that awaits you as an *Apex*. Our *Vis'* skills are designed for our survival, and you have all you need in your previous form to do that. So, your extra skills as an *Apex* must mean something, a forewarning of something big."

Her mother's words made her stomach clench. Ysobella just voiced the niggling worry that had been growing inside of her with every new skill she discovered about herself.

Every living thing on earth evolved with the abilities and traits designed for their survival. The pack leader that emerged among them was the one who honed those skills and traits to the fullest. The fact she had all these attributes, these powers that were so unusual... so seemingly unnecessary, made her think there was a purpose to it.

Being an *Apex* was thrust upon her with no warning. She believed the purpose for her emergence would knock on her door with the same suddenness. And she might not have enough time to perfect her new abilities before she would be required to use them.

Jacob got into the shower to wash the scent of sex and blood from his body. His lady guest for the night lay unconscious in the guestroom. She was not a drinker, so after sex, he drugged her using flavoured water. This second alternative was more enjoyable than spiking alcoholic drinks. Not that he was complaining. Sex was preferable, and she was beautiful in face and body.

The quick shower did its job. It cleaned him up and cooled him down. He got out of the cubicle, wiped his wet body with the thick, white towel, then wrapped it around his waist. He wanted to check on his donor, to make sure there was no adverse effect on her when he harvested a portion of her liver.

He inspected the woman lying naked on top of the sheet, the cut on her abdomen now a mere red gash. By all indications, she healed like all the others. In about four to six hours, when she woke up, she would not know any different.

She had a bit of a fever earlier, so he left her uncovered, to allow the icy blast of the air conditioner to lower her temperature.

As he walked closer, her similarity to someone struck him. He bent over her and inspected her face. He thought about it for a while, then recognition came to him.

She reminded him of that woman in the restaurant, the one who was with the human boyfriend. It surprised him he could still remember her. He never did. Even with this woman who shared his bed and her organs, he'd be hard pressed to recognise her if he encountered her in public tomorrow.

It might be because that woman was the only one that ever turned him down. No doubt because of the man she was with. It was inevitable that one of these days, he would encounter her again. Their community in Manila was small. And when that happened, he would make sure he got her. And not just be for her liver.

Katelin had been reviewing the historical information about the *Apex* of old. She had cancelled her appointments and dedicated the day to research. Her daughter Ysobella's gut instinct was always on point, and she worried about Yuana's reckless flight lessons.

Like Ysobella, she believed her granddaughter's emergence as an *Apex* and all its accompanying powers had a specific purpose. Yuana had to be prepared for it.

Their archives covered over six thousand years of their history and there were corresponding momentous events in the lives of their kind that followed every emergence of an *Apex*. Those events, the *Txandictus,* or the *Shift,* as their history called it, grew in magnitude every time. And the *Apex* of the day took on the leadership mantle and ushered their kind through the *Shifts*.

In two instances, the *Apex* refused to live up to their role, and it threw the *Viscerebuskind* into turmoil. The first of the two *Shifts*, their kind handled the crisis by coming together. It resulted in the founding of the *Supreme Viscerebus Tribunal*. And the *Tribunal* enabled them to overcome the second *Shift*. It strengthened the *Tribunal*'s mandate.

One crucial piece of information they wanted to find out was the powers of the *Apexes*, and how they used them in the past. But this information was scarce. Mentions of it in poems, ballads, and folklores were written by bards, but the historical account did not back up the flowery words. She could only note them down, but not as facts.

Her daughter Ysobella had every right to panic – the *ZeNading* killed some *Apexes* in the past. She could not find a definitive purpose of *ZeNading* apart from the amazing bragging value it gave an *Apex* who mastered the skill.

Katelin sighed and flexed her back to ease the stiffness caused by the long hours of reading. Her brain throbbed with information.

Then, she realised – every *Apex* who emerged after the *Txandictus* was believed to have been forced into *Ortus* because of the severity of the *Shift*. Those *Apexes* took on the leadership mantle out of necessity.

The *Apexes* that preceded the *Shift* were mere figureheads of the Tribunal. Except for the two *Apexes* who created the *Shift* themselves. And those two battled against the *Tribunal* for control.

Her granddaughter emerged as an *Apex* out of the blue, with no *Shift* on the horizon to trigger her *Ortus*. The *Txandictus* that would follow Yuana's *emergence* could happen in the next ten to twenty years, as their history showed. Yuana would have enough time to train her skills to prepare for it.

Or she would engineer the *Shift* herself.

Either way, the Tribunal would resent Yuana's *emergence*. And the De Vidas would face the biggest political and personal challenge in their lives as a family, to protect her.

Roald grabbed his towel and mopped the dripping sweat off his face. Their training was so intense his muscles locked up. He could feel the micro tremors in them, an indicator of fatigue. He rolled his shoulders to loosen his back. The pain bothered him less than his frustration with his performance during the training.

It seemed like no amount of training would enable him to match the speed and the strength of an *Aswang*. And it angered him. *How could I defend myself from something like that?*

He did not want to be reduced to carrying a gun on his person all the time. He did not own one, had no license to carry the weapon. And he had less training in using a gun than in *Kali* and *Karambit*. It was doubtful an attacker would give him time to draw a gun.

Mateo walked into the locker room, patting the sweat off his face. Roald tried to hide his anger by making a show of untying his shoes, but his careful movements did not deceive Mateo.

"You did well out there, Roald. I am very impressed," Mateo said, sitting on the bench.

He looked up from his preoccupation. "Thank you, sir. I am glad to hear that," he said. He tried to keep a lid on his feelings and push the bitterness in.

Mateo's gaze settled on him, studying him. "But you are not glad..." It was a statement.

"I think I could do better..." He did not want Mateo to think that he was not grateful.

"Yes, you could. But that takes time. If you continue this and do it with consistency, you will be better. And if you keep at it some more, you would be better than the day before that. The question is, are you willing?" Mateo's gaze was challenging.

"How long do I have to train? How many weeks, months, years?" His frustration coloured his question.

"What standards are you aiming for, Roald?"

"The highest..." He could not admit that he wanted to be good enough to kill an *Aswang*. He did not want to offend Mateo.

Mateo's smile was understanding. "Roald, I made a commitment to you, to train you with everything I got until you become as good as my best *Iztari*. I will not renege on that. I also told you that with a highly trained *Iztari* like myself, with my natural strength and speed, you will have a hard time beating me," he paused, and added, "but against a normal *Vis*, you can hold your own very well. Trained *Iztaris* are infinitely less common in our society."

"Is that a fact, sir, or are you just saying that to make me feel better?" Another validation was always welcome.

"I would never lie just to make people feel better," Mateo said, slapping his shoulder as he walked off towards the shower cubicle.

"Let's hope that my first unfortunate encounter with an *As*– a *Vis* is someone who is not an *Iztari,*" he said in jest.

Mateo paused with a strange look on his face, but it was gone in an instant. "You have more than a fair chance if carry your *karambit* with you. In your hands, the blade would be lethal," Mateo said and disappeared into a shower cubicle.

"Yeah, especially if your *karambit* is dripping in ChrysaDonna," Daniel commented as he came in. He, too, was drenched in sweat. Daniel had finished his sparring session with one of Mateo's deputies.

"ChrysaDonna? Is that a plant?" That piqued his interest.

"Yup. A combination of two plants. Tanacetum and Belladonna. Every *Vis* learns to avoid those plants when wounded," Daniel's muffled response came from behind his towel as he patted his face.

"Why? What does it do?" he asked.

"*Vis* are super healers. Their wounds mend fast. *ChrysaDonna* slows the process down as Tanacetum thins the blood and Belladonna dilates the blood vessels," Daniel said, as he rummaged in his gym for his clothes. "Are you showering?" Daniel asked, unaware of the importance of the information.

"Oh, yes!" Roald replied and jumped up. He felt energised with the new knowledge. And he was going to meet with Yuana for dinner after. He wanted to smell good for her. This time though, he wanted to leave early to pass by a friend's herb, oils, and candle shop.

I have a ChrysaDonna to procure.

Daniel combed his wet hair absentmindedly. He mused over the training, the first intense session since his *Mejordia* traits surfaced. It still amazed him: the power, speed, and strength. He sparred with his father's best *Iztaris,* two of them, and he could keep up. They were both better skilled and more experienced, but he held his own. It was a heady feeling.

He glanced at the empty locker room. His father should be waiting for him outside. Roald had called out his goodbye earlier, leaving in a rush; probably running late for his date with Yuana.

His training preoccupied him. He did not even see how Roald coped during the sparring session with his father.

Mateo Santino would be an unrelenting and exacting trainer. This was his father's act of contrition. And his integrity would never allow him to quit unless he found himself forgiven, maybe not even then. Daniel's worry was Roald's absolution was not assured, despite all his father's efforts.

"Hey, Dan. Are you not done yet? I'm starving, and we have a reservation at 7:30." His father's voice broke through his thoughts.

"Coming..." he yelled back. "Geez, Dad. What's the hurry? It's not our first date," he said as he rushed out to meet his father by the entrance.

"No wonder you have no girlfriend, you're too slow," Mateo shot back as they hurried to the car.

"You only speak so condescendingly about my lack of dates because you are dating."

His father grinned at him, his face alight with a secret joy Daniel had never seen in his face before.

"So, when do I meet this... woman?" he asked as he unlocked the car. His father slid into the passenger seat.

"Soon, when enough time has passed," Mateo replied, but the smile on his face remained.

"How much time do you need?" Daniel found his father's meaningful smiles and evasive ways intriguing.

Mateo had taken undue interest in the passing traffic. "As much time as necessary."

"Oh, you have *time*..." That was one solid clue. "So, she is a *Vis*?" Daniel wracked his brains for clues as to the identity of the woman.

"Yes, she is." His father's grin returned. And it looked spontaneous and boyish.

Incredulous, he stared at his dad – who was behaving like a juvenile.

"If this woman could make you smile like a Cheshire cat, I'd say it's time to meet my future stepmother, father dear," he said. And he meant it.

"Watch the road, Dan," Mateo said instead.

His gaze swivelled at the road, but there were no oncoming cars. He frowned at his father's attempt to change the subject. Mateo had the grace to look contrite. But the time for introduction between him and this mysterious woman was his father's call.

Daniel sighed. "How did your sparring with Roald go?" This was a safe enough topic while he negotiated the busy road.

"Oh, he did very well. Your friend has natural talent and skill." His dad sounded proud and smug.

"I'm glad. Roald seemed driven to excel on this. It's almost manic." Daniel wondered if his father noticed.

"His phobia rules him, and he's doing his best to face it, to control it. I'm glad that he found a way to handle it. And even more glad that I can help," Mateo said.

"Dad," Daniel stopped his father before they walked into the restaurant, "thank you for doing this."

"I have no choice, Dan. Like Roald, I'm driven to do this. And he would probably give up on himself long before I would." Mateo's mouth firmed.

"I know, Dad." For his father's sake, he hoped Roald would forgive him.

"Mind you, I am enjoying the process. Possibly more than Roald does."

He shrugged. "Well, he's doing it for protection. Fear as the underlying motivation will not induce joy."

'I'm five minutes away. Meet me at the lobby?' Roald's text message informed her. Her phone rang a second later.

It was Kazu.

"Good morning, Yuana." His cheerful voice came through.

"Good morning, Kazu."

"Yes. I called because I want you to know that our training tonight will require about five hours. Can you be away for that long?"

"Well, we train at night, so... it should not be a problem." The training sounded intense. In the past, their training ran for two to three hours at most.

"I will see you later, Yuana," Kazu said, satisfied.

A jolt of an unknown sensation struck her in the chest. She was still rubbing it away when she walked out of her room to the kitchen.

Her thoughts shifted to the breakfast she would prepare for her and Roald. The strange gut instinct and the evening's training with Kazu were forgotten.

Roald's protesting muscles reminded him of the intensity of the training. He groaned as he parked in front of Yuana's building. He was ten minutes early for their usual breakfast at Yuana's unit, but he wanted more time to spend with her.

Last night's dinner date was the first in two weeks. The romantic setup reminded him he had neglected their relationship. He had been so driven to train, the dinners they spent together in the past fortnight were just that – eating together. It was not the quality time he promised himself he would always have with her.

Yuana was setting the napkins and the silverware on the table when he stepped into her unit. It smelled of butter, pancakes and bacon. And coffee. Yuana's special coffee. His mouth watered.

He snagged her by the waist and planted a warm kiss on her neck, nuzzling it. He loved her scent, so distinctly her.

"Morning, love," he murmured.

She turned in his arms and kissed him on the mouth. "Morning."

He ushered her into the chair and pushed her down. "Sit down. I will get the food," he said.

"You look upbeat today, Ro?" Yuana said, her gaze assessing as she sipped on her coffee. Her eyes followed him into the kitchen.

"Upbeat and aching." His sore bicep twitched against the weight of the orange juice jug as he lowered it to the table.

"Training was hard?" She looked up as he approached with their plates.

"Yes, but I am pleased with the outcome." That was true. He was getting better every time.

"That's good." Yuana's smile was proud and indulgent before she brought a forkful of pancake into her mouth.

"And I got a bottle of *ChrysaDonna*," he said, watching her reaction. He wanted to know if the adverse effects of Tanacetum and Belladonna oil were as common knowledge as Daniel claimed.

She looked confused. And suspicious. "Why?"

"Added protection for... my *karambit*," he said.

Yuana's expression went blank, but he could tell that she was onto him.

She smiled. "So, did you get it in the oil form or the drops?"

"Essential oil. I was planning to use it to polish the *karambit* to keep it rust-free."

"Yes, I thought so," she said, her smile widened.

Her eyes glittered with knowledge, then she tucked into her food with gusto. He reached over, picked up her free hand, and kissed her palm. It was too early to gush about how he felt about her. And too syrupy, even for him.

Half an hour later, Roald escorted Yuana to the elevator of the De Vida building, then got back into his car and drove off to his office. His mind on his first meeting for the day; the body aches and pains ignored.

He did not notice the car parked right across the street, the watchful eyes of its driver, and the malicious glimmer in them.

17

YUANA BOUND

Jacob Montejo could not believe his luck. He had spotted the woman he had been wanting to find for a long time – the first to ever turned him down.

She was still as stunning as he remembered, seated in the front seat of her human boyfriend's car. He almost approached them two intersections ago but stopped himself.

He followed them instead. The human boyfriend drove her to the front of the GJDV building. They walked hand in hand into the lobby and exchanged kisses. The couple seemed still very much into each other. He would need to eliminate the competition first before he could have her.

Then the boyfriend returned to his parked car and drove off.

Jacob pulled into the drive and stopped right where the boyfriend's car parked earlier. He felt a malicious glee at his action. It was symbolic of what he wanted to do – supplant the feeble human in her life.

Jacob got out of the car, brimming with his usual confidence. His youthful handsomeness could get him any information he wanted. He adopted a genial demeanour, a pleasant smile pasted on his face as he approached the reception desk. Two *Erdia* females manned it.

"Hi..." The appreciation on both women's faces was clear as he approached the desk.

"Yes, sir, how can we help?" The younger of the two, the more assertive individual, spoke. They were both wearing the company uniform of slate grey two-piece slacks and blouse accented by a red belt and a plastic-moulded red and yellow chrysanthemum pin. Nameplates identified them.

"Sandra, I have an appointment with one of your team members tomorrow, but I lost her business card. I came here to get her information." He put on a twisted smile to project regret. "Fortunately, I just saw her walk in a couple of minutes ago. Would you be able to tell me her name?" He infused a pleading note in his voice and looked into the eyes of the girl.

Sandra blushed. "How long ago, sir?" Her voice thinned into a higher pitch.

He smiled at her. "About two minutes?"

The girl searched the system, flustered, the red in her cheeks now crept to her neck. "Sir, there are eight girls who registered in the past five minutes. Some of them were visitors, some were employees..." she said, apology in her tone.

"Do you remember what she was wearing, sir?" The other girl piped in.

"She did not pass by this desk to register. She was with a guy when she came in." He was annoyed, but his smile never wavered.

"Ah, that should be Ms Orzabal, our VP for Sales and Marketing," Sandra said, her face lightened up. "She came with her boyfriend. The tall guy, right?" she asked, making sure of her facts.

He nodded. "Yes, that's her. Ms Orzabal. Thank you, Sandra. I hope to see you tomorrow when I return for my meeting." He said and winked at her. The silly girl giggled and reddened a bit more. The other girl rolled her eyes.

Back in his car, he dialled the landline printed on the brochure he took from the reception desk. The operator answered and connected him to the office of Ms Orzabal. Her secretary picked up the call and insisted on taking a message. Undeterred, he waited in the coffee shop at the ground floor of the building. She would need to eat, eventually.

Two hours later, his persistence paid off. Ms Orzabal walked into the coffee shop at half past ten. She paused by the entry to greet the staff and then sat at the corner table. Her hair was tied in a loose bun, wispy strands framed her small face. She wore light make-up. He waited for her to finish her phone conversation. He did not want to annoy her just in case she remembered him from last time.

Once her coffee was served, he approached her table. When she looked up, he saw a flash of recognition in her eyes. She remembered their last encounter. "Yes, can I help you?" Her formal tone confirmed he would have to extend considerable effort to change her first impression of him.

"Ms Orzabal?" He pretended he did not remember their last meeting.

"Yes." Her tone was clipped, her body held aloof, civil, cold.

"I was told GJDV has a corporate program for employees. I would like to see if it will work for my company's employee benefit program." That program was a stroke of luck.

"Yes, we do. Would you like us to present to your employees?" Her polite facade remained.

"Of course, but maybe you can tell me more about it first? So, I can determine if it fits us." He wanted more time to charm her and change her mind.

"Sure, give me a moment. Let me call for some materials."

She stood up to make a call outside the shop. He took a seat at her table to wait for her. He could not help but smile in satisfaction. His ploy worked. He watched the captivating Ms Orzabal finish her call and walk back in.

He got up as she neared, a gentlemanly gesture meant to impress her.

"Please take a seat, Mr..."

"Jake Montejo," he replied and offered his hand. Ms Orzabal grasped his hand in a firm handshake.

"Can I offer you coffee, Mr Montejo? While we wait..." Her insistence to address him formally meant it would not be easy to get a date with her.

"Thank you, Ms Orzabal, but I am good," he said, sitting back and giving her an engaging smile.

A well-dressed young woman carrying a laptop approached them.

"Ah, Lyndsey, thank you for coming. Please take a seat," Ms Orzabal said, smiling at her staff. "Mr Montejo, this is Lyndsey Gomez, she's my Corporate Sales Director. Lyndsey, Mr Montejo here inquired about our Corporate Memorial Plan for their employee benefits program and would like to know more about it to see if it is suitable."

A ringing started in his brain at her statement. He expected Ms Orzabal to do the presentation herself, rather than the newcomer. He thought he had her cornered.

"Mr Montejo, you are in excellent hands with Lyndsey. I would have to leave you, as I have another meeting. It is nice to meet you and thank you for considering us." Ms Orzabal inclined her head and, with a quick nod at him, walked away, taking her coffee with her.

Fury bloomed inside of Jacob at her dismissal. He wanted to snarl at the smiling assistant in front of him and drag back the woman who just left. But he controlled himself. He did not want to give away his ploy. He sat through the assistant's digital presentation with gritted teeth. Half an hour later, his jaw ached. His patience was worn thinner than hair.

It was now a matter of personal pride to get Ms Orzabal. As for her human boyfriend, he would have to be removed from the picture. The man might even be useful. Grief could make people susceptible to manipulation. And for ditching him like that, he would use her own assistant to accomplish his goal.

His next step would be to find out human's identity and where to find him.

Yuana's annoyance at having her quick break interrupted by an arrogant *Vis* faded by the time she reached the stairway. The coffee stop after a marathon meeting was her way to think and relax. She would have to accomplish that through the walk along the corridors back to her office.

As she passed by the security office, the Head of Security, Aleister stopped her. "Ms Yuana, can you spare me a moment for verification?"

She sighed inwardly. This was a routine procedure. Her great grandparents' position in the *Tribunal* required constant tracking and tight security to all the members of their family.

"Sure. What is it about?" she said.

They paused by the hallway.

"Can you tell us about the guy who approached you at the coffee shop some minutes ago? Was he a *Vis*?" Aleister asked.

She nodded. "Yes, he's one of us. His name is Jake Montejo. He asked about the corporate memorial plan program of GJDV. I left Lyndsey to deal with him." Her previous irritation at the said man's unwelcome interruption returned.

"Okay. Did you know him?" Aleister asked, taking down notes on his tablet.

"I would not say that, but I encountered him a few months back, in a restaurant. I found him rude and arrogant even then," she replied.

"Okay, that would explain his interest in you when you walked in. He must have recognised you," Aleister said, the slight frown on his face eased.

"He acted like he did not remember the event when he walked to my table and introduced himself." She thought back to Jake Montejo's behaviour. "Or he could have been pretending."

Aleister frowned. "Was he trying to pick you up that first time?" At her nod, "Speaking as a man, Ms Yuana, it would be impossible to forget the event if a beautiful woman shot you down," he said.

"Oh, well. No harm done. That's why I had Lyndsey deal with him." she shrugged. "Is there anything else?" she asked.

Aleister shook his head. "That is all, Ms Yuana. Have a great day."

"Thank you, Aleister," she said and walked on.

She appreciated the security their company and the *Tribunal* provided her and her family, but they could be overly cautious. Now it planted a seed of alarm in her mind.

Should I warn Lyndsey about Jake Montejo?

Nah, she'll find out soon enough. Plus, who knows, maybe she likes his type.

That night, Yuana prepared for her training with Kazu. She did not make dinner plans with Roald to allow herself the five hours Kazu asked for. She would catch up with Roald and Daniel after.

She told her parents that she would fly tonight, and they made her promise she would not do *ZeNading*.

"Don't worry, Mama," she said, unable to promise straight on. Luckily, they took that as an agreement.

Half an hour later, she was airborne, and on her way to meet Kazu in midair somewhere over Pasig. She found him soon after. And as was their usual practice, they landed on the rooftop of the tallest building to talk.

"Good evening, Kazu." She folded her wings around her.

"Good evening, Yuana," he said. "You look stronger than when I last saw you. More confident." He sounded satisfied.

She smiled. Kazu's folded batwings reminded her of padded capes of old. "I have been flying." She did not want to mention her own efforts in *ZeNading*.

"That's good. How high have you flown?" he asked.

"About thirty thousand feet."

"Are you ready?" Kazu asked, a smile of satisfaction on his face.

"Yes," she said, swallowing down the twinge of fear. "So, how do we do this?"

He nodded. "We will fly straight up, very high until the atmosphere becomes thin, and then we regain our human form. As we plummet down, at two hundred meters, we shift to our *Animus* and fly straight back up. We will do it seven times." Kazu's gaze glittered with intensity.

Seven times? "In a row? No break in between?" The thought made her breathless.

"No break." Kazu's nod accompanied his words.

Oh, flock!

"Okay." She nodded, but she felt shaky inside.

"Shall we?" Kazu asked.

She took a deep breath and took flight. Kazu followed. The power of his flapping wings stirred the air behind her. Her heart pounded in her chest, protesting the pressure. They flew higher, and higher – ten thousand, fifteen thousand feet.

There was an incoming storm, the clouds were heavy with moisture. They both emerged on top of the clouds, and they flew some more still. Twenty-five thousand. Thirty-five. At forty-five thousand, breathing became difficult. The pressure squeezed at her lungs and her heart felt too big for her chest.

A sting struck at the base of her neck. Her hand automatically went to it and encountered a small protrusion.

A projectile? A dart? Where did this come from?

Her vision clouded as she looked at the small metal tip in her hand. Dizziness assailed her; her limbs became heavy. And before she had time to panic, everything around her faded.

Kazu saw Yuana's form go limp and fall. Quick as a flash, he snagged her by the waist and carried her back to their launch point.

He laid her down and checked her pulse – still strong. Her wings had retracted, and she was losing her *Animus* form by the second. He unzipped his *morphbag*, pulled a sarong from it, and covered Yuana's body to protect her modesty as she regained her human form.

From inside, he took out a bottle of antiseptic, a clean white towel, surgical clamping scissors, and a sapphire blade. With quick movements, Kazu pushed aside the sarong to uncover Yuana's abdomen. He applied antiseptic just below her rib cage, right above her liver.

He made a three-inch-wide cut on her skin. A sliver of red blood followed the progress of the blade staining her alabaster skin. The metallic scent floated to his nostrils. He pressed the instrument deeper into the layer of skin and flesh until he could see the organ. Kazu sliced a small piece off and popped it into his mouth, gulping it down.

He staunched the flow of blood by pinching Yuana's wound tightly together. Her skin covered the gash like a wave washing over the beach. Within seconds, any sign of the incision vanished as Yuana's *Apex* super healing abilities took effect. He wiped the blood off until there was no trace of what he did to her.

Kazu sighed. He had accomplished her part of the oral *Aztarimar*. It was now time to complete his. He poured the antiseptic onto his hands, the scalpel, and the towel. He dabbed on his side.

The sharp sting made him wince. The dark blood that oozed from the cut disappeared into the jet-black skin of his bat *Animus*.

Kazu sucked in a deep breath to steel himself for what he needed to do. With his left hand, he dug into his cut and pulled out a bit of his liver. The hand holding the blade trembled as he sliced a sliver off.

For a few minutes, he focused on his breathing to shut the pain away. The closing wound tingled as tissues and nerves reconnected and healed the cut, reminding him of what he needed to do.

With the bit of his liver still held in his palm, he moved closer to the unconscious Yuana. He opened her mouth and dropped the small chunk down her throat. The delicate line moved in a instinctive swallow, a drop of blood tinged the corner of her mouth.

He breathed a sigh of relief. The *Aztarimar* was complete. The merging of the dual *Apexes* had begun.

Panting, he pressed his hand to his side; the right side of his torso hurt. He slumped against the concrete. He needed to heal. The next two hours would do that. Kazu closed his eyes and allowed the chilled night air to cool down the fever building in his body.

Yuana woke up to the violent tremors that shook her. Her vision focused on the unfamiliar terrain. The cold, hard and dusty floor against her back made her realise she was in her human form, completely naked. Only the thin material covering her protected her from the elements.

She rolled onto her right side. A sharp pain inside her ribcage took her breath away. There was soreness in her abdomen area like she did a thousand sets of crunches.

She surveyed the area to get her bearing. Fluttering fabric caught her eye. Kazu, in a light kimono, stood by the corner of the building, watching the ground below. She sat up and wrapped the flimsy fabric – a sarong – around her. It must have belonged to him.

Kazu turned towards her. "Stay there, Yuana." His gentle tone reached her as he walked closer.

"What happened?" she asked. The last thing she remembered was flying high.

"You lost consciousness and fell. I caught you and brought you down here. You were unconscious for a long time. It worried me," Kazu said.

"But what could have happened to me?" She had flown that high before, and she did not have any problem.

"It could be a combination of factors. The altitude, the scarcity of oxygen, the thin atmosphere, and if you were nervous already when you flew, your heart was under enormous stress," Kazu said, a concerned gaze running over her from head to toe.

"Does that mean I cannot do it?" Disappointment crept into her.

He shook his head. "No, it means that we have to try again. Just not tonight. It is late, and you must be tired," he said in a gentle tone.

She *was* tired. And sore. There was an echo of pain under her right rib cage. "Why do I hurt here?"

"I snagged you by your torso when you plummeted. I must have bruised you internally." There was a note of apology in his voice, his hand going to his own side. "Can you fly?" Kazu asked.

"I think so," she said. Chilled to her core, she had to focus to transform, but she was strong enough to fly. She flexed her wings as they sprouted behind her back. There was nothing wrong with her except the soreness in her middle and a slightly weakened feeling.

"Go home and rest, Yuana. Let's do this again in a week," Kazu said.

She nodded and took flight. With a last glance at Kazu as she circled the rooftop before she flew away, she saw him limp a little towards the sarong that fell off her. She watched as he put them in the *morphbag* he wore around his waist. Despite the distance, she thought she saw a glint of something glassy or metallic inside his bag.

The drizzle reminded her she needed to head home. The sooner, the better. Her internal clock told her it was almost midnight. She needed to hurry, or she would be late for her night out with Daniel and Roald. With a burst of energy, she flapped harder and flew towards home.

Her eagerness to go out to dinner with Roald and Daniel waned a few minutes later. The idea of a long bath seemed much more enticing.

Kazu remained on the rooftop, his eyes closed. Images of Yuana's thoughts reached him. This time, the images came clearly, like watching through her eyes. He heard her thoughts and felt her eagerness to come home and get ready for her night out.

It was time to test his influence over his *Aztarima*. With a deep breath, he sent *aural* commands to Yuana.

A long, hot bath is rejuvenating. A good night's sleep is necessary.

He sensed Yuana's resolve waver a bit but reinstated itself.

It seemed her mind was not as susceptible to suggestions as he thought. The second *Apex* possessed a stronger will than he expected. He tried once more.

You're tired. And grimy. Nothing matters but to rest.

He felt Yuana waver and slide into the suggestion. Her thoughts shifted towards resting. He had imprinted on her. The *Aztarim* was a success. Yuana was now bound to him, although she did not know it. He had accomplished what he set out to do to ensure the success of their joint destiny.

Beginning tonight, he could prepare her for the *Txandictus* without her knowledge. It was for her own good, and for the benefit of their kind.

Satisfied, he removed his kimono and shape-shifted back to his *Animus*.

It was time to go and rest.

Yuana landed in her outdoor garden silently. She went into her unit via her bedroom, naked and covered in grime. She did not realise how dirty she was until she saw the water run grey around her.

A thought kept niggling in her head about taking a long, leisurely bath. Uneasiness shadowed it. Like a there was something she needed to do but couldn't remember. A skirmish between taking a quick shower or a slow bath occupied her. The quick shower won.

As soon as she stepped out of the shower, she felt exhausted. Visions of her comfortable bed bombarded, the urge to go to bed strong. But the undefined, niggling sensation was close behind.

She squeezed water from her hair, her mind hunting for the cause of the shadowy feeling, then she remembered – Roald and Daniel were waiting for her.

"Oh, shit!" She ran dripping into her bedroom and grabbed her phone. Three text messages.

'How was the flight? Knock when you're back.' – Mama.

'Yu, we moved venue. We're going to the bar next door to your building,' – Daniel.

That was fifteen minutes ago.

'Hon, are you close?' – Roald.

Five minutes ago. *Whew!* She had time. She sent her reply to Roald.

'I just got home. A quick shower. I will be there in fifteen minutes. Are you still next door?' – Yuana

'See you. Yes, still next door.' – Roald.

Yuana pulled on a dress, tied her damp hair in a loose bun and applied light makeup. Then she dashed out, phone in hand, and rang her parents' doorbell. Her dad opened it.

"You're back! And... you're going out again?" Her father took in her attire.

She hugged him and kissed his cheek. Her mother sat on the couch, an anxious frown on her face. She gave her mother a tight hug and a kiss. A gesture of reassurance. She would rather avoid her mother's questioning now.

"Are you okay, Yuana?"

She nodded. Her heart lurched at the thought of telling her mother what happened earlier.

"I'm good, Mama. I'm just running late. Daniel and Roald are waiting for me." Her mother did not respond but kept a steady gaze on her. Yuana knew she couldn't get out of telling her what happened in her flight lesson. "Can I tell you and Papa tomorrow? Right now, the boys are waiting for me."

Her mother sighed, nodded, and kissed her cheek. "Okay. Have fun."

As she rode the elevator down, she thought about what to tell her parents. She had never been good at lying. But if she told them what happened, they would panic. And they had every cause to do so. If it wasn't for Kazu, she would have died.

An indistinct image flashed inside her head as she walked out of the elevator. It was gone before she recognised what it was. A text message reminded her she had somewhere to go, and Roald waited for her.

She walked on until the signage of the bar came within sight. Her ribcage twinged. It was not pain, it was similar to a gut feeling, except it came from her side. It felt... peculiar. With a sigh, she brushed it off her mind.

Roald threw his gym bag at the boot of his car. He was visualizing the gruelling *Kali* session he just had with Mateo, running the new set of hand-to-hand attack and deflect combinations in his mind.

Mateo had him spar with one of the *Iztaris*, so he could pit his skills against someone whose style was different. The change in the venue added a new challenge. Mateo wanted to take out the familiarity of a routine out of their training. And it roused his competitive nature.

Roald took out the *karambit* from his bag to put it on. It had become a habit for him to wear it for protection, but he had to take it off earlier. He had polished it with the ChrysaDonna oil this morning, a routine practice since he bought the oil. The knowledge that he had added a layer of protection gave him more confidence. He slipped the *karambit* around his neck. He was due for brunch in the Aurelio residence.

As Roald shut the car boot, a massive blow struck his side, throwing him against the car next to his. A quiet crunch in his ribs and a piercing pain in his torso told him it broke upon impact. The pain took his breath away and buckled his knees. He knew the broken bones pierced his lungs, making it hard to breathe.

A man stood over him, a malevolent grin on the stranger's partially masked face as he kicked his injured side with a force that made Roald ball up in pain. Adrenalin surged in his veins, making him numb.

The guy lifted his leg back to stomp on his stomach, but Roald rolled away. Enraged the stranger bent and grabbed him by the collar, then lifted him off his feet. By his attacker's strength, Roald knew he was being assaulted by an *Aswang*. An unusually strong one.

On instinct, he grabbed the *karambit* hanging on his neck and with one quick movement; unsheathed the knife and slashed at the guy's side.

The sensation of blade slicing flesh confirmed that his stroke connected.

His attacker staggered back. Surprise wiped the bloodlust from the man's eyes as he clasped his wounded side.

Rage triggered inside Roald, giving him the surge of energy to struggle to his feet. He was going to defend himself despite his unsteady legs and tortured breath. Roald's vision wavered but he fought to keep himself conscious.

The masked *Aswang* looked at his bleeding wound in disbelief. A flash of fear showed in the man's eyes as he realised that he was not healing fast. The stranger turned and ran away towards a red car a few parking spaces from Roald's. It backed out and zoomed away, the screech of tires echoing in the parking lot.

Roald propped himself against his car, trying to memorise the plate number. The pain in his chest was excruciating. His legs gave way, and the terror of the *Aswang* attack flooded his brain as the sound of the departing car faded with his consciousness.

Daniel was dialling Yuana's number when the screech of a departing car diverted his attention. Then Roald came into his view, staggering, hands around his middle, his right hand held a bloody *karambit*. Roald took two unsteady steps before he crumpled to the ground.

With Yuana forgotten, Daniel sprinted towards him, Mateo's running footsteps following closely behind. Roald's face was ashen, his breathing shallow, raspy and laboured; he must have sustained broken ribs and punctured lungs; his chest cavity was filling with fluid. Roald would drown in his own blood if he did not get to the hospital soon.

"Dan, let's take him to the hospital." Mateo's urgent voice penetrated Daniel's terror-filled brain. He lifted Roald into his father's van, and together they sped away from the parking lot. Daniel's heart pounded hard, his fear for Roald paramount.

"Dan," Roald's weak voice penetrated the fog of dread in his mind. He looked down and saw Roald's struggle to stay conscious.

"Hush, bro. Save your strength. We are on our way to the hospital," he said, as Roald coughed blood, freaking him out even more.

"No... Dan... Red... Maz... da, K... G... Y... 4... 7..." Roald whispered before he lost consciousness. Frantically, he searched for Roald's pulse. Nothing. His brain screaming NO! With trembling fingers, Daniel took a deep breath and felt for it again. His heart jolted in relief as he detected a faint heartbeat in Roald's neck.

Their arrival at the hospital could not come any sooner. Everything happened in a blur. The scene of Roald being wheeled to the emergency room reminded him of Yuana.

By coincidence, the phone in his pocket rang. It was Yuana.

"Hey, D! We got cut off. What time are you and Roald coming here?" Yuana's cheerful voice floated through the line.

He took a deep breath, "Yuana, Roald is in the emergency room, we took him here in the hospital just a few minutes ago."

Daniel heard Yuana's intake of breath. In a shaky voice, she asked which hospital. And without further words, the line went dead. Yuana was on her way. He was glad there were no tears, no panicked questions that required answers. He was not up to it.

Roald mumbled something earlier. He wracked his brain, trying to remember it. *Red Mazda. KYG... KGY... 47... 74?* It was amazing Roald had the presence of mind to get the plate number and tell him just before he passed out. Daniel typed the information on his phone so as not to lose it.

Fury grew inside him, making his head pound. He would make sure that they found the bastard who did this to Roald. He glanced at his father and recognised the same rage and determination on his face. Mateo treated Roald like a son, and to Daniel, he was a brother. That evil attacker made the mistake of messing with his family. Between his father and him, the man would rue the day he harmed Roald.

"Did you see what happened?" Mateo asked, handing him a cup of coffee.

"No... I was calling Yuana," he said, sighing.

His father sat down beside him. "It was not a random attack."

"Why do you say that?" he asked. The definite statement intrigued him.

"Roald has an imposing physique. He's tall and muscular. He looks strong. No one will pick a fight with him on impulse. Since there is nothing in the scene that indicated any crime Roald might have interrupted, we can assume the attacker targeted him," Mateo said, his eyes narrowed as if he was running his mind through the site of Roald's attack.

"Perhaps we need to have the site examined." He offered a token contrary opinion, wanting to be objective.

Mateo nodded, conceding, "I already gave orders to the *Iztaris* to search the area, so we will know later."

"But your initial assessment is that Roald was targeted?"

"Yes. The only crime Roald could have interrupted is carjacking. I doubt it because he had time to stow his gym bag away," Mateo said. "If he walked in on the perpetrator, we would have found the gym bag near him," he added.

He found it amazing his father took on that much information in those frantic seconds. He did not even recall anything except Roald's ashen face. *And... the bloody karambit in his hand.*

"Dad, Roald's *karambit* had blood on it," he said.

"Yes, I saw. I took it off his hand earlier. I had it sent to the lab to be tested for DNA," his father assured him, patting him on the back.

"He fought back. With Roald's skill, the only thing I can think of that could have allowed such damage done to him is if the attacker surprised him with a heavy, blunt weapon," he said. Damage like broken ribs required tremendous force or a solid weapon. His anxiety for Roald faded as he focused on analysing the situation.

"I agree. Roald is way too skilled to be beaten just by anyone if he saw the attack coming," Mateo said. "There is no sign there was more than one attacker. The running feet I heard just before we saw him came from one person," he added.

"So, perhaps the guy was going to carjack Roald's car, or the one next to his?" he asked, expanding his speculation. He could not remember what type of car was parked beside Roald's.

"Perhaps, but, if the perpetrator can afford to drive a Mazda, then it is possible that he was not there to steal a car," his father supposed.

"Or the Mazda could be stolen as well," he said.

Yuana's voice cut their discussion short. "Dan! Where is he?" Yuana's face was pale with distress.

In her dash towards him, she tripped into his arms. Daniel held her steady, but he kept his expression calm. "Roald is in the emergency room. Don't worry," he said, rubbing his hands up and down Yuana's arms in comfort.

"What happened?" she asked, her hands gripping his shirt front.

"We do not know. I saw him stagger and collapse. We rushed him to the hospital immediately." Daniel did not want to share his theory about the attack when it was based on mere assumptions.

"What was his injury?"

"The doctor has not told us yet, but from what I have seen, I would guess he had broken ribs." He left out the punctured lungs, and possibly other organs as well.

Yuana nodded, but he could tell that it did not work. Yuana paced the hallway, her shoes making clicking sounds reminiscent of her Aunt Ximena. He tugged at her arm to stop her and pulled her down to a chair.

Ten minutes later, Ximena came to the waiting room, her composed face and demeanour made both himself and Yuana feel better. Ximena hugged her grandniece close.

"Don't worry, Yuana. Dr Rodriguez is the best. Roald will be fine," she said, smiling at Yuana, her confidence, contagious.

"Thank you, Tita Mena," Yuana said.

"I have arranged Roald's room already. Why don't you guys wait there?" she said.

Yuana shook her head. "No, Tita. I want to be here when Roald gets out of surgery," she said.

"Yuana, the procedure will take hours. There is nothing you can do here for now. Go to Roald's room, it will be more comfortable." Ximena's voice was firm, brooking no arguments.

Yuana frowned and hesitated. And Daniel could not fault her. He felt the same.

"Yuana, what does Abuela always say about worrying?" Ximena's gentle question made Yuana sigh in resignation.

"That it is premature suffering." Her response was grudging.

"Okay then, go to Roald's room. It's 808," Ximena said, finality in her tone. "And I mean all of you. All of this worrying is not helping, and it is adding unnecessary negative energy to the area." Ximena eyed him and his father, too. She handed the key to Roald's room to Mateo.

They had no choice but to comply. Ximena came with them. As they sat around the sterile hospital suite, Yuana blurted out, "Roald's parents! Have they been told?"

He shook his head. "No, they don't know yet. It did not enter my mind to call them. And I do not have their phone number. Do you?"

Yuana sighed. "Perhaps it's better to tell them in person," she said, dejected.

"We can send someone to their house. Don't worry," Mateo said, patting her cheek. "Do you know their address?"

Yuana nodded.

Half an hour later, Ysobella and Galen arrived, carrying a picnic basket and containers of food, their countenance confident, soothing, and determined.

"If the mountain does not brunch at home, we will bring the brunch to the mountain," Galen declared, his tone light, as if what happened was a mere hiccup in their day.

Yuana's grim expression lightened. She went to her father's arms, and Galen kept her there for a long time, as fathers do when they comfort their little girls. Yuana looked scared and vulnerable, and it made Daniel's heart clench.

"Let's eat, people. Let's not put all these to waste," Ysobella said, laying out the food on the table. They came equipped with paper plates and disposable cutlery.

The smell of bacon and sausage made Daniel's mouth water and reminded him he had not had breakfast, but it was the sight of the pancakes and strawberries that did it for him. He took a plate, speared a couple of pancakes, and picked up a handful of strawberries. Ysobella poured syrup and squirted cream over his food. Like her daughter Yuana, she knew his food preferences.

The conversation topics were light; they avoided the discussion about what happened to Roald. Nobody wanted to speculate and add to the anxiety everyone tried to hide from everybody.

Daniel marvelled at the ease with which Yuana's family dealt with each other during tension-filled hours. He had always thought having a big family would mean a noisy and hectic existence. He did not expect the quiet camaraderie, the automatic sharing of support that did not need words to be expressed. Maybe this was the advantage of having a limited social circle. It forced them to rely on their family members, and such reliance would establish roots so deep into each other that verbal cues were unnecessary. The De Vidas had years of practice.

Of all the *Vis* traits that had awakened in him, Daniel could only hope *Project Chrysalis* was right in assuming he also inherited *Vis'* longevity.

If they were wrong, and he was still human in that aspect, when he died, his father would be alone. Mateo was an orphan with no other known relatives. At that moment, the idea of leaving his father behind was heartbreaking.

Now, he was glad that his father was dating. Hopefully, the lady would be someone his father could fall for, the one who could be with him for the rest of his long life.

18

TRAIL OF THE ATTACKER

Two hours later, a knock at the door broke the cadence of their conversation. Everyone abandoned the façade of calm they wore. All eyes swivelled to the door. Mateo opened it.

It was the doctor. Yuana shot to her feet as soon as the doctor entered.

"Dr Rodriguez, how did the operation go?" Ximena asked.

The doctor smiled, and a chorus of sighs echoed in the room.

"He has multiple broken ribs, punctured lungs and liver, but the operation was successful. We siphoned the fluid from his lungs and repaired his ribs. All he needs to do is to rest and recover." The satisfaction in the doctor's tone reassured Yuana like nothing else.

"Can we see him, Doc?" she asked. She was impatient to see for herself that Roald was well. The tension in Daniel's body told her they shared the same sentiment.

The doctor nodded. "He's in the recovery room. But only two at a time, please. He is resting, so try not to disturb him. We will move him to this room in about two hours."

Daniel accompanied her as they followed the doctor to the recovery room. Yuana found the doctor's walking pace too slow for the sense of urgency riding her. She would have run if she knew where the room was.

When they reached their destination, she pushed past the doctor to get in. Her heart trembled to a stop when she saw Roald on the bed. He had tubes attached to his mouth to aid his breathing, drips were connected to his hands. They wrapped wide swaths of bandage around his torso. His face was pale, his lips dry.

She touched the hand nearest to her. It was cold, but his pulse was strong. And for the first time in the past hours, she was reassured that he would get better. Tears threatened to break through, but she stopped herself as Daniel was in the room, and she did not want to lose control.

When she glanced at him, she noted the clenched jaw. Daniel's throat bobbed up and down as he swallowed his emotions down. He looked enraged. Daniel was as affected by the incident as she was.

They both sat down beside Roald's bed. She had kept her hand on Roald's. Touching him was comforting. She knew that Daniel and his father avoided discussing what happened earlier, but she could not stand the restraint anymore. She wanted her answers.

"Dan, what happened?"

"We do not know yet," Daniel replied, sighing.

The undertone in his reply made her rephrase the question. "What do *you* think happened?"

That gave Daniel pause. "Yuana, this is all conjecture. We will not know until we've had a thorough investigation," he said.

"But..." She wanted the unvoiced information in Daniel's mind.

"Okay... Dad and I think that someone attacked Roald on purpose." There was caution in Dan's voice.

"Attacked on purpose? By whom? Why?" It was the last thing she expected to hear. It made little sense. *Who would attack Roald?*

"We do not have the answers to that yet. But Dad already sent *Iztaris* to investigate the scene. I think he ordered the guys who sparred with Roald earlier. They were still at the gym when that happened. It is personal to my father. And to me."

Fury blossomed in her heart. "Find him, Dan. Make him pay. Break every bone in his body. And when you're done, give him to me and I will make sure my face would haunt his dreams for the rest of his life." The rage in her was deep and primal. The desire to thrust her claws into the mystery man's chest and pluck his heart out was overwhelming.

The same anger reflected in Daniel's eyes. "We will, Yuana. I promise you."

They moved Roald to his private room two hours later. He stirred but lapsed into sleep immediately after. Yuana decided to stay. Daniel followed suit, to keep her and Roald company. The rest of her family went home with a promise to return the next day.

After half an hour, the lead *Iztari* assigned to investigate brought Roald's things and his initial findings. He found Roald's car keys and mobile phone underneath the car. A further proof the attack was a surprise. There were no scratches or other clues on or in the car itself.

She got in touch with Roald's parents as the *Iztari* reported they were out of town. They were in Hongkong for an Architectural convention where Alecsandro Magsino was the keynote speaker for the last day of the event.

Yuana reassured them Roald was fine, the surgery ended well. With the promise to take care of their son, they agreed to finish the event.

She withheld the details of the attack and told them it was a road accident. She did not want them to worry since the attacker was still at large.

Mateo entered the room just as she got off the phone. He brought copies of footage from the cameras in the parking lot which captured the attack in its entirety.

It showed the Red Mazda was two cars behind Roald's dark blue Benz. It seemed the driver followed Roald into the lot and parked nearby. The unknown man waited for two hours until Roald came out of the gym.

The attacker had a slight build, and not as tall as Roald. He wore a loose hoodie and a mask that covered his eyes and nose. He approached Roald from behind, while the latter was preoccupied with putting away his gym bag in the boot. The punch on the torso threw Roald sideways against the car nearby.

Yuana's stomach clenched as Roald fell to his knees. There was no audio, but her brain supplied the thud of each kick on Roald's ribs, the imaginary crunch of broken bones, and every pained gasp.

The images were grainy, but the viciousness of the man's assault was clear. The footage, taken from several cameras and multiple angles, showed everything except the assailant's face.

Her breath stopped when she saw Roald's attacker lift him off the ground. No mere human could have done that. Roald was much bigger, much taller than his mugger. His unusual strength gave away a very important clue – Roald's attacker was a *Vis*.

Incredulous, she looked at Dan and Mateo. They were both as shocked.

They watched Roald fight back, saw the assailant drop him as Roald slashed him along the ribs. The assailant staggered back, clasping his wound. Roald struggled to his feet, his stance defensive, *Karambit* clasped in his hand.

The stranger paused, seeming perplexed, and to their surprise, he turned and ran away out of camera range. He was outside the frame when a car pulled out and sped away.

Roald hobbled to his car before he collapsed in a heap. Within seconds, Daniel came into the frame, followed by Mateo. Daniel immediately picked

Roald up and at the edge of the frame, she saw the side of Mateo's van opening. Daniel lifted Roald into its interior. She watched as the van sped away.

Yuana didn't realise she was crying until she felt Daniel wipe the tears from her cheeks. Grief and fury threatened to explode her heart. She blew it out through pursed lips as she tried to hold back the tears. Daniel pulled her into his arms, offering empathy and comfort.

"Shh... don't cry, Yuana. We will get the wretched *Viscerebus* who did this to him. I promise you," Daniel murmured, vehemence barely leashed.

She nodded, trying to keep her sobs down. Her shoulders shook with the effort. "He could have died, Daniel. If you were not there at the right time, that man could have killed Roald."

"Shh... stop, Yuana. Roald needs you now more than ever," Daniel pulled away, holding her head in his hands, his thumbs wiping the flow of her tears. "Don't let this break you."

That stopped her tears. Daniel misunderstood. Her wrath bubbled over. "These are tears of rage, Dan. Make no mistake. The ruler of hell himself could never induce such fury in me."

Yuana brushed her tears with the back of her hand and pushed away from Daniel's arms. She realised with a start that Mateo was still in the room. The grim expression told her Daniel's father was as furious as she was.

"Let's review the facts. Maybe we can find more clues to his identity," she said. Seething fury overtook her grief. Impatience to catch the attacker drove away her anguish at watching Roald get beaten.

"Okay. Let's examine what we overlooked. Here's what we know," Mateo said, enumerating the details that they had.

"As far as I am aware, we are the only *Viscerebus* acquainted with Roald," Daniel said, his tone speculative. "And I am sure no one in your family has any cause to harm him."

"So, you think his attacker was a stranger?" she asked. The idea seemed implausible.

"Yes, he could be," Daniel replied, although he did not seem as convinced by his theory.

"But what is the motive? Why would a complete stranger attack Roald with such viciousness? It looks... personal." The images were fresh in her mind, making her insides quiver.

"It may not be personal to the attacker, but to the one who sent him," Mateo said.

"What do you mean, Tito? That someone sent a *Vis* thug after Roald?"

"Some of our kind work for humans as paid henchmen. They're called *Katyrrians*. They are hired to rough up, or sometimes kill, humans at the behest of other humans," Mateo said.

"What? Isn't that against our laws?" It was the first time she heard of this.

"It only becomes illegal to the *Tribunal* if their activities reveal our existence. The humans usually do not know that the *Katyrrians* are *Viscerebus*," Mateo said. "So, if the crime they commit falls within the realm of explainable human acts, our *Tribunal* will not intervene. But that does not exempt them from human laws and prosecution," Mateo added.

"Won't the incarceration of our kind expose us? Or do we supply *victus* in human jails as well?" she asked. The intricacies of the interwoven lives of humans and her kind were unknown to her.

"No. The longest stay of our kind in human jail would be three days. We transfer them to a *Viscerebus* jail to complete their sentence. But only if this is possible, if not, they are executed," Daniel said.

"So, it's possible that a human who has a grudge against Roald sent a henchman to attack him?" She wracked her brains for any person who Roald might have mentioned in passing. But nothing came up. "I can't think of anyone. Not a competitor, angry shareholder, or any disgruntled employee. Has he mentioned anything to you?" she turned to Dan.

Dan shook his head. "No. Roald is not the type who makes enemies. And our industry is not that cutthroat."

"The guy was wearing a mask. Does it mean he thinks Roald would recognise him? Or was that for the benefit of the surveillance cameras in the lot?" she asked.

"We won't know until the DNA result from the knife comes out," Mateo said. "That will take some time. Our quickest lead would be the car registration trace. Let us hope it was not a stolen vehicle."

"And let us hope the blood from the knife will lead us to the perpetrator," Daniel added.

"Yes, let us hope his blood is on our records," she sighed. They needed to find more clues.

She looked down at Roald's prone form. He looked vulnerable and helpless. He came so close to death just hours ago. One of their kind had attacked Roald. And for the first time in her life, she understood the hate the humans harboured against the *Viscerebus*.

"Don't worry, Yuana. We will post an *Iztari* guard to protect him 24/7..." Mateo said, the hand on her shoulders warm and reassuring.

Her heart brimmed with gratitude to fate for making sure help was within seconds of the incident. And a deep-seated appreciation for the stature of her name, and the presence of friends like Daniel and his father.

The ties that bound her to Roald had grown stronger. The ties of love, and now, of vengeance.

Kazu opened his eyes. His frustration reached a level that disrupted his usual calm. He had been trying to access Yuana's mind for the past two days. He could see through her thoughts well enough, but he found it impossible to penetrate it, let alone impose his influence. Not when powerful feelings ruled her.

Yuana was turning out to be a challenge. She was not as malleable as all his other *Aztarimas*, his imprinted disciples. All of them, he imprinted *aurally*, and he controlled them easily. Yuana was the only one he had to imprint orally and was proving to be the hardest to handle. Maybe this was a drawback of the oral process, a side effect. Or it might be because she was an *Apex* herself.

The man who occupied her heart was now in the hospital, and Yuana's concern for him kept her closed to his influence.

Kazu faced two choices: be generous and allow her to allay her worry about her boyfriend's wellbeing, then get her back to training afterward; or he could erase the man from her life – unfortunate collateral damage to his goal to prepare Yuana for the coming *Txandictus,* the tectonic shift in their world order.

The latter option offered a permanent solution, but it could delay Yuana's training because she would grieve. And she would be impenetrable while beset by such emotions.

When he lost his parents, it took him years to recover. It might take Yuana as long to mourn. The *Shift* had already begun, Yuana had to be ready before the year ended.

He would spare Yuana a few weeks to take care of the human and regain her equilibrium. Her emotional commitment to their unfolding destiny was crucial. That would only be achievable through a free mind and an open heart.

He would be patient.

Roald woke up to a dry throat and a fuzzy brain. He tried to look around, but he was too weak to even lift his head. Early morning sunlight brightened the room. The hum of the air conditioning was the only sound.

A warm hand atop his own drew his attention to Yuana's head resting on the bed. Nightmare-laden dreams seemed to have replaced her normally peaceful sleep; there were furrows on her brows. And she looked tired.

He scanned his surroundings, trying to understand where he was, what happened, why he seemed to be in a hospital.

How long have I been here?

His head hurt, trying to remember. His torso ached. He glanced down at the source of his discomfort. His chest was bare, but tight bandages bound his ribcage. And the memories came back to him like water from a broken dam. It was too overwhelming to make sense.

The door to his left opened. His body tensed in alarm, putting him on guard. He automatically reached for his *karambit* under his pillow, but a sharp pain in his ribs made him gasp. And it drew the attention of the intruder. It was Daniel, who looked concerned.

"You're awake," Daniel said, walking to his side.

"Yes," he squeaked, huffing the pain away. Cold sweat beaded his forehead.

"You're in pain?" Daniel asked, his hand on the control of the drip attached to him.

He nodded. Daniel adjusted it, releasing more morphine to his drip. Within moments, the sharp pain dulled into a faint throbbing.

Daniel pulled a chair and placed it by the bed, facing him.

"I'm glad you're awake now. We were anxious," Daniel said, his glance rested on the sleeping Yuana.

"How is she?" he croaked, his tongue was as thick as wood and as dry.

Daniel reached for a bottled water by the table, unscrewed one and gave it to him. His hand seemed boneless; it trembled with the effort to lift it to his lips. Daniel helped him.

It was a small sip, but the water soaking the parched tissues of his mouth and throat was akin to a downpour after a drought. Roald sighed at the pleasure of it.

"How is she?" he repeated his question. His prime concern was Yuana's welfare.

"She's fine. Understandably worried about you. And uncharacteristically aggravated. She's furious at the man who did this to you." Daniel replied in an emotionless tone.

He recognised Daniel's usual tack when he did not want to show his true feelings. The flat statement confirmed that. And Roald felt touched by it. He would not point it out, though, out of respect to his friend's sensibilities and his lack of energy for banter.

"My parents, were they told?" His mother would freak out.

"Yes. But we convinced them to finish the convention. They are flying in today. So, expect them here later," Daniel said, handing him the bottled water again. He accepted it and sipped some more.

"I should expect a flood of tears later, then," he said, sighing.

"By the way, we told them you were in an accident. We have not told them what happened to you," Daniel said.

"Thank you. That was the right thing to do, or my mother would overreact." Thinking about his mother's melodramatic reactions was enough to sap his energy.

Daniel's demeanour turned serious. "Do you remember what happened, Ro? There are holes in our theories because we are missing information."

"I am not sure if I remember everything," he replied, trying to recall. "Ask me questions. I will try to answer them."

Yuana stirred, turning her head away, interrupting their conversation. Roald touched her hair. But she was still asleep. He worried she would wake up with a stiff neck in this position. Daniel seemed to have the same thought.

Daniel scooped Yuana into his arms and laid her on the daybed at the other end of the room. He watched Daniel get a sheet from the closet and cover her with it. Dan went back to claim Yuana's seat, ready to question him.

"Thank you, Dan," he said, grateful for Daniel's concern and care for Yuana.

"Don't mention it. I could hardly let you lift her yourself when you cannot even carry the water bottle and manage the distance between hand to mouth," Daniel replied with his usual dry humour.

Roald smiled. That was true. He was weaker than a newborn chick.

"Okay, tell me what you have about my attacker. Perhaps it will help me remember details," he said. He felt apathetic. Maybe it was an effect of his fatigue. Daniel needed answers, and he would provide as much as he could.

"We can analyze facts later. It is too much information to process. Just answer my questions," Daniel said.

He nodded. Daniel was right. He was tiring already, and they had not even started yet.

"Did you recognise your attacker?" Daniel asked.

He shook his head. The memory of the man's face came easy. "No, he was wearing a mask," he replied.

Daniel received the information with a nod. They must have known this already.

"Did you recognise his car?"

"I think it was red... A Mazda," he replied. He remembered seeing the guy getting into the car.

Again, Daniel nodded. "You gave me a plate number; do you still remember?"

He thought about it for a while. Nothing. "No."

Daniel took out his phone and showed him what looked like incomplete plate numbers. *KYG... KGY... 47... 74.*

"Which one seemed more correct to you?" Daniel asked.

"I do not know..." His memory of the plate numbers drew a complete blank.

"Okay." Daniel did not seem fazed by his lack of recollection. "Last question. Is there anyone who might hold a grudge against you? Enough to want to have you attacked."

"No. I do not have enemies," he replied, drowsily. His eyes were getting heavy.

"Yes, I thought so, too," Daniel said, his voice fading.

Daniel weighed if it was a good idea to ask Roald about the details of the actual attack, but Roald had fallen asleep again. With a sigh, he stood up and looked at the two people dearest to him.

For the first time since he discovered and awakened his *Vis* traits, he found a purpose to use them. And he felt a deep satisfaction he could physically take on the coward who attacked Roald. He would hunt him down, no matter how long it takes.

Their only viable clue was the car. With a surge of impatience, he paced the room at his helplessness to make a move, to follow a lead, so they could begin looking for the Roald's attacker.

A gasp and a sudden movement from the corner made him turn – Yuana bolted upright, her eyes wild with agitation.

Alarmed, he sat beside her. "Yuana? Are you okay?"

"Dan, you need to go to the Mazda distributor. You should be able to get a list of all the red Mazdas sold by them." She gripped the neckline of his shirt, her pupils dilated.

"Yuana, they could have sold hundreds of units." *Is she in the throes of her dream?*

"The plate number should tell us the year it was registered! The first three letters correspond to a specific year. Your dad should be able to find out from the Land Transportation Office." Yuana's voice rose in intensity.

"You are right..." Her suggestion was a brilliant one. "I will take care of it myself." It gave him a surge of energy and made him feel powerful.

"Let me know what happens, Dan," Yuana's frantic entreaty brought his focus back.

"I will... Now, Yuana, you need to eat. Have you had your *victus*?" He warmed her cold cheeks in his hands.

Yuana sighed. "Yes, Tita Mena gave me some yesterday." Her voice lowered to a whisper. She seemed to have remembered that Roald slept nearby, and she did not want to rouse him. She moved toward Roald and stood over his bed, caressing his cheek. "Has he woken up?"

Daniel walked over to her side. "Yes, he did. We had a quick conversation earlier. He's going to be okay, Yu."

"Why didn't you wake me?"

"You were exhausted. You needed your sleep," he said, smoothing her hair back.

"How was he? What did you talk about?" she asked, leaning against him, towards the comfort that he presented. Daniel placed his arm around her shoulders, a force of habit.

"He's fine, a bit disoriented. But that is to be expected." He kissed the top of her head, glad that Yuana seemed to cope well. "And I asked him a few questions about his attacker," he added.

Yuana looked up at him, alertness had replaced the leaden expression in her eyes. "What did he tell you?"

"Well, he did not recognise his assailant, because he was wearing a mask. He remembered the red Mazda, and he does not know of anyone who would want him harmed," he said. "And then... he fell asleep after," he added.

"So, where are we in our theories? Which one is the most likely?" Yuana sighed.

"Leave this to me, Yu. I will take care of it. Just focus on Roald," Daniel said, squeezing her to him. "Later, when his parents arrive, I want you to go home and rest. You have been here for two days."

"I cannot do that, Dan. I am sure they will come here straight from the airport. They would be tired from the travel." Yuana sounded weary. He knew she was dreading having to explain the circumstances to Roald's parents.

"I can take over for you if need be. I will look after Roald if his parents want to rest. Go home. I just want you to take care of yourself," he said, grasping her chin when she opened her mouth to disagree. "Don't argue or I'll call your father and mother."

"Oh, okay..." Even her grudging acceptance sounded exhausted.

"For now, let us order breakfast. We will eat while Roald is asleep." He handed Yuana her phone so she could do the ordering. "I will call Dad to send someone to the Mazda dealership and call the Transportation office." He brandished his phone to reassure her.

Yuana's smile of gratitude soothed his anxiety.

Meanwhile, fifteen kilometres away...

Jacob Montejo examined the faint scar on his ribs in his mirror. It had been there for two days, and no sign of fading. As he touched the raised tissue, the fear that he felt when it did not heal immediately came back to him. The shallow wound should have healed in ten minutes. But it took his body half an hour to close the gash. And worse, it left a mark.

Did his harravis habit affect his healing ability? It seems impossible because his Vis traits are magnified by the viscera of another Vis.

Memories of the attack came back to him – his surprise at getting injured, his panic at the non-healing cut. He could swear the man was a mere human, but maybe he needed to learn more about his nemesis. There should be no more surprises next time – if the man survived the last one.

He wondered about the root of all this – Ms Orzabal. *Is she a De Vida?*

She held an executive level position in the company, so she could be a relative, a family friend, or someone very good at her job. Either way, she would be close to the prominent clan.

Linking himself to the most powerful *Vis* family in the country would be a coup. He would surpass his dead brother's achievements. Harri had two goals in life – to stop him from being a *harravis*, and to become a *Patriarch* to restore the Prowze name to its former prominence. Harri failed in both.

Their kind was too stupid to realise what a loser his older brother was when he was alive. It was the only thing Harri succeeded in – preserving the respect of the *Tribunal* members in their former *Gentem*. And denying him his revenge. And he would take all that away from Harri's memory by being a *Patriarch* himself.

Ms Orzabal could be his fast track to prominence. Through marriage. But only if she was a De Vida. It was not worth sacrificing his freedom otherwise.

Daniel and Yuana opened the door to a frantic Cielo and Alecsandro Magsino. Roald's mother hugged her. His father walked straight to Roald's bedside, looking down at his sleeping son. There was a grim, focused expression on his normally preoccupied countenance.

"How did it happen, Yuana?" Cielo asked as she approached Roald's bedside, pulling her with him.

"Um... we do not have the exact details, Tita. Let's wait until Roald wakes up," she said, evading the question.

Cielo's eyes widened in alarm. "He has not woken up?" She could see the panic gears grinding inside the older woman's head.

"He did already, Tita," she said hastily. "He has woken up, and we have spoken to him, but he's still fatigued," she explained.

"Okay," Cielo said. Pacified, she patted her son's hand, avoiding the swollen part where the IV tubes were once attached. They had removed the blood drip from Roald; his blood count had normalised.

"Thank you for taking care of him, Yuana," Sandro Magsino's deep voice rumbled just above her ear.

She looked up at Roald's father, at the face so similar to his son, only older.

"There is no need to thank me, Tito. There is nothing I would not do for him," she said.

"What did the doctor say about his condition?" Sandro Magsino asked, glancing at both Daniel and her.

"Some broken ribs, a punctured lung, but all is well. He needs to take it easy for the next six to eight weeks," Daniel replied.

Cielo Magsino's sigh of relief was dramatic, Yuana had to suppress a smile.

"So, he needs to remain in bed for that long?" Cielo Magsino asked, her maternal instinct out to the fore.

"No, Tita Cielo. The doctor said that while he needs to avoid strenuous activities and lifting heavy things, he should move about, to prevent mucous build up in his lungs." It would drive Roald crazy if his mother forced him to lie in bed for that long.

"And it will help him heal faster, Tita, if he is mobile. I believe he would be discharged tomorrow," Daniel interjected.

"Does he have to sleep upright like that?" his mother asked.

"Yes, Tita. The doctor advised it," she said.

"Okay," Cielo Magsino's fears were mollified.

"Tita, will you be staying here tonight?" Daniel asked.

"Of course! And we are prepared for that," Roald's mother replied, almost excitedly. She pointed at a small overnight bag she placed on a chair.

That made Daniel smile. "Tita, I'm going to take Yuana home, she has not had a proper rest since Roald was admitted here."

"Really? Then, by all means, she needs to go home and rest," Cielo Magsino said. "Go on, Yuana, we will take over for now. Come back tomorrow when they discharge Roald."

It seemed she had no choice. With a hug to Roald's parents, Yuana picked up her bag and followed Daniel out of the room.

Just outside of the door, Mateo was waiting. His eyes were bright with repressed excitement, a paper held in his hand.

"Dad! You've got news?" Daniel's exclamation prompted her to shush him. Roald's parents might overhear.

"Yes. Let us discuss it somewhere else," Mateo said. They followed him to his van. Father and son drove her home.

"So, what have you got, Tito?" Her heart pumped hard in excitement.

"Your hunch on the Mazda dealership paid off. There are three red Mazdas that were sold within the two-year period. Given that we do not have the exact plate number, I thought I will show you the names on the list. It might make sense to you." He handed the list to them.

She snatched the list from Mateo's grasp and scanned it. Her sharp intake of breath made both Mateo and Daniel lean closer to her.

"What?" Mateo asked?

"I don't know the other two names, but this one, I recognise..." she said, pointing at the last name listed. *Jacob Montejo.*

Daniel took the list from her hand, examining the name. "How do you know him?"

"He came to my office a few days ago. He introduced himself as Jake Montejo," she said. "And he asked about our corporate employee benefits program."

"How did Roald meet him?" Mateo asked, frowning.

"I am not sure if Roald ever met him, but I have encountered him twice. The first time, I was with Roald," she said, trying to recall the details of their first meeting.

"And?" Father and son had the same gleam in their eyes.

"Well, the first time happened months ago. It was in a restaurant where Roald and I had dinner. He approached my table and tried to pick me up when Roald was in the men's room," she said.

"And I guess he did not like being rebuffed?" Daniel asked dryly. Yuana could be very direct. A man with a fragile ego would be crushed.

"I think so. He insulted Roald, so I was a bit... harsh," she admitted. She felt a twinge of guilt. *Perhaps if I was not so harsh on him...*

"Yuana, don't you dare blame yourself!" Daniel's irritated tone jolted her away from her thoughts.

"Am I that transparent?" she asked. She realised just how much Daniel knew her. Either that or she was too easy to read.

"No, I just know you," Daniel replied, a tone of impatience in his voice.

"Did he meet Roald?" Mateo's question brought them back to the issue at hand.

"No, there was no encounter between them, but he definitely got a good look at Roald then. He was two tables away. He left the restaurant with a *Vis* woman he picked up there," she said. Her memory of that night's events became clear.

"How about the other day, in your office? Was there a chance that he saw Roald there?" Mateo asked.

She shook her head. "I do not think so. He was at the ground floor coffee shop and approached me just before midday. Roald dropped me off two hours prior." She was now seeing Jake Montejo's action through a different lens.

"He came to my office using the guise of business, Tito. Aleister said he seemed to have been waiting for me. It was not a coincidence he was there. I think he went after Roald to get back at me because I turned him down twice," she said, her conviction about her conclusion strong.

Mateo and Daniel were quiet, both thinking on her words. There were so many questions running around her brain.

"He must have seen you and Roald together and followed you to GJDV. That is how he found out where you work, Yuana. And I suspect he followed Roald as well," Mateo said. "The DNA sample should confirm if he is Roald's assailant."

"Is he in the system? If not, we need his blood sample," Daniel said.

"If we do not have it. I will get it for you," she said, her heart aflame with fury.

Daniel's frown had the dawning of suspicion. "Yuana... what are you planning...?"

"He is after me, Dan. I can get close to him." She hardened her tone on purpose.

"You are not going anywhere near him. I will not let you. And I am sure Ro will agree with me," Daniel said vehemently.

"Roald cannot disagree if he does not know. Besides he's too weak to argue at the moment." Burgeoning anger flared in her heart. She would not be dissuaded.

"He is dangerous, Yuana. If he finds out what you are after, he might hurt you too," Daniel said, his disapproval of her plan clear.

"Dan, I am not going to challenge him to a cage match. I'm simply going to charm him into lowering his guard and steal some of his genetic material." For the first time in her life, she was glad that she had the physical attributes to disarm men and lull them into complacency.

Alarmed, Daniel asked, "How do you propose to *steal* genetic material from him? And what kind of *genetic* material are you referring to?"

She drew back at the implication of his question. "Eww... not *that* genetic material, Daniel. My family will break *my* ribs if I ever do that. Have some faith in my capabilities." she said, exasperated.

"Sorry... I just... well, he was after your charms, after all..." Daniel mumbled, and had the grace to look apologetic.

"Okay, so what is your plan, Yuana?" Mateo asked, shaking his head at the juvenile exchange between his son and her.

"He came to my office pretending he was interested in our employee benefits program, so I will give him what he wants. I will handle his account myself," she said, sitting back. "I think he wants the opportunity to dazzle me, so I will give him that."

"Yuana, I will not allow you to be alone with him," Daniel said angrily, "so if that is what you have in mind, forget it!"

"I agree with Daniel, Yuana," Mateo said. "Senora Margaita and Senor Lorenzo will feed me my own liver if I let you do this without a backup," he added.

Mateo was right. "Okay, you have a point there, Tito. So, how do we do this?" she conceded.

Twenty minutes later, they hammered a firm strategy before they reached Yuana's condo.

Yuana's assistant, Lyndsey, would set an appointment with Jake Montejo. Yuana would make the presentation to his employees. She would bring coffee for both of them, and one of their *Iztaris*, disguised as the building's cleaning crew, would steal Jake Montejo's cup afterward.

Simple plan.

19

WRATH OF THE APEX

Jacob Montejo smiled at his reflection in the glass window of his office. A sense of satisfaction filled him. Ms Orzabal's assistant just called him to request an appointment on behalf of her boss. The beautiful Ms Orzabal would present to his employees their corporate package.

He confirmed a meeting tomorrow.

She must not have been that torn up over what happened to her boyfriend if she was working like usual. Maybe he did her a favour by putting her human boyfriend in the hospital, or the morgue.

He wondered what happened to his victim. It would be odd to ask... *what's her face...* Lyndsey... if she knew anything. The assistant might just mention his query to Ms Orzabal. It would raise suspicions because he was not supposed to know.

No matter... he wanted Ms Orzabal, and it looked like he was going to get her. If he was lucky, it might be as soon as tomorrow. He needed to plan his move. If she was a De Vida, she would need proper wooing.

If she was not, she would still be useful in making connections with the De Vidas.

He chuckled to himself. Perhaps if she proved to be entertaining enough, he would woo her for a bit. It could be a welcome diversion, a change from his usual pursuits.

Who knows, I might be good at it?

Yuana glanced at Daniel, who sat beside her with a grim expression. His jaw clenched so hard, the line of it so sharp, she thought he could open cans with it.

Worry lined Daniel's forehead, and his concern touched her, but this was her plan, and she was determined to see it through. She yearned to crush the man's balls in her hands. And if he annoyed her enough, she might just use her talons to rip them off.

The car stopped briefly. A light knock on the window startled her. A uniformed staff outside held two Styrofoam coffee cups. Daniel lowered the window and took the cups from him, handing over folded bills for payment. They marked the cups Y and J.

"Here's the coffee, Yu. I had it pre-marked at the coffee shop to make it easy for our guy to identify the cup he needs to bag. Make sure you use the Y cup," Daniel said, his expression getting darker by the minute.

"What kind of coffee is this?" she asked, raising the cup for Jake Montejo. She wanted Daniel to look at her.

"Flat white. He has a penchant for that. He ordered that twice while he waited for you." Daniel's jaw tightened even more.

She sighed. She reached out and touched Daniel's jawline. Daniel's eyes flew to hers. "Can I borrow this? It's so sharp, it's positively a deadly weapon." Daniel's frown deepened at her attempt at levity.

"This is serious, Yu. It could get dangerous."

She nodded. It was no use arguing with Daniel when he was like this.

Daniel sighed, resigned. "Our guy should be on the 26th floor now. He needs to be seen cleaning the premises so as not to arouse suspicion. You will see him when you get off the elevator. He will greet you both good morning and ask if you want coffee. Your response should be, 'No, thanks, I have a mocha here,'" he added.

The car slowed and halted in front of the building. Daniel stopped her from getting out for a last-minute assurance. "We will park across. If things don't go according to plan, just come out to the front. I will be here."

"Daniel, don't worry. I can handle myself," she said and stepped out.

She had dressed the part today. Corporate, yet sexy. Her fitted skirt had a side slit up to mid-thigh for movement – to dazzle or knee an offending groin. Her shoes had slim but sturdy heels. She wanted to charm, but she was prepared to fight. Daniel had no idea just how physically capable and mentally prepared she was for this.

She had seen how vicious Jake Montejo was, but one thing she noticed, his punch was not that of a trained fighter. His physique was not that of a warrior. If he got too close, she was confident that he would not have the instinct to block a punch. Not from a woman. He would not expect it.

As she walked across the lobby towards the lift, Jake Montejo approached her from the side. Creep that he was, he waited for her. She schooled her face to remain pleasant as she greeted him.

"Good morning, Mr Montejo. Coffee?" she said and offered him the cup with a J on it.

He noticed the letter and gave her a delighted grin. He gladly accepted it. "Oh, thank you, Ms Orzabal. This is very thoughtful of you," he said. The smug smile remained on his face.

"Yours is flat white. I had to have it marked so I don't mix up the drinks," she said, an equally charming smile on her face.

"How did you know?" The distasteful, smug smile on his face widened.

The slime ball! She suppressed the urge to gag.

"I like knowing our client's preferences, Mr Montejo," she replied. "I asked the coffee shop where we met what you ordered," she added, adopting a coy and apologetic smile.

Satisfaction sparkled in the depths of his eyes. Her target was pleased with himself. She felt tempted to throw the hot coffee on his face. It took extreme self-control and the knowledge that the shmuck was eating out of her hand to not do so. Jake Montejo was so convinced of his own appeal that he did not suspect anything.

They took the elevator, and it surprised her when he pressed 10th floor button rather than the 26th.

"I thought your office is on the 26th floor." Her tone was calm, but her mind raced.

"Let's go to my private office first. The presentation room is not ready yet, but it would be in half an hour. We can enjoy our coffee here in the meantime," he said and ushered her out as the door opened on the 10th floor. She had no choice but to follow him.

Now that is a wrinkle in their plan. How are they going to secure his cup?

She would have to adapt to this and come up with an alternative plan. She also needed to tell Daniel where she was, or he would panic.

Jake led her to a well-appointed two-bedroom unit. It was finished in black and white tones with teal accent. A painting of a fox hidden among a bush with purple flowers, a bat and a raven hung prominently on the wall.

The man has taste.

"Take a seat," he said, patting the sofa beside him. That condescending motion sparked a temper in her, but she restrained herself. She sat on the opposite couch and feigned coyness.

She felt her phone vibrate in her bag. It must be Daniel. He must be worried since she did not show up on the 26th floor.

"Can I use your bathroom?" she asked in a jolt of inspiration.

"Sure, that way, first door to your left," Jake said, pointing to a hallway. With a smile, she got up and left him.

Once inside, she checked her phone and saw she had seven missed calls from Daniel. He must be frantic by now. She was about to dial his number when she realised she could hear Jake Montejo's movement in the living room. The sound-proofing of the room was not ideal.

She sent a text message instead. *Room 1018, his unit.* And to give her team the time to position themselves, she refreshed her make-up. Jake Montejo lounged on the couch when she got back to the living room. There was a glimmer of malice in his eyes despite his benign smile. Her gut tingled in warning.

"What time is the presentation again? I allotted only a couple of hours for this. I have another appointment after." She wanted this situation back under her control.

"In another fifteen minutes." His response was dismissive. "How long have you been working with GJDV?" That change of topic startled her. Her instinct against revealing information to strangers, *Vis* or not, kicked in.

"Three years." It was technically true. She worked with their other companies and subsidiaries in the past.

Jake Montejo nodded, but there was a frown of disappointment on his brow. And that made her wonder what he was up to. As she observed him, she realised she had not seen him sip from the cup, so she raised her cup to him, a toast to prod him to drink up. His smile widened, but he complied.

Her coffee was no longer hot, just a comfortable lukewarm. She sipped slowly, keeping her eyes on him, challenging him to do the same. To drink more, to deposit more genetic material on the cup. And he did.

A strange feeling rose from her chest, a cold, numbing sensation that grew outwards, making her heart pump harder. She understood the reason for his smugness. He drugged her.

Suddenly, she felt scared. She could see him through her fading vision, watching her. Predator to prey. There was no doubt in her mind this was Roald's attacker.

She closed her eyes, and something inside her rebelled. She would not let him victimise her as well. Her pumping heart doubled its beat with her growing fury as she fought the drug.

At the back of her mind, an idea sprouted. With the last of her waning strength and consciousness, she shape-shifted into her *Animus.*

Heat bloomed in her gut, spreading outwards, chasing the numbness away, creating a pins-and-needles sensation in her limbs. And with it, her mind cleared. The *syne-morphosis* burned away the drug in her system.

She felt the heat at the back of her eyes and focused the tingling sensation on her fingers. Her *Animus* possessed her core. As she marvelled at the surge of power her form provided, she felt Jake walk closer, his breath warm along her jawline. She held still as she waited for his next move. Her eyes were closed but she could see him as clearly as if she was looking at him.

Jake's mouth landed on her neck, his intention clear. She shoved him away, her eyes opened. He staggered back, surprised that she was conscious. Jake froze, snared by the gleam of fury in her red eyes. With a growl, he lunged at her. Quick as a flash, she swiped at him with her talons, creating three deep gouges on his cheeks, throwing him against the wall.

At the same moment, the door crashed open, and Daniel rushed in, his expression murderous.

Faced with an angry, well-built adversary, Jake Montejo ran. He turned towards the open verandah, jumped down into the overhanging ledge two floors down, and another. And the next. He landed on top of the structure that covered the front drive of the building. On his last leap to the ground, he was in his animal form, a large dog. He scampered away, leaving his clothes on the pavement.

Daniel turned back to her. Black fury on his face, he breathed hard. She thought he was going to rail at her.

"Are you okay?" he asked through gritted teeth and tight jaw.

"I am fine, Dan. I could have handled him... But thank you for coming to my assistance anyway," she said.

Daniel gulped, swallowing his rage. He took her hand and inspected her talons, still wet with Jake Montejo's blood. Questions in his eyes. "What is your animal form, Yuana?" he asked, bewildered. She could read what was on his mind; Daniel had never seen anything like it.

"I will tell you later, Dan. For now, get your DNA storing kit, and get his blood from these," she said.

Daniel took a deep breath. "Right," he said and dug out from his *morphbag* a glass vial with a long-stemmed cotton bud inside. He swabbed the blood and tissue from her talons. The cotton bud came away soaked. It was satisfying to know she hurt the bastard.

She stood up; her talons retracted as she washed her hands in the sink. Daniel watched her the whole time.

There was a quick knock on the front door. Daniel let a guy into the room with a small nod. This must be the *Iztari* tasked to pick up the cup. Like all *Iztaris*, he had the build, the agility and the movement of a soldier.

Daniel pointed to the cup. It overturned, coffee still dripped from it, creating dark brown stains on the cream rug under the coffee table. The *Iztari* nodded and took out a plastic bag from his *morphbag* and picked up the cup with it. The man threw a glance at her when he noticed the blood drips on the rug.

Daniel handed him the vials next. "Those are blood samples," he said.

At the guy's questioning look, "Yuana swiped it off his cheeks," he added. A tinge of dark pleasure in his tone.

"Oh," was the *Iztari's* surprised response. "So, what's next?" the man asked when Daniel said nothing.

Their original plan was just to secure the cup for the DNA material. Now, they had the cup, blood, and the target seemed to have run away.

"Send those to the lab for the DNA test. Send for a team, we will have the guy investigated for..." Daniel glanced at her, unsure of what to say.

"He drugged me, and tried to molest me," she supplied.

Daniel's scowl was back in a flash, even darker than before. "Okay. Let's hunt the guy down. And let us start here," he said. The *Iztari* nodded and pulled out his phone to call a team in.

Daniel got up and pulled her to her feet, out of the unit and toward the elevator. They stood in total silence. His jaw so rigid, she was half afraid it would lock. She dared not tease him, afraid he would explode.

His grip on her hand remained firm as he tugged her toward their waiting car. Their first stop was to pick up Mateo, and then on to the hospital. As soon as the door closed on them, Daniel turned to her.

"Now, tell me exactly what happened. Leave nothing out." Daniel's piercing gaze was unblinking.

"Well, he was there by the elevator when I entered the lobby. I did not expect him to whisk me to his unit ..." she said.

Daniel huffed with annoyance. "You should have called me immediately," he said through gritted teeth.

"When do you think I could have done that, Dan? Just before we got into the elevator? I did not know we were going to his unit. Inside the elevator? There was no signal. Just before we entered his unit? That would have been odd," she said with extreme patience, but a trace of sarcasm was unavoidable. Daniel's protective instinct had surfaced, and it made him unreasonable.

He sighed. "I'm sorry, Yu... You are right, of course." Daniel raked his hair with his fingers. "Please continue."

"We chatted a bit. And I asked to use his bathroom so I could call you. But the soundproofing of the room was poor; he would have heard our conversation. So, I texted you instead. I spent a few minutes fixing my makeup to give our guy time to get into position," she said.

She realised Daniel took a while to get to the unit. "What took you so long?"

"I rushed in the moment I got your text, but they asked me to register at the reception desk before they would let me in. And there were three other people before me," he replied, scowling at the remembered nuisance. "So, what happened next?"

"I think he put the drug in my coffee while I was in the bathroom," she replied.

"Yes, you said he drugged you. But... how did you avoid it? Did you pick up the scent before you drank the coffee?"

Daniel's confusion at finding her not just conscious but in fighting form enough to injure their target was understandable.

"Actually, I was too distracted to notice. He was not drinking his coffee, so I raised my cup to a toast, so he had to comply and drink his coffee. In exchange, I had to do the same. I fully ingested the drug," she said.

"And it did not work?" Daniel was perplexed.

"It worked. It was a fast-acting drug. I was losing consciousness within seconds," she said, recalling the moments, "but something told me to *synemorph* to my *Animus,* so I did. And the transformation burned away the effects of the drug from my system."

Daniel looked at her, awed. "I didn't know you could do that. Is that normal?"

"I don't know. I have never heard of it happening before myself."

"So, what happened next? You said he attempted to molest you..." Daniel's jaw had tightened again.

"Well, he kissed my neck, and I was revolted. So, I pushed him away. But he charged at me, so I swiped him across the face. He was lucky I did not take his eye out," she said, remembering it angered her once more.

"Yuana, your claws earlier – those did not belong to any land animals I know of. Definitely not panther claws. Those looked like eagle talons," Daniel said, leaning closer. "I may not have the skills to shapeshift, but I know very well that *Viscerebus* cannot transform into winged creatures... so, explain."

She reached for the console and raised the transparent soundproofing barrier between them and the driver. Daniel's eyebrow rose.

"Dan, this cannot go beyond the two of us..." she said. Daniel frowned, but he nodded. "I am an *Apex*." The shock on his face would have been funny, if being a super shape-shifter was a joke. She waited for Daniel to recover.

"An *Apex*? You are an *Apex*?" Daniel couldn't seem to grasp the idea. She nodded. "The once-in-every-two-hundred-years kind of *Vis*?" he asked.

Again, she nodded. "Yes, the super shape-shifter. The direct issue of the genes of Aetos and Prometheus. The apogee of our kind," she joked. Daniel's incredulous expression struck her as funny.

"How long have you known?" Daniel's brows rose higher. He looked thunderstruck.

"Not too long ago. I found out while I was in Mindoro."

"Does Roald know?"

"Yes. He discovered my secret, so I had to tell him," she said. "And don't start throwing tantrums about me not telling you. I wanted to keep it a secret from everyone except my family until I am ready," she warned.

"Well, I was going to point out that you have known me far longer than Roald, but he is your boyfriend, so he outranks me." Daniel's joke was an olive branch.

"Keep the information to yourself. Apart from my family, Roald and you, nobody else knows," she said.

That was her version of apology.

Roald woke up to the sharp scent of oranges, then the familiar tinkling notes of his mother's chatter and the deep baritone of his father. The voices of his parents acted as background noise to the inner babble in his head.

He would have to deal with his mother's hovering presence later. Hopefully, they would not ask about the "accident" again. He had told them he did not remember the details, and he did not want to lie to them too often.

He was impatient to be home and to deal with what happened to him. To find out who attacked him and why. More and more details were coming back to him. One thing that kept him thinking was the nagging feeling he had seen the man before. His movements were familiar. He just could not remember where they previously crossed paths.

The door opened and interrupted his thoughts. Yuana and Daniel came into the room. Yuana's gaze was on him the moment she stepped across the threshold. Her smile widened when she saw him awake. She rushed to him, dropping a kiss on his mouth. Her lips were warm and soft. And tasted of cinnamon and mint.

"Good morning, my love," she said against his mouth. "Are you ready to go home?"

"Yes, since yesterday. Were you able to sleep well?" he asked.

Yuana nodded. The light in her eyes told him she had something to say, one she couldn't blurt out while his parents were in the room.

"Papa, why don't you take Mama to a lunch date? The Wild Orchid Café is a block away. Yuana and Daniel can take care of me while you enjoy a good meal." He appealed to his father, knowing he would pick up on his meaning.

His father regarded him closely. The nod of agreement implied that Roald would need to give him a long explanation later. One they would both keep from his mother to protect her. He nodded back in acknowledgement.

As soon as his parents left the room, Daniel and Yuana pulled a chair close to his bed. The weight of suppressed information was heavy and almost palpable.

"Okay, you two. Have we found out who attacked me?"

"Yes. His name is Jacob Killian Montejo. He targeted you because of Yuana," Daniel said, glancing at her.

"Who?" The name was unfamiliar. "Where did I encounter him?"

"Remember that one time we had dinner at Anton's. A man approached me while you were in the men's room. I rebuffed him. And we think he did not take it well," Yuana said, trying to jog his memories with the details.

He thought about it, trying to recall the said date. Then it dawned on him. And it clicked. "The guy who left with a woman he picked up at the restaurant..." he breathed. "He was my attacker," he said with certainty.

Yuana and Daniel blinked at the confidence in his statement. Yuana gripped his hand. "Are you sure?"

"I recognised his walk. He had a way of walking that was distinct."

Yuana and Daniel exchanged glances, loaded with the meaning that made him wary. "What? Is there something else I need to know?"

"We just need the DNA matched, then we have solid proof," Daniel said.

"The DNA from the *karambit*?" He remembered slicing the bastard's torso with it.

"Yes. If that matches the sample that we got from him. We can prosecute him."

"I'm confused. You got a sample from him? Aside from the blood in the *karambit*?"

"Yes. We ran the DNA from the *karambit*, and we are waiting for the results of that. But just in case his DNA is not in the system, we got a sample from him. If the two samples match, it's a sure thing." Daniel explained.

"Hang on, Dan... How did you find him if we had nothing but an unidentified DNA?"

"Yuana here got a brilliant idea to check on Mazda dealership regarding red ones sold in the last two years. We knew the car's registration period because of the first three letters in the plate number," Daniel said, smiling at Yuana, a proud light in his eyes.

"And it yielded three names. One of them I recognised because he was in my office a few days ago, pretending to be interested in the GJDV corporate employee benefit program. He introduced himself as Jake Montejo," Yuana interjected, her tone casual. "I remembered him from that night, so when I read his name on the list, we made the connection."

He watched the emotions that crossed Yuana's face and noticed the guarded look that Daniel threw at her. They were hiding something that could upset him.

"How did you get the DNA sample from him? I doubt he volunteered it considering what he did to me," he looked at Yuana. She couldn't lie to him.

"Well, we set up a trap. Yuana made an appointment to present to his employees this morning. We brought two coffees and Yuana gave one to him. Then we sent one of our guys who posed as a cleaning crew to retrieve the cup. And we succeeded," Daniel interjected, and his quick response made him more suspicious.

"It did not go as planned, did it?" His intent gaze at Yuana.

The quick, exchanged glances between the two, confirmed his guess. "What happened, Yuana?" he persisted.

Resigned, Yuana sighed. "Yes, it did not go as planned, but it turned out fine in the end." His silence prompted her to explain further. "Instead of taking me to his office, he took me to his unit, sixteen floors down. I went along with it, but I messaged Daniel where I was. Jacob Montejo... drugged my drink..." Yuana held up a hand at his enraged gasp. "But it did not work. When he tried to touch me, I struck him across the face. And Daniel burst into the room right on time."

Her delivery of the facts was rushed and Daniel's nods were brisk as she related the last bit. The two looked nervous that he would explode.

"So, you were not hurt?"

Yuana leaned over and kissed him on the lips. "I was not harmed at all. Not a hair in my head." She smiled, patting her locks for emphasis.

He glanced at Daniel for confirmation.

Daniel nodded and chuckled. "Yes. She was unharmed. You should have seen the guy. Yuana sliced his face open."

"What? She did? How?" That was unexpected.

"With my talons," she said, wriggling her fingers in the air.

"You shape-shifted into your... form?" He was unsure if Daniel knew of her *Apex* nature.

"Only the necessary body parts," Yuana said, wriggling her fingers once more.

"So, where is the guy? Did you apprehend him?" He glanced at Daniel.

Dan shook his head. "No, he ran away. He got scared when he saw me. He jumped off his verandah, and into the ground. But we are onto him. With the tracking skills of the *Iztaris,* I am confident we will catch him soon."

Roald didn't know what to think about that. "So, what do we tell my parents?" he asked after a while. He would need to explain to his father the details later.

"Tell them the details if you want. Just don't tell him about your attacker being a *Vis*. Tell them we know who the guy is, and the authorities are looking for him," Daniel said.

"Or you could stick to the accident story. That the authorities have discovered the identity of the guy who ran you over with his motorcycle. You could say the police are looking for him," Yuana suggested.

"The accident story is easier to explain. And less for my parents to worry about. The truth will make them fear another attack since he is still at large," he said. But a terrible thought entered his head, and he met Daniel's gaze.

"Don't worry, bro. We have deployed a group of *Iztaris* to guard you and your parents until we catch Jake Montejo," Daniel said.

"How about Yuana? Is she guarded as well?" He remembered the viciousness of the man and his strength. He wanted to make sure that his attacker would not have any opportunity to ambush Yuana. She remained the object of his attacker's desire.

"Ro, she is a De Vida and the great granddaughter of the *Matriarch* and *Patriarch* of this *Gentem*. She was well guarded prior to this incident, even more so now," Daniel assured him.

Thank God for privileged parentage, Roald thought and heaved a sigh of relief.

Rapid heartbeat thumped against Jacob's ears and chest. His lungs felt scored. He was running faster than he ever did in his life. His muscles trembled to the point of pain, but he couldn't stop until he found a safe place. Somewhere to hide, think and plan until it was dark enough for him to make his move.

He was scared out of his mind. His encounter with Yuana Orzabal terrified him in more ways than one. The more reasonable fear was the fact that by now Yuana Orzabal must have reported him to the *Iztari* office for what he did. The possibility of her connecting him to the attack on her boyfriend was now a certainty. That would be disastrous. His attack on a human would reach the *Tribunal*, then he would become an object of an intensive *Vis* hunt.

His less reasonable apprehension, which petrified him more, was the woman herself. She partially transformed. It wasn't something normal *Viscerebus* could do unless they were pregnant and only during dire circumstances. She transformed before the circumstances became dire, and she didn't look pregnant.

When she fixed those red pupils on him, terror rippled all over his body. She was a small, slim woman, maybe half his weight, it was unexplainable how she intimidated him with just one look. He panicked and lashed out. A childish reaction that got him a slashed face from her talons.

A shiver ran down his spine at the memory, and his heartbeat picked up. Jacob shook his head to dispel the image from his mind.

He would need to hide until things clear up. *But where?* It wouldn't be possible to go back to his unit. It must crawl with *Iztaris* now. As a *harravis*, he was stronger than most *Vis*, but faced with a couple of well-trained *Iztaris,* he would not prevail.

He needed to access his funds and set up a new lair somewhere. He could handle *harravis* habit for a month, then he would need to hunt. This time, his hunting days would be restricted. While there were no signs of his past crime because of his strategy, he wouldn't be able to lure his victims as openly as before. The *Iztaris* would put out a notice about him among their kind. He would have to re-think his moves.

Right now, his immediate concern was to find clothes before he transformed back into his human form. Walking around in his *Animus* was exhausting, but he could not go around naked as a man. It would attract attention both from the humans and his kind. The *Iztaris* would search for him in both forms.

His best bet would be to go to the affluent residential areas in the city. Stray dogs, especially his size, would attract attention as well. He ran along the hedges, trying to remain inconspicuous.

From a distance, he saw the entrance to a gated subdivision. He slipped past the guards and trotted in leisure. Here, he could just be a lost pet on its way back to his master's home. He ambled along the pavement, looking for clothes hanging outside, and a corresponding open gate.

Jake Montejo was unaware that his life was more in danger than he knew. He did not know there was another pair of eyes who witnessed his attack on Yuana. He did not know that Yuana's emotions and recall of the events have been transmitted to another person – him. Yuana's *Aztarim.* And at this moment, his fury against the bastard who attacked his *Aztarima* was uncontainable.

Kazu followed Jake Montejo's movements from overhead. The only thing stopping him from snatching the idiot right now was daylight. With his long-distance vision engaged, Kazu followed his target's progress as his dog form slipped through the gate of a high-end subdivision. His prey would no doubt look for clothes and shoes to wear so he could regain his human form.

Kazu flew above the clouds to avoid detection. He had spotted the highest rooftop in the subdivision, where he would lie in wait until the sun set. In the meantime, he tracked his prey's movement as he circled above.

He remembered his wrath and alarm when the coward drugged Yuana. His view of the attacker's face blurred as her consciousness wavered. His admiration for Yuana's willpower overruled his fear for her welfare. He felt her struggle to fight the effects of the drug, then her own fight instinct kicked in. Transforming into her *Animus* was an inspired action, and a welcome insight into her powers. And his.

His admiration doubled when she single-handedly stopped the predatory idiot. If he had been there, he would have severed the brain stem of Yuana's attacker rather than just slash his face to ribbons. It was still satisfying to watch.

So, he would hunt the moron down himself and eliminate him. Jake Montejo would no longer pose a danger to Yuana and her *Apex* nature before the morning came.

As Kazu expected, his prey waited for the cover of darkness to steal clothes and a pair of running shoes. He watched him transform and get dressed as he skulked out of the gate and walked toward the entrance of the subdivision.

Kazu smiled in wicked satisfaction. In a flash, he swooped down and snatched up his target. Jake Montejo's yell of surprised terror spooked some pets nearby. It was dark and he was too fast for anyone to see clearly what happened.

His prey stopped trying to break away from his hold when they reached five hundred feet in altitude. Jake must have known that it would be fatal to fall to the ground from that height. His efforts were futile, anyway; his feet would never touch the ground alive.

Jake Montejo seemed frozen in fear, but his muscles trembled as Kazu flew them both higher. At twenty thousand feet, his prey went limp with terror when Kazu threw him high up in the air like a ragdoll. Jake Montejo flailed, his screams of sheer panic unheard by anyone at that height.

Kazu's sharp bat claws swiped up, slicing him up like a butcher, opening Jake's abdomen from belly to chest. Their gazes met a fraction of a second as Jake plummeted to the ground; Kazu's eyes gleamed with triumph, Jake's wide with shock.

Headfirst, Kazu dived and grasped the man's exposed viscera with one clawed hand, ripping the heart out. He caught the dead man by the neck with his other, unconcerned with the trail of blood. It would dissipate before it reached the ground.

Kazu flew to his destination – his victim's apartment building.

Jake Montejo's lifeless body landed with a quiet thud at his own verandah. Not a single passerby on the street below the tenth-floor apartment noticed.

Savage satisfaction filled Kazu as he chewed on the heart he held and flew away, the taste of blood and texture of the tissue familiar and welcome.

He had forgotten how good it was to flex his powers when necessary. The *Iztaris* would find Jake Montejo's body in the morning. Yuana would not have to worry about him anymore.

No additional cause to delay her training to prepare her for the looming *Shift*.

The Txandictus is afoot and Yuana could use every single moment that she has before it is upon them.

20

THE DUAL APEX

Roald limped behind Yuana as she carried the breakfast tray to the dining table. He had refused to eat in bed. He was tired of being treated like a patient. His mother's disapproving gaze followed him. Like Yuana, she wanted him to stay abed, but he insisted.

"Here you go, Ro. You must eat all of this since you made me carry this tray back here," Yuana said as she placed the plate of omelette in front of him.

"I expect you and Mama to join me, mind you." He pulled a chair for her.

"You know very well I don't eat breakfast, my son." His mother kissed his forehead. "I will leave the two of you to enjoy. I will be late for my pottery class." His mother gave Yuana a peck on the cheek, grabbed her bag, and went to the door. "I will be back after lunch," she said as she closed it shut behind her.

Yuana watched his mother stroll out of his condo with a fond smile. Cielo Magsino was a kind woman who liked everybody. His mother and Yuana had different personalities, but she saw Yuana as a perfect complement to his character.

"Did Daniel say what time he's coming over?" Yuana asked as she laid an omelette plate on the table.

"Should be anytime now," he shrugged, pouring her a cup of coffee.

Right on cue, the doorbell rang. A grim-looking Daniel walked in. Without words, Daniel beelined to the coffee pot and poured himself a cup, then sat down in silence. Roald glanced at Yuana, but she seemed at a loss herself.

"We found your attacker," Daniel said in a flat tone, his eyes glittered with a strange light.

"Jake Montejo?"

Daniel nodded. "Yes. The *Iztaris f*ound his body on his verandah this morning."

"His body?" Yuana was frowning. "He's dead?"

"Yes. He was disembowelled and missing a heart."

Yuana's shocked gasp echoed his. Daniel's expression carried the trace of his disbelief at Jake Montejo's demise.

"He was killed by an *Aswang*?" Terror struck Roald's heart as the memories of the attack came back to him. He did not realise his hand had closed on the *karambit* hanging around his neck until Yuana's hand touched his.

"Yes. Only a *Vis* can do that to him. But the question is how? The front door of his unit was untouched. Hell, nothing inside his unit was disturbed! The sliding door was still locked from the inside." Daniel's frown cut deep, as if he still could not wrap his head around the fact.

"His killer attacked him in his verandah? How did he get back to his own unit? Didn't we seal his front door?" Yuana's questions came out in a furious stream.

"Yes. And we installed an alarm by the front door. It wasn't triggered. And he couldn't have entered through the verandah itself. It was on the tenth floor, and his *animus* was canine. Dogs are not exactly known for their climbing abilities," Daniel said, bewildered.

"Do we know the time of death?" Yuana's face wore a focused, analytical expression.

"Sometime around seven p.m.," Daniel replied. "There were a lot of humans walking along the street that time of the night, and no one heard anything."

"Whoever killed him... must be a very strong *Aswang*," he blurted out. The memory of the attack rushed to the surface of his mind like a freight train. It had been resting at the back of his consciousness since he woke up in the hospital.

"What do you mean?" Daniel's frown deepened. Yuana's gaze swivelled to him.

"I have sparred with your father, Dan, and two other *Iztaris*. I know how strong you guys are. Jake Montejo is not as trained or as buff, but he was exceptionally strong," he said. "I only survived that attack because I had this blade, and he was not expecting it." His hand gripped the *karambit* tighter on impulse.

"Stronger than my dad and the *Iztaris*?" Daniel echoed softly. He pulled his phone from his pocket and dialled it. "Dad, can we run a blood test on our dead perp? We think he's a *harravis*."

"My attacker is a *harravis*?" Roald's brain reeled. He thought he had neutralised the threat of the *Aswangs* to him. It seemed that it was not so.

"If Jake Montejo is a *harravis*, how did a mere *Vis* manage to kill him?" Yuana asked. "Or perhaps there were more than one?"

"A cursory inspection of his body showed few signs of struggle. No defensive wounds. There were minor bruises on him, some strange marks on his neck, some discoloration on his shoulders, and the massive, open wound on his torso, from abdomen to chest, where his heart was torn out," Daniel said after his brief conversation with Mateo. "It looked like it was a quick kill. It might have taken him by surprise."

"But how did he end up on his verandah?" Yuana asked.

Roald listened to Yuana and Daniel discuss the case, his heart pounding so hard it was deafening. His brain whirled in panic as he tried to calm himself, to have logic rule over the emotions that were controlling him right now.

"What could kill a *harravis*?" He did not realise he voiced the question aloud until both Yuana and Daniel turned to him.

"Trained *Iztaris* could," Daniel replied, his gaze on him keen.

"Do you think trained *Iztaris* did?" He did not think that Daniel believed so.

Daniel sighed and shook his head. "Not anyone from our team. But a team of *Venatoris* turned *Erne* could."

"*Venatoris*? *Erne*?" he and Yuana asked in unison; his was confusion, hers was surprise.

"*Venatoris* are former *Iztaris* turned private investigators and bounty hunters. *Ernes* are vigilantes."

"But why would a *Venatori* or an *Erne* come after him?" Yuana asked.

"I don't know. We have not even raised that possibility until Roald asked the question."

"Perhaps he had a lot of enemies. Powerful ones. And they sent *Venatoris* or *Ernes* after him," Yuana speculated, her brows knitted in concentration.

"Isn't it a strange coincidence that he got killed the same night of your attack?" Daniel asked Yuana.

"It could be a mere coincidence, no matter how strange it was. Maybe, he was already being followed and what he did to me made them nervous. It would bring the *Tribunal* over his head. And they did not want to be exposed," Yuana said.

"That's a possibility..." Daniel conceded.

"So, does that mean that whoever killed Jake Montejo would also go after Yuana?" Roald asked. The concept was frightening to him.

Daniel paused, his gaze turned inward as he pondered on the possibilities. "I think the death of Jake Montejo would be enough for them."

"But we do not know that for sure," he said. Yuana's warm hand touched his arm, a reassuring smile on her face.

"Don't worry, Roald. The *Iztaris* would never stop the investigation until we find out the full story." At his worried frown, she added. "Don't forget that I am a De Vida, and my great grandparents occupy the highest position in this *Gentem*. I will be fine."

He nodded, but the gut feeling that Jake Montejo's death was anything but simple remained.

Yuana got off the phone with Daniel. He asked her to meet him and Mateo at her aunt's laboratory. It had something to do with Jake Montejo's DNA result. Her initial urge to call Kazu and arrange for a flight lesson became a secondary concern.

An image of a frowning Kazu flashed in her mind. He seemed annoyed. She shook her head at the thought. She must miss being on air more than she realised. Her mind had been imagining Kazu's disapproving reaction.

With a quick word to her assistant, she left her office.

Ten minutes later, she and Daniel sat dumbfounded, staring at her Aunt Ximena.

"Did I hear it right, Ximena?" Mateo asked, his disbelief echoed their own.

"Yes, Mateo. The *harravis* who murdered the dead mother and her foetus is the same one who attacked Roald and Yuana. The DNA results confirmed that."

"Holy *Prometheus!*" Daniel whistled under his breath.

That surprised her. Dan never used the name of the *Viscerebus* God in the past. He was turning more like them every day.

"So, what are the facts about our dead *harravis*?" Íñigo asked.

"His name is Jacob Killian Montejo, a businessman, logistics..." Mateo enumerated, but Ximena interrupted him.

"Wait, what's his previous *Gentem*?" Keen interest glittered in her aunt's eyes.

Mateo glanced at his notes. "Hmm, I am not sure. It says here 'Singapore', but his last recorded *victus* receipt there was decades ago. 1996 to be exact." He flipped another page. "He had been availing his sustenance here, 300 grams at a time, as a visitor or as a transient entrepreneur. And he availed of them from different Sustenance Supply centres in Metro Manila."

Her aunt frowned as if she held information that linked to the current facts. "Which logistics company was he connected to?"

"EasyMove, it's a human-owned company," Mateo replied, his tone speculative.

Ximena shook her head in disbelief. "He's the younger Prowze. He had a falling out with his older brother, Harri, when Jacob turned to *harravissing* like his father. And even more when he threatened Ellowyn's life, Harri's wife. He broke off contact after the death of Harri and Ellowyn. It seemed he had not stopped *harravissing* as the blood test showed he was deep in the habit up to the day he died."

"Tita, how did you know all that about him?" Her mind was blown away that her aunt had a connection with Roald's attacker.

Ximena's smile was sad. "Their mother was a school friend. I was to be their *Amadrina*."

Stunned silence enveloped the room.

"I am sorry, Tita. That is tragic. Was he the last Prowze?" Yuana said. She did not know what to say.

"Technically, he was." There was a mysterious glint in her aunt's eyes. "Harri and Ellowyn are on a protective *Tramway*."

"Oh..." It seemed even Jake's brother wanted nothing to do with him, Yuana thought.

"His demise might have ended the hunt for Roald's attacker, but it also raised more questions," Íñigo said, forewarning in his voice. He exchanged a loaded glance with Ximena.

"Such as?" Mateo asked.

"First, our initial question before we knew who he was. How did he find out about the cure for *VM*? Second, how did he maintain his *harravis* habit all these years? There were no *Viscerebus* disappearances or murders reported in those periods." Íñigo's directed his gaze at Mateo.

"You're right on the second mystery. There were no reported incidents of death or disappearance of our kind that I know of. Not here, and not anywhere. The global *Iztari* reports would have showed that. Ironically, the *Brogen Protocol* which requires the practice of sharing information among the *Gentems* was formulated because of their father, Johan Brogen Prowze's case."

"I think the most crucial question that should be asked is – who killed him? And how did it happen?" Yuana asked the group. "Whoever engineered the slaughter of Jacob Montejo is a dangerous nemesis," she added.

Would he, she, or they stop at Jacob's death?

Kazu zoomed up to forty-five thousand feet above his apartment, his presence shrouded by the darkness of the night. His eyes closed, senses focused on the images being uploaded to his mind. Jacob Montejo's recent memories flashed in his inner eye like snippets of a movie played in reverse order.

His breath lodged in his throat as the heavy air whooshed past his body. He was falling, his chest an open chasm...

His terror as he looked down at the rapidly vanishing ground from under him as he was carried up, the tightening of his heart and lungs as the air thinned, he panted as he breathed in...

Ms Orzabal's face as she slashed him across the cheek, the sting of her talons as it scraped skin and flesh...

His fear as he looked at the warm blood flowing out of his cut that refused to heal...

The pain of the blade cutting his side... His satisfaction as he kicked the human boyfriend of the luscious Ms Orzabal...

The woman lying naked on his bed, the open wound that closed and disappeared into flesh, leaving just a red gash... the exhilaration as the power of the woman's liver coursed through him...

That last memory...

Kazu's eyes shot open. His heart pounded at the information. The bastard was a *harravis,* and his manner of procuring *Aswang* liver was singular. And that was interesting.

He closed his eyes again to probe deeper into the memories of Jacob Montejo. But the rest were fleeting and unclear.

It seemed the shock of his death had erased Jacob Montejo's memories until the most recent. It was a pity, but it was enough.

Yuana opened her eyes to a dark room, her night vision engaged. She was confused for a second as she looked around. She had felt herself falling from a great height, the sensation of the rough and hard ground under her feet as she ran on concreted pavement, then stared at her own face, saw her talons swipe at her, and the pain of that slash. A naked woman on a bed.

A strange dream.

Maybe her subconscious recalled that flight when she lost consciousness. And the talon slashing must have been when she struck Jacob Montejo. But what about that running on a pavement in her previous *Animus*? She must be in her former animal form, judging how close the ground was to her face.

Where did the memory come from? She had never run in her *Animus* in any city. And who was that woman?

Her gut tingled with a sensation akin to a warning. It was a niggling and unsettling, like a reminder of a missed clue, as if she was looking for something that she could not remember what.

She closed her eyes once more and summoned sleep, coaxing its return by calming herself. She breathed in and out until she faded back into slumber.

Ximena swallowed the pain in her heart. She wasn't looking forward to making the call, but it was only proper. She dialled Harri's number.

"Auntie Ximena, this is a pleasant surprise..." Harri's voice came through clearly, as if he was next door. She heard Ellowyn's tinkling laugh in the background, followed by a chorus of faint meows.

"Harri, I'm afraid my call does not bring good news..."

The sobering in Harri's voice was audible. "Tell me, Auntie. It's about Jacob, right?"

"Yes... He's dead, Harri."

The gasp that came through the line was not unexpected. The silence that followed was grave and Harri's deep inhale was heavy.

"How did it happen?"

"Someone from our kind killed him... We do not know who or how it happened. But we will find out. That I swear to you."

"I understand... Did... Jake suffer?"

"No. There were no signs of struggle. We think he didn't see it coming."

Another long silence followed, then Harri sighed. "Thank you, Auntie Ximena. I appreciate the call."

"Harri, just one question..."

"Yes?"

"Did you ever mention to Jacob about the... cure?"

"No. I have never spoken to him since we *Tramwayed*."

"Okay. Let me know what kind of arrangement you want me to do for Jacob."

"Give me a day, Auntie."

"Take all the time you need, Harri. I will take care of his body for you."

Roald stretched his obliques, testing for soreness. There was still a slight twinge. His doctor said he should ease into his training.

He turned to see Mateo watching him. A knowing look in his eyes.

"There is no need to rush yourself into a hospital re-confinement, Roald. Another week would not make much difference."

"I can handle it, sir."

Mateo shook his head and laid a hand on his shoulder, palm warm as he gave it a gentle squeeze. "No. You will be worse off if you have a relapse. But I understand your need to do something because you are feeling helpless."

"It's been weeks. We still do not have any idea who killed Jacob Montejo." Roald did not know why he raised that issue.

"Your attacker was very careful with his movements because he was a *harravis*. There were no obvious clues as to who killed him." Mateo's tone was confident, but he evaded Roald's gaze. Roald waited for his trainer to meet his eyes.

"What do you think Jacob Montejo was hiding? His *harravis* hunting strategy? A trail of victims?" Roald knew he hit the mark by the micro change in Mateo's expression.

Mateo didn't respond outright. Roald knew the older man saw his determination to find out the truth. His heart beat in overdrive at the combined rage, frustration, and panic. The truth felt like a looming monster, but he preferred to stare it in the eye than wonder where it was, what it looked like and when it would attack.

Mateo sighed. "There are no traces of any victims. No missing persons report, no mysterious disappearances. You must understand that with our kind, it is impossible for the latter because of our need for *sustenance*. The *Tribunal* record and track all movements of our people."

"So... you are more interested in how Jacob Montejo secured *Aswang* viscera?"

"Yes, and if there are more like him. Maybe those who hunt the way he did killed him. And they did not want him caught and revealing their secret."

The revelation was like a kick to the chest. *There are more of them, much stronger and much faster?* His heartbeat sped up, deafening him. "How can I prepare for that? How can I defend myself?" he breathed.

Mateo's jaw clenched. "Roald, Jacob targeted you because of Yuana. It was an isolated event. *Harravissing* is a capital crime against our kind, and it is punishable by death. This is our fight. It does not involve you."

That was a logical statement. Those people Jacob Montejo tangled with would not waste their time with a human like him. But Yuana's great grandparents were the *Matriarch* and *Patriarch*, the highest positions of power a *Viscerebus* could occupy. They might go after her.

Mateo preempted his concern. "It would be perilous for them to touch the granddaughter of the *Chief Iztari*. The entire force would hunt them down. She is also the great granddaughter of the *Matriarch* and *Patriarch*. That would bring the might of the whole *Tribunal* on them. That is public knowledge. I think they would not make that mistake, especially if they want to keep their activities hidden," Mateo said.

His heart lightened a bit, but the knot that rested in his stomach remained. He realised his fear was not just for Yuana.

"I would still prefer to continue my training, sir." He could not voice out his desperation, and why it was imperative for him to resume.

Mateo looked at him, his gaze intent. "All right. But we will do this gradually... It would be counterproductive if you relapsed, Roald."

He wanted to protest, to insist, but Mateo was right. His trainer gave him a small smile. "I will teach you something we never teach the *Veilbound* humans. Unless the time is right, and the situation calls for it."

The possibilities Mateo's statement implied made his pulse race. "What is it? And why now?"

"The situation calls for it and the time is now." His mentor walked towards the training floor. He followed.

"Am I learning a new technique?" he asked as he unsheathed his training *karambit*.

"In a manner of speaking." Mateo brought out a silicon dummy, much to his surprise. "I am going to teach you how to kill an *Aswang*."

Yuana watched Roald practice on the dummy to the point of mutilation. He had been striking the silicon representation of a human body repeatedly. At the same places in its anatomy.

Roald stabbed the dummy at the base of the skull and slashed sideways, a perfect stroke to sever the brain stem. Then he struck at the chest cavity, where the heart would be. The succeeding curved cut would carve the heart out of any one of her kind.

She knew who taught him. She didn't know whether to be grateful to Mateo for teaching Roald the techniques on how to kill them.

Roald's focus on the activity was fierce, grim determination flashing in his eyes. Fear drove his ferocity to master the strokes.

It is time I lessened one of his fears.

“Where are we going, my love? And why the blindfold, it’s already dark.” Roald asked as she led him to her outdoor garden. With his sight covered, she transformed into her *Animus*. She didn’t want to frighten him.

“Do you trust me?” She took his hand, the part of her that was still human. He squeezed her hand in response.

She held his fingertips and skimmed them lightly over her feathered arm. Roald’s fingers stilled. She waited until he moved them closer to her arm again, a frown on his forehead.

“Are you...?” His voice was a whisper.

“Yes.”

She held her breath as Roald touched her arm, travelling up to her shoulder, to the curve of her clavicle. With his left hand, he pulled the blindfold from his face. The dark depths of his eyes glittered as he took in her partially transformed face and the crown of feathers on her head.

Yuana kept her eye colour and face human so he would not be too shocked at the change in her appearance. His gaze travelled to the feathered mounds of her breasts, down to her feet. His fingers were light as he touched the iridescent blue-black plumes that covered her from head to toe.

“Where are your talons?” he asked. She almost heaved a sigh of relief.

The dark red talons manifested by the time she held one up. Roald jerked in alarm, but he recovered his composure. He examined the wickedly sharp tips. His pulse throbbed in his throat. And she picked up the slight scent of panic in him. She waited for the fear to grow in his eyes, but Roald took a deep breath and continued his exploration.

“Show me your wings?” he asked.

Hope bloomed in her chest. Her wings sprouted and unfurled, wide and high over her. It made Roald step back. But he steadied himself.

As he stood there gaping at her form, she detected a change in him. His anxiety changed to excitement.

“Would you like to fly with me?” She hoped he would say yes.

He nodded.

She stepped behind him, enfolded him in her arms. Roald’s arms snaked over hers, his wrists wrapping around hers. She understood his need to feel secure.

“Ready?” she asked. At his quick nod, she took flight. With her chest to his back, she could feel each thump and thud of his heart, the in and out of his shallow breaths, and every tensed muscle in his body. She would not fly very high tonight. Roald might have trouble breathing in the thin air.

On and on, she flew. Her destination was fixed. Ten minutes in, Roald’s body loosened as his trust in her flying capability, her strength to carry his weight, grew. Their flight took less than half an hour. Roald's body stiffened when he realised where they were. They landed in front of his family's beach house in Mataas na Kahoy.

"What are we... why here?" he asked. She did not reply. She pulled him towards the tree house. Her wings retracted by the time they reached the front steps of the structure that haunted his childhood dreams. "Yuana..."

The door was locked, but she wrenched the padlock off. In the middle of the square room, by the edge of the child's bed, she turned and faced him. Roald's eyes followed the slow vanishing of the feathers from her head as her hair replaced the plumes and tumbled over her shoulders and back. His gaze fixed on her shoulders as the dark blue-black hue lightened to creamy human skin, to her breasts now revealed.

His gaze travelled to her navel, now all human, down to her delta of Venus. Roald swallowed; desire flared in his eyes as he stared at the triangle of flesh, now throbbing in response.

"Yuana..." he rasped.

"Underneath all that, Roald... it is just me," she said, her voice a mere whisper. "Here... feel me..."

Goosebumps now covered her body, both from the chill in the air, the aftermath of her transformation, and the thrill of what was to come.

She tugged at his hand and brought it to her core. A shiver ran down her form as his icy fingers explored the heated and moist flesh. With a groan, he pulled her flush against him. They were chest to chest, belly to belly; his belt buckle pressed against her abdomen. His kiss was devouring, frantic, conquering. His fingers buried in her drenched core.

Roald's nose flared in response to the fragrance of her arousal. His strokes turned deep, then shallow, in and out. Her hips reacted instinctively, offering herself to his exploration. The strain of tempering her strength added to the torturous exercise. She had to be careful; he was human.

Her lower abdomen clenched in agony at the mind-blowing pleasure of his touch as she thrust against his fingers. Her initial plan to seduce him, to make him forget the old memories and replace it with new ones, faded into the liquifying heat of her quest for release.

Roald pulled his mouth from hers to allow them both to catch their breaths. His fingers pulled out from inside her, and she groaned in protest. Roald's breath was shallow and tortured, his lungs working hard, his gaze glittering. The fingers that travelled across her shoulder blades were feather light yet intent. And she understood his silent request.

Her wings sprouted; the blue-black feathers contrasted with the texture and paleness of her skin. Roald's warm palms lingered on the flesh of her back, where her human skin blended into the plumes of her wings. His breath hitched, and his heart rate accelerated. Roald's pupils were dilated.

The dark depths were pools of passion. She unbuckled his belt and undid the buttons. Roald's moist palms paused in their explorations, closing on her shoulders as he waited for her next move.

She pulled his shirt up and out of the waistband of his pants, scattering the buttons on the ground. Roald did not notice; his eyes blazed. She backed him closer to the child bed until the backs of his legs bumped into it. She pressed against his erection. It was thick, veined, hard, and palpitating in excitement.

She stepped onto the edge of the bed for better access to his velvety, turgid member. She rubbed her wet core up and down against the length of it. The pleasure made her shiver. Roald wobbled, his hands going to the wall behind him to steady himself against her movements. Her wings spread wide behind her for balance.

Roald's body arched against her, her hands resting on his shoulders. Sweat covered her body as she stimulated herself on him. When she couldn't take it anymore, she raised herself on a tiptoe and impaled herself on him. Her abdomen spasmed as the delicious sensation enveloped her. Roald's groan was feral. One hand now clasped her butt as he pressed into her. They were now fused at the groin, panting in unison.

Roald's hand grasped her head and brought their lips together. Their tongues duelled in sync with the thrusting of his hips. Her back hit the wall, her wings splayed wide against the wood, as Roald's thrust became deeper and shorter. It seemed endless and not enough. At the point of her peak, he lifted his mouth from hers.

"Yuana, can you...?" he rasped, his eyes burning into hers.

She understood. She closed her eyes and *syne-morphed* into her full *Animus*. Roald gasped and thrusted deep, grinding into her as he reached his peak.

Her climax washed over her at the intensity of pleasure written across his face. She came and came in a flood of release. Her scream echoed in the small square room.

Sometime later, it could have been hours, she roused herself from his arms, naked in her human form. They were both drenched in sweat. And the room was heavy with the fragrance of their lovemaking. The steam that coated the glass walls faded as the temperature inside the treehouse cooled.

Roald stirred and levered himself up, then kissed her damp forehead.

"Thank you..." he said against her lips, his tone and touch reverent.

The sweetness of his gratitude squeezed at her heart. "You are welcome..."

The kiss that followed was soft, full of appreciation and wonder. "Did you do that to exorcise the ghost of this playhouse out of me?" he asked as he nibbled on her lower lip.

"Yes... did it work?"

He nodded, a smile on his lips. "It did... but..."

"But?"

"It seems that I have developed a fetish for feathered creatures..."

She giggled. "Should I keep chickens, geese and turkeys away from you and your... fowl habit?"

Roald's laughter reverberated in the glass and wood structure. And her heart absorbed every vibration of his joy.

21

THE IMPENDING SHIFT

Fari Wolff placed his pen down. The paper in front of him displayed a chaos of scribbled notes, his thoughts even more so. The new directive surprised him.

An unfamiliar feeling of guilt constricted his heart for a moment as he reviewed the written instruction, but his inquisitive, scientific brain won. This would be the biggest challenge in his career, and he could not resist it.

To synthesise the *Visceral Metastasis* gene and turn it into a serum was the kind of an ambitious goal that could carve a scientist's name into the annals of their history.

It would be the first biological weapon of their kind. One that would both empower and endanger the *Viscerebus* recipient. But the human application intrigued him more. If they succeeded, it would shift the balance of power between humans and *Viscerebus*. And it would be to their favour.

His brain made rapid calculations on how he would organise the second team to conduct the experiments without exposing their work to his other team, who were hard at work at synthesising liver cells.

They must never know the value and the danger of each other's projects. It would take one moralising employee to a break the secrecy of the program. It would put his project in jeopardy.

Ximena's distinct staccato footsteps echoed as she entered the lobby. Íñigo followed close behind. He carried their presentation to their biggest donor for the *Altera Project*. This individual had been part of the program from the beginning. The amount of his donation added credibility to their endeavour and triggered the rest of the donations. He remained anonymous to everyone in the *Tribunal*, except to them.

Today was the first of their regular bi-annual meetings for the year.

The restaurant host escorted them to a private room. Their donor saw them the moment they entered the room. He always faced the door, so she expected it.

"Good afternoon, Mr Mori. Have you been waiting long?" She held out her hand with a smile.

"Not long, Ms Ibarra. You are always prompt; I just like being first in the room." Mori smiled back and clasped her hand with a familiar, warm, and firm grip. "How are you, Mr Araya?" He offered his hand to Íñigo.

"All good, Mr Mori," Íñigo replied.

They sat down, and ten minutes later, their drinks were served. Mori leaned back, his fingertips tented, a speculative gleam in his eyes.

"So, how is the *Altera Project* coming along? Can we treat the *VM* infected among our kind yet?" Mori directed the question at her.

"We are now doing confidential clinical trials with the serum. Right now, it has sixty per cent efficacy. We are working on increasing that to eighty, then to one hundred per cent." She was confident that they could achieve their goal.

Mori's smile was satisfied. "And when do you think your team could achieve the one hundred per cent?"

Her smile widened. "Before the year ends..."

Mori's eyebrow quirked. "That confident, huh?"

She exchanged a glance with Íñigo, who wore an assured smile on his face. "Yes. Sooner if we can get more volunteers for our *Vis* trial. We need to reach the required number to get the approval from the Medical Board of the *Tribunal*," she replied.

"What was the highest efficacy that your trials achieved?" Mori asked.

"With twenty-two per cent of the cases, we achieved eighty-five. We think it had something to do with the age of the source foetus. We are validating our assumptions," she said.

Unknown emotion flashed in Mori's eyes. It was sharp, almost like triumph. Unease fluttered in Ximena's stomach.

Maybe it was my imagination, just a trick of light.

Mori's smile returned. "I am very pleased with the development of the project."

"Does that mean that we could expect your continued support?" Íñigo asked.

Mori's smile widened. "Of course. The iron is hot, we need to keep pounding."

Íñigo raised his glass. "Let's toast to that."

As she watched Mori through the sparkling bubbles of her drink, the remnants of her initial unease faded with the sharp bite of the champagne streaking down her throat.

Aristo poured a glass of wine and sat back, slipping off her high-heeled shoes. The joy that suffused her after the date with Mateo faded. The conversation with Mori banished it. Or rather, the reminder of their goal and what she needed to do pushed it aside.

She had more recruiting to do. And Mateo would have been a perfect recruit. But a part of her wanted to keep him separate from her mission. Like a haven one could go to at the end of a long day at work. Mateo felt like that to her.

But for now, she needed to resume her mission. The sooner she completed it, the better. Her next target was a chain of human-owned hospitals. It would accomplish what they wanted right under the noses of their *Tribunal*.

For now, the Grand Plan should be her priority.

END

GLOSSARY

Alta – or High Society – the traditional, informal societal hierarchy among the *Viscerebi* communities. It functions just like the human communities' counterpart. The most active members of the Alta are usually the social climbers who want to reach the highest level.

Amadrina – second mother or godmother. A female Viscerebus who offers herself to another female Viscerebus as a surrogate mother to the latter's child should something happen to the biological mother.The responsibility of an Amadrina is equivalent to full motherhood. Female Viscerebus seldom offer themselves as one, as the law considers this as a legal agreement. An Amadrina signs on the birth certificate of the child. And in certain circumstances, in the child's interest, an Amadrina's right is superior to the father's. (*See Baughan vs Edris*) The Amadrina's right over the child ends at eighteen, unless the Tribunal deems the child unable to take care of himself or herself.

Animus – Heart or Instinct Animal or Spirit Animal – the true animal form of a *Viscerebus*. All Viscerebus have one, although not all will discover theirs. An *Auto-morphosis*, or reflexive transformation usually reveals to a *Viscerebus* their Animus. Some *Vis* transform into one animal all their lives and discover later that their *Animus* was a different form. In some *Viscerebus* families, it was part of their tradition to deny sustenance to the child of twelve to force an *Auto-morphosis*. This is usually done under the supervision of the adults. The practice lost favor over the centuries because it often results in injury to the child and usually the said child elects to transform into the animal hunting form they habitually turn into anyway, thus defeating the object of discovering their Animus. Now, the term is used erroneously by modern *Viscerebus* to refer to their animal form, whether it is their true Spirit Animal or just their hunting form.

Apex – A super shapeshifter. A very rare Viscerebus that can transform into a winged animal, either chiropteran (bats) or avian (birds) form. They can transform fully, or partially. Other special Apex skills that has been manifested by previous ones are : echolocation and sound blasting, magnetic field manipulation. Natural facial alteration for disguise, a skill Apex Kazu Nakahara discovered. For an Apex that become skilled in turning on their brain's theta waves, they can read other people's brainwaves and influence it. Studies show the full skill set of an Apex has not been fully revealed yet because new skills keep getting discovered by each successive Apex.

Aquila—the other name for the giant eagle named *Aetos Kaukasios*, one of the two primary mythical gods to the *Viscerebus*. The other is *Prometheus*. The *Viscerebuskind* attribute the beginning of their race to the two gods. According to the legend, Zeus sent Aetos to devour the liver of *Prometheus* every night as his eternal punishment for giving fire to the humans and for tricking Zeus to choose a less valuable sacrificial offering from them. The *Viscerebus*' need to eat viscera is attributed to the saliva of Aetos believed to have contaminated the liver of *Prometheus*, which was used by the latter to create the *Viscerebus*.

Aswangs – The Filipino term for *Viscerebus*. Of all the countries in the world, the existence of the *Viscerebus* is the most entrenched in the Philippine culture for these reasons: First, the Filipinos had the most aggressive campaign against them. Humans formed hunting teams called *Venandis* whose sole purpose was to kill *Viscerebus*. The Filipino Venandis were the most experienced. The practice, which started as a family endeavour, became traditionally and habitually passed on to the next generation. There are still active, albeit lesser number of *Venandis* operating in the country. Second, the superstitious nature of the Filipinos allowed them to believe that Aswangs still existed, albeit in exaggerated and erroneous form. Many books have been written, and movies made featuring Aswangs as evil creatures, usually depicted as the minions of the devil. Like every culture, the existence of the *Viscerebus* has been relegated into myth and lore, and the term Aswang is used as a blanket term for almost every man-eating and blood sucking ghoul in the country.

Auto-morphosis – also known as *Reflexive Transformation* is the involuntary shapeshifting into the animal spirit of a *Viscerebus*. The vital instinct to hunt and secure *Victus* or *sustenance* triggers this transformation. The vital instinct is triggered when a *Viscerebus* fails to consume human viscera for more than three days. It is possible to induce an Auto-morphosis through practice and meditation. Some *Viscerebus* do this to discover their *Animus*. This is opposite to voluntary or conscious shapeshifting, also known as *Syne-morphosis*. The difference is that Auto-morphosis is induced by *Vital Hunger*, and the latter is a natural skill of every *Viscerebus*.

Aztarimar – the practice of imprinting one's aura into another. From the root word *Aztarna* (to imprint) and *Arima* (soul). This is an almost forgotten skill that each Viscerebus has. There are two ways to do it: a) *Aural*, where the *Aztarim* (the giver, the imprinter) creates trust with the Aztarima (the receiver), and then connects with the Aztarima telepathically without the knowledge of the *Aztarima*. The practice is similar to meditation and requires a lot of mental skill and focus from the Aztarim. This is the preferred manner of the Aztarim if they have a hidden agenda and does not want the Aztarima to tap into their own Aura. However, this is not fool-proof as a Viscerebus with a strong will and mental control can prevent the Aural connection if they wish, and at the same time tap on the Aztarim's aura. b) *Oral*, where the two individuals are reciprocally both the Aztarim and the Aztarima. This is done by exchanging a small piece of each other's liver and consuming it. They are automatically connected to each other. This would require mutual and voluntary agreement between both parties. The process require both parties opening their own bodies, slicing a tiny piece of each other's liver, exchanging it and consuming the other party's liver. Aztarim is a way to force a ***Dignus,*** which is a perfect aural and reciprocal connection achieved between two Viscerebus. This is a very old practice and the modern Viscerebi abandoned this for so many reasons.

Calyptratus (Ca) – the form stabilizing gene. The second of the two primary *Viscerebus* gene. This pairs with the *Metamorpho* gene. This enables the *Crux* and is responsible for keeping a *Viscerebus'* human form.

ChrysaDonna – a concoction comprising of two herbal plants; Bladonna and Tanacetum. Combined, it doubles the slow-healing potency that Bladonna or Tanacetum alone can provide. Iztaris carry an essential oil or ointment version of it during battle as an offensive tool and blade maintenance. The formula was a well-guarded secret in old days and forbidden to be sold without permit. It was restricted to the Iztaris. Progressively, time has loosened the restriction when the need for it lessened as battles between

Viscerebus practically stopped. Harravirring and Harravissing are considered capital crimes punishable by death, so the encounters between Viscerebus became unnecessary. It was finally lifted in the early 1900's when the use of ChrysaDonna lost favour as the risk outweighed the benefits. Accidental injury during blade training and maintenance became a more serious concern if one was using the concoction on their blade. Other oils became more popular, especially sunflower oils. Today, Viscerebus-ran apothecaries and lifestyle shops no longer carry them. Someone who wanted a ChrysaDonna would have to secure both oils and concoct it themselves.

Emergence – or ***Ortus***, the human term used when Apexes discover their authentic form, also known as Animus. The Apex can induce emergence by forcing an Auto-morphosis or reflexive transformation. Part of the traditional Auto-morphic rituals include the excited wish of a child to "emerge as an Apex" which normally results as disappointment as Apexes, or super shapeshifters, are extremely rare.

Equubus – or Tikbalang in Pilipino. They are a very rare kind of *Viscerebus* whose *Animus* are horses. Unlike a normal *Viscerebus*, their need for human viscera is not as frequent. They only need the 50-gram human liver every month to stabilise their human form as opposed to an average *Viscerebus*. And they can only take liver unlike most of their kind who can take heart and kidney as well.

Erdia – an Erdia is a half-blood, born from a Male *Viscerebus* and a Female human. Erdias are very human in their nature except they are slightly stronger, faster, and live longer than their human counterparts. They may inherit some enhancement on their senses, too. They don't inherit the shapeshifting and need for human viscera, though.Most Erdias who use their enhanced strength and speed become athletes. Erdias who inherit superior sense of taste and scent usually become renowned chefs, perfume makers and other profession that maximizes their abilities.The knowledge of the Erdias about the *Viscerebuskind* would depend on whether the *Viscerebus* father tells his offspring. If the Erdia was told, they would be bound to the *Veil of Secrecy* just like their parent, and they become part of the *Viscerebus* world. A significant number of Erdias are unaware of the *Viscerebus* world because the *Viscerebus* father abandon them from infancy. These Erdias, being *non-Veil-bound*, are treated as human. They live normal human lives, unaware of the existence of the *Viscerebus*.

Eremite—or hermits, are Erdias born with hyper-enhanced senses. The senses of some Eremites are sometimes stronger than a Viscerebus. Eremites are offsprings of an Erdia and a Viscerebus, but they are very rare, with a ratio of one in every 50 million. And even rarer would be an Eremite with a gift of foresight, an attribute of Prometheus.

Erne – are Viscerebus vigilantes. They usually work in secret and targets corrupt influential Viscerebus. Ernes are considered criminals, thus they work under the radar. They usually are former Iztaris, and are known to have reluctant ties with the department.

Gentem – (nation in Latin) – the current country of residence, or the immediate, previous country of residence of a *Tramwaying Viscerebus*. A Viscerebus can have between six to ten Gentems in their lifetime. This is not to be confused with *Patriam*, which is the country of birth of a Viscerebus.

Gorzati – this is the fatal result of a shape-shifting effort gone wrong. When an Viscerebus force themselves to transform into a winged creature, a skill only possible for an Apex, or a natural-born super shape-shifter. Their efforts causes a monstrous transformation and severs the body in half when the Viscerebus take flight. This results to the eventual death of an Viscerebus.

Harravir – also known in the Philippines as *Tiktiks*. They are *Viscerebus* who hunt humans for their *victus,* or human viscera. They mostly exist in rural, uncivilised, and remote areas. They are the same as the modern *Viscerebus*, except they have not adopted the modern way of surviving without killing humans. In most circumstances, this was because they have not heard of the existence of the *Tribunal*.

Harravis—also known in the Philippines as ***Wakwaks***; are Viscerebus that hunts other Viscerebus for their viscera. The Harravis' fundamental goal is to consume Viscerebus organs, as it is far more potent than a human's. The Viscerebus viscera makes the Harravis stronger and faster than a normal Viscerebus, and they remain so for as much as sixty to ninety days. The Harravis practice can also be addictive as it raises the dopamine level in a Viscerebus. And like drug use, regular and sustained Harravissing habit drives the Harravis to hunt more often and at shorter intervals.

Heraldaketa – or the Transformation, a local *Tribunal* Journal published by the *Supreme Viscerebus Tribunal* for the *Viscerebi* communities. These are usually released by each local *Gentem*. Currently, in some Gentems, the Viscerebi simply refer to them as the Journal.

Iturrian—the source. The term used for the pregnant woman who provides, voluntarily or involuntarily, the foetus growing in their belly as a treatment for Visceral Metastasis. The receiver, or the VM-inflicted Viscerebus who takes the treatment, is referred to as the *Ontzian*, the vessel. The act is called the *Messis,* or the harvest. All three terms are used in a hushed voice as the practice itself is not openly sanctioned by the Tribunal.

Iztari – the law enforcement of the *Supreme Viscerebus Tribunal*. They are embedded in the human armed forces, police, and security industry. It is a way of hiding in plain sight, acquiring military training, and gaining knowledge on the human military and police system. The Iztaris' main mandate is to implement strict adherence to the *Veil of Secrecy*. They are deployed to either a) hunt *Harravirs* or *Harravis,* b) implement the *Veil* procedures, c) defend humans or other *Viscerebus* from *Harravirs* and *Harravises*, d) find and secure other *Viscerebus* families or tribes.

Jaurdinas – or *Blue Generals*. From the term, Jaun (lord) and Urdina (blue). They refer to a leader who commands a group of warriors, soldiers or fighters. As opposed to *Zuriahjas*, who is someone who has vast influence over a group of people by virtue of position, education or achievement. Examples: presidents or prime ministers, politicians, or heads of corporations, civic leaders, etc.

Kali – also known as *Arnis de Mano*, or *Eskrima*. This is a weapons-based form of Filipino martial arts which includes sticks, knives, bladed weapons, open hand, and other improvised weapons made from regular household or personal items. The names Arnis and Eskrima, was thought to have been borrowed from the Spanish invaders, but the art had long existed in the island prior to the arrival of the Spanish forces in 1521.

Karambit – also known as Kerambit, is a small curved knife with a fingerhold, and the blade resembles the shape of a tiger claw. The weapon was originally an agricultural tool, but had been refashioned as a fighting weapon. It was unclear who invented the weapon. It could have been the humans, and it was later adapted by the Viscerebus, or a vice versa. Due to its portability, the Iztaris took to the Karambit and it became one of the primary weapons of the force. It became a part of the standard issue in an Iztari's arsenal. The weapon is used primarily for close combat to incapacitate an opponent to submission, not to kill a Viscerebus. The addition of

Bladonna, or Belladona oil into the blade made the weapon devastating. It became a standard practice for a Karambit-carrying Viscerebus to coat and polish the blade with the said oil.

Katyrrian – or henchmen. They are male or female Viscerebus who hire out their services as henchmen/women to humans. Their job includes intimidation and sometimes elimination of their human targets. The Tribunal usually look the other way if the methods of the Katyrrian fall within the explainable human acts. Their actions become illegal in the Tribunal's eyes once it endangers the Veil of Secrecy. The Katyrrian, however, is not immune to human laws. The Tribunal would allow the Katyrrian to suffer the penalty of human incarceration if it is possible to supply them with human viscera. The first step is to transfer the convicted Katyrrian to prisons controlled by the Tribunal, but if this is not possible, the Katyrrian becomes a danger to the Veil. The Katyrrian is usually executed by the Iztaris by the order of the Tribunal.

Kxalyptra - pronounced as "calyptra". A symbol of the *Veil of Secrecy.* These items are placed in the location when a social event organized by a *Viscerebus* includes *non-Veil-bound humans*, or humans who are not aware of the existence of the *Viscerebuskind.* This serves as a warning and a constant reminder to the Vis in the venue to keep to the Veil.

Manananggal – a Philippine mythological monster referring to a self-segmenting Viscerebus. Officially called a ***Gorzati.*** The legend of the Manananggal was born when some humans found dead winged Viscerebi with their lower half missing. The lack of knowledge created a myth around the Manananggals and they were considered a different kind of Viscerebus.

Manyaxi – a female *Viscerebus* who has a very active *Vital Instinct* or *Vittalis,* yet unable to achieve absolute transformation due to a mutation in her genes. She is unable to *syne-morphose*, and only able to partially shapeshift during *auto-morphosis*, sprouting claws and fangs necessary to secure viscera.

Mejordia – or, Mejor Erdia (better Erdia) are half-bloods born from a Male Harravis or Wakwak and a female Erdia. They are a genetically stronger version of an Erdia. To become a Mejordia, a child must be conceived during the forty-eight hour window that a Viscerebus first ingested viscera of another Viscerebus. (*See Erdias*). A habitual Harravis can only conceive/create a Mejordia child once, as it is only possible in the initial ingestion of the Viscerebus viscera.

Messis—the harvest. Originally, this refers to the harvesting of the human viscera, or *Victus*. But the use of the term has lost favor because humans who overhear the term would ask for explanation. The term now refers to the illicit act of securing amniotic fluid from a six-month-old foetus from within the womb of the mother, also referred to as the *Iturrian*, the source. The amniotic fluid is the only treatment that stays the progression of Visceral Metastasis in the body of an infected Viscerebus, also referred to as the *Ontzian*, or the vessel.

Metamorpho (Mm) – the shape-shifting gene, one of the two primary *Viscerebus* genes. This enables a Vis to transform. It comes with another gene, *Calyptratus,* as its pair. The two are linked. This gene triggers the *vital instinct* and *auto-morphosis*. This gene and its pair are the two genes could only be passed on from mother to child.

Morphbag – an aero-dynamic bag, usually made of leather and worn around the waist or across one shoulder. It is designed to carry the light clothes, shoes and other small personal effects like money, wallet or mobile phone of a Viscerebus when they plan to shape-shift. Its invention is attributed to a medieval itinerant tanner named Morpheus, who got tired of getting chased out of villages for emerging out of the woods naked, or covered in leaves after every hunt.

Odorius – the superior scent gene is a tertiary gene, or a selective-inclusive gene which means it can be passed on to Erdias in weaker form. Apart from giving the Viscerebus a strong sense of smell, this enables the internal recognition and cataloguing of the chemical signature of the plants in the brain of the Vis, Mejordia, Eremite, and in certain rare cases, Erdias

Painlokaas - a bait. This refers to a person that was purposely trained to entrap someone. Usually deployed by the Iztaris. The term was adopted later on to mean field spies, or intelligence operatives whose main objective is to put their target in a compromising position to enable blackmail.

Patriam—(Latin for country)–refers to the country where the Viscerebus is born. This is their country of origin. We should not confuse this with ***Gentem***, which is the current country of residence or previous country of residence of a Viscerebus before they left for their Transit. A Viscerebus does not have any specific nationality like humans do since all Viscerebus relocate at least five times in their lifetime. They are instead referred to in their Patriam. For example, a Viscerebus born somewhere in Spain is considered of 'Spanish Patriam'. A family of Viscerebus may be of different Patriams if the offsprings are born in different countries.

Prometheus – A Greek Titan and the god of creative fire and the creator of men. He was the son of Titan Iapetus and the Oceanids, Clymene. His siblings are Atlas, Epimetheus, Menoetius. He is known for his intelligence. He is also credited as the creator of human arts and sciences, and a champion of humankind. His name meant "Forethought". According to the *Viscerebus* legends, while he created humans out of clay, Prometheus made the first *Viscerebus* couple from his own liver, the soil and rocks of the Caucasus Mountain where he was bound and tortured. With his DNA, the *Viscerebus* inherited godlike traits of super strength, speed, senses, healing abilities and long life. Prometheus also imbued them with the ability to shapeshift so they can hide themselves from Zeus. It was said that he created them out of his need for companions to distract himself from the pain and the loneliness during the regrowing of his liver every night. During the day, the first *Viscerebus* were in their animal form, a feline, and a canine, but they transform into their human form at night to keep Prometheus company. This is also why cats and dogs were regarded as the closest companions to humans.

Supreme Viscerebus Tribunal – or the SVT. This is the primary ruling body of the *Viscerebus*. It is composed of previous and current *Matriarchs* and *Patriarchs* from different *Gentems* all over the world. SVT functions as both as the main legislative and judicial body of the *Viscerebi*. The execution of the laws, however, is the responsibility of each *Gentem's Tribunal*. Members of the body meet bi-annually, where laws proposed by members are discussed and voted on. The main mandate of the Tribunal is to oversee the compliance of every *Gentem* in the upholding of the *Veil of Secrecy*.

Syne-morphosis – voluntary or conscious shape-shifting. This is opposite *Auto-morphosis*, or reflexive transformation; which is induced by *Vital Hunger*.

Txandictus – the Shift. This is the momentous event, strongly connected with the Emergence of an Apex among the Viscerebuskind. The Shift either immediately precede or follow the Emergence, or the Ortus. These events brings in a change in the way of life of the Viscerebi. The Apex becomes the natural leader that ushers the Viscerebi through the successful shift in their history.

Veil of Secrecy—the inviolable law of the *Supreme Tribunal* to keep the existence of *Viscerebus* a secret from *non-Viscerebus*. The Law made exceptions to a) Human spouse; b) Human kids. However, the exceptions apply only if the above people prove themselves loyal to the *Viscerebuskind* and to the Veil. The strict adherence to the Veil guides every interaction of a *Viscerebus* with humans and *non-Veil-bound Erdias*. The violation or breaking of the Veil entails severe punishment that can result to the death of the human or the *non-Veil-bound Erdia*, and the violator is expected to execute the punishment within a prescribed time-period.

Venatori – a private law enforcement force, usually former Iztaris. They could be hired directly by a Viscerebus, but they normally work with the Iztari department when the latter is short on staff, or if the target requires special skills. Venatoris are a combination of private investigators and bounty hunters in the human world.

Victus – colloquially called as *sustenance*. This is the blanket term for human viscera: heart, liver, and kidney, that a *Viscerebus* must consume regularly to keep their *Vital Hunger* at bay and prevent involuntary transformation to their animal form. This term had become less popular than its colloquial counterpart as humans who overheard ask question what it means. The *Tribunal* encourages the use of the term *sustenance* in a public setting to avoid the questions.

Visceral Metastasis—the cancer that can only be transmitted to another Viscerebus at certain conditions. The disease attacks the viscera and the blood vessels. A Viscerebus can contract the disease when they consume an infected Viscerebus viscera. The disease can be transmitted to a woman if the infected male has sex with a female Viscerebus within forty-eight hours of initial infection. And if that woman was pregnant at the time of the intercourse, the disease will also infect the foetus in utero. Past the forty-eight hours, the disease is no longer transmittable. An infected woman, however, will transmit it to all her offspring. However, if the Viscerebus is born with the disease, their VM is transmittable every time they have intercourse with another Viscerebus. The disease cannot be passed on to humans or Erdias.

Viscerebus/Viscerebi (pl.)—or *Viscera-eaters*, colloquially known as *Vis*. They are a different species of human. They live two to three times longer than humans; are stronger, faster, and have quick healing abilities. Physically, they look exactly like humans, but they can shape-shift into a land-based predator. The Viscerebus need to eat human viscera to stabilise their human form. To normal humans, they are monstrous man-eaters.Viscerebi are known by many names in many cultures. And the descriptions vary because of the dilution of the truth specifically engineered by the *Tribunal* to bury the existence of the *Viscerebus* under myth and lore. The common thread among these lores is the shape-shifting and the viscera-eating. Most modern human societies have completely ignored the lores, but the belief persists in some pockets of rural communities all over the world. This is especially true in Asian countries, particularly the Philippines, where stories about *Aswangs*, the local name for *Viscerebus*, are still told to this day.

ZeNading – short for *Zenith* and *Nadir,* or peak and rock bottom. The Apex practice of flying to the highest height, transforming back into their human form and plummeting to the lowest possible point, then returning to their Animus, and recovering just before hitting the ground. ZeNing was the used by the old Apexes as a display of mettle, courage, and might.

Zuriahja – or *White Generals*. From the term, Zuria (white) and Rajah (prince). They refer to educated and highly placed leader who commands a group of individual; one who has vast influence over a group of people by virtue of their position or achievement. Examples: presidents or prime ministers, politicians, or heads of corporations, civic leaders, etc. As opposed to a *Jaurdina*, or Blue Generals, which refers to military leaders.

Zurugatzen—another word for ***Absorption*** - the practice of Viscerebus, Erdias, or some Veil-bound humans to offer voluntarily their own viscera upon their death. They offer it for the consumption or absorption by a select loved one, usually a maximum of four individuals. The dying party must voluntarily surrender his or her organ for the magic to work. They practice this because of the belief that the departed one will be part of their loved ones forever. The *Zurugat* (receiver), once they ingested or absorbed the organ, allows them access to the flashes of memories of the *Rugat* (root or original owner, the giver).

RISE OF THE VISCEREBUS

WORLD OF THE VISCEREBUS BOOK 3

AUTHOR'S NOTE

This second edition of Rise of the Viscerebus was made because I realised just how amateurish my first effort was.
We have included a Glossary of Terms in this edition. I apologise to the readers of the first edition.
I invite you to let me know if you were one of those, and I will send you a FREE digital copy of the Glossary of Terms.
Please send me an email at ozmarigranlund@gmail.com

ACKNOWLEDGMENTS

My eternal gratitude to:

My son, Joshua. It's a blessing to have someone as smart as you as my child. You challenge me to be a better writer, a better mother, and the kind of human you would be proud of.

My beta readers, for attacking the material and not me. Your generous and honest feedback helped whip this book into a better shape.

But most especially to you, Johanna W, for the objective opinion and for pointing out plot holes and character flaws.

And to my BFF, Caca J, for the kind words, the constructive criticism, the suggestions and the encouragement, and for being a staunch supporter.

Finally, to my two cats, iO and Laki, for sitting with me during the long hours of the writing process.

PROLOGUE

Manila, 1996

In a dark alley behind a nondescript building on the poor side of the city, a man waited anxiously under the shadows cast by the awning above the backdoor of a clandestine abortion clinic. He was waiting for two clients. The first would be the *iturrian*, the source, the second was the *ontzian*, the vessel. He was tempted to light a cigarette to help him tolerate the stench of uncollected garbage, animal piss and excrement just a few meters from him. But he also did not want to give his location away. It was difficult to do as he was very nervous.

A taxi pulled up at the entry of the alleyway, and a pregnant woman got off the car. She paused by the entry, nervously looking around. Her neck craned forward as she tried to peer deep into the dark depths of the lane in front of her. He darted from under the awning and the only light source in the alley, and waved frantically, but quietly, to the woman.

Still, the woman did not move; she looked more scared now than earlier. He must have appeared very suspicious, so he relaxed his face into an innocuous smile and approached her.

"Ms Matilda Gomez?" he asked, his tone even. The woman nodded. Relief registered on her face.

"Mr Brion?" she asked and took a tentative step forward.

"Yes. You are late. Was it the traffic?" he asked, took her elbow, and walked her toward the backdoor of the clinic.

"I had a hard time getting a taxi," she replied.

"Okay, let's get you ready," he said. He paused by the backdoor and groped for the hidden doorbell by the side of the panelling. He lifted the protective cover and pressed the button. Seconds later, they heard footsteps coming down the stairs.

A scrub-wearing woman, much like what one would see in a proper hospital, opened the door. She smiled at the pregnant woman and gave him a terse nod. The nurse would take it from here. She ushered Ms Gomez upstairs to prepare her for what could be a harrowing night for the *iturrian*. The door closed once more on him.

With the source in place, he sent a text message to the *ontzian* to inform him they could do the *messis*, the harvest, within ten minutes. He hunkered down with his cigarette. If he was lucky and things go well, his job would be finished in an hour.

The room was dimly lit and smelled of antiseptic. Matilda could feel herself relaxing, as she imagined walking out of this place hours later, no longer pregnant, her life back to normal. Her husband, when he returns from his overseas posting, would not know any different. She truly wanted to move on from this mistake and intended to make it up to him, even though he would not understand why.

From the corner of the room, she watched a man putting on the green scrub. The nurse who attended her said he was the doctor. There was something about him that unsettled her. As he came closer to her bed, she had a sudden jolt of premonition. She felt threatened and scared and would have bolted upright if she was not so drowsy.

He did not make any menacing gesture, but—it was his eyes—all black, glittering, and intent, and on his face, a certain maniacal hunger.

"No..." she weakly raised her hand to ward him off, but the drug had taken full effect and she lapsed into unconsciousness. Her own protest faded with her.

The man carefully pushed the hospital gown and revealed Matilda's distended belly. He laid his hand on it, felt the pulse of the foetus growing there. It was strong and healthy, a perfect source. He slowly stuck out his tongue, and it stretched down long and thinned into the size of a straw. The pointed tip speared through Matilda's belly button; it made her belly spasm.

Both nurses turned away. They could never get used to this scene, an *aswang* feeding on amniotic fluid and foetus blood. It was too gruesome.

His tongue penetrated deeper, and the man started sucking the fluid from the sac, his eyes closed in enjoyment. The distress of the foetus was discernible by the violent movement it made. The undulation was visible in the belly of Matilda. Within minutes, the movement quieted. The foetus was dead.

A few minutes later, the man withdrew his bloody tongue and retracted it into his mouth. He wiped his face with the sleeve of his scrub, and turned away in satisfaction, only to turn back when the vital sign monitor started beeping. They hurried to the patient's side and noted she was dying by the pallor in her skin. She looked almost bloodless. They both frantically tried to revive her for long minutes, to no avail.

"What are we going to do?" the man asked, a worried frown on his face. They shrugged. Humans were fragile creatures, they die easily. While this was an unfortunate event, they had dealt with it a few times in the past. They knew what to do.

"Bury her in the plot of land they advised you to have ready for such a time like this. Help us with the body and let us take her down to your car. Then Mr Brion will assist you," the older nurse instructed him in a calm tone. He nodded and moved to help.

1

THE MEETING

A*nother day, a slightly different dollar. Quite a cliched expression, but apt.*

Yuana pushed the last button through the hole of her silk blouse and glanced at her reflection with little focus. She picked up her handbag, and her laptop as a reflex action. Just like she did every day for several years.

She sighed. Her schedule was so predictable, so uninspiring.

Although, there was a welcome variation to her routine today - a participation at a tech event later in the day. It was part of her job as their company's Head of Marketing. Maybe it could offer something more stimulating.

She told herself there was nothing to complain about. Her family was wonderful, they did not lack money; her work offered challenges enough that allowed her to exercise her creativity, but everything felt superficial. She was living on the sidelines of her own life. It might be great, but it was handed to her. She did nothing to earn it. She was restless, and deep inside, dissatisfied with herself.

Her introspective mood carried through breakfast. Her mother noticed.

"So, what global issue are we solving today, Yu-Yu? Global hunger or world peace?" her mother asked. She lowered her coffee cup, one eyebrow arched in inquiry.

"None of those, Mama. I was just feeling... low energy, I guess..."

"You mean you're bored," her mother said dryly.

She smiled. "Not precisely. I am just wondering if there is more to my life than being the Head of Marketing of GJDV, your daughter, a De Vida." She shrugged.

Her mother's head tilted to the side as she looked at her closely.

"In your heart of hearts, Yu, if you can have anything in this world, what would it be?"

"I do not know, Mama," she replied honestly.

Maybe it was time to think about what she truly wanted in life.

On the car ride to the event, her mother's question rang in her head repeatedly.

What is it I wanted above all else?

What is missing in my perfect life now?

What is the one thing that called to me, yet I could not seem to find?

Yuana's palms felt clammy, and there was a faint sensation of moisture in her scalp. She was not used to being on stage, but this was part of her function in the company.

I am here to sit as a panellist, and not to make any presentation. I can do this.

When they called her name, she put on a false display of confidence, and pasted a big smile on her face. Loud music and claps accompanied her ascent as she climbed up the low steps, her photo displayed on the three enormous screens onstage. As she took her seat, hundreds of expectant and curious faces stared at her. Her heart pounded in sync with the deafening introduction song as other guests were introduced.

It took ten minutes before her heart settled into a calm enough state for her to enjoy the topic. Being in public eye was something her kind were discouraged from doing for centuries.

The thirty-minute Q and A session for the topic "Sexy Tech for Unsexy Industries" ended well. The questions thrown at her were all about their company's distinct business model - they develop, operate, and maintain a chain of funeral homes and memorial gardens across the globe.

The morbidness of their offerings - memorial plan products, mortuary and forensic pathology services entranced the audience. Most people do not think about mortality until death knocked on their doors and touched their lives.

Her co-panellists were surprised by Grupo Jardin De Vida's keen interest to adopt the latest technology for their operation. It seemed to them incongruent for a company that dealt with something as fundamental as death. Yuana preferred to call it life and afterlife care.

Her pride in their company must have shone through because she received enthusiastic applause from the crowd. She had always believed they provide valuable services not just to their kind, but even to the human communities they lived in.

As she descended the stairs back to her seat, some members of the audience approached her - a mixed combination of startup founders interested in bidding for her business, members of the organising team who congratulated her and made introductions to other notable participants, and some guys who were just interested in getting her number.

Roald watched from a distance as Ms Yuana Orzabal got surrounded by well-wishers. He saw her picture earlier in the event app as a panellist for the topic and made it a point to attend and listen to her. He wanted to know if she had the brains to match the beauty. And he was not disappointed.

She drew the eyes of every participant in the ballroom. She was articulate, witty, and beautiful to boot. Her face glowed with health; her eyes sparkled with life. It was bemusing to hear her talk about death and sending a body to eternal rest, while her presence was electrifying. The contrast was fascinating.

He intended to meet and impress her, but queuing up to get her card with the rest would not cut it.

"Hey bro, are you considering queuing up to meet Yuana? You've got mad competition," Daniel taunted.

"Yuana? You know her?" He picked up on the familiarity in Daniel's tone.

Daniel nodded. "Yes, our families have been friends for decades."

"D, you got to introduce me to her," he cajoled.

"No way, bro. She's a good friend. Plus, she is not interested in romantic relationships," Daniel refused laughingly.

"Hey, we are best friends, and I am a good man... Come on, bro, I just need an intro," Roald pressed.

"Bro, save your effort for the other girls. There are plenty of women here who would be easier to win. Yuana will shoot you down."

"Come on, D. You never had a problem being my wingman before. Why the reluctance now? Are you and her...?" The thought dismayed him.

Daniel shook his head. "Normally, it would not be a problem. Yuana and I even had a long-running gag of setting each other up with the worst potential blind dates. But you are both my good friends, and I do not want to be in the middle if things go wrong between you."

"D, let me worry about that. Come on, do me a solid favour here, I will give you anything you want, just introduce us. It's that simple," Roald persisted.

Daniel sighed. "All right. Just an intro. But you owe me big time, bro. And if she spurns you, don't come running to me for hugs," he warned.

It was a seamless and impressive production, she thought, as she scanned the hall. All the big names of the tech world; Google, Facebook, Amazon, Microsoft, Apple, and Tesla, were there.

The digital presentation, the equipment, and all the technological whiz bangs she expected from the industry did not disappoint.

She was walking the exhibit hallways and examining the products in the booths when she heard someone call her name.

It was Daniel!

A wide smile on his face made her smile as well. She had not seen him for a long time, yet it felt like no time or distance passed between them. It was not surprising since he had been a friend of hers since they were teens.

"Hey, Yu! You looked good on that stage, woman."

His teasing smile was wide as he walked towards her, his arms outstretched, poised to give her a bear hug. It should not have surprised her to see him here since he owned an Internet of Things company that automated household appliances and connected it to the internet.

"Hey, Dan! If I knew you would be here, I would have declined their invitation to sit on the panel."

He gave her a big, warm hug, a buss on the cheek, and a playful peck on the jaw as he made an audible sucking sound. It made her laugh, and she swatted him playfully on the cheek to make him stop.

"Ha-ha! Found anything you like yet?" His eyes twinkled in mischief.

"Still looking. There is a lot of exciting technology here, though," she said. She took his offered arm as they walked on.

"You were looking for something in data analytics, right?" Daniel asked, one eyebrow raised.

"Right. Data science, and anything that can keep track of our clients, their social presence, buying habits—all that lovely digital stalking stuff," she joked.

"Well then, let me introduce you to someone in that field. His company is doing just that." He steered her towards a tall, good looking, and smartly dressed guy standing not so distant from them.

She threw Daniel an accusing look. She sensed a setup, but said nothing, as they were already within earshot of the guy. Daniel had a habit of setting her up on dates with unsuitable guys as part of an ongoing private joke between them. Although he had not done so for the last few months.

"Yu, meet my friend, Roald. He's one of my closest friends in the industry, and I have known him for over five years. We met at the Web Summit in Ireland, and we have hung out regularly since then. Roald, this is Yuana Orzabal. Their company, GJDV, is looking for tech in the data science and analytics field." A hint of laughter touched his voice.

Roald held out his hand in greeting, which she shook briefly. She kept her expression blank and polite. This one had a distinct air about him that was not present in other men Daniel foisted on her in the past. His eyes twinkled, and possessed a pleasant, approachable aura. It was a welcome contradiction to his obvious self-confidence.

She realised he enlisted Daniel's help to wrangle a personal introduction. Clever move, but it was not going to work. She elbowed Daniel's side surreptitiously, his stomach muscles contracted as her elbow hit his funny bone.

It was her way of warning him he would get a talking to from her later.

Roald could tell that she knew he was more interested in her than as a potential client and was already on her guard. This woman was as perceptive as Daniel had warned him about. He would have to up his game.

"It is my pleasure to meet you, Yuana," he said. His deliberate use of her first name was to establish his friendly intention.

Her eyebrows raised infinitesimally.

"Thank you. So, Roald, what exactly do you do in the data science field?" she asked.

It was a pleasant question, but business-like. She immediately labeled him into her friend zone. The question gave him a chance to impress her with his credentials.

"My company, Buy-O-tech, designs algorithms. We track consumer decision-making and buying triggers based on their social behaviour. Then we combine the social media footprints of the consumer and their friends. We measure their actual purchases against the events in their life, etc."

He paused, then added, "Our system analyses all these data and finds commonality. Then we look for any patterns. In short, we try to zero-in on their buying triggers," he said, happy to discuss his technology.

"Isn't everyone's buying trigger based on emotion?" A small frown appeared in her forehead.

"Yes, but which emotions? When and how do these emotions trigger the actual buying? This is what we are trying to find out," he replied.

Yuana's eyebrow quirked and gave him a brief nod in agreement. "Okay, that sounds interesting."

"It would be my pleasure to show you a demo of our system. How about we do it over dinner?" he suggested. He caught Daniel's effort not to snigger.

"Lunch would be preferable," she replied.

She easily sidestepped his intention. Roald inclined his head in concurrence. Daniel's grin was grating. He would have elbowed Daniel in the ribs, too, if he was close enough.

"You have a unique sounding name, how do you spell it?" she asked, changing the topic.

"R-O-A-L-D, from Roald Dahl, the writer. My mom's favourite." He liked her focus on his name. It felt more personal.

"He's my favourite too." Her quick admission was friendly, but still distant.

Her gaze was assessing. He smiled wider in response, in the friendliest and warmest way he could manage.

"I grew up with his books. My favourite among them was Fantastic Mr Fox," he said.

"Really? I would have thought it was The Twits," she quipped.

Her smile was challenging. That made him laugh. She was indeed a fan of the writer.

She's got wittiness in spades, too.

He was utterly captivated.

An hour later, Roald was still grinning. She was as smart, as sharp as he first thought her to be. She was fiery yet cool and collected, had a wicked sense of humour, and her quiet self-confidence intrigued him. He won a minor victory during the chat. He secured another meeting with her. A Friday lunch to talk about her data science needs.

Granted, it was lunch and hardly romantic, but he intended to use it to his advantage.

Daniel enjoyed the banter between the two. He watched Roald's effort to move past the business-only barrier Yuana erected. Roald had turned on the charm, but it bounced off Yuana's well-placed armour.

Maybe Roald needed to be reminded that Yuana was formidable, and unlike the lightweight women he dated in the past, he might just get friend-zoned by her.

No doubt a first for Roald. But if there was a woman who could achieve that, it would be Yuana. For as long as he had known her, all her relationships had been casual and non-committal. And her reason for keeping it so remained compelling, one that not even Roald's charms could break.

Contrary to Roald's expectation, lunch was not the success he envisioned it to be. He used every tool in his arsenal, yet she remained unaffected.

Oh, it was an engaging and stimulating lunch; she bantered with him, laughed at his jokes, came back with witty zingers, but she remained coolly distant, unruffled by his efforts, and seemed determined to keep it at that. She treated him like a friendly acquaintance, and while it was aggravating, he understood her reserve. They just met, after all.

The harder he tried, the more she withdrew. He knew then if he kept doing what he was doing, he was in danger of getting written out of her appointment book. So, he adopted a friend-only demeanour for the rest of the meal.

He ventured to ask something personal during coffee to determine why she preferred casual dating. "So, I am curious, why are you still single?"

She laughed and replied, "I did not realise there is an expiration date on being single. What is the usual shelf life of a single woman?"

"Sorry, that came out wrong. What I meant was you do not lack any admirers; I saw that at the tech event. They flocked to you like bees to blossom, and I am sure that was not an isolated occurrence. Wasn't there anyone interesting enough to qualify as a boyfriend?"

She shook her head.

"Why not?" he asked.

"Because they were all bees, and I am no blossom. And most unfortunately, the bees could not tell the difference." She punctuated the statement with an elegant shrug.

He did not understand what she meant, and it galled him to think he was just one of the bees. However, on the bright side, she had given him a forewarning, and he doubted she afforded all the other bees the privilege. He had a leg up over all the others and must use this to succeed where they failed.

As he leaned back against his office chair, he remembered Daniel's warning and realised he needed to change tack. If she wanted to be friends first, he would give her that. Maybe this friend zone could be his back door, and he could convince her to date him after she had seen his true character.

Yuana came out of the lunch meeting entertained. Once he got the hint that she was not interested in a romantic relationship with him, his flirting efforts turned to a more down-to-earth harmless charm. She found him funny, smart, knowledgeable, and generous with his ideas. He was fascinating in his energy, his passion for his work, and his willingness to share what he knew.

It was surprising to find out his tech ideas came from helping in his mother's home décor shop during his university years. Roald claimed he had wanted to earn his own money so he would not need to ask for extra from his parents to pay for his social activities and hobbies, like video games and sword-making. That impressed her. According to Daniel, Roald came from a well-off family, and did not need to work.

An incident during lunch made an impression on her and revealed something interesting about Roald's personality. They served her salad with an extra unwanted garnishing—a live caterpillar in her lettuce. Just before he called the server over, he gently lifted the creature out with a spoon and moved it to a leaf in a bush growing outside the restaurant. When he came back, she asked him why he did that; he explained they would probably kill the creature in the kitchen, and he wanted to give it a better chance of changing into a butterfly. Roald had an innate kindness in him, and she liked that.

It was a pity he was not one of their kind. It would have been too easy to engage in something more involved with him than just friendship. He was far too charming for her peace of mind, so she decided she would not date him, casually or otherwise.

In the succeeding months, Roald took every opportunity to strengthen his bond of friendship with Yuana. He wanted to get to know her, to learn about her quirks, her preferences, her ideals, her principles. His initial motivation for this friendship was to mask his true intention to woo her, but he realised he wanted to be her friend, almost as much as he wanted to be her boyfriend.

She seemed content to keep their relationship platonic, yet he could tell the attraction between them was mutual. After over six months of friendship, he had yet to convince her to date him. He did not want to push hard for it because, despite the flirtatious banter that had become a staple in their interaction, there was no firm sign from her she was ready or willing to date him. He did not want to make it awkward between them by asking her. She was strong-willed enough to turn him down.

He found her independence unique and alluring. She did not weigh herself down with the masculine energy other women seemed to think was required to achieve their autonomy. Yuana did not see the need to engage in the traditionally male activities other self-proclaimed independent women adopted to show their empowerment.

Instead, her brand of self-sufficiency was a blend of femininity, gentle firmness, open-mindedness, and grit.

Slowly and unwittingly, it became a mission for him to become someone she would need and rely on. He wanted to be someone she could relax with, would allow into her life, into her heart. He wanted to be a presence constant in her day, a permanence in her night.

In the few instances where they met socially, and there were very few as she had little interest in such affairs, he kept a friendly presence. He was protective but not territorial, especially when other men flocked to her side. She had an aura of elegant approachability, but she kept them all at an arm's length with ease. Seeing how she dealt with those guys made him want to cross the friend zone barrier badly. He did not want to be in their number.

Once he tried to rouse her jealousy, but that did not turn out well. Yuana, being herself, gave him a wide berth to entertain his date, who was less than pleased at his inattentiveness. It strained his considerable patience and self-control trying to be present and pleasant to a perfectly great lady who did not interest him, while the object of his affection was being present and pleasant to other guys on the other side of the room. It had been such a trying night he would never repeat the exercise.

He became her technical consultant for the technology she wanted and helped her find the software development company who would design the GJDV app. Being around her work hours would be a constant reminder of him in as many facets of her life as possible.

His campaign started by claiming her lunch hours on weekdays. He would either invite her to lunch or drop by with packed food in tow. She was a foodie, and the strategy allowed him to find out her food preferences and dining habits. And it further cemented his presence in her life.

Daniel teased him he was bordering on stalker territory. He reasoned that his motivation to be close to her was not to control her but to sow the seed of the idea he was worth the risk, that being with him would be easy.

He discovered Yuana had an affinity for nature, trees in particular. His love for outdoor activities melded well with her interests. He indulged her love of nature, of the woods, the pristine lakes, and rivers. Now and then, Daniel got invited to their outings either by himself or by her. They became a trio, or more like a two plus one.

He had a hunch that Daniel always agreed to join them when invited because Dan enjoyed watching him suffer through holding himself in check during those outings.

All this time spent with her had a dual benefit of getting to know her and of showing her who he was. The bonus: her time spent with him was less time spent with another man.

Yuana was brushing her hair absentmindedly as she thought about how much Roald got under her skin with his constant friendly presence in her life. He was attentive and supportive, funny, and creative. He was both eye candy and brain food, which somewhat annoyed her because it became harder to lump him together with all the other guys.

What she needed now was a break from the temptation Roald posed. She could very well fall in love with him if she was not careful, and she would rather not do so. Being a female *viscerebus*, it would be hard for her to form a committed relationship with someone outside of their kind. She did not want to face the same choice her mother had to make with her father decades ago—to leave him and cut him off from their lives abruptly and completely.

If she fell in love with Roald, leaving him would be devastating. She was not confident in her own fortitude to live away and hidden from the man she loves while keeping tabs on him and his life from a distance. She did not have her mother's endurance and self-sacrificing nature.

Thoughts of her mother gave her an idea of how to achieve the distance she needed. Her mother was scheduled to fly to Europe for the GJDV directors' forum. They could meet up with her great-grandparents in Amsterdam, who would attend the annual gathering of the Supreme Viscerebus Tribunal. It would be the perfect opportunity and environment to mix business and family bonding. The trip would give her time to rest her mind and her emotions and perhaps set to right her skewed internal compass.

Maybe the European air would clear the cobwebs out of her confused brain.

Roald gave himself one last cursory glance at the mirror, before rushing to grab his keys. He would meet Yuana at the newly finished medical arts wing of the St. Michael's Hospital. The inauguration tonight required formal attire. The hospital board commissioned his father to design it. He was his father's plus one. Coincidentally, GJDV was the major donor of the new wing; Yuana would represent the company.

He was raring to see Yuana. He had not seen her for ten days because she travelled for business. The time zone difference limited their phone calls, so he had to content himself with text messages which took her hours to reply to. It took every ounce of his willpower not to follow her to wherever she was, but that would have driven her away. No mere friend would drop everything just to follow a friend across the globe.

He arrived ahead of Yuana, so he positioned himself near the entrance so as not to miss her the moment she did. He took deep breaths to slow his heartbeat down, to appear calm and relaxed when she arrived. It would not do to behave like an excited dog when she showed up.

Five minutes later, from his vantage point, he saw Yuana emerge from a sleek, royal blue car, wearing a flowy, bright yellow gown, with a high slit that parted to show her leg when she slid out of the car, her feet encased in dark purple heels. Her dark hair was slicked back to one side and a cascade of curls on the other.

She was breathtaking.

His already elevated heartbeat picked up its pace. And at that moment, seeing her now, he realised with a vengeance the reality he and Yuana could never be "just friends". He had always known he wanted more than friendship from her, he never comprehended until now how much, and how he wanted it unequivocally.

Yuana was looking forward to the event. It is the most strategic project of GJDV this year. The hospital wing would be a valuable addition to their portfolio of investment and influence. A necessary tool to further secure viscerebus' *Veil of Secrecy* in the most efficient way possible.

She was also glad Roald would be here. They had not spoken properly for ten days. She missed his easy-going presence, the jokes over lunch, their stimulating banter. It would be great to catch up. The recent trip afforded her renewed confidence that she could manage her reaction to Roald. Just being with her mother and great grandparents reminded her what she had and what she would endanger if she broke the *Veil of Secrecy* by marrying a human.

Walking into the lobby, she took a glance down her dress to check for wrinkles. Her stride faltered in mid-step when she saw Roald advance towards her. The intensity of his gaze made the smile on her lips waver. Her breath caught in her throat as it hit her - how much she'd missed him, how vital his presence had become in her life. It shook her to her core, and she panicked. She had an urge to run. Only Roald's warm hands on her upper arms kept her in place.

There was no smile on his face, his jaw tight. She felt a frisson of alarm as she met his gaze. She was trapped and unable to formulate an escape plan.

"Good evening, Yu," Roald said, his voice husky, his dark eyes intent.

"Good evening, Ro," she replied. Her breath caught in her throat.

He didn't respond, merely kept looking at her, like he wanted to say something but did not know how to begin, or if he even wanted to speak at all. She would rather he didn't. The tension broke when someone called Roald's name.

It was a man who had Roald's height and facial features. Architect Magsino, Roald's father.

Roald took a deep breath, a frown on his face. He sighed and took her hand, then led her to where his father beckoned them closer. His father stood with the hospital director and some other people Yuana did not know. Up close, Roald's father had the same smile. The crinkles at the corner of his eyes expressed his delight as they approached. She could imagine how Roald would look like when he aged.

"Ah, finally. I am very pleased to meet you, Yuana." The timbre of his voice was identical to Roald's. His silver-tinged hair had the same texture as his son's. Father and son were so alike, except for the lips. Roald's was fuller.

"The pleasure is mine, sir. Roald told me so much about you." Roald's father would serve as her barrier for tonight. Until she regained her emotional footing.

Her only believable form of defence was to focus all her attention on Architect Magsino. They were both invited to cut the ribbon for the new wing. Roald's father would test her stock knowledge on design and architecture.

Her sparkling interest in the topic was a mask, as she hid behind the beaming countenance aimed at the father. All the while, she studiously avoided the son's unwavering attention.

Roald stuck by her side the whole evening. He contributed little to the surrounding conversation. He kept a steady focus on her until she became uncomfortable under such concentrated scrutiny.

When the hospital director came over to introduce his son, Jon, and daughter, Melinda, she escaped Roald's attention. Jon offered to get her a drink. She suggested they get it from the bar together.

Roald had no choice but to stay with the director's daughter while Yuana went away with the director's son. He was fuming inside. His already aggravated temper, caused by the stress of holding himself in check the whole evening and trying not to kiss her senseless, was further rubbed raw by her choice to distance herself from him.

He could not proclaim himself as her boyfriend, to call her his, no matter how much he wanted it. No right to stop her from accepting attentions from other men, no right to feel protective. And absolutely no right to show everyone they belonged together.

He took a deep breath and glanced in her direction and saw her still chatting with the director's son, laughing at whatever joke the man told. To an onlooker, she appeared carefree, but he caught the surreptitious glance she threw his way, and that was not lightheartedness in her eyes, it was distress.

What was she afraid of?

The look compelled him to take off the friend-only mantle. He had achieved his goal to get through her armour. He was sure of that. Whether she would allow him to go to the next level was unclear. But this would be the time to press his advantage while she was feeling overwhelmed. Tonight, they would have their reckoning. She might erect a new wall in the morning, and he could not allow that.

He scanned the crowd for his father. Luckily, he was close by. Time to free himself. He escorted the director's daughter to his dad under the pretext of introducing them. And thus accomplished, he turned on his heels and hurried to where Yuana was still using the director's son as a shield against him.

Yuana's mask of cheerfulness slipped when he touched her elbow. Her reply to Jon's question about the projects of the GJDV Foundation faded in mid-sentence. She swallowed like her throat had gone dry.

"Yu, can I speak with you for a moment?" he asked. The polite question was for the benefit of the director's son. For a split second, he thought she would deny him, but she nodded.

He led her to the most secluded corner he could find in the crowded lobby, a small space behind a pillar. Yuana gave him a bright smile that did not reach her eyes. She was pushing him back to the friend zone, and this annoyed him a little more, for he had absolutely no plans of going back there.

"Yu, I value you as a friend, so I want to give you a fair warning. Beginning tomorrow, I shall start wooing you."

"Roald... I..." The direct declaration took her by surprise. "I do not get into romantic relationships..."

Her unconscious use of his full first name was not a good sign.

"Yuana, I cannot hang around you pretending I do not want more than friendship from you. I cannot do it anymore. I want the liberty to show you I care for you." His tone was as firm as his resolve.

"Roald... I..."

Her eyes were enormous pools of uncertainty and panic. A slight sheen of perspiration glistened on her hairline. He had never seen her so flustered and vulnerable; but he could not haul her into his arms; he did not have that right... yet.

"Just let me woo you, Yuana, give me a chance to win your heart," he urged her. "No commitments," he added, giving an inch back so she would say yes. He was desperate himself.

"Okay," she said after a moment. She could not meet his eyes.

He released the breath he had been holding while he waited for her answer, and with the exhalation, his tension eased. He would not kid himself into thinking the coming months would be an easy siege to win her heart. Yuana would make it challenging for him, he was sure of that.

He feared something was preventing her from being free to love and receive love. And whatever it was, he intended to battle it by showing her how dependable he would be, how reliable being loved could be.

Later that night, in the privacy of her bedroom, Yuana replayed the events of the evening and reexamined how she felt about it. If she was honest with herself, there was excitement and fear, and something akin to a release. She tried to recall in all her dating years if she had ever dated anyone that got this close to her. Roald was the first guy who managed to. The prospect of what could come out of it was both welcome and unwelcome. The contradiction was unsettling.

She was not inexperienced in handling men, so her panic could have come from facing something she was unprepared for. She never noticed Roald had breached her emotional barrier. Definitely a first.

Her grandmother's words of wisdom rang in her head: *'worry is just premature suffering'*. Her grandmother was right. She was over-reacting. Who knows, this wooing might even be enjoyable?

She had a natural buffer, a pre-ordained defence against falling in love—being a *viscerebus*. She could not hide what she was if she embarked on a committed relationship. And nothing could induce her to give her heart to anyone, considering the consequences. Not even Roald.

The Tribunal had very strict laws against the casual revelation of their nature and their kind to the humans. The consequences of breaking the *Veil of Secrecy* should she fail to restore it at the prescribed time frame was not worth testing. She would be forced to take fatal action against Roald, and it was not something any viscerebus would be glad to do.

She had to be tactical about this. Her best defence strategy was to learn more about how Roald thinks as a man, so she could marshal her own defences. In this aspect, Daniel would be the best person to ask. She should call him in the morning, as it was too late at night.

But hell, Daniel introduced them, so he was partially responsible for the quandary she was in now. And if this would keep her awake, he would have to suffer with her. She picked up her phone and dialled Daniel's number.

"Hey, Yu, anything wrong?" Daniel's throaty mumble floated through the line. He yawned.

"Not yet, but you will help me keep things right," she informed him dryly.

"Okay... what did I do this time?" Daniel asked, wary.

"You introduced him to me... and he's determined to escape the friend zone," she said. It annoyed and alarmed her in equal measure.

"Who? W-what?" The sound of a rustling bedsheet as Daniel shifted was audible.

"Roald told me directly he will woo me. And I don't like it."

Daniel's chuckle annoyed her even more.

"Sorry, Yu... But what is the problem exactly? You never had difficulty keeping them within the friend zone before."

"Well, Roald is not like the others. He refused to be just friends," she said. Daniel's obvious enjoyment of the situation irritated her.

"Okay, so what do you want me to do?... Where and when shall I bring the shovel?" Daniel was trying to soothe her ruffled feathers.

"Oh, be serious, Daniel!" Her sharp rebuke, and the mention of his full name, no doubt sobered him up.

"Okay. Why didn't you just tell him you are not interested? That friendship is the only thing you can offer."

"I did... He... would not accept it," she replied with a heavy sigh.

"So, how can I help, Yuana? What do you want me to do?" he asked.

"What is his usual strategy, his usual wooing moves? I need to be ready."

"I cannot tell you," Daniel replied.

"Why not? A bro code of some sort?"

"No. In the five years that Roald and I have been friends, I have never known him woo any woman. So, I do not have any clue on how he does it."

"Why do you think he wanted to woo me? I was perfectly happy just being friends."

"Well, you were unattainable, a challenge, and most men will find such a challenge nearly impossible to resist," he said.

"Maybe I should just sleep with him one time, to get it over with," she grumbled, half-joking.

"No, don't do that. It will not push him away." Daniel's reaction was quick.

"Oh, don't be daft! I have no plans of sleeping with him just to stop him from wooing me. That's like giving him the trophy before the competition even begun," she snapped.

Her sharp exhale interrupted Daniel's chuckle.

He cleared his throat. "I think Roald is serious about you. Roald is like a male version of you, not a player, but not into serious relationships either. I believe he's angling for a forever-kind of love affair like his parents," he added, his tone laden with forewarning.

"Well, that doesn't help," she said sharply.

"Yuana, just remember the very reason you had no serious relationship. That should help you avoid all the emotional traps Roald will set on your path."

"True..."

"It worked for you before, it would still work this time. Although, I have to admit when Roald sets his mind into doing something, he is a determined fellow. He will not give up that easy, so you have a battle in your hands," he said.

"Oh, damn! This is going to be a problem..."

"Well, there's a possibility he could be bad at wooing; it's his first time after all. He could end up doing something that would make you cringe."

"One can only hope so," she said. That did not seem likely, as Roald had never done anything that induced a cringe from her.

A lengthy silence on the other line made her wonder if they got disconnected.

"Do you want me to talk to him?" Daniel suggested after a while.

"Do you think he would listen and stop?"

"Perhaps... But do you really want him to?" he asked.

A heavy sigh escaped from her. "I do not know..."

"Well, you can always preempt the heartbreak and do what all the other women of your kind do in instances like this. Go and disappear. He can't woo you if you are not here, can he?" he said.

"I will not let him drive me away, that would give him power over me for the rest of my life. And you know how long our kind lives..."

She realised she had been looking at this the wrong way. She saw herself as a helpless victim, a passive recipient of Roald's wooing efforts, which placed her in a weak position. What she should do would be to approach this like a competition. Her wits against his. This idea appealed to her, and even better, it made her feel powerful.

Daniel was wrong. It would be Roald who would have a battle in his hands.

2

THE SIEGE AND THE SACRIFICE

Roald's courtship started the following day.

Yuana arrived at the office, looking forward and expecting her usual coffee, but saw something else instead. On her table lay an enormous box, wrapped in silver and blue. A small silver card attached had a message that read:

Good morning, Yuana.

Let me engage your senses today.

~R.

Intrigued, Yuana opened the box and gasped. There was a layer of fragrant, bright yellow champacas. Her favourite flowers. The familiar heady fragrances of tea, vanilla, hay, and peach assailed her senses. A small blue card with a message accompanied the flowers—

Poetry is not the blossom, but the scent of the blossom.

~R.

Wow! Flowers and poetry. Impressive start!

Enthused, she saw two silver ribbons protruding opposite each other from under the layer of Champacas. She lifted it with care. Underneath was a box of mint chocolates. Again, her favourite. A small silver card accompanying it said:

I taste a liquor never brewed– Emily Dickinson.

~R.

That, too, had the two silver ribbons she could lift out. She did and was delighted to find a book. It was the "Good Omens" by the late Terry Pratchett. The accompanying blue card said:

My sight may have been the first of my senses you captured, but it was merely directed by my heart.
~R.

She was now beyond impressed - Roald accomplished all this within a few hours. He was proving to be a challenging combatant. And this was just day one.

Should I worry?

Not quite.

She then noticed a small digital recorder in the corner of the box. When she pressed play, Roald's deep voice floated in the air. "*You're welcome... Dinner tonight?*" The last silver card that accompanied it said:

Say yes. The sense of touch depends on it.
R.

That made her laugh. She was more than energised; she felt challenged.

Roald would make a good general, judging from how rigorous the campaign he launched to make her fall in love with him. His strategy was multi-faceted, and his actions were well executed.

The Four-Senses, her name for Roald's signature gift box, came in regular schedule. Its contents were always unexpected and varied. The only constant in those boxes was the digital recording of him asking for a dinner date. She could only marvel at the amount of research he had done to find out the things she liked.

At one point, a box came with a bottle of neroli-based perfume for scent. Another one contained gorgonzola and red wine for taste. One was most touching because it had a beautiful snow globe with a small ceramic figure of a man and a woman with dark hair like hers. The scene portrayed a park in the middle of winter, and the music it played was the most beautiful she had ever heard.

Another box came with a Halloween theme, her favourite holiday. It was the middle of the year. His note said:

Anything you desire that is within my power to give is yours.
R.

Their former activities before he began this formal pursuit of her remained the same. Roald knew when to be professional and platonic. And when she was feeling relaxed, he would turn on the charm. In short, he kept her emotional footing unbalanced by being friendly and companionable one moment, funny and playful in another, and the best and worst of it—intense and seductive.

She had to admit to herself she could lose this war to Roald if she did not take care. And she had no one to blame because she unknowingly provided him an ally — her willingness to enjoy the effects of his actions.

It was time to end it. For both their sakes. Tonight, she would have to tell him to stop. The longer she delayed, the harder it would be.

Yuana kept postponing the 'speech' throughout dinner. She justified every delay with flimsy reasons until she ran out of courses, and it left only the dessert. She counted down while she stirred cream in her coffee, then laid her spoon aside.

"Roald, this will be our last date." She adopted a formal tone. Roald must understand she meant business.

"And why is that?" Roald sat back, a small smile on his face.

That confused her. She expected a stronger reaction from him.

"I am tired of this wooing business; I want it to end. I just want us to remain friends." She was as firm, as calm as she could project herself to be.

"You agreed to give me a chance to win your heart, remember? Are you breaking your word?" he asked. His tone was gentle, his expression, deadpan.

"I agreed, and I gave you a chance. But that chance has run out." She tried to keep her façade of calm and decisiveness in the face of Roald's composure.

"I have not won your heart yet. And I promised myself only when I succeed would my wooing end." He said it lightly, but the seriousness of his intent was there in his eyes and the edges of his smile.

"Roald, be reasonable. I told you I do not do romantic relationships. And you promised no commitments. Are you going back on your word now?" Her tone had risen an octave. Her pulse thudded against her wrist.

"Yu, I am not asking you to accept me as your boyfriend, all I am asking from you is to allow me a chance to win your heart. It should be up to me to decide if I won it or not, when to stop and give up."

His reasonable tone was causing her panic to surface. "This is interfering with my life now, Roald. It is becoming more complicated, and I dislike complications." She did not want to be forced to threaten him with the complete severance of their ties.

"You are a strong, independent woman, Yuana. If I cannot win your heart, no amount of effort on my part will accomplish the impossible. Those efforts would not have interfered with your routine or your life," Roald reasoned.

She did not know what to say.

"I think I am getting to you, that my efforts are paying off, that I am making headway. That is why it's complicating your life," he added.

"No, of course not!"

"Well then, my wooing should not be an issue," he shrugged.

She heaved a sigh of frustration. She could not fault his logic. Maybe she would have to try another approach.

Roald let out a slow breath of relief. He survived Yuana's first attempt to put him back in the friend zone. He had been expecting something like this from her almost every week. At one point, he worried she was going to threaten him with cutting off their ties if he persisted.

He was glad the threat did not come, because he would have no choice but to respect her wishes no matter how much he disagreed. That would be excruciating, especially since she had unwittingly admitted how affected she was by his efforts.

Yuana could not seem to get past the first page of the digital marketing proposal in her hand. Her thoughts were with Roald and how to cut the strengthening bond between them cleanly before things got any deeper.

If she did not engage in his courtship efforts, there was very little chance of him winning her heart.

Why not stop seeing him altogether?

Easier said than done. The problem was, she did not want to stop seeing him.

Maybe her mother would have some wise counsel for her. After all, she went through the same thing with her father a long time ago.

"Come in, Yu. Do you need anything?" Ysobella asked without looking up from the document. Her mother was busy signing some policies.

She walked in and sat down by the small coffee table in the corner of her mother's office. They usually sit there when they discuss non-business issues. Her choice of seat piqued her mother's interest.

Her mother pressed the intercom button and requested coffee for both of them, then sat down on the chair next to her.

"Okay, what is our mother-daughter topic for today?" Her mother's casual demeanour showed she had already guessed what it would be about.

Their family always checked the background of every person any of the family members interacted with for over three occasions. Somewhere in their security department, there would be a dossier on Roald. She was certain her mother had reviewed that file at least once.

"Mama, how did Papa win you?" she asked.

Her mother's surprise was momentary, then her expression turned introspective; a slight smile curved her lips. Her eyes flashed at the beautiful memories triggered by the question.

"Through friendship, intelligent conversations, little acts of affection, and a lot of laughter."

Oh, fuck, I am doomed!

It was the same strategy Roald was using on her, and it touched the same vulnerabilities she had inherited from her mother.

"Was there ever a point you thought of stopping everything before things got serious, before you fell in love with Papa?"

"No. You see, Papa and I were friends. We both did not have any intention of getting into a serious relationship. We had priorities and compelling reasons not to get into one. His was to become an excellent doctor. He was an orphan, and he worked very hard for everything he achieved. I had no interest in dating human men, knowing what happened to your Aunt Ximena, plus I loved my work. So, it caught us both unaware. We did not realise until it was too late, we were already in love," Ysobella recounted.

"You friend-zoned Papa and still fell in love..." she sighed.

"Yes. Your father crept into my heart quietly and steadily, unlike what Roald is doing to you, a full-on assault," her mother said. "Yuana, you are in a better position to control your own path. You know of Roald's intention. You can make pre-emptive decisions."

She nodded, but she was unconvinced by the strength of her own control.

"Mama, what is the best way to... avoid getting involved?" She could not admit to her mother her emotions were already engaged.

"Stop seeing him and find a distraction to occupy your thoughts," her mother suggested.

That was going to be hard. She would have to wean herself from craving Roald's presence first.

So how would I start the weaning?

First, she would stop going on a date with him. This way, he could not say she did not keep her word to allow him a chance to win her heart. After all, it was not the gifts that affected her so; it was his physical presence.

Ysobella took out the huge grey leather binder from the unlocked bottom drawer of her desk. Her talk with Yuana reopened the dam of memories she thought she had buried deep. She never succeeded. Those memories remained on the surface, covered by the thinnest veneer of normalcy.

This binder contained every scrap of information and photos she had of Galen's life since she left him. There was not much as he was a private person. The last entry was a clipping from the Baltimore Sun newspaper dated over two years ago. It was an announcement of the engagement of Dr Galen Aurelio and Dr Natalie Holtz.

The sight of the clipping generated the familiar ache in her heart, a mixture of regret, jealousy, and yearning.

Is Galen happy now?

Did the marriage enable him to move on from their disastrous past?

Had he finally secured the family he never had and always wanted? A family I denied him.

There was no use torturing herself further. She flipped to the other newspaper clippings of Galen. They were articles about his medical missions and coverage of his speaking engagements in the medical forums. Every mention of his name in the paper she had collected like scraps, like the proverbial crumbs that lead to home.

The hurting in her heart intensified. She flipped unseeing to other pages, trying to control the tears that welled in her eyes. With a measure of control back, she looked down at the page opened on her lap. And lost her tenuous grip.

Her back rigid at the effort to stop herself from sobbing, tears dripped on a cellophane-covered paper. The memories attached to the twenty-six-year-old document came rushing back at her like a runaway train.

May 10, 1993

She had been on her feet for the last thirty-two hours of hospital duty, and it exhausted her. She rested her back against the wall while she waited for Galen to drive around the front. They were to have a quick lunch and then he would drive her home so she could take a nap before their dinner later.

They were going to fly to Italy the following day for a month-long holiday. She was ticking off the list of essentials in her head, trying to remember if there was something she had forgotten to pack when Galen pulled into the driveway of the hospital.

Too tired and preoccupied to pay attention to the sly smile on Galen's face, she slid into the passenger seat. She was asleep by the time her head hit the headrest, but awoke to the gentle touch of Galen's hands on her face half an hour later.

"Where are we?" she asked.

Galen kissed her temple and murmured, "Your apartment."

"Are we not going to lunch?" She had struggled to open her eyes.

"If you are starving, we can have lunch, but you look like you need sleep more," he replied.

"I would rather sleep," she murmured.

"Sleep it is then," he said.

He reached over to release her seat belt.

She roused herself determinedly; she did not want to tempt Galen into carrying her to her apartment, as he was inclined to do now and then. He came round to her side of the car to open her door and assist her with her things.

Galen walked with her to her unit, with all her medical files and books, and deposited them at her dining table. He turned her towards the bedroom, peeled off the lab coat from her shoulders, and hung it on the coat rack just behind the bedroom door. He then unzipped her dress from behind and undressed her with clinical efficiency until she was down to her underclothes. She stepped out of her shoes with a grateful sigh.

With gentle hands, he pushed her down to the bed and pulled the covers over her and tucked her in. He leaned over and nibbled at her lips gently, a habit of his that was more soothing than arousing. He then left her bedroom to let her sleep.

Hours later, she woke up refreshed and hungry to dimly lit and fragrant surroundings. The light and scent of cinnamon and magnolia came from two candles at the corner of the room.

Thirty-five minutes later, she was inspecting herself in the mirror when she heard the key in the front door. Galen had arrived. She picked up a small evening bag from her wardrobe and proceeded to the living room.

She stopped in her tracks as she stepped out. An amazing sight greeted her. The room was dim, illuminated only by white fairy lights strung all over the walls and a dozen candles all over. All the red candles carried the same scent as the ones in her bedroom. The coppery red cloth that covered the dinner table set off the formal looking white china set for two and the centre-piece of dozens of white roses.

She looked up in confusion at Galen. Her heart hammered in a deafening beat. The feeling of dread crawled into and penetrated her armour-clad heart.

Galen took her hand and led her to a chair and sat her down. His smile was almost shy. He was nervous, she realised, and it made her heart sink. Galen sat down across from her and poured them both a glass of champagne. She could see he was waiting for her to speak.

"What is this, Galen? What is the occasion?" she asked, trying to sound flippant. She hoped this was something else and not a proposal.

Galen looked at her, reached inside his suit pocket, and handed her a thick, embossed silver envelope.

She took the envelope. Her heart thudded louder as she slowly opened it. Inside was a beautifully prepared and filled up marriage license. Galen's signature was bold and firm. A blank space awaited her own signature. Her mind in a whirl, her throat too thick for words, her eyes focused on the document.

"Bel, please say something," Galen implored.

She smiled weakly; Galen's uncertainty tugged at her heartstrings. "Sorry, it completely surprised me. I don't know what to say..." she had said.

"I understand, I was too absorbed in the setup and the setting that I didn't stop to think how shocking this would be for you," he said sheepishly.

"It's okay. It was certainly creative... I hope you are not hiding the priest in the closet..." she joked, outwardly calm and cheerful, but she was crumbling into pieces deep inside.

"No... no... not quite. The marriage license is my way of proposing to you, my signature on it signifies my lifelong commitment even now. Your signature meant the acceptance of my proposal. You can take as much time as you need to decide when the actual ceremony will be. For now, I just want your commitment to us, my love," he explained.

Serious plea for acceptance, for confirmation, replaced the ever-present twinkle of mischief in his eyes.

"I can't sign this... I have no pen," she whispered.

The relief on his expression was almost comical as he hastily fished his silver sign pen out from his inner breast pocket and handed it to her.

She uncapped the pen and deliberately, beautifully signed the license. There was a brief pause when they both looked at the signed license, the import of the moment indelible. Galen stood up, drew her into his arms. His lips descended to hers, and his murmur of "My Bel," was as deep, as intense, as sealing as the kiss that followed.

The pain of the recollection, of the regret, longing, and the undying wish in her soul for the outcome she would rather have, but did not come to pass, washed over her again. She allowed herself to grieve once more, to allow the free flow of tears to wash the pain away into a dull, manageable ache. As she regained control of her emotions, her heart felt lighter.

She closed the binder and slid it back in the bottom drawer, locking it away this time.

Yuana went back to her own office with a plan. Roald was familiar with her work schedule and her preference in the lack of social activities, so the first thing she needed to do would be to apply a drastic change to it.

She started by scheduling late afternoon and dinner meetings with clients and their subsidiaries. She also pushed her weekly meeting with Roald and the IT team earlier in the day. Lunch with Roald became shorter as she moved her marketing team sessions to early afternoon.

As to her Friday and Saturday nights, she needed to create a girl squad immediately. She spent her youth travelling the world, so she did not have a group of high school or university friends to bank on. To do that, she had to get in touch with the women she met at the course of her work in the past two years.

By the end of the day, she had two groups of girlfriends and booked all her Fridays and Saturday nights for the next two months.

She had limited her encounters with Roald to twice a week, both for purely business reasons. For every other night, she scheduled team-building time with her sales and marketing team. She had eliminated all other opportunities for date nights.

In the end, she felt the satisfaction of a job well done and a sense of loss. With a sigh, she left for home early. She needed a pick-me-up, and only her family could do that.

Roald's frustration reached a boiling point.

Three weeks, countless invitations and attempts to take Yuana out, to spend time with her, all turned down because she had previous engagements. At first, he thought she made it up. But her secretary gave him a glimpse of Yuana's schedule when he dropped by her office unannounced with some pastries and coffee in tow, hoping to surprise her. Yuana was at their south branch for a meeting.

She still took his calls, but their conversations were rushed because of her tight schedule. He asked her point-blank about if she was avoiding him. She denied it.

What a load of crock!

She found a more effective way to guard herself, and it was exasperating. Seeing her with regularity was his small reward for not being able to hold her or kiss her. Now that had been taken away from him and his frustration had reached a catastrophic level.

He paced in his living room for half an hour, then decided he might as well go out to blow off some steam. A much better option than moping and thinking of her and all the ways she had thwarted his best-laid plans. No one was more resistant to loving than Yuana. But he was already too emotionally invested, so he had no choice but to persevere. He grabbed his keys and got into his car. He would decide on his destination en route.

Ten minutes later, he took the first sip of the craft gin and tonic he ordered. No use telling himself to stop thinking about her tonight; it had the exact opposite effect on him. He hoped she was as distracted and as full of thoughts about him as he was about her. It would serve her right for choosing to have a business meeting over having dinner with him.

He was still grumbling when the object of his obsession walked into the bar with an older gentleman. Yuana didn't notice him as she was busy laughing at what the gentleman was saying. The man was elegant, fit, good looking, and about fifteen years older than him.

He directed Yuana to the chair he pulled for her, his hand on the small of her back. The familiarity in their interaction told Roald Yuana was open to this man. Something he had yet to achieve. His heart tightened, his gut wrenched at the sight, and a corrosive emotion came over him.

This did not look like a meeting, it looked more like a date.

Inside, he seethed. The flavour of acrid jealousy in his throat. The precariousness of his position in Yuana's life became all too stark. His back muscles were rigid with the effort to stop himself from hauling Yuana out of there, far away from this man who seemed to have succeeded where all of them failed.

He should walk out and away, but his body refused to move.

He watched Yuana excuse herself from her date and walk towards the ladies' room. By reflex, he got up and followed her. Possessiveness and the desire to have his suspicion allayed drove him.

He waited by the hallway of the comfort rooms and positioned himself at the corner where Yuana would not see him when she came out. He didn't want her to panic and duck back inside where he couldn't follow.

Yuana was putting her phone inside her purse when she walked past him. Her head snapped back up as something triggered her awareness a split second before his hand closed on her elbow and spun her around.

Surprise, excitement, gladness, and longing flashed in quick succession across her beautiful face.

His wrath vanished upon seeing her open expression. He also saw with clarity what he meant to her. His heart was full to bursting with the same emotions, and he was helpless against the pull of his attraction to Yuana.

Nothing else mattered now except the need to kiss her. He drew her into his arms, one hand cradled the back of her head as he guided her face towards his. He could not take his eyes off her soft, plump lips. Compelled, he brushed her lower lip with his thumb to tamp down the ferocious need that coursed through his veins, to give her time to pull away.

But she did not. Instead, her exhaled breath quivered in anticipation, and this was permission enough for him. He sealed her lips with his, demonstrating the enormity of the passion, the craving, the burning desire to make her feel what was in his heart. And when she kissed him back with equal fervour, he poured all the yearning of his soul into the kiss.

He angled her head to deepen the kiss, to savour her better, to imprint himself into her as deeply as he could, and to absorb her into himself as fully as possible. This woman was his better half. He was as certain of it as his own breathing.

The kiss could have been just a few seconds, and yet it felt like an eternity. An eternity that was insufficient. He could go on kissing her, but she broke the kiss, panting, trying to regain control. His arms tightened around her. His wordless statement to her that the pretence was over, and from that moment on, they belonged to each other.

And this was the end of their cat-and-mouse game.

Yuana laid her cheek on Roald's chest, breathless and feeling entirely boneless. She needed some time to pull herself together. There was no denying the truth. Not to him, not to herself. She had fallen in love with Roald.

At that moment, she received the answer to the question she asked herself many times before — the one thing in life she wanted above all else was in her hands now. Yet she would not be allowed to keep it. Not with him. She made the same mistake her mother made and there would be hell to pay.

"No more games, Yuana, okay?" Roald said over her head.

His chest vibrated beneath her cheek, his arms wrapped around her, gentle yet unyielding. When she did not respond immediately, he pulled away to look down at her face.

"Okay," she said. Her eyes closed briefly. It was easier to hide her dread if he could not read it in her eyes.

"No more running away. You are home now," he said, his voice reassuring, yet wanting reassurance.

She nodded. She could not voice out the real reason she would never allow herself to find a home in his arms, in his heart. For now, like her mother, she would take advantage of the small sliver of time afforded her by fate. She was hopeful it would be long enough to sustain her for the rest of her very long life.

With a sigh, she pulled out of his arms — Uncle Iñigo was waiting, and Aunt Ximena might be there already.

"Come, join us. My Uncle and Aunt must wonder where I am now," she said.

She glanced at her own reflection in the mirror on the wall. Her face was flushed but acceptable.

Her Uncle... a relative, not a date. And Yuana was going to introduce him to them.

Roald smiled, reassured and joyful. He accompanied Yuana back to the bar with a spring in his step.

Later that evening, for the first time since they met, Yuana allowed him to drive her home. He made huge strides today; he met her relatives, and now he had the right to drive her home.

His own drive home was like the beginning of his life. He went to bed thinking of all the things he could do to show Yuana the benefits of having him as a partner, as an integral part of her life. He vowed to make sure Yuana would not find any cause to regret giving him her heart.

Peace and well-being settled on him. It was like finding something vital he never knew was missing until found. She felt like home, his lifetime goal, and her happiness his achievement. And for the first time in his life, he understood what profound gratitude was like.

Roald was unaware that for Yuana, their new status did not bring absolute joy. It was laced with a sense of doom, and a sense of hope.

Was there any way to change their destiny?

Any way that could help Roald accept my nature as an aswang?

If he did, would he be able to get past the fact that for the humans, I would always be an evil creature of the night, a literal man-eater, a monster?

Would he be able to adapt to my way of life and live among my kind?

Would it do me any good if I avoided the same fate that befell my mother?

For Roald, their entire relationship would be a lopsided one. He would be the only one making the sacrifices, while she would reap the benefits of his love. He would have to accept her regular consumption of raw human viscera, her shape-shifting nature that may pose a danger to his life, their children that would all be aswangs like her, and the responsibility to keep everything a secret until the day he dies.

She would outlive him by at least a hundred years. Her natural long life which she used to consider a blessing now felt like a curse. When Roald dies, she would have to live the rest of her lengthy life with just the memory of their life together, bereft of him.

That would be her punishment.

Perhaps there was merit to following her mother's footsteps - to enjoy as much time with Roald as she could, to make every moment memorable for him. And to make enough of them to tide both of them over until their inevitable parting. There was value to what her mother did. She made the sacrifice by keeping him ignorant of the truth: his woman was a fearful creature of lore — an aswang.

Hopefully, it would be enough for Roald, as it seemed to have been for her father.

Roald got up early. He was too elated to stay in bed, his body too full of adrenalin. He was trying not to send an early text message to Yuana. She could still be sleeping, and he did not want to disturb her.

He ended up doing a two-hour gym session, and yet he was still pumped. He was contemplating his boyfriend strategies for the day when Daniel tapped him on the shoulder.

"You look possessed, bro!" Daniel commented, his gaze assessing.

"What do you mean?" Roald asked, his thoughts still on Yuana.

"You have been grinning for the last ten minutes, for no apparent reason. So, what's up?" Daniel's eyes narrowed in suspicion.

His grin grew wide. He was too happy to be bothered about being mocked by Daniel. He did not respond as the recent development in his relationship with Yuana was too new and personal to share.

But Daniel picked up on it. His eyebrows raised in disbelief. His expression was so telling, it made Roald laugh. Without words, Daniel slapped his back and walked away, leaving him to savour his happiness.

Daniel still couldn't believe Yuana and Roald were now a couple, especially since the cost would be so high for her. And for Roald, although he did not know it yet. They'd reached a point where, no matter which path they chose, there would be sacrifices and heartbreak for both of them.

Yuana risked a lot, and it would only be because she had fallen in love. The one thing Yuana yearned for, a loving relationship, was now at hand but would never culminate to the end she deserved. And he felt responsible because he introduced them.

All kinds of emotions he would rather not have assaulted him. He was pained, concerned, and confused. His former casual existence now no longer possible. He was in the middle of it, and he had no one else to blame as he placed himself there, albeit unintentionally.

He wavered between calling Yuana or waiting for her to call him. Knowing her, she would be torn between living for the moment and preparing for the eventual end. For aswang to human relationships, the Tribunal rules may bend, but it would not change the outcome. To a viscerebus, the *Veil of Secrecy* was paramount. It must be above friends, above family, above all else. And there would be harsh measures if the *Veil* was not maintained, measures that would be literally life and death.

He told himself he may be overreacting. There was still a possibility their relationship could wind down into the natural fading of affection that ends up in friendship. They were casual daters, both of them.

Somehow, though, the scenario rang hollow.

The same scenario played in Yuana's mind. She had been convincing herself the best outcome of her relationship with Roald would be to enjoy it, build wonderful memories together, and then let the intensity wane into friendship. One they would both cherish and count among the most memorable of their lives, and nothing more. She could steer them towards that end, after all, their passion could not burn hot forever. Time would reduce it to a mere ember.

She was deep in thought, staring unseeing at her coffee when she felt her mother's hand on her shoulder.

"A peso for your thoughts?" Ysobella asked, her tone gentle.

She smiled up at her mother. If only she could stir the heat away from her life the way she was doing with her coffee.

"It's worth more than a peso, Mama."

"Okay, so I raise it to ten." Her mother sat down beside her.

"Raise it to a hundred?" She took a fortifying sip of her coffee and welcomed the scalding heat of the beverage on her tongue.

"Oh, that serious, huh?" Her mother's eyebrow rose.

"Yes," she replied with a heavy sigh.

"So, out with it, Yuana. What's bothering you? Matters of the heart?"

"Mama, how would I go about having a relationship with Roald and end it in benign terms, one that would not leave a scar?" Her interest in her coffee dissipated with the swirling steam that rose from her cup.

Her mother looked at her. "Living a life always leaves a scar, Yuana. That's what memories are. You cannot avoid it. Neither can Roald."

"Is there a way not to leave a lasting mark?" *A way where it would not hurt so much?*

"It is not up to you how deep or how lasting the mark will be on Roald. That is on him. But the scar on you, how deep this experience would mark you, how long you will nurse the wound, that is your province."

Yuana's eyes flicked up as she realised her mother was not just talking about Roald. Her mother's own scars were deep and enduring.

"Why do you nurse yours still, Mama? Why not let it go?" If this was the life she would face, she would like to prepare for it.

A sad smile curved her mother's lips. "It's a reminder that once, I fell completely and irrevocably in love. And the pain that came with the reminiscing is the measure of how much capacity I have for love. That is my badge of courage." Her mother sighed. "I would like to think that I did something selfless at one point in my life."

Was there a timeframe for forgetting, for getting over a heartbreak?

"How long do you intend to keep reminiscing, Mama? When will you let go?"

"I let go two years ago, Yuana. But, like any habit, it will take time, and time will make it easier."

Time would, hopefully, make things easier for her and Roald, too.

The ride to the GJDV's office was a quiet one. As always, whenever Galen's name or their history together got discussed, the memories of those times would resurface. The pain that came with the recollection had dulled, but the regret was still as strong as ever.

Ysobella leaned back against the backseat and closed her eyes, trying to stem the flow of those past moments, but it kept coming just the same.

June 12, 1993

She woke up from a nap, yet she still felt tired. It could be jetlag, since she just returned from a month-long holiday in Italy with Galen. She fiddled with the dazzling aquamarine ring on her finger, the engagement ring Galen gave her a month ago, and thought about the signed marriage license stored in her safe. True to his word, Galen never mentioned the document since, but the implication that it was just a matter of time was as present in both their minds as an unvoiced question.

As she fixed herself a cup of coffee, a mixture that included some dark chocolate and mint syrup, she recalled all the days of the past month. She allowed herself to spend it with Galen, as full of joy as possible. It would be a full compensation, albeit a poor substitute for all the years she would lose later. It was her bribe to herself to buy more time with him. They were glorious, bittersweet days, and it gratified her to have them.

She had instructed the covert Iztari team who trailed them to take as many pictures as possible, for those photos would be her lifeline, her tether to Galen and the life they could never have.

Maybe she could squeeze more time with him, a few more months. She needed to break up with him before they announced a wedding date. It would save Galen the embarrassment of a cancelled nuptial.

As she got up, a wave of nausea assailed her, and she ran to the bathroom. In the middle of the waves of dry heaving, a realisation washed over her. Every spasm wrenched from her gut, a punctuation, a corroboration of her suspicion. She did not need a test to confirm it; she knew all the symptoms.

She was pregnant with Galen's child.

Fate had not favoured her wish for more time with Galen. Her clock had run out. The open suitcase she intended to unpack was now a cruel joke. There was no need to do that now. The growing life in her belly decided for her.

Tomorrow, she would erase all the traces of her life here. She must disappear. Galen would never know about the child.

With a heavy heart, she dialled the GJDV security team head, and informed him the Relocation plan would begin today.

The click of the phone sounded like a death knell, and she gave in to the grief crushing her heart, tainting all the joys she had hoarded in the past month.

Three days later, she found out from the report she received from the covert security team leader who trailed Galen, that Galen spent those three frantic days looking for her.

Visions of Galen's pain and desperation broke her heart anew.

She was a fighter by nature, and people who knew her would never think her a martyr. Yet here she was, willing to relive the pain of those last days again and again, willing to get hurt every time. This was the only way to atone for what she did to Galen.

Her form of self-flagellation.

Yuana agreed to meet with Roald for lunch; their first as a couple. This would be an important one. It would set the parameters and the tempo of their relationship. To steer them to a benign parting, it was crucial that their pace was one she dictated, and not the headlong manner Roald would most likely lead them into.

Five minutes later, her secretary ushered Roald to her office. The warmth in his eyes, the smile on his lips made her heart skip a beat. He looked happy, and there was an answering gladness in her heart. He leaned down to kiss her; she turned and offered her cheek instead, conscious of the people around who were watching them with interest.

Roald chuckled, but did not argue.

"Shall we?" she asked, impatient to talk to him and set her rules. She wanted to establish control as soon as possible.

"And we shall," he replied, beaming.

Arm in arm, they walked to the elevator that took them to the Japanese restaurant on the ground floor of the building. Once ensconced in a private spot, with the view of the vast greens of the Jardin De Vida, she faced Roald.

"Ro, I have a request to make," she began. She did not want to lose her nerve, and that would be inevitable if she waited until later.

He picked up on the seriousness in her expression, and his smile faded. "What is it?" he asked. His back straightened, like he was preparing himself for something unpleasant.

"I am not used to this... Can we take it slow?"

"Is that all?" Roald looked disbelieving at the simplicity of her request.

She nodded.

He reached over, closed his hand over hers. His tight grip on her hand communicated his relief. "We can go as slow as you want, Yuana. You set the pace, and I will follow," Roald said, his gaze and tone warm and understanding. "You can take as long a time as you need until you are comfortable with the idea of us." His eyes softened in sympathy and sincerity.

"Thank you for understanding..." Her relief was shallow. Roald had no idea what she was setting up for them.

"I will always try to understand you, Yuana. I know something is stopping you, a fear that you do not feel comfortable sharing with me yet, and I accept that. So, I will wait until you are ready." His words sounded like a promise, one that he seemed intent to keep.

Those words gave Yuana hope, the kind she had never even contemplated before. But it was only day one of their couplehood. It was too early to tell how this would progress, and too early to predict the end. As her grandmother used to say, *'worry is just premature suffering'*, and she had suffered enough, so she would give her concern a rest for now.

With a temporary decision reached, her heart lightened, and she couldn't help but give Roald a beaming smile which chased the serious expression from his face. Surprise replaced it. Then his eyes smouldered.

Taking heed of her own request to take it easy, she smiled him an apology, and flipped open the menu, forcing Roald to follow her lead.

Behind the menu, Roald could only shake his head. She heard him mutter, "You might just be the death of me..."

Oh, Roald, I hope not. You do not know how close you are to the truth.

2019

He watched Narcisa, his six-months pregnant girlfriend, dust the furniture around the rented condominium unit. His focus was on the size of her belly and thought of the foetus living and growing in it. The ultrasound results confirmed the foetus was healthy. All its organs fully formed, as expected.

He had already prepared the remote mountain lodge he had rented to harvest what he needed. His heartbeat quickened with the prospect that his cure was at hand. He would, at last, get rid of the Visceral Metastasis that plagued him. A disease that had been passed on to him by his father. Anger suffused him again at the thought of his father who caused all this. Johan Brogen Prowze's execution for that crime was not enough for the misery he bequeathed his sons.

Narcisa interrupted his thoughts to ask what he wanted for dinner. He could not be bothered, so he told her so. His girlfriend's fawning nature irritated him. Her simple provincial mind bored him within a few days of meeting her. There were several times he wanted to show her how annoying she was but stopped himself as it was part of his plan to pretend to be in love with her so she would obey him without question.

She was but a human pawn for his goal, a host for the only cure for his visceral metastasis.

Tomorrow, the messis would begin. Narcisa would go out early to buy some items he instructed her to get. He would leave half an hour later and pick her up at the meeting point he had prearranged. She had no clue he set it up so no one would see them leave their building together. He had already established his alibi when he advised the front desk to watch an eye out for Narcisa for a few days while he was away.

He engineered the last-minute invitation for her to join him to limit the possibility of her telling anyone she would spend time with him in the next few days. And he also did not tell her their destination as an extra precaution. She didn't bother to ask him, her trust in him complete.

He should feel guilty about what he was about to do to her, and to the foetus in her belly, his own offspring, but he did not. The child was conceived to provide the only cure for his disease. He was not heartless, though. He planned to make it as painless for her as possible, so he prepared some natural anaesthetic to keep her asleep and unconscious the entire time.

With a deep breath of anticipation, he relished the coming of tomorrow. Soon, he would live his life unhampered by this death sentence of a malady. The bitter irony of the disease was not lost on him.

Both the cause and cure stemmed from the consumption of the viscera of his kind.

3

THE FALLING

Roald watched his girlfriend of two weeks come down the stairs wearing leggings, a short, loose cotton shirt and running shoes. She carried a small travel bag. Yuana's long dark hair was set in a high, loose bun. Fresh and relaxed, she gave him a quick kiss good morning, and handed him her bag, then proceeded to the kitchen.

The bag was surprisingly heavier than he expected. Yuana carried it with such ease he thought it contained nothing but light clothes. She must be a lot stronger than her slim frame suggested.

They were going to Caliraya today for a weekend getaway. Their first ever as a couple. He had booked a beautiful lake-side property. He wanted everything to be comfortable, enjoyable and romantic.

Ten minutes later, she came out with two thermal mugs and handed one to him. Her beaming expression went straight to his heart, as it always did. He would have kissed her properly right there and then, but Celia came into the living room with a set of fishing poles and gear. She handed it to him, and he accepted it with a quick glance at Yuana. It seemed his girl had some fishing activities in mind during this trip.

Another half an hour and they were on their way to Caliraya. It would take about two hours to get there, but he was looking forward to a leisurely drive. They would take a scenic route, a perfect start to a romantic getaway.

They had gone out of town and on nature trips before, but this would be the first time he would have Yuana all to himself for a good forty-eight hours. His heartbeat rioted at the idea. He had to remind himself that this could end up being a torturous weekend for his self-control. Yuana's request to take things easy meant she still dictated the pace of their relationship. When they would become intimate rested on her decision.

Yuana was hyperaware of Roald during the drive. The beautiful scenery barely registered in her consciousness. Thank Aquila her thermal mug contained ginger tea rather than coffee. Caffeine would have been disastrous to her nerves.

The atmosphere on this trip was dense with anticipation and excitement. They were both trying hard to remain relaxed, to pretend this trip was just like their previous nature trips.

She would have found it funny if the atmosphere between them was not so thick with tension. The air between them so charged, thunder and lightning would not have surprised her.

She half wished Daniel accompanied them on this trip, like their other out-of-town trips in the past. He was a perfect foil, an effective barrier between her and Roald. But she also wanted to spend the time with him, just the two of them, as most normal couples do.

Why am I nervous?

She had been with men before. *What is so different now?*

She glanced at Roald. His profile to her as he concentrated on driving. His fingers on the steering wheel tapped in sync with the music. She did not even realise they had background music.

What does Roald have that impinges on my psyche?

Why can't I keep a distance from him?

Her heart quickened as she looked at him, her lungs needing more air, and she had to restrain herself from reaching out and touching him. Her mind could not seem to explain it away.

Roald sensed her gaze and glanced at her. Her breath caught when her eyes met his, unable to smile back when he did. His eyes blazed at whatever he saw in hers. There was a split-second pause before they both quickly averted their eyes. Their breathing hitched.

She knew now what made it so different this time—her heart was engaged, and that made her vulnerable as she had never been in her life. Emotions akin to panic, relief and wonder combined ruled her. It was a stunning, terrifying, and exhilarating feeling all at once.

Roald gripped the steering wheel a little tighter to steady the tremors in his hand. The look in her eyes, the fire in them, shook him. Her reaction showed him it affected her too. It gave him hope that maybe this trip would induce Yuana to commit more to him than before.

She continued to withhold something crucial from him, and while he wanted it very much, he wanted her to have no reservations when she finally let go.

He stole a glance in her direction; she faced ahead. Her shoulders were tensed. There was a stiffness in her jawline, and her hand gripped her thermal mug. Her inner struggle was visible to him and his heart ached for her.

He reached over and soothed the hand that gripped the mug, loosening her fingers. This was his way of telling her that all would be fine. After a while, she released the mug and turned her hand over until they were palm to palm. Their fingers interlinked; they were in accord.

And his heart purred.

All at once, the tension eased, and the awareness between them changed. It became more fluid, like a river that found its course.

Two hours later, they were being shown the beautifully designed lakeside villa that he rented. It was airy and well-lighted. The grounds were landscaped with pink bougainvillea, low palm trees, ferns, and small flowering bushes. Two huge ylang-ylang trees flanked the driveway. The boughs were thick with the yellow blooms, their heady scent greeting them as they walked around the grounds.

The side of the house that faced the lake was all glass. A wide covered patio led to an infinity pool, a short boardwalk, and a jetty. There was a red speedboat at the end. The first floor featured an open planned living room, kitchen, and dining area. The second floor housed three bedrooms, the middle being the master bedroom. A long verandah connected the three bedrooms. There was also a jacuzzi at the corner with a small bar attached to it.

The caretaker paused by the middle of the main bedroom and asked him where the luggage would go. He advised him to leave it where it was. He wanted Yuana to decide their sleeping arrangement. And he would give her the time and space to decide, without the presence of a stranger.

The caretaker left them to their privacy to buy the items in the grocery list he had provided the man prior to their arrival. An awkward silence pervaded the room. Yuana was standing in the middle, looking at the bags. He could guess what she was struggling with in her mind.

"Yu, I am going downstairs to check if they delivered the items I ordered for the bar. I will let you decide our sleeping arrangements while we are here. You can have this room. You can decide where you want me to sleep. Just put my bag there," he said.

He gave her a peck on the cheek and left before she could reply. The magnificent ornate four-poster bed in the room was giving him ideas, and it was not the right time to have those.

Bemused, alone and standing in the middle of the room, Yuana took a deep breath to steady herself. Roald had left the decision in her hands, and she was not sure if she liked it. Part of her just wanted him to decide for them, but she appreciated the reason he didn't want to pressure her. He had promised to let her set the pace of their relationship.

Do I want this?

She wanted this from the very beginning, perhaps from the first time she met him.

Am I ready?

With this level of soul-deep intimacy, where all of her would be laid bare—there was no way one could ever be ready for such an experience.

But if she was going to squeeze every joy out of them being together, if she was going to create beautiful memories for Roald, now would be the right time.

With that realisation, she made a firm decision. She picked up his bag. Roald would find it where she intended for him to sleep.

Yuana found him by the bar, mixing them a craft gin and tonic. He figured she needed to relax. He didn't want their stay here to be stressful for her. And he could do with something that would loosen his strung-out nerves and muscles.

He handed her a glass, and she accepted it with a smile. They both took a sip, enjoying the refreshing wash of the lemon, cinnamon stick, and juniper berries on their tongues. The icy burn of the drink down their throat released the tension in their bodies. They sighed in unison.

"What do you want to do first?" He held out his hand to her.

Palm to palm, they ventured out to the front patio, which was conveniently opened for them by the caretaker. The guy's hosting experience was obvious. He knew how to set the atmosphere. There were flowers in the vases, nuts, dried fruits, and chips in sealed glass jars on the bar and the coffee table, fresh fruits on the dining table.

"I want to do so many things, but I would like to explore the lake first.

This place is so beautiful," she breathed. Her expression was soft and wistful. He nodded, willing to do anything she wanted to do, even if it was just to sit on the couch and watch tv.

"Let us go boating later, to explore, and maybe to fish. The sun is too high, and it is almost lunchtime," he suggested.

"Okay," she said with a slight smile. Her expression serene. She seemed contented and at peace. And this perplexed him.

Had she decided? And more to the point, what did she decide on?

This would drive him to distraction, guessing what was next. And he couldn't ask her without putting pressure on her. If she decided against it, his asking might change her decision, and he did not want that. He wanted her wholehearted participation. If she had chosen in his favour, the asking might make her self-conscious, and he definitely would not want that.

He was right. This woman, more than his match, would be the death of him.

Lunch was scrumptious. Benny, the caretaker, turned out to be an outstanding cook. He served them fresh fish encased in salt and baked to perfection, along with freshwater prawns sautéed in ginger, chilis and pumpkin puree; fresh garden vegetables: grilled eggplant and okra topped it off.

Roald made sure that every item on the menu was her favourite. He wanted her to know that her everyday comfort, her happiness, was central to his life.

After coffee, when the sun had cooled down, they spent the afternoon cruising around in the lake, with Benny pointing out every notable point. They went home at sunset. Benny wanted to have time to prepare dinner. The air had turned crisp and cool.

They walked hand in hand along the boardwalk and sat outdoors by the infinity pool. Their feet dangled in the water as they waited for dinner time. Yuana had a faraway look. Her gaze turned towards the horizon. He wondered what she was thinking, and if it was the same thing that consumed his thoughts.

"Do you like it here, Yu?" He wanted to know what was on her mind.

"Yes, I do. I love it. Thank you for taking me here," she breathed. A slight colour tinged her cheeks.

"And I love making you happy. So, you'd better get used to it," he said.

And he meant it. His first order of business when they got back home would be to check out properties there. This could be the site of their future holiday home.

She smiled at him; her eyes glittered with a message that he dared not interpret. Again, he was tempted to ask her, but stopped himself for the same reason earlier. Just then, Benny approached to tell them dinner was ready, and he served it on the table by the pool.

Roald helped her to her feet and led her to the table. Their dinner was light and simple but finished with a rich chocolate dessert and red wine. Benny left them to enjoy the night in privacy and retired early in the caretaker's flat at the corner of the property.

The mood was as mellow as the wine, the night fragrant with ylang-ylang and lake water. He watched Yuana's relaxed face. But the fire in her eyes burned hot in contrast with her demeanour, and it fuelled the flame in his belly. He had to take several slow, deep breaths to temper his reaction to her. He wanted her to decide, at her own time, to give him a sign. And if a sign was coming, he hoped it would be as blatant as she could make it, because he doubted his ability to pick it up in his current state.

Yuana stood up, interrupting his thoughts as she pulled her shirt off. He was too stunned to react as he stared at the curve of her back, as she dropped her shirt on her chair. She toed her shoes off and threw him a glance over the shoulder.

"I'm going swimming. Are you coming?" she asked. Her eyes twinkled; her smile enticed.

"Are you all right, Yu?" he asked, worried for a moment she was drunk.

"I feel wonderful, and in the mood for swimming." Her smile deepened. "Coming?" She asked again as she peeled her leggings off and jumped into the pool in her underwear. She had swum across the pool before he recovered his composure.

He took his clothes off and joined her. He cut through the water to her end, where she had one arm draped over the edge of the pool, her chin propped on it, her gaze on the glistening water of the lake. The cricket song, accompanied by unfamiliar bird calls, and the repetitive soft lap of the water over the bank accentuated the serenity of the evening. The scent of wet earth and ylang-ylang perfumed the air.

He did not know what had absorbed her concentration from across the lake, but whatever it was, it gave him the opportunity to observe her face undisturbed. Her profile was irresistible to him. The plump curve of her lips, the fine arch of her brow, the slim line of her neck, all communicated delicacy and softness, and yet, she had an inner strength that he could not fathom. A sense of mystery that he could not comprehend.

Yuana shivered when the icy breeze from the lake swept towards them. Unwilling to break the magic of the evening, he moved behind her, her back to his chest, his arms caged her body for a second before he wrapped it around her. His lips rested on the side of her temple as he enveloped her with his warmth.

He did not want to speak, he just wanted to savour the warmth and texture of her body curved into his. She melted into his heat as she huddled closer into him. Her sigh of contentment struck straight to his soul and strengthened the ties that bound him to her. She turned and looped her arms around his neck. He looked down at her, waited for her to make a move—to give him a sign.

She lifted her lips to his and nibbled at his bottom lip, then soothed the light bites with her tongue. She repeated the action a few more times without haste. He held still for a moment, giving her the liberty to do what she wished for as long as she wanted, but his self-control splintered in an instant. His groan of surrender made her giggle. He cut it short when he clamped his lips over hers.

The kiss was languid, deep, and drugging, slow, and intense. Her plump lips cushioned his own, as his tongue explored her mouth. The velvet licks of hers duelled with his and sent shock waves to his gut. His brain became fogged with sensations, with her taste, her scent, her touch, her essence. It was not enough, but he could not assume more than what she was giving him now.

He ended the kiss to rein in his craving, to give her time to decide. He was not sure if alcohol fuelled her actions, and the honourable part of him wanted her sober, her choice made with a clear head and a willing heart.

She smiled at him and said, "It's chilly now. Let's go in."

He nodded and loosened his hold on her. They both swam back to the other side of the pool and got out. The chilled air made her shiver as she collected her clothes and the dessert dishes on the table.

He stopped her. "I will take care of the dishes. Go in and shower."

He took the dishes from her hand. When she hesitated, he gave her a gentle push toward the house. She complied and hurried inside.

As he placed the dishes in the sink, he realised he volunteered for this task not just because he wanted her comfortable, but because he didn't know where he stood. The kiss, while incendiary, was not a clear enough sign for him, and he didn't want to assume.

He stopped outside the door of the master bedroom and listened. His heart pounded as he stared at the doorknob. He would be disappointed if his bag wasn't there. He erred on the side of caution and moved to the room next door. And with bated breath and figurative fingers crossed, he opened the door and looked. His bag was not in this room.

There is another room to check.

He moved to the other room, his breath held, as he opened the door. The sight of the empty room blanked out his mind and weakened his knees at the clarity of her decision. Straightaway, his desire surged at the certainty that Yuana had chosen to spend the night with him.

It took him long moments to process that he did not know how to proceed. He was like an untried boy on his first sexual experience. It unsettled him. With his own heartbeat ringing in his ears, drowning all the other sounds around him, he entered the master bedroom quietly. The sight of his bag on the luggage rack confirmed his conclusion, and his heart thudded against his chest.

The muted sounds of the shower penetrated his hearing. Images of Yuana showering flooded his mind's eye. And his already tightly held breath hitched further. The door to the bathroom was ajar, and he didn't know what to make of it. He wasn't familiar with her habits, so he did not want to assume it was an invitation.

With care, he dropped his shoes and shirt on the luggage rack, while trying to decide what to do. He heard the sounds of Yuana finishing her shower; she turned the water off. The brief silence that followed was an eternity as Yuana emerged from the bathroom.

And his breath stopped altogether.

Barefoot, naked, her long hair sopping wet. The dripping rivulets travelled down along her curves and left moisture beads in their wake. It was all over her shoulders and her face glistened with it. A long, white bath towel clutched in her hands as she patted her face. The rest of it hung between her bent arms, shielding from his gaze, her stomach, and the rest of the sweet valley between.

Her eyes, visible above the towel, were on him. The fire in them blazed hot with a challenge. She looked like a woman on a mission.

For a moment, he felt like a prey.

Yuana's heart hammered so fast, she could not think beyond the desire that pooled in her core. She decided hours ago and had been in a state of anticipation since. But she played it cool as she did not know how to proceed, how to tell Roald without sounding contrived.

She had left the bathroom door open, with what she hoped was an invitation he would pick up on, but it wasn't clear enough for Roald. It seemed he was keeping his promise to follow her pace. She would have to make the first move.

He stood bare-chested by the bed when she came out. His sharp, indrawn breath was an echo of hers. He stood transfixed by the sight of her, just as she stood frozen at the sight of him. She had seen him shirtless before, but tonight was different.

Roald swallowed as his eyes travelled along her body, taking in the sight of her sopping wet and naked. She was immobile, caught in his gaze as it moved back to her face. The raging flame in those eyes reached out to her. His desire was almost palpable, his frame rigid with tension.

He took one step closer, then another, until scant inches separated them. His body heat reached out to her, his breath on her face was warm. She could smell the slight scent of chlorine on his skin.

"Are you sure of this, Yuana?" His voice was quiet, deep, and gruff. His eyes never left hers.

"Yes." Her own voice was gravelly, her throat seizing up.

His lips moved closer, almost touching hers. "Last chance to change your mind... There is no going back after this," he murmured against her lips.

"Do you want me to change my mind?" She crossed the scant inch between them and pressed her lips to his.

And that was the trigger that unleashed Roald. With a groan and a brief expression of relief, he pulled her into him and sealed her mouth with his. One of his hands cradled her nape, and the other rested at the low of her back. Both arms tight bands around her, an unbreakable and welcome prison. Her hands were flattened against his hard chest, the towel trapped between them. As their kiss deepened, his shoulders hunched, his arms tightened to press her closer into him, as if he was trying to absorb her.

They ate at each other's mouths. Her blood thickened in her veins; her heartbeat rampaged in her ears. Roald broke the kiss. His lips travelled across her jaw and neck, the growing bristles on his chin abraded her flesh. His lips settled on her lobe as he lightly nipped it; it sent shivers up her spine. Her core turned liquid, her knees buckled. An involuntary moan escaped her lips.

The tip of his tongue soothed the tortured flesh, and it travelled back to the corner of her mouth. He lifted his head. The thumb of the hand that held her nape moved towards her lips, massaging it softly. His eyes darkened, pupils dilated, as he watched her swollen lips throb in reaction.

He drew in a shaken breath. "Jesus, Yuana..." He groaned as he swooped on her lips again.

The kiss was ravenous, almost violent. But just as abruptly, he broke the kiss and moved to her collarbone, his mouth rubbed, then sucked and licked at the vulnerable line from shoulder to her cleavage. She was melting inside like a hot chocolate, her ability to think liquefied with the sensation Roald was subjecting her to.

Roald's questing hand encountered the trapped towel between them. He loosened his hold on her and whipped it away. He discarded it to the side and left her naked in front of him. His indrawn breath as he appraised her body, locked her own breath in her lungs. With reverence, he stroked his knuckles down from the dip that connected her clavicle to her throat to the valley between her breasts.

In response, her eyes closed as she followed the sensation of his hand as it travelled down her body. Her belly spasmed in anticipation when it rested on her belly button. Her arrested breathing synced with his touch.

When her shoulder blades touched the cool wall, her eyes jolted open; Roald had backed her against it. His mouth was on hers again, and gave her deep lashes of his tongue, as his kiss turned gentle but intense. Her eyes closed again as she drew breaths from serrated lungs. It was like drowning. His own gasps for air fuelled her excitement further.

His weight settled on her, and the button of his jeans pressed against her. She was naked against his half-clothed self. It spurred her on. Her hands fumbled at the buttons at the waistband of his jeans.

A hand stopped her. "Wait, Yuana... I won't be able to control myself..." he groaned; his face pained.

"It's a challenge for you then," she breathed, undeterred. He had no hope of stopping her.

"I want to make it last forever," he said, his eyes closed as he tried to control himself. His hand still on hers, holding it flat against his waistband.

"We can have the forever later, I have no patience for it now." She wrenched the button off his jeans. His surprised look at her ferocity and strength reminded her of her nature and his. She gentled her action. He pressed into her in response, his hardness imprinted on her flesh.

Before she could react, quick as a flash, he turned her to face the wall and pressed against her back. She gasped at the shocking sensation of the cool wall on her sensitive nipples. Behind her, Roald kept his palms flat on the wall, his weight pressing her body against it, his hips undulated into her. The movement aroused her further.

Then his lips landed at her nape and rained small kisses and quick licks down her spine, vertebrae per vertebrae. Goosebumps raised on her flesh, her back arched in response. His lips stopped at the last bone, his hands were gentle as he cupped and caressed the cheeks of her bottom, his thumbs grazed the underside of her feminine folds. He brushed the sensitive seam with light and repeated strokes. Her insides clenched. He paused what he was doing, and she almost whimpered in protest.

He turned her forward, her eyes opened at the swiftness of the move. Roald was on one knee in front of her. He looked up at her. His eyes blazed with passion and hunger. His warm tongue traced the shape of the under-curve of one breast. Her fist clenched. Then he did the same with the other. His gaze never wavered as he watched her reaction, as he learned what would elicit the most ardent response. His tongue continued its foray down to her belly button, and past that. She sucked in her breath. The muscles of her stomach tightened as she waited and hoped for what was coming.

But Roald resisted the temptation her writhing body offered, and his lips and tongue moved to the hollows of her inner thighs. From her hipbone down, his kisses traced a fiery line at the edge of the delta of her desire. It drove her crazy. He repeated it on the other side, and it pulled a whimper from her lips. Her plea for completion came out in a sob.

When he finally gave her what she was asking for, he kissed her feminine core like he would her mouth. Deep, slow, exploring licks and laps, his lips soft and insistent. Her juices flowed, her hands grasped his head in reflex, as she held him in place. She could not stop herself as she pressed him deeper into her, while her hips arched towards him in a blatant offering of herself. It was an encouragement, a plea for what she wanted so badly.

Her inner thigh muscles trembled, her knees weakened, her stomach tightened.

"Ro, please..." she implored.

He lifted his lips from her flesh, and with stunning speed and fluid motion, he scooped her up and deposited her into the middle of the bed. He stripped off his own jeans in record speed, his face dark with passion and determination. Roald loomed over her before he lowered himself between her parted legs, his arms hooked under her knees.

Then the velvety tip of his erection, hard as steel, prodded her feminine lips slick with her own juices. She held her breath as she waited for him to penetrate.

"I'm sorry, Yu, I cannot wait..." he groaned against her neck before he breached her in gradual, relentless degrees.

The slick slide was like an eternity with the slowness of his entry. It made her aware of every silken inch of him. They both exhaled in relief as he pushed in. Her breath held as he stilled when she absorbed his full length. They were groin to groin, and she felt full everywhere. Then his hip flexed, and it made her gasp. Roald groaned and started a slow pull out, a reverse journey within her. Her own inhale of excitement echoed his own as he pulled out almost to the tip.

Again, and again, he repeated the movement. His back muscles were like velvet steel in her hands. His breath caught when her hands touched the hard cheeks of his bottom as she grabbed it for purchase. She responded and met his thrust. Her legs wrapped high up his back as she arched into his downstrokes. His lips captured hers in a kiss so combustible, his tongue mimicked the measured thrust of his hips.

Over and over. He stroked in and out, his face strained with the effort to prolong the moment. The cord of muscles on his back knotted. A slight quiver ran through his entire body, just as the tremors in her abdomen signalled the inevitable peak, their breaths in unison against each other's lips. The slow, deep glide was delicious, her insides turned slicker by each entry and withdrawal. It was both too much and not enough. She wanted more of it.

"Deep and slow, Ro... more..." she heard herself implore him. It was so good; her heart was expanding to bursting point.

Both their breaths quickened, their heartbeats in tune as the blaze raged on. Roald's long strokes shortened, faster and faster, tighter and tighter. And at the last second, he pressed as deep as he could go, his groin pressed so hard into hers she felt fused to him. Her core quaked and waves of sensation burst forth from where they were joined. A floodgate of emotion rushed at her, from her, and carried her away. She could not find purchase, and it left her consumed, her energy sapped.

When her awareness returned, her emotions were so high, she could cry. She felt undone to her very core, raw and exposed, and there would be no recovering from it.

Roald slumped over her body, his weight a heavy but welcome load. Their limbs felt boneless and melted into each other. She was enveloped by him, surrounded by his presence. She relished it. Her arms went around his neck and claimed him. It was glorious and poignant at once. His arms tightened, slow and unwilling to move and withdraw from her. They remained locked in each other's arms until their breathing evened out, and their bodies cooled.

As the air turned chilly, their bodies no longer protected by the heat of their passion, Roald shivered. She rubbed his naked back to warm him. He rolled off and took her with him, then tucked her to his side, and pulled the covers on top of them.

After a moment of silence, he kissed her temple and sighed, "I am sorry, Yu. I lost my head," he whispered.

"No need to apologise. I was not exactly in control of my faculties as well," she murmured.

"Give me a moment to recover, and I promise to do better," he said, a teasing note in his voice.

"Give me that same moment, and I will require you to do better."

He laughed softly, kissed her ear, and levered up on his elbow to smooth the damp hair from her face. There was tender satisfaction on his. He rubbed her lower lip with his thumb for a moment as he scanned her face, then he bent and kissed her with reverence.

"Know this, Yuana..." he said, his voice serious. Propped on his elbow, his eyes fierce, his expression solemn— "You have my heart, irrevocably, completely..."

Her heart reacted in response.

"And you have mine," she replied. It took everything in her to keep the sadness from her voice.

"I am glad to know that..." His arms drew her closer into his body as he laid back down. "After tonight, there is no going back," he said, his tone possessive.

"Yes, there's no going back..." her soft reply.

There would be no going forward either...

And her heart broke anew.

4

THE DE VIDA DILEMMA

Roald was excited about today's lunch. Their second anniversary was coming up. And he needed to fish for some information from Yuana about what she might appreciate as a gift. He also wanted to gauge if she was ready to move their relationship to the next level. At thirty years old, he was ready to marry, and there was no one else in this world for him but her.

Normally, he would pick her up from her office, but since her meeting was in the building next to his, they agreed to meet instead. He could not help but smile at the memories this place evoked. This was the venue of their first dinner as a couple.

After two of the most blissful years of his life, no one could fault him for wanting to level it up now. He wanted to complete his happiness by asking for her hand in marriage. He could give her, perhaps, a year of engagement, and then they would get married.

He was watching the door for Yuana's arrival when Daniel entered with some friends in tow. Daniel waved at him in greeting. He waved back. Dan separated from his two companions and approached his table.

"Hey bro! Long time, no see!" Daniel joked. They were at the regular tech meet up the night before.

"I know, you gained weight since I last saw you." He thumped Daniel on the shoulder.

Daniel laughed and patted his flat stomach, "It's the Guinness last night, they're a killer."

"Here for a meeting?" he asked. The two guys who came with Dan, now seated at a distant table, were looking in their direction.

"Yeah, they're founders of a complementary IoT. We are checking if we have synergy," he replied. Dan looked around and noted Yuana's absence. "Waiting for Yuana?" he asked.

He nodded. "Yes, she's on her way. She's coming from a meeting in the building next door."

"Okay. I shall say hi later when she arrives." Daniel was about to join his own party, when impulse prompted him to stall his friend.

"Dan, I'm planning to ask Yuana to marry me," he said in a suppressed tone despite his excitement.

Daniel looked at him in surprise, his face wiped of all other expressions. He had the impression Daniel was not in favour of it but was too polite to say so.

"Weren't you guys taking it slow?" Daniel's tone was tentative.

"It will be our second anniversary in less than two months, Dan. Surely, two years qualify for slow." He felt defensive about his position.

"That seems like a big jump. Why not live together first?" Daniel asked.

"Yuana is not in favour of that. Believe me, I asked multiple times, both in jest and in earnest." He had asked her more than a dozen times. He thought it was the surest way to convince her he was excellent husband material, but she opposed the idea. Her family, according to her, did not approve of such arrangements.

"Do you think Yuana is ready?" Daniel asked, rational as ever. His comment was spot on, a testament to how well Daniel knew Yuana. And it gave him pause.

"Ah... You got me there... I'm not sure. She seems content with what we have."

"Well then, I suggest you test the water a little, and not ask her outright. That will save you the awkwardness on your second-anniversary dinner," Daniel said, with his usual dry humour.

Yuana's arrival saved him from replying, a sweet smile on her face when she spotted him. They both faced Yuana as she approached. Their body language signalled identical warm welcome.

After an exchange of hugs and some teasing banters, Daniel left them to their privacy to join his party seated at a table across the room.

Daniel spent the first half of his lunch meeting distracted with thoughts of Yuana and Roald. If Roald asked for Yuana's hand in marriage, it would be the beginning of the end of their relationship. He wanted to tell Roald so, but he was in no position to warn him. He was not supposed to know. And he could not speak for Yuana. This was between the two of them.

He witnessed how happy the past two years had been for both of them.

It seemed the perfect middle ground for Yuana's situation. Their relationship was something Yuana needed, and Roald's marriage proposal would stop all that.

He hoped Roald would listen to him and be careful about this marriage business. Even if Yuana, for some miraculous reason, married him, Roald had no idea what he would get into. Roald knew nothing about living with an *aswang* or marrying one and having children that would all be *aswangs*. The mental, emotional, and physical toll it would require from Roald would be beyond anything he could imagine. He himself, an *erdia*, a half-blood child of a male aswang, and familiar with living the viscerebus life, refused to get into it.

The more fundamental concern for him, though, was Yuana. Her life was about to turn bitter, the one thing she avoided for so long was now upon her. And the knowledge pained him.

He was not a dessert person, but to soothe his anxiety for his two friends, Daniel ordered Murder by Chocolate and a strong coffee to settle his nerves.

A decision he regretted later; caffeine was not exactly calming.

"Home, miss?" Her driver's question jolted her from her thoughts. He was looking at her from the rear-view mirror.

She nodded. "Yes, please."

He nodded his acknowledgement, and soon, they were on the road.

She settled back against the leather seat. The hum of the running car provided the background noise that cancelled the sound of the busy Manila traffic. Her brain returned to its previous preoccupation as they travelled towards home.

The scene at lunch replayed in her mind on a constant loop since she got back from it. Any normal woman would have been happy to find out her man was thinking about marriage, that he wanted their lives linked forever, and yet, to her, it felt like an indictment.

Roald did not ask for her hand outright; he made a casual comment about it, but the effect of that comment was jarring. She had smiled and replied it was too serious a topic to discuss over lunch. He laughed and dropped the subject altogether. But this did not reassure her. His proposal was imminent, she was sure of it. He may even spring it on their anniversary, less than two months from now.

The timer to their relationship had counted down. The deadline to make the choice - to leave him or to break the *Veil of Secrecy*, was now upon her. A choice she could not make from day one, despite thinking about it from the beginning.

Perhaps her family would have insights, solutions, different options...

Yuana sat down in her usual seat at the distinct square table that sat eight. The rest of her family walked into the dining room led by her grandfather Edrigu, who held a bottle of a good Bordeaux. They would have liver for *sustenance* tonight, judging from the wine her grandfather decanted.

Her mother and grandmother were talking about an upcoming party hosted by a new family who joined their *Gentem*. Her great grandparents were discussing a new Tribunal ordinance proposal that needed more study. They were all waiting for Aunt Ximena to arrive from the hospital.

Their family conversations, as usual, were engaging. Tonight, however, her concern was interfering with her ability to integrate herself into their midst.

By the time the small cooler that contained their *victus,* the daily sustenance arrived, everyone was ready and waiting by the dining area. They passed the raw liver around as they all took their individual portions. That done, they sat down to dinner.

Their routine always followed the same flow: easy banter throughout the meal, all serious topics were not to be discussed until dessert. Her great grandmother insisted on it.

As the leche fritas were served, Yuana tapped her wineglass with her dessert spoon to signal she had a serious business to discuss. All eyes turned to her, expectant and encouraging. It gave her the courage to pose her concern straight on.

"Mama, Roald brought up the subject of marriage over lunch today."

The table became quiet. Her family exchanged glances. They all understood the gravity of the subject.

Abuelo Lorenzo, her great-grandfather, reached over and gave her hand a reassuring squeeze.

"What do I do?" she asked when no one said anything.

"We have measures in place, but it will all depend on the steps you will take when the proposal comes," her Abuelo Lorenzo said.

"I do not know which step to take, 'Elo. Roald may not be like us, but I love him, I trust him, and I think he can handle our truth. That he can accept it..."

Her Abuela Margaita's gaze was gentle. "Yu, we understand how you feel, and you are not the first in the family who had to go through this. We really like Roald, but this is beyond love, beyond trust. We need assurance that he could uphold the *Veil*. But the more crucial question for you — would he adapt to our way of life?"

"I believe he can handle it, 'Ela. He loves me..." She heard her own desperate plea for them to support what was in her heart. Although she had her own doubts, she needed for them to give her the answer she wanted to hear.

"We know, we have seen how he treats you, how he looks at you. But can that love withstand the truth of our nature? And beyond that, will he be able to live in our world?" her grandmother Katelin interjected, her face reflecting worry.

"Yuana, do you realise Roald's life will never be the same the moment you tell him?" Aunt Ximena's expression was grim. Out of everyone, she looked most concerned. It was understandable. Of all the women in their family who had the misfortune of falling in love with a human, she suffered the most.

Everything they said, Yuana already knew in her heart. She was looking for a justification to allow Roald into their lives. But the consequences of doing that, if it did not work out, would be fatal to the De Vidas. And to every single one of her kind.

"So, Yu, is Roald capable of all that?" her grandfather Edrigu asked, his gaze probing, his brow furrowed. She was his baby girl, and knowing she would go through the same painful path her mother did, hurt him.

"I'd like to think he can, but, in all honesty, I am not sure." How could she predict how Roald would react to a truth that could shake the foundation of everything he believed to be true?

"Can you not delay this? Give it more time? Is there a need to rush the marriage?" Her mother's tone was gentle and sympathetic. She, of all people, knew what lay before her.

Yuana sighed. "I guess I can delay it. I suspect he will not propose until our second anniversary, and maybe I can delay it further by having a long engagement..." Her mind wanted to grasp at something that could keep Roald in her life for as long as possible.

"Yuana, no. Don't use the long engagement tack. It will be more painful as he will expect a wedding. It will crush him when you break it off, eventually. I should know..." Aunt Ximena cautioned; her mouth thinned into a bitter line.

"Don't jump the gun, Yu. Sure, you discussed it earlier, but you need not decide tonight. It seems to me he mentioned it to you because he wanted to gauge your eagerness to get married. He hasn't formally proposed yet, right?" her mother asked.

Yuana shook her head. "No, but I dread the time when he does. I cannot say yes, and I do not want to say no... I'm not sure I can say no..."

"Well, *apo*, since he hasn't asked you, you do not need to think about it yet. Let us enjoy the dessert. There is not much we can do for now," Abuela Margaita said. Her ever-practical side on display as she tried to lighten things up.

Everybody nodded. But the leche fritas remained untouched on their plates. The coffee went cold in their cups. And with a deep sigh, her grandfather Edrigu opened another bottle of red wine.

The following day, Ysobella got to work distracted. She was worried for her daughter. Yuana would face the same dilemma she struggled with twenty-eight years ago. She had chosen to keep the *Veil*, to protect their kind, and walked away.

She hurt the man she loves, one who loved her very much. Galen would have been a devoted husband and father to Yuana had their situation been normal.

She still thought about the what-ifs now and then. And it never failed to bring her down. And like before, she pulled herself out of her misery by the reminder that her life was good. She had a wonderful daughter and a loving family.

That should be enough.

As she stepped into her office, her assistant Luisa greeted her with her cup of coffee, made exactly how she liked it. Luisa set her coffee down on her desk and handed her a white, embossed business card. She sat down without looking at the card.

"Ms Bella, a visitor is waiting for you in Meeting Room One, a certain Dr Galen Aurelio." Luisa pointed to the card in her hand.

Dr Galen Aurelio.

Her brain reeled. It knocked the breath out of her lungs.

How did he find me?

After all these years?

Luisa was still waiting for her answer.

"Okay, I will be right there. Make him some coffee," she instructed, her mind still blank.

Luisa nodded and left.

Her heartbeat was deafening, and it became harder to draw breath. Her mind, no longer blank, was now in churning chaos.

What did he want?

Why is he here?

She found herself in front of the door of Meeting Room One with one dominant thought - to see Galen again.

The narrow pane of glass by the side of the door gave her a partial view of the man who owned her heart. He looked the same, albeit older, his thick hair peppered with silver strands. His jawline, still as cut, his shoulders as wide as she remembered. The ache in her belly intensified.

She watched him pick up the cup and take a sip. The surprise on his face after the first sip made her realise Luisa made him *her* coffee. And it was exactly as he preferred it, how they used to enjoy it in their distant past.

He cast a searching glance towards the door and noticed her. He froze.

She saw both recognition and confusion and knew he was questioning his own vision. She had received that look from people only a few times in the past, and it had always made her feel defensive.

With a deep breath, she stepped into the room with a smile. Her external mask donned—the façade of Ysobella Orzabal.

"Good morning. I'm Ysobella Orzabal, how can I help you?" she said in a pleasant tone, her hand held out in a handshake.

Galen hesitated a bit, but took her hand, and clasped it longer than necessary as if he was trying to determine who she was just by the touch of her hand.

"Dr Galen Aurelio," his brief reply.

He continued to stare at her. She could tell that he was trying to assess how old she was— thinking that she was too young to be Isabel; she could be Isabel's younger sister or daughter. She looked far too similar to Isabel Gazcon. His former fiancé.

"How can I help you, Dr Aurelio?" she asked, a smile still plastered on her face.

Her stomach still clenched. She knew what Galen wanted to ask from her. The same questions she faced a few times in the past from acquaintances who used to know her in her youth.

"This may seem untoward and strange, but are you related to Isabel Gazcon? You look so much like her." Galen's hands trembled a little.

He released her hand with reluctance. Ysobella was glad he did. She was half afraid that he would be able to feel the racing pulse beating in her wrist.

"Please take a seat," she said, feeling the need to sit down herself.

They both did.

"Why are you looking for Isabel Gazcon, Dr Aurelio?" Her calm tone belied the state of her composure.

"I will be blunt, Ms Orzabal, as I am a desperate man. She and I almost got married at one point, at least until she left without a word. And I have been looking for her for almost three decades." Galen's blunt reply gave her pause.

"What brought you here, to my office?" How he found her was still a big question.

"It was a lucky coincidence. Yesterday, as I waited for my driver to pick me up in front of the hospital, I saw a familiar face across the street. The face of the woman I had been searching for all my life—and it was you. I had my driver follow your car all the way to this building. I sat there for a long time, trying to decide what to do. This morning, I decided to call in cold."

Galen's tone was flat, but the emotions in his eyes flashed with meaning so clear she could read the hope he felt then, his disappointment now, and the resurgence of the hope that he would finally discover where Isabel was.

And at her silence, he continued, "You carry a similar name. Is she your mother?" His gaze fixed on her face.

"She is not here, Dr Aurelio. She retired in solitude in Spain." Her standard response was one that every one of her kind prepared and practised for, designed to evade the question and direct it to another matter.

"I must see her, Ms Orzabal. It is why I came back to the Philippines. It is my sole goal in this life left to me." Galen's voice intensified.

"What do you mean by 'life left to you'?" She frowned.

"I am dying, Ms Orzabal. Prostate cancer. And I want to spend the rest of my life with her if she will be generous enough to allow me."

The revelation took her breath away. Galen was dying. She did not realise just how vital it was for him to be alive and well in some part of the globe, and how much that knowledge sustained her over the years.

"Tell Isabel I will not ask about the past, why she left me. We do not have to discuss it. I just want to be with her." His plea vibrated with determination. "Is she married, Ms Orzabal? To your father? Is your father still alive? Is this why it is not possible to see her?" His anguish was unmistakable.

That could have been her exit. She could have ended it right there if she had confirmed 'Mr Orzabal' is alive and married to Isabel Gazcon.

All she had to do was nod. But she shook her head instead, unable to speak.

Buying time to compose herself, and on impulse, she took his hand. "Come back tomorrow, Dr Aurelio. Let me ask her first."

Galen's face lit up with hope. He stood up and pulled her in for a hug full of gratitude. Her heart sank. The dilemma has come back to haunt her.

With a vengeance.

Ysobella worked all day in a daze. She had called her Aunt Ximena for advice. They called the family for a teleconference over lunch. Food was delivered at Ysobella's office, while Ximena dialled their group chat window on Ysobella's laptop.

One by one, the family members came online, except Yuana. They left her out of the call on purpose. Ysobella preferred to tell her daughter face to face later.

"Oh, Bella, what is the emergency? Are you okay?" her grandmother Margaita asked. She sat with her grandfather, Lorenzo. They were getting ready for lunch at home.

Her mother and father came online next. Her mother, Katelin, was putting away some papers her father, Edrigu, had signed.

"Oh, Bella, you seem worried, what is the matter, Hija?" Her dad noted her distress.

"Pa, Galen found me."

"What?" Their reaction came in unison. No one was interested in lunch anymore.

"How?" her grandfather asked.

"He came here this morning, 'Elo. He thought I was Isabel Gazcon's daughter, and he begged to see her." She could not hide the plea in her voice.

"What did you say to him?" her grandfather asked.

All eyes were on her.

"I told him Isabel Gazcon is spending her retirement in Spain." She felt like she was standing on a precipice, a temporary holding place before she had to make the jump.

"So, what is the problem?" her father asked, aware that something else was coming.

She did not know what to say, or how to say it—what was in her heart now that she was facing the De Vida dilemma once again. But her family waited with patience for her to speak again.

"You face the choice again..." her mother guessed. A knowing glance reflected in her eyes as Katelin recognised the pain on her daughter's face.

"He is dying, Mama. Prostate cancer. His only wish is to spend the rest of his life with me." She could not suppress the sob of agony in her voice.

"Oh..." Her family's surprised reaction was identical. They exchanged looks between them. Everyone understood the gravity of what was facing her. They had watched her suffer the last time.

"What do you want to do, Bella?" her grandmother asked.

"I love him, 'Ela. I never stopped loving him. And I do not think I have the heart to walk away again. Not this time." Her chest ached with the effort to control her emotions.

"So, what are our options? Maybe you can stay with him for a while?

Spend time with him until... the end..." Her father suggested, his pragmatic nature on the surface.

"I do not know how long he's got, and I do not want to hide the real me from him this time, Papa. He needs to meet his daughter. I want him to know about Yuana before he finally leaves me." A hint of defiance coloured her tone, but she could not help it. At this moment, Galen's needs were more important than every other consideration.

No aswang could live with a human for more than a few weeks without revealing their true nature. To live together with a secret that big would be a near-impossibility.

"You know the dangers, Bella, what is at stake. We all advised Yuana last night to take it easy, to take her time until she is sure. So, I pose the same question to you - how sure are you of Galen?" There was a gentle caution in her grandmother's voice.

It calmed the manic thoughts in her head. As usual, her grandmother brought back her ability to think beyond her feelings.

"Ela, my heart tells me I can trust him. But I will not jeopardise us, so I will try to reveal as little about us as possible. Perhaps I will start by talking to Yuana. She deserves to meet her father." That decision, at least, felt right.

"Okay, Bella. We will discuss this later, over dinner," her grandfather said wearily.

And a unanimous nodding of heads closed the family meeting, for now.

That night, the De Vidas lingered over dinner. The dessert was served in time for Yuana's arrival close to midnight. Her daughter came home late from her dinner with Roald.

The De Vidas greeted Roald warmly, almost like a member of the family. He was a solicitous boyfriend to Yuana, and they knew how much love there was between the two. This worried all of them, but they could only brace themselves for the pain the youngest member of their clan would go through when the time to choose came. They could only be there to protect her, help her pick up the pieces and start anew. Just as they had done for generations.

They watched discreetly as Roald tried to prolong the night. The young couple displayed their reluctance to part. It did not matter that Roald would see Yuana in just a few hours, as it had become his habit to pick her up in the morning to drive her to work. They all suspected Roald bought his condominium unit because it was a mere ten minute drive from their compound. With Roald gone, Yuana went to the kitchen with her family. There was time enough to discuss during coffee and dessert.

"Are we discussing Roald?" Yuana asked, as she sensed that something was amiss. She looked around the table. All eyes were on her.

"Not really, Yu-Yu, but it's the same dilemma," Ysobella replied carefully, gauging how to broach the topic to her daughter.

"What do you mean, Mama?" Yuana's brows knitted, her dessert spoon poised over her dish.

"Your father is back, Yu... He found me this morning..."

"What?" Yuana's mouth fell open, her gaze darted to everyone around her. Her face reflected a gamut of emotions at the news. "How?"

Yuana knew her father's identity, had seen the photographs, read the reports and newspaper clippings of Galen, had heard the stories about him. Her shock must have come from the idea of meeting him. With the action that her mother took decades ago, it was a given that Yuana and her father would never meet.

"He came to my office this morning, looking for Isabel Gazcon. He thought I was the daughter of Isabel Gazcon..." She related everything that transpired in her office to Yuana.

It stunned Yuana. "What did he want? Why did he go looking for you after all these years?" Yuana asked, breathless. The glitter in Yuana's eyes reflected the suppressed joy that bloomed in her heart for the chance to meet her father.

"He said he has been searching for me for years. And he came to the Philippines as he needed to find me." Her own longing and the repressed dread bled into her voice.

"Why? Why did he need to find you?" Yuana's brows furrowed deeper. There was wariness in her daughter's tone.

"Your father is dying, Yuana. He begged me to take him to Isabel Gazcon. And he wants to spend the rest of his life with me." Her throat felt tight as tears pooled in her eyes.

"Oh, Mama! I am so sorry..." Yuana launched herself from her seat and hugged her.

When her daughter drew back to look at her face, understanding dawned in Yuana's eyes. Her daughter read what was in the deepest recesses of her heart. Time and distance changed nothing. She loved Galen with all of her being then, and she still did, perhaps even more so.

As she wiped her tears, she read the thoughts that registered on her daughter's face. The similarity of their situation, the timing, could not have been more obvious.

Yuana looked around and saw the grim faces of her family. They all witnessed how much her mother suffered from that break. And how much this recent encounter with her father broke open the dam of emotions her mother kept bottled up inside ever since.

Her grandfather pressed a white handkerchief into the palm of her mother, who dutifully used it to dry her cheeks. Her grandfather stood behind her mother's chair and stroked her back, imparting comfort and strength.

When her mother calmed down, she sat back down on her chair and asked, "So, Mama, what is your plan? What are you going to do?"

"I want to introduce you to your father, Yuana. If you allow it. I want to make it up to him for all the years I have stolen from both of you."

Her heart leapt at the idea of seeing her father, of finally getting to know him.

"You stole nothing from me, Mama. You did what you thought was the right thing to do. And yes, I want to meet him too." She hugged her mother again, too full of emotion to say anything else.

"So, Bella, what is the plan?" Katelin, her grandmother asked. Her family appeared to be well-apprised of her mother's decision, and they were just waiting for the details.

"I will take it slowly. I will start by introducing Yuana to her father. Hopefully, it will suffice, and I would not need to go further than that," Ysobella replied.

There were collective slow nods all around, except her great grandmother, who was staring at her mother. There was understanding and worry in her gaze.

They waited for her father in the VIP corner of the coffee shop at the GJDV building. Yuana was both excited and scared. What she knew of him and their relationship was from the stories her mother told her, some pictures of them together, old letters, newspaper clippings and articles. He was a top-notch neurosurgeon based in New York, and he was supposed to be married. Now it would seem that the marriage was over since he came looking for her mother on the last days of his life.

An elegant, matured man walked through the front door of the coffee shop. Yuana recognised him because he looked like the photos she had seen over the years. Photos her mother collected to keep tabs of him as he lived his life on the other side of their world. But even without her visual knowledge of her father, she would recognise him by the tension that entered her mother's body when he entered the room.

For a split second, it surprised her to see he was much older than she expected. His hair flecked with silver, his face dignified and lined with experience. Then she remembered her father was human and not a viscerebus. He would age faster than their kind.

The wait staff greeted him, and after a brief exchange, he was led towards the VIP room where she and her mother sat waiting. Galen Aurelio looked as apprehensive and excited as both of them. Her mother was at the edge of her seat.

"Ms Orzabal. Thank you for this." He smiled at her mother and extended his hand. She took the offered hand, and he enveloped it between his.

"Thank you, Mr Aurelio. This is my daughter, Yuana." Her mother gestured towards her. Her smile was tight as she held out her hand. Meeting her father was more nerve-wracking than she thought it would be.

Galen smiled into her eyes and enclosed her hand with both of his. "It is a pleasure to meet you, Yuana. You look as beautiful as your mother."

Her heart tightened in her chest. Her father did not know he was clasping his own daughter's hand.

"Please take a seat, Mr Aurelio." Her mother gestured towards the seat between them. The service staff came in with three steaming coffees and some small sandwiches and set them down on the table. Her mother had ordered them for the occasion.

The staff drew the wooden blinds closed to give them privacy as they left. They sat in tensed silence for a few seconds. The ticking of the clock seemed loud, the coffee and sandwiches ignored.

Her mother broke it, "Can I call you, Galen, Mr Aurelio?" There was a tiny tremor in her voice. She seemed unsure on how to start the discussion, and setting the names straight was the easiest path to it.

"Oh yes, please. It will make me feel young to be on a first name basis with you young ladies," he replied.

Her mother's smile did not reach her eyes.

"So, what did Isabel say? Did she agree to see me?" Galen asked, looking at her mother.

Her mother looked back at him; tears pooled in her eyes. She took a deep breath, closed her eyes, and replied, "She did... She's here."

Galen sat up and glanced at the door, but no one was coming in. He looked back at Ysobella and saw tears streaming down her cheeks and realised the truth. He saw past the close similarities in her features, the acknowledgement and shared memories in her eyes. This was his Isabel, in the guise of Ysobella Orzabal.

He pulled her out of her chair and enclosed her tight in his arms. The feel of her against his chest triggered all the memories of their past. Her scent was the same, and she held him just like before. He had his Isabel back.

His own. Finally.

Awareness pricked at the back of his head as he remembered Yuana and realised why she was here. Yuana was crying too, and he dared not believe what was going through his mind, the conclusion it was forming.

He eased Ysobella out of his arms to gaze into her eyes. "Is Yuana mine?" he asked. Ysobella confirmed with a quick nod, her gaze apologetic and apprehensive.

He smiled at her, dropped a kiss on her lips, and turned towards the daughter he had just met. A gift he did not expect. He held out his arms, and after a slight hesitation, Yuana went to him. He enfolded her in his arms, his heart so full of love and gratitude, it was almost impossible to contain them.

His eyes closed at the glare of the bright sunlight rays that penetrated the slits between the curtains. He felt the heat of the rays against his face. It felt like a miracle was bathing his soul with warmth. His heart was full to bursting.

Sometime later, they sat down and fortified themselves with the cooling coffee. They were all exhausted from the emotional upheaval. There was silence while they nibbled on the sandwiches and processed their own thoughts and feelings.

Ysobella sighed and glanced up from contemplating the bottom of her cup, to him. He looked back in response.

"I know you have questions, so ask away. I promise to answer everything I can—" Ysobella's words were a mere breath.

As he looked at her, all the unanswered questions were running rampant in his mind, answers he was aching for yet afraid to receive, clarifications that may be painful to hear, so he asked the easier questions first.

"How is it you look as young as when I first met you? You didn't seem to have aged at all."

He thought he saw a slight flicker of panic in her eyes, but her smile was sweet. He must have imagined it.

"Genetics, healthy living, diet, exercise, medical procedures, the whole shebang," she replied. "I will tell you more about the whole shebang when the time is right," she added, a sad-looking smile on her face.

"Okay." He lifted her hand and pressed a kiss on it. He understood she was not ready to open up to him yet. The same reason that made her run away from them years ago remained. And he was determined to know what it was, to eliminate it, because he did not want to die without receiving her heart in full, just as he would make sure she received his.

He turned to his beautiful daughter, who was misty eyed while watching them. He examined her face and wonder expanded his heart. This young woman with very youthful looks, the perfect mix of his features and Ysobella's, this girl that was life's ultimate gift to him.

"This explains why my daughter is stunning. Thank god for the wonderful DNA you obviously shared with her," he said.

Yuana's short and embarrassed laugh escaped her as she dabbed her eyes with an embroidered handkerchief.

"Did you tell her about me?" He turned back to Ysobella and asked with no rancour in his heart.

Ysobella sighed and nodded.

"Yes, I told her as much as I can, although I must admit I did not want to build you up too much in her mind, as I was convinced, I would never see you again. I did not want her to miss the father she would never meet," Ysobella said in a slow, tentative tone, as if she was cognisant of the pain those words might trigger in him.

She was right. A slight measure of resentment rose in him, but he quashed it on purpose, as he had no more time for anger and resentment. He needed to squeeze as much love and sweetness out of the remaining days of his life.

"So, what is next, Bel? I am not sure what your plans are but... be warned I will accept nothing less than us being together." His tone had hardened. He wanted her to know his full intent.

Ysobella smiled and replied, "I intend for us to be together, Galen, you and me, and Yuana. As a family. But I hope you will allow us to ease into it and not jump headlong. We haven't seen each other for twenty-eight years, and you have just met your daughter."

Impatience rose in him. He felt possessive and greedy for the time and presence of his Bel and Yuana in his life. He wanted them with him every hour of the day. Especially since his clock was running out. But he understood the awkwardness created by those years of separation. So, he would be patient, up to a point.

For now, he agreed.

"Would you allow me to schedule activities for us? I want to spend as much time as possible with you and my daughter." He looked at his woman and child, and gladness suffused his heart and spread all over him.

"How about we make breakfast or lunch a family affair, so we see each other every day?" Ysobella suggested.

"Yes, I would love that. But I want dinner to be our special time, Bel."

"Let's start now and spend lunch together as a family. The beginning of the rest of our lives. Now, allow me some time today to cancel all my commitments." Ysobella said in a fervent tone.

That was a reasonable request.

"Fair enough." He smiled back at both of them. He glanced at his watch and saw it was close to lunch. "It is almost lunch. What is our game plan? Where do we eat?"

For him, he'd just started to live. The past decades were on pause, and now that he'd found his Bel, his life could begin ticking on again, joyful, and meaningful.

"Can you tell us about you, Sir? What have you done in all those years? Do I have any brothers and sisters?" his daughter asked. The questions were full of excited curiosity.

He reached out and touched his daughter's hair, felt the silkiness of her tresses. He was still trying to take in the reality of his beautiful daughter sitting in front of him.

"Call me papa, if that is okay with you?"

Yuana nodded, a smile on the plump lips she inherited from her mother.

"I never married, Yuana. I spent my time working and looking for your mother. This year, I retired..." He glanced at Ysobella; he was not sure if she told their daughter about his cancer.

"I know about your cancer, Papa. Is there anything that could be done?" Yuana said.

"I'm afraid I have run out of options. I have checked every conceivable medical cure science can offer, including those not available to mere mortals. Remember, I am a doctor." It was poignant that his remaining time on this earth would be the happiest and the most heartbreaking.

"Did you ever have any other relationship after us?" Ysobella asked. It told him she would not begrudge him if he had, because she was the one who walked away.

He weighed how much of the truth he was going to share with her. "I tried, Bel. After two years of looking for you with no success, I thought it was time to move on. I even had two long-term girlfriends. They were both doctors too. But work was always in the way, and my heart wasn't in it. We parted ways as friends." And that was the truth.

Ysobella's eyes widened, then a line of pain appeared around her mouth. Her eyes brimmed with emotions that seemed like they might explode but she held on to her self-control.

It moved him.

"I stopped looking for your replacement five years ago, Bel," he added, unable to stop the need to push her over the edge.

"I didn't even look for yours, Galen."

The image her words created made his heart expand in magnitudes he could not fathom. Her pain was as excruciating as his, her wound as fresh. His throat tightened, unable to say anything. Restrained by his daughter's presence, he could not haul her into his arms. He lifted her hand to his lips instead and crushed a kiss at the centre of her palm.

The kiss contained every promise, every apology he could offer, and every restitution he would collect from her for the time they were apart.

Yuana watched in silence, aware at this moment she was outside of their thoughts. Her parents were so in love then, but unable to be together. This was what she and Roald would face, their situation so similar. The enormity of the pain she and Roald would go through had unfolded right before her eyes, and she did not know if she could put both of them through that.

That evening, a subdued De Vida family came one by one to the dining room. The setting of the table was extra special. It was a momentous occasion, and they would decide on something important tonight.

There was no bantering over the steak and kidney they were having, the steak barely touched, and all of them nursed a glass of burgundy. Everyone was waiting for Ysobella to speak.

All eyes swivelled to her when she placed her glass down, their gaze solemn.

"I need to spend as much time with him, and it might affect our routine..."

"Do you have a plan? How can we help?" Margaita, her grandmother asked. The realities of their lifestyle, the challenge it posed to them over the centuries, were all too present. And it had to be faced every time. As the matriarch of the De Vida clan, her grandmother always took the lead.

"He wanted to spend as much time as possible with me and Yuana. Practically every hour of the day," she replied. She wanted them to hear her willingness to give Galen what he needed.

"Even dinner time..." Her grandfather Lorenzo's remark was not a question, but an acknowledgment of the fact.

She was sure her grandparents had already discussed this earlier. They always functioned as a team. And they both knew what was in her heart.

She nodded, confirming what they guessed.

"So, what's the plan?" Ximena, her aunt asked.

As usual, her supportive aunt was as willing as the rest of the family to accommodate her request. They just needed to ensure it would be safe. As the one in charge of the logistics of their victus, she would orchestrate all the changes needed to ensure this would work.

"I will take a light load at the office. I will go there only when necessary. Uncle Íñigo can handle my work in the meantime. I will live with Galen, so we can spend breakfast or dinner with him. Lunch will be with Yuana. This way, I can eat here either breakfast or dinner..." Her voice trailed off. She suddenly realised how difficult this would be to orchestrate.

"It is far better for you to stop by here before your dinner with him, during cocktail hour, perhaps. We can adjust our sustenance time, or the manner of how we take it, we just have to be careful. You can dine here now and then so we get to know him, and vice versa," her grandfather suggested.

"You can even bring him here during weekends. For an entire day. It would make this family affair more traditional," Katelin, her mother suggested.

Her parents wanted to assess the man their daughter had given her heart to. One who might be the first-ever non-viscerebus part of the De Vida clan, even if it was only temporary.

Her parents exchanged glances. Her father's expression told her he saw this partial integration of Galen Aurelio into the family leading to more.

Edrigu Orzabal, their *Gentem's Chief Iztari*, was in favour of bringing Galen more closely into their midst but wanted to determine the potential danger it might pose to the family. Her father, notwithstanding his position in the local Tribunal, had their security as his key priority.

"Mama, won't Papa ask why you left?" Yuana voiced the one nagging question in her head as they were discussing the plans. Their family was loving and given that they would welcome and accept Galen, the question of why she left would not be far behind.

"He said he wouldn't..." she replied. But uneasiness crept back in.

"He might not ask, but he will always wonder," Ximena said with forewarning.

"Yes, he will. And I am not sure what to say to him yet, but I will try to delay the truth until the very end. Hopefully, being happy together will be enough." She wanted to reassure everyone, despite knowing she was hoping in vain. Galen was not the type to leave issues unresolved.

And just like that, they found the simple solution to her logistical problem without exposing the family and their daily habit of eating raw human organs. It was a simple plan, one that might work for them.

The limited time available to Galen assured the exposure would be temporary. Maybe they could create a new procedure out of this, one that may even work for Yuana's situation.

She could tell that Yuana felt hopeful for Roald and herself, their relationship, their future, for the first time in a long time.

That same night, Yuana helped her mother pack her essentials. There was no need to pack a lot, as her father's hotel was not far. They had decided Yuana would stay at home to allow her father and mother time with each other, but they would meet for lunch without fail, and spend weekends and several activities together.

They worked in silence for a few moments, but Yuana could not stand it. She voiced out what was bothering her, "Mama, how much time do you and Papa have?"

"Not long enough, Yu-Yu. He could live to be a hundred, and it's still not going to be long enough." Her sigh was deep. "I will always be left behind. Our kind always is when we fall in love with people like your father..."

"Is there a way to make Roald, and Dad, like us? Any old folklore or myth, perhaps?" It was a silly question, but she had to ask.

Ysobella shook her head, a small sad smile on her lips. "None that I know of. We are born this way." She shrugged. "And even if there is a way, would they want to? Voluntarily and whole-heartedly?"

They both know maybe Galen and Roald would say yes because of love, and because they would not understand exactly what they were getting into.

"I wouldn't ask Roald, Mama, even if I am sure he would say yes."

"Well then, Yuana, we must endeavour to make their lives with us the happiest ever. This way, our love for them will be worth the pain it will cause them."

Without further words, they finished packing Ysobella's small luggage. Tomorrow, her mother would move in with her father. And the morning would bring something new for the De Vidas. No one in their past had ever come back with such compelling reason for them to even consider exposing what they are.

For Yuana, tomorrow felt both scary and exciting, and it felt inevitable.

The air in the well-lit embalming room was thick with the smell of antiseptic. Two men, both dressed in light blue poly laminated scrubs, goggles, mask, blue wellington boots, and gloves, occupy it together with a newly deceased body of a woman lying on the embalming table.

The atmosphere in the room was light despite its morbid purpose. One man was humming *'Born to be Alive'* as he cleanly took out the liver, kidney and heart from the body brought down to the mortuary not more than half an hour ago. His work took mere minutes, his movement practised and economical, his skill clear as he wielded the scalpel.

Once finished, he separated the organs and placed each into small iceboxes lined with clean, white china trays. The boxes were on a low table beside him. All three were numbered. He placed the heart in the first box, and the kidney and liver in the other two. Once done, he peeled the gloves off, dropped it in a sanitised container, then closed the lid of the iceboxes. He then motioned to the other guy to take over the body.

Then he stepped out, taking the ice boxes with him. His destination would be the embalming room next door. He had harvested *victus* from six bodies already and had six more to do before his day ends. Today's organ harvest would be given to the *Eastern Sustenance Delivery team* in charge of distributing them to their recipient.

With the first man gone, the other man started preparing the embalming fluid with a mixture of formaldehyde and several other chemicals. He picked up on the song the other guy was humming, and he ended up humming it himself. Soon, the sound of the embalming machine filled the room as he worked with the body.

The sight of the fresh liver earlier made him hungry, motivating him to move faster. The liver was his favourite sustenance.

5

THE FAMILY

Galen woke up early and had been pacing the living room of his suite for two hours as he waited for the clock to strike nine. He would meet his wife and daughter for breakfast. In his heart, Bel was his wife, and he would make sure it became a legal reality this time.

It was hard not to regret the lost years, or blame himself for failing to pursue a more exhaustive search in the Philippines. He would have found her earlier.

There were still twenty minutes to go before nine, but he could not stand it anymore. He went down to the private room in the breakfast outlet of the hotel.

Yesterday, he'd spent the afternoon looking for gifts for his two loves, to mark the day they officially became a family. He had wondered if Ysobella was still partial to emeralds and if their daughter took after her. He realised he knew no one he could ask about his wife and daughter.

In the end, he got his girls matching necklaces of platinum and emerald. He wanted it bespoke, but there was no time, so he had offered the top end jeweller a considerable incentive to convert beautiful emerald earrings into pendants. The twin necklace would be ready by noon.

Ten minutes to nine, he saw Ysobella's car pull over to the front of the hotel lobby. He saw his Bel alight, followed by his daughter. They were both wearing light silk dresses, his Bel in blue, and his Yuana in lavender. The two women held hands, as if to fortify each other, and together, walked through the lobby doors, where he was waiting in breathless anticipation.

His daughter was beaming; Ysobella's face was calm, but her eyes blazed with emotion. There was an answering lump in his throat. His eyes never left Ysobella's. He didn't even realise he met them halfway, as he pulled them both into his embrace. They embraced him back as tightly. He kissed their foreheads and marched them towards their reserved breakfast outlet.

He felt like a schoolboy, unable to contain his excitement as he sat them both. "I've ordered the breakfast for us; I hope you do not mind. There will be something for everyone."

The silly grin would not leave his face.

"We do not mind, Papa. Everything will be great, I am sure... How was your evening?" Yuana asked.

She wanted to calm her father down and give her mother a chance to recover from her emotions. Her mother was never speechless until now.

"I didn't sleep a wink, otherwise, a splendid night." Her father's eyes darted between her and her mother.

He could not seem to get enough of staring at them. The intensity of his gaze made her mother blush. The intimacy of that exchange made her feel like an interloper into their world, where only the two of them inhabit.

Mercifully, the food arrived, and it was a veritable feast.

It appeared her father ordered everything on the menu and more. A lady wheeled in a trolley laden with the hot coffee pot and three mugs, a small sauce bowl with melted chocolate, and an even smaller one containing mint syrup.

Startled, she watched her father prepare coffee just like how she and her mother preferred their cup. Her dad served them their cup like he had been doing it all their life.

"Thank you, Galen," her mother said with uncharacteristic shyness.

The smell of the coffee infused the room. She could see this was an old, shared experience between her parents, one that encapsulated all the sweet memories of their relationship, one that sustained her mother over the years. This was how her mother introduced the brew to her. Now, she understood the value of it.

As she cradled her own cup in her hands, the hot bottom of the porcelain warmed her fingers, she thought of all those nights when her mother sat alone. She always had the same coffee in her hands, her face wistful. Her mother must have been reminiscing about their old memories together and dreamed of all that could have been between them.

They were contented for now as they savoured their coffee in silence. Breakfast was a lighthearted affair, an unspoken understanding that the hard questions would come later.

It was surreal to be sitting here with her father again, to have their second chance, arranged by fate in a neat package of a breathtaking beginning and a heartbreaking ending. One her mother accepted with both hands and a very open heart.

The courage it took, the strength it required from her mother, took her breath away.

In the past three hours, she discovered much about the man who stole her mother's heart. Her father exhibited a wicked sense of humour. His anecdotes about life as a surgeon had them laughing. His interests varied from physical pursuits like sports to intellectual ones.

He beamed throughout; his eyes crinkled at the corners when he laughed. His voice was deep and had a natural rasp to it. He was attentive and affectionate. She saw what her father was like when he was younger and why her mother fell in love with him.

Galen Aurelio, apart from being good-looking, was a magnetic man. He also had the natural ability to read through her mother's often enigmatic aura. They were well-matched.

While her father talked about his life and every other subject under the sun, he seemed to avoid any mention of their separation. It seemed a conscious effort on her father's part, which meant that it was at the surface of his mind, and he was just giving them time. Her mother's plan to avoid the truth until the very end had no chance of succeeding. She was sure the reckoning would come much sooner than later.

A text message from Roald reminded her she was to meet him for lunch. He informed her he would be fifteen minutes late. She did not expect their breakfast to roll into lunch, and for a moment, she was tempted to invite him to join them. She decided against it. To introduce him to her father would add roots into their connection and would make a clean break harder to achieve. The thought dampened her happiness.

"Mama, I have to leave you two lovebirds alone. I need to meet with Roald, and I have to pass by the office first... Is it okay, Papa?"

Her father nodded, too happy to be upset. She suspected the prospect of being alone with her mother was more than adequate compensation for losing her company for a few hours.

"No problem, Yuana. But make sure this Roald guy is worth giving up your time with me..." He teased and chucked her under the chin. She kissed him on the cheek, did the same to her mother and picked up her bag.

Roald found Yuana gazing out into the vast, well-manicured grounds of the GJDV garden. The mini lake glistened at a distance. A wistful expression on her face. But he was far too excited to share his news with her.

Lost in her thoughts, it startled her out of her reverie when his lips landed on her shoulder. She swivelled; one eyebrow arched. She knew by instinct he had something wonderful to share with her.

"You've got delightful news?"

"Yes, I closed my Series A round! I got Access Capital's confirmation they will invest the final one million US into my company!" He pulled her out of her chair into his arms and swung her around.

"Congratulations! I knew you could do it!" She was as breathless as him.

He set her down on her feet and kissed her. His lips warm and gentle, the kiss brief but intense. His arms still locked around her, he contemplated her flushed cheeks.

"That was why I was late. They asked for a last-minute call..."

"It's okay. I will always wait for you," she replied softly.

She seemed surprised at her own words, like she did not mean to say something dramatic but could not help herself. He frowned, his eyes searched hers. Yuana had always withheld a bit of herself from him. He was aware of this from the beginning, and it was a driving desire to tease it out of her until she was open to him. In the three years they had known each other, he thought he was succeeding, until the other day when he mentioned marriage.

He saw the familiar panic flare in her eyes. It was a kind of fear that resembled desperation, and it scared him. But then she teased him and remained quite relaxed during the meal. He thought he just imagined it and pushed it out of his mind. Now, the same niggling feeling was back. But he would not push, he would be patient.

"You seem bothered today. Did something happen?" He tilted her chin up when she glanced away. "Tell me."

"I met my father yesterday. He found my mother." Her response was almost a whisper, but it shocked him.

"Wow! Really? That's big."

"It is. It has been twenty-eight years since my parents last saw each other." Yuana looked sad and subdued.

"How do you feel about this? Are you okay?"

She nodded. Then a soft smile appeared on her lips and it widened, her eyes, misty. His heart clenched at the sight.

"Yes, it was like a surprise gift. It was unexpected, but it was a wonderful welcome thing." There was wonder in her eyes that glittered with emotions.

"When did you meet him yesterday? Why didn't you mention it to me last night?" He wanted to be the first person she would go to when momentous events in her life happened and was a little disappointed that she did not.

"I'm sorry. It was overwhelming. And I was more concerned about my mother. She had never stopped loving him."

He kissed her forehead in apology. *I am a selfish heel.*

"So, what was he like?" He might need to impress this other significant man in Yuana's life.

"Oh, he's wonderful. He's smart, funny, charming, and very handsome." She sounded like a girl in her teens, describing a matinee idol.

"So, when are you meeting him again? Is he visiting? Or staying here?" He was very curious now. He needed to find out how to approach the guy who would be his future father-in-law.

"We had breakfast with him this morning. Mama is moving in with him, but I will stay at home because we all agreed they need their time together alone. But he insisted on seeing me and having meals together every day." Her words came out in a rush, her delight was obvious.

"That's understandable, since he hasn't seen both of you in almost three decades. So, how long is he staying here?"

"He's planning to stay here, in our lives, for the rest of his... And I hope it is going to be a long life." The sadness that had touched her eyes earlier returned. "He is dying," she added, and there was a catch in her voice.

"Oh, I'm so sorry, Yu." He wrapped her in his arms once more. His heart ached for her.

He realised he would need to give her time to get to know her father better. And that he could not press for marriage yet, at least not for the next few months.

Yuana needed to be a daughter first, for both her parents, more than be a woman for him. As for himself, he needed to be her man during the coming days.

What's a few months, anyway, when they have a lifetime together?

Within his arms, as her cheek rested on his hard chest and inhaled his scent, Yuana was both comforted and saddened. Her mind kept wandering between her parents and her own situation with Roald, her heart vacillated between hope and despair.

Maybe with the return of her father to her mother, there would be a way for her and Roald to skip the separation part, avoid the pain Roald would be subjected to.

If fate would not be kind to her, then she and Roald would be in for a lot of suffering. But for now, she should not think about it.

Her father's entry into her life should take precedence.

Galen sat in comfort, coffee in hand, on the lush sofa in Ysobella's office. He watched her sign the mountain of documents on her table. Ysobella told him they were memorial plans, and they needed signing so they could issue the policies to the buyers.

He was relieved when he found her, happy for having her and Yuana back into his life. He felt light and happy for the first time in decades. As he contemplated his next steps to convince her to move in with him, the need to find out why she left him in the first place rose in his mind. He tamped it down as he promised her in the beginning that he would not ask about it. And he knew this outcome came about fast because of that promise.

He did not want to break his word, but the need to know had grown stronger. He was sure Ysobella still loved him, maybe as much as he did her. And pushing for the truth this early might make her retreat from him again, so it was more important to secure her promise not to leave him again.

With his strategy fixed, he became certain what his next step would be.

He watched her finish the documents. Her assistant Luisa came and took the stack that she signed, then left the room. The atmosphere turned electric as they realised they were alone.

Galen unfolded his tall form from the couch and approached her. He could see the slight nervous tension in her body, how she was using the worktable as a shield between them. Galen smiled at her. He had no intention of allowing walls, physical or emotional, to come between this woman and himself ever again.

Time and distance had done that to them for twenty-eight years, but even that did not sever their connection, no matter how hard she tried.

Ysobella's heart rate quickened at the expression on Galen's face. She felt like a cornered prey as Galen walked closer. He leaned on her desk and loomed over her.

"All done for the day?" he asked, looking down at her with a trace of relish.

She nodded and busied herself with putting away her stuff into the drawers as she tried to slow her heartbeat down. Earlier, she went through the motion of signing papers with her mind abuzz with mixed emotions.

Excitement, apprehension and dread made her signature less and less graceful as she signed document after document.

Meeting her family tonight was more important. They would try her grandfather's plan - to proceed to their house to introduce Galen to her family, have some cocktails, then dinner. It was stressful to think that her family would meet Galen tonight, but not as nerve-wracking as the idea that Galen was going to meet her clan.

But it was the after-dinner plan that was making her jumpy. She felt like a teenager anticipating her first kiss. The idea of her moving in with him afterwards stole the breath from her lungs every time she thought about it.

Then add her anxiety over the question she was still unprepared to answer - why she left him. He would ask it, and it would be a lot sooner than she would be ready for. She could see the unvoiced question in his eyes every time and sensed his effort to stop himself from asking.

Galen halted her jerky movements with a touch. He lifted her chin to peer into her eyes. "Are you afraid of me, Bel?" he murmured, his voice low. His breath smelled of coffee and mint.

"No... just nervous, I guess..." It was time to face the music. "Let's go?"

She stood up, moved to collect her bag from the side table beside her work desk, and turned expectantly at Galen.

For a split second, he seemed like he wanted to press her, but let it go.

Margaita was satisfied with the spread in the tapas bar. The Spanish wine selection from their cellar would pair well with them. It would be a casual evening, as formality might just make everyone nervous, and trigger questions that could not be answered satisfactorily, much less truthfully.

Tonight's sustenance would arrive in half an hour, and everyone would be home by then.

Everyone was worried about the outcome of tonight's event. The last time they allowed a human into their clan was two hundred years ago. While this would be a temporary situation, the danger to their clan would be real. As the Matriarch of the *Philippine Gentem*, her decision to allow her granddaughter to bring a human into the family was dangerous, and borderline irresponsible.

But her granddaughter's happiness was at stake. Her support was not even in question.

While the choice was hard, the family agreed they would support Ysobella for this brief grab at happiness. They all witnessed how she suffered when she broke up with Galen years ago. If it was not for Yuana, they were sure Ysobella would have given up.

And in all those years afterwards, Ysobella never moved on from Galen. She stopped dating people outside of their kind, and they harboured hopes she would fall in love with someone else, but it never happened. Her heart remained aloof, disengaged.

And now, it seemed like her great-granddaughter could be on the same path. Maybe the return of Galen into their lives would prepare Yuana for what she would face when the time to choose comes.

Lorenzo came into the dining area as she was checking the decanters for the red wines. Her preoccupation was clear, and her husband understood what was distracting her. He took the wine opener from her hand and took over the decanting of the Rosado and Rioja.

Ximena, their oldest daughter, was on her way and should be home in five minutes. She would have their sustenance at hand, a job that was usually Ysobella's would be Ximena's or Katalin's for the unforeseeable future.

"Are you ready, *Cara*?" Lorenzo asked. Familiar admiration filled his eyes. She smiled back at him, her own gaze appreciative of him and the love they shared despite more than a century of being together.

They heard the front door open, followed by the voice of Yuana. Roald would be with her, as it was his usual habit to drive her home. Hand in hand, they walked out of the dining room to greet their great granddaughter and her boyfriend. Yuana and Roald both turned in their direction as they entered the living room, welcome on their faces.

As they reached the young couple, Roald took her right hand and bent down to touch his forehead to her knuckles. "Mano po," Roald said. He repeated the gesture to Lorenzo. This act of respect was the first thing that endeared Roald to them the first time they met him. And he had been consistent in his respectful manner for two years.

"Good evening, Señor and Señora Ibarra," he said.

"Good evening, Hijo," Lorenzo replied. She nodded her acknowledgement. They said nothing more. They were not sure if Yuana had invited Roald to join them, or if she kept the event within the family.

While Lorenzo engaged Roald in conversation about his tech business, she threw Yuana a questioning look - *did she invite Roald to the family cocktail event?*

At the uncertainty in her great granddaughter's eyes, she decided for her. She was certain Yuana would introduce Galen to Roald at a certain point, anyway. It would be better not to create tension between the two young lovebirds while Yuana was buying time for both of them.

Yuana's turmoil would make the Galen situation harder to deal with as a family, especially for Ysobella and Yuana. It was best to deal with one situation at hand. The fate of Yuana and Roald's relationship could wait.

She turned to Roald, and with an inclination of the head, said, "Hijo, I hope you would join us tonight. We have a special family cocktail, as Yuana's father will finally be introduced to us."

Roald was surprised and threw Yuana a questioning glance.

"She didn't know, Roald. It's a last-minute plan," she said.

Yuana threw her a grateful smile.

"It would be my pleasure, Señora. But allow me to go home for a quick change, I am not dressed for it," Roald said. He appeared thrilled at the opportunity to meet Galen Aurelio.

"You look fine, Hijo. But if you feel you need to, the cocktail is in 20 minutes. Will you have enough time to change?" Lorenzo asked.

Her husband did not think it a good idea to include Roald tonight, but he trusted her wisdom, so he would defer the questions till later.

"I can make it, Señor. I live only a few minutes away," he said with a confident smile. He gave Yuana a quick peck on the lips. "See you in a jiffy, Yu." He hurried out to his car.

Yuana gave her a hug. "Thank you, 'Ela. I am so glad you read my mind."

"You're welcome, Yu-Yu." She touched Yuana's face, to ease the slight frown on her great granddaughter's forehead. "Take your mind off it for now. We need to deal with your father first. There is no rush, so delay as much as you can. And while you are at it, enjoy each other. Squeeze every ounce of joy that you can while it lasts and make him as happy as he can be while you are together. It is the least you can do for him..."

Within the circle of her arms, Yuana stood in silence thinking on her words. She could see that it was the most viable path for Yuana for now. She knew that her great granddaughter would never put them in danger on purpose. A breakup with Roald would devastate her. Her family was vital to Yuana, but Roald had become vital to her life, too.

They turned around towards the sound of an unfamiliar car at the front driveway. Yuana's parents had arrived.

Immediately after, the sound of Ximena's car followed. They could hear them chatting in the entryway as the door opened. At the sound of excited chatter, her youngest daughter, Katelin, and her husband, Edrigu, both came out from their room and leaned over the railing to confirm that their daughter Ysobella and Galen had arrived.

They rushed down to meet their visitor.

Four generations of De Vidas offered a warm welcome to Galen Aurelio and admitted him into their midst, but not into their inner sanctum, yet.

Galen would have to prove himself to them first.

The living room was awash in excitement. The introductions were brisk. Her father interacted well with her family. Nita, their long-time housekeeper, brought out the drinks, followed by her daughter, Celia, who was carrying the canapes. And in the middle of the merry crowd, her great aunt Ximena slipped into the kitchen with the small cooler of sustenance she carried home daily.

These were the people she would endanger if she broke the veil. Her great grandparents, her grandparents, her aunt, her mom. And everyone who was part of the GJDV company along with their household staff, who had been serving the De Vidas for generations. All part of her extended family.

Tonight was a celebration for her parents, so she would stop her miserable thoughts and enjoy with the rest. With resolve, she pasted a smile on her face as she waited for Roald to return.

One by one, members of her family slipped to the kitchen to take in sustenance. When it was her mother's turn, her father reached out a hand to stop her, a quick gesture of inquiry. Her mother murmured a response that satisfied him. She herself was just waiting for Roald's arrival before she took her turn.

Soon enough, she heard Roald's car pull over. He'd showered by the looks of his damp hair and wore a charcoal grey round-necked shirt, dark grey coat, and distressed jeans. He looked like the successful tech entrepreneur that he was. Roald hesitated at the door. He appeared uneasy and out of place in their family gathering.

She met him as he crossed the doorway, held out her hand to him and pulled him into the living room towards where her father was chatting with her grandfather, Edrigu. They were talking about their shared love of Kali.

"Papa, I would like you to meet someone." She touched her father on the elbow to get his attention. He turned, beaming, then his gaze moved to the tall guy beside her.

"Ah, so this is the famous boyfriend, Roald," he boomed.

Her father seemed happy to meet the man who had taken a significant position in her life. He extended a hand to Roald.

"It is my pleasure to meet you, Sir," Roald replied and grasped the extended hand.

"It is my pleasure as well, young man. My daughter seemed to have chosen well."

On that score, she was confident her father would have no cause for complaints. With Roald's left arm still around her, a possessive hand rested at the low of her spine. He glanced down at her. His eyes told her that no words could convey the depth of his feelings for her.

And a lump of emotion lodged in her throat.

Galen caught their exchange and noted their body language. Her father's knowing look told her it warmed his heart to see his daughter would be in excellent hands.

When her father started engaging Roald in a conversation, she took it as a cue to take her sustenance. Celia had been giving her signals for the last ten minutes. She reached back on Roald's hand resting at the small of her back and squeezed it, then eased out of his arms. He looked down at her in inquiry, and she pointed to the kitchen. He nodded in acknowledgement and let her go.

On her way to the kitchen, she thought... this could work.

Celia was waiting for her and handed her a small bowl containing sustenance, a slice of a human heart.

"Yu-yu, here you go," Celia said, her own bowl set by the sink.

"Thanks, *Manang*! Have you had yours?"

Celia nodded.

Yuana swallowed the slice and took a gulp of red wine to wash the smell from her breath.

Five minutes later, she walked back to the living room, refreshed and strengthened, ready to enjoy the company of her family with Roald.

By the threshold of the kitchen door, Yuana noticed how her family seemed to meld well with her father and Roald. This scene should be enough to make anyone in her position feel happy, but dread hovered ever-present in her consciousness.

Roald was chatting with her mother, who stood beside her dad, her father's arm around her waist as he kept her close. She observed from a distance; she did not make any sound or movement, but Roald seemed to have sensed her presence. He turned towards her; their eyes locked. They were thinking about the same thing.

They both wanted the kind of love her parents have for each other. Timeless and boundless, undimmed by distance and years of silence.

He extended a hand towards her; he wanted her within his reach, as if he missed her. She walked towards Roald, needing the same thing, and they both sighed as their fingers touched.

As the evening progressed, Galen noticed how close Ysobella's family were, how attuned to each other's thoughts and feelings. They were warm and friendly, and their care for each other deep and genuine.

He had met no one whose great-grandparents were still this active, this youthful. Ysobella's grandparents could still be mistaken as her mother.

While they exuded a casual, lighthearted vibe about them, he sensed a brittleness in that façade. There was a mystery lurking in Ysobella's family. He realised this may have something to do with the reason Ysobella left him years ago.

As the night deepened, Ysobella's nervousness increased. It was ridiculous. She was a grown, experienced woman of sixty-five, not a debutante on her first date, or worse, like a virgin on her wedding night. She had not been celibate, so there was no reason to be uncertain.

What made this so difficult?

Because my heart is in it.

That was what made all her sexual encounters in the past casual, why it made no impression on her. It was all a meaningless act. This time, as it had always been with Galen, her heart was more than engaged. Since the beginning, he had owned half of it.

Her mother, Katelin, must have sensed her nerves were as taut as a violin string. The family already knew, and they all supported her decision to spend time with Galen, but having seven pairs of eyes watch her leave with him tonight would be a bit nerve-wracking. Her mother engineered an exit that made her choice very natural, almost commonplace.

Aunt Ximena quit the event first. She announced she had an early start the next day for a surgery scheduled at nine a.m. That was a signal for everyone to wrap up. The living room started emptying in the next half hour.

Her grandparents followed suit and announced they needed their beauty sleep. There were exchanges of hugs and kisses as the three prepared to leave the living room with the stragglers. Her parents lingered on, finishing their drink to help wind down the evening.

Roald took his cue and finished his drink. "Yu, I need to be going as well." He turned to the rest of the party, said his thanks, and bid them goodnight. Yuana walked him to the front hallway and entry door, as was their habit every night.

With Roald gone, Yuana said goodnight to her grandparents and then to her father. They agreed to meet for breakfast every day at her father's hotel. He had chosen a hotel that was conveniently close to their office and home. Finally, she kissed her mother goodnight and whispered good luck in her ear.

For Ysobella, the breakfast conversation, and the departure of Yuana, made her decision to leave with Galen tonight less awkward. At least until she realised she had not discussed it with Galen at all. Now, it seemed like the wrong time to ask Galen if he was okay if she moved in with him.

What if he said no?

It struck Galen he did not know how tonight would end, as he had not discussed it with Ysobella earlier. He was far too preoccupied with the joy of being with her the whole day he took for granted how it would end. They discussed their daytime activities and interaction but realised now he should have at least clarified with her what the plan was after dinner time.

The night was at an end, and more than a few minutes of lingering would make things more awkward. So, he winged it, hoping he read Ysobella's intent well enough.

He turned to Ysobella, and with feigned casualness and calm, said, "Shall we say good night to your parents so they can rest?"

His statement was open to her interpretation on purpose, and he hoped she would agree with him. She nodded, uncertainty in her gaze. So, he pressed on and decided for both of them.

"Thank you for the lovely evening, Mr and Mrs Orzabal. It has been a pleasure to have met all of Bel's family." He shook Edrigu's hand firmly.

"It was a pleasure to have met you too, Galen." Ysobella's father's grip was equally firm.

He shook Katelin's hand, and they both thanked and wished each other good evening. With his arm around Ysobella's shoulders, he turned to her, and said, "Shall we?"

He hoped his meaning was as clear as his intention. She nodded.

"Yes, let's go." Her smile made his heart leap.

He expected her to ask for a few moments to pack some personal items, so it surprised him when she moved towards the foyer. He followed, and only then did he notice two elegant suitcases standing by the door. His heart leapt higher at the thought his Bel had decided since last night to move in with him. His Bel was as impatient to resume their long-interrupted life together.

And gladness pervaded his soul.

Edrigu watched Galen all evening.

The man appeared to be decent, intelligent, honest, dignified, and truly in love with his daughter. His background and credential remained as impeccable as before, when he first met Ysobella in the US. Probably even more so now as he had become a world-renowned neurosurgeon.

He had Galen's background rechecked and updated since he resurfaced into his daughter and granddaughter's lives. The Iztari network in the US came up with nothing negative about him so far.

Earlier, Galen was startled when he realised something about the De Vidas. As Galen's eyes scanned everyone's faces, deep speculation on his face, Edrigu thought Galen was getting closer to the tipping point.

The man would ask questions soon. He would give it forty-eight hours at the most before Galen demanded an explanation about the peculiarity of the De Vida clan.

The drive to the hotel was blessedly short, because Ysobella had turned quiet, and it made him uneasy. She seemed to dread the rest of the evening, and the atmosphere between them became filled with tension.

Soon enough, they arrived at the hotel. He introduced her as his wife to the front desk when he asked for a second card key. It came out so naturally. Perhaps because he had always seen her as his spouse, but the reminder of the lost years pained him.

The trip to their room, her hand held in his, was tensed. Inside their suite, as they waited for their luggage, she stood in the middle of the living room. Her body telegraphed unease as she perused her surroundings. Galen stood by the entrance as he weighed what tack to take to ease the tension between them. Since they left her house, she was on edge. Her body vibrated with unleashed energy held tight.

A knock on the door announced the doorman with Ysobella's luggage. Galen directed him to bring the luggage into his bedroom. The second bedroom in the suite would remain unused, or at least reserved for Yuana when she stayed over. Their life as man and wife would begin as soon as he had sorted whatever was bothering Ysobella.

After the doorman left, he found Ysobella, still standing in the same spot, looking flushed and more uncertain than ever. He walked towards her and pressed her down to sit on the couch. He sat beside her and held both her hands in his, warming them.

"What is the matter, Bel? Why are you so nervous?"

He wanted to know what was bothering her, and how to make it go away. And he could not help unless he found out what was making her so skittish. He leaned close to her until their foreheads were almost touching.

"I am not sure... I just am." Her honest reply made him smile.

He took her face between his hands to ensure she would not avoid his gaze, so she would not misunderstand his intention. "Bel, we will do nothing you are uncomfortable doing. I am willing to wait. Just don't make me wait too long. We have wasted enough time."

She took a deep breath and nodded.

"For now, I just want to have you with me, hold you while you sleep, and fall asleep with you. Is that okay?"

Again, she nodded.

"And know this — nothing you can tell me would make me not want to be with you. Not even if you and your family run a criminal enterprise, or have bodies buried in your backyard, or torture kittens and puppies for a hobby. Nothing. Do you understand?" His eyes never wavered from hers. He needed to make her believe he meant it.

Ysobella's inward sob told him he struck so close to the truth. And she would like to believe he meant the words. Tears blurred her vision. Her jaw was taut as she struggled to stop herself from losing control. Her secret must have been such a burden, too monumental for her to tell him.

Galen saw her inner struggle, and it pained him: he could do nothing about it, except pull her close into his embrace, run his hands up and down her back to soothe her as she sobbed on his chest. It was heart wrenching.

The intensity of her distress convinced him she had suffered as much, if not more, when she left him. And in that instant, her tears washed away every transgression she had committed against him when she left. However, the need to know the reason grew, making the urgency more unbearable.

Nevertheless, he endured, continued to hold her until her tears subsided and her body had gone limp. The outpouring of emotion exhausted her, so he scooped her up in his arms, sat down on the couch with her on his lap, and cradled her like a baby. They stayed like that for a long time, contented for the moment.

Galen could feel the thoughts whirling around in Ysobella's head. He did not want her thinking and stressing herself again, so he jostled her a bit to break her train of unhappy thoughts and focus her attention on him.

"Bel, why did you pretend to be somebody else during our first meeting in your office?"

He kept his tone relaxed. He was curious, and he wanted to start with the simple questions first. She tensed for a moment, but to his relief, she relaxed back into his arms.

"It seemed the most natural thing to do when you didn't seem to recognise me. You surprised me," she admitted.

He shifted her from his arms so they were face to face.

"I know I promised not to ask, and I won't. Not tonight, but will you consider telling me why you left me, at least before I die?" He asked in all solemnity. He was not beneath emotional blackmail.

She took a deep breath and nodded.

That would do for now. And for tonight, it was enough that she would be in his bed and in his arms, just as she had always been every night in his dreams.

Ysobella sighed, grateful for the brief reprieve. She could never keep her truth from Galen for long. He would wear her down, and she would weaken because he deserved the truth.

Do I really believe Galen's love for me and Yuana will be enough to keep the family secret safe?

Is it worth the risk?

Do I have it in me to do what I must if my trust in Galen turns out to be a mistake?

6

YSOBELLA'S SECRET

Yuana rubbed her dry eyes. The clock on her wall showed it was five a.m. She had been lying awake since she decided to tell Roald the truth about her. She could not subject Roald to a lifetime of questions in his head and inflict a perpetual wound to his soul if she disappeared like her mother did.

It was excruciating to watch the joy, longing, regret, and guilt in her mother's eyes whenever she gazed at her father, and she felt her pain like it was her own. While her mother survived the aftermath all those years ago because of the family's full support, she did not want to walk that same path.

What she saw in her father's eyes as he regarded her mother was another matter. It echoed the same joy and longing, but there remained the questions and the fear her mother might disappear again. The emptiness in her father's eyes when he talked about those lost years was beyond bearing. It sounded like a bitter and joyless existence.

She would not subject Roald to the same torture. When they part ways, she would want him to move on properly, if not completely, from her, from them. Roald must be able to live a full life afterwards. She did not want him to spend decades pining for her, she would do enough of that for both of them.

In her heart, Roald would do nothing to hurt her and her family. He may even try to adapt to their ways in the beginning, but to be bound by the *Veil* would ask for too much.

The question was when and how to tell him.

The other challenge would be how to make him believe. It would be impossible to accept something he did not think existed. As a technical guy, he would need solid and irrefutable proof. To do that, she would have to reveal more than what they could bear. To reveal more meant the danger would be greater. That proof would be harder to deny and dispute later.

The question of when was the other matter. A few months? Years? Her father's situation with her mother might take time, and Roald would never wait that long. Unless she was mistaken, she was sure her mother would tell her father the truth. To divulge their secret to two potential witnesses, both respected individuals with unimpeachable reputations that could corroborate each other's claims against them would be irresponsible and dangerous.

She would need to discuss this with her mother, and then the entire family.

How will I get private time with Mama when Papa was always by her side?

She needed to strategize. She was due at breakfast with her parents in a few hours. Roald would pick her up soon, so there was little time to get herself ready.

Roald was looking forward to this morning. Yuana's father invited him to join them for breakfast. He thought of declining, as he felt this should be between Yuana and her parents. But then, he could make Galen an ally in his quest to ensure the highest probability for Yuana to say yes when he proposed. Galen had limited time on this earth, and could not afford to waste it. Galen needed to see that he was good for his daughter, that he would be there to protect Yuana in his absence, that he was necessary to Yuana's happiness. So, the more activities they shared, the better it would be for his cause.

He pulled up in the driveway of Yuana's house, and it surprised him to see her already waiting for him by the front door. A frown of impatience written on her face. He did not even have the time to get out of his seat to open the door for her; she went straight to the passenger seat, opened it and slid in. He stopped her hand as she reached back for her seat belt.

She turned to him, inquiry in her eyes. He leaned in and kissed her. "Good morning, Yu," he murmured on her lips.

That took her out of her preoccupation. She kissed him back with a smile on her lips.

"Good morning, Ro." The preoccupation had faded from her face.

"So, what seems to be the hurry this morning?" he asked.

She was pale, but the kiss gave her a flush on her cheeks and plumped up her lips. He soothed her lower lip with his thumb.

"Sorry, I was just excited about this breakfast." Yuana's smile was bright. But tension creased her brow.

"Me too. I want to impress your father. And I hope you will put in a good word for me..." His joke earned him a grin.

They shared a conspiratorial smile like two people working on a secret plan together. A twinge of guilt hit him; he had a hidden agenda. This was an opportunity to advance his cause.

Breakfast was in her father's suite. The smell of hot coffee and croissant welcomed them as they entered. Her father's well-appointed suite had a stunning view of the city and boasted two spacious bedrooms and a wide-open living room that connected the dining and the kitchen. There was a faint scent of lemongrass in the air that reminded her of spas.

The food came in the middle of their first cup. There were Spanish omelettes, lots of hot bread, fresh fruits, and crepes. It was a relaxed affair, like they had been doing this as a family for a long time.

As discussed between her and Roald, she took the lull in the conversation as her cue to take her mother aside for the conversation.

"Mama, Papa said I have a bedroom here, can you show it to me?"

A minute inclination of her head was a signal her mother had no problem interpreting. They had exchanged it for years, a part of their silent language between mother and daughter.

Her dad glanced at her and her mother with a smile, oblivious to the conspiratorial nature of the room tour.

Roald picked up the hint and engaged Galen in a conversation about kali. He shared the same interest in the martial arts as the rest of the De Vidas. Both men watched their women stand up and leave the table to walk towards the second bedroom in the suite.

She followed her mother towards the verandah and closed the door behind them. Her mother seemed to read what was on her mind.

"Mama, I know you are planning to tell Papa." Her mom did not contradict her statement. "How will you do it? What is your plan?"

"I do not know, Yu. But I cannot hide it from him when the time comes. And the time to tell him grows closer every day." Her mother sat down with a heavy sigh.

"Mama, I am thinking of telling Roald," she blurted out. She was beyond thought, she had decided. And the "how" was the reason they were going to have this discussion.

Silence reigned.

They were both aware that they would put their family and their kind in danger by exposing their nature. But the risk of that had become the easier option than parting ways with the men who owned their hearts. They were mother and daughter, destined to go through the same path at the same time.

"Yu, I thought I would reveal it little by little," her mother said after a while. She sounded unconvinced by her own proposition.

"How will you do it, ma? Start by showing him what we eat? What we look like when we are hungry? What we do when we hunt?" She could not keep sarcasm and sadness from her tone. That side of their nature would scare the bravest of men.

"Those are excellent suggestions..." her mother replied, her tone unsure.

"Is it wise to tell them both at the same time?" This bothered her most, but it had to be asked.

Ysobella's head jerked up. Her mother almost said no. To tell her father was dangerous enough, another person knowing would increase the risk. Both Galen and Roald were prominent and credible people. Plausible deniability would become nonexistent when one could corroborate the tale of the other.

"Yuana, it's very dangerous to tell them both... you know that..."

"I know, Mama. It is also easier for everyone if I just do what you have done, what the others in our clan have done for centuries; to just disappear for a few years... but..." Her voice quivered and broke off.

There was sympathy in her mother's gaze. She reached out and smoothed her hair.

"Why would you tell Papa? Are you very sure of him?" She could not help but ask. She wanted to shore up her defences, her reasons on why it was okay to tell Roald this early.

"I want your father to be happy, to take only sweet memories about us with him. But I am sure he will ask for the truth, and he will not rest until he gets it. I'm scared it will traumatise him when he finds out, and I can only cushion the blow, make the pill sweet..." Tears pooled in her mother's eyes. "I trust him, Yu-yu. And he has proven his constancy by finding me after all these years. I am certain he won't harm me or you, that he will keep our secret close to his heart. But that was not the question you wanted to ask, was it?"

Her mother's statement made her heart ache with pride for her father and envy for her mother's unwavering faith in him. But her direct gaze made her flinch inside; she was asking her the same question about Roald.

"I trust Roald, Ma. I do not think he will do anything to hurt me, I also believe he will protect our secret..." She had to defend Roald and their love. She needed her to agree so she could convince herself that a happy ending was possible.

"I do not fault your trust in Roald, Yuana. I agree, we can trust him, he will not hurt you, and can even be relied upon to keep our secret. But telling him, just like telling your father, has a bigger risk to them. Can we risk the damage to their psyche when they find out the truth about us? That the women they love were *viscera-eaters*, that our entire family is?"

The statement hit her with a thud to the chest. That did not even enter her mind, she was so focused on what their laws required if Roald failed. She did not consider the emotional toll it would exact from Roald just for learning the truth.

"What am I going to do, Ma? I want to tell him. I do not know if I can live the rest of my life without him, with just the thoughts of the what-ifs as my companion. Papa's return to our lives made me hopeful and made the option of leaving untenable." Her chest ached now; her throat hurt.

"I understand, Yu-yu." Her mother patted her cheek. "Perhaps we can mitigate the risk? Let me tell your father first, gauge his reaction, and we can decide after that."

It was not a perfect solution, but it was better than nothing.

Without words, they got up to rejoin their men in the dining room where their shared laughter could be heard. The lighthearted mood did not change as they sat with them. Both men, with little thought, draped a protective arm around the shoulders of their ladies.

The two men had come to an understanding and formed a solidarity in a common goal, so they were pleased with themselves. The food was delicious, and company was brilliant. All was right in their world.

Galen watched Ysobella tidy up in the living room while they waited for the housekeeping to come and pick up the remnants of their breakfast. She was deep in thought about something, and it made him uneasy not knowing what it was.

He was still half-convinced she would bolt in the middle of the night and disappear from him again. He reminded himself that this time it would be different because he had met her family. It was not like the first time when his only connection to Bel was Bel. Last time, when she disappeared, there was no way to trace her. He did not know where to start.

Galen decided he would spend the day wooing his Bel, much like what he would have done back in the day. His only goal when he came to the Philippines was to look for her. He didn't have any plans beyond locating her. It was sheer luck he found her a mere week after his arrival. But he was flexible and quick on his feet, so he would improvise.

He gently pulled her away from the task she was doing and enfolded her in a loose embrace. "How would you like to show me Tagaytay today?"

He had heard of the beauty of the scenery, and that it was very romantic. He planned to implant his presence in Bel's every waking and sleeping moment. His Bel had a romantic soul, and a love for nature, so Tagaytay would be perfect.

"I would love to, very much," she replied with a smile, running her fingers along his collar. He remembered she loved volcanoes and had a certain affinity for it. It somewhat represented her, normal, calm and peaceful on the surface, yet it hid explosive secrets underneath. One he was uneasy to find out, but had accepted that he must.

"Then we shall spend the day in Tagaytay, my love." He smiled, pleased that she agreed to his suggestion.

His hands unlocked from behind her and slid up her sleek back. His fingers travelled over her familiar form. He kept his touch light; he did not want to alarm her. His right hand moved upward to cradle her nape as he manoeuvred her for his kiss. The touch of his lips was slow, gentle, and exploring. He wanted her to remember, to appreciate the sensations, and to get used to his kisses again. This was part of his strategy— to keep reminding her so she would never forget, so she craved him again, just as he had never stopped remembering or craving for her all these years.

Hand in hand, they walked out of the room. He kept them palm-to-palm during the drive most of the time. The warmth of her hand in his soothed his soul, reassured his mind, and calmed his heart from the fear of losing her again.

During the drive, he discovered that this compulsion was as vital as a kiss and a hug. He looked back at all the women he had a relationship with, trying to remember if he had ever had this driving need to link his fingers with a woman. He never even wanted to in the past, even avoided doing it because it made him feel uncomfortable.

The revelation astounded him — that the act of holding hands was a more profound expression of intimacy. It was the melding of souls; akin to a surrender; the veritable handing over of his heart into the hands of this woman for her keeping.

He now wanted to make sure he would live longer than was fated for him. Before he found her again, his goal was just to see her before he died, but now, he wanted to live longer for her, for their daughter. The universe owed him this. He would make sure he collected.

It was a scary thought to contemplate the power Bel held over him, a power he gave her himself. And Bel knew it. He could feel it. She would never hurt him on purpose, and that was the operative word—on purpose.

It was clear whatever made her run away the last time would be the only reason that would force her to hurt him again. And only by shining the light on it would the threat be eliminated.

He told her last night nothing could make him stop wanting to be with her, and he meant it. But he started thinking her reason for leaving him must be bigger than any normal social obstacles, criminality including.

He began playing scenarios in his head of what could be worse than being a criminal or being crazy enough to torture small animals. And in each possibility, he asked himself if he could get past it. It was a yes, to all of it.

He was certain about his own heart, but braced himself for whatever horrendous truth it would be. It made him anxious.

With Yuana and Roald gone, she was alone with Galen and the resolve to create a strategy for the revelation. All kinds of possibilities and scenarios played in her head.

Nothing came to mind that seemed to be the right way. Her decision earlier to stop obsessing about how and just allow the situation to take its natural course was proving hard to do. Every time she had a moment to think, she could not help but strategize. And it was close to driving her insane. She could not seem to come up with the correct steps to take, and worse, it made her anxious and tainted her moments with Galen with unnecessary preoccupation.

What Yuana half-joked about earlier had merit. It would not make sense to Galen if she told him point-blank: the De Vidas are aswangs, and there were more of them in the world. He would need proof. Irrefutable evidence that could be most shocking to Galen, and most dangerous to their kind.

But for Galen to live in their world, their lifestyle, he must know everything. He had to see what they are, what they are not, and why they are not the monsters legends made them out to be. Hopefully, since Galen was born and raised in America, he did not grow up with the old lore about her kind. Without that fear, she could use logic to reveal and explain the viscerebus nature.

Now, the critical question would be the how. Maybe if she dropped little clues, it would give her an inkling on how he would behave when handed the big truth.

The car finally arrived in Museo Orlina. Their shared love for arts and museums made this the natural choice. Anticipation flowed in her blood as she got out of the car. The visit was the first for both of them.

For two hours, the various galleries in the museum engrossed them. It featured stunning glass sculptures and various other contemporary art exhibits from local and foreign artists. As they emerged from the lower floor onto the roof deck where the coffee shop was located, a breathtaking view of Taal volcano greeted them.

The mixed scent of fresh lake water, green grass, hot coffee and cakes perfumed the air. Their seat in the corner table closest to the verandah afforded them privacy and the best view on the deck. Galen ordered some coffee, cake, and fruits.

"Do you mind if we have a leisurely merienda here? I would like to savour the moment—the view, the ambience, you..." Galen whispered. His warm breath tickled her palm as he planted a kiss on it.

His gaze glittered with boyish charm and seduction. It made her blush. At her age, she should not blush anymore. Galen, however, looked pleased at the high colour on her cheeks. He reached out and traced the reddening patch with a fingertip.

"No, I don't mind. The weather is pleasant," she said, her voice fading.

Her vain attempt to change the topic and break the heat of the moment made Galen grin. Thankfully, the server arrived with their order, and for a few moments, she busied herself with pouring them coffee and serving Galen some cakes. It gave her some time to gather her composure back.

"So, what is next on our agenda for today? Do you want to drive around, or are you content with just sitting here and enjoying the view until sunset?" She felt compelled to fill the silence with conversation.

"I am happy to sit here for as long as you want, Bel. I am satisfied for now, but not content yet," he said.

His words carried the forewarning of the things to come, of the things he would demand from her. She nodded because she understood.

"I know, Galen. And perhaps the time has come for me to answer your questions. So, I will try to give you as much of the truth as I can. All I ask is for you to be patient with me if I cannot answer all of them now." Her heart hammered against her chest - the door to the truth was now open, and there would be no going back.

"As long as you tell me all, eventually. I can give you time, Bel, if that is what you need."

He reached for her hands. He needed her touch to reassure her and calm his rampaging pulse. A part of him was afraid the truth might be too much to overcome.

She took a deep breath and squared her shoulders, like she was about to face a firing squad. Galen felt her tension and dread from the one question that mattered the most, the crux of everything that embittered their past. And his heart clenched in response.

"Did you know you were pregnant with Yuana when you left me?" He caressed her knuckles, a gentle, reassuring motion.

Her fingers unclenched. It seemed the question was something she could answer.

"Yes, I found out the day I left you... That made me leave you that day." The reply came out of her in a half whisper. The rasp in her voice carried remembered pain.

"But why? I asked you to marry me..."

Ysobella's eyes flashed in panic. She looked away. And he understood. Impatience rose in his gut. He wanted to press her, but his earlier promise stopped him.

"So, it wasn't because you did not want to marry me?" All those years, he thought she bolted because she did not want to commit to him, that her love was not as deep as his.

"No, not that. It was never that... It will never be that." Her eyes held a kind of pleading.

"So, will you marry me if I asked again?" He wanted reassurance it would not be like the last time.

"Yes." Determination flashed in her eyes, her tone almost challenging.

His heart expanded at the sight, but the thorn of that mysterious reason remained. And it was still causing pain.

"So, how long are we going to avoid the real reason you left, Bel? How long do you want me to wait before I can ask the question? And before you can give me the truth?" He could give her time, but he needed a timeline. The wait would be easier to bear if there was a date he could mark off on his calendar.

She lifted his knuckles to her lips. It was a request for one last minor delay. "Tonight, I will tell you. In our suite, the truth requires complete privacy."

It was his turn to kiss her knuckles. "Okay." He would grant her the few hours of reprieve she asked for. "What do you think of Roald?" he asked.

The change of subject made Ysobella smile. It was a mixture of relief and gratitude.

"I like him. He loves our daughter, perhaps as much as you once loved me," she replied.

He shook his head in a slow, emphatic movement. "No, I disagree very much. One, I still love you as much, perhaps more now than before. Two, he cannot possibly love her as much as I love you. I have twenty-eight years of proof in my favour." He was only half-joking.

Ysobella laughed. "Enough of the buttering up, Galen, or I would be too slippery for you to hold." She appeared pleased, flattered, warmed by his words. A blush tinged her cheeks.

"Sorry to disappoint you, Bel, but no amount of butter can do that..." He grinned. He missed the banter between them.

"So, what do you think of Roald?"

"Oh, I like him. As a man, I can appreciate the depth of love he has for our daughter. But as a father, I wish he would go away, at least, until I am ready to relinquish her. I mean, I just found her. He had a three-year advantage over me, so it should be my turn now."

Approval crinkled the corners of her eyes, the curved plump lower lip invited thoughts less amusing.

"Tell Yuana that. I am sure she would want to spend time with you too. I think the only reason she hasn't intruded into our daily activities was that she wanted us to have this time together first."

"Really? She does not feel awkward about me as her father, a stranger she just met who now demands to be part of her life?" He was unable to hide his excitement at this revelation.

"Oh yes. I know our daughter very well... And you were not a stranger to her. I told her all about you, and we kept tabs on what you had been doing all those years."

"You kept tabs on me? Since when? For how long?" The barrage of questions and the rush of emotions the statement generated swirled together like a tornado in his mind. It was impossible to grasp, it made his head spin.

"About a year after I left. I had every intention to keep the break clean, like what the others in my family did in their time, but I could not do it. By chance, I saw your picture in the newspaper, when you were part of the group of surgeons who travelled to the medical mission in Tijuana. I clipped that article, told myself it would be a onetime thing..."

Others in her family? Tijuana? She was there?

He turned away to deal with the rush of fury that surged in him. At her; she knew where he was, that she was in the same city, but still stayed away; at himself for the missed opportunity.

He fought against the flood of recalled memories of that mission. It was a break from the frantic search for her, from the frustration of losing her, from the pain of knowing she left him on purpose. He spent a year searching for her in the US, in every hospital and clinic, and then did the same in the Philippines, but he did not find her. It did not help that she'd given him a false name.

The fury raged in him, but he swallowed it back to force it down. She was still bound by the same reason for leaving, and he could not have known then that she was there.

"You were in Tijuana at the same time?" His voice hoarse, his throat had gone dry.

"I was. And I hung around Tijuana until your medical mission ended, hoping to see more newspaper coverage of your group. But there was only one..." Her quiet sentence made him turn to her once again.

He knew she saw the flash of anger in his eyes, noted the hardening of his jaw as he pushed it away. He knew she understood and would have welcomed it had he expressed it. She deserved it. And perhaps, if he had railed at her, both of them would have felt better.

"Was Yuana with you in Tijuana?" He forced himself to ask, even when knowing the details would hurt.

She nodded, unable to put to words her response.

"Where was she born?" Questions about how Yuana was as a baby hovered in his mind.

"She was born here, Galen. We went to Tijuana that summer because I needed to get away and to be closer to where you were without being in the US."

Her admission was a balm to his wounded heart.

"Tell me about your life, Bel, after you left me. I need to fill in the missing details in my head about your life, about Yuana's, what you did, what kept you busy when you were away from me."

Again, she nodded. She understood the emotions that drove him.

"We lived all over the world. I flew to England the day I left you and settled in a minor city in the northeast. I would not allow myself time to think about you, or I tried my best, at least. Work became my solace until the seventh month of pregnancy. I flew back here to give birth to Yuana and stayed for another six months. Before we settled in Bizkaia, on a whim, we flew to Tijuana. For one quick stop... It was to be my last attempt at letting go. Yuana and I lived in Bizkaia until she turned six.

"We moved to Cape Town after and stayed there for another six years. Then it was Oslo and Melbourne. And finally, Yuana and I came back home four years ago." Her voice was flat as she glossed over the hard details.

Her description of the past twenty-eight years was dispassionate and casual, but he saw through the façade she had erected over her own emotions. The effort she exerted to control herself and how exhausting it had been, was visible in the slight tremor in her voice, the line of pain in her mouth. For now, the itinerary of those years would suffice, the rest could follow. He would get it out of her soon enough.

"I have one more question, Bel, and then we can stop our Q and A if you want to. Is that okay?" he asked. He did not want to stress her more than necessary. The revelations today had already been more than what he expected to get from her.

"Ask away." Her back straightened.

"When did you stop collecting all those articles about me?"

This vanity question was something vital to soothe his aching heart. The knowledge that she kept tabs on him, the thought that she held on, had a powerful effect on him. It was stitching close the wounds of his heart.

Ysobella looked at him, a sad smile on her lips. "I stopped five years ago."

"Why? After all those years, why did you stop?" he pressed.

"You got engaged, Galen, and I thought it was only fair to let you live your new life without the spectre of me hovering at a distance. Selfishly, I also thought it was time for me to let go." Ysobella had lowered her eyes to the table napkin she was twiddling with for the last half hour. She seemed reluctant to voice her admission.

He stilled her fidgeting fingers and trapped them in his hands. He waited until the uncomfortable silence grew. Her gaze caught in his as he held her head between his hands, and pulled her over for his kiss. Repressed emotion was released in the kiss that was slow and lingering. It was incongruent with the violence of the feelings he held inside.

Her sigh blew warmth on his lips as they pulled apart.

"She never stood a chance, Bel. She was smart enough to recognise she would never have my heart, and courageous enough not to settle for anything less than she deserved. So, she called the engagement off after two months."

"Are you still friends with her?" Ysobella's voice was soft, unsure.

It seemed she took pity on the unknown woman who became ensnared in their lives and got her heart broken because of it. She was collateral damage to their tangled love affair.

"Yes. We worked together in the hospital; she heads the Pediatrics department. We formed a strong friendship after the breakup," he replied.

He saw a flash of jealousy in her eyes. Perhaps she was jealous of the days and nights he spent with his former fiancé in her stead; those little quiet moments of shared joys and pains, the exchange of ideas, fears and dreams. Those moments that they both valued and cherished when they were together.

"What did you do with those clippings? Do you still have them?"

He could not let go of the thought she kept him in her heart all those years. Just like he did her, despite his desperate efforts to exorcise her from his soul.

"I kept them in my desk drawer. I will show them to you one of these days, I promise."

Galen wanted to ask more questions, but he had promised her just one more question, and he had asked more than one. He kissed her shoulder and pulled her close. This would suffice for now.

Little by little, he had made her open up to him. Tonight, he would know the real reason why she left, why she chose to suffer away from him. The thought of the looming truth made him fearful and hopeful at the same time.

Again, he asked himself what could be bigger than his love for her and their daughter that would be enough to be a deal-breaker, that would cause him to turn away from them? His mind came up empty. This unknown truth that forced his fierce Bel to give him up was worrying.

The worry intensified into fear.

Ysobella sent a message to her family to inform them she and Galen would not be coming to dinner. Normally, this would not cause much alarm to her family, as this happens occasionally when one of them travels out of the country. Their structure so well organised worldwide, the supply of the sustenance anywhere would not be a problem. Her absence would be a concern because she told them she would reveal the truth to Galen tonight. Her decision was a dangerous one.

For them. For Galen.

It was seven p.m. when they reached their hotel. Galen ordered steak, some salad and wine while she took a bath to calm her nerves. She was as taut as a violin string. She was both hungry and without an appetite.

When she moved to the bedroom to get dressed, she noticed flickering lights in the living room. The room was full of red and white candles. Galen had set up the dining and living room with dozens of huge candles — some waist high. Galen had recreated the setting of that fateful night decades ago. She emerged from the bedroom with her heart hammering.

She looked at him, speechless. He grinned at her reaction.

"I had the concierge source for them while we were in Tagaytay... I remembered you liked candles. Do you still like them?" he asked. The crinkles in his eyes smiled, his deep dimples prominent on his cheeks. It made him look boyish.

"Yes." She picked up the nearest red candle and the scent of cherries wafted to her nostrils. Cherry and cinnamon candles. His action warmed her and made her braver for the task ahead.

"Hmm... you smell deliciously fresh. And sweet." Galen's voice was husky as he nuzzled the side of her neck. He tugged the neckline of the bathrobe aside to give him better access. "Are you hungry?" His question suggested that he wished otherwise as he nibbled at her collarbone.

His suggestive question was tempting, and she even considered that her revelation might be more palatable to Galen if they slept together first. But her truth might be repugnant to him, and it could taint the experience into something nauseating. She did not want to give him an additional source of nightmares.

Her stomach protested at the thought of eating. Perhaps the wine would help bolster her courage and dull the senses.

"Wine first? And let me get dressed." She felt vulnerable in her robe, aware that she was naked underneath.

He walked over to where the wine and the glasses were. She rushed back into the bedroom. Her pulse had picked up. When she walked back to the living room minutes later, Galen was waiting for her by the couch with two wine glasses. He handed one to her as she approached him.

She accepted the glass and swirled the red liquid in it watching streaks of the wine run slowly towards the centre of the glass. She took her time sipping and savouring the vintage as she searched for the best way to start the conversation. Galen watched her go through the ritual as he sipped his own glass.

She took the seat across from him. Galen's eyebrow quirked at her action, but he said nothing.

"Galen, what would you consider a deal-breaker?"

"Funny you asked that. I have been asking myself the same question since I found you. And I cannot think of any. As I told you already, you can be an animal-torturing killer, a psychopath, and I will still choose to be with you." Galen's reply was firm, his gaze direct.

She contemplated her options on how to broach the subject further. An idea came to her.

"What if I told you I was born a man, and that I am a transgender? Would you still feel the same about me?"

Her question jolted Galen upright. His expression was blank for a moment, but she saw alarm, denial, and dismissal flit in split-second succession across his face.

"Bel, I struggle to imagine you being a transgender because of Yuana. Unless you lied, and she is not mine..." His tone was half-joking.

"She is yours. But humour me anyway... Imagine I am a transgender woman and ask yourself if you can accept me, if you can love me as much as you do now," she persisted.

Galen paused for some moments to think about what she asked him to do. The silence dragged, every second, suspenseful. The frown on his face, the flash of his eyes held her transfixed.

She could see his attempt to imagine her being a transgender, but she could not read what he saw in himself as he examined his heart.

"Bel, I cannot see past the love in my heart now. It is hard for me to dig deeper into the what-ifs of this premise because I know you are a woman." His sigh deeply. "Perhaps I would not have fallen in love with you in the first place then because our relationship would not have progressed past friendship. All I know is that I love you and imagining you to be a transgender did not make my love disappear." His voice deepened as his intensity increased.

"Throughout the years, I have gone through every imaginable reason I could come up with on why you left me. I had used those same scenarios to justify my anger at your disappearance, used them to convince that it was good riddance, and yet, here I am, I still searched for you, still wanted you. As far as I know in my heart, nothing you can tell me can change that." Galen's colour was high. His eyes flashed with anger, and maybe, frustration.

She stared at him, indecision and despair fighting for dominance in her mind. The battle infused tension in her jaw and every line of her body. She fought against the desire to cry and break down.

"Just tell me, Bel, trust my love for you. Trust I will not do anything to hurt you with the revelation you will give me today," he pleaded. Galen gripped her fingers tight.

A deep breath for fortification and a last attempt to inject more courage into herself, she nodded. "Okay... Will you promise to keep an open mind, to give me the benefit of the doubt, even if what I tell you seems impossible? For I swear it will be the truth."

"Of course, it is the truth, you would not have left me otherwise," he said bitterly, a grimace on his face.

She inhaled deep and took the mental step across from secrecy to full admission.

"Galen, do you know what *viscerebus* are?"

He shook his head, but a slight recognition crossed his face. The term must have sounded familiar.

"Do you know what *aswangs* are?" He blinked at the term. He recognised it, but he looked perplexed. She added, "I... my entire family... and your daughter... we are *aswangs*."

"*Aswang?* As in the supernatural creatures that eat people?" His eyebrows rose, perplexed.

He stared at Ysobella intently, unable to take in what he just heard. His eyes darted all over her face, searching for signs she was kidding. She seemed sincere in her declaration; it confused him.

Ysobella nodded slowly. Tears pooled in her eyes.

"Yes, Galen, in the olden days, our kind eat people or at least specific organs of people that we need to consume to survive."

Aswang? Abruptly he stood and walked away towards the dining table where he left the wine bottle. He downed the contents of his glass in one gulp, poured himself another, and downed that one, too. His emotions played catch up with his thoughts.

Ysobella's face fell as if her world crashed. There was the pain of rejection and fear in her face. She must have stood up when he did, as she flopped down on the couch as if her knees had gone weak. She fixed her gaze on him, her body tensed with anticipation for his reaction.

Galen could not define what he was feeling, disbelief being forefront. Ysobella would never use such an alibi to justify her disappearance as she knew him very well. He was a man of science, where scientific proof would be a prerequisite before he forms an opinion. That she had to implore for an open mind from him meant she truly believed herself to be an *aswang*. The doctor in him kicked in. His brain began running through similar symptoms and medical information that might explain this.

"All of you? Your entire family?" Galen asked.

He needed a catalogue of behaviours and symptoms before he could make a diagnosis. His rational self demanded it. Science could explain even miracles. Every malady and behavioural anomaly, there would be a corresponding treatment.

"Yes, all of us, including Yuana." Her quiet response sounded like defeat, her sigh, a resignation.

Galen moved from the dining table closer to where she was and sat across from her. Ysobella released a relieved breath.

"Where, how do you get the organs?" He asked, although he dreaded the response.

"We do not kill people if that is what you are asking. No one in my family ever killed anyone. Our kind has not needed to for centuries." Her reply was defensive.

Our kind? She believed that there were more of them outside her family?

Then a thought entered his head. "Your business..., does that have anything to do with your being an aswang?" GJDV dealt with dead bodies. It would be the most logical way to get access to human organs.

"Yes. Through our company, our operation, we harvest the liver, heart and kidney of a deceased human. We only get what we need and only when we need it," she replied. Ysobella fell silent, allowing the information to sink.

"And the family of the deceased never finds out about it..." He understood it, and the simple brilliance of the setup.

"They never do. But we make amends to the family by providing exemplary service, and to society by providing free burial services to people who cannot afford it. It is our way of making restitution," she said, her expression even, like it was all very matter-of-fact.

"How long has your family been *aswangs*?" This could be a congenital malady, or a strange belief system. It may be a form of Clinical Lycanthropy, or Renfield syndrome, or some kind of undiagnosed dysmorphia that ran in her family.

"For as long as my great grandparents can remember, and for generations beyond that."

"Do you know how it happened, how it began?" His medical mind abuzz, he thought of the causes that may have led to this.

"No one knows exactly how it began, but our best guess is mutation. The cause is a specific mitochondrial gene. Our being an aswang is a hereditary trait passed on from mothers to their children," Ysobella replied, a frown on her face.

His reaction baffled her. Then her frown cleared as she realised what he was doing. He was trying to diagnose her.

"It is not a disease or a mental disorder, Galen. I can give you undeniable proof." Her voice rose higher. Her face crumpled with heartbreak at his reaction; tears glistened down her cheeks.

Galen wanted to argue, to reason it away, but he stopped himself as he remembered his promise to have an open mind. For a better diagnosis, it was best to let her speak, and provide all the information that he needed.

"I'm sorry, Bel. The doctor in me kicked in. Please continue..." He leaned forward in his seat, his intention to listen with attentiveness. He wanted her to be comfortable and more open with him.

"What else do you want to know?" she asked. Prudence and frustration coloured her voice.

"You mentioned that heart, liver and kidney are the only human parts you eat. You called it sustenance. Why?" He did not want to offend her, but the key to her ailment seemed centred on those organs.

"We do not know why those organs. For centuries we have tried to find out. We are still trying. Our metabolism is different. We are stronger, faster, and we heal quicker than humans. We also age slower and live longer."

Galen blinked: his mind raced back to the first time he saw her again — her youthful looks. But current plastic surgery techniques could have contributed to it. However, Ysobella seemed certain. The level of her belief in her statement was intriguing.

"Animal organs are very similar to ours, so why humans?" he asked.

"Animal organs can serve as a temporary substitute, but there's a limit to how much we can consume. It makes us sick if we have too much of it. Why human viscera? That is the part we are still trying to find out," she said. "All we know is the effect of human heart, liver and kidney to our body. It energises us. It strengthens us."

"What does it do to you if you do not consume those?" He wanted to know if there were physical effects or if it was just psychological.

"It feels like when a normal human is starving, but worse. We behave like anyone in need of food, one will be desperate for it and will do everything to eat. The difference is that our *vital instinct* takes over, and we cannot help but hunt."

"Hunt? What do you mean? How do you hunt?" He was more than intrigued at the layers of Ysobella's declaration.

"We... shape-shift into an animal, whichever animal suits the environment." Ysobella had averted her eyes. She sounded unsure, unwilling to answer.

"Do you only shape-shift when you're hunting?" This could be the way for her to realise the truth, that this was a psychological problem.

"I can shape-shift when I need it, when I want to. The only time I have no control over it is when I miss my victus past the point of bearing. My *vital hunger* takes over, inducing an *auto-morphosis*, or *reflexive transformation*." Ysobella's head snapped back up, her eyes focused on his face. Her expression cleared and brightened.

"Do you want to see?" Her question came out in a whisper. Her pupils glittered with purpose.

He almost said no. But this was the perfect opportunity to observe how deep her psychosis lie, and maybe this would shake her out of it.

He took a deep breath and nodded. "Alright."

Ysobella stood up and walked towards the centre of the room, unbuttoning her dress at each step. His mind froze as he saw her undressing. His pulse quickened as the silk dress slithered down her legs and pooled around her feet. With her back to him, she unhooked her bra, peeled it off one creamy shoulder, then another. She dropped the item on the coffee table. The tiny clasp on the strap hit the glass top, and the sound reverberated in his head. When she bent down a bit to slip off her underwear, Galen's heartbeat galloped to a degree that each thud was audible and tangible.

Ysobella turned around and faced him. For a moment, his brain refused to move past the reality that he was looking at the naked version of Ysobella. The colours were high on her cheeks, the rosy tint spread down to her neck and shoulders. She looked self-conscious but she did not turn away from his intense perusal.

When the blood reached his brain, he noted Ysobella's toned body, her breasts still firm and high, her butt still tight. Her body had not aged a day since he last saw it this close twenty-eight years ago. When his eyes caught hers and his gaze travelled back to her face, he was even more transfixed by what he saw in them.

There was apprehension, sorrow, determination, and acceptance. Like she feared his reaction but had prepared herself for what was inevitable.

Ysobella swallowed, then turned sideways. He saw a miniscule tremor at the base of her spine, and it travelled up every vertebra to her nape, and back down. A flush of colour started from her sacral region accompanied by a growing heat and it spread all over her body. Her skin vibrated. The colour and texture changed, from flesh tone to a black, glossy sheen. Her long hair retracted into her scalp; the dark brown shade darkened into the same midnight hue. She dropped to her hands and knees; her spine mutated to conform to a four-footed form.

Galen could not believe what was in front of him. Ysobella's naked human form had changed into a black panther. It happened in a flash, but his mind played the details in slow motion. His first internal reaction was to doubt what he saw, but it was undeniable.

The panther sat there, a few feet away, its yellow cat eyes trained on him. Its sleek body seemed poised to pounce. He could not think, much less speak. He just saw his beloved Bel change into an animal; a powerful predator capable of killing him if she wished. If he had not seen it happen, it would be impossible to believe the animal in front of him was a woman. There was nothing to hint of any human form in the cat sitting across from him.

But those yellow eyes drew back his gaze and held it captive. From its depths he recognised her in the uncertainty and the tears that pooled in its feline eyes. And the once unseen hint of his lovely Bel was now visible to him.

"Bel..." It was the only thing he could say, his voice choked.

Upon hearing her pet name on his lips, Ysobella's panther head bowed. Her chest ached with the pressure of the emotions she held back. Her body returned to its human form. Crouched, she dropped into a fetal position to hide her nakedness. She felt exposed in every way. Tears pricked at the back of her eyes, but she squeezed her lids shut against it. She did not know what would happen next. She had laid her reality bare to him. *Would he walk away?* Misery cloaked and chilled her.

She did not hear him approach, but his warm hands cupped her shoulders and lifted her until she sat on the floor with him. His arms enveloped her, rocked her. Tears of relief, uncertainty and grief burst out of her like a dam. The burden of the decades of separation resurfaced in waves, battering her.

He wiped her tears, hushing her. He murmured everything would be all right. And his words made her cry even more. As he seemed to realise, he could not stem her tears. He cradled her head into the nook between his shoulder and jaw, his warm hands rubbed soothing circles on her back.

"Bel, please do not cry... It is breaking my heart... please..." His plea vibrated in his chest; his voice pained.

Her sobs subsided after a while. She found hope because she was in his arms. His voice was soothing as he reassured her over and over that everything would be all right. Her tears had stopped flowing a while ago, but she did not want to leave his arms. If he was going to walk away after this, she wanted to prolong the moment. This could be the last time he would hold her like this. This was the core of the matter for her, not just his acceptance, but if he would stay after what he discovered.

She felt wrung out like a mop, deflated and limp. She lifted her head from his shoulder, and he pushed away from her to look into her face. He wiped the tears from her cheeks; her lashes damp.

"Are you all right?" he asked. Concern was thick in his voice.

She replied with a single nod. She had no more energy to talk, and it was now in his hands to continue the conversation. He seemed at a loss. Galen stood up and held out his hand to help her up. She had forgotten she was naked until icy air hit her and goosebumps rippled down her body. She shivered. He bent down and picked up her dress and handed it to her.

With a sigh, she pulled her dress up to cover herself. Her body ice-cold to the core, a normal aftermath of every shape-shifting back into her human form. It would take a few minutes for her body temperature to return to normal.

Once dressed, Galen led her back to the sofa where her wine glass sat unfinished. He picked it up and handed it to her. She followed his silent instruction and downed the contents of the glass. Galen had moved to the bar and poured himself a cognac. He took a sip as if he needed the exercise to collect his thoughts.

The emotional release depleted her; she could not move or say anything. She sat huddled in the corner; the armrest cushioned her back. She waited for Galen to speak. The decision was his to make.

"Why a panther? It doesn't seem to be what the environment called for."

The question was not what she expected; it gave her pause.

"I am partial to big cats. And I have shape-shifted into a panther more times than any other feline form." She realised Galen was delving into the issue with a light hand.

"When and why did you ever need to shape-shift?"

"Sometimes as a self-defence, or when I am in an area where being an animal would be better, or if I want to experience a place in a different viewpoint," she said.

He took her response in silence but had to gulp his cognac down. Her transformation had alarmed him. And she could understand that. It had shaken his perception of reality.

Galen stood up and poured more cognac in his glass, his movement abrupt. Some liquid sloshed out and spilled on his fingers. He downed the contents and poured himself another measure. Galen walked back and sat beside her. His body language communicated impatience... and repressed fury.

"Bel, why did you leave me? I need to know why you didn't just tell me about you being an *aswang*. Did you think I would reject you if I found out?" His voice was raw, pained, and furious.

She was taken aback. This was what Galen needed to hear more than anything else.

"It is not a simple answer, Galen. Part of it was the uncertainty of your acceptance. Another was the fear the truth would scar you for life. We all have heard the scary stories about aswangs. Imagine if you find out it was true, and the woman you fell in love with was one. It would be traumatic. I didn't want you hurt that way." Her explanation was insufficient even to her own ears.

Galen's jaw tightened; his eyes flashed with anger.

"I got hurt anyway, Bel. And the experience traumatised me when you left me without a word. So, I cannot say which choice would have been less destructive to my psyche."

The bitterness in his response struck at her heart. The anger spoke of the never-ending longing he felt for her during those years they were apart, his efforts to tamp it down, and his failure to do so.

"I got hurt too, Galen. Perhaps as much, if not more, than you. You had the benefit of anger to cushion the blows, I didn't. I had guilt. It was my constant companion all those years. But I had to break up with you because to tell you would be to endanger my family and our kind. Our laws were all rooted on keeping our existence hidden." She needed for him to understand that her choice was difficult.

"Why did you just disappear like that? I spent the first months in frantic search of you, all the while driven mad by thoughts that something horrific happened to you."

The dark frown and gruffness contained all the remembered pain, the sleepless nights, and the torture that he went through. Each syllable abraded her already-injured heart. Her mind supplied the image of his suffering. Her mangled heart continued to pump in pain.

"I did not have the strength to face you and break up with you. I didn't think you would have let me go. And I would not have been able to resist you and walk away." Her throat constricted, her voice a mere whisper.

"You are right. I would not have let you go..." Galen agreed.

He had straightened up, his back rigid. He was the same determined, unrelenting Galen that she knew. The old Galen would have put up a fight, and it seemed he had not changed.

"Galen, now that you know what I am, what is next for us?" It was hard to ask him directly, but the wait was unbearable.

"Ysobella, have you not learned anything from all this? I found you after twenty-eight years after you walked out on me without a word. You are the only thing in my bucket list, my last dying wish, and you still doubt me?" His irritation was palpable in the sharp response.

The vehemence in his statement stunned her; it kept her mouth shut. But her heart expanded to bursting, and tears of gladness pooled beneath her lids. She wanted to smile, but emotions squeezed at her heart that made it impossible to do so.

Her expression must have penetrated the cloud of fury surrounding Galen, as the irritation that darkened his face vanished. He yanked her close, cupped her head between his hands, and kissed her with a fierceness that almost hurt. She tasted all his frustration. Her tremulous sigh of relief gentled his mouth, and the kiss turned slow, deep, exploring. He imparted all the vows and promises in his soul, in the pressure of his lips on hers, the way he angled her face to deepen the kiss. He ate at her mouth like a starving man. It had been too long for both of them. And this was the first time there were no more barriers between them.

The ringing of the phone was jarring, ending the kiss before they were ready. Galen cursed out loud, and a shaky laugh escaped her. Galen seldom used colourful terms.

It was the room service, calling to ask if they were ready for their food. Galen glanced at her, as he mouthed *food*.

She nodded briskly. "Yes, please... I'm starving."

Galen sighed and confirmed with the staff on the other side of the line.

She was so happy and light she could float on air. Everything inside her unlocked and all her senses awakened to life. Her smile as she looked at him must have been radiant, for Galen answered with a beaming one. Now, they found all the missing pieces of their soul, his and hers. They were, at long last, one and whole.

There would be adjustments for both of them. Most of it from Galen's side, but the confidence he exuded strengthened hers. Galen was aware of the challenges, but the foundation of their love was strong, so they would prevail. Of that he seemed certain.

And his certainty powered hers.

Iztari Pereiz and his team tracked their target into a remote village, nestled between a river and a mountain. Based on the report, the target was one of their kind who still hunted humans. The *harravir* had taken a child from his bed in the middle of the night. The villagers found the body of the boy in the woods, a kilometre from his home, missing a liver, kidneys, and a heart. They had deduced by the amount of human viscera taken from the body; they were dealing with more than one harravir. Or one who hunted for a family or a small clan.

They scoured the area in stealth and travelled upwind to avoid detection. One of his team members picked up the scent of the target and radioed it to his team members. The team then converged at the site.

And in the cover of darkness, they waited. They saw a man emerge from a clearing; his scent confirmed to them he was an aswang. He had not changed into his hunting form yet, so they followed him, making sure they kept themselves hidden.

After a half an hour of tracking, they followed him into the next village and watched him transform into an enormous dog, as he prowled the edge of the cluster of houses. Their target checked for homes with any open doors, or any humans out and about. It was already seven in the evening, and most people in this remote part would already be indoors as soon as the sun set.

Then, from the other end of the village, two drunk men came tottering into their view.

The big dog kept to the shadows as it crept closer to the men and prepared to pounce. The two drunk guys paused in their tracks, one of them turned to the bushes to throw up.

They assumed their target would grab the one who was throwing up as he was in a more vulnerable position, but their target went for his companion. They all sprang into action, net in hand, to stop the attack. The victim gave a long shriek as the big dog clamped its jaws into his neck. The impact of the attack knocked him down like a log. Two of Iztari Pereiz's teammates threw the net into the dog, while Iztari Pereiz pried his jaw open and loose from the victim's neck.

Captured, the dog thrashed against the net that was holding him down. The victim was barely alive. Blood spurted from the bite on his neck. Iztari Pereiz spit on a white cloth that he pulled from his backpack, then pressed it down into the neck of the victim. He wanted to stem the flow of blood and his viscerebus saliva would help.

His barfing companion was still spewing his guts nearby, unaware of the attack.

The victim's shriek and the noise of the thrashing dog attracted the residents of the nearby houses. One by one, gas lamps flickered on, providing illumination to the three Iztaris. Iztari Pereiz sighed. They would have preferred a quieter operation.

Soon, the village leader, an old gentleman, came out of his home and approached them to ask what was happening. Their prepared speech mollified the entire village since the incident was very easy to explain away—that someone had reported a rabid dog loose in the area, and the government deployed them to catch it to protect the villagers. Their target was smart enough to keep his hunting form. It would have been a monumental problem if he panicked and transfigured back into his human form.

Amidst the barrage of thank you's, there was also a volley of aghast comments about how scary the situation was, how fearsome the big dog was, and how lucky that they were there and saved the life of the village brew master. The Iztaris took the 'rabid' dog, who had turned docile now, away from the village.

The target knew he had been caught by aswangs. He could tell by their scent, but he did not quite know who they were, why they were wearing military garb, and what would become of him.

Meanwhile, the brew master's barfing companion fell asleep by the roadside, unaware of what happened. He would not find out till morning.

7

A TASTE OF THE ASWANG LIFE

Morning dawned early for Yuana. Her mother sent her a text message the night before to inform her breakfast this morning would be for her and her parents. Their discussion would be about Roald and her decision to reveal herself to him. Her father took her mother's revelation very well, and she was optimistic about her chances, but the request to exclude Roald did not bode well.

She had informed Roald today would be a family day for her, and she would miss their lunch together. Roald understood, but still insisted on picking her up and dropping her off at her father's hotel since he would not see her the entire day.

Dinner would be at the De Vida's home. The family had been told about her father's reaction to their secret. There were still some concerns, but they were optimistic and would give her father a chance. They trusted her mother's judgement and supported her in this decision, but they all know there were safeguards in place.

Just in case.

And what would come after when the just-in-case scenario happened was a greater concern for her mother, and for her. No Viscerebus would ever wish it on their worst enemy.

Yuana's usual bright and sunny disposition were missing that morning. She seemed preoccupied, and in a hurry. Her kiss goodbye to her grandparents was a quick peck on the cheeks and a distracted wave. She gave him just enough time to greet her grandparents good morning before she tugged his hand toward the car.

Roald pulled the car over to the side as he exited the gate of Yuana's house and turned towards her. He did not like that something bothered her.

"Good morning, Yuana." He leaned over and kissed her on the cheek. "Tell me what is wrong and why you look so pensive again today."

Yuana looked startled, leaned over and kissed him briefly on the lips and murmured, "Good morning, Ro." The smile that followed was dazzling.

That confused him. *Did I imagine her earlier mood?*

She moved back toward her seat, but he prevented her by holding her in place. His right hand rested at the back of her head as he continued to kiss her softly, savouring her. Her cinnamon-flavoured lip gloss plumped up her lips and tempted him to nibble on the luscious flesh. He indulged for a few moments before he let her go.

Satisfied, Roald turned the machine back on and resumed their trip to Galen's hotel. That kiss was a splendid way to start the day, and he made a mental note to make it a habit from now on. Then he remembered he was giving up his lunch hour today with her, so that would entitle him to another kiss later.

In his opinion, it was a fair trade.

Her parents both looked at peace. Her mother beamed at her from a distance, her father's pupils twinkled with joy and mischief. The truth freed her mother from the burden she carried for decades. And she was happy for them and filled with hope for her own future.

Will I have the same luck with Roald?

Her father walked toward her with his arms outstretched. He pulled her close when he reached her, and hugged her so tight that it lifted her off her feet. He swung her around twice, his delight infectious. She was laughing like a child when he put her down.

"Good morning, my sweet," he said, his voice a deep rumble in his chest. "How is the fruit of my loins doing this morning?"

She gave him a mock grimace, "Fruit of your loins? Really, Papa, did finding out the truth about us traumatise your vocabulary?"

Her father threw his head back and laughed. "Ah, you are indeed your mother's daughter. You inherited her quick wit." Her father chuckled.

He seated her down on his left, her mother already seated to his right. He behaved like the head of their family, whose heart was full, and soul at peace, unbothered by the spectre of any future difficulties.

Over a basket of hot croissants, freshly made omelettes, and cups of coffee, they opened the conversation about her situation with Roald. Her mother set her cup down, reached over and covered her hand resting on the table. It was time to discuss her revelation strategy.

"So, Yu-yu, what is your plan?" her mother asked without preamble.

Her father turned toward her. She guessed her mother had briefed him about it. And now he would be in on their secret and the reason for it. He looked as apprehensive as her mother with the idea of an exposure to another non-aswang.

"Yuana, putting your lives in jeopardy does not sit well with me..." Her father's frown was more than emphatic.

"I trust him like Mama trusted you, Papa..."

Her father grimaced. "Touché."

"How will you tell Roald?" Her mother's asked gently.

She had not planned for the *hows* yet. She was more anxious about whether it was possible. Her father's reaction was a very good indicator.

"I have no idea, Ma. How did you tell Papa? Perhaps I can do the same?"

"Ah no! Definitely not." Her father's vehement reaction surprised her. Her mother threw him a tilted glance, an elegant eyebrow arched inquiringly.

"It's not the... right strategy..." Her father's vague and flustered response was confusing. "There has got to be other ways to reveal herself... to that boy... I will not permit it." A tone of paternal protectiveness was thick in his voice.

She had no clue what her father was talking about. She and her mother watched a gamut of emotions race across her father's face, from alarm to defensiveness and back. Then her mother burst into laughter. Galen threw her an annoyed glance.

What the hell was going on?

Her mother dabbed at the tears of mirth from her cheeks. "Your father would rather you... reveal yourself in another way, my dear. He's being a protective dad," she said, patting the corner of her lids with a napkin. "He finds my way... too revealing..."

"Oh!" And that made her chuckle. It was a unique experience to be self-conscious about nakedness. But her father was human, and he was not used to it.

"How long have you known this guy, my sweet?" Galen interjected, slight annoyance for being the object of jest between mother and daughter was still in his voice. He wanted them to focus on the subject at hand.

"Three years, papa." She was glad to be discussing this with him, glad to get a human viewpoint from someone in love with an aswang.

"How well do you know him? How much do you trust him?"

Her father's concern was understandable since he had just met Roald.

"Well enough, Papa. As I told you earlier, I trust him. But we are talking earth-shattering revelations here..."

Galen nodded in understanding. "I think he is an upstanding fellow, actually. I like him."

His father's words warmed her. She wanted his support, his honest assessment of Roald's character. She would have a blind spot for Roald because her feelings were engaged.

He and Roald were on the same boat, and if Roald accepted what she was, both of them would go through the same challenges.

"Pa, how did you feel when you found out about us?" she asked.

"It shocked me. I could not believe it. Not because I thought your mother was lying, but my logical brain refused to accept at face value what she told me. I was busy diagnosing her symptoms, because I wanted to find a medical explanation on why she was certain she was an aswang. It comes from being a man of science, a doctor..." His shrug was apologetic. "But never did I consider leaving your mother or you, regardless of what the truth was. Even when I was so convinced it was a psychological problem, my primary motivation was to find the treatment for your mother."

"So, when you saw with your own eyes definitive proof, what was in your heart?" If she could peek through her father's soul, she would. She was desperate for validation.

"Apart from the initial shock of seeing your mother transform her beautiful self into a panther, it was just a matter of convincing myself that what I saw was real. My feelings didn't come into it because I already knew nothing changed in how I feel about her." His response came out slow and contemplative, as if he was reliving the moment, and what he went through.

Yuana's heart lurched and expanded with hope, with a fervent prayer that Roald's feelings and reaction would be like that of her father.

"What do you think, Galen? What you have observed of Roald, is it safe to tell him?" Ysobella asked. Her mother echoed the same question in her mind.

"I do not know enough about him to form a firm opinion, Bel. But to his credit, our daughter trusts him, and I am convinced he loves Yuana very much. It is my love for you that will ensure I will do nothing to harm you, our daughter, and your family. It might be the same motivation for him." Her father's words were thoughtful.

"You think he will take it well, Pa?" She had to ask. She needed every assurance she could get.

"My sweet, he might just take it well. And maybe... he and I can adapt to your way of life together..."

His eyebrows rose high, as if his own suggestion surprised him. And it had merit. He and Roald could go through the experience together. It could make the process easier for both of them. It might even be fun.

Immense gratitude for her father bloomed in her chest, tears pooled in her eyes. She hugged her father tight on impulse. Behind him, her mother's smile was wide, as if she thought the idea was marvelous and would solve many problems.

It also improved the odds of success for Roald. The danger of having two reputable men corroborating each other's claim no longer existed by her father's vow to keep the secret safe. And she knew he would keep the *Veil*.

The hug surprised Galen, but he returned it by instinct. He was glad he could do this for his daughter and it made him less guilty for not having been in her life before this. No matter how much he told himself no one would blame him since he was not aware she existed until four days ago, he still felt pained about his absence in her life.

"Okay, it is settled then. You will tell him. How?" he asked after Yuana moved from his embrace.

He still did not like the strategy Ysobella used when she told him. He did not even want to entertain the thought. This was his daughter they were talking about.

"Perhaps we can tell him together..." Yuana said.

It was obvious to him she was going to cajole them to help her. Having her mom to back up her revelation, and her dad to reassure Roald it was okay to be in love with an aswang might help matters a lot. And it might be enough, and there would not be a need for any disrobing and transformation.

"Yes. We can do that. When do you want to do this?" Ysobella asked.

"How about tomorrow, at dinnertime?"

"Perhaps you should tell him during the day, my sweet... With us, not with the family. I am sure he has heard stories about aswangs growing up. It might intimidate him to be surrounded by all of you, especially if you all transformed into predatory animals..." A small shiver ran up his spine at the thought.

"You have a point there, Papa. Okay, I will tell him we will have lunch tomorrow with you and Mama. Shall we do it here?" Yuana's voice had perked up with relief now that they had made a plan.

"Yes, it would be best. We have more privacy here. What are his favourite dishes? We might as well feed him properly."

"You make it sound like he is on death row, Pa." Yuana grimaced and pouted.

"Well, in a manner of speaking, it is the end of something in his life. Plus, some say that one is much more likely to accept an immense shock when one's stomach is full," he added.

"Who said that?" Ysobella asked, laughing.

"I did. Just now."

They ditched the plan to do a city tour of Metro Manila in favour of a long and leisurely discussion about being an aswang and the De Vida way of life. Galen seemed eager to know as much as he could. He processed every tidbit of information like a true man of science.

"So, Grupo Jardin De Vida is an international conglomerate..." There was amazement in Galen's voice as he took in the information about how the viscerebus thrived in the world where they remained the minority.

Ysobella nodded. "We have investments in other funeral homes and memorial gardens worldwide, just as some of our partners who operate a similar setup in their country are investors in GJDV. We share resources with our kind when they are here, the same way they share theirs when we are abroad. But in some operations, instead of investments, we have partnerships." Pride for their company blossomed in her.

"It is amazing how your kind banded together and adapted current technologies. It seemed so seamless. I can imagine how your kind could live anywhere in the world and keep your existence a secret..."

Galen's low whistle made her grin. Yuana was smiling as well. Her daughter must wonder if Roald would think the same of their kind's achievement.

"It started about five hundred years ago, and we learned through experience how to perfect the system. Our Tribunal's goal was to ensure that we could continue to live and thrive with the humans. Your fear of our kind was well-founded, but it no longer exists. Not in the past two hundred years, and yet that fear remained a powerful driver of violence towards our kind."

Galen's analytical mind needed answers, and she was more than willing to provide it to him. If he would adapt and take to their way of life, then it would be best to equip him with the right information.

"Your *Tribunal*, it sounds like most governments, or an organised religion," Galen mused.

"That is an apt description. Like any innovation, it was borne out of necessity. In our ancient past, it was a violent existence for us aswangs. While we prey on humans for survival, they hunted us to defend their own. And we also had to deal with the predation from *our* own kind."

"Your own kind? What do you mean? *Aswangs* eat other *aswangs*?"

Galen's surprise was not new to her. The humans always assumed that they were the only nemesis of the *Viscerebi.*

"Yes, papa. It is not so different from humans killing other humans. We refer to aswangs that hunt humans as *harravir*. Here in the Philippines, the local name is *tiktik*. The aswangs that hunt our kind, we call them *harravis*, or as it is known here as *wakwak*," Yuana interjected.

"So, you had to battle hunters from two fronts..." Galen paused as he contemplated that. His eyes darted between her and Yuana.

"Yes, our kind had to. The constant hunting from humans and our own kind decimated our numbers, so our ancestors formed the *Supreme Tribunal* with the sole purpose of ensuring our survival," she said. The system was much more nuanced and complicated to explain in one conversation.

"How does the Tribunal work?"

"It's simple enough. Each *Gentem,* or a country, has a local *Tribunal* composed of twenty-four to thirty-six individuals, headed by a pair of leaders, called a *Matriarch* and a *Patriarch*. They implement the Supreme Laws in their country and make sure that the system works. They are also the representatives to the *Supreme Tribunal*, which is a gathering of all the Local Tribunal heads. The supreme law is centred on keeping the *Veil of Secrecy* intact at all times. The system takes all the aswangs into the fold and takes care of them. This was the only way to make sure we remain a secret. The established enterprises all over the world, like GJDV, ensure we have the resources to do so."

Galen nodded, a focused expression on his face as he thought about what she said. He frowned as a concern surfaced in his mind.

"So, is it part of your rule not to marry humans?"

"There is no rule against us marrying humans, as we need to procreate. Only the women can pass on the genes of an aswang, so the Tribunal encourages that. What the law forbids is the revelation of our existence. Common practice dictates that if we fall pregnant from a union with a human, that we leave the man behind..."

A heavy silence ruled for a moment.

"Bel, you broke the law when you told me..." Galen had begun to understand. "Is there a consequence to this?" His frown deepened.

"If you keep our secret safe, the *Restoration Plan* will not kick in. We have seven days to rectify the leak. If the *Rectification* fails, then it becomes the responsibility of the transgressor to bring the Restoration Plan forward." Dread for the remaining possibility dropped like a lead weight to her stomach. The vigilance over Galen, and soon over Roald, would be lifelong. Both men would never find out.

Galen's eyes narrowed in concentration. She could feel the question forming in his brain, and she wished he would not ask.

"What is the *Restoration Plan*?"

"The transgressor... me... would have to restore the *Veil of Secrecy*. And the most expedient way would be death..." she breathed, "I would have to kill you, Galen."

Galen gasped; his eyes widened. They both stared at him, watched as the full comprehension of the enormity of the risk and the supreme trust they gave him dawned on him. He swallowed as emotion overwhelmed him. He pulled them both into his arms, his breath laboured.

"Do not worry, Bel, I will never put you through that. I swear to you. And if, by mistake, it happened, you would not need to do the act, I will spare you that," he said in a fierce promise, sealed by a kiss on both their foreheads.

Tonight, he would face the family at dinner. Galen understood that this would be a test for her family to see if he could handle the fundamental instinct of a viscerebus. His reaction would determine if her family would trust him to keep the *Veil* intact.

She wished her heart was as confident that he would prevail, but her anxiety persisted.

Margaita sat in her favourite thinking chair with a glass of red wine in hand. Her forehead knitted in contemplation when Lorenzo walked into the room. For a few moments, he observed his wife worry over their granddaughter and great granddaughter. Being Punong Ina, the matriarch made the matter of the revelation so much more complicated because it was rife with political consequences and repercussion.

But as a De Vida, family would always be a priority. There was no question about their acceptance of Galen in their midst as they judge his trustworthiness. In the meantime, for Ysobella and Yuana, they would welcome Galen with warmth. He might well be the first *non-Erdia* human taken into their fold. Perhaps, if this worked, it would set the precedent.

At the sound of Galen's car, his wife stood and joined him. They waited for Galen, Ysobella and Yuana to come in. They entered all three abreast. The joy in the faces of their granddaughter's family lightened the tension-filled mood in the house.

A short time later, Katelin and Edrigu came down to join in the gathering. His son-in-law, Edrigu was more restrained, as he observed Galen's interaction with the family. His daughter, Katelin, was more open and relaxed as she conversed with the man her daughter had chosen and risked the *Veil* for. Katelin had the most optimistic mind-frame in the family.

Ysobella stood and watched while her parents engaged Galen in a probing conversation. There was a line of stress in his granddaughter's smile. The stress of the evening weakened her earlier joy.

"How are you doing, Bella?" he murmured to her as he handed her a glass of Barbaresco.

Ysobella glanced up at him and took the glass with a grateful smile. "Thanks, 'Elo..."

"You look worried..."

She took a sip before she replied with a tiny nod, "A little bit... Is Aunt Ximena here yet?" There was a slight tremor in her hand.

"Ah, you missed sustenance last night... Don't worry, she should be here soon. And she's going to bring liver..." He patted her hand in reassurance.

Ysobella grinned. "We could have testicles tonight and I would not notice it."

"Fortunately, human testicles do nothing for us." He grimaced. "The idea alone makes me want to give up being a Vis."

Ysobella's chuckle was worth the mild discomfort.

True to form, Ximena's car pulled up at the exact time. They all turned towards the front door as Ximena entered with the familiar icebox that carried the victus, a human liver they would have for tonight. Nita rushed towards her and took the icebox to the kitchen.

Ximena joined them, accepting a glass of wine from Edrigu. A quick buss on the cheek of her mother and all the women in the room, a brief exchange with Galen, then she flopped herself on the sofa, and kicked off her high-heeled shoes, unconcerned about etiquette.

His first born looked tired.

"Long day, *Cara*?"

"Yes, Pa. I just came back from Havensville Antipolo to see how the three families we brought in from Talim Island were faring. The entire clan needs comprehensive training and indoctrination. They were so deep in the old ways. They were desperate and dangerous." Ximena's explanation, while addressed to everyone, her eyes were on Galen. She was testing the man.

Galen stayed silent.

"Havensville is one of the housing communities we put up for our kind, Galen. We provide them with homes, education, and employment. We also provide them their sustenance, so they do not have to resort to hunting humans," Katelin interjected.

Katelin saw the question in Galen's expression and his hesitation to ask, so she volunteered the information. It was predictable of her. His second daughter was the peacemaker of the family.

"You moved them from Talim Island... so how were they living before you brought them in?" Galen's question was of pure curiosity. He seemed keen to understand rather than pass judgement.

"They were hunting humans. This family had been moving all over Rizal and Quezon province for decades, trying to survive. This was why it took us this long to track them. They don't know about the *Tribunal* and what we do, so we brought them in." Katelin's gentle and matter-of-fact explanation was the perfect tenor to adapt.

"Were they glad about this... move?" Galen asked.

"This family was, as they were almost decimated. They used to number up to thirty, but they are down to eight now. The years of hunting by the venandis took a toll on them," Edrigu said. He had taken out the hand that was in his pocket earlier. A sign that his son-in-law had relaxed.

"*Venandis*?" Galen's eyebrow rose and glanced at Ysobella.

Edrigu nodded and replied, "Venandis are humans that hunt our kind."

"Oh, that makes sense. The humans will organise to fight back," Galen said, looking proud. "So, what do we call those that hunt the *harravis*?"

Edrigu's smile deepened. Galen's unconscious use of the pronoun "we" revealed his intention and determination to be part of their family. And that reassured every single De Vida in the room.

"That would be the *iztaris*. They are our kind's version of special forces. Our primary mandate is to implement the laws that keep the *Veil of Secrecy* intact. That includes stopping harravirs, rehabilitating them, and eliminating harravises." Edrigu's response was simplified. A wise move, as they still needed caution at this point.

"Papa is the *Chief Iztari* in the country," Ysobella added.

"Chief? How many iztaris are there?"

"There are about thirty to fifty in every city, depending on the size of the territory," Edrigu replied, taking a sip of his wine.

Nita's entry into the living room interrupted their conversation. She carried a wooden tray with a beautiful cloche made of darkened glass. They all turned towards her. The slow steps she took seemed prolonged. The item inside the cloche became the focus.

This was a genuine test of Galen's resolve.

Without being told, Galen seemed to know what it contained. His posture straightened, as if he was bracing himself for a blow.

Nita placed the tray down on the tall cocktail table that was set up in the room for the evening. There was a brief pause that felt like hours, everybody's eyes on Galen. Margaita broke the tension by lifting the cloche and revealed fresh, human liver on a wooden platter. Beside it was a sharp carving knife and fork, and several dessert forks. She handed the cloche to Nita, then took the knife and fork and started carving half-inch slices of the raw liver, blood pouring out of the cut, coating the knife bright red.

Galen was transfixed. The scent of raw flesh and fresh blood did not faze him. His profession prepared him well for this experience. But he was unsure how he would feel when they ate the viscera, so he steeled himself. He did not want to show any adverse reaction; he did not want to offend. This was the test, not the revelation Ysobella made yesterday.

His stomach quivered when Margaita placed the carving knife and fork down on the side of the tray. Seven bloody liver slices lay in its center. Margaita then took one of the dessert forks and speared one slice and brought it into her mouth. She tipped her head back and slid the slice onto her tongue. Galen's stomach clenched tighter as he saw the raw liver disappear into her throat. There was no mess, not a drop of blood on her lips.

Lorenzo followed suit. Then one by one, they took their turn swallowing the liver slice in the same manner. Katelin patted the corner of her lip with a napkin to remove a blood drop. Galen's stomach knotted at each swallow. Bile rose into his throat as he struggled to control his gag reflex. It nauseated him. Cold sweat dampened his brow and trickled down his back. Mercifully, not one of them made eye contact with him.

Except Ysobella.

He knew she could see how he was trying to stop himself from throwing up; and noted the sweat that glistened on his top lip, his cheeks and brow, his white knuckles that held his glass in a death grip. She had not taken her liver slice yet. He knew she wanted to see how he would react to seeing them eat it. Misery lined the stoic facade she displayed. Her distress deepened as his skin turned grey in gradual degrees throughout the whole thing.

When Yuana stepped close to the tray to get her slice and moments later slid it down her throat, he could not hold it. He muttered a quick, "Excuse me," and rushed to the powder room without waiting for a reply from anyone. He closed the door and retched until his throat was raw and he could taste his own bile.

Ysobella watched in helpless anguish as Galen rushed from the room. She could feel everyone's stare — the sympathy, understanding, support, and it made her want to howl in pain. She could not subject Galen to this every time she and Yuana needed to sustain themselves. Tonight, she would not partake to spare him.

Uncomfortable silenced reigned in the room as they tried to ignore the sounds of Galen dry heaving in the nearby comfort room. Every wretched sound was a stab to her heart. Her stomach churned in reaction. By the end, she was swallowing hard to fight off her own nausea.

The powder room door opened, and Galen emerged. His face was pale and damp from splashing water on his face. He looked sheepish and apologetic as he patted himself dry with a handkerchief.

His gaze fell on her. And she could not mask the anguish on her face. Galen's expression changed to dismay. The tears she tried to hold back spilled down her cheeks. Galen rushed to her and pulled her into his arms.

"Shh... Why are you crying, Bel?" He wiped her tears with his thumbs.

She took a deep breath to stem the flow of tears and smiled at him. "I am okay, just being dramatic." She pulled out of his arms, conscious of the spectacle they made in front of the family. She motioned for Nita to take away the wooden tray where her liver slice lay untouched.

Galen stopped Nita as she was about to pass him by, his questioning frown upon her. "Are you not having your sustenance?" He tipped her chin up to peer into her eyes. She shook her head.

"It's okay. I don't have to." She turned away.

"Hey... Bel, it's okay. Go have your slice," he insisted when she hesitated. "I want you to take your sustenance."

"I do not want you to..."

"It's okay, go take it... I promise I won't look." His teasing was true. She knew he would prefer not to see the act.

Ysobella gave him a slight smile, her heart grateful. "Yes, close your eyes."

Her efforts to tease him back were weak. She passed her fingers over his lids, and he closed them. She turned her back to him, and with quick movement, speared the liver slice and swallowed it.

The whole De Vida clan watched the scene unfold and saw Galen display the depth of his love for Yuana and Ysobella, his determination to belong, his willingness to do whatever it would take to adapt. The tension that gripped all of them for days now eased and faded. Galen was on his way to making history in the De Vida clan.

Ximena's heart squeezed hard; her throat tightened. Her niece was lucky with the man of her choice. Unlike her. Galen had the fortitude. Unlike *Martin*.

"So, are we all ready for dinner? I am starving, I could eat a human," Katelin quipped.

At Galen's startled expression, everybody laughed. Including Galen.

Later that night, while they were preparing for bed, Galen remarked to Ysobella, "I guess it is safe to say the old myth that declared garlic and salt can kill aswangs is not true... The garlic mushrooms served earlier were superb."

Ysobella laughed.

"Yes, that was a pure but useful myth. Some of our kind in Aklan encouraged the belief in the human communities. It helped identify the villages who had vigilant venandis among them. The copious amounts of garlic bunches that hung on windowsills and doorways signalled the intensity of the fear in the village. The higher the fear, the more likely it was they have active venandis protecting the village. Our kind learned to stay away from such villages as a matter of self-preservation. So, the belief that we are afraid of garlic became a maxim to the humans."

"And the salt? How did my kind come about the idea that salt is an aswang killer?"

She found Galen's curiosity in the superstitious belief about their kind amusing. His scientific brain had turned it into a study in sociology.

"We avoid salt, because it can slow our ability to heal, but not enough to pose a fatal danger to us. How did the humans find out? We are not sure, but we think maybe in one of the old skirmishes between some unfortunate aswang and humans, someone threw salt on a wounded aswang, and it made the aswang flee. I mean, have you ever experienced putting salt on an open wound? I'd recoil as well."

Galen chuckled. He seemed happier since he had passed the first night of witnessing the most gruesome side of their nature. Sure, it was stomach-turning, but as he had said, as long as he did not watch them do it, he could move past it.

This would work, they could succeed at this.

She felt relief and gratefulness flood her veins as he pulled her closer into his embrace and kissed her. A full night of loving was in order.

Meanwhile, Yuana stared at her ceiling, still wide awake. Her father passed the test with flying colours and convinced the family of his sincerity and loyalty to her mother. They all now believed this would work. She was thrilled for her father and mother.

They did not discuss Roald's situation because everyone focused more on the immersion of her father into their world, and it was not the right moment for such a discussion.

She worried for a while when her father turned grey during the ordeal, and she felt fearful when he threw up. But then, her father proved his mettle and rallied after that.

Now, she wondered if Roald would do as well. Her father was a doctor, used to seeing, smelling, handling raw flesh and blood. Yet the act of eating the raw liver turned his stomach.

Roald had no such medical training. This would be more challenging for him, more gut-wrenching and stomach-turning.

What if he can't handle it?

This would be infinitely more traumatic for him. Maybe sparing him the truth would be kinder, better for him and his psyche.

8

PRELUDE TO THE PAIN

Her ringtone woke Yuana up. She fell asleep at dawn because of exhaustion. Groggy, she groped for her phone. It was Roald.

"Good morning, sleepyhead..." His voice low and concerned.

She neglected to call him the night before as was their normal practice every day for the last two years.

"Good morning, Ro..." she rasped, her lids refusing to open. Her eyeballs felt dry and irritated.

"Are you all right?" Roald's question was sharp. He seemed alarmed.

Perhaps she sounded under the weather. At this hour, normally, she would already be up and about.

"I am good, just overslept," she murmured.

"It's a good thing I did not show up at your door this morning. When you did not call last night, I assumed you might want a late start this morning..."

"Thanks, Ro. You know me so well..."

"Would you like to sleep some more? I can call you later."

She sensed he wanted to probe but stopped himself.

"No, it's fine. My brain is awake now. A shower will perk me up." She stretched her limbs to get her blood flowing. "I can be ready in an hour, or so," she added.

"Yu, there is no urgency to get up. You need not be in the office if you are not up to it. I can come by later when you are ready."

"Okay..." It was easier to agree with him than argue when he adopted the brook-no-argument tone. "I will go to the office later today. I think I can be ready in... a couple of hours," she said, after glancing at the clock. It was past nine in the morning. Her usual work hour began at eight.

"Good. Rest well and I will see you later," Roald said and hung up.

Roald's call brought back the reasons that kept her awake all night. It cleared the cobwebs of sleep from her brain. Perhaps a bath to soothe her nerves would calm her into a decision.

Under the thick spray of warm water, the choice that had been see-sawing in her mind all night came back. There would be considerable pain in either choice.

Which one would leave a less indelible mark on Roald's heart?

Her own pain and the wound it would leave in her soul did not matter. She had accepted this last night. She closed her eyes against the water flowing over her face.

If only it could wash away the obstacle that nature placed between her and Roald.

Two hours later, she was still as torn. Roald would come to pick her up in five minutes. She needed to present a more pleasant front to him. He was much too perceptive. She chose a bright red dress, one flowy and light to mask the turmoil inside. Her outward appearance no longer reflected the sleepless night, concealer hid the dark circles under her eyes.

Her great grandmother sat at her favourite chair in the living room when she came down. She was reading a history book, *'The Age of The Enlightened Despot.'* Her Abuela's passion was history. She called it useful gossip. A slight smile on her lips welcomed her as she came down the stairs.

"Good morning, Yu-yu. You had a bit of a lie-in this morning..." her Abuela commented as she bent and planted a kiss on her forehead.

"Yes, 'Ela. Too much excitement last night. She gave her the brightest of show of teeth to mask her disquiet. She was not feeling up to any confession or heart-to-heart conversations at the moment.

"Is Roald coming to pick you up, or are you taking your own car?"

"Roald is picking me up. We will have lunch with Mama and Papa today."

"It's a pity the boy is not our kind... He's a good man..." Her Abuela's words made her wince.

As if on cue, they heard Roald's car pull over. She remained seated on the arm of her Abuela's chair as she waited for Roald to come in.

"Good morning, Señora," Roald greeted Margaita, bending towards her raised hand, and touched his forehead to her knuckles.

"Good morning, Hijo," Margaita responded warmly.

Roald then shifted to her, scrutinising her face. She was sure he was searching for signs of fatigue.

"You look fresh, relaxed, well-rested and glowing." He gave her a satisfied smile and offered his arm to her, "Shall we?"

She linked arms with him. "Sure, let's be off," and with one last peck on her Abuela's cheeks, they left Margaita to her book.

The drive was uneventful. Inwardly, Yuana's brain and heart were engaged in a battle for supremacy. She had called her parents earlier to tell them of her vacillating decision. They advised her to just let things unfold, that they would follow her lead.

There should not be any pressure to reveal anything to Roald today. There was no looming deadline, except her own mental clock. A few more weeks of delay would not make much difference, she told herself often, yet the sense of urgency would not let her be.

Roald could not put a finger on it, but despite Yuana's serene expression, something weighed on her. And this bothered him. It never sat well with him that Yuana withdrew deep into herself, as she would do now and then. In the three years they had been together, no matter how convinced he was of the love between them, that small invisible barrier she erected remained. And one of his goals in life was to break that down.

Perhaps her father would help him. Galen would need *his* help to get to know his daughter better and may be the key to weakening that last blockade that prevented Yuana from giving all of herself to him.

They arrived at Protogenis, a Greek restaurant chosen by Yuana's parents for their lunch. The server ushered them to a secluded private room that overlooked the garden. Cosy, airy and well illuminated, the glass doors, when closed, shut the noise from the main dining area. There were several layers of lace curtain which when drawn provided limited to complete privacy.

Within a few minutes of their arrival, the restaurant manager ushered Ysobella and Galen into the room. The couple held hands and giggled like newlyweds. A sudden jolt of envy hit him. This was the future he wanted with Yuana — an enduring love and burning passion for each other, a veritable heaven on earth.

Galen pressed a kiss on Yuana's cheeks, then shook his hand. Yuana gave her mother a hug, and he bussed Ysobella's cheek. After a few exchanges of pleasantries, they sat down.

Galen ordered a bottle of rosé, a Chateau Miraval, and favourite of both mother and daughter. The weather was warm, and it seemed a perfect wine to start their lunch. They feasted on light salad, pasta, and seafood, the specialty of the restaurant.

Their conversation was light, pleasant, and entertaining. Roald didn't let it show, but he sensed Yuana's disquiet throughout lunch. She became withdrawn as the hours progressed. Sure, she laughed at her father's jokes and took part in the conversation, but there was a not-quite hidden desolation in her.

At one point, he glanced at her by instinct, and the look in her eyes sent a jolt to his gut—she appeared to be memorising his features, like she was planning to say goodbye. It was gone in an instant. He thought he imagined it, but the dread remained.

And this frightened him.

While he enjoyed and valued the time spent with Yuana's parents, he was impatient for it to end. He wanted to uncover what troubled Yuana. It had been growing and creating a divide between them, which grew wider every day. That invisible thin barrier had been thickening.

He thought back to when he first noticed it. It was when he first mentioned marriage. Perhaps she panicked because she did not want to get married yet. He could give her more time.

Don't jump to conclusions, Roald. Maybe the issue was about work, or her parents.

But her parents noticed Yuana's mood as well, as they glanced at her often during lunch, and then exchanged a quick glance between them. There was question and concern in their eyes. And that added to his unrest.

What is bothering her?

The finale of the meal was rich revani and hot Greek coffee. The syrup-soaked dessert paired well with the bitter tang of the dark coffee.

While Galen engaged Roald in a discussion about technologies in the medical field, Ysobella stared at her daughter over the rim of her coffee cup. Yuana had been quiet for most of the meal, her smiles, superficial. The decision had been weighing on her only child.

If only she could take on her burden. But this was a choice only Yuana could make, the consequence she would have to bear. As a mother, she could be there during the storm, to give comfort and help pick up the pieces if she falls apart.

Yuana *looked* serene, relaxed even, but she sat at the edge of her seat, like a cat poised to flee. Galen and she waited for their daughter to make the choice, her timing unknown to them. It was inevitable though, and the sooner the better.

All the signs of Roald's forthcoming proposal were all there. She suspected the only reason Roald had not done so yet was because of the untimely appearance of Galen in their lives. He was being considerate of Yuana. But he would not wait long. And now that Roald had met Galen, she was certain Roald would recruit Galen into the act.

As a mother, she hoped that if Yuana chose to tell Roald, he would rise to the occasion, just like her Galen. After last night, Galen would prevail over anything.

Every one of them had put their trust in someone they loved, and for various reasons, their trust was misplaced, but as far as she could recall, based on what her great grandparents had told her, those instances ended in the eventual Restoration Plan being brought into effect. And it had been shattering to the people involved.

She pondered if every single one of her relatives who opted to reveal themselves to their loved one were as confident about their decision, and as elated as she was over the knowledge that her trust was well-placed.

Then the unwelcome thought intruded in her mind: they must all have felt the same elation, and then the devastation when they realised they made a mistake, and they would need to pay for that mistake with blood on their hands. The blood of their loved ones. She shook the image out of her mind.

Galen would be... was... the first human taken into their circle, and he would remain there. She was sure of that.

But will Roald turn out to be the second?

Or will Yuana be another one in the family who will have to Restore the Order?

Yuana sipped her coffee just to mask her inner turmoil. That was not the best choice of beverage when her nerves were as taut as a drawn bow. Roald's proposal would come anytime now. She could almost hear and read Roald's thoughts every time he looked at her father—he would involve him, take him in as an ally to make her say yes.

Who am I protecting with this decision, really?

My heart?

Or Roald's?

If the Restoration would take place. She would not have the strength to kill him.

Yuana excused herself from her parents to visit the ladies' room. Roald pulled the chair out for her. After she closed the glass door of the private room behind her, he turned to Ysobella and Galen. He had to do something. If Yuana would not tell him, perhaps her parents would. They loved her as much.

"Tita Bella, something is eating at Yuana, and I am concerned about her. Has she mentioned anything to you?" This was not the time to be timid.

Ysobella and Galen were both surprised and exchanged a quick glance. More tension infused him. What bothered Yuana was significant, and her parents both knew what it was.

"Why don't you ask her?" Ysobella said.

The gentleness of her response implied a kind of sympathy that added to the foreboding that crept into his heart. Ysobella then excused herself to follow Yuana to the ladies' room, and Roald could only nod weakly.

There was pity in Galen's gaze when they met his. Yuana's father tried to distract him by asking about his tech business. He did not want to talk about anything except Yuana's problem, but realised he needed the time to recover his composure.

Whatever Yuana would say later would require a calm mind.

As Ysobella expected, Yuana sat at the pristine and comfortable waiting area just inside the ladies' room as she deliberated on the options before her. Her daughter seemed nowhere near to making any choice. Yuana had run out of time, and she wanted to tell her that.

She sat beside her daughter and put her arms around her shoulders. Yuana gave her a dejected glance. There was no need to say anything.

"Roald asked us what was bothering you," she said without preamble.

A spark of life glowed in Yuana's eyes, "He did?"

She nodded.

"Should I tell him, Mama? Or do I do what you did to Papa?"

"My darling, you know I cannot make that decision for you. The only thing that can help you make the right choice is the outcome, and regrettably, outcomes happen in the future, and we have no way of knowing in advance. Either decision will hurt," she replied. "Choose the route that will offer a better chance at a full life for you, for Roald."

Yuana took a deep breath and straightened. She kissed her on the cheek and stood up. Arm and arm they walked back to the private room where the two men waited. Her daughter seemed to have decided on her course.

"Papa, can we go to your hotel suite after this?" Yuana asked Galen as soon as they entered. Galen and Roald were both on their feet as they came into the room.

Galen's nod was automatic, a question conveyed in the slight narrowing of his eyes. Roald, however, was focused on Yuana's face. The firm determination of an unpleasant decision made etched in the angle of her chin and jaw. That she averted her face seemed to unnerve him. Roald's jaw tightened, but he kept silent.

For now, her daughter had closed herself off from Roald, and the young man did not like it. Roald was determined to break the barrier that her daughter placed between them. The boy did not know what he would face later.

A better chance at a full life.

Yuana's decision was going to be based on that premise. She hoped Roald would see it the same way.

The ride to Galen's hotel was quiet and fraught with tension. Galen offered to drive them all in his car. Galen's driver drove Roald's car back to the hotel.

He and Yuana sat at the back. Not knowing what was torturing Yuana was excruciating. He was certain it involved him and their relationship. He only hoped it was not something he would be powerless to fix. Everything else was fixable.

Yuana held herself distant from him, her spine rigid as she sat. He did not like the emotions the distance roused in him, as if Yuana was severing their connections. He battled the frustration and the hurt that gripped his heart, but he would not let her do that.

Not today. Not ever.

He lifted Yuana's right hand from her lap, his much bigger hands covered hers. She stiffened and tried to pull away, but he tightened his hold, and she relented. Her fingers softened, her palms warmed and melted into his. Her wall crumbled a little, and it pacified the savage beast in his heart for the moment.

Their interlinked fingers gave him hope and bolstered his confidence.

He wanted to remind her with his touch that her pain was his to bear. And the distance would not make the bearing easier.

Soon enough, they arrived at Galen's hotel. He released her hand as he descended from the car, but claimed it back when he helped her out. Her hand was clasped in his until they reached Galen's two-bedroom suite. He did not care if her parents witnessed his desperation, his vulnerability to Yuana's power over him.

There was no casual conversation on the way up. The tension was so thick the other guests in the elevator shot nervous glances their way during the minute-long ride.

Galen opened the door to his suite, and they followed him into the dining area. Roald released her hand and pulled Yuana into a chair. She sat down and he sat beside her. He wanted her to feel his presence throughout the wait he was forced to endure. Her parents did the same; Ysobella sat close to Yuana.

Yuana turned to him in a determined move. Yet she did not seem to know how to start. Tears sparkled in her eyes, and it squeezed at his heart. On instinct, he caught her hand and trapped it between his.

"Yuana, just say it. It will be fine, I promise you." That was his hope, anyway.

Her deep breath shook, a tremor in her voice. "Roald, I need to tell you something about me..."

There was a lengthy pause as she struggled with her next words.

Roald felt his heart thump faster in panic, that he had to lighten the mood. "Don't tell me you were born a man, Yuana," he joked.

"What? No!" Yuana frowned, confused, especially when it elicited a snort of laughter from Galen, cut short by a sharp glare from her mother.

"Sorry..." Roald mumbled. "You are making me nervous, Yuana. Just tell me what it is." His heart hammered against his chest.

"Roald, I want you to believe that I love you very much. And that will not change no matter the outcome." Her voice thickened with emotion; tears welled in her big brown eyes.

Panic sparked in him. A declaration of love at the beginning of a discussion did not bode well.

"I know that, Yuana. I believe that. And I love you as much, so just tell me."

All this was making him more apprehensive and that her parents were in the same room, at the same table, made his misery more acute. He was convinced she would leave him for a cause too big for them to overcome.

The hand he held clenched in tension. "Roald, I... I am not human like you," she sobbed the words.

But it barely registered. He could not believe what he heard.

"What? What do you mean, not human?"

His analytical brain could not compute what she'd just said. He glanced at both of her parents' faces, trying to anchor his mind into something real. Ysobella's face was gentle in sympathy, Galen's was blank.

"I'm a *viscerebus*... an *aswang*. My entire family are..." she whispered. Tears ran down her cheeks.

The word struck terror in his soul, and he did not know why. His confusion doubled, he felt staggered. It was the last thing he would have expected her to say.

"Yuana, I do not understand... why are you saying this?"

His bewilderment numbed his earlier panic. He just wanted her to give him a logical explanation, a statement he could dissect, solve, put a structure to. Something he could do something about.

"Is it because you are not ready to get married? We can wait for as long as you want..." He would supply her with any plausible excuse he could think of. Anything within the realm of acceptable reality.

She shook her head, then bowed. "No, Roald. It is not about that... I want you to know what I am before we even consider marriage." The sobs made it hard for her to speak.

"Yuana, what you are is the woman I love. That is what you are to me. The rest does not matter. There is nothing else we need." He could not express his plea for her to take it all back, or at least logically explain why she called herself an *aswang*.

Yuana stared at him and understood what he wanted her to do. Her demeanour changed as she took a deep breath, her back ramrod straight. Grim determination was etched in every line of her neck and jaw.

"Roald, I am an *aswang*. I wish I can take it back. I wish I can say being an aswang is a euphemism for some medical condition that can be cured. That with the right and enough treatment, I will no longer be one. But that's not the case. I, and my family, are all *aswangs*, and we have been for centuries."

Her voice had firmed, her declaration, calm, but his brain couldn't seem to grasp what she said.

Galen grimaced at Yuana's statement. Ysobella threw Galen another sharp glance, as if able to read his thoughts. And this confused him more.

They knew what Yuana was talking about?

"Yuana, how can you be one? They do not exist. They are folklore, just one of the fantastical creatures in our mythology..."

The despair in him grew. He was afraid Yuana suffered from a psychosis that required medical attention. But he could deal with her mental illness and support her through it for the rest of their lives.

"We exist, Roald. And I can prove it." Her voice intensified, a tinge of frustration in the heightened pitch. She pulled her hand from his grasp and stood up.

Her father shot to his feet, and he followed suit.

"Mama, Papa, can you leave us?"

"Ah, Yuana... no, I draw the line on you getting naked..." Galen exclaimed, paternal protectiveness rising to the surface.

"Galen, relax... and shut up." Ysobella's gentle admonishment stopped him, a restraining hand on his arm. She tugged at him, but Galen refused to move and intended to stand his ground. Ysobella pulled at him. Galen relented and allowed her to pull him toward their room, an expression of surprise at the hand that led him away.

As the door closed behind them, Yuana turned to him. They were now standing face to face, just inches apart.

"It's all right, Roald. Whatever your decision after I show you, I will accept. I only ask that you keep everything I told you and what you will witness, a secret. You cannot expose us. It is dangerous, and fatal... to us..."

A trembling right palm rested on his cheek. It was an act of love and comfort, to prepare him for what was coming. The gentle action made him more anxious.

"Yuana, you do not have to do this..."

He did not know what he was denying her to do. The terror must have reflected in his eyes because Yuana's hand stilled.

"Roald, I can stop here, and we can forget this conversation ever happened. But our relationship cannot progress. Everything has changed, and there is no going back. Without you accepting this truth, there is no future for us. Without it, you cannot accept me. And this acceptance is crucial to us being together, for you to join me in my world, because I won't be able to survive in yours." Her voice broke, but he could not mistake the finality in her words, the desolation in her posture.

"Yuana..." He did not know what to say. His chest hurt like his ribs were being ripped apart.

"You can walk away now, go home, think it over. Or you can stay, keep an open mind and let me prove to you what I am. The choice is yours," Yuana said in a calm but determined voice. Her decision clear in the firm lift of her chin.

He sank back into his seat, his knees weak, his mind a jumble of tumultuous thoughts. It was so unlike him, as his one great skill was making a quick analysis of any situation, listening to his gut, and making a decision. Those skills failed him today, at the moment when Yuana and their future were at stake.

Yuana decided for him. She pulled him up and out of his chair and led him to the door of the suite. His steps were wooden, but he did not resist.

She opened the door, gave him a light but lingering kiss on the lips, and with a gentle push she closed the door on him.

He stood outside, faced with the closed door of Galen's suite. His soul in chaos, but the need to run was overwhelming. The terror was familiar, like a long-forgotten emotion, a monster that used to haunt him, and had come back to life.

It was paralysing.

His ear pressed against the door; Galen tried to listen in on what was happening in his living room. There was no discernible sound from outside. He looked back to confer with Ysobella, who sat on their bed, one elegant leg crossed over the other, watching him.

"I cannot hear a thing," he whispered.

She nodded. "Roald left, Yuana let him go." Her confident assertion confirmed that her keener sense of hearing was able to pick up the sounds in the other room much better than him.

Galen opened the door and found Yuana still standing by the front door, her back rigid, taking deep breaths to calm herself. And as soon as she saw him, she lost control, her face crumpled, and she burst into tears.

He rushed over and enfolded her in his arms, offering comfort to the wonderful brave young woman who had just gone through something he probably wouldn't have the strength to do himself. Seeing her broken made him understand what his Bel must have suffered when she left him, and whatever remnants of anger and resentment he harboured in his heart vanished completely.

Ysobella stood by the bedroom door as she watched them both, heart-warmed by the sight of father and daughter together, but her eyes gleamed with concern and heartbreak for their only child.

With a sigh, she walked closer and embraced Yuana from behind. Yuana became sandwiched between the two adults who would do everything in their power to make things better for her, including taking on her pain if that was possible.

Roald trudged up to his condo unit, consumed by his own thoughts and emotions. He did not know how he got home without running over anyone along the way. His phone rang off the hook, but did not bother to pick it up. He was shell-shocked, like his psyche was detached from his heart and body.

He went to the sidebar in his dining area and poured himself a measure of cognac. The fiery trail of the spirit down his throat defrosted the icy chill that covered his heart and thawed the feeling back into him. And with the thawing, the remembered chaos and pain followed.

How did such an enjoyable lunch turn into this nightmare?

Yuana's claim upended his well-ordered world and shook the foundation of his existence.

Why would Yuana claim to be a mythical creature?

Either she believed it, or it was an alibi to drive him away somehow. As a deterrent, the latter makes little sense to use as an excuse - it was too far-fetched and the least effective one to stop their impending marriage. It was far more plausible she believed herself to be an aswang.

He poured another measure of cognac into the glass, took the bottle with him, then slumped his exhausted frame onto the couch. His thoughts restarted; his brain resumed its usual pace. He was ready to analyse and put order to what happened earlier.

In all that muddle, one thing was clear to him - Yuana thought that being an aswang made it impossible for them to be together. She wanted to protect him. This was the last barrier he needed to shatter. And the only way to do this would be to listen to her, to keep an open mind. And perhaps he would make heads or tails on what caused her mistaken pronouncement.

Then he remembered she emphasised they could only be together if he accepted her and adapted to her world, that it would be impossible to move forward without it. He would give her whatever she needed, listen to her, and adapt to the circumstances until he guided her out of this psychosis that clouded her reality. He would do everything necessary for them to get over this hurdle, because if there was something he would never accept or adapt to, it would be the loss of Yuana.

Yuana would need strong proof to shake her out of her belief. He would let her talk, take notes and get clues, and then he could research about it and find the proof to present to her. She could have a psychosis that remained untreated for years. In the three years they had been together, Yuana had exhibited no telltale behavioural signs or symptoms of any mental issues.

It came out of nowhere. So, maybe, it was buried in her subconscious and his offer of marriage triggered it to the surface.

Dinner would be strenuous tonight. She was not up for the questions, or worse, the concerned glances her family would throw her way throughout dinner. She had cried long and hard earlier, but her tears still hovered under a fragile facade. A word or a look would shatter it.

She would rather stay in her room and curl up in a ball to soothe the ache that bloomed in her insides since Roald left. Today, she learned a heartbreak was not a quick pain like a stab or a bullet shot, but a long, lingering, expanding kind that intensified hour by hour. It was like poison spreading all over her body, and there was no stopping it.

She still held hope that Roald would not stay away too long, that after the initial shock had dissipated, he would call her. But she had to prepare for the outcome that Roald may not come back.

Maybe this was the best outcome. She did not reveal verifiable information that could endanger their kind, but it was alarming enough for Roald to walk away.

This could be the middle ground for them, a less painful option.

That had to be better than the others.

Her father's heartbeat was steady in her ears. His scent, which should be new to her, was familiar. He smelled of juniper berries and moss. Being curled up between her parents gave her a measure of comfort. She could sense her mother's concerned gaze; her pain and exhaustion must be visible to her.

The drive to their house was cheerless and short. As they pulled up in front of the drive, she pushed herself up into a sitting position and uncurled her legs from under her to find her shoes. It would cause alarm if she walked into the house looking like death was upon her. She would need to make herself presentable.

Her mother's gentle hand stayed her fidgety one as she rummaged in her bag for a mirror.

"Would you prefer your dinner sent to your room tonight, Yu?"

Bless her mother's sharp instinct for reading her so well. She shook her head. "I am not hungry, Mama." Food was the furthest from her mind.

"Okay." Her mother nodded.

She took the moment her parents gave her to check her reflection in her hand mirror. She was as wrung out as a used mop. Her emotions raw, her mind in a whirl. Blessedly, her eyes were no longer puffy. She would pass muster.

One more deep breath, and she got out of the car, braced herself for the quick moment that it would take for her to say goodnight to her family and take herself off to her room.

Dinner ended earlier than usual, Katelin noted. Each one of them had masked their concern for the youngest member of the clan when she kissed everyone goodnight. Yuana opted to go to bed early, without dinner, and more worrisome, without sustenance. This was the first time she had turned down that which was vital to their survival. They did not badger her because she needed time to herself and she had about two days before her vital hunger kicked in.

They all guessed that things did not go well between Yuana and Roald. It must not be too bad because there was no forewarning from the three for serious consequences the family would have to face. They hoped they would not need to deploy the Restoration plan. They had not needed to for decades.

Katelin worried about her granddaughter. It would be the worst outcome if Yuana was forced to end Roald's life herself. Her granddaughter possessed a sweet and sensitive soul, and it would destroy her to do so.

She was tempted to ask Ysobella about what happened when Yuana left the dining room, but her mother shot her a warning glance, one that everyone caught. That was a clear non-verbal instruction from her, the Matriarch. They would not discuss the issue in front of Galen. A quick hand signal from her informed them all — the discussion would be for the following day, nine a.m.

And their topic would be the Risk Reduction and Intervention Plan, the *RRIP*. They would not allow Yuana to reach that point of catastrophe. She was far too young to carry the memory, the trauma of taking the life of someone that could very well be the love of her life. It would not be a good way to live the rest of the long life their kind had been blessed, or cursed, by nature to possess.

Edrigu's figure emerged from the adjoining bathroom, his hair damp from the shower. It was a quick one, and she could guess why - her husband wanted to speak to her. He harboured the same thought that niggled with persistence in her brain since Yuana asked to be excused. The thought refused to be banished and stayed in both their heads the whole evening.

His eyes hunted for her on their bed, but shifted to the window where she sat, when he found their bed empty.

"We have something to discuss," he began.

"Yes, I know."

Edrigu stared at her. She was sure that he recognised the seriousness of the topic by whatever grim expression graced her face.

Meanwhile, in another room, Margaita and Lorenzo were discussing the same thing—the De Vida *RRIP*—and the last time they implemented it. It did not end well for Martin, and the emotional toll for their daughter, Ximena, was crushing.

Their eldest daughter had been paying for the consequence of her choice for over fifty years. And there was no sign of Ximena forgiving herself soon.

With heavy hearts, they discussed the merit of setting up the preemptive actions they might have to deploy to protect their great granddaughter. They would hold a big family meeting at home tomorrow.

Without Galen.

Without Yuana.

And not so far away, Roald had been pacing.

He turned over in his mind several possibilities and justification on why Yuana believed she was an aswang. The presence of her parents in the room, their silence while Yuana made the claims, baffled him.

Did they understand what she said?

How can they accept it?

How can they support it? Or even encourage it? They were both doctors.

And he wished he had the mind to ask earlier. None of it made sense. His stomach muscles clenched ever tighter as the evening progressed. He sipped his drink, welcoming the slow burn as it travelled down his throat, trying to shake the sense of disconnect in himself.

The chaos in his mind, his heart and his gut created unbearable tension all over his body. He flexed his shoulders to relieve the tension there, then took a long deep breath to release the pressure that had not left his chest since he quit Galen's condo.

Hours later, he gave up drinking cognac as he dissected his own thoughts; the spirit did not help at all.

His exhausted mind gave way to sleep around dawn, but just as he fell into sleep, an idea murmured deep into his subconscious...

What if Yuana was telling the truth?

That night, a long dormant nightmare that used to plague his childhood came back with a vengeance.

Yuana could not summon the energy to get up. The clock on her wall showed it was almost noon. On normal days, by this time, she would be at her weekly meeting with her team, an activity she considered crucial.

Today, she had no enthusiasm to care about anything, or do anything. Not even to think. She overslept, and yet she was still exhausted. She only wanted to sleep, to get a respite from the pressing weight on her chest, to numb it.

For just a few more hours...

There was a soft knock on the door. Yuana closed her eyes and pretended to sleep. When she did not answer, her mother entered, approached the bed and sat by the edge. Yuana kept her breath steady, even as her mother caressed her hair. She did not want to talk, did not want to be reminded.

She wanted peace, she just wanted Roald.

Her act must have been convincing, because her mother got up after a while and left. She would be back to check up on her again later. That was her mother's nature.

She was certain her mother and the entire family had already been told what happened last night. And they had discussed what to do next. It should worry her, because the next steps would involve the Tribunal.

But she could not muster the motivation to care.

Ysobella retreated from her daughter's room. Her child was suffering, and she felt helpless. Yet she could do nothing about it. Galen had been furious about the situation last night, but the one thing that mellowed his rage was Yuana's action. Their daughter snuggled close to him like a child, and Galen's heart melted. He was grateful to be there to comfort his daughter.

The De Vidas had a meeting earlier about the circumstance with Roald. They did not include Galen in the meeting because her grandparents deemed it too early for him to know the inner workings of their society and the Tribunal.

During their meeting, they decided they would implement the RRIP—their Risk Reduction & Intervention Plan as a proactive move, albeit at a slower pace. But the RRIP's Final Wave would only be deployed on her go-signal. She had spoken for Roald, on Yuana's behalf. She believed, or hoped, that Roald would come around.

For the moment, at her request, they all agreed to give Roald some time, a chance to prove himself worthy. For Yuana's sake, she wanted to give her daughter a chance at happiness. She just hoped her faith in Roald would prove worth it.

With a sigh, she proceeded downstairs to wait for Galen.

Galen arrived just before lunch at the De Vida home. He would meet Ysobella there. He wanted to check on his daughter. Nita opened the door for him, greeted him like a part of the family. He followed her to the living room where everyone congregated.

All of them except Yuana.

It was not a good sign.

After exchanging handshakes with the men and buss on the cheeks with the ladies, he kissed his Bel last on both cheeks and murmured, "How's Yuana?"

Her absence concerned him, but it did not surprise him she was a no-show. Ysobella glanced upstairs.

"Should I go to her?" he asked, uneasy. "I am clueless about this... fatherhood thing."

Ysobella gave him a slight smile. "Perhaps she will come down for lunch, for you."

Yuana did not come down for lunch. Nita came back from her room, lunch tray still full, and informed them Yuana was not hungry and would rather sleep. Seven pairs of eyes exchanged worried looks all around. Every single one of them fought the impulse to go up to Yuana's room.

No one did. Lunch had the thick air of false ease. It was a good thing the menu featured light dishes. It was hard to eat anything on an already tight stomach.

He expected the family to discuss Yuana and Roald's situation, but no one brought it up. The grim expressions on the faces of the older men and the disquiet in the women meant something was afoot. He wondered if the board meeting that Ysobella attended earlier was truly about business. It annoyed him they excluded him from the discussion of Yuana's future; he was Yuana's father, after all. Perhaps his new family had not learned how to share yet, and old habits were hard to break.

During coffee and teatime, he excused himself to see Yuana.

He knocked, and when she didn't respond, he opened the door a crack. Her room was dark, her blackout curtains prevented the daylight into her bedroom. His eyesight hunted for his daughter in the room, as he called out her name in a whisper.

He found her in the middle of her bed, curled up like a child. With no response from her, he tiptoed to her bedside and looked down at his daughter. Yuana was deep in a fitful sleep. She was in the middle of a painful dream. A slight frown creased her eyebrows. Tears leaked from the corner of her lids; small sobs escaped her. His paternal heart ached. He wanted to wake her up, but she quieted after a shaky breath, and settled into her slumber.

Yuana tugged at his heartstrings. His only daughter. This young woman who made Ysobella's bitter exile sweet would be his Bel's solace when he left this earth. His daughter, the other half of the sole reason he wanted to extend his life past his prognosis.

He needed to talk to Roald and knock some sense into him. And if that did not work, he would make the boy pay for hurting his baby girl.

The object of Galen's outrage had a terrible night. Roald woke up more anxious than the night before, caused by the nightmares that felt familiar. It filled his dreams with horrific interwoven images of him frozen and helpless as he watched Yuana attack faceless individuals, of him eating raw and bloody human organs — of their newborn child turned into a monster baby attacking a faceless nurse.

One particular portion of his dream bothered him the most, but he could not remember the details. What jolted him awake was the primal scream of a child, a child that might have been him, yet separate. He sat up, sweaty and panting. His heart pounded so hard against his chest he feared he was having a heart attack.

Thoughts of Yuana came to him. He was a heel for not texting her to assure her he was still there, that he would not leave. That he just needed some time to sort himself out.

He must phone her.

Two hours later, his anxiety reached fever pitch. He could not contact Yuana, or she had decided not to pick up his calls. And this disturbed him so. He wanted to go to her, but his emotions were in such a disarray that seeing her might do more damage than good. The state of his emotion was so precarious.

He checked his emails for want of something to do, and when there was nothing that required his immediate attention, he just exited his inbox. He had no motivation. Nothing seemed to matter. His future did not interest him like it used to. It was like his mind and heart anaesthetized him from life. The sense of impending doom had not left him since yesterday, and it was mounting in intensity like a looming deadline.

He was about to dial Yuana's number again when his phone rang; it was the reception.

"Mr Magsino, you have a visitor, Dr Galen Aurelio... Do I send him up?"

Galen is here?

Alarm bells rang in his head.

Is he here because he was mad at him, or did something happen to Yuana? She had not been answering his calls.

"Yes, please send him up."

He opened the door for Galen at the first knock. And judging from the grim frown on his face, he was more angry than worried. Either way, his presence would bring unpleasant news.

Galen pushed past Roald and walked into his living room. He looked like he wanted to throttle him and knock his teeth down his throat. Galen had the right to be protective over Yuana. As her father, he could pummel him to the ground, and he would be justified. But at the moment, Roald did not care.

"Is Yuana all right? She was not answering my calls." His first concern took precedence over Galen's wrath.

The worry in his voice must have taken the edge off Galen's anger, for his mouth twisted in annoyance.

"Humph, serves you right! I would ignore your calls too, if I was her," Galen said, exasperated.

His eyes bore into him, and he must have seen the signs of a sleepless night on his face, as Galen's sigh sounded resigned.

"So, what is your plan, Roald?"

He was not clear what Galen was asking from him. Or why Galen seemed more interested in his relationship with Yuana, rather than the state of Yuana's mind. Galen appeared to have accepted Yuana's impossible statement that she was an aswang like it was the truth.

"Sir, why does it seem like you are supporting Yuana's statement she is an aswang? Why are you not alarmed that she made those pronouncements? You are a doctor; does this not bother you?"

Galen's brow rose. His mouth opened as if he was about to say something but stopped himself. A long sigh preceded his statement. "The issue between you and my daughter is not a medical one. It's a test of faith in each other."

Galen's cryptic response confused him.

Why was Yuana's father not concerned about her mental health?

"What do you mean? Did she say those things to see if I would stick around? I cannot believe that Yuana would resort to something so petty. It's not like her. And she sounded serious... Was she?"

Galen kept silent; his probing gaze so prolonged it made him uncomfortable. Yuana's father seemed to have seen something inside him that changed his expression.

His sigh was deep, "It is not my thoughts or feelings that matter in this, Roald. It's yours, and more to the point, what you believe." A small, sad smile twisted Galen's lips. "You and Yuana need to finish this. The sooner, the better. If you want your relationship to move forward, there is no other route but that," he said. "Hopefully, your path won't end up diverging."

Roald could only nod.

And the anxiety lodged in his chest grew.

Roald spent the next couple of hours trying to contact Yuana, but to no avail. Her father told him she was resting in her room, but she could not have been sleeping all this time. The growing urgency to speak to her, to reassure her and himself all was well between them was making him frantic. He told himself maybe she just needed some space, some time for herself. Perhaps he needed to give her that much, for now.

He spent another two hours see-sawing between wanting to give Yuana more time and trying to contact her. He had been sending her text messages until he realised the phone recording stated her phone was out of reach. Her phone was off. She would not receive the text messages or the missed call notifications.

Finally, he could not take it anymore. He grabbed his car keys and rushed out of his unit. Securing Yuana was the most important thing. Together, they could triumph over any obstacles. Apart, they would have no chance.

Ten minutes later, his car pulled up in front of the De Vida's driveway. It was half-past nine in the evening, so he was sure the family finished dinner already. He was uncertain what kind of reception to expect from them. The De Vidas would know the discord between him and Yuana. He hoped they would not find it disrespectful for showing up this late.

Nita opened the door for him. While the De Vida's housekeeper displayed slight surprise, her amiable manner toward him did not change. It was an encouraging sign.

"Is Yuana in?" he asked.

She hesitated, but led him to the receiving area, through the anteroom to the main living room. She bid him to wait. When she returned, Katelin was with her.

It was disconcerting to gaze into Katelin's less than cheerful face. But she did not look angry.

"Good evening, Mrs Orzabal, I am here to see Yuana."

"Good evening, Roald. Yuana is in her room. I am not sure if she is up to seeing anyone, including you." Her candid response hurt.

But his feelings did not matter at the moment. "Is she all right? I have been trying to call her the whole afternoon, but she hasn't been picking up my call." He just wanted an assurance that Yuana was fine. If she would not see him, at least her family could reassure him.

"Please come and sit down, Roald," Katelin said. She gestured towards one of the plush seats in the living room.

He complied.

"We are concerned about her. She stayed in her room the whole day, she did not eat, and she refused to talk to anyone... What happened between you and Yuana?"

He had the impression Katelin already knew, and she wanted to hear from him, find out his side of the argument. Her face was emotionless, and she seemed ready to give him a chance.

"I do not mean to be disrespectful, ma'am, but I do not think it is right for me to discuss this with you until Yuana and I have sorted it out." He could only apologise, but he would not betray Yuana's confidence unless she told him it was okay. "And I'm worried about Yuana. Is it possible for me to see her?" he added.

Katelin's blank face softened. She stood up and motioned for him to follow her up the stairs, through a long corridor that overlooked the vast living room. Yuana's room was at the end of the hallway. Every door was heavy, ornate, and antique-looking with distinct carvings. Each door had a unique design, but he had no time to inspect or admire it.

They stopped at her dark hardwood door with carvings of trees and birds. Katelin softly rapped on the door. There was no answer, so Katelin knocked again.

"Yuana, *hija,* Roald is here."

For a moment, he thought Yuana would not respond, that she would ignore his presence. But the door opened a crack, then widened. Yuana emerged from the dark, her eyes swollen, dark circles underneath. They were big and tortured in her pale face. The sight took his breath away. His heart squeezed tighter as he noted her gaunt face. She had lost weight in the two days they were apart.

By instinct, he took a step forward, to take her into his arms, but she stayed him with an outstretched hand. The act of rejection hurt, and he retracted his own hand and rested it on his chest. He rubbed the jolt of pain in his chest away.

In silence, Yuana opened the door wider to let him in. He came in and stopped in the middle of the room. It would have been in total darkness except for the light that spilled through the opened door. She had drawn the heavy blackout curtains closed. Not a single lamp, or a candle was lit, which was strange because Yuana loved being surrounded by lighted candles.

Yuana had a short, murmured conversation with Katelin before her grandmother walked away and left both of them. Then she stood still, surrounded by the light from the hallway. She stared at him, then flicked the light switch on the standing lamp by the side of the door, bathing the room with soft illumination. She closed the door shut and walked towards the end of her bed. Her eyes never left his as she sat down. Her exhausted sigh made his heart ache a bit more.

"Are you ready to listen to my truth?" She sounded resigned.

"Yes, but not until we have taken care of you first. Your father said you haven't eaten in days."

Unable to help himself, he crossed the room and pulled her into his arms. Yuana resisted for a moment, her body rigid. He knew she wanted to keep the emotional wall she built during the past days between them. But he was determined to offer her comfort and make her feel the longing in his soul.

After a while, she yielded and relaxed into his warmth. The tensed muscles of her back eased, her body moulded into his. His own sigh of relief was deep. It was like coming home.

A short eternity passed. Then she pulled away, a tired smile on her face.

"I am okay now. I am ready to talk when you are."

He shook his head. "No. Tonight, you will eat first, then sleep. We will talk tomorrow. I will come back here to continue the unfinished discussion between us." He pushed the tousled hair off her face. Yuana needed care for now. "Understood?" He kissed her forehead to soften the command.

She nodded. "Okay."

As Roald drove back home, he felt better, more reassured about his relationship with Yuana. Yet his apprehension remained stronger than before. He told himself this time he knew what they would talk about. Unlike the other day, when surprise overtook him. Next time he could control his reaction, and the situation.

She had promised to provide proof, and he should look forward to that proof.

So, why do I feel anxious about seeing it?

Its presence would help him determine what mental issues were plaguing Yuana, and the absence of credible proof might help open her eyes.

Never had he perceived the dawning of another day with such trepidation and anxiety.

Meanwhile, Yuana went to bed calmer, and despite having some soup and bread, she did not feel revived. Her resolve to settle the issue in the morning strengthened. Not having to guess the status of their relationship was freeing.

She had the foretaste of life without Roald, and it was an unpleasant experience. And a big part of it was the uncertainty.

Roald's visit tonight lifted some weight off her chest. He proved he would not just leave. But tomorrow, she would know for sure if he would stay and what her future would be.

Roald's logical brain would not accept her words alone. He would need a proof he could not discount. Only shape-shifting would achieve that. The one irrevocable proof she had would also be the most dangerous and damaging.

Still, there was hope. Roald came to her tonight. She would keep that hope in her heart.

For now, she needed her rest. Perhaps a good night's sleep would cure the slight tremor that plagued her body.

The light of the moon provided extra illumination for a small woman. She was tracking the footsteps of the wild boar she was hunting. Her sun-browned skin dry and wrinkled, her curly hair thick on her head. She was an experienced hunter. Her responsibility to her human tribes-people was to provide them with food. This had been her task for the last ninety years. In exchange, they sacrifice their dead and their sick for her needs. One could say it was a fair trade, but she did not like it.

The Tribunal now provided her sustenance. There was no need for her tribes-people to sacrifice anyone to her. They offer her the organs of their dead now and then as a gesture of gratitude.

She shook herself out of her thoughts; she had a boar to capture. Their tribe needed the food as the recent drought devastated their cultivated fields, leaving nothing for them to sell or to eat. She needed to provide for them.

She could smell the wild boar, hear its snorts and the rustling of the leaves as it hunted for something to eat. The boar was big and would need strength and cunning to catch and subdue. *Should I shape-shift?* If she got close enough to the boar, her human form was better equipped to handle the boar than her dog form.

She moved closer to the wild boar, taking care not to alert it to her presence. It had found some tubers and was busy digging it out with its tusk. She crept closer to her prey. At ten yards away, with a burst of speed, she sprinted to it, grabbed its hind legs and swung the boar against the nearest tree, bashing its head. The boar did not stand a chance.

The animal could feed the tribe for two meals; she needed two more to assure three days' worth of food. She was scenting her environment, trying to pick up the odour of any nearby potential prey, when she scented another *Aswang* in the area. Someone she was not familiar with. She had not encountered other aswang in this part of the woods for decades.

This was curious.

She was looking for the aswang by scent when she heard the zing of a travelling bullet a millisecond before it hit her at the back of the head. She was dead before she hit the ground.

From behind a tree, the unfamiliar aswang stepped out to approach the fallen aswang that he shot. He laid the hunting rifle down beside the body. He inspected his prey for a moment, noting she must be a middle-aged, maybe a hundred to a hundred fifty years old. It was hard to tell with these indigenous people.

He took out his hunting knife and with quick, practiced movements, disembowelled his prey. His mouth watered when he got to the heart. This was his favourite organ. He sat by the root of the old tree where she dropped dead and enjoyed his spoils in leisure.

He felt the energy of another aswang course through his veins, and satisfaction suffused him. The risk of the crime was more than worth the reward for this kind of power.

Sometime later, he cut up the remaining organs and placed it in a collapsible ice bag to preserve them. The kidneys would be good for another eleven hours, and the liver another twenty-nine. Then he took out the folding shovel he carried in his backpack and started digging. He needed to bury her body so no one would find her. And the iztaris would never know there was an active harravis predating in the area.

9

YUANA, THE VISCEREBUS

The day started at half-past nine in the morning for Yuana. She still felt weak, and the tremor in her body had not dissipated. A tight ball of muscles ran up and down her spine. It rested at the small of her back where it shot sharp jolts of pain that jerked her upright. It took several deep breaths to relax her back until the spasm faded.

Her entire body ached, like some sort of malady.

Did I sleep in a bad position last night?

Once the pain disappeared, she continued to dress. She pulled on a light, flowy, and silky summer dress over her head. The dress was appropriate for later. It would be easy to pull off. With her hair tied in a loose bun, she proceeded downstairs to the breakfast room.

She was on her second cup of tea when her great-grandparents came down, their fingers intertwined. It was bittersweet to see their instinctive display of love for each other. It was something she wished for herself and Roald.

"Good morning, 'Ela, 'Elo." She greeted them with a smile. She knew they worried for her, and she wanted them reassured. They smiled back at the greeting, bent down and gave her a kiss on the cheek.

"Did you sleep well, Yu-yu?" Her 'Elo surveyed her pale face and touched the slight grey circles around her eyes. But he smiled in satisfaction.

Yuana gave her Abuelo a quick nod of confirmation. "Elo, Roald is coming at lunch today, to finish our talk." She wanted them informed. And she needed their help.

They exchanged quick glances and nodded their acknowledgement.

She understood they would let her take the lead on this, but their support was unequivocal.

While her great grandparents had omelette and toasts, she continued to have tea to calm her nerves. She had no appetite, and the tremor in her body returned and had intensified. The muscle spasms restarted. The knot at the base of her spine reformed and travelled up her back in a slow roll, tightening the muscles along the way. It had now rested at the base of her skull.

She regulated her breathing in silence, to will it away. Her great grandparents might get alarmed. It seemed her body was unaccustomed to emotional distress; it had no previous practice. This was the first real one she had ever experienced, and it was major.

"Yu, we want you to know that we readied the Risk Reduction and Intervention Plan. We placed the First Wave team of iztaris on alert, but we will not deploy them until your mother gives us the signal."

The information made her heart jump. This was no longer just between herself and Roald and their relationship. The hypothetical danger to Roald's life was now a reality.

She could only nod. "I understand, 'Elo. It is our law, after all. You had no choice. It would cause concern in the Tribunal, your position as Patriarch and Matriarch would be in jeopardy."

"But we are not so tied to the law that we cannot give the youngest of our clan some special privileges. It is within my call as Matriarch to allow your Roald a chance to redeem himself. Take your time if you are not ready for a full revelation today, because the RRIP's deployment would only kick in once you do." Her great grandmother smiled at her encouragingly.

"Thank you, 'Ela. But I am ready to do it today. I do not want to wait. I think my nerves can't take it..."

She grimaced as another spasm hit her. A soft gasp escaped her. She clenched her hand to stop the tremor, a smile pasted on her lips so as not to worry her elders. She regulated her breaths to will the spasms away, but they kept coming in waves, increasing in frequency and intensity.

Her great grandfather stared at her, noting the sweat on her brow, the strain of pain around her mouth. His hand shot out and closed over her clenched palm.

"Yuana, you are having a reflexive transformation episode. You're about to auto-morphose." Her great grandfather's voice was as tense as the hand that covered hers.

Her great grandmother's gaze became alert as it swivelled to her.

"What do you mean, 'Elo?" She tried to calm the tremor in her muscles and stop the spasm that travelled up and down her back. The pain of it robbed her of breath. She was panting within a minute.

"You haven't had sustenance for two days, and your vital hunger is growing. Your bones and muscles are preparing to transfigure, but your crux, your inner control is preventing it, hence the tremors and the spasms. If you don't get sustenance soon, you will be too weak to fight your vital instinct and it will overpower your crux, and you cannot stop the transformation. Our vital instinct will ensure that you hunt, to secure sustenance," her great grandfather explained as he watched her fight off the transfiguration.

Without sustenance, she had a few more hours before she shape-shifted into her animus. She never had to fight off her vital instinct before. She had no experience or practice; her crux was not that strong.

Her great grandmother's conversation over the phone with her Uncle Íñigo floated to her. She asked for help. Her 'Ela walked back to the breakfast room to the sight of her hyperventilating in an effort to stay the spasms and the tremors.

"Yuana, relax... Take long slow breaths in... long slow breaths out. Focus on your breathing, not the spasms or the tremors. Just focus on your own breaths..."

Her 'Ela's voice was as soothing as the warm hands that enveloped her clammy ones. She obeyed, slowed her breathing, and within a few minutes, the spasms subsided, the tremors abated.

"Thank you, 'Ela," she breathed. Wisps of loose hair had stuck on her sweaty neck and face. She was drenched.

"You're welcome, Yu. Íñigo is coming with victus in about an hour. Can you hold on until then?" Her calm voice was reassuring. Her gaze travelled all over her face, and she looked satisfied colour was back on her cheeks.

She nodded. She was glad she would be better soon. It would not do if she shape-shifted into her big cat form in front of Roald without warning.

And worse, what if my vital instinct took over my animus, and I attacked Roald, being the only human in proximity?

"Eat, Yuana, even if you have no appetite. You need protein in your system to boost your strength," her great grandfather said.

As if on cue, Nita came into the room with some slices of beef, cooked medium and sautéed.

She complied, recognising now she was hungry on both fronts. Her physical hunger was easier to satisfy than her vital hunger. If it would help stave her vital instincts from kicking in, then eat this beef she would, until Uncle Íñigo arrives.

Roald also got up early, for a different reason. He spent the morning researching online about the malady that Yuana could suffer from. He discarded a few of the listed symptoms. So far, the closest he found was Clinical Lycanthropy and Renfield Syndrome.

Clinical Lycanthropy might be the best explanation for Yuana's psychosis. Those who suffer from it were convinced they turn into wolves or other animals. If those patients assumed themselves to be werewolves, it was not a stretch for Yuana to believe she was an aswang.

Those diagnosed with the disease sometimes barked or howled like wolves, but as far as he knew Yuana never behaved or exhibited animal behaviour. She had been perfectly and beautifully normal until her pronouncement.

As for the Renfield Syndrome, Yuana had not exhibited an obsession to drink blood or any other behavioural patterns associated with the syndrome. They had been together almost daily for three years, and she had shown no signs of paranoia, let alone the desire to drink blood which seemed to be the primary component of the malady. His stomach turned at the idea. He was glad to strike that one out.

The research, while not conclusive, gave him hope. If it was a medical condition, it just needed treatment. Maybe her condition was rare that she believed herself to be a mythical monster rather than a normal animal. But it did not matter, because if psychiatry sessions could treat Clinical Lycanthropy, then her psychosis was treatable.

It was a relief to hold the results of his extensive research. The pressure on his chest eased to a degree he felt almost the same as before. Thank the tech gods for Google and Reddit. With the relief came the realisation he was famished. He had not eaten a proper meal for what seemed like an eternity, so while he printed his research materials, he made himself breakfast.

After eating, he planned to take a shower and drive over to Yuana's as agreed. He was due there at eleven a.m.

Hours later, his mood was buoyant, even excited, as he jumped into his car, briefcase in tow, to drive himself to the De Vida home.

Since ten a.m., the whole De Vida clan, except Ysobella and Galen who were still on their way, gathered in the living room. They scattered around, each trying to project calm in the tension-filled morning.

Not one of them knew how the day would unfold as Yuana never discussed her plan. And on top of it, she was in danger of involuntary shapeshifting because her vital instinct was triggered. Even now, they watched Yuana calming herself down, trying to keep her crux in control, to delay the shift for as long as possible.

Íñigo had not called yet. The sources he worked on this morning were not appropriate, so he called all their other branches to see if they could find what Yuana needed - fresh human viscera. The location had to be less than an hour away. They also had to make sure they were not taking away from other aswangs.

Ximena realised they needed a plan just in case Yuana transfigured. Her vital instinct to hunt might override her control.

"Mama, Papa, we need a place for Yuana to rest while we are waiting for Íñigo, just in case she transforms. We need to make sure she is away from Roald and Galen..."

Margaita and Lorenzo both nodded and scrambled into action.

Her great grandfather led her to the entertainment room. It was a spacious room, with twelve well-upholstered maroon leather seats and padded cream walls for better sound quality. This was her favourite. It had a lingering smell of butter popcorn courtesy of the automatic popcorn machine in the corner. There was no obvious movie screen on the wall, instead, it would descend from the ceiling via remote control. Her grandparents commissioned it for watching movies and playing games. It was perfect to keep the noise in and out.

Her great grandmother sat with her to keep her entertained and distracted from the tremor and the spasms. They sat in companionable silence, breathing in and out in unison to keep her focused on her breathing.

The reflexive transformation and all the burning sensations that kept coming in waves all over her took precedence. She had never experienced this before. She never had to go without sustenance and worry about having her vital instinct kick in to the point of desperation. And if Uncle Íñigo did not come soon, she would have firsthand knowledge of the desire that drove their kind to hunt humans.

Already, the tremors were getting harder to quiet, the knotted ball of muscle at the base of her spine more difficult to subdue. Her skin tingled, creating goosebumps, and her stomach muscles twisted into knots. Her transformation was imminent.

Will I shape-shift into my favourite animal, or will my vital instinct decide what form I will turn into?

"It is likely you will turn into the animal you most often shape-shift into," her 'Ela replied.

"Did I say that out aloud?" It startled her. But she was glad to focus on something else.

"Not so loud, but yes, you did." A reassuring smile on her great-grandmother's face.

"Likely? What other animals can I turn into aside from my usual go-to panther?" She knew very little about this impending process.

"It seemed that De Vida women have a partiality for sleek felines. Your grandma Katelin's animus is a leopard." The idea amused her great-grandmother. "So, why a panther? Like your mother?"

"Yeah, well, a panther is sexy, 'Ela. And it is easier to hide in the dark when your coat is black." She was curious now what her great grandmother's spirit animal would be. "So, what is yours, 'Ela? And how about 'Elo's?"

"I shift into a wolf. Your aunt Ximena's animus is also a wolf. Your 'Elo is a bear."

Interesting. "So, what other animals will I transform into?"

"It's hard to tell. Your grandfather used to transform into a fox until he discovered that his true animus was a dire wolf. Mine had always been a wolf, and it was the same when I auto-morphosed."

"But why do we have two spirit animal forms? Shouldn't we just aim to transform into our animus in the first place?"

"In the olden times, we didn't choose our spirit animal. The adults force an auto-morphosis while the child is young, and the child's first transformation would usually be their animus. Later on, we discovered we can master our transformation skills, and we learned to shift into many other animals. And children learned to choose their form to some extent. Times changed, and soon, our kind trained to transform with the animal form of our choice, rather than what our spirit dictated."

"So, what is the likelihood of my animus being wolf like yours, 'Ela?"

Her Ela shook her head. "Not a chance. You have a natural affinity for feline beings. Your spirit animal was a panther, your animus, if it is not a panther, would most likely be one within the cat family."

"Ah... I like my current animal form. I am used to it. Can I keep it even if I transform into another cat?" She felt regret at having to give up being a panther.

"You can always shift into your old form. But your true animus will be the most natural and powerful form for you. You will have more synergy with its attributes and powers. You will know the difference when it happens."

"I feel foolish. I have been an aswang since birth, transformed multiple times. Yet I still have a lot to learn about being one."

"We all do, my dear. The modern times had limited us to the rudimentary layer of our being. We allowed ourselves to ignore and forget our elemental power deep inside. Just like most of our kind transform only into their chosen animal form, very few do in their spirit animal. And majority of our kind would die without knowing and experiencing their animus."

"Well, if there was a silver lining to this excruciating process, it would be the unravelling of my true animus."

Her great-grandmother nodded, smiling.

"Ela, shouldn't I be wearing an impedio?" She recalled the use of the contraption that all of them were required by the Tribunal to have for such a time like this.

Her Abuela shook her head. "If you were alone, or if your companions would not be able to restrain you, then yes, you should be strapped in one. But with all of us here, there is no need for it." The confidence in her voice was enough to reassure her.

Voices from the living room streamed through the door left ajar by her great-grandfather, who went out to join the others. The voices of her mother and father were in the mix. She heard them ask for her and her Aunt Ximena's reply, pointing to where she was.

Her mother and father rushed in and hugged her. Her father's face lined with concern. "How are you, sweetie?" he asked, his gaze scrutinising.

"I'm okay, Papa. I..." she gasped.

A sharp stab of pain from her gut to her chest jolted her out of his embrace, cutting her voice off. The spasm at the base of her spine restarted hard and fast, the force of it bent her over. She clutched her stomach.

It alarmed Galen to see the spasming knot of muscles run up and down his daughter's back while she was bent over with what appeared to be severe stomach pain. He panicked for a split second, not knowing what to do, then his doctor side kicked in. He moved to examine Yuana, but Ysobella held him back. Her eyes were wide with urgency as she pulled him out of the room, closing the door behind them.

"Where are we going? Yuana needs me." He tried to resist Ysobella's pull, but her strength prevented him from going back to the room.

"You need to be away from her as she might shape-shift by reflex." Ysobella kept pulling him farther away from the room.

"Why do I need to stay away from her? I have seen you transform."

"That was different, Galen. Mine was a voluntary transformation. Yuana had taken no sustenance for the past two days, and her vital hunger has surfaced. When it takes over, her vital instinct will force her to hunt, and she might be too weak to control it. When that happens, she will go for the closest human around."

Terror struck his soul. The thought of his daughter attacking a human was too big a shock to take in. He never thought of his Bel, his daughter, or the whole De Vida clan as savage man-eaters. Despite their penchant for human organs, they were as sophisticated as the most affluent people he had met. Being told and almost witnessing a display of this nature of an aswang was jarring.

The front door opened, and an older gentleman walked in. He went straight through to the living room, like he was a part of the family. He had a peppering of grey hairs on his temple, and his smart, casual clothes fit his toned physique. The guy must have been a decade older than him.

"Thank god you're here, and just at the nick of time!" Ximena said as she jumped up from her seat.

She took the familiar ice box from the hands of the stranger. Nobody seemed to have thought of introducing the new arrival to him. All eyes were on the icebox that Ximena had rushed to the kitchen. Galen did not need any explanation of what it contained or what it was for. In this matter, he was in sync with the aswangs in the room.

Katelin hastened to the entertainment room, and the sounds of Yuana's gasp of pain and heavy breathing echoed in the living room.

He shot to his feet; paternal instinct overriding his sense of self-preservation. But Ysobella's grip on his arm prevented him from going to his daughter. Ysobella was strong; the power of her physical capability to restrain him was clear. Another aswang trait that separated them from humans like himself.

The doorbell rang loud and there was a synchronised swivelling of heads towards the main door, all breathing suspended. Roald had arrived.

After a split-second pause, Edrigu sprung from his seat to open the door for Roald.

Roald came into the room carrying a briefcase. He looked nervous and became more uneasy when he saw the entire family gathered. He searched for Yuana among them. Unsure of what to do, he stood just at the edge of the room.

"Is Yuana here, sir?" Roald inquired.

Edrigu nodded and motioned him to a seat but said nothing else. He threw a side glance at Katelin, which she understood. Katelin got up and walked past Roald towards the entertainment room.

Roald remained standing where he was.

Just as Katelin opened the door, the sound of agony rang from the room. And to Roald's ears, it was unmistakable; it was Yuana. The briefcase fell out of his nerveless fingers, and without a thought, he rushed towards the entertainment room. The terror in the sound and fear for her propelled him.

What he witnessed rendered him speechless. Yuana was on all fours in the middle of the room, Margaita on her knees beside her, calming her. Yuana was heaving, her back arched, her spine rippled. A ball of muscles travelled from between her shoulder blades down to her lower back, the movement stark under her silk dress.

Even from a few feet away, he could see the feverish flush that covered her body. The heat wave she generated reached him. Her skin vibrated, it changed colour and texture. Her smooth flesh-toned skin darkened into glossy jet black...

Stunned and shaken, he did not remember being pulled in haste out of the room. He found himself seated on the couch; a glass of dark liquid thrust into his hand by Galen. When he looked back toward the entertainment room, he saw Lorenzo and Edrigu disappear inside the room. The door closed behind them, shutting out the sound.

Vaguely, he looked around. All eyes were upon him, their expressions grim. He felt as dazed as someone who suffered a massive blow to the head; he could not think. Galen's hand steadied the glass, the liquid in it sloshed by the tremor of his hand, spilling some on his fingers.

"Drink, it will help," the older man directed him.

Steadying himself, he took a sip. It was brandy. He was too bewildered to note its quality. The drink spread warmth through his chest. The fiery trail it created along his throat was the only thing that anchored him to reality.

Galen looked at the young man he had liked from the first time they met and felt extreme pity for what he was about to face. He could recognise a kindred spirit in him, a shared experience. The abrupt manner of Roald's discovery of Yuana's secret shook the boy far more than when he found out about Bel's hidden nature. And this was worrying.

A chorus of sighs of relief broke from everyone's lips when the kitchen door opened and revealed Nita bearing the wooden tray that Galen had nicknamed the organ-bearer. She hastened to the entertainment room.

The moment the door was ajar, a chilling animal sound echoed from the inside. It was something he did not recognise; it sounded like a cross between a human scream, a panther roar, and a bird call.

Yuana may have transformed. He just didn't know what she turned into.

The wooden platter was an answered prayer. For the moment, Yuana quelled her transformation, but it took every ounce of energy in her body to do so. Panting, she looked up, her body covered in sweat despite the air-conditioning in the room. Nita rushed the platter over. An entire heart, sliced in inch-thick portions, fresh and bloody, lay in the middle. Her trembling hand reached over for a slice; her instinct took over.

An overwhelming sense of well-being washed over her as she consumed all of it. It was beyond normal satiation of a physical hunger and thirst. It was an explosion of sensation that suffused her from head to toe. Like water poured over a flame, it extinguished the burning pain in her middle. The sliver of a human heart encapsulated her fundamental need for human organs.

Free of the tremors and the spasms at last, she leaned back in her chair. Her hair was damp, the natural waves more pronounced. Her muscles ached with the strain; her lungs felt raw. The exhaustion fled her body like smoke dissipating in the air and was replaced by an electrifying energy that made her whole body tingle. Its power radiated outward to the top of her head and to the tips of her fingers and toes. The chilly air made her shiver and raised goosebumps in her skin. Nita dropped a warm blanket around her shoulders.

"Thank you, Nita," she said as Nita leaned over to plant a kiss on her forehead.

Nita lifted her bloody fingers and wiped them clean with a warm, wet hand towel. With that done, she took the platter away with her.

Yuana sat still for a moment to temper the energy that coursed through her veins. Movements in the room caught her attention as she noticed her 'Elo and grandfather. Their presence reminded her Roald would be here soon. She must look a fright. She pushed herself off the couch.

Katelin pushed her back to her chair, "Calm down, Yuana. We can handle Roald for you for a while. Take a few more minutes to collect yourself."

There was caution in her grandmother's tone, and that made her frown.

"Meet with him when you are ready, and only when you are ready." Her great-grandmother, in contrast, was the picture of composure and serenity.

She nodded, although they averted one crisis, she would need to deal with the original issue at hand. It was impossible to remain calm.

"Yuana, Roald saw..." her grandfather Edrigu said in a quiet voice.

Her stomach dropped. Her 'Ela and grandmother looked up in surprise.

"What did he see, Lolo?" A sense of foreboding was back.

"He saw enough, Hija," Her grandfather's response was gentle, his gaze apologetic.

"How did he take it?" Her heart ached for Roald. She would have preferred a better way for him to find out.

"He's still outside with your father and mother," her Lolo replied.

The lack of a direct answer was answer enough. Roald did not take it well.

"I didn't think this through, Lolo. I don't know what to do," she admitted, "Any suggestions?"

Edrigu considered the question, "He's a logical sort, very technical. So, appeal to his logic, if he is still willing to listen."

Is Roald still willing to listen?

She was hoping he would be.

There was only one move forward. She could start with finding out what part of the myth Roald knew and believed. Other proof could come later, if needed, to support her explanations about their kind, and how it was to live like them, how similar and dissimilar they were from humans.

Bolstered by a semblance of a plan, she picked herself up and smoothed her skirts down. With her shoulders straight and head held high, she walked towards the living room.

Her elders followed suit.

A gamut of emotions bombarded him when Yuana walked into the living room. She looked pale, but there was a fierce light in her eyes, her expression serious. His heart's elevated heartbeats had not slowed down yet, but it galloped faster at the sight of her.

The earlier images of her on her knees, the spasming muscles running down her back, her vibrating skin, and the howl he heard, all came rushing back. The dread morphed into terror. He wanted to run, but her gaze held him in place.

"How are you?" she asked him and touched his cheek.

He laid his hand over hers in reaction and felt his own icy skin. No doubt because of shock. Her warm fingers anchored him to the present. There was dampness in the roots of her hair, the clamminess of her skin contradicted the heat of her hand. And yet the knot in his chest stayed, and the sensation of being in a nightmare remained.

Her family sat themselves in a half circle on the long sofa, the middle seat empty. She led him to sit across her and her family before she took the vacant seat. This was an explicit statement of both support and instruction from them.

"What do you think you saw, Roald?" Yuana asked without preamble.

His terror grew like a cloud overhead. He did not know how to describe what he witnessed. He was unsure if he imagined it.

"I am not sure, Yuana..." he rasped. Half of him wanted her to reassure him he just imagined it.

"I was transforming, shape-shifting into my animal form. I did not want for you to find out that way," she sighed.

"Your animal form?" he echoed, baffled, his panic rose.

"My hunting form. Our kind shape-shifts into animals so we can hunt for human prey. That's what aswangs did in the old days. We no longer do that." Yuana's voice was calm, even, and dispassionate.

"What does that mean? Being an aswang?" He was desperate to receive lucid information his thinking brain could handle. Something his mind could understand. Anything that made sense to him.

"It means I have to consume human liver, heart or kidney with regularity to survive; that I transform into an animal whenever I want or need to. It means I live thrice as long." Her voice increased in intensity, but not in volume.

"Why are you saying this, Yuana?" He wanted her to retract all of it.

Yuana's eyes flashed. "Because I want you to understand exactly what you will sign for if you choose to be with me. And what you will leave behind."

Roald's heart sank deeper at every statement she made. There was no need for proof. He realised he believed her. The presence of everyone in the room was confirmation. His brain felt like exploding. He cradled his head between his hands, trying to ease the throbbing that had begun earlier, and had now doubled.

Anger sparked in the depths of Yuana's eyes.

"And, Roald, it means our future kids will be *aswangs*. Like me..." Her words sharp. It cut through his heart like a hot knife. "They will eat human organs, transform into predatory animals... They will all be like me."

His head snapped back up. Horror enveloped him. That was too much to take in. He stood up and walked out. A new terror screamed in his head. His legs were too shaky for him to run, but his heart was ready to burst with the enormity of his panic.

Yuana watched Roald walk away. Anger and grief cloaked her soul. If their relationship would end, it was best that he severed it himself.

Seconds later, Roald's car zoomed away. Silence dominated the room. The whole De Vida clan, including her father, didn't know what to say. Tears ran down her face as she tried to keep the devastation in. Her shoulders shook with the effort not to howl.

Roald failed the test.

That night, Galen and Ysobella spent the night at the De Vida mansion. Yuana needed her family now more than ever.

Galen was unaware of the exact plans of the De Vidas, but he suspected they had contingencies for cases like this since it was paramount to their survival as a species to remain hidden. He would give Roald up to forty-eight hours himself to adjust to his new reality, and then he would whip him into shape. He did not want his daughter to end up with the burden of having to kill Roald herself.

If it came to it, he would be more than happy to do it for her.

Beside him, he could sense Ysobella was trying hard to suppress her rage. There was a hardness in the lines of her face. He had never seen her angry, but the set of her jaw showed him how formidable his sweet wife could be.

He touched her clenched fist, and Ysobella let out a deep breath.

"I asked the family to give Roald two chances to redeem himself. He's blown his first chance. For Yuana's sake, I will keep to that arrangement. But *Holy Prometheus*, Galen, I wanted to pluck his heart out and crush it with my bare hands for hurting our daughter..." The fury made her voice tremble.

"If it comes to that, you will have to give me the honour, my love. I'm giving him two days to come to his senses, then I will come after him."

Ysobella stared at him. Tears glistened in their depths, out of anger, frustration, and heartbreak.

As planned, Edrigu sent a message to Dr Sanchez to prepare her team. Lorenzo would meet the iztari teams tomorrow, for their individual task assignments.

He would update Roald's dossier. He would deploy the First Wave team of iztaris.

Hopefully, for the sake of Yuana, their deployment would not go further than the Second Wave.

10

THE FIRST WAVE

Roald didn't realise it was already morning until the doorbell rang. He did not want to answer it. He just wanted to be alone, but the ringing was incessant. It became obvious after ten minutes of the constant peal of the doorbell whoever was on the other side of the door was not going away.

He dragged himself off the couch, still wearing the same clothes he had on yesterday. His limbs were stiff from sitting for so long. He peeked through the peephole — Daniel. He opened the door while trying to recall if they had set an appointment today.

"Dude, what took you so... long... What the heck, Roald? You look terrible!"

Daniel looked him up and down. He was sure that Dan noted the rumpled clothes, the shadow of beard on his face, the dullness in his eyes, the exhaustion. Daniel had never seen him like this, but he did not care.

He returned to his couch and dropped back on it. His head was still pounding, his mind and body drained. He felt heart-heavy and soul-weary. The dissonance in his mind and heart was so great he had no words to describe the anguish he was in.

"Bro, c'mon, talk to me. What is wrong?" Daniel persisted and followed him to the living room.

He saw alarm on Dan's face. But he did not have the energy to respond and converse at the moment. And even if he did, he did not know how or where to even begin. He still could not believe it himself.

His dry, tired eyes hurt. He had not slept since he returned from Yuana's house. He was beyond miserable.

Roald sighed, then he heard Daniel walk to his kitchen and putter about. Soon, the hiss of steaming water and the smell of coffee permeated the room. And something in him thawed. His mouth watered at the fragrance of the brew, but he kept his eyes closed. He did not want to encourage conversation.

"Come on, Roald. I will not leave until you tell me what is wrong," Daniel called over from the kitchen, with the badgering tone that he was familiar with. There was no avoiding Daniel's presence. He roused himself and sat up straight.

With two cups of hot coffee in hand, Daniel approached and placed both cups on the coffee table. His friend sat across him and waited for him to say something.

He reached for the cup that Daniel brought and took a sip. The bitter, toasty flavour and the heat of the coffee cleared the cobwebs from his brain.

Perhaps if he went out with Daniel to whatever appointment they had for the day, it would give him respite from the quagmire of emotions that was twisting him up inside and loosen the knot in his chest and stomach.

"Are we supposed to go somewhere today?" He met Daniel's assessing gaze over the swirling steam of the coffee.

Dan shook his head. "No, we have no plans. I came by to ask for your advice and feedback on the pitch deck I prepared for my Series A."

Daniel fished out a memory stick from his pocket and placed it on Roald's coffee table.

He could only nod. He felt depleted, yet restless; dog-tired, but unable to sleep. The glare of the sun aggravated him and made him nauseous.

"So, are you going to tell me what happened?" Daniel persisted.

"I am not ready yet." He sounded strained and disoriented, even to himself.

"Okay," Daniel relented. "But if you need to talk about it, just give me a holler. Go get some sleep, your face would put a zombie to shame."

He nodded, leaned back, and closed his eyes once more.

Daniel could see the damage to Roald's psyche. He was grief stricken. The misery that enveloped him was severe. He had thought, or rather hoped, Roald and Yuana would tire of each other in due course, that their relationship would cool down, that their breakup would not be this devastating. He did not expect Roald to be this shattered about it.

How long will it take Roald to climb out of it?

He should call Yuana and check how she was doing. She must be as devastated as Roald. But he had a job to do, and that required watching over his friend and preventing further damage to Yuana. And to Roald.

They continued to sip coffee in silence. Daniel understood Roald was not ready and was still in shock— more likely in denial. For now, he would be a sympathetic friend and allow Roald the time to come to terms with what he discovered.

After half an hour of companionable silence, he patted Roald's shoulder in a silent gesture of sympathy and farewell.

He had a preliminary report to write.

Roald could not sleep, no matter how hard he tried. When Daniel left, he had drawn the curtains closed to darken the room, but his thoughts still would not slow down. He laid there for hours, unable to fall asleep.

More than thrice, he considered working. He scanned his email inbox, trying to find a message that would motivate him to do something, but for the life of him, he could not rouse himself to do so. He lost his appetite for food, his work, his life.

He caught sight of the red car-shaped memory stick, a miniature Ferrari, on the coffee table. Maybe reading something colourful like Daniel's pitch deck would help serve as a distraction or even an impetus for him.

He reached for his laptop stored under the coffee table, turned it on, and plugged the memory stick in. He clicked on the only file, and it opened into the elegant visuals of Daniel's company - Domestech's investor's deck.

Ten minutes later, he failed to make headway on the material. His laptop screen had darkened into a snooze because of lack of activity. All he gathered from staring at this deck was that the corporate colours of Domestech were the same shade of burgundy and silver of Daniel's father's company. The words, the graphs, the visuals did not make any impression on him. After another ten minutes, he gave up altogether, and closed the lid of his laptop.

He looked around his unit, and contemplated if drinking some cognac would help today, as it did not offer him any solace yesterday.

An hour later, his second shot remained untouched on the coffee table. He had not slept for over twenty-four hours, and he knew his body needed sleep, but nothing seemed to work. Every kind of distraction he tried had not worked so far. In the past, when he was in a troubled state, all he needed was... Yuana.

The thought of her sent a streak of agony through his heart. He should not think about her. Not today, not yet. If he did, it meant he would have to deal with what happened, what changed, what loomed in their future. And what was driving him to the edge of panic...

To take his mind off Yuana and the impending decision he knew he needed to make, he hit the gym. Working out always engaged his brain, and he figured this was better than drinking.

Edrigu received a message from the First Wave Team. They reported they were all in position; the *Breach* was in place, but not yet triggered, and that Roald was just about to go over the edge, his reaction a little more pronounced than projected. The revelation had hit Roald hard.

Edrigu replied and gave his instruction to his team. Roald's actions could bode well, or be disastrous for them, a first in half a century for their clan.

Yuana did not lock herself in her room this time, but spent it walking around in a daze in the garden or sat in solitude at the library. She seemed disinterested in doing anything at all.

Tomorrow, Ysobella and Galen would take Yuana to their estate in Mindoro, at the foot of Mount Halcon. She needed to get away, to be closer to fresh air and the sun, and to give herself the space to run around in her animus to vent.

Nita left early for Villa Bizitza to prepare the house and the household team for Ysobella's family. The trip served two purposes: to distract his granddaughter and to keep Galen away from their activities on implementing the RRIP. Galen need not know the details of their operation. He was still under observation and not integrated into the family yet.

Two weeks on, Roald came back from the now usual three-hour gym session. His six-foot frame more toned than it had ever been in all his life. But the gruelling workouts that allowed him to escape for the past days lost its diversionary value. He needed to find an alternative or a supplement to it.

He sat down to have a tall drink of lemonade, replacing the lost liquids the backbreaking work-out squeezed out of him. It was moments like this, when he did not have a task that required his focus that the forced restraint he placed on himself crumbled under the avalanche of emotions.

For the past sixteen days, he was like a zombie. He filled the days with physical activities, meetings that never held his interest, and nights going out with Daniel. He refused to deal with the core of his unease, was postponing the inevitable, because something about it scared him. But he kept telling himself he just needed more time to figure out why he felt so disordered.

He missed Yuana, and the need to hear her voice was getting stronger every day. It all contributed to his disquiet. But he had no business calling her until he sorted out his views and feelings about her... nature. He needed to deal with the panic whenever he thought of her being an aswang. He did not want to lose Yuana, but he was uncertain how, or if he could even get past it.

His sleep, when it came, was troubled by recurring nightmares. He was not eating well, his appetite shot. And his mother worried about him. She called every day since he and Yuana failed to show up to the opening of his mother's new shop. She knew something was wrong, but he could not open up to her.

How would one tell their mother that her future daughter-in-law was an aswang?

Ten days ago, she'd showed up unannounced to his condo, took one look at him and guessed in an instant what was wrong. She worried most about his lack of appetite and his inability to sleep. He blamed the nightmares, but instead of being mollified, she worried even more.

Her mother booked appointments for him with a psychiatrist, but he kept cancelling on her. Her mother persisted, and for some reason, the doctor kept allowing the reschedule.

Now, he was bone tired, his emotions and mind stretched taut, and he had developed a permanent chest ache. Their company doctor found nothing wrong with him physically, so it had to be psychological.

Maybe it was time to obey his mother's and take Daniel's advice. He needed professional help.

Yuana fared little better.

She accomplished her days on autopilot. Her mind, in one hand, was full of imaginings of Roald coming around, accepting her like her father did with her mother. And in another, preparing herself for the future without Roald.

She knew her despondency, her lack of energy and interest in anything directly resulted from her depressed state. Her family insisted that she focus on her well-being, and not to worry about anything else. It gave her permission not to bother with anything else but herself.

Her parents were enjoying themselves, at least. But their concern for her marred their joy. So, she spent time out in the woods to give her parents opportunities to be alone, and not watch her mope around the house.

The decision to get away and go to the Villa had been a good thing. Nature soothed her disquiet. She spent hours walking in the forest that bordered their land and running long distances at night in her panther form. Her lone treks into the woods worried her father. Not even a display of her strength compared to humans appeased him. It took her mother's instruction to take two of their aswang household staff to shadow her, to convince her father to let her go out.

The mountain had been hers alone during her outings. It was easy to avoid the human hikers. She could smell and hear them some distance away.

But the setting sun always reminded her the respite was temporary, and there were people expecting her and a reality waiting for her back home.

As she looked out into the vast expanse of their land from her bedroom verandah, across the lush undulating green at the base of Mount Halcon, she felt a measure of peace. It reminded her of her youth and the days when she had no cares but her childhood curiosity. The enormous and ancient trees beckoned to her, as if they sensed she needed healing. And while in their midst, time had no influence.

With her hair drying in the natural air, the hem of her purple wrap dress stirred in the breeze, the whisperings of nature called to her. The sun sank behind the mountain peak. It would be dark soon.

Then a familiar, soft whirring sound blew in with the wind. It came over the horizon. The sound grew louder. She knew what it was before she saw the familiar Dynali H3 helicopter the family owned. It was flying in from their Calapan branch, carrying the sustenance for the household.

With the helicopter's arrival, her parents would expect her to come down to the living room soon. To join them in the cocktail hour that they had taken a habit to before dinner. Maybe a glass of G&T would stimulate her soul for a few hours.

Ysobella got off a phone call with her father, who informed her of the First Wave team's action so far. They had deployed an iztari in Roald's condominium tower, another in his gym. Two others were tailing him in shifts.

Roald had been suffering as much, if not more, as Yuana. And he had been drowning his pain in physical activities, mental challenges, and a lot of trivial pursuits. It softened her anger against Roald. It gave her hope for her daughter.

The sound of the approaching Dynali helicopter broke her reverie. Their sustenance was here. She turned to see Galen dressed in smart casual clothes, looking elegant and ready for dinner as he came out of the adjoining bathroom. They would have cocktails first, as was their custom. As part of the compromise with him, the cocktail hour afforded her and Yuana the ideal occasion to consume their victus out of Galen's sight in consideration for his stomach.

"So, what did your father say?" Galen asked as they descended the stairs to the living room.

"Not much. Just updating me of what was happening at work." She shrugged.

She felt uneasy not telling him everything, but her parents requested she not to divulge the iztari operations until it was necessary.

Yuana sat on the couch, her expression pensive, as she contemplated the cinnamon stick, orange peel and basil leaf garnish on her clear drink. Gone was the lifeless expression that graced her face over the past few days. This was an improvement.

She glanced at Galen and noticed a similar approving glint in his eyes. They agreed. This version of Yuana was better. They both pasted a pleasant expression on their faces; presenting a cheerful facade to their daughter helped reduce her anxiety.

"How was your walk in the woods, my sweet?" Galen asked and kissed his daughter's cheek.

"I went to the beach today." Yuana smiled, there was a twinkle in her eyes. She seemed more upbeat, not so melancholy.

"Oh. Did anything interesting happened?" she asked.

"Yes, I met some of our kind from the Lantuyan tribe. It surprised me to find out that our aswang kin live in open and cooperative existence within the human Mangyan community. Does our Tribunal know?" Yuana's gaze focused on her, keen interest in its depths.

She nodded. "Oh yes, the Tribunal knows. It was your 'Ela's grandmother who secured the permission from the Supreme Tribunal two centuries ago."

"Oh..." Father and daughter's remark came in unison.

"Their relationship with the tribe's people is unique. While it deviated from the Veil of Secrecy law, the SVT granted them an exception. The reason behind it was their tribal practices, which remained unchanged to this day. The tribe considers the aswang among them as divine. In return, the aswangs use their skills to provide food for their tribes-people. It is a symbiotic relationship. And if one or two ever thought of claiming there were aswangs in their tribe, the modern humans would never believe it. They will dismiss it as a folktale."

"Isn't that ironic, mama, that an unsophisticated tribe has more freedom than us, the civilised kin?" Yuana's mouth turned up in a slight curl.

"That is fascinating," Galen said, one eyebrow arched in keen interest. "How big is this tribe? And do they know about us?"

She nodded. "The Lantuyan aswangs is a small group, just seven of them. Our company employs them to do a thorough search of the island for other aswangs. One of their covers is as guides for hikers during the limited hiking season in Mount Halcon. Some of them work the grounds of Villa Bizitza together with some human Mangyans. We need a few to cover the property, as it is twenty-hectares."

Galen's eyes widened. "Oh. So, all of them work for companies owned by your kind?"

"Well, a few of them work with the city hall of Calapan, where a small community of lowland aswangs live and work with the GJDV branch in Calapan. Part of their benefits, just like all aswang employees of the company, is the daily ration of sustenance. The Tribunal provides for every one of our kind," she replied.

"Your Tribunal certainly functions better than any human governments that I know of," Galen said.

"It's a matter of survival. We have no choice, Papa," Yuana said with a tinge of bitterness.

One hundred forty-nine kilometres away, Roald stared at the photo of the psychiatrist his mother had chosen for him on his phone. He had done some research on her and found her credentials top notch. He had checked the top in her field of study and his search kept leading him to Dr Emme Sanchez. She was the preeminent expert in this field of psychiatry.

The vice in his heart loosened. If he would spill his guts and Yuana's secret to a stranger, at least it would be to a medical professional. She would have the skills and experience to help him. And any information he divulged, the doctor-patient confidentiality would protect both Yuana and him.

Dr Sanchez would think him crazy for giving credence to Yuana's claim, but he was not concerned about being believed, he did not need the validation. What he wanted were some answers to the questions in his head and what steps he could take to find relief from his inner torment.

For now, he would take a shower and meet Daniel at the bar across the street. His hours of avoiding his own thoughts would end tomorrow, so he might as well take advantage of the remaining hours. Hopefully, tomorrow he, and by extension, his mother, would find satisfaction from the session.

Dr Emme Sanchez felt a certain sense of grim satisfaction as she put the phone down. It was apparent their RRIP, deployed for the second time in her lifetime, worked as predicted. The subject had called her to confirm their appointment set for tomorrow at lunch. The Breach was flawless, as expected.

She typed the message: *the yarn is on the spindle,* and sent it to the First Wave team to trigger the next step in the plan. She opened the file waiting in her laptop - Roald Magsino's dossier. The more she knew about him before their session tomorrow, the better.

Roald Magsino's case would not be a repeat of the last time. She would not have another De Vida suffer from her mistake. Death would be a better alternative for this young man should he fail the test.

The first one, decades ago, a man who did not deserve what he got, ended up with a fate worse than death. She contributed to the horrific fate of imprisoning his mind into a never-ending nightmare. Both she and Ximena were still paying for what they did to him fifty years on.

This was the most personal case she has ever had to do as a psychiatrist since then. She would do better for this one.

Maybe Roald Magsino was to be her penance, her atonement.

Daniel arrived half an hour early at the bar where he and Roald agreed to meet. He ordered a whisky while he waited. He had just met with the First Wave team. They discussed each other's updates. The software he deployed on Roald's laptop channelled him to the office of Dr Sanchez, as they meant for him to do.

He felt a deep sense of guilt for introducing Roald to Yuana three years ago. If he had not, his friends would not be in this predicament. He should have recognised Roald was smitten the first time he saw Yuana. His friend's firm resistance to diversion and discouragement was a dead giveaway.

Roald would have met Yuana that day, anyway. Roald would have found a way.

Despite Roald's firm interest then, he also never thought it would turn serious. Yuana always put a barrier between herself and the men she dated, and understandably, too. And Roald was the quintessential perpetual bachelor. He assumed Yuana and Roald would end up as friends, like how most of Yuana's flings ended up being.

He remembered the teenage pact he made with Yuana when they first became friends as teenagers; he could be her perpetual boyfriend shield to protect her from falling in love. It seemed like a marvellous idea in the first few months until Yuana released him from the pact because it hampered both their dating lives.

Perhaps they should have taken the pact more seriously, and they would not face this now.

Maybe it was providential because it positioned him to help Roald get out of this as unscathed as possible. At least, with his mind or his life intact.

It was to Roald's credit he never mentioned to him Yuana admitted to being an aswang. He had kept the information to himself, even if he was having a hard time accepting it. Roald had kept Yuana's secret for weeks now. There was no doubt in his mind Roald believed Yuana, even if he was still in denial. And tomorrow, they would find out from his session with Dr Sanchez to what extent that belief was, and if Roald could keep it a secret for the rest of his life.

He was halfway through his whiskey when Roald showed up. Tonight, he had a job to do, and he had better do it well if he would ensure that Roald lives and remains sane.

Roald pulled up the bar chair next to Daniel and ordered a cognac. A brief exchange of small talk passed between them as Roald waited for the bartender to pour his drink. The man was still busy making cocktails for another customer.

"Dan, how long have you known Yuana?" Roald asked out of the blue as he received his drink from the bartender.

Oh, fuck! He hoped Roald would pass this test.

"I've known her awhile. We met in Oslo during a holiday. She was fifteen, I was eighteen. Then we became close in Melbourne. I used to live there, and she was studying there. So, about thirteen years... why?" He kept a casual tone.

Roald did not answer, his focus was on the glass in his hand as he swirled the contents.

"How come you never dated her, Dan?"

Roald's eyes were now on him, watching his reaction. He was sure Roald was trying to find out if he knew about Yuana's nature.

He smiled. "Oh, we did, briefly, when I first met her. We dated for a few months, but we ended up as dear friends, and that is what we remained to be." He felt a twinge of remembrance in his heart at the memory.

It was true, and he was sure that if they had continued dating, perhaps he would have fallen for Yuana as Roald had. He would have been a better individual for someone like Yuana. Being an Erdia, there would be no need for the soul-destroying revelation as he was aware Yuana was an aswang. And he was already part of their world.

What stopped him was not wanting to have aswang kids. He did not want them to have the same rootless existence that every aswang had to endure, the constant move to avoid making long-term friendships that left social footprints, the recurring predicament every female aswangs would go through when they fell in love with humans. He wanted normal kids, and a mate he could live with, grow old with, die with.

Roald had no readable expression on his face, so he could not quite guess what he was thinking. There was no response from Roald, instead he was back to contemplating his glass. He took a sip, and then said, "I took your advice, Dan. I will see the psychiatrist that my mom found for me tomorrow."

The change of topic made his heart skip a beat.

"Really? That is good..." He injected surprise in his voice.

Roald nodded.

"So, what happened between you and Yuana, bro? You seemed really broken up about it. Did you guys part ways?" He was reluctant to push the issue, but he had a job to do.

"No! We are still together." Roald's quick denial spoke volumes.

He heaved a brief sigh of relief. "So, what is wrong? What went so wrong that you need a psychiatrist to put you to rights?" he persisted, trying to prompt Roald into telling him what he already knew. He could see the internal battle Roald was going through, wanting to open up, yet resisting to. Perhaps out of pride, self-preservation, or hopefully, out of love for Yuana.

"Yuana told me she is an... *aswang*..." Roald said, unable to look at him.

"What? An... *aswang*?" He feigned emphatic surprise. "Do you believe it?" he asked, injecting incredulity in his voice, and felt guilty for the pretense.

"That is why I need to see a psychiatrist," Roald said.

Roald's inability to answer a direct question confirmed his assumption that Roald believed Yuana's declaration, but it terrified him to look deep into himself.

"Is the psychiatric visit for her state of mind, or yours?"

"I do not know, bro." Roald's reply came after a deep sigh and a big swallow of the cognac.

He patted Roald's shoulder in encouragement. He was certain that pressing Roald further about it would make Roald suspicious over his undue interest in the subject.

"Okay, bro, if there is anything I can do to help... I can do research for you, if you want." He was hoping for Roald's demand to keep the information secret between them.

"Bro, let's keep this secret just between us, please. I want to protect Yuana," Roald said, his voice low and quiet.

"Of course." The relief was beyond words. Roald was unaware that he just upped his own chances to live with that request.

Roald might never know that Daniel was bound to the same *Veil*, and that he had never been so glad to make such a promise in his life.

By ten thirty the following morning, Edrigu, Lorenzo and Margaita were ready at the conference table. Their focus was on the small secondary screen where they were watching Daniel test their access to the cameras set up at the Session Room Three in the clinic of Dr Sanchez. Daniel was broadcasting online from the Technology Department of the iztari office across town. Mateo Santino, one of their senior iztaris and Daniel's father was also present.

Two minutes later, the wide primary screen flickered to life and reflected a clear transmission of the digital cameras installed and camouflaged in Dr Sanchez's office.

The whole technical set up included a powerful microphone and noise cancelling sound system. They could listen to every conversation in Dr Sanchez's office.

Satisfied and ready to begin, Edrigu rang Dr Sanchez to tell her they were live. She raised a thumb to the digital camera located across her seat. It was one of the six installed in the rectangular room. They disguised this camera as a power indicator by the light switch.

With everything ready, they all sat down to wait for Roald's arrival for his appointment.

Roald arrived ten minutes early. Dr Sanchez saw it on the screen of her laptop. She saw him approach the receptionist. The receptionist had instructions to take Roald to Session Room 3 as soon as he arrived. It was a room reserved for aswang treatments and all aswang related cases only. The sole room connected to the iztari office.

Dr Sanchez rose from her seat when the door opened. It was her receptionist.

"Doctora, Mr Magsino is here," Sara said, then stepped aside to allow Roald to come in.

"Thank you, Sara. Good morning, Mr Magsino."

She noted the signs of sleeplessness and exhaustion on his face. He was a handsome young man, tall and confident. He was fit and healthy, apart from the slight dark circles and the dull sheen in his eyes. Pain underlined the mild smile. The boy was in emotional distress.

"Good morning, Doctor Sanchez. Thank you for seeing me despite the many cancellations. I assure you; my mother did her best to make me go." Roald shook her offered hand.

"You are welcome, Roald. And do not worry about it. Your behaviour was normal. Men resist shrink visits more than women. I am glad you came anyway, as this will be valuable for the medical journal I am writing."

She smiled and bid him to take a seat on the plump beige leather couch. Roald sat on the edge, his posture rigid.

"Can I offer you a drink? Or some light sandwiches, perhaps?"

He looked like he needed food. He declined the sandwiches but accepted the chamomile tea.

After the secretary placed the tea set and a platter of finger sandwiches on the coffee table between them, Dr Sanchez poured them both a cup. Roald regarded her with curiosity and a tinge of suspicion.

"Am I what you expected?" she asked with a smile.

"I'm sorry. I did not mean to stare. You look... younger in person." Roald's answering smile was apologetic. He sat deeper into his seat, his back still ramrod straight.

"I would thank you for the compliment if my looks were my doing. I inherited it from my parents. So, good genes count a lot."

Roald relaxed, and he slid further into the couch. They sat in silence for a few minutes. She picked up a slice of finger sandwich and took a bite. She was not hungry, but she wanted Roald to eat. And as she expected, he took one as well. She let him eat a couple more before she set her cup down on the table.

She turned on the digital recorder to begin her patient consent spiel. Roald set his own cup down.

"Before we start, I want you to know I always record all my sessions because I need to review it multiple times later, so I can do proper diagnosis. This recording shall be confidential and will only be between you and me. But in extreme cases, where I will need outside assistance, I will only share it, with extreme discretion, with the relevant third parties. These instances are, first, if I believe there is an imminent and violent threat towards yourself or others; second, if there is a need to facilitate client care that will involve other providers and sharing information is necessary for your treatment... Do you agree to this?"

She paused and waited for him to accede.

His agreement was a salve to her conscience as she would share this with people who would be in imminent danger if he revealed to others what he knew, and lethal violence may come his way if he did.

He nodded. "Yes."

Her words seemed to have met his approval. The tensed line in his mouth relaxed. He liked the idea of anonymity. That boded well for him.

"All right, shall we begin?"

After a long deep breath, he nodded. She nodded with encouragement and set the digital recorder down on the table between them.

"So, tell me what is on your mind, Mr Magsino?"

Roald began with what he must have thought to be the safest door to open - his observation that his girlfriend of two years seemed like she was withholding something from him. He recounted the days prior to the revelation. His tone was almost dispassionate as he focused on the facts. Roald seemed to avoid any mention of how he felt about it.

With gentle leading questions, she pried the details of the day of the revelation. He related it like a story he saw in a movie or read in a book. His words were careful and minimal.

When he reached the day of the revelation, he hesitated and looked torn between continuing and stopping.

"She made a claim... a revelation..." Roald paused.

"What was her claim? What kind of revelation?" she asked.

Roald had never mentioned Yuana's name. It was a good sign. He was protective of her. His love was still strong.

"She said... she was an *aswang*..." Roald's jaw tightened at the mention of the word, and fear flashed in his eyes.

"Okay. And how do you feel about it?"

"It could not be true... I think she was just misguided. Or perhaps she suffered from a form of clinical lycanthropy..."

She had no trouble reading between the lines of Roald's statements, the unconscious peppering of justification, rationalisations, and hidden entreaties for help.

"I am worried, Doctor Sanchez. It affected my sleep... my girlfriend could not be..."

It was very significant Roald had not asked her yet if there was a treatment for Yuana's malady. Roald was not conscious of his tacit admission that he believed Yuana. The session was about his own fear. But she had yet to determine whether he was appealing for help to overcome it so he could adapt to Yuana's nature, or to move on from them.

Her most crucial task was to find out if his mental state could withstand the terror of the truth. Only then the second question could be asked - whether his love would overcome his deep-seated fear of aswangs. His trauma ran deep. It was at the level of a phobia. All the signs were there.

And that was not good.

Across the distance, just like Dr Sanchez, the First Wave team were focused on the session. They were all looking for signs in Roald's behaviour that would confirm he would be a danger to their existence. The sessions would guide them on what methods to take to neutralise any threat he might present to their kind. The result would be the same, like all the others before him - he would pose no harm to them, either by nature or by their design.

For the De Vidas and the iztaris watching this exchange on their screens, it was notable that Roald never once mentioned Yuana's name to Dr Sanchez. He referred to her as his girlfriend. Despite being in a safe environment, Roald was still protective. If he continued to do this in the succeeding sessions with Dr Sanchez, this may just turn out well for Roald.

To Margaita, it was also clear Roald's anxiety sprung from a deep trauma. It was more than just a boyhood fear from horror stories told by the adults when he was young. She flicked open the printed dossier of Roald, checked the data that detailed his background, his family and childhood.

This required a closer look.

An hour later, Dr Sanchez wrapped up the session by posing a question to Roald.

What was it about the revelation that bothered him the most?

Roald winced when he heard this, like bumping a wounded knee at the corner of a table by accident. But he left Dr Sanchez's clinic feeling easier. This was an improvement from the grim existence he had been living with for the past week that felt like an eternity. The session gave him the sense that a light at the end of the tunnel would soon become visible to him. Perhaps in a few more sessions onward.

Their next session would be three days later, at three p.m. He declined the eleven a.m. time slot, an automatic reaction to keeping his lunch hour free - for Yuana.

His own instinctive thought startled him into admitting to himself he was missing Yuana. Badly.

Perhaps a call would not hurt. She was still his girlfriend, after all.

Roald stared at his mobile phone, trying to think of what to say to Yuana when she picked up. Maybe he should text first. She might be in a meeting or something.

He was re-reading his text for the umpteenth time, but the words seemed inadequate. It read impersonal, not to mention presumptuous, since he had not texted or called her for days.

So, how will I know it's the right time to call her without sending the text?

He called Yuana's office. Her secretary, Sochi, answered the phone.

"Hi, Sochi, is Yuana free to talk to me?" he asked. His heart hammered like a drum, he was certain it was audible to Sochi.

"Hey, Roald. She's not here. She's on leave for over a week now, didn't she tell you?" Sochi's surprise rang clear through the line.

"Hmm... no, I was on leave myself. Would you have any idea when she will be back?" Not knowing Yuana's location made his heart drop into his gut.

"It was an indefinite leave, so I do not know when she will return. But she's with her parents." Sochi's voice was controlled and speculating.

"Thank you, Sochi. I will just call her mobile." His stomach tightened; dread burned it like acid.

Yuana had told him about how her mother left her father without a word twenty-eight years ago. And that Yuana might do the same to him was something his entire body raged against.

It took him a few minutes to calm his panic down before he dialled her number. Again, and again. For hours. She was not picking up. Finally, an automated message echoed from the line: her phone was out of reach.

Fear settled inside him, leaden and cold. He pushed the possibility that Yuana left him out of his mind. He had those three years together with her that he could bank on. He refused to believe that Yuana would cut him out of her mind, her heart, her life with such drastic ease. Time spent together may provide him some leeway, but time would also erode his advantage fast.

He needed to sort himself as soon as possible. This development brought back the question that Dr Sanchez put forward earlier.

What was it that bothered me so much about Yuana's revelation?

Her dark blue shoes made staccato beats on the tiled hallway floor of the psych ward. Its steady rhythm belied the beating of her heart. She always had mixed feelings when she visited this part of the hospital. A mixture of longing, regret, and massive guilt.

And yet she would come twice a week, like clockwork.

What compelled her to walk this way, without fail, was patient seven in the special wing of the ward. As she neared his room, she took a fortifying breath to shore up her heart against the familiar surge of the emotions that would assail her once she saw him.

For fifty years, this had been her routine, a twice-weekly dose of emotional pain and restitution. It was a heavy price; one she continued to pay and would keep on paying.

Like her usual practice, she viewed him through the small glass panel in his door for a few minutes. As expected, he was busy painting. It was the only thing that occupied his time, his only focus in the fifty years in that room.

She watched him wield his brush like a maestro, fluid and effortless, his enormous talent clear. His tortured soul showed in the colours, the strokes, the technique applied in his paintings. The trauma that ruined his mind communicated to the world through his art. The paintings were all dark, grim, horrifying, yet compelling. He painted with only one theme —*Aswangs*. With one ruling emotion—horror.

The effects of the treatment he got for not keeping the *Veil of Secrecy* intact, the mixture of mind-altering drugs and trauma had broken his mind beyond repair. For half a century, she asked herself whether death was a kinder fate. Her cowardice to end his life brought him to this state, a breathing shell of the man she loved.

She punched the key code on the door pad and the lock snapped open. She entered as quietly as she could. Not that it mattered because he never seemed to notice anything outside his line of vision. She approached him and stood beside the easel. He stopped painting and looked at her.

"Hello, Martin," she breathed. His blank eyes looked back at her. No sign of recognition, no emotion. And that was the most painful of all. Those eyes used to gaze at her with such passion, deep love, and adoration.

She looked down at the painting that had occupied him for the last month. This one took longer than the others. He used to finish a painting every three weeks. By the look of it, this one still had a long way to go. It appeared to be in its early stage, just big splodges of black, grey, red, and other melancholy colours.

She collected all his work, the payment for each one she deposited in an account in his name. She had hoped to give the account to him when he got better, so he would have the funds to support his art. He had a small fortune to his name. But he had not gotten better. The money lay untouched in his bank account for half a century.

He looked every bit his age of eighty-five, deep lines etched on his gaunt face, this man, who owned her heart and soul. His time was running out, and she could almost feel grateful for that. She wanted him to achieve the peace of mind that her kind had stolen from him. Taken from him because of her.

She sighed and turned to leave, and was halfway to the door when she heard him whisper, "Mena..."

She looked back in surprise, her breathing held. But he was still painting. Then she saw it from a distance and realised he was painting... her.

11

FULL CONTACT

They watched the sun set in the horizon, the colours of the surrounding sky changing from bright yellow to deep orange. There was a certain quiet power at this time of the day. For an aswang, it was symbolic of their own physical change.

Yuana glanced at her parents. Both were holding a wine glass, poised for a sip. Her father's free hand rested on her mother's. The way they looked at each other displayed an enduring love she envied and coveted. Their displays of affection were now a common sight to her. It was bittersweet to witness since this could have been hers and Roald's ending.

While the uncertainty of their situation hurt, she could not find it in her to blame Roald. What she was expecting him to accept was difficult. This was the longest time since they met, they had no contact. It was hard to bear, but she had no choice. This trip was both a prelude to her future and a chance to clear her mind.

Can I survive the life my mother lived when she left father years ago?

Her mother had her then, a daughter to take care of, a motivation to live for. She did not have that. Only her family and her work. The tramway would separate her from her family, and her work would not be enough. She knew that now. Her soul needed a higher purpose to get her through the rest of her long life.

As the sun disappeared behind the mountain peak and daylight bled into night, their only illumination were the dimmed lights from the living room, making the millions of stars overhead visible. The stars seemed to twinkle in harmony with the cricket song and night bird calls. And she felt, once again, the pull of her nature, her spirit's need to unite with the land. To run in the woods and experience the night in all its mysteries.

Her mother had the same impulse glittering in her eyes, but the warmth of her father's hand rooted her. And for her mother's sake, she stood there beside her parents, in her human form.

"Bel, is there a difference in how aswangs perceive the night?" Her father's question came out of the blue.

They both glanced at him. Her father seemed attuned to her mother's thoughts. She threw Yuana a questioning gaze and she understood her mother's intent.

Her father's question was a testament that he had taken another step to acceptance, the further integration of his life into their world. Seeing their display of humanity in daylight and very human settings was one thing, to be with an aswang in the middle of the night, in darkness and within their hunting ground was another.

"Do you want to come with us into the woods, Galen? We can show you..." Her mother's invitation had the flavour of a dare.

He smiled at Ysobella; the dare was accepted.

"Yes, I would love to." He relished the adventure. To know all the facets of the non-human side of his wife and daughter in their natural habitat was essential to his adaptation to their world.

They grinned at him and stood up in unison. He followed them down the stairs by the side of the verandah and out into the vast expanse of the garden. The thick, dewy grass cushioned their shoes, dampening them. They walked further into the woods that bordered the foot of Mount Halcon. The growth of the trees thickened as they walked deeper. The forest floor was damp, and it muffled the sound of his steps.

Only his, as the two ladies were light on their feet.

The canopy above added another layer of darkness, muting the glow of the full moon, but his eyesight had already adjusted so he could still see Ysobella to his right and Yuana to his left. They both took a hand. He paused as they did.

The women inhaled slow and deep, as if taking on the entire forest into their lungs. He copied them, his eyes closed on instinct, and the muscles in his body loosened. He noticed the sounds of rustling as a small animal moved among a patch of dry, dead leaves and broken branches on the forest floor, the chirping of crickets, the mournful call of an unknown bird and the whistling of the wind as it travelled through the leaves in the trees above them.

It was mysterious. It was magical. And supernatural.

He opened his eyes, and the trees seemed to glitter around him. Thousands of fireflies darted all around them. He turned to Ysobella. She was watching him. Her dark eyes were gleaming, so black that it was almost alarming. Her irises were dilated to absorb more light, enabling night vision.

"How far can you see in this darkness?" he whispered, unwilling to break the spell that lingered in the air.

"About two hundred yards," she whispered back. "There is a mouse deer over there..." She pointed to the trees in front of her. He squinted to see, but failed, so he just took her word for it.

"And a tamaraw with her young bull just to your left, Papa," Yuana added, as she pointed to the gap between the trees across from her. They both followed her direction. His vision could not penetrate past the wall of darkness. Ysobella squinted.

"I cannot see it, Yuana." He felt somewhat silly about his human inadequacy.

"And I can barely make it out," Ysobella said, a little amazed. "You have a much better vision than me... Must be the age difference."

Yuana looked surprised.

They walked deeper into the woods; hands still linked. At one point, Yuana paused and turned to her right. "Let's go to the river, Mama."

Ysobella nodded. She angled her head, trying to pick up the sound of the river.

"This way, Ma. I can hear the water." It seemed Yuana's hearing was also keener than her mother's. Never mind his.

They followed Yuana's lead, and about two hundred fifty meters on Ysobella paused. "I can hear the water now."

Ysobella glanced at him. He shook his head; he could hear nothing. They walked on, and another three hundred meters on, he picked up the sound of the rushing water hitting rocks and soil.

"Aha! I can hear the water."

That made both mother and daughter chuckle. They continued on.

They stopped at the edge of the river, the sound of the rushing water louder now, the scent of vegetation in the surrounding areas more intense. Yuana closed her eyes and sniffed at the air. She seemed focused on picking up the distinct smells, her lips notching up into a knowing smile as she identified the scents. As if she was cataloguing them all in her head. It was fascinating to watch. Her mother was doing the same thing.

He was going to copy what they were doing, when Yuana angled her head to the right, a slight frown on her face. Her nose must have picked up something peculiar. Yuana glanced at her mother, waiting for her to react.

A second later, Ysobella's brows knitted. Her lids snapped opened, mother and daughter's gaze locked.

"I smell a man, mama. I do not recognise him," she murmured. Her mother nodded.

"He's not one of our staff..." Ysobella confirmed. The two women faced toward the source of the mysterious odiferous man.

Minutes later, a tall figure emerged from the trees bordering the other side of the river. He was wearing a dark shirt and jeans, his raven hair long. He was barefoot and walked in a fluid motion. The stranger had a rugged, almost wild aura about him, like a hunter. His almond-shaped eyes assessed them with interest. He looked Japanese.

The man stopped by the edge of the river and gave a friendly wave. He seemed to regard them with the same curiosity as they did him. It must have looked odd to encounter three people, dressed in clothes more suited in a city, out in the middle of the woods in the dead of the night.

"Good evening..." Galen waived at the stranger, surprised that another soul, apart from them, was out there.

"Good evening." His accent confirmed he was Japanese. He looked to be middle-aged.

"He might be Mr Nakahara. The Japanese straggler who went into hiding at the end of the war. The one our family was collaborating with in this area," Ysobella informed them in a sotto voice.

"Are you Mr Nakahara?" Ysobella asked. And the older man nodded and smiled.

"I am Ysobella, this is my daughter, Yuana, and Galen, my husband." Her introduction of him, an acknowledgement of what they were to each other, made his heart swell.

Mr Nakahara walked a short distance back and signalled his intention to jump across the narrower channel. He landed with a soft thump on their side of the river.

It astounded Galen. The gap was too wide for any normal human to jump across, and the height the other gentleman achieved was also impossibly high. He realised this Japanese gentleman was an aswang. He never thought about there being foreign aswangs.

Mr Nakahara drew near and held out his hand to shake theirs. Galen would have bowed to him, but Mr Nakahara seemed to have adopted western ways. After the exchange of more pleasantries, Ysobella asked the same question that was playing in Galen's head.

"What brought you out tonight, Nakahara-san?" Ysobella asked excitedly. The story of Mr Nakahara fascinated her.

He felt a slight twinge of jealousy. There was something self-assured and wise about this older man. Nakahara was attractive. His demeanour and aura, elemental.

"Exercise, I often run around in these woods at night," he replied. He was looking at Yuana with profound interest.

"In your human or animal form?" Ysobella asked.

"I enjoy testing my senses and skills in both forms. It is good to keep them sharp," he replied in Japanese-accented English, his gaze still fixed on their daughter. Ysobella and Yuana noticed Nakahara's interest. It was not strange or creepy, just very concentrated, and it intrigued both women.

"How long have you lived in the area, Mr Nakahara?" Yuana asked.

This elder gentleman piqued his daughter's interest. She was establishing rapport with the Japanese gentleman, a skill her daughter was good at. Nakahara's gaze was fierce and speculative. He seemed as keen on establishing rapport with her.

"Since 1942. The war ended, and I stayed," Nakahara replied, shrugging.

"Why? Didn't you want to go home to your family?" Yuana's eyebrows quirked.

"My family died in Nagasaki when the Americans dropped the atomic bomb. No reason to return." A quick, nonchalant response.

Since World War Two?

"Oh... And you've always stayed here? In Mindoro?" Yuana was as surprised as he with Nakahara's response.

He wondered how old this man was. He looked mid-fifties, but given that he was an aswang, he could be over a hundred.

"Yes, here in Mount Halcon. This is my home. I love it here. The Mangyan aswangs are friendly. They helped sustain me after the war. When there was fighting, it was not a problem, but with the war finished, no more source. And I did not want to kill innocent people. So, they come and share their sustenance with me..." Nakahara said with a grin.

His Ysobella appeared touched by his story, and proud of what their Mangyan kind did for a stranger who, by all intents and purposes, was an enemy.

"I read somewhere... Didn't they send a search party here, looking for you?" Galen asked. He remembered seeing the article years ago.

Mr Nakahara's smile was mischievous.

"They did. They spent a week looking for me. I was watching them the entire time, and I stole some of their supplies. Especially the nori... I miss nori." The man chuckled at his recalled memories.

"How did you evade them?" he asked.

"I transformed into a dog, as a pet of one of their Mangyan guides..." he replied. His eyes glittered with mirth.

Feeling more comfortable with him, they sat down on the nearby trunk of a fallen tree. Mr Nakahara remained standing but was back to staring at Yuana again. Unable to quell her own curiosity, Yuana asked him pointblank.

"Mr Nakahara, why do you look at me with such intensity?"

"Forgive me, but I can sense a similar spirit in you..." He bowed to her in apology.

"What kind of spirit?" she asked.

"In time, Ms Yuana, you will know." A mysterious smile spread across his lips. "Have you discovered your animus yet?" Nakahara asked after a brief silence.

That gave them all pause.

"No, not yet," Yuana replied.

"You should find out, it will reveal your true self, and maybe the path of your soul," he said. And with that, Nakahara walked away. He glanced back at them with a brief wave of farewell before disappearing into the woods.

Her brows knitted in bewilderment. Yuana turned to her mother, a questioning look on her face. Her mother just shrugged, as if it was not important that day.

"So, Yuana, what do you transform into?" He was interested as he did not get to witness it that day.

"I can show you, Papa..." Yuana teased.

"No... no... I don't want to see you naked. Just tell me," he blurted, alarmed at the thought. That made Yuana chuckle.

"There is no need, Papa. Just close your eyes. It takes less than a minute. But I have to remove my clothes prior to transformation. It is impractical to be running around as a predator wearing a dress, shoes, or jewellery."

"It is also easier to get dressed after, when it is all in one place, quicker if you do not have to hunt for a missing shoe," Ysobella said, dryly. It made him laugh.

For Kazu Nakahara, meeting the young lady brought him excitement and anticipation of what was about to unfold once she discovered herself. It may take her a while, as she remained unaware. Maybe he could help facilitate her *emergence*. She would need plenty of time to learn about herself and her powers.

The young lady would be in for a monumental surprise. The key thing was that she had no choice. Her animus was unfurling from her core. Hopefully, she would embrace it and fulfil her full potential.

It was crucial to the big shift that was about to come.

Meanwhile, in Manila, Katelin was busy with her immediate task - searching the record system of their Local Tribunal. She was looking for any reported incidents of accidental human exposure or aswang attacks in Santo Tomas, Batangas between the period of 1989-1999. Roald was born and spent his childhood there. Her mother was sure Roald had a close encounter with an aswang when he was young, and Dr Sanchez concurred in her first assessment.

Nothing showed up in Santo Tomas, so she expanded her search and added the places where Roald's parents have roots. And that included the province of Laguna and Quezon. She got lucky when two events caught her attention. One was in Pagsanjan, Laguna in 1993, and another in Mataas na Kahoy, Batangas in 1994.

Katelin focused on the Pagsanjan event first. It detailed a gruesome Restoration of Order Campaign that involved three of their best iztaris, Benjamín Carrión, Troy Villegas, and Felix Coronadal. The ROOC was against a group of harravirs who had been terrorising the area for months. The report said the team got into a violent clash with a notorious band of harravirs led by Major Felipe Ona, a retired scout ranger, and an excellent tactician. Apart from the Major, the harravirs were an uneducated poor family of four, loyal to their leader, and had been serving him when he was still a soldier. Major Ona kept them in his employ when he retired.

Their band started their illicit hunting three years after Major Ona retired. The attacks appeared indiscriminate until a pattern emerged. Every full moon, they would kill a pregnant woman. It meant one of the harravirs had Visceral Metastasis, a lethal form of cancerous growth that affected aswangs. The only known treatment to halt the growth of the disease was the amniotic fluid of a foetus. Whoever it was, he must have attacked and ingested the viscera of an infected aswang. This meant the afflicted aswang was likely a harravis and more dangerous. Major Ona turned out to be the afflicted harravis, and had been one for years, but his symptoms did not show until twenty years later.

The iztaris had a hard time tracking and apprehending them. They used an unwitting pregnant woman as bait. They watched over her for weeks until Major Ona's group went after her. Their faulty intelligence pointed to a group of three harravirs based on the statements of the witnesses in the previous attacks. It was Major Ona's strategy to expose only three to the actual hunt to fool the iztaris into sending a small group, thus improving their odds of winning should the Iztaris catch up with them. In reality, there were five of them, so they outnumbered the iztari force from the very beginning.

The last encounter was a bloodbath. Felix Coronadal died when the harravirs ambushed him. They tore him to pieces and ate his liver, heart, and kidneys. It was pure luck that Ben Carrion and Troy Villegas heard the ambush over their walkie-talkies, and with another stroke of luck they found the mangled remains of Coronadal before they encountered the group. When they saw the body, they knew that the raw viscera of their fallen buddy powered the harravirs. They now faced a group of harravises, a much stronger and faster adversary.

Carrion and Villegas outmanoeuvred the group by setting traps and waiting through the night until they caught two. The strategy turned out to be their saving grace, because after the second harravis got caught in the wolf pit, he called for help to his companions and revealed their number.

By dawn, they were in a death match with Major Ona and the remaining two. The fight took over an hour and well into the daylight; the area rang with the sounds of bolo striking bolo, metal cleaving flesh. They could not use guns because of their proximity to the village. Gun shots would have brought the humans into the skirmish area to investigate. The other two harravises were strong but had no combat training. The iztaris dispatched them with relative ease. But it took both of them to defeat Major Ona. He was a skilled bolo fighter, and the aswang viscera powered him. In the end, the coordinated attack and complementary skills of both iztaris prevailed.

The incident was the first in over a hundred years where a ROOC ended up with all aswangs killed. The harravirs could not be rehabilitated, they were almost feral and had been brainwashed by Major Ona. With the number of humans and aswangs Major Ona's group killed, they had permission from the Punong-Ama for complete elimination of the targets.

The Sanitation Team burned the bodies afterwards. The Social Sanitation strategy implemented in this case was to let nature run its course. They were sure that convincing the actual victims the attack didn't happen would not work and instead worsen the situation.

They created a story that a small group of wild boars attacked the villagers, and the military came and hunted the sound down and circulated it in the neighbouring towns. Soon enough, the incidents were reduced to folktales and rumours.

This event was notable as it influenced the change in their standard procedure when deploying iztaris during ROOC operations against harravirs and harravises.

Tomorrow, Katelin would call on both gentlemen and interview them. One of the attacks by Major Ona's band may have been the event that traumatised Roald. Perhaps iztari Carrion and Villegas could shed light on minor instances that did not make it to the report.

Ysobella, Galen and Yuana came back to the villa at two a.m., still pumped with adrenalin. Galen had asked them to show him what it was like to be an aswang, and the closest way was to show him what they could do. It turned into a demonstration of strength, skill, and speed—a hunting exhibition in her human form rather than her animal hunting form.

It was thrilling to listen to the sound of a potential prey, to pick up its musty smell that gave away its location. Yuana's prey was a wild boar, foraging on the forest floor. With her heart beating hard in her chest, she tried to recall everything her grandfather taught her when she was young. She crept up closer, sprinted at full speed, grabbed the animal by the hind legs and bashed it against the trunk of the nearest tree.

Her lack of experience showed. The boar was stunned, but it struggled and fought her. She did not want to bash its head against the tree again and ended up twisting its neck. She had never killed any animal that way; it took her a while before she succeeded. The boar's tusk slashed her arm during their tussle, but she did not feel the pain. Her first hunt since childhood, and the beat of the blood in her veins, was primal.

Her father took the boar from her. He regarded her with a mixture of paternal pride and awe.

"Oh, the boar gored you?" Her mother inspected the long gash on her arm.

She shrugged. "It's shallow. It will heal in a few minutes."

They took the wild boar home. Her father wanted roast boar for dinner the following day. He had told Yam-Ay, the lady in charge of the household, that she was to preserve a tooth as he wanted to make it into a pendant, a memento of his daughter's hunting prowess. It made her smile. Her heart warmed by her father's adoration as she washed her wound and the boar's blood from her hands over the kitchen sink.

The hunt, while exhilarating, stirred something inside her. And the sensation had not left her since. It was a certain disquiet, a restlessness of the soul.

That night, despite the physicality of the evening's activities, one thought kept her awake. Discover her animus. What Mr Nakahara said to her about herself earlier had piqued her interest.

Roald endured a similarly sleepless night. His bed sheets in a messy heap behind him as he paced in his bedroom. He had done push-ups to tire himself to sleep. All it did was give him tight shoulder muscles. He had been dialling Yuana's number all day and night, but her phone line remained out of reach.

He even gave in and called Daniel. It would serve no purpose to hide his concern.

"Dan, Yuana is out of reach. Do you know where she is?"

"Sorry, bro. I don't..." Daniel's low voice was understanding.

His chest tightened. "Do you know anyone who can tell me where she is?"

Daniel's sigh was deep. "Have you tried calling her home?" Dan sounded like he doubted the efficacy of his own suggestion.

"I have not... I am not sure if her family would help me." Stating the obvious tasted bitter in his mouth.

"I will see what I can do, bro, but I cannot promise anything."

He nodded, even if Daniel could not see it, for his own benefit.

All kinds of scenarios ran through his head after he hung up of Yuana hurt somewhere, of her finding somebody else who would accept her fully. The battle between heart and mind raged inside him: the need to ensure he did not lose Yuana, the fear that he already had, the instinct to reach out to her, and his apprehension that he would not overcome this. It was driving him crazy.

Would I have pursued her so single-mindedly if I had known then what I know now?

Memories of when he first met her flashed back in his mind. The jolt of electricity that struck his heart when she came onto the stage was as fresh to him as if it happened yesterday. She was beautiful in her navy-blue flowy dress, but he had met a fair number of beautiful women before.

Physical attributes were not reason enough for his attraction. What set Yuana apart were her eyes. The sparks of energy, passion, playfulness, and suppressed power were clear in that one side glance she threw in his direction as she passed by him. It was an unseeing gaze, not directed to him, and yet it captivated him.

He had wheedled Daniel for an introduction. Half of the guys in the room were in a literal queue to shake her hand as she came down from the stage after the panel. He was certain he would make a better impression on her consciousness if a common friend introduced him to her.

He was so determined to succeed then, would not leave without meeting her. It cost him a Sonos One speaker three days later, a payment to Daniel for giving him Yuana's mobile phone number.

Would I have pursued that introduction had I known?

Daniel warned him then she was only interested in casual dating. He now understood why. The twinge in his gut intensified. His desperation to make certain Yuana was still his, rose like acid from his stomach. He could overcome anything for as long as he and Yuana remained together. He could not envision his future without her or bear the thought of not having her in his life.

So, why am I having a hard time accepting Yuana's nature? What am I scared about?

Sleep, when it finally came to him was disturbed, full of disjointed images of Yuana, a dark moonless night, the treehouse of his childhood, a flash of light, and a monstrous figure bent over a prone woman covered in blood.

His own scream of terror woke him up. Sweat poured down his back, his heart hammered out of his chest. The images were so vivid he still felt like the child he was in the nightmare. The tears on his wet face were real. The terror had left him shaking.

He recognised the treehouse. His father built it for him in their holiday home. But he did not recognise the face of the woman lying in a pool of blood, nor the man crouched over her. His hands and face bloody, a terrible rage reflected in his eyes. The nightmare felt familiar, like he had dreamt of it before.

Had my subconscious fused an old dream with my current concern about Yuana and merged them?

He got dressed in a daze. The question Dr Sanchez asked him to think about was now an incessant echo in his head.

What was it about Yuana's revelation that bothered me?

He could not answer it.

Do I believe Yuana?

A thud of realisation hit him in the chest. He did, one hundred per cent. And he feared what that meant.

He sat on the edge of his bed and picked up the business card of Dr Sanchez lying on his bedside table. Hopefully she could spare him a few minutes today.

Katelin, Margaita, and Lorenzo sat in the secret briefing room as they waited for the rest of the group to arrive. Edrigu arrived five minutes later. The screen connected to the private covered parking lot located across the street flickered to life.

They watched Ramon, the loyal and long-time driver of Lorenzo and Margaita, escort a group of people to the car repair shop beside the parking lot. He steered them down the stairs to the underground pathway that connected to the briefing room disguised as a granny flat attached to the principal house.

General Mateo Santino led the group, followed by his son Daniel, *Iztaris* Ben Carrion and Troy Villegas. Security cameras all the way to the primary room covered the group's progress through the hidden hallway. Within seconds, they emerged from the utility room of the granny flat into the living room where they all sat.

Daniel looked around the room. His interest captured as he noted all the well-concealed security equipment that peppered the cosy surrounding.

"Gentlemen, now that we are all here, let us move to the meeting room."

Lorenzo got up and proceeded to what appeared to be the bedroom. The group followed him. The door opened instead to a sound-proofed room, equipped with a wide screen and computer system, and a conference table that seats eight.

"So, what do you have?" Lorenzo sat on Margaita's right after he pulled a chair for his wife. The meeting had started. Everyone sat down, laptops got turned on and files opened. Mateo took the floor.

"Punong-Ina, Punong-Ama." He nodded at Margaita and Lorenzo, as a greeting and a sign of respect, then continued on. "We deployed five people, one leased a condo unit on the same floor as Mr Magsino's, all listening devices planted in his unit now. The second one acts as the subject's social shadow for his day activities, and a third one for his evening activities. For his workplace, Daniel will cover it. The fourth and fifth iztaris will shadow his parents. We had bugged their home as well."

"Is there anything we need to worry about?" Margaita asked, a slight frown on her face.

"Nothing yet, Punong-Ina. But we expected this given the depth of the relationship between Mr Magsino and your great-granddaughter, plus the level of emotional maturity of the subject. We predict he would be very reluctant to share this information to his social circle for fear of derision, not just for himself, but for your granddaughter too," Mateo replied.

This was welcome news for the family. For the sake of Yuana, they did not want him harmed. Not unless it became necessary.

"Okay. How about the issues I mentioned earlier?" Katelin asked. She addressed Iztari Carrion and Villegas.

"As far as we had gathered, Mrs Orzabal, the witnesses had no connection to Mr Magsino or his family," Ben Carrion replied. "They were all residents of Barrio Balanac as we keep an extensive record of all those witnesses. We have kept close track of them and their families over the years. As far as we know, they have not crossed paths with the family of Mr Magsino."

"It's a pity that we do not have the same extensive records on Roald." Katelin sighed.

"What are we looking for, Mrs Orzabal?" General Santino asked.

"We are certain Mr Magsino had a traumatic experience with an aswang when he was young, that perhaps he had seen an aswang attack during his early childhood," Edrigu explained.

"There was no reported incident in his place of birth, Santo Tomas, Batangas, that coincided with the timeline," said Katelin. "So, I searched in the nearby environs. And the only thing worth noting seemed to be the Pagsanjan incident in 1993 and the Mataas na Kahoy incident in 1994. The Mataas na Kahoy incident did not seem to be the right event as it was a simple extraction of a pregnant single mother aswang and her child."

"Ah, I remember that case. I led it," Mateo quipped. There was a slight grimace in his expression.

Daniel threw his father a sideways glance of surprise.

"Can you tell us more about that event, as the reports provided little detail?" Katelin asked.

"Nothing much to tell. A tip reached the office about a near attack of a pregnant aswang in Mataas na Kahoy. By coincidence, I was in Lipa City for a three-week holiday with my late wife's family. They assigned the case to me as the lead since I was already there. It took about a week to trace her. We found her by accident. There was a reported tiyanak attack that evening in Balete. We thought those were two different incidents, but the tiyanak turned out to be the lady's three-year-old son. The lady was about seven months pregnant. She was suicidal and intended to starve herself and her son to death. She caged herself and her son in the rented house where they lived. But the child ripped through his cage and attacked the neighbour." Mateo's description was dispassionate and dismissive.

"Wow! The report never detailed that," Katelin uttered.

"Carlo Quizon, the second lead, was bad at reports," Mateo said.

The location seemed to have triggered something in Daniel's recollection; he sat up straight, an urgent look on his face.

"There must be something to this, Dad. If I am not mistaken, Roald's family has a rest house in Lipa. I remember they had a company budget meeting in that house, because he invited our gang to follow and join them for a weekend swimming party. I cannot remember why I could not join them, but the place could be in Mataas na Kahoy," Daniel said, a lilt of excitement in his voice.

"Why don't you ask him so we can confirm?" his dad suggested.

Daniel did. He dialled Roald's number, who answered within two rings.

"Hey, bro, what are you up to this morning?" Daniel asked in a pleasant tone, his phone on speaker.

"Hey, D! I'm just about to get to the car, I'm on my way to my doctor," Roald replied.

This was a surprise to all, as they knew that Roald's next appointment with Dr Sanchez was the following day.

"You feeling okay, bro?" Daniel asked, a frown on his brow.

"I'm okay, bro, just another session with the shrink." Roald's reply was nonchalant, oblivious to the crowd listening to their conversation.

"Okay. Hey, bro, don't you have a rest house in Batangas?" Daniel kept his tone as casual as possible.

"Yes, in Mataas na Kahoy, why do you ask?" Roald asked.

"Well, I was thinking of places where my team and I can do the mid-year budget, and I remembered you did yours two years ago at your place... Can I borrow it? If it is okay with you."

"Oh sure, when? We may need to have it cleaned and prepared. We have not been back there for over a year."

"I will let you know; we are still planning it. Thanks in advance, bro."

"You're welcome," Roald replied, and he hung up.

Silence ruled for a split second as the call ended. Daniel looked at the group, waiting for reaction.

"Okay, let us look into that rest house. It may lead to something," Edrigu said and glanced at Mateo, whose face was grim. Mateo nodded.

A message came from Dr Sanchez. Edrigu turned on the system in Session Room 3. Minutes later, they had live audio and video access to the session and saw Roald enter the door. Dr Sanchez stood up to greet him. Roald sat on the couch, Dr Sanchez in her usual seat.

"Thank you for seeing me today, Doctora. I know you're busy and I really appreciate you made time for me at such brief notice." Roald's voice was pleasant.

"It's my pleasure, Roald. It is additional research material for my medical journal." Dr Sanchez's smile was gentle.

After tea was served, and short pleasantries exchanged, Dr Sanchez bid Roald to relax, and said, "So, tell me what's on your mind." Her calm facade was admirable being that the group eavesdropping on their conversation were all tensed.

"Your last question had been on my mind since I left our last session... on what bothered me most about my girlfriend's revelation..." Roald paused. "I think I fear it, about her being an aswang, and I do not know why..."

"Are you scared she will hurt you?"

Roald paused, then shook his head. "No, not that. I'm not scared of her."

"You said you feared something. What was that something?" Dr Sanchez prompted him.

"I had a bad dream last night. That question was the last thing on my mind before I fell asleep... The certainty that I fear aswangs, what she is, came to me when I woke up. What exactly I am scared about, I do not know, except the fear was there."

"Tell me about your dream..." Dr Sanchez asked.

"It's a mix of images... but it was the emotion that came during and afterward that stayed with me. It felt familiar... and recurring. I was a child in my dream, and I saw a woman lying on the ground, blood pooled all around her, and a man crouched over her, his hands and face bloody..." Roald's terror was clear in the tremor in his speech.

"Did you recognise anything in those images? Places, the woman, the man?"

"The place — I'm certain I was on my tree house, the one my dad built for me when I was young. It used to be my favourite playhouse when I was a child," Roald's brows knitted as he scoured his memories.

"How about the man and the woman?"

"No, I do not think I know them. I may have, but just do not remember, but it felt like they were strangers to me."

"So, in your dream, the event happened at your place?"

Roald shook his head. "No, the bloody scene was outdoors. It happened in the garden of the house next door. My treehouse sat atop an ancient mango tree beside the perimeter wall. It was made of wood and glass and offered three views. It overlooked the lake, our garden, and the front lawn of the neighbour's house."

Dr Sanchez nodded and jotted down notes as Roald talked.

"You said the woman was lying on the ground, bloody... was she dead?" she pressed. At the nod of Roald's head, she continued, "And the man, what was he doing?"

There was a long silence from Roald, his eyes closed, as he tried to dredge up details from the nightmare. Sweat beaded his upper lip, his face in a grimace of terror as the images came back to him.

"It looked like he was... eating her, and he looked savage." Roald's response was a hoarse whisper.

"What time of the day did it happen?" Dr Sanchez asked, her interest keen.

"Night, it was night." His reply came quick.

"Was there a moon that night?"

"No, it was dark, but I remember a flash of light, and the man looked up at that flash, and that's how I saw his face." Roald's shiver was visible, even on the screen.

Dr Sanchez stared at Roald. "What do you think he was?"

They all waited for Roald's answer with bated breath, but he kept silent.

"Could it be you assumed him to be an aswang, because he looked like he was eating her?" Dr Sanchez said, her suggestion gentle.

Roald stared back at her. His indecision clear. Then he sighed, "Yes, it's possible. I am sure my nanny at that age used aswang stories to scare me into behaving, to make me eat my greens, or abide by my bedtime schedule."

"Do you think the event in your nightmare actually happened?" Dr Sanchez asked gently.

"I am not sure. Maybe I need to speak to my parents. If it happened when I was young, I must have talked about it then."

"Yes, that is a good idea. It may just be an irrational fear borne from an unusual event that got melded into the scary stories your nanny or any of your elders were telling you then," Dr Sanchez said. Her demeanour was composed and non-judgmental. Roald's shoulders relaxed. "Will you keep me updated on that?"

Roald nodded.

"Do you believe your girlfriend is an aswang?" she asked.

This was a crucial question, and his answer would determine the course of action she and the rest of the people listening in on the conversation would take.

"Yes... I think I do... Or at least I think I did." Roald's quiet rasp was tortured. The verbal admission seemed to have unlocked something in him. His shoulders straightened.

"Doc, do you think my girlfriend is an aswang?" Roald asked, his gaze focused on Dr Sanchez. It appeared that he needed some validation, a professional opinion.

Her smile was enigmatic. "I cannot make that assessment, Roald, as she is not my patient. You are. I would have to speak to her myself to make any diagnosis. She could very well believe herself to be one, and that is a different kind of neurosis," she replied.

"I thought the same at first, Doc, until I saw..." Roald stopped in mid-sentence.

"What did you see?" she prompted.

They had briefed Dr Sanchez of the event. The good doctor was fishing for Roald's genuine thoughts about what he saw. It would determine how convinced Roald was, and if there was a space for them to plant reasonable doubt.

"I saw her changing... her colour, her skin texture. I felt her temperature, the heat haze from her skin..." Roald's voice was wondering, the tremor audible.

"What did she change into?"

"I did not see beyond that. They pulled me away."

"What was your state of mind that day, the previous night, or a few days before? Were you well rested? Were you eating well?" Dr Sanchez asked.

"No, after the first discussion about it, I was not sleeping well, barely ate," he admitted.

"So, it is safe to say your anxiety level was high, right?" He nodded. "There is a possibility you misinterpreted what you saw?"

"It is a possibility, Doc, but right now, I am sure of what I saw." Roald's insistence was emphatic.

"Okay. We will take it as it is." She nodded, her expression placid and placating. "What do you plan to do with that knowledge? With your relationship with her? What is next for the both of you?"

"I am working to get our relationship past my fear," Roald replied, sounding less certain of the outcome.

"Have you spoken to her since the revelation?"

Roald grimaced. "I haven't had the luck. Her phone has been out of reach for days now. I also want to be completely sure of my mind, my heart. If I am to convince her we have a future together, I need to know how I can deal with this."

To his hidden listeners, the statement was a welcome relief.

The session ended with Dr Sanchez giving Roald permission to call her anytime if he had any more concern about his fear of aswangs. They had established that he had some trauma about aswangs, and it was affecting his perception of his girlfriend's nature. The following day's session was cancelled. Instead, they would have an on-call consultation from then on.

Roald left the clinic with a more relaxed countenance. The frown on his face eased, and his steps were more purposeful. He told the doctor that his next stop was to find out where his girlfriend was so he could get to her.

They knew he would come to the De Vida house.

The session yielded many investigative points for the team. The most obvious one was for them to go back to Mataas na Kahoy to find the house the Magsinos owned, find out if the episode Roald detailed in the session happened, and if it was an aswang-related one.

With all the tasks assigned, Lorenzo dismissed the group. They had achieved excellent progress in this case, and judging by how Roald behaved in the sessions, the future for him and Yuana was looking up.

The team left the briefing room in batches suffused with enthusiasm.

Everyone except Mateo.

He was going back to Mataas na Kahoy tomorrow. And it filled him with foreboding. The memories of his last visit to the area were best forgotten and left undisturbed. But he would not defy a direct order from the Patriarch. So, he would go with Edrigu in the morning. He had a feeling he knew its exact location.

He hoped it was not the one beside the lake house he rented for a few weeks in 1994. His past and the family secret he kept from Daniel for twenty-five years had caught up with him.

With a heavy heart, Mateo bid the De Vidas goodbye. Daniel followed him, unaware that his life would soon be upended.

Roald slowed his car down at the corner street to allow half a dozen vehicles to cross. He could see the main gate of the De Vida compound from where he was, a mixture of trepidation and anticipation in his veins.

A familiar dark blue BMW pulled out from the car repair shop across from the De Vida compound — it was Daniel's. That was odd. Daniel's house and office were nowhere near the area.

Two minutes later, he pulled into the driveway of the De Vidas. Nita showed him to the living room where Katelin and Edrigu De Vida waited to meet him.

"Good afternoon, sir, Ma'am." He recognised nervousness in his own voice.

Edrigu had a spark of satisfaction in his eyes. He must have found consolation in his discomfort.

"Good afternoon, Hijo," Katelin replied with a gentle smile.

He appeared miserable and tired, but her reception emboldened Roald, so he took a deep breath and ploughed into the purpose of his visit. "Ma'am, I am here to ask for help. I need to find Yuana."

His directness made Katelin blink, and she threw a glance at her husband.

"Why do you want to find Yuana?" Edrigu's quiet question told him clearly that they would protect Yuana to all ends.

"Sir, I want to make things right with her, and I cannot do that if I cannot locate her and talk to her." He would not discuss what was in his heart with anyone but Yuana.

Edrigu looked at him for a long time until he felt uncomfortable, but he refused to look away. He wanted Yuana's grandfather to see his determination and the sincere desire to fix matters with their granddaughter.

Finally, Edrigu spoke, "Villa Bizitza, Baco, Oriental Mindoro."

He was dumbstruck for a split second but understood Edrigu was giving him permission to try his luck with Yuana.

"Thank you, Sir." He grabbed Edrigu's hand and shook it with uncharacteristic vigour.

"Good luck," Katelin said, her face serious.

After a quick farewell to the couple, he rushed back to his car.

He had a travel plan to make.

12

THE APEX

Despite not finding sleep till dawn, Yuana woke up full of energy. The last thoughts before she fell asleep remained foremost in her mind. It was a nagging inner voice to discover her animus.

Roald still pervaded her consciousness, but her preoccupation to find out this hidden facet of her nature diverted her from her heartache. A new door was before her, one that could lead to a different path, an option that was never on the table before.

Her parents were at the ground floor verandah, enjoying a bottle of rosé, probably a Graci Etna Rosato, her mother's recent favourite. Her mother laughed at whatever funny story her father regaled her. It was the happiest she had ever seen her. Her father's eyes sparkled with joy, passion, and satisfaction; his own lips deepened with a smile.

As usual, seeing them this happy evoked a mixed feeling in her; gladness to see her parents contented, and envy her own relationship did not pan out the same way, no matter how similar their situation was. Some people were luckier than most.

She stood by the stairs for a while, unwilling to break the happy circle, when they noticed her and beckoned her over.

"There you are, my sweet. Come and join us. The rosé is chilled to perfection." Her father waved her over.

She walked closer, gave them both a hug and sat down. She poured herself a glass of the rosé. There was slight tension in the air, like suppressed energy poised to explode. Both her parents looked excited. Her mother was beaming, but there was a nervousness in her gaze.

"So, what is it, Ma? Pa?" she asked.

A twitch appeared at the corner of her father's mouth, and it widened into a grin. His excitement was that of a boy on Christmas morning who discovered he got everything he wished for.

"I proposed to your mother... and she said yes!"

"You did?... She did?... Oh my god!" she squealed, jumping up to hug her mother.

Her own heart overflowed with happiness for them. Perhaps the adage was true, that for every end, there was a fresh beginning, and that genuine joy was born out of genuine pain. Her parents found their joy and a new beginning after twenty-eight years of pain. They were ecstatic. Her family was now whole, and that was enough for the moment.

"When is the wedding?"

"We haven't discussed the details yet, but I want to get married on the tenth of May. It was the day he first proposed. I want to pretend there was no time wasted between us..." Her mother's face glowed.

"May tenth it is..." her father murmured. He picked up her mother's hands and dropped a kiss on her palms. Heat rose to her cheeks. She felt like an intruder in their circle.

"We can tell the family when we return. I will plan the wedding, Mama. It will be fun."

It was something to be excited about, and she was glad. She could set aside her concern for her own relationship. Her parents' happiness was a balm to her sore heart. "Let me raise a toast to the most beautiful parents a girl could ever wish for..." Her glass raised.

"To the family I have always wanted and now have..." her father said.

"To a love that was lost and now found..." her mother's voice cracked.

Their glasses met and clinked. It was an emotional but heartfelt toast. Silence followed as all three of them dealt with the feelings the moment created.

"It was not really lost, was it, Bel? We just got... misplaced, you and I," her father said. His tender gaze turned to her mother.

"Yes, you are right..." Tears pooled in her mother's eyes.

Yuana swallowed the lump of emotion that formed in her throat, constricting her heart as she witnessed the enormity of her parents' love for each other.

"Shall we toast to that then... To misplaced loves that found their way back..." she said, wanting to lighten the mood.

They raised their glasses in agreement.

The bottle of rosé was consumed in a series of toasts until the air cleared and became easy and cheerful again.

"Have you heard from Roald, Yuana?" Her father's gentle question came out of the blue.

"Not yet, Papa. But then, I have not turned on my phone since we came here," she replied.

"Why not? Do you not want to talk to him anymore?"

"I do. Yet I am afraid to turn it on and only to find out he has not tried to contact me at all," she admitted.

"I doubt that very much," Galen scoffed. "I have seen the boy's torment. It would surprise me if Roald was not beside himself looking for you."

"We have been here for over a week, Pa, why hasn't he showed up here yet?" The underlying bitterness seeped in her tone.

"He doesn't know where we are, Yuana. Our office did not, as well, and even if they did, our SOP would not allow them to divulge that. And the family will not tell him unless they believed it would be the best thing to do," her mother said.

As if on cue, the phone rang. It was Edrigu calling. After a brief exchange, Ysobella looked at her with a smug smile on her face.

"Your grandfather just called to inform us he just gave Roald the address to the villa, that he might show up anytime."

Hope filled her heart, and it lifted her spirits.

"There you go, Yuana. I told you so..." her father said confidently, but she heard the sigh of relief under his breath.

"I am glad he is coming here. Then I would not have to go through the inconvenience of flying to Manila to beat him within an inch of his life," his father said in a sotto voice to her mother.

She smiled.

The news put Yuana in anticipation the whole afternoon, and after a few hours, left her overwhelmed. Her mind kept playing scenes of reconciliation and rejection one after the other. It was like being on an emotional roller-coaster. Finally, she could not take it anymore. She went for a run in the woods.

An hour into her sprint deep in the forest, the afternoon sun had already descended low on the horizon. It gave the surroundings an auburn gleam. The breeze blew through the trees and cooled the sweat-dampened fabric of her shirt. She proceeded to the riverbank where they met Mr Nakahara the night before. The persistent thought about her animus led her there. It did not surprise her to find the gentleman seated on the same fallen tree trunk, meditating.

She watched him for a while, noting the lightening at the hair on his temples. There was a rugged yet serene air about him, like a well-worn pair of jeans. He exuded mystery and wisdom, no doubt brought about by his war experience and years of living in the mountains. He could be the same age as her grandfather, but he looked more hardened and battle-tested. His sun-browned skin made him appear younger, as well.

She approached him with care, not wanting to disturb him. She planned to sit by the bank until he was done, but he spoke, his eyes still closed. "Good afternoon, Ms Yuana."

She came closer and sat down beside him on the fallen trunk. "Pleasant afternoon, Mr Nakahara," she said.

He opened his eyes and stared at her, a slight smile on his face. "You are here to find out about your true nature, yes?"

She nodded. "How? I do not want to starve myself just to induce an auto-morphosis. I almost had one of those. It was not a pleasant experience. And I have no plans to repeat it."

"Reflexive transformation may be the usual way, but not the most ideal, or the only way," he said.

That was intriguing. "What other ways are there?"

"Meditation is one, but that takes a long time to master, and I sense you are impatient." His focused gaze was knowing.

"Yes, I want to know now. Is there a faster, less painful and easier way to discover my animus?"

"Faster? Maybe. But it is not easier, and it requires considerable effort to achieve. Are you willing to do whatever it takes to *emerge*?" Challenge glittered in the depths of his dark eyes.

Her heart thundered in her ears. "Is it worth the effort to find out? Most of our kind lived until their end without knowing their true animus and still had a full life."

He smiled. "Most of us do not have the potential that you have. When you emerge, you will discover more than your spirit animal."

"Will you teach me?"

He nodded.

"I can teach you now... Are you ready?"

Am I? She took a deep breath. "Yes, I am. How do we begin?"

"You need to increase your heartbeat to a degree that you can hear it, then you transform with no form in mind. You just let it happen."

Nakahara's soft instruction crawled into her heart like a mist on a moonlit night.

"Transform with no form in mind? How can I do that?" Nakahara's method was counter-intuitive to what she was taught.

"You focus on your heartbeat, not on your form," he said. "That is why raising your heartbeat is crucial."

"Raising my heartbeat? How? Like through... running?"

"Yes, running hard. Very hard. Until you can feel your blood pounding in your ears.

She thought of where and how long she would have to run to achieve the feat. She ran for over an hour earlier and she did not achieve that, so she needed to run faster and harder.

"Okay, I can do that."

With a glance of goodbye to Nakahara, she ran at full speed away from the river and toward the foot of the mountain where she planned to run uphill until she achieved the required audible-heartbeat state.

And run she did.

Air whizzed past her hair and face as she zigzagged around the trees in her path. She jumped over fallen trees, boulders, and low branches; her sight focused on the inclined ground ahead. Her legs burned, but she quickened her pace still.

In her peripheral vision, she saw wild animals, ground and tree dwelling alike, scamper away from her path. Still, she kept the punishing pace and speed, knowing that if she slowed down, she would have to start again.

She was not sure how long and how far she had covered, but she pushed herself to run longer. Farther and faster, even as her lungs felt scored by the effort to breathe and bring oxygen to her muscles. She sprinted until she could not, anymore.

Until her heartbeat drowned out the sounds of her surroundings.

She stopped and looked around, her senses on high alert. She was on a small hilltop; the sun had set, and the horizon was darkening. Behind her, she could see Villa Bizitza from a distance. With that as the last picture in her mind, she pulled her yoga pants off, her shoes and her top. She closed her eyes to begin her transformation, her focus on her heart beating loud in her ears and strong in her veins.

The familiar tingling started at the base of her spine and spread all over her body until it reached her fingertips. Her core generated heat, expanding outward, enveloping her from head to toe. She focused her mind on her heartbeat until she became a passive observer of what was happening in her body. She waited for her spine to bend her to all fours, but the familiar sensation started on her shoulder blades instead. Her bones stretched out, growing outwards. She opened her eyes when her skin vibrated, saw the start of the transformation from her human form to whatever animal she would turn into.

In the waning light, it surprised her to see that her skin had turned from her normal flesh tone into a familiar yet unfamiliar midnight dark sheen, and into a texture that she had never seen before. In the countless past transformations, shiny black fur had covered her body.

This time, the black fur transformed into something else; small, downy, glossy feathers of dark blue-black, or dark violet. She flexed her hands and saw the long and thick talons that replaced her nails. Her hands did not transform into paws. And she was still upright.

The stretching pressure on her shoulder blades turned into a familiar spasm that halted into a jolt. She looked back and saw a black arch over her shoulders and head. She reached back to touch it, unable to believe her own conclusion.

Wings! I have grown a pair of wings!

She flexed her shoulder blades, and the wings moved like an extra pair of arms. Enthralled, she unfurled both wings and tested the range of motion that she could make. She expanded them wide and flexed to test their strength.

An imposing figure hovered over her, startling her. The figure landed with a soft thud nearby. She took an involuntary defensive step backward, ready to fight, until she recognised him.

It was Mr Nakahara, in his animus form, winged like she was.

His wings, however, were bat-like. Dark, glossy fur covered his humanoid form. It was hard to tell in this low light what exact colour it was, but it looked black. His features were unmistakable despite the now dark colour of his skin. He had claw-like hands with dark talons like hers. She did not feel threatened by him, although he looked intimidating.

He walked closer to her. His eyes glowed. "Ah... Your animus is avian..."

She was too overwhelmed to respond to him. Her wings flexed and spread wide, caught a strong breeze, and lifted her a few meters up into the air. She staggered back onto her feet and folded her wings back.

"Do not use your wings yet, Ms Yuana. You need to learn how to fly first..."

His smile was full of satisfaction. He walked a slow circle around her as he inspected her full form. He stopped in front of her, a friendly, almost paternal, expression on his face.

"Why did I transform into this? It is unlike anything I have seen, or known..."

Her own form mystified her. She did not just turn into a bird, which was unusual enough as their kind could only transform into land-based animals, she turned into what looked like an avian humanoid. And judging from the form that Mr Nakahara had taken, his animus was a... bat-man.

"Ms Yuana, you and I, we are an *Apex*..."

"An Apex? I'm an *Apex*?" she breathed, still unbelieving.

Mr Nakahara remained quiet.

"But... That's not... possible... I can't be?"

"You need no other proof than your current form. Winged-creature transformation is impossible to achieve for any normal aswangs. Only Apexes, the super shape-shifters, can achieve this."

She nodded, her brain still in a scramble. She knew what an Apex was. Their history talked about previous Apexes in past centuries. They were very rare, and only one in every two hundred years would emerge in their midst of the two hundred fifty million strong aswangs.

No one in her family knew of any that ever existed in their lifetime. To be one was mindboggling.

Why me?

Apart from being a De Vida, she had no exemplary achievements of her own, no notable physical or intellectual contributions to their kind. She did not deserve to be an Apex or suited to be one. She realised with a jolt that Mr Nakahara being an Apex meant there are now two in their lifetime. And that was even more rare.

"How come no one knew you are an Apex?"

"I choose not to let anyone know. I do not want the responsibility." His response was guarded. But she understood.

"What responsibility? What are we supposed to do as Apexes?"

"You will know soon enough, when you expose yourself..."

"Why reveal yourself to me?"

"I believe you and I have a destiny to fulfil. So, we have to work together. But at the very least, I want to help you achieve your potential. It is up to you. But once you are ready, I offer my assistance to train you... in due time..."

Her mind buzzed with confusion and questions. It elated her in a way that she now knew what her animus was, but she was uncertain how she felt about being an Apex. Everything that happened was so unprecedented in her existence as a human and an aswang.

"So, what is next for me, Mr Nakahara?" she asked, needing guidance.

He took her hand in his.

"You rest, you think, you test your wings, then you decide," he said, the friendly smile back on his face.

She sighed and nodded.

"Damn, does that mean I need to walk back? I cannot fly yet, and I think I am too tired to run," she muttered to herself.

Mr Nakahara grinned.

"I will fly you back," he said. "But only this one time..." His eyes twinkled.

She grinned and picked up her yoga pants to put them on. Her taloned feet distracted her. She felt taller, similar to being in high heels, only this time, the height was because of her bird claw feet on perpetual tiptoe.

Not bad.

She picked up her top and pulled it over the feather-covered mound of her breast. The back of the shirt bunched over her shoulders where her wings sprouted from her shoulder blades. On instinct, her wings shrunk into her back, and she returned to her human form. She pushed her bare feet into her shoes and turned to find Mr Nakahara with his back to her as he took in the view and waited.

"All done," she said.

He held out his hand and scooped her into his arms. Then his powerful bat-like wings opened, and lifted them into the air. The flight was not as smooth as she assumed it would be. The beating of his wings created an up and down motion as they cut through the wind to generate the lift. He flew close to the treetops to avoid being spotted. Old habits for survival die hard. This was what she could expect, she supposed, when she learned to fly on her own.

The flight did not take long, and soon, Mr Nakahara landed at the edge of the forest.

"Thank you, Mr Nakahara. How can I get in touch with you?"

"You're welcome. If you need me, you can find me by the river. I would know when you are there."

"Okay... So, I shall say goodnight..."

"Ms Yuana, please do not tell anyone about me. I have hidden my nature for decades for a reason," Mr Nakahara said gravely.

Her nod was solemn. "Don't worry, Mr Nakahara. It is not my secret to tell. I will tell no one."

"Call me Kazu. We will work together closely. Nakahara is a long name to say, Kazu is shorter." He smiled.

"And call me Yuana. Thank you again, Kazu."

And with that, she turned to walk the rest of the way to the villa. From behind, she heard the *thwack-thwack* sound his large wings created as he flew away.

As she neared the compound, she saw two of the Mangyan aswangs that were tasked to follow her every time she left the house. They looked relieved when they saw her approach. She had forgotten about their usual habit of tailing her. No doubt they lost her in the woods and were anxious.

"I am sorry, Kuyas, did I worry you?"

"It worried us, Miss. You ran so fast. We cannot keep up," they said, almost in unison.

"Sorry, I forgot you were following me, I did not mean to," she said. "We can keep it a secret, if that would make you feel better... I will not tell Yam-Ay," she teased.

Their eyes widened, and they both nodded, vigorously.

"Okay then, I shall go inside now. See you tomorrow." She walked straight to the kitchen. She was hungry and in need of food and sustenance.

Her parents were in the living room, looking all cuddly and affectionate with each other when she came in.

"Kids, kids, stop that... You're being a terrible role model for me," she said in mock disgust.

They both turned around with an identical shamefaced expression.

"How was your run, Yuana? You were gone awhile," her mother said.

"It was good, Mama. Can we eat first? I am starving and what I need to tell you and Papa requires sustenance."

Their eyebrows rose.

"Is it serious?" her mother asked.

"It may be. I can't believe it myself still." She was already halfway up the stairs on her way to the room.

"Okay, I will have the food and the sustenance prepared. Are you showering first?" her mother called after her.

She was ravenous but preferred to eat feeling fresh. Her shower was quick. She dressed and combed her wet hair back; she would not bother with a blow drier. Food was first in her order of business.

Her father was in her parents' room when she came down to the kitchen, the victus ready for both her mother and herself to wolf down. It had become a practice in their household to ensure her father would not see them eating raw viscera in consideration for his stomach. With their aswang needs met, they went to the dining room to wait for him, but he was already there, picking at the appetiser. He was as famished as she.

Dinner atmosphere was light and quick, with all of them starved. Her confession would wait until dessert. For complete privacy, she requested for it to be served in the entertainment room. Five minutes later, the dessert trolley was wheeled and stationed in one corner of the sound-proofed entertainment room. They sat down with slices of the dark purple ube cheesecake, lava cake and hot beverage in hand. Her parents looked at her with anticipation.

"Mama, I know what my animus is, I have transformed into it earlier..." She was uncertain how to break the information to her parents.

"Oh, so what was it?" Ysobella asked, puzzled at the importance she placed on finding her spirit animal.

"It's a raven..." she replied, as she watched her mother's expression.

"A raven? How can your animus be a raven?" As expected, Ysobella was baffled.

"Why can't she have a bird as her animus? Can you not transform into any kind of animal you want?" asked her father.

"She cannot be a raven because we can only shape-shift into land-based animals. It is impossible for us to transform into any winged creature, unless you're an..." The meaning of what she said dawned on her mother. "*Apex...*" Her head whipped back toward Yuana, unable to say anything, her expression incredulous.

"What's an Apex?" Galen asked, intrigued. His eyes darted between them.

"A super shapeshifter, Papa. One that can transform into a winged animal," she replied for her mother, who was still speechless in shock.

"And I gather it is extremely rare?" One eyebrow quirked; his gaze focused on her mother's dumbstruck expression.

"Yes. One in every two hundred years," Ysobella said in a throaty voice.

"Wow!" Her father swivelled in her direction.

"You are an *Apex...*" Ysobella said in wondering, still unable to believe what she heard.

She nodded. "Yes, Mama, I turn into a raven... I think."

"You think? You are not sure?" her father asked.

"Well, it could be a crow, I can't tell the difference." She shrugged.

"Can you show us?" Ysobella requested in a whisper.

Yuana understood why her mother wanted to see for herself. She needed to validate what her brain could not process-the fact her daughter was an Apex.

She stood up. There was no need to undress for this as she had chosen a dress with a low back. With enough room for her wings to sprout out without constraints. She expected she would have to show them.

Galen forgot to worry about seeing his daughter naked. He was as caught up in it as Ysobella. The transformation, while he had seen it before, was still mesmerising. However, the heat haze surrounding Yuana, her vibrating skin, the change of her colour from human tone to dark bluish sheen was something else.

Wings grew out from behind her and loomed bigger over her shoulders and past her head. The stark contrast between her skin now covered in small dark and glossy fan-shaped contour feathers, and the light-coloured dress was dramatic. The dainty, flowy dress was incongruent with the black-red talons her fingernails turned into.

Her hair had transformed into an aerodynamic crest of semi and filo plume feathers that fanned around her face. It gave her a majestic and intimidating look. It reminded him of a monkey-eating eagle, and it looked like the feathers could flatten close to her scalp when in flight.

The skin on her face was the only thing that kept its human colouring and texture, but on her eyebrows grew a pair of bristle feathers. It made her appear as if she had very long eyelashes. Even her eyes turned black, like raven's eyes, with no visible iris. The effect was menacing and spellbinding. Yuana looked formidable in her avian humanoid form.

Her father's mouth hung open.

"Oh, *holy Prometheus*!" Ysobella breathed out her amazement.

She approached Yuana, touched the soft, downy, feather-covered arm and then her face, as if contrasting her new reality with the old one.

"How do I look, Mama?" Yuana asked, her voice soft and vulnerable, yet proud.

"You look magnificent, Yuana," Ysobella replied, sounding proud and overawed. "You are an *Apex*... The first one in our recorded history for over two hundred years..."

Galen felt an answering pride and something grand inside his heart.

Yuana inspected herself in the bright light. The blue-black sheen of her feathers, the dark red talons on her hands and the jet-black ones on her feet fascinated her.

He handed her his cell phone. "Take a picture of yourself," he urged.

With the camera open, she did. She saw her face for the first time in her raven humanoid form. Her eye area had an iridescent, dark feather growth that made her look like she was wearing glittery goth make up.

It surprised Galen when her flesh-coloured face changed to match the rest of her body.

"Wow! You can do that?" He could not help but exclaim.

Yuana shrugged one shoulder. "So, it seems. It could be useful for a full camouflage."

"True..."

He took the phone from her and moved back to take a full body shot, then handed it to her to view the photo. Yuana's mouth dropped open.

"*Holy Aquila!* I look terrifying..." she breathed.

"Yuana, do you understand what being an Apex entails?" Ysobella asked. It interrupted Yuana's preoccupation with her own form.

"No, mama. Except for its rarity, I know very little about being an Apex. I mean, what is the purpose of being one apart from the ability to transfigure into a winged creature?"

"Let us ask your great grandmother, she might provide us insight on this. In the meantime, what do you want to do?"

"I need time to process this. Let us not tell anyone yet, Ma, Pa? I need to think."

"Okay, take your time. Let's find out everything we can about it before we let our world know of your existence..." Ysobella said.

And he could not agree more.

Yuana turned back into her human form. The process was as quick as a blink.

It must have been the loss of the wings, but in his eyes, Yuana looked deflated. Things just became more complicated for his daughter. She now had to deal with the appearance of her father in her life, with the uncertainty of her relationship with Roald, her Apex capabilities, and what it meant to her as an aswang.

His daughter's plate was overflowing, and there was nothing he could do to help.

And for the first time in the longest time, another first in a day full of it, he was glad the dessert tonight had the chocolatey kind.

Roald was busy with the arrangements for his trip to Villa Bizitza, Baco, Oriental Mindoro. There were no available flights to Calapan the following day, so he would take the bus, the ferry, and hire a car in Calapan City to drive to Yuana's holiday home at the foot of Mount Halcon.

He did not want to wait another day.

In his head, he rehearsed what he would say to convince her not to give up on them if she had not ended their relationship yet or give them another chance if she did. Either way, he would not go home without Yuana back in his life. No other outcome would be acceptable. With determination, he went to bed early; he wanted to be at Yuana's house before dinner time.

Roald was on the road by seven a.m. He wanted to make sure he had plenty of time for the eleven-a.m. ferry to Calapan City. The knot in his heart, a constant reminder of what was at stake. His head played scenarios of how he would win Yuana back. He pushed any thoughts of failure away. He would not consider the possibility of losing her.

The long, quiet journey provided him with plenty of thinking time. Memories of their time together surfaced like buoys: echoes of the days when he wooed Yuana, how much effort it took for him to get close to her, to make her open up — how he had to learn to be a friend to her first. He thought those were the most torturous moments of his life as he watched other men flirt with her while he acted as her wingman.

How wrong he was then. That could not have compared to what he was going through now.

More images floated into his consciousness; eight months since they first met, he had launched a stringent campaign to win her heart. Multiple times during the courtship she tried to discourage him, but that had the opposite effect. There were many moments in those months he almost gave up and accepted that he would never win her, but those glimpses of pain and longing in her eyes when she thought he wasn't looking kept him going.

He could understand now why she was so guarded then, why she did not want to gamble her heart away. And it was the same reason she tried very hard to keep him at a distance, why she tried every trick in her book to put a wall between them, to keep herself apart from him, because she was protecting both of their hearts.

And she was doing it again. But like before, he would not let her succeed. They could not protect their hearts from each other anymore. It was too late.

Another car was driving along the Star Toll, with Mateo and Edrigu on board. As their destination drew closer, Mateo's gut tightened at every kilometre covered, in direct contrast to his loosening grasp on the closely held secret that he had kept for over twenty-five years. He was still hoping this incident had nothing to do with his past, that it was unrelated.

That it was just a bitter coincidence.

An hour and a half of driving in complete silence, they turned right into the entrance to Mataas na Kahoy. They slowed down at the junction to allow a truck loaded with rebars to turn the corner when Edrigu saw a police officer walking down the street. He rolled down the window on his side of the car to ask about the Magsino home. Daniel had told them it was in Barangay Manggahan but did not know its exact location.

The instruction given by the police officer was not very clear except that it was a grey house at the end of the street with an enormous mango tree and a glass treehouse on it. It was the crucial confirmation that it was the house they were looking for. The police officer offered to have them assisted, but Mateo declined it, much to Edrigu's surprise.

"It's okay, officer, I know where it is." Bleakness enveloped his heart now. It dashed the hope he was holding onto. With grim determination, he drove to the house of his nightmare. Sure and true.

He knew that his precise knowledge of the house's location was not lost on Edrigu. As a friend, Edrigu would give him the space to stew in his own thoughts and allow him the silence that he needed.

Five minutes later, they stopped in front of the Magsino's house. A concrete six-foot high wall and a dark blue metal gate enclosed it. They parked in front, and both got out. The house was empty and locked up. They did not have the key, but that was not a problem for them. They glanced around to make sure no one was in the vicinity. With that assured, they both vaulted over the wall with ease.

"I will take the inside of the house, you do the outside," Edrigu said.

He replied with a quick nod and walked towards the front lawn where the tree house was.

Mateo paused by the foot of the incline as he looked up at the structure. This kid's play area was no traditional tree house, its unique use of wood and glass a direct give away that a prominent architect designed it.

The strategic placement of the glass windows he suspected was for the adults to see what young Roald and his playmates were doing inside. The main house was elevated and must have provided an unobstructed view of the interior of the treehouse.

He walked the wooden board incline that wrapped around the base of the tree and lead to the doorway. He took in the interior of the beautiful playhouse. The room was square; the floor was hardwood. Play mats must have protected it at some point.

As Roald had described it, three walls of the room were almost floor to ceiling plexiglass. Hard wood panes about an inch thick and two inches wide framed and bisected the glass, giving it a French window design. It acted as both decoration and support. The treehouse looked like a square gazebo perched on a tree. The only wooden wall had a furniture set against it. It looked like a low child's bed, judging from the shape under the white sheet that covered it.

By the foot of the bed, there was a low table with shelves built under it. Above the table, and fixed on the wall, was an empty built-in bookshelf. He could picture it full of children's books and toys. The two parallel glass walls — one faced the main house, and the other faced the neighbouring property.

He moved closer to the dusty plexiglass wall that looked out at the front lawn of the neighbouring house. The sinking feeling that had pervaded his being since they left Manila had settled low in his stomach. He felt numb as certainty had severed the last thread of denial that he did not know he still harboured.

He was the man Roald saw that night, and the boyhood memory that haunted his nightmares was true. The grief of that night rushed back. His jaw ached with the effort to control himself from howling. The deep breaths that he took did not help. When the release came it made his shoulders shake.

He took another deep breath to collect himself and straightened his back. There was still work to be done.

"What happened that night, Mateo?" Edrigu's quiet voice startled him. He did not hear him approach.

"It did not begin or end that night. And that one night cannot explain everything." The weight of his misery was a bitter taste in his mouth.

"Explain, then. I will listen," Edrigu said, his voice low.

"Remember the 1987 battle with the Moros, the one headed by Lt. Colonel Enrico?" At Edrigu's nod, he continued. "Do you also remember why the Tribunal executed him?"

"Yes, I was not part of the judging panel then, but I remember it well. It was for abuse of power for forcing his aswang soldiers to commit harravis practices," Edrigu replied.

He nodded.

"Both Major Ona and I were part of his battalion. He forced us to go harravis to save our lives and our troops. For most of us, it was a onetime thing we had to do to survive. But Lt. Colonel Enrico wanted to continue the practice and turn all his aswang soldiers into full harravises, so I blew the whistle on him. I thought that was the end until Major Ona started his active hunting party in Pagsanjan in 1993. After he was killed, they autopsied his body, and confirmed he had Visceral Metastasis. He had been hunting pregnant women to stay the progress of the disease. He used the hunting party as a cover for his own need to secure amniotic fluid. I would have ignored his Visceral Metastasis diagnosis if I did not recall Lt. Colonel Enrico's autopsy also revealed he had the same disease." His voice broke, unable to continue.

"You have *Visceral Metastasis*?" Edrigu prompted, shocked.

"Yes, I had myself checked, and the results came back positive. They gave me two years to live. It devastated me. My wife was pregnant with our baby girl, and Daniel was just five years old, so the next thing I did was to prepare to die and ensure the future of my family. There was no way I would kill women and babies regularly just to prolong my life."

His distaste for the act was still fresh.

"But my wife decided otherwise. That night, we had dinner outdoors by the garden. Daniel was in bed by then. She brought up again her earlier suggestion to sacrifice our unborn child for my cure. I would not have it. She told me her doctor diagnosed her with cardiomyopathy, and giving birth to our baby might kill her, so I needed to survive for Daniel. Still, I said no. I wanted a second opinion for her because she needed to live for both our kids. But she gave me no choice."

The ball of pain that he thought he had got rid of resurfaced with a force of a tsunami, threatening to obliterate his control.

"Her last words to me were *'Do not waste my sacrifice, promise me you will survive'*... right before she shot herself in the head."

He closed his eyes at the avalanche of buried emotions and the vivid images of having to open her up and eat his own child's viscera. It was beyond description. It made his stomach turn. Bile burned his throat, and he swallowed hard to push his nausea back.

"And you had to do as she asked," Edrigu said. His grim expression and taut jaw conveyed that he understood the torment Mateo went through, the devastating loss of his wife, and having to kill and consume his own child.

"Yes. I found out from her doctor after her burial that she did not have cardiomyopathy..." He forced himself to breathe out the fury he was feeling. "She made me eat my daughter, Edrigu."

The anger at the act she forced him to commit under this pretext was still raw in his heart. He realised he was still angry at his late wife, and had not forgiven her for what she did to him and to their family.

"She decided long before that night, Mateo. She planned it. Did she suffer from depression during her conception of Daniel?"

The question gave him pause.

"Yes." He looked back at Espie's pregnancy with Daniel and remembered that she suffered from postnatal depression months after Daniel was born.

"That may have been the trigger, why she did what she did... Does Daniel know?" Edrigu asked.

"No." He sighed. "I told myself that I will tell him when we are both ready, when the right time comes. But I have never found the right time to do so. I guess I have never been ready. I am not sure how I will tell Daniel, without destroying the image of his mother and father in his mind."

Edrigu sighed. "If there was a way to keep the truth from Daniel, I would not be averse to helping you do that, but this might not be possible, given the circumstances."

"I know... Perhaps it is time."

"You would have to tell him, Mateo, the sooner the better, before he finds out during the briefings. You owe that much to him," Edrigu said.

"I know." The rhythmic tip-tapping of a small branch against a glass wall sounded like a countdown to a deadline.

He would prolong the time, if he could, but he had no choice.

13

THE FORK IN THE ROAD

Yuana spent the first few hours of the morning examining her animus from front to back, head to toe. In the natural sunlight, her feathers were more dark blue-violet than black. The contour feathers that covered her body had an iridescent quality to it. The violet hue in the feathers gave off some dark red, green and gold at certain angles.

She loved her Apex form, her wings in particular. It was a superhero fantasy come true. She discovered her wings were flexible; she had wrapped them around herself like a blanket and used them like an extra pair of arms. They were so big that when stretched, the wing tip touched the high ceiling.

It was a pity that once she learned how to fly, she would have to limit her flight to remote locations and moonless nights.

She had tested the talons on her feet earlier and grasped items with them like birds of prey do. To test the grip strength, she played tug of war between her hand and feet talons and discovered that her feet talons were as strong as her hands.

Last night, she researched as much as she could find about ravens, crows, eagles and hawks. In daylight, she did not look like a raven as she had first thought. She was a combination of various bird species.

Would I inherit birdlike powers apart from flight?

Maybe I should research about Apexes.

She picked up her bathrobe and threw it over her shoulder. Her human form was back by the time she tied the robe tie around her waist. She sat down on her reading couch and logged into their viscerebus archive.

Her research about Apexes yielded fascinating, but superficial information. Past Apexes transformed into a chiropteran form, like Mr Nakahara.

Her avian form was rarer. There had only been a single recorded avian Apex, and he turned into something similar to a snowy owl. It made sense as he emerged from the Alps. Perhaps her colour had to do with being able to blend into her surroundings.

She was only the second avian Apex in history.

In their recent past, the Apex had served as a figurehead, someone the aswangkind rallied behind, like a unifying royalty, during some momentous change in their society. Those previous Apexes were not required to rule, as the Tribunal still did that. There was nothing that showed what else the Apexes were good for. It seemed they were just figureheads.

Like a modern monarch?

She was not sure if she wanted that role - all the trappings of authority, but without real responsibility or accountability.

Hmm... perhaps there were some documents in the Vivliocultatum that could provide more information. Her great grandmother may be able to secure access to the Viv from the Supreme Tribunal.

An entry in the system caught her attention: *The Dawn of the Dual Apex.*

What?

She clicked on the link. It opened to an article about the written works of Aiden O'Cuinn, an Apex who lived during the medieval times. He was the chieftain of their clan and known as a poet. He had written ballads and poems and recorded much of the momentous events in his life. Just before he died, he wrote an unfinished ballad called *The Rise of the Viscerebus.* And there, he predicted the coming of the two Apexes.

It read:

When the era of the Two Apexes born in the same lifetime dawns, it will be the beginning of the cataclysm. The first will emerge at the same moment the seed of the great crisis is sowed. The second will rise to signal its turning point. Two have to become one to overcome, for as long as they remain separate, the enemy prevails.

The text said the first Apex was a forewarning of a great crisis. And the second one would signal the turning point of the crisis. The first pointed to Kazu Nakahara, and the second, to her as they were the first two Apexes ever to exist in the same lifetime. The rest of the words seemed to suggest they would need to fight some enemy.

She was not a warrior. No training for it, either physically or mentally. She was unsure if she could handle the responsibility of leading all the aswangs in the world. Kazu may have a point in keeping his identity a secret.

After reading that, she was leaning towards anonymity herself.

It was during brunch when a call came through from Calapan. The iztari team who tailed Roald informed them he had boarded the eleven a.m. ferry from Batangas Port to Calapan City. They expected him to arrive in Calapan by one thirty. He had booked a car from a local travel agency, so Roald should get to Villa Bizitza by around three in the afternoon.

Ysobella instructed Yam-Ay to prepare the guest room. She had a feeling Roald would not be going back to Manila tonight. Knowing his determination, he would not give up on Yuana easily.

It was unnecessary to inform Yuana about the call or she would twist herself into knots. She would know soon enough. Plus, it would be more romantic if there was an element of surprise.

Daniel arrived home midafternoon, much earlier than usual. It was rare for his father to ask him to dine at home on a Friday evening. Friday and Saturday nights are prime time for people his age. But he could not say no. He sensed it was important to his father. His voice had sounded flat, a sign that something was bothering him.

His father was in the living room, slumped on the sofa, scotch in hand, his mother's photo album set in front of him. And this alarmed him even more. His father would only drink scotch one day a year - the death anniversary of his mother and his unborn baby sister. And that would not be due for another five months.

Instinct prompted him to sit with his father. Maybe it was time to share the burden of whatever drove his father to drink himself into a stupor once a year.

Daniel poured himself a measure of the scotch. His father looked at him with tired, red-rimmed eyes. He looked defeated. This was distressing because even in those annual drunken days of the past years, he was in pain but never this beaten, like a general who lost a war.

They continued to drink in silence for a while, both unwilling to break the mood, waiting for the other to speak. Finally, his father put his glass down, rubbed his eyes, and sat up straight from his earlier slump, like a soldier deciding to fight one last battle despite the odds.

"Daniel, have I done well as your father?"

The question astonished him; he did not know what prompted his father to ask it.

"You did very well, dad, more than I could ever hope for." They had a relaxed father and son relationship, more like buddies.

His father's pupils darkened and glittered with intensity; his jaw clenched tight. "I need to tell you something that I wish with all my heart I could spare you from. All I ask is that you do not judge me too harshly." His voice was rough, like the scotch had scorched his vocal chords.

Daniel felt a kick to his heart.

His father sat back on the sofa, the glass of scotch cradled in his hands, his profile to him. He could see his throat forcing down whatever emotion he wanted to control. Seeing his father this distressed made him nervous.

"In 1987, when I was still a Captain, I was part of an anti-insurgency campaign in the mountains of Lanao against Moro rebels. Someone tipped them off, and they ambushed us, killing half of our troops. They trapped us in an unfamiliar terrain and surrounded us. It was a very dangerous situation, their number double than ours, and they knew the area well. To survive, our commanding officer, Lt. Colonel Enrico, an aswang, commanded a group of us to turn harravis to save ourselves and the troops. We consumed the viscera of our fallen aswang comrade to get out of there. And we succeeded. It saved us, including the human troops," his father said in a flat tone.

Mateo inhaled, then took a swig of the scotch. Daniel sat still as he waited for his father to continue. There was no doubt the story was very important.

His father cleared his throat. "When we got back to civilization, our Commanding Officer wanted to turn us fully into harravises, to make it part of our Standard Operating Procedure as a battalion. My fellow officers and I disagreed, so I turned in my CO to the Tribunal. They found him guilty, and he was executed. I thought that was the end of that. Twenty years later, that one incident came back to haunt me..." he broke off. Fury reddened his face.

"What happened, Dad?" he asked, a sense of foreboding in the air.

"Do you recall the Pagsanjan 1993 incident and the head perpetrator, Major Ona?" Mateo asked instead, the quiet question ominous.

Daniel nodded.

"He was one of the company leaders under Lt. Colonel Enrico and was part of our battalion in the fateful 1987 clash. After they killed him in the Pagsanjan campaign, his autopsy confirmed he had Visceral Metastasis. My former CO's autopsy revealed he had the same disease. It was too much of a coincidence, so I had myself tested..." His father's voice quavered.

"And?"

"And it was positive." His father's grim reply was like a lead ball in his chest.

"You have *VM*?" His heart sank.

"No... I no longer have it. I was cured," Mateo replied. His voice cracked.

"How? I thought it was an incurable disease."

"It is, but there is one cure... the viscera of a foetus, specifically one with the closest DNA to the afflicted."

There was pain and panic reflected in the depths of his father's eyes. A chill invaded Daniel's body. "What does that mean?"

"Your pregnant mother shot herself in the head to force me to..." his voice broke, "so I can be cured..." Mateo swallowed a few times to force the lump of emotions down.

The silence was uncomfortable as the cloud of confusion cleared. Daniel's chest tightened to the point of bursting as the truth sank into his comprehension.

"You... ate... my...?" He reeled back.

The image of his father eating his baby sister was repulsive. He jerked away and rushed to the guest comfort room, his stomach heaving. All those gory and horrendous stories about aswangs as told by every human adult in his childhood, stories he considered a joke, became a horrifying reality.

Waves of excruciating sensation enveloped his body, varying degrees of disgust found its way out of his gut and radiated all over his skin as he heaved over the toilet bowl. He could not comprehend where his pain was coming from, his heart, his head, his soul.

His stomach emptied; he had no strength to get up from the floor. The stark proof of his father's nature hit home for the first time in his life. He grew up knowing this; it did not matter to him, or so he thought. This information made him see the non-human part of the only parent he had, the man who had the most influence in what he was now. And he realised he had not accepted his father's aswang side, that he avoided the core of that truth all his life.

This was why he never allowed himself to fall in love with aswang women, not what he kept telling himself about wanting to spare his future children, but because it repulsed him. And this sickened him, to come face-to-face with his own intolerance. And yet, even knowing his own failing, the fact remained that it revolted him.

Part of him wished he had never learned the truth, or that he could just forget. But this was his father waiting outside, not some stranger he had no love for. He could not just walk away from this. They both needed to live with this truth. He pushed himself up and trudged back out to the living room where his father waited for him.

"What now, Daniel?" his father asked, not looking at him, his head bowed.

"I do not know, dad..." He slumped beside him on the sofa.

He could no longer look at his father and see just that—his father—now, he was an aswang who ate his baby sister. Images of his father opening his mother up came bubbling up from inside him. He closed his eyes tight to will it away.

"I understand..." Mateo said. He sounded disheartened and resigned, as if he expected this, but was unprepared for it. He recognised the pain that accompanied the feeling of rejection that his reaction generated. His father's grim expression, the lines of misery around his mouth and eyes, told him he had broken his dad's heart. And his own chest quivered with the same agony.

He shot to his feet and walked out, unable to process the emotions and thoughts that churned in his guts and heart in front of his father. He felt a thundering of rage directed at anything and everything: at his father, the aswangkind and their nature, at himself, and at the situation that had placed him in an impossible position.

Hours later, Daniel was nursing his sixth glass of vodka and getting increasingly frustrated because the mind-numbing state he had been expecting since the fourth glass had so far eluded him. Tonight, his mind remained intractably sober and active.

Why tell me now?

He was contemplating the bottom of the glass through the transparent spirit, when he realised the connection — Roald.

Oh, holy fuck!

It was his father who traumatised Roald when he was young. Roald saw his father's heinous act from his treehouse.

Damn!

Another sin to feel guilty about.

Another load on my already over-burdened conscience.

He sighed and chugged the drink in one swallow and grimaced at the spicy burn of the liquid down his throat, then poured himself another one.

Anyone in his position deserved to numb the pain and confusion with alcohol for a few hours.

Roald, with steadfastness, kept his thoughts positive throughout the one hour and a half ferry ride by going through all the photos of Yuana and himself together on his phone. There were very few photos of her, he realised. He never noticed before, never needed them, because she was his, then.

He groped for the small ring box in his pocket and pulled it out. The cushion cut, eight carat emerald that would be the centrepiece for Yuana's engagement ring was exquisite. She had a unique taste in jewellery and a traditional engagement ring design would not suit her. He wanted this one, and their eventual wedding ring to be a collaborative effort.

The ring was a non-issue in their conflict, though. The chief obstacle remained - whether he could live with her aswang side and her world. He could not answer it with a clear yes, but he knew in his heart that he had accepted what she was. And he would dedicate his life to finding a way to reach the point where everything about her otherness no longer bothered him.

This idea occupied his thoughts during the three-hour drive to his destination.

Roald slowed down and paused by the gate of Villa Bizitza. His pulse raced. Now that Yuana was close by, all the days he missed her hit him like a ton of bricks. This woman who could both be infuriating and adorable in two seconds flat, be fire and ice in a smile or a word, the softness to his hardness, and strength to his weakness. Even now, she was the only person who could ever present him with a dilemma impossible for his brain to decide on, so he allowed his heart to do it for him.

He rang the bell at the gate and waited. Thereafter, a small person opened the walk-in gate.

"Yes, Sir?" the dark-skinned man inquired. He looked like a Mangyan.

"I am here to see Ms Yuana Orzabal," he said with a confidence that he did not have.

"Okay, sir. Ms Orzabal is waiting for you," the man said.

"Yuana?" he asked, startled. A jolt of optimism speared through his heart.

"No, sir, Ms Bella," the man clarified, instantly deflating the hope that ballooned in him.

The man moved to open the gate, leaving Roald with no choice but to go back to his car and drive it inside the compound.

A vast, well-manicured lawn flanked the drive on both sides. There was a profusion of ornamental bushes and flowering plants that made the gardens appear like an explosion of colours. Huge, ancient trees stood like well-spaced sentinels that surrounded the house and shielded it from outside view. The drive curved to reveal the circular driveway, similar to their house in Manila. The building was about two hundred meters from the gate, made of wood and distinct granite accents.

It surprised him to see the same man who opened the gate for him was at the front of the house, waiting to open the door for him. The man bid him to follow and brought him to the living room, where Ysobella and Galen were waiting for him by the couch.

Yuana was nowhere in sight.

"Good afternoon, *Tita, Tito.*"

He felt awkward and vulnerable. Yuana's parents could very well send him home before he could see her.

"Good afternoon, Roald. What brought you here?" Galen asked.

There was no animosity in Galen's greeting. It boded well for him and his cause.

"I am here to make it right with Yuana. Can I see her?" His breath held; his heart pounded.

Ysobella and Galen exchanged a glance. Ysobella's expression was serious, Galen's was impish. Ysobella turned to him with an impassive face. "Give the car key to Yam-Ay, she can have your bag brought up to the guest room."

She directed his gaze to a small, dark-skinned woman who appeared silently and unnoticed beside him, startling him. He fished the key from his pocket and handed it over to the woman, who bustled past him toward the front door where his car was parked.

"Yuana is in the morning room," Galen said, "hmm... that way." He pointed to a hallway to his right.

"Thank you, Tito, Tita." He nodded his thanks to both and walked towards the morning room, where Yuana was.

To make right what he ruined, to reclaim what he lost.

The morning room was bright and cosy with its country-style decoration. The breeze that blew through the French window ruffled the lavender-coloured curtains and stirred the cinnamon and vanilla flavoured air. Beyond was a verandah with white outdoor wicker tables and chairs. They were empty.

He moved closer to the window to find Yuana when he noticed the coffee cup on the corner table, and an open book lying face down on the seat. It was a Roald Dahl Collections book, one that he gave her on her birthday.

He moved to the verandah to seek Yuana and found her standing on the steps that led down to the lawn. Her hands tucked into her pockets; her gaze fixed on the mountain range ahead. He stood there for a while, thinking how to approach her, when she stiffened and whirled around.

For a moment, they were both frozen in time, their eyes locked on each other, their breath held.

"Roald," she breathed out his name.

And that was the impetus that jerked him back to the present and propelled him to her. He hauled her into his arms and buried his nose in her fragrant hair. He missed her with every fibre of his being, from the top of his head to the tips of his toes, all his senses clamoured for her. The need to kiss her warred with his need to keep her in his arms. He would not risk looking into her face or he would not be able to stop himself from claiming her lips. He had no right after the way they parted last time.

"I missed you," he murmured in her hair, his arms locked around her, unwilling to let her go.

"I missed you too," she breathed.

Her scent shot straight to his heart. He allowed himself the luxury of being wrapped by her presence, the warmth of her body.

She rested in his embrace a few moments more, then pushed herself out of his arms. He was reluctant to let her go. She walked back up to her seat, set her book aside, and sat down. He followed her lead and sat across from her. His gaze never left her.

Her sigh implied a multitude of emotions. "Why are you here, Roald?"

"I want to make everything right between us, Yu. I want us back." He wanted to say more, but words would not come.

"Which 'us' do you want back, Roald? Our old 'us' is gone." The sadness in her voice squeezed on his heart.

"No. Our 'us' never went away, Yuana. Circumstance may have changed, and time may have come between us for a short while, but you and I remain the same—we are one," he insisted.

He had to stop himself from reaching over to her clenched hand. But the invisible barrier created by the past few days was almost tangible and thickening by the second.

"Did you take my *aswang* nature in consideration when you refer to 'us'?"

Her gaze was sharp and intent but he glimpsed the spark of hope and wariness in its depths. An answering hope bloomed in his chest.

"Yes, I did... carefully, torturously, and I am resolved to accept everything that comes with it." He heard the intensity in his own voice.

"Everything?" she asked. Her eyes glittered. "What do you see in our future together, Roald?" She challenged him to lay down his expectations.

"Us, together, facing whatever comes. Adjusting to each other, to the circumstances, but always committed to handling whatever life will throw against us."

He did not have a clear picture of what their future would be like, or how hard it would be for him, but he did not care. He just knew how life would feel without her.

Focused on him, she got up and walked to him, sat on his lap and laid her head on his chest. She drew out a deep sigh. Tension left her rigid spine, her warmth melted into him like a tired child needing a cuddle.

He responded by instinct. His arms wrapped around her, and he rocked her in a soothing rhythm. The movement was for him as much as for her. Peace settled in his soul, knowing she had not severed their connection, that she had not given up on him, and she had banked on the love between them as he did.

Tears of relief and gratitude pricked behind his closed lids. He squeezed them shut to keep it in. He felt an enormous gratitude to the universe.

"Did it really take less than a month for you to accept me and my nature?" She sounded disbelieving.

"No. It took just less than a month for me to accept I cannot live a joyful life without you in it. I can work on the rest for as long as you and I are together."

Yuana smiled. She seemed satisfied by his response.

"What's next? How do we proceed from this?" she asked.

He understood what she meant, as they could not ignore his struggle about her nature, but he was resolute in taking his time to find the cure for her. She was half human. There might be a way to separate her from her... otherness.

"We can go on as usual, let us not dwell too much on our differences. Let us just focus on where we are similar, our goals, our core values. I will try my very best to adjust to the situation."

Yuana frowned and became thoughtful. "We could stretch the status quo until you have adapted to my world. We could apply the same arrangements we have in place for my father..." She brightened at her own suggestion.

"Oh... You have a special arrangement for your father? What is it?"

"Nothing drastic. We avoid doing some of our... practices in front of him." She shrugged. "How can I make it easy for you? What can I do?"

He smiled and kissed her forehead. "Be patient with me. Help me understand the things I do not."

"Okay." The brief reply encapsulated her intention to do everything in her power to help him succeed.

"And Yuana... please promise me..." he said. His hands cupped her face and made it impossible for her to look away. "... you will never leave like that again..."

She nodded, her eyes teared up, and she swallowed as if her throat was too thick with emotion.

"I cannot fix what we broke between us if you leave. Promise me..." he repeated.

"I promise," she whispered.

His gaze became focused on her lips, his thumb rubbed her lower lip, a prelude to a kiss, his way of asking permission, of giving her the time to say no. A tremulous breath was her response, and that was all he needed. He closed the distance between them and touched his lips to hers and shared an evocative, deep sealing kiss that spoke of penance and forgiveness, of passion and love, of vows of commitment asked for and given.

The kiss was both familiar and new. Their future flavoured it, certain and uncertain. And it tasted of Yuana.

He lifted his head, looked lovingly at her face, smoothed her hair back. His hand came to rest at the back of her head.

"You have my heart, Roald Magsino," her voice cracked. A beaming smile spread sweetly on her face.

He felt an answering jolt of joy in his heart. "And you have mine, Yuana Orzabal, and everything else that you might need. You only have to ask."

EPILOGUE

Edrigu reached home, soul tired. Roald should have reached Villa Bizitza by now, and he felt optimistic that all would be well between him and his granddaughter. Regardless of the outcome, the team would shadow him for the next few weeks until they were convinced he posed no threat to their safety. The bugs in his premises would remain until they were fully satisfied that it was safe.

A tinge of worry surfaced in his mind as he remembered Mateo. He wondered if his friend was able to speak to his son, Daniel.

How did Daniel react to the revelation?

Kazu flew overhead toward the Villa Bizitza compound, high enough not to be visible to anyone on the ground who might look up by coincidence. He circled the house a few times. Yuana must join him, so he could fulfil what he vowed to do.

Just a few more months and his destiny would unfold.

Their training had been continuous. They had to be better than the *Iztaris*. The go-signal was given yesterday, and their plan set in motion. With grim satisfaction and a small amount of regret, came the acknowledgement that the *Tribunal* was unprepared for what was coming to their doorstep.

The fate of the viscerebuskind is about to change.

WORLD OF THE VISCEREBUS GLOSSARY OF TERMS

These are the Viscerebus terms mentioned in the novel.

Animus (Heart or Instinct Animal) or Spirit Animal — the true animal form of a Viscerebus. All Viscerebus have one, although not all would discover theirs. An Auto-morphosis, or reflexive transformation, usually reveals to a Viscerebus their Animus. Some Viscerebus transform into one animal all their lives and discover that their Animus was a different form.

In some Viscerebus families, it was part of their tradition to deny sustenance to the child of twelve to force an Auto-morphosis. This is usually done under the supervision of the adults. The practice lost favour over the centuries because it often resulted in injury to the child and usually the said child would elect to transform into the animal form they habitually turn into, thus defeating the object of discovering their Animus.

Now, the term is used erroneously by modern Viscerebus to refer to their animal form, whether it is their true Spirit Animal or just their hunting form. (*See Auto-morphosis. See Spirit Animal, Reflexive Transformation – World of the Viscerebus Almanac*).

Apex – A super shapeshifter. A very rare Viscerebus that can transform into a winged animal, either in chiropteran (bats) or avian (birds) form. They can transform fully, or partially. Other special Apex skills manifested by previous ones are echolocation and sound blasting, magnetic field manipulation. Apexes can also turn on their brain's theta waves and read other people's brainwaves or influence it.

It is said that the full skill set of an Apex has not been fully revealed yet because new skills keep getting discovered by each successive Apex, and each would depend on the core strength of the individual. (*See Apex Shapeshifting – World of the Viscerebus Almanac*)

Aquila—the other name for the giant eagle named Aetos Kaukasios, one of the two primary mythical gods to the Viscerebus, the other is Prometheus. The Viscerebuskind attribute the beginning of their race to the two gods. According to the legend, Zeus sent Aetos to devour the liver of Prometheus every night as his eternal punishment for giving fire to humans and for tricking Zeus to choose a less valuable sacrificial offering from humans. The Viscerebus' need to eat viscera is attributed to the saliva of Aetos that contaminated the liver of Prometheus, which was used by the latter to create the Viscerebus.

Aetos was the offspring of two other Titans, Typhon and Echidna, the father and mother of mythical monsters in Greek Mythology. (*See Prometheus. See Origin – World of the Viscerebus Almanac*).

Aswangs – The Filipino term for Viscerebus. Of all the countries in the world, the existence of Viscerebus is the most entrenched in the Philippine culture for two reasons:

First, the Filipinos launched the most aggressive campaign against the Viscerebus. Their Venandis were the most experienced. The Venandi practice, which started as a family endeavour, became traditionally and habitually passed on to the next generation. There are still active, albeit lesser number of Venandis operating in the country.

The superstitious nature of the Filipinos allowed them to believe that Aswangs still existed, albeit in exaggerated and erroneous form. Many books have been written, and movies made featuring Aswangs as evil creatures, usually depicted as the minions of the devil.

Like every culture, the existence of the Viscerebus has been relegated into myth and lore, and the term Aswang is used as a blanket term for almost every man-eating and blood sucking ghoul in the country.

Second, the local tribes in the country were also the first to accept the Viscerebus into their midst and established a collaborative and symbiotic relationship. Native Viscerebus in the Philippines were the only one sanctioned by the Tribunal to work openly with the human tribal members. Their Veil-binding applies only to humans that were not part of the tribe. (*See Venandi*)

Auto-morphosis – also known as *Reflexive Transformation* is the involuntary shapeshifting into the animal spirit of a Viscerebus. The vital instinct to hunt and secure *Victus* or *sustenance* triggers this transformation. The vital instinct is triggered when a Viscerebus fails to consume human viscera for over three days.

It is possible to induce an Auto-morphosis through practice and meditation. Some Viscerebus do this to discover their *Animus*. (*See Animus, Victus, Crux, Reflexive Transformation, See Shape-shifting – World of the Viscerebus Almanac*)

Crux—is a subconscious inner control of a Viscerebus to stop or start shape shifting. A Vis can call forth their Crux into consciousness to prevent a reflexive transformation. A Crux is strengthened with practice or meditation. This is similar to human willpower. (*See Auto-morphosis, Reflexive Transformation, See Shape-shifting – World of the Viscerebus Almanac*).

Emergence – the term used when Apexes discover their authentic form, also known as Animus. The Apex can induce emergence by forcing an Auto-morphosis or reflexive transformation. Part of the traditional Auto-morphic rituals include the excited wish of a child to "emerge as an Apex" which normally results as disappointment as Apexes, or super shapeshifters, are extremely rare. (*See Animus, Apex. Auto-Morphosis. See history of Apexes – World of the Viscerebus Almanac*).

Erdia—an Erdia is a half-blood, born from a Male Viscerebus and a Female human. Erdias are very human in their nature except they would be slightly stronger, faster and live longer than their human counterpart. They may inherit some enhancement on their senses. They don't inherit the shapeshifting and need for human viscera.

Most Erdias who use their enhanced strength and speed become athletes. Erdias who inherit a superior sense of taste and scent usually become renowned chefs, perfume makers and other professions that maximise their abilities.

The knowledge of the Erdias about the Viscerebuskind would depend on whether the Viscerebus father tells his offspring. If the Erdia was told, they would be bound to the Veil of Secrecy just like their Viscerebus parent, and they become part of the Viscerebus world.

A significant number of Erdias are unaware of the Viscerebus world because the Viscerebus father abandon them from infancy. These Erdias, being non-Veil-bound, are treated as human. They live normal human lives, unaware of the existence of the Viscerebus. (*See Eremite. See Mejordia, Veil of Secrecy – World of the Viscerebus Almanac*).

Gentem—(nation in Latin)–the current country of residence, or the immediate, previous country of residence of a *transitting or tramwaying* Viscerebus. A Viscerebus can have between six to ten Gentems in their lifetime. This is not to be confused with ***Patriam***, which is the country of birth of a Viscerebus. (*See Patriam – World of the Viscerebus Almanac*)

Harravir—also known in the Philippines as ***Tiktiks***. They are Viscerebus who hunt humans for the *Victus*. They mostly exist only in rural, uncivilised and remote areas. Harravirs are the same as the modern Viscerebus, except they have not adopted the modern way of surviving without killing humans. In most circumstances, this was because they have not heard of the existence of the *Tribunal*.

Most modern Viscerebus sustain themselves without needing to kill humans because the Tribunal provides the *Victus* required by every Viscerebus. The practice of Harravirring is a capital crime in the Viscerebus world and may be punishable by death.

To prevent the commission of the crime, in very rare circumstances, a Viscerebus can use a temporary alternative using pork or beef organs. But this is not advisable and should only be used in emergencies. Consumption of animal organs can make a Viscerebus sick.

A captured Harravir may be rehabilitated, educated and integrated into the Viscerebus communities, but if this is not possible, they are executed by the Iztaris.

Harravirs are the prime enemies of the Venandis, which are humans who actively hunt Viscerebus victimising human villages and communities.

(*See Tiktik, Venandis. See Maniniktik – World of the Viscerebus in Almanac*)

Harravis—also known in the Philippines as ***Wakwaks***; are Viscerebus that hunts other Viscerebus for their viscera. The Harravis' fundamental goal is to consume Viscerebus organs, as it is far more potent than a human's.

Viscerebus' viscera make the Harravis stronger and faster than a normal Viscerebus, and they remain so for as much as sixty to ninety days.

Harravis practice can also be addictive as it raises the dopamine level in a Viscerebus. And like drug use, regular and sustained Harravissing habit drives the Harravis to hunt more often and at shorter intervals.

There are perils in this practice as consumption of the viscera of another Viscerebus enables the transmission of Harravis diseases. Most notable and deadliest is the Visceral Metastasis.

A Harravis power or diseases is transmittable to another Viscerebus through sex within the first forty-eight hours of infection. Harravissing is a capital crime in the Viscerebus world and is punishable by death. (*See Visceral Metastasis, Wakwak*).

Impedio – a leather vest and chain contraption meant to restrain a Viscerebus from attacking humans during a reflexive transformation. And when appropriate, a muzzle is part of the set. It is strapped tightly to the body of the Vis, the chains attached to it are to be attached to a strong foundation like a wall or a huge tree. Every Vis is required to own one, and carry it with them if they travel to remote places, especially if they travel for more than three days.

The modern Impedio has a Tracking Device that is automatically triggered when the Distress Transmitter is turned on. The Distress Transmitter can be activated manually, or automatically by the change of the heartbeat in a Vis during complete transformation.

The transmitter sends signals to the nearest Iztari office, indicating that someone is in need of human viscera. The Iztaris are then deployed to rescue the unfortunate being.

It is considered illegal to activate a Distress Transmitter as a joke or a prank. The punishment consists of a huge fine, and a demerit point on their record. (*See Auto-Morphosis, See Demerit System -World of the Viscerebus Almanac*)

Iturrian—the source. The term used for the pregnant woman who provides, voluntarily or involuntarily, the foetus growing in their belly as a treatment for Visceral Metastasis. The receiver, or the VM-inflicted Viscerebus who takes the treatment, is called the *Ontzian*, or the vessel. The act is called the *Messis,* or the harvest. All three terms are spoken in a hushed voice as the Tribunal do not sanction the practice. (*See Ontzian and Messis*)

Iztari—the law enforcement of the Supreme Viscerebus Tribunal. They are embedded in the human armed forces, police and security community as a way of hiding in plain sight, acquiring military training and gaining knowledge on the human military and police system.

The Iztaris' main mandate is to implement strict adherence to the Veil of Secrecy. They are deployed to either a) hunt Harravirs or Harravis, b) implement the Veil procedures, c) defend humans or other Viscerebus from Harravirs and Harravises, d) Find other Viscerebus communities.

The Iztari system is unique, as there are no ranks among the Iztaris. However, there is a Team Head appointed when a team is deployed. The only figure of authority is the Chief Iztari. Iztari office employs both Viscerebus and Erdias with the right skills. The Erdias are office bound and do analyst and research tasks rather than fieldwork.

Only the Viscerebus may go on field because of the inherent danger of dealing with a vicious Harravir and Harravis. Iztaris are well-trained and well-equipped for combat. The Iztari office uses the latest technologies that the human and the Viscerebus kind can offer. Ten percent of the Viscerebus population are Iztaris. (*See SVT – World of the Viscerebus Almanac*).

Messis—the harvest. Originally, this refers to the harvesting of the human viscera, or *Victus*. But the use of the term has lost favour because humans ask for explanation when they overhear it. The term now refers to the illicit act of securing amniotic fluid from a six-month-old foetus within the womb of the mother, also referred to as the *Iturrian,* the source. The amniotic fluid is the only treatment that stays the progression of Visceral Metastasis in the body of an infected Viscerebus, also referred to as the *Ontzian*, or the vessel.

Messis, as a practice originated from the traditional Harravir acts where an infected Viscerebus hunt for pregnant human females. At the implementation of the Veil of Secrecy, the practice became illegal. It evolved into using abortion clinics to secure the treatment for the infected.

The practice remains hidden. The Tribunal tolerates it but does not openly endorse it. (*See Ontzian and Iturrian, Visceral Metastasis*)

Ontzian—the vessel. The name used to refer to the VM-infected Viscerebus receiving treatment by sucking the amniotic fluid of a six-month-old foetus from the mother's womb. (*See Messis and Iturrian*).

Prometheus—A Greek Titan and the god of creative fire and the creator of men. He was the son of Titan Iapetus and the Oceanids, Clymene. His siblings are Atlas, Epimetheus, Menoetius. He is known for his intelligence, as the author of human arts and sciences, and a champion of humankind. His name meant "Forethought".

According to the Viscerebus legends, while he created humans out of clay, Prometheus made the first Viscerebus couple from his own liver, the soil and rocks of the Caucasus mountain where he was bound and tortured.

With his DNA, the Viscerebus inherited godlike traits of super strength, speed, senses, healing abilities and long life. Prometheus also imbued them with the ability to shapeshift so they can hide themselves from Zeus.

It was said that he created them out of his need for companions to distract himself from the pain of having his liver eaten every day by Aetos, and the loneliness during the regrowing of the organ every night.

During the day, the first Viscerebus were in their animal form, a feline and a canine, but they transform into their human form at night to keep Prometheus company. This is also why cats and dogs were regarded as the closest companions to humans. (*See Apex, Aquila. See Origin story – World of the Viscerebus Almanac*)

Reflexive Transfiguration – also referred to as *Auto-morphosis*, the involuntary transformation or shape-shifting into the animal spirit of a Viscerebus. The vital instinct to hunt and secure sustenance triggers this transformation. This instinct, in turn, gets triggered when a Viscerebus failed to consume sustenance, weakening the Crux, the subconscious and internal control of a Viscerebus to retain their human form. Once weakened, a Viscerebus' human form becomes unstable. Once sustenance is consumed, Crux control is regained, and the Viscerebus can shift back to their human form with ease.

It is possible to induce a Reflexive Transformation through practice and meditation. (*See Auto-morphosis, Impedio. See Shapeshifting – World of the Viscerebus Almanac*)

Spirit Animal – or Anima Mea (Soul), also called *Animus* (Heart or instinct)—is the true animal form of a Viscerebus. They are usually revealed during an Auto-morphosis or Reflexive Transformation. All Viscerebi have one, although not all Viscerebi can discover theirs. For example, a Viscerebus can transform into a leopard all his/her life and discover that his/her Animus is different. (*See Animus, Auto-morphosis*).

Supreme Viscerebus Tribunal – or the SVT. This is the primary ruling body of the Viscerebus. It is composed of previous and current Matriarch and Patriarchs from different Gentems all over the world. SVT functions as both as the main legislative and judicial body of the Viscerebi. The execution of the laws, however, is the responsibility of each Gentem's Tribunal. Members of the body meet bi-annual, where laws proposed by members are discussed and voted on. The main mandate of the Tribunal is to oversee the compliance of every Gentem in the upholding of the Veil of Secrecy. The SVT is the ultimate rule of law for the Viscerebi. (*See Veil of Secrecy. See 5000BCE Constitution, Implementing Rules and Regulations – World of the Viscerebus Almanac*).

Sustenance– or *Victus*. The blanket term used by Viscerebus to refer to human viscera that they take regularly. This is crucial to stabilising the human form of a Viscerebus. This is the term used by modern Viscerebus, as the term does not invite unnecessary questions and explanations. (*See Victus, Crux, Auto-morphosis. See Reflexive Transformation, Vital hunger*).

Tiktik – is the Philippine term for ***Harravirs,*** which are Viscerebi who hunt humans to survive, (also referred to as Human-Hunting Viscerebi), they mostly exist only in rural, uncivilised and remote areas. They are the same as the modern Viscerebi, except they have not adopted the modern way of surviving without killing humans. Most modern Viscerebi sustained themselves without needing to kill humans. The practice of Harravirring is considered a crime in the Viscerebus world. (*See Harravir*)

Tiyanak – a Philippine Mythological name for a monster that adopts the form of a human baby. According to legends, it lures a human to pick it up by crying piteously, but it transforms into a blood-thirsty monster once a human picks it up. Humans usually encounter them in remote areas like the woods. In reality, they are a baby Viscerebi, or a ***Tzikiavis,*** who had reflexively transformed due to hunger.

A baby Viscerebus cannot achieve full transformation because of immaturity and inexperience, and they end up looking like a baby-sized, fanged and clawed monster. Humans who were attacked by a hungry baby Viscerebus assumed Tiyanaks differed from a Viscerebi. The legend was created thereafter. (*See Tzikiavis – World of the Viscerebus Almanac*).

Transit—also known as *tramway*. The program of relocating a Viscerebus and his/her family to maintain the Veil of Secrecy. A Viscerebus can be under a Life Transit, a mandatory, scheduled relocation every thirty years; or a Forcible Transit, unscheduled relocation because of the Viscerebus' violation of the Veil. A Forcible Transit is equivalent to an exile in human government.

A tramwaying Viscerebus is required to cut contact with any of their *non-Veil-bound* human or Erdia friends, relatives and connections. But they can keep contact with other Viscerebus and Veil-bound Erdias friends, relatives and connections.

A Transitting Viscerebus may keep his or her old name and profession or may take on a new one. The new tramway location must be in a different country or continent. A Transitting Viscerebus can return to their *Patriam* or previous *Gentem* after 100 years to ensure that any human they had a relationship with before are already dead. Visits to the Patriam and previous Gentems are permitted on brief holidays and only once every ten years. Veil of Secrecy restrictions apply. (*See Gentem, Veil of Secrecy. See Patriam, Transit Program – World of the Viscerebus Almanac*)

Veil of Secrecy—the inviolable law of the Tribunal to keep the existence of Viscerebus a secret from non-Viscerebus. The Law makes exceptions to a) Human spouse; b) Human kids. However, the exceptions apply only if the above people prove themselves loyal to the Viscerebuskind and to the Veil.

The strict adherence to the Veil guides every interaction of a Viscerebus with humans and non-Veil-bound Erdias. The violation or breaking of the Veil would entail severe punishment that could result in the death of the human or the non-Veil-bound Erdia, and the violator is expected to execute the punishment. (*See SVT, or Supreme Viscerebus Tribunal. See 5000BCE Constitution – World of the Viscerebus Almanac*).

Venandis – are Human Viscerebus-Hunters, also referred to as **Maniniktik** (or those who hunt Tiktiks or Harravirs) whose primary aim is to eradicate the Viscerebi as a means of defence and survival. Over the centuries, Venandis have died out because of the effectiveness of the Tribunal's campaign to have the humans believe the Viscerebus are just figures of lore and myths.

However, there are still some small pockets of Venandis in the world who work in secret. These are usually a small family of Venandis who kept the belief by passing on the training from parents to children. (*See Types of Aswang hunters – World of the Viscerebus Almanac*)

Victus – colloquially called as *Sustenance.* This is the blanket term for human viscera, heart, liver and kidney, that a Viscerebus must consume regularly to keep their Vital Hunger at bay and prevent involuntary transformation to their animal form.

This term had become less popular than its colloquial counterpart as humans who overheard ask question what it means. The Tribunal encourages the use of the term *Sustenance* in a public setting to avoid the questions. (*See Sustenance, Crux, Auto-morphosis, Reflexive Transformation, Vital Hunger*)

Visceral Metastasis—the cancer that can only be transmitted to another Viscerebus at certain conditions. The disease attacks the viscera and the blood vessels. A Viscerebus can contract the disease when they consume an infected Viscerebus viscera.

The disease can be transmitted to a woman if the infected male has sex with a female Viscerebus within forty-eight hours of initial infection. And if that woman was pregnant at the time of the intercourse, the disease will also infect the foetus in utero. Past the forty-eight hours, the disease is no longer transmittable. An infected woman, however, will transmit it to all her offspring.

However, if a Viscerebus is born with the disease, their VM is transmittable every time they have intercourse with another Viscerebus.

The disease cannot be passed on to humans or Erdias.

The disease can take at least 10 years before it manifests the symptoms. And it can take as much as thirty years to some. The symptoms are like a human kidney, liver, heart disease and leukaemia. Once diagnosed, the primary treatment to stay the progression of the disease is the amniotic fluid of a six-month-old human foetus.

The only cure is consuming the viscera of a foetus that is a close blood and DNA relation to the infected. This means siblings or child of the infected. This cure is highly confidential and requires prescription/endorsement of a Viscerebus doctor and sanctioned by the SVT's Matriarch and Patriarch. It also requires the complete agreement from the donor, which is either the siblings, parents, or the mother of the child.

Most of those infected will never have themselves checked by the Viscerebus doctor, because it is tantamount to a confession that one has a Harravis habit or was infected by a loved one. Harravissing is a capital crime and punishable by death.

Apart from natural causes, the leading cause of death for a Viscerebus is the disease. And because of the Veil of Secrecy which inhibits the availability of the treatment, Visceral Metastasis is considered a death sentence. (*See Iturrian, Ontzian and Messis*).

Viscerebus/Viscerebi (pl.)—or Viscera-eaters, colloquially known as ***Vis***. They are a different species of human. They live two to three times longer than a human, are stronger, faster, and have quick healing abilities.

Physically, they look exactly like humans, but they can shapeshift into a land-based predator. The Viscerebus need to eat human viscera and stabilise their human form. To normal humans, they are monstrous man-eaters.

Viscerebi are known by many names in many cultures. And the descriptions vary because of the dilution of the truth engineered by the Tribunal to bury the existence of the Viscerebus under myth and lore. The common thread among these lores is the shapeshifting and the viscera-eating.

Most modern human societies have completely ignored the lore, but the belief persists in some pockets of rural communities all over the world. This is especially true in Asian countries, particularly the Philippines, where stories about Aswangs, the local name for Viscerebus, are still told. (*See Aswang*)

Vital Hunger—the term used to refer to the need to consume *Victus,* or *sustenance.* The sensation is similar to physical hunger, but it pertains to the need of a Viscerebus to secure sustenance to keep their Crux strong and prevent an Auto-morphosis. This manifests if the Vis has neglected to consume sustenance for at least three days. This triggers the *vital instinct* to hunt, which triggers the Auto-morphosis, or reflexive transformation.

The symptoms are usually a loss of energy and physical weakening of the Viscerebus. Some Vis develop physical hunger like symptoms, like shaking and trembling. Vital hunger itself is not painful, but the accompanying pain comes from the battle between the body's Crux and the vital instinct. (*See Auto-morphosis, Crux, Reflexive Transformation, Vital Instinct*)

Vital Instinct—the basic survival instinct of a Viscerebus drives the need to consume *Victus,* or human liver, heart or kidney. This is interchangeable to the term Vital Hunger. This surfaces when a Viscerebus fails to partake of human viscera for over three days. At this point, there is a battle between the Vital Instinct and the Crux of the individual.

The stronger the Crux, the longer the Viscerebus can control the transformation. However, inevitably, the Vital Instinct wins, thus forcing an Auto-morphosis, or the reflexive transformation into the Viscerebus' Animus. Once the Vital hunger is quenched, it restores the Crux control of the Viscerebus. (*See Crux, Auto-morphosis, Reflexive Transformation*).

Vivlioccultatum—the hidden archive and library. This is a massive structure that contains the original works, written history, books, manuscripts, arts of the Viscerebuskind made by the masters and notable members of the race.

Works are collected for its preservation and in compliance with the tenets of the Veil of Secrecy. The Vivliocultatum was established in

202AD. The Tribunal mandated the owners of works that can prove the existence of the Viscerebuskind to surrender them and forbids the replication of those materials. Those works were taken and stored in the Vivliocultatum.

In several, but rare instances, original owners were allowed to make a replica of their material for their own collection. However, they can replicate only works that can pass off as an artistic expression of myths or legends. Replication of such works require the highest permission from the Commission of Art in SVT.

The Vivliocultatum also became the repository and archive center of all the records of the local and the Supreme Tribunal.

The location of ***The Viv***, as it was colloquially called, remains a secret. But one thing is sure, it is located underground. Every year, the SVT organises an exclusive exhibit for their kind to view selected works in various notable museums in the world under the guise of cultural artifacts. (*See SVT, or Supreme Viscerebus Tribunal, See 5000BCE Constitution – World of the Viscerebus Almanac*).

Wakwaks – the Philippine name for ***Harravis,*** is a Viscerebus that hunts other Viscerebus for sustenance. The latter's fundamental goal is to consume Viscerebus organs as it is far more potent than a human's. One Viscerebus liver can sustain a Viscerebus for 3 months. The consumption of a Viscerebus viscera makes the Harravis stronger and faster than a normal Viscerebus, and they remain so for forty-eight hours. The practice of Harravissing is considered a capital crime in the Viscerebus world and is punishable by death. (*See Harravis*)

Note: *All novels in the World of the Viscerebus series contain a glossary of terms used in the book. The full glossary of terms and other information can be found in the WORLD OF THE VISCEREBUS ALMANAC.*

ABOUT THE AUTHOR

She was born in a province known for butterfly knives, strong coffee, and feisty people, where one grandfather nurtured her with stories of myths while another took her trekking. By the age of three, she had acquired an incurable reading habit. She collected fairy tales and developed an affinity for herbs, spices and trees. As an adult, she became an entrepreneur and a proud sales professional. Finally, she stopped dilly-dallying and answered her calling.

To learn more about Oz Mari Grandlund and discover more Next Chapter authors, visit our website at www.nextchapter.pub.

World of the Viscerebus - Books 1-3
ISBN: 978-4-82419-606-4
Hardcover Edition

Published by
Next Chapter
2-5-6 SANNO
SANNO BRIDGE
143-0023 Ota-Ku, Tokyo
+818035793528

24th July 2024

Milton Keynes UK
Ingram Content Group UK Ltd.
UKHW041234251124
451300UK00023B/141

9 784824 196064